THE DROW THERE AND NOTHING MORE

THE DROW THERE AND NOTHING MORE

GOTH DROW™ BOOK THREE

MARTHA CARR

MICHAEL ANDERLE

DISRUPTIVE IMAGINATION®

LMBPN Publishing
PMB 196, 2540 South Maryland Pkwy
Las Vegas, NV 89109

First US Edition, June, 2020
Version 1.01, January 2021
eBook ISBN: 978-1-64202-985-7
Print ISBN: 978-1-64202-986-4

THE DROW THERE AND NOTHING
MORE TEAM

Thanks to the JIT Readers

John Ashmore
Allen Collins
Angel LaVey
Daniel Weigert
Deb Mader
Debi Sateren
Diane L. Smith
Jackey Hankard-Brodie
Jeff Eaton
Jeff Goode
John Ashmore
Kerry Mortimer
Larry Omans
Paul Westman
Peter Manis
Veronica Stephan-Miller

If we've missed anyone, please let us know!
Editor
The Skyhunter Editing Team

DEDICATIONS

From Martha

To everyone who still believes in magic
and all the possibilities that holds.
To all the readers who make this
entire ride so much fun.
And to my son, Louie and so many wonderful friends who remind me
all the time of what
really matters and how wonderful
life can be in any given moment.

From Michael

To Family, Friends and
Those Who Love
To Read.
May We All Enjoy Grace
To Live The Life We Are
Called.

CHAPTER ONE

Cheyenne Summerlin rolled over in her bed and reached for the stack of pillows she'd grown used to grabbing in her sleep. Instead of pillows, her hand slapped down heavily on air, and she almost rolled onto the floor.

Her first instinct was to keep from falling. Her hand lashed out, and the force of her newly unlocked telekinesis threw her back onto the small bed while splintering the wooden floor beside her with a crunch. The halfling drew her hand back and pushed herself up to sit in the narrow twin bed, blinking herself awake.

Where the hell am I?

In two seconds, she recognized the massive bookshelf against the wall and the desk against the window. Cheyenne groaned and vigorously rubbed her cheeks.

Still at Chez Summerlin. I did everything I could to stay out of here.

The halfling blinked at the ceiling and tossed her childhood comforter off before slipping out of bed. When her gaze fell on the shallow crater she'd blasted into the floor, she winced. She stooped to drag the black area rug from in front of the bookshelf to the divot in the floor, covering it relatively well.

Eleanor's gonna find this the next time she cleans in here. Right now, I'm pretty sure a dented floor is the last thing on Mom's mind.

Cheyenne slipped into her clothes from yesterday, then grabbed her phone off the nightstand to check for messages. There was nothing. "So, Corian found nothing, or he's just too busy to bother. Fine."

She shoved the phone into her back pocket and froze when the sounds of soft laughter and clinking glasses carried toward her from down the hall. Tilting her head, the halfling opened the door to her old bedroom and glanced at the breakfast room at the back of the second story. The doors were open, and she caught a brief glimpse of Eleanor walking across the room before the woman disappeared.

They sound awfully happy, considering what's going on right outside.

The halfling shuffled down the hall, running her fingers through her tangled black hair. A few strands caught on her septum piercing, and she grimaced as she fought to free her face from her hair. Then she reached the open doors to the breakfast room and raised her eyebrows.

They'd rearranged the chairs to face the long, curved wall of windows so Ember could roll her wheelchair up to the very center. In the cream armchairs on either side of Cheyenne's fae friend sat Bianca Summerlin and Eleanor, both of them dressed and ready for the day.

Eleanor had just sat back down in her chair but turned with a grin when Cheyenne cleared her throat. "Good morning, sleepyhead."

Bianca shot the woman an amused glance before raising her Bloody Mary to her lips. "We thought we'd let you sleep in this morning, Cheyenne."

The halfling smirked. "It's only seven-thirty."

"Correct." Bianca drank. "I do hope that's not nearly as late as you normally sleep. Doesn't your earliest class start at eight-thirty?"

Cheyenne shot the back of her mom's head a playful frown. *If it was anyone else, I'd wonder how she knew that.*

"Not anymore." The halfling crossed the wide room toward the three women enjoying themselves and the now-less-peaceful view of the valley behind Bianca Summerlin's home. "I think I started to tell you last night. My schedule's changed a little." She stopped behind Ember and put a hand on her friend's shoulder. "You doin' okay in here with these two?"

The fae looked at her over her shoulder and smirked. "I think I can hold my own."

Eleanor chuckled. "And she didn't even join us for a Bloody Mary."

"I had enough to drink last night, thanks."

Bianca sat back in the cream armchair and lifted her chin. "I admire a woman who knows when to say no, despite her saying no to *me*."

Ember shot Eleanor a worried glance, and Bianca's housekeeper waved her off, whispering, "She's joking. Mostly. You're fine."

Cheyenne headed toward the breakfast cart Eleanor had rolled into the breakfast room every morning for as long as she could remember. The woman had laid out her usual spread: buttered toast with a variety of jams in tiny jars, hardboiled eggs, an assortment of fruit, and a French press, now empty, next to a matching set for cream and sugar. The Bloody Mary tray, of course, sat on a side table beside the cart. The halfling reached for a slice of toast.

"I would very much like to hear how your class schedule has changed, Cheyenne," Bianca muttered after another sip of her morning cocktail. "Seeing as that is news to me."

Spreading strawberry jam on her toast, the halfling glanced quickly at her mom, who only stared through the curving wall of windows. "My professors decided all our time was better spent if I taught undergraduate classes instead."

Eleanor choked on her drink and pressed her napkin to her lips. Bianca shot her a quick glance, the corners of her mouth twitching into a tiny smile. "Do *you* think it's time better spent?"

Cheyenne shrugged and took a huge, crunchy bite of toast. "It alleviated a lot of scheduling issues."

Bianca leaned forward in her chair and turned to look at her daughter for the first time this morning. The halfling hunched over, keeping the crumbs in her mouth, and pulled a napkin from the tray. She didn't speak again until she'd swallowed her food. "Sorry."

Her mom leaned back in her chair, satisfied with Cheyenne's return to proper etiquette. "As long as it works for you. That's what matters."

"I always thought you should've been teaching those classes anyway," Eleanor added, twirling her straw in her Blood Mary.

"I *could* teach my own graduate classes." Cheyenne caught Ember's amused glance and forced herself to look out the window to keep from laughing. "Right now, I'm teaching stuff I learned halfway through high school, but it'll get me my degree, so I was fine with making the change."

"Not *happy* with it?" Bianca took another sip of her drink.

"Not quite, but it's better than nothing. At least I get to choose what I teach. That was part of the deal—a fairly loose lesson plan."

"I'm glad it's working for you." Nodding, Bianca returned the majority of her attention to the view.

Cheyenne didn't miss the slight flare of her mom's nostrils as the woman's gaze once again fell to the huge scar of jagged black stone jutting toward the house from the tree line. The halfling looked across the acres of well-manicured lawn Bianca called her backyard and studied the FRoE agents who'd camped out there overnight. *She is not happy about that, but her irritation is way better than leaving her exposed to whatever else might come out of that new portal.*

She couldn't help but try to make light of it. "How's the morning entertainment?"

Bianca rolled her eyes. "Not entertaining in the slightest, Cheyenne. You know how I feel about this entire arrangement."

"I do." The halfling took another bite of toast.

"I also am perfectly aware of the necessity." Bianca tilted her head and rested it gently against the back of the armchair. "That doesn't mean I have to like it."

"The morning doesn't quite start off the same way with such a different view," Eleanor added. She glanced at Cheyenne and raised her eyebrows.

That's code for Mom woke up on the wrong side of the bed. Can't blame her.

The halfling scanned the breakfast cart for coffee cups, and Eleanor seemed to read her mind in an instant. "Oh, Cheyenne. Let me pull another cup out of the cabinet for you."

"I can get it."

"No, no. It's not every day we get to see your smiling face first thing in the morning." When the housekeeper saw Cheyenne's deadpan expression, she snorted. "See? Lovely. And I might as well make myself useful when our routine's been interrupted as it has been. Pull up a chair, sweetheart. I'll get you some coffee."

"It's dangerous for me to argue with you this morning, isn't it?"

Bianca choked back a small laugh as Eleanor pushed out of the armchair. "Your mother seems to think that's funny, but I'll tell you right now that you're absolutely right. We all have a job to do." Eleanor turned toward the back of the breakfast room and shrieked.

"Eleanor!" Bianca nearly spilled her cocktail in surprise. "What in the world?"

The housekeeper stared with wide eyes at the dark circle of light appearing midair just inside the double doors. Cheyenne whirled to see the conjured portal opening even wider, then Corian stepped through into Bianca Summerlin's house.

The halfling's mother leaped to her feet, her tall bloody Mary glass clenched tightly in one hand, which she extended out to the side as if to keep the suddenly-appearing nightstalker away from her drink. "What is *that*?"

Shit.

Cheyenne leaped forward, giving Eleanor's shoulders a brief, gentle squeeze as she passed the woman. "I got it, Mom. It's fine."

"Wait." Corian stared with glowing silver eyes at Bianca Summerlin, the tufted points of his ears twitching in confusion.

"Out." Cheyenne pointed into the second-floor hallway as she stormed toward him.

The nightstalker blinked rapidly and shook his head before finding the presence of mind to cast an illusion spell. The feline features of his face flashed briefly before shifting into those of a human man with blond hair and a slight flush creeping up the sides of his neck.

"Cheyenne," Bianca warned, not moving as she stared at Corian, the cat-man who'd just appeared out of thin air in her breakfast room.

"I'll take care of it. Be right back." The halfling shoved Corian backward out of the room, spinning him before pushing him farther into the hall.

He kept trying to steal glances over his shoulder at her mom, who glared at him, one eye twitching until Cheyenne pulled the French doors closed behind her.

"What were you *thinking*? You can't just open a portal wherever you want. Especially not in *this* house."

The nightstalker snorted and shook his head, unable to wipe the surprised smile off his human-looking lips. "Good to see you too, kid. I got your text."

CHAPTER TWO

"That was seriously delayed." Cheyenne folded her arms and raised an eyebrow. "I texted you almost twelve hours ago."

"What can I say? I was busy following that name."

"Did it lead to a person?"

"Oh, yeah. And then some." The fiery light of triumph glinted behind the nightstalker's eyes, even through his illusion. "And I stopped by your apartment. You did it, Cheyenne."

The halfling's eyes widened when Corian withdrew her drow legacy box from behind his back. The runes glowed with a soft golden light all over the copper surface, every layer locked into place and now forming a much larger pattern of runes she still didn't understand.

"I did it," she muttered, staring at the lockbox.

"My guess is your run-in last night with those things from the in-between did the rest of the work for you."

Cheyenne's fingers tingled with warm energy when she took the *Cuil Ani* from her mentor's hands. "So, all it took was for me to almost die fighting off those things on my own. Good to know."

Corian snorted. "Open it."

"Are you crazy?" The halfling shot a quick, cautious glance over her shoulder at the closed French doors and lowered her voice. "I can't open this here. One Border portal and a team of FRoE agents in her

6

backyard is about all the magic my mom can handle. You pushed her tolerance over the edge when you popped in unannounced like that."

"I didn't know she was there. I was looking for *you*."

"Obviously." She brushed her fingers over the locked layers of the puzzle box and nodded. "I need to go clear up that mess first."

"What mess?"

"Hey, when Bianca Summerlin stands from her chair and shouts in surprise at the first nightstalker she's ever seen, there's a mess." Cheyenne tapped her temple. "It's all up here, but that makes it even more important to deal with it as soon as possible. And then I have to take Ember home and make sure she's good before I start running around opening drow legacy boxes."

"That's your friend?" When the halfling nodded, Corian's human-looking nose twitched in a very catlike way. "Smells like fae in that room."

"Well, there's nothing wrong with your sense of smell." She glanced at the closed doors again. "You really need to go. I'll call you when I'm back at my apartment."

He flashed her an oddly feral grin for his human illusion and nodded. "You'd better. And hurry, kid. The real work begins now, and L'zar will want to know as soon as possible."

"Yeah, he visited me last night in my head." Cheyenne's lips twitched into a smirk. "He's not very happy with you for going off on your own little mission, by the way. Apparently, you're supposed to be my babysitter."

"Very funny." The nightstalker's fingers worked in a quick series of precise patterns, and the dark circle of a new portal opened in front of him. "Call me as soon as you can."

"Yep."

Corian glanced at the *Cuil Aní* in Cheyenne's hands one more time, then stepped through the portal back to wherever he'd come from. After the circle of dark light disappeared with a soft pop, Cheyenne darted into her childhood bedroom and tossed the activated lockbox on her unmade bed.

Last thing Mom needs to see is the one thing L'zar left her that night besides me.

She quickly returned to the breakfast room, knocked lightly on the doors, and turned both handles to push them swiftly open again. "All taken care of. Sorry about that."

Bianca and Eleanor had both sat down again in the cream armchairs. Bianca's long, calm inhale sounded particularly loud in the silent breakfast room. "I accept your apology, Cheyenne. And I expect that little mishap to be the first and last of its kind."

"It will be, Mom. I promise. It shouldn't have happened in the first place."

"I should think not."

Cheyenne pressed her lips together and met Ember's gaze when the fae girl looked over her shoulder. *I left Ember right in the thick of Mom's rage. Time to get out of here.*

"You ready to head out?"

Ember gave her a thin smile and rolled her wheelchair back before turning around smoothly. "Ready when you are."

"Yeah, I think it's time. I'm gonna go check in with those agents outside, then we'll head home."

"Sounds good." Ember glanced at Bianca, who stared straight ahead through the curving wall of windows. "Thank you for inviting me up here, Bianca. And for your hospitality."

The woman of the house didn't move an inch. Ember glanced at Eleanor, who gave her a sympathetic smile. When the fae looked at Cheyenne, the halfling nodded toward the open doors.

The second Ember started to wheel forward again in her chair, Bianca's hand shot out and settled lightly and briefly on the fae girl's forearm. Ember stopped to look at Cheyenne's mom with wide eyes.

"You are always welcome here, Ember. That's not an invitation I hand out lightly."

"Thank you."

Bianca extended her hand, which Ember took after a second's hesitation. "It was a pleasure to meet you."

"You too. Thanks again." As soon as Bianca released her hand, Ember wheeled forward again.

Eleanor stood from her chair. "I'll see you out."

They got to the open doors together before Bianca called after them without moving from her chair. "Eleanor, please bring up some tea. A strong Earl Grey, if you don't mind."

"Of course." The housekeeper turned and dipped her head, even though Bianca couldn't see it. Then she ushered Cheyenne and Ember out into the hall and closed the French doors softly behind her. "Not one of our better mornings."

Cheyenne raised her eyebrows. "I noticed. Mind if I take the wheel, Em?"

"Take all of them." The girls shared amused glances, then Cheyenne grabbed the wheelchair's handlebars. She sucked in a sharp breath and glanced at the puncture wounds in her palms. *I need to start keeping that darktongue salve on me all the time.* Gritting her teeth against the sting, she pushed Ember toward her room.

"I'll meet you down there," Eleanor said as she headed down the wide, sweeping staircase to the main floor.

"Thanks, Eleanor."

The woman waved her off with a noncommittal hum, then Cheyenne stopped outside her room and darted inside to grab the legacy box. She took a quick look at the unmade bed, tucked the box under her arm, and made the bed in less than thirty seconds with a quick shake of the comforter and a re-propping of pillows. When she returned to the open hallway of the second floor, Ember shot her a small, knowing smile.

"What?" Cheyenne shrugged. "It was bred into me, all right?"

"I didn't say anything."

"You didn't have to." The halfling grabbed the box from under her arm and dropped it in her friend's lap. "Will you hold onto that for me? I need my hands."

Ember stared at the *Cuil Ani* as Cheyenne wheeled her toward the Chez Summerlin elevator. "This looks different."

"That's because it is."

"*Did* you?"

"Yep. Apparently, this halfling's all grown up and ready to claim her legacy, whatever that means." Cheyenne pushed the single call button on the wall beside the elevator. "As soon as we're home, I'm heading off with Corian to open this thing and figure out what the heck that legacy is."

The door opened slowly, and the halfling wheeled her friend inside before punching the button to take them down.

"You should open it now."

"I really shouldn't." Cheyenne snorted. "Whatever's in there was meant just for me. Obviously. There's already been enough craziness in this house for one visit, and if that box starts up its weird light show and who knows what else, I don't want you, Eleanor, or my mom anywhere near it."

Ember removed her hands from the box and raised them in front of her chest.

"Relax. I'm pretty sure it won't do anything until I open it."

"Yeah, that's reassuring."

The elevator shuddered a little when it reached the ground floor, then Cheyenne pulled Ember out and into the industrial-sized kitchen. Eleanor stood at the stove over a boiling kettle of water and gave the girls a brief, distracted smile over her shoulder. "I'll be right there. Just making the tea."

"No problem. We're not out of here just yet." Cheyenne took them along the side of the kitchen and out the swinging doors into the open hall that ran down the side of the house. "Okay. You got it from here?"

"Still working on super-tight spaces." Ember grabbed the wheels of her chair and nodded. "There aren't a lot of those here."

"Good. I'll be right back." Heading toward the front door, Cheyenne turned back and pointed at her friend's lap. "Don't lose that box. Kind of important."

Ember's eyes widened, and she stared at the drow legacy box in her lap as the halfling slipped out and closed the door swiftly behind her.

Cheyenne stopped for a moment to take a deep breath of the fresh morning air, then shook her head. *It's too early for a heaping helping of FRoE attitude.*

She jogged down the wide, curved stone steps at the entrance to the house, then headed around the garden and down the other set of stairs toward the backyard. When she stalked out from beneath the jutting balcony of the veranda, she could feel her mom's gaze shifting to fall on her. Cheyenne didn't turn around or look up. *Give her enough time, and she'll get over it—as long as these guys do their job and keep her safe.*

Rhynehart and his team were up and ready for duty, though some of them still sat in the grass, nursing their tin cups of instant coffee. The portable camping stove or whatever they'd used had been put away already. *Wouldn't put it past one of these guys to light up a ball of fire in their hand and use that instead.*

"How's it going out here?"

Rhynehart turned from glaring at the currently inactive portal ridge to glaring at her. "Good morning to you too."

"It's not, really. I just want to make sure it's not about to get any worse."

He gestured toward the black columns of jagged, glistening black stone that cut a straight line from the little FRoE camp to the forest. "Kind of impossible, don't you think?"

"As long as you and your guys keep back whatever else might come through this thing so it doesn't get to the house or my mom, I'll count that as not getting worse."

"Well, you can make your report, then, halfling." Rhynehart raised an eyebrow. "This thing's been as silent as the grave since we got here."

Cheyenne looked up at the top of the stone pillars. "No flashing lights?"

"Nope."

"Okay. That doesn't mean it won't still happen."

"Kid, I know what a portal is, at least the kind I'm used to regulating on the reservations. What I don't know is how the hell this thing got *here*."

The halfling shook her head. "I really wish I had an answer for you."

Rhynehart turned again to study her longer than two seconds. His scowl remained, but his irritated glare had softened into understanding. "We'll hold out here until we get the order to pack up and ship out. I have a feeling that won't be for a while."

"Yeah, me too." Cheyenne studied the portal ridge one more time, then met the man's gaze and nodded. "Thanks for being here."

"It's my job. Otherwise, I wouldn't be."

"Right. I know." She nodded at the agents scattered behind their team leader. Some of them looked up to meet her gaze with a brief nod. Most of them minded their own damn business. "Call me if anything changes. And I know you have my personal number, so don't bother asking about that dinosaur phone you guys gave me."

Rhynehart smirked. "If anything happens up here, you'll be the first to know. After I make the calls I gotta make to *keep* my job. Orders and all that."

"Sure." The halfling turned to head across the lawn, paused, and glanced at him one more time. "Good luck."

"Yep." Rhynehart shifted his folded arms and sniffed, gazing at the portal ridge.

With a quick nod, Cheyenne stalked back toward the house. Her gaze flickered briefly to the wide wall of windows on the second floor that curved in the same line as the extended veranda below. The morning sun glinted off the windows, so she couldn't see anything in the breakfast room.

But she's watching. That's what she does. Watches and waits, only this time, she won't be able to do anything if something happens. That's a first.

The halfling hurried under the veranda and around the side of the house to jog back up the steps. *If I play this right, Mom won't have to lift a finger.*

CHAPTER THREE

"All right. Let's get outta here." Cheyenne left the front door open a crack.

Ember shrugged. "I'm just waitin' for my chauffeur."

"Very funny."

Eleanor hurried back down the staircase, her face flushed. "I wasn't about to let you two slip away without saying goodbye."

Cheyenne stepped willingly into the woman's open arms, anticipating the crushing hug Eleanor never failed to give. The housekeeper's arms closed gently around the halfling instead as she murmured into Cheyenne's ear, "She loves you and only wants what's best for you."

"I know." The halfling hugged Eleanor back and smiled when the woman pulled away and held her at arm's length.

"It's been very good to see you so much lately. This should happen more." Eleanor's smile disappeared, and she blinked quickly before letting out a tiny, choked-off laugh. "Not *exactly* like this, of course. I'm not sure how much more she can take before I'm cleaning up shattered glass off the floor of every room."

"You've got plastic tumblers still, right?"

The housekeeper chuckled. "Yes, Bianca Summerlin drinking cocktails from a plastic tumbler. When that happens, be ready for the world to end."

For some reason, the words made Cheyenne's insides squirm. She covered it with a tight smile. *The world's not ending. Not this one.*

"Thanks for everything, Eleanor. As always."

"I wouldn't have it any other way." The woman patted Cheyenne's cheek, then turned toward Ember with an even warmer smile. "It was so nice to finally meet you, Ember. I know it's already been said, but I'm allowed to make my own invitations. Any time you want to come back, you just make Cheyenne drive you right up here, got it?"

Ember laughed and accepted Eleanor's hug as the housekeeper bent over to wrap her arms around the fae girl. "Thank you. I had a great time."

Eleanor raised an eyebrow as she straightened and patted her gray hair back into place.

"Yeah, even with everything that happened," Ember added. "It's good to get out."

"I've been saying that to the woman up there for twenty years. Maybe she'll listen if she hears it from someone else." The housekeeper winked, then turned to head back up the stairs. "You drive safely, do you hear me? None of that reckless fast-car nonsense."

Cheyenne walked backward toward the door, spreading her arms. "Can't make any promises."

"Oh, get out of here." Chuckling, Eleanor went up the steps.

The halfling held the door open for her friend, and Ember wheeled herself to the threshold before pausing.

"You want me to help?"

"Nope." Ember tightened her grip on the wheels. "Let me try."

"Sure."

The wheelchair rolled back an inch, then Ember lurched forward and pushed herself out onto the landing. The wheels caught for a split second on the metal liner of the doorway, and she tipped forward before pale violet light flashed around the wheels of her chair. She hovered two inches off the ground and slowly lowered to the stone landing, her knuckles white around the rims.

"You still got it." Cheyenne stepped outside and shut the door behind her. "I don't think it's going anywhere."

"Just had to check." Ember grinned. "This is wild."

"I have a feeling it's gonna get wilder." The halfling stopped at the edge of the first step, folded her arms, and considered the wide, curving stairs in front of them. "What about now?"

"Yeah, definitely." Ember nodded quickly and pulled the drow lockbox farther into her lap. "I'm not going to try to conquer a whole staircase."

Chuckling, Cheyenne grabbed the chair's handlebars and spun her friend around before tilting her back onto two wheels. "It's more like half a staircase, but I get what you mean."

They moved down the steps as gently as possible. When the halfling's black Vans crunched on the gravel, she kept pulling back to get Ember to the passenger side of her brand-new Porsche.

"Easier to go down than up, isn't it?"

"Was that supposed to have some kind of double meaning?"

"I'm talking about stairs, Em." Smirking, Cheyenne opened the passenger-side door and helped her friend transfer into the seat with a practiced ease they'd nailed down over the last few days. Then she folded the chair and took it to the trunk before sliding into the driver's seat. The engine started with a push of the button. "So, that was my mom and my home life, packed neatly into fifteen hours."

"I like her." Ember shrugged. "Even with the giant rocks sticking up out of the ground and you fighting off monster things."

"Well, that part was new."

"Still. Your mom's incredible. I don't know anyone else who'd just stand there and watch all that while sipping a drink."

Cheyenne laughed and buckled her seatbelt. "She tried to hide it, but I saw her sneak a few swigs here and there."

"Can't blame her."

"For knocking back booze like she was?" The halfling shifted into drive and took off slowly around the huge gravel circle in front of the house. "No. Can't blame her for that." *For other things, but who's keeping score?*

She drove down the long gravel drive and the gentle incline down the hillside away from Bianca Summerlin's estate. After everything that had happened in the last fifteen hours, silence was definitely golden. Neither of them said a word until Cheyenne turned onto the frontage road that would lead them out of Henry County, Virginia and back toward Richmond.

"So." Ember cleared her throat and stared at the puzzle box in her lap. "That guy back there who showed up out of nowhere."

"Never seen a nightstalker before, huh?"

The fae's eyes widened. "That was Corian?"

"That was Corian." The halfling let out a long, slow breath. "His timing's bad about fifty percent of the time. He's basically saving my ass the other half."

"And he brought you this box?"

"Yep. Said the breakfast room smelled like fae, too, so now he knows who you are."

"Oh, jeeze." Ember rolled her eyes. "It's always the smell."

"Hey, for me, it was the ears." Cheyenne flicked her High Voltage Raven Black-dyed hair and shook her head. "Glad I don't have to worry about that anymore."

"Not when you're wearing that thing, huh?" The fae nodded at the Heart of Midnight pendant around Cheyenne's neck, the thin silver chain studded with retied knots.

"Oh, that. I was thinking more along the lines of having a lot more control over what I look like these days, but yeah. This thing's about worn out anyway."

"I've got plenty of chains if you need a new one."

"No, I meant the pendant. Apparently, it has a shelf life. But I'm pretty sure—" The buzzing phone in her back pocket cut her off, and she shifted to pull it out before glaring at the screen. "Brace yourself. This might get weird."

"Who is it?"

"Sir himself." Cheyenne rolled her eyes and accepted the call.

"Where the *fuck* is he, halfling?"

She pulled the phone emitting the shouting voice away from her ear and shot a quick glance at it. "If you mean Rhynehart, he's still at my mom's. Where you ordered him to be."

"Rhynehart? I'm not talking about Rhynehart!" Sir barely turned away from his phone to let out a stream of profanities. Ember looked at Cheyenne with raised brows, and the halfling shrugged. "I got a call from Chateau D'rahl this morning. L'zar Verdys pulled his second disappearing act in the last twenty-two years. Know anything about it?"

Shit. She scowled at the road. "No, I don't know anything about it. I'm not his keeper."

"You're his goddamn daughter, Cheyenne. I want to know where that lunatic drow is. Besides the guards on Alpha Block with cat shit for brains, you're the last person who talked to him."

"I have no idea where he is. Remember that giant *opening* that showed up out of nowhere at my mom's house? That's where my focus has been lately."

"Well, re-focus!" Sir let out a deep growl. "I want to see your number on my screen the first time you catch a reeking whiff of that sono-fabitch. You hear me?"

"Kinda hard not to when you're shouting."

"Figure it out." There was a loud slam and a click, then the line went dead.

Cheyenne pressed her lips together and tossed her phone into the cubby under the dashboard.

Ember eyed her warily. "I'd ask what that was about, but I heard the whole thing."

"Yeah, the dude's got serious anger issues. L'zar's out."

"Why?" The fae cocked her head in consideration. "I mean, besides the obvious part about not wanting to spend any more time behind bars, but wasn't he supposed to be protecting you from something by staying *in* the prison?"

"That's what I thought." Cheyenne swallowed. "But I passed the drow trials. That means I'm not another dead drow kid he's trying to groom for his rebellion, so the prophecy's been blasted to smithereens."

A dark-gray blur streaked with white darted down the road toward them. It passed so close to the Panamera that it knocked the back end sideways.

"Shit!" The car fishtailed on the narrow frontage road, and Cheyenne jerked her foot off the pedal, rocking the steering wheel back and forth to correct the swerve. She got the thing straightened out in seconds and glanced into the rearview mirror. "What the hell's going on?"

"Woah." Ember pushed down on the seat with one hand and braced herself against the window with the other.

"You okay?"

The fae had gone white, and she heaved a shaky breath. "We almost went off the road."

"But we didn't."

The streaking blur backtracked and whizzed past Cheyenne's window before stopping two yards in front of the car. The halfling slammed on the brakes in a spray of gravel and fine dust, rocking her and Ember forward against their seatbelts. The second she recognized L'zar Verdys standing in the middle of the road, his white hair strewn wildly around his grinning face, Cheyenne slammed her palm on the horn and counted to five.

He didn't flinch.

She dropped her hand into her lap and shifted into park. "What the fuck?"

Ember's mouth worked silently until she found her voice. "Who's that?"

"Our escaped convict."

The fae whipped her head toward Cheyenne and whispered, *"That's L'zar?"*

The drow in question tossed his hair out of his eyes and stepped calmly toward the driver's side window. Cheyenne glared at him until he rapped gently on the glass with the back of his hand, then slowly rolled the window down. "What are you doing?"

L'zar ducked his head to peer at his daughter and her friend in the passenger seat. "Looking for you. That's fairly obvious. It took me forever to track you down, Cheyenne. Take off that damn pendant, will you?"

Can't argue with an order straight from the top, can I?

Without breaking her father's gaze, the halfling jerked the chain around her neck, which broke as easily as ever, and tossed the whole thing into the cubby with her phone. "Why were you tracking me?"

The drow sniffed the air delicately and peered around his daughter at Ember. "Your car smells like fae."

"L'zar!"

"Oh, come on. Aren't you going to introduce us?"

"No. You're standing outside my car in a prison uniform looking like a full-on drow for everyone to see. What are you doing?"

"I came to help you. Which you're going to need more than ever from here on out." His gaze fell on the copper rune-studded legacy box in Ember's lap, and those glowing golden eyes widened. "You did it."

"Yeah, I did it. Trials completed and passed with flying colors, just like saving my own life. You can't *be* here."

L'zar blinked, his grin widening, and slowly lifted his gaze from the box to his daughter's face. "I'm pretty sure I've just proven I can be wherever I want, Cheyenne."

"Are you *trying* to get locked up again? No, don't answer that. I got off the phone with the FRoE's head honcho two minutes ago. They're pissed that you're out again."

"Naturally."

"And they think I know where you are."

"What did you tell them?"

Cheyenne gave an exasperated grimace. "The truth, which was different two minutes ago. I'm sure they have a whole team of freshly geared operatives just itching to find you. So far, you're making it really easy."

"That's fine." L'zar glanced at the legacy box one more time, and his grin widened. "We'll just go back to your place."

"*No!* That's the first place they'll look for you. It's not a secret anymore that I'm your daughter."

"Have you opened it yet?"

"Seriously, enough with the box."

His long, slender slate-gray fingers clamped down on the open window as he leaned closer. "Have you?"

"Not yet. I'm smart enough to save that for somewhere private and safe. Which apparently you've forgotten all about."

"I want to be there when you do."

Cheyenne shrugged. "Fine. I'm calling Corian when I get home, and we'll deal with it then. You should go find *him* and get out of the open before you bring down a whole bunch of shit I don't need on both our heads."

L'zar didn't move, so the halfling slipped her finger under the automatic window button and rolled it up. The corner of the drow's grinning mouth twitched as he stared at Cheyenne with wide eyes. A tiny bit of pressure from his hands stopped the window with a mechanical whine.

Cheyenne jerked her hand off the button and gritted her teeth. The next second, her pale skin and dyed-black hair were replaced by the purple-gray flesh and bone-white locks she shared with her drow father, and a burst of violet sparks erupted from her fingers and crackled across L'zar's hands. He withdrew them slowly from the window, chuckling as he took a step back from the car.

"Go find Corian," Cheyenne said as she rolled up the window. "He's probably at the warehouse. I'll find *you* when I'm ready."

The window slid into place, and the drow convict smiled. "I can't wait."

Shaking her head, Cheyenne shifted into drive with a quick jerk and took off down the frontage road toward Richmond.

"Holy shit." Ember swallowed and glanced at the legacy box in her lap. "And I thought *I* had dad issues."

"It's all relative, right?"

Ember barked a laugh as Cheyenne reached for her phone and pulled up Corian's number. He answered on the second ring.

"That was fast."

"I'm not back yet. Just called to give you a heads up. I'm not the drow who needs a babysitter. You've got an old friend heading to the warehouse right now, FYI."

"He's out?"

"No, Corian. Chateau D'rahl's taking him on a field trip on account of his good behavior."

The nightstalker growled into the phone, "What an idiot."

"Took the words right out of my mouth."

Corian's sharp laughter made her pull her phone away. "He just couldn't wait any longer, could he? Damn. Don't forget to call me when you're ready to join the party, kid."

"That would be impossible. I'll be home in less than an hour."

"Good." Another laugh burst through the line, then Corian hung up on her without another word.

Cheyenne tossed her phone back into the cubby and shook her head. "Here we go."

CHAPTER FOUR

Cheyenne opened the front door to the loft apartment she and Ember shared and stepped inside to hold it while Ember wheeled herself through. "Sorry I have to bail right back outta here."

"You're not bailing." Ember picked up the legacy box and held it out toward the halfling with a smirk. "It's your destiny or whatever."

"Ha." Cheyenne took the box and turned it over, studying the bigger symbols created from all the tiny runes now locked into their correct positions. "It better have more for me than a crazy-ass drow and a bunch of pissed-off FRoE on my heels."

"Fingers crossed."

The girls shared a wry laugh, and Cheyenne set the box down on the armrest of the couch before heading into her room. She pulled off her shirt and took a quick whiff. *A shower. Tonight. That's final.*

Her pants dropped on the floor, then she headed toward the glistening black dresser with the silver skulls for knobs on the drawers and rifled through her clothes. She picked a maroon shirt with black fishnet from chest to collar and black skinny jeans. Cheyenne tugged it all on, then shrugged and crossed the room.

The brown glass jar of Yadje's healing salve was right where she'd left it in her backpack on the floor, and she twisted off the lid before taking a tentative sniff. *Smells awful. Hurts even worse.*

She dipped a finger into the pale, taffy-like salve, twirled it around to get rid of the stringiness, then set the jar down on her black velvet comforter. Grimacing, the halfling smeared a bit of darktongue goo on the palm of one hand and grunted. The grunt turned into a growl as the salve did its work, burning through her hand and bringing tears to her eyes as it sealed the fresh wound from the inside out.

"You okay?"

"Just healing myself," the halfling shouted into the living room. "No big deal."

Ember's wheelchair rolled with a soft rumble across the floor and she stopped outside Cheyenne's bedroom. "Healing yourself?"

The halfling nodded toward the jar on the bed. "Free salve from a friend. Apparently, people pay with their own organs or something just to get this much." She lifted her goo-tipped finger with a shrug, wiped it off on her other hand, and smeared the rest of it over the hole in her other palm. "Oh, dammit."

The fae chuckled. "No pain, no gain, right?"

Cheyenne whirled around to shoot her friend an exasperated glance. "The last time someone told me that, I was barely conscious and strapped to a hospital bed that wasn't anywhere near a hospital with handcuffs that turned off my magic."

Ember wrinkled her nose. "Trigger identified."

With a snort, the halfling looked down at her puncture-free hands, then grabbed the jar and screwed the lid back on tight. "A blast from the past. Trust me, you could call me every derogatory term in the book, and it wouldn't sound as stupid as when Sir says, 'Good work, halfling.'" The accuracy of her impersonation made her laugh, then she shrugged back into her black jacket, grabbed her backpack, shoved the salve back into the bottom, and nodded at the living room.

With a raised eyebrow, Ember wheeled backward out of the doorway, and Cheyenne closed the door behind her. "Time to open that box, I guess."

"Let me know how *that* goes."

The halfling looked over her shoulder at her friend as she headed for the puzzle box on the couch. "Don't I always?"

"Doesn't mean I'm any less curious about whatever special prize is in there."

The *Cuil Aní* joined the darktongue salve at the bottom of her pack, then she zipped it up and slipped the straps over her shoulders. "I wouldn't be surprised if it was a bomb or something. One last test, right? If L'zar's halfling kid can walk through fire and magical shrapnel, *then* we'll know she's ready."

Ember let out a laugh. "You'll be fine."

"I know. I just wanna get this over with." Cheyenne headed to the door and paused. "You good here, Em? Like, we have food and stuff?"

"Hey, the fae who's getting her magic back doesn't need a babysitter either." Ember pointed at the door. "Get out."

"Yeah, okay. Call me if anything weird happens, huh? Just in case."

"Seriously, leave."

Smirking, the halfling slipped out the door, closed it behind her, and pulled her phone out of her back pocket as she headed down the hall toward the elevator. *I can't remember the last time I talked this much on the phone in one day.*

Corian picked up as the elevator doors opened. "You ready?"

"Yeah. I'm heading down to my car right now. You guys all at the warehouse?" The doors closed, and the halfling heard muffled laughter in the background. "Corian?"

The line went dead, and she stared at her phone. *Everyone's crazy today.*

A dark circle of light bloomed in the air in front of her. The next second, Corian's feral grin greeted her. His hand snaked out to snatch her wrist, and he tugged her through the portal and into Persh'al's warehouse in DC.

Staggering forward, Cheyenne jerked her wrist out of his grip and glanced behind her. The portal was gone. "Come on, man. Seriously?"

"I know you like your car and everything, kid." The nightstalker chuckled and folded his arms. "But this is one of those things that really can't wait."

"Yeah, I get that part." The halfling glanced around and found Persh'al, Byrd, Lumil, and L'zar gathered in front of Persh'al's tables of computers, all of them grinning at her like insane magicals.

"Right on, kid." Byrd slow clapped until Lumil slapped his hands down and shook her head.

"Uh, thanks?"

23

"The trials, Cheyenne." Lumil folded her arms and nodded, the dark scar encircling her green neck glinting in the warehouse lights as she pursed her lips through a smile. "We weren't sure you'd get there."

"I was." L'zar had changed into someone's loose black pants and gray button-down shirt, probably Persh'al's. The pant legs were a little short.

Persh'al scoffed. "Oh, yeah? So sure that you played drow prisoner for twenty years longer than you had to?"

L'zar glanced at his friend and raised an eyebrow. "I knew the second she came to see me in *the Dungeon*." The drow's eyes widened as he mocked Chateau D'rahl's best attempt at a high-security visitation room.

Cheyenne slipped her pack off her shoulders and headed across the warehouse to set it on the table. She stopped when she saw the magical with cracked silver skin like scales tied to one of the rolling desk chairs with yards of tightly woven nylon rope. His hands were bound behind his back with a magical zip-tie pulsing with electric blue light, and his face was scraped, bloody, and grotesquely swollen. She could see that much, even with his chin dropped to his chest. "Who's that?"

"Huh?" Persh'al looked up at their scaly prisoner strapped to the chair and shrugged.

"Forget about the magical beneath the ropes, kid." Corian nodded at Lumil, who jumped to attention and took off to wheel the unconscious lizard-looking guy across the warehouse toward what turned out to be a dark supply closet. The chair's wheels squeaked with every rotation until the goblin woman shoved the magical into the closet and pulled the door shut with a bang.

She dusted off her hands and marched back to the group with a satisfied nod.

Cheyenne stared at the closet door, then slowly turned toward Corian. "Is that the guy with all the O'gúl tech?"

"We can talk about that later." L'zar clasped his hands behind his back and stepped forward. "I want to watch you open the *Cuil Aní*."

The eyes centered on her made Cheyenne's skin itch. She cast them all a dubious glance, then finished her trip toward the table and set her backpack down. "Any way you guys can make this a little less creepy?"

No one said a word.

"Okay." She unzipped her backpack and slowly drew out the legacy box, all of its thinly carved runes now glowing with a bright inner light.

Persh'al sucked in a sharp breath, the box's light casting a dazzling reflection in his yellow eyes. Byrd's mouth fell open, and Lumil didn't bother to elbow him in the ribs to shut it.

Turning the box over in her hands, Cheyenne shrugged. "It's not like this thing has a latch or anything."

L'zar cleared his throat. "*Palimé.*"

"What, now?" The halfling raised her eyebrows.

"That's how it opens, Cheyenne. That word from your lips." L'zar's eyebrows jerked up and back down again as he dipped his head. "Do it."

The halfling scanned the five magicals watching her like a pack of starving wolves before returning her focus to the drow legacy box. *Here goes nothing.*

"*Palimé.*"

The *Cuil Ani* warmed quickly in her hand, though it didn't get too hot for her to hold this time. The glowing runes emitted a brilliant flash of gold light, then the whirring mechanisms inside clicked and whined, moving faster and faster.

Seriously, if this is a bomb, I'm throwing it at L'zar.

The sliding layers forming the top of the box pulled away from each other to jut over the outside, and after they'd separated, Cheyenne blinked at the thing inside.

"What is it?" Lumil whispered.

The halfling glanced at the goblin woman, then reached into the legacy box and picked up the large gold coin lying on the bottom. She lifted it and cocked her head as she lowered the puzzle box to her side. "A coin?"

L'zar's wild, predatory grin returned. "*Yes.*"

She waved it in a small circle. "This is ridiculously anticlimactic."

"Only until you know what that coin is for."

The warehouse fell silent. Cheyenne dropped the coin back into the box and set it down on the table beside her backpack. "So, what does this drow coin buy me?"

L'zar chuckled and exchanged glances with Corian. "It's not just a coin, Cheyenne. That is the next step in claiming your legacy."

"I thought the thing inside the box *was* my legacy."

"Part of it, sure." The escaped drow convict drew his fingers through his bone-white hair and inhaled deeply through his nose. "The *Cuil Aní* is just a guide through your trials. That coin, your *marandúr*, is the token of your legacy. Normally this would be done in Ambar'ogúl, where you'd present it to the Crown and assume your station as a fully dedicated drow."

"Ha." Cheyenne glanced at the coin. "Looks like we're out of luck with that one. No way is that gonna happen."

L'zar's golden eyes blazed. "Oh, but it is."

CHAPTER FIVE

"What?" Cheyenne glanced at the other magicals gathered around her and pointed at her drow father. "Someone needs to tell this guy he's lost his mind."

Corian dipped his head. "Just listen."

"In order for you to claim your true power and what's rightfully yours by birth, Cheyenne, that *marandúr* must be placed in the Rahalma altar in the courtyard of the Crown's fortress." L'zar steepled his fingers and pointed them at her. "And you're the only person in either world who can do that."

"No. Sorry."

Lumil grimaced. Persh'al rubbed his bald, orange-speckled head beside the neon-orange mohawk sprouting out of it. Byrd turned toward his fist and forced out an uncomfortable cough.

"It isn't something you can turn down." L'zar's smile faded, but the intensity of his gaze on the half-drow remained. "You don't have a choice."

"Right. Because the Crown *wants* me to claim this new legacy."

"It's the same legacy, Cheyenne."

"Whatever. The drow in power over there has been sending magical nutjobs after me for weeks to stop me from completing the trials." The halfling folded her arms and shook her head. "You're right. I don't have a choice, 'cause no way in hell is she gonna let me just waltz into her fancy castle and stick a coin on some whatever-it's-called."

"The Rahalma. The drow altar."

"Sure. You said she has every drow on that side come to *her* to pass their trials, right? I broke the rules by passing mine over here, and she knows who I am."

"That won't make a difference once you deliver that coin."

Cheyenne glanced at the now-tense magicals surrounding her and blinked. "Did everybody forget about the new portals opening up and the shipments of O'gúl war-machine parts her people have been smuggling over here? Because that seems a hell of a lot more important than me dropping a coin on an altar."

The corners of L'zar's mouth twitched as he stared at her.

Oh, he's pissed now, huh? Join the club.

"Cheyenne." Corian's low voice cut through the tension. "Those two things aren't mutually exclusive. We'll deal with the portal issue as we can, and we're working on the war-machine issue." He glanced at the supply closet. "Needless to say, the road to claiming your legacy is gonna be a little bumpy."

"No shit."

"But you taking your *marandúr* into the Crown's seat of power and returning it to where it belongs will do far more for this war than anything we can achieve from over here. If we time it right, it might even stop the devastation before it begins."

"It's already happening." Cheyenne swallowed. "A portal opened in my mom's backyard and brought those things right to her. You said the war's already started."

"That was nothing compared to what's coming."

She frowned at her nightstalker mentor, then glanced quickly at L'zar and had to look away. *That stare is freaking me out.* "I thought the *marandúr* was mine. What do you mean I have to put it back where it belongs?"

Byrd chuckled and spread his arms. "Because you're—"

"Because you're my daughter, Cheyenne," L'zar finished for him. The goblin cocked his head and looked at the floor. "Because the Crown of Ambar'ogúl has dipped itself in pestilence, and I mean to root it out. As my daughter, it falls to you to do the same."

"No." The halfling slowly shook her head, her dark human eyes burning into his golden drow gaze. "I'll help with this war if that's what it comes to, and if taking some coin to an O'gúl altar is how I have to do that, fine. But I'll do it because *I* choose to, not because I'm your daughter."

L'zar's eyes narrowed, and he stepped toward her on long, swift legs before setting a slender hand on her shoulder and giving it a little squeeze. "If that's what you need to tell yourself, I guess it's a good start."

Then he crossed in front of her and headed toward the sunken brown couch that looked like it hadn't been moved or cleaned in decades and flopped down onto it, lifting both legs to sprawl across the cushions.

Cheyenne scowled. *He doesn't know the first thing about me because he doesn't want to.*

When she glanced at Corian, the nightstalker was studying the sprawled L'zar Verdys, who looked like he could have been sleeping if neither of them knew better. Then her mentor met her gaze, frowned, and gave her a curt nod.

"So." Byrd clapped his hands together and rubbed them vigorously. "We getting back to the interrogation, or what?"

"Not when he's passed out like that." Lumil punched the goblin man in the shoulder.

"Oh, right. Like you don't have anything up your sleeve to pound him back to consciousness."

"You know what? Maybe my fists need a break. You ever think of that?"

"No, because you never *give* them a break."

As the goblins bickered, Persh'al turned toward his computer monitor to type furiously while code Cheyenne couldn't read scrolled across the screen.

Corian approached Cheyenne with his hands thrust into his pockets and spared a final glance at L'zar. "This is a big deal for all of us, kid. Especially him. He doesn't show it, but he's proud of you too."

"I didn't come here for anyone's approval."

"I know."

Cheyenne pulled her gaze away from her motionless father and nodded at the *Cuil Aní*. "What is that coin, really?"

"Exactly what we said it is. The old laws still stand, Cheyenne. I know you've heard that so many times, it's probably lost its meaning."

She snorted. "It didn't have any to begin with."

The nightstalker nodded. "It will. But we're not exaggerating when we say you taking your *marandúr* to the Rahalma on the other side will help us protect the humans over here and all the magicals who came Earthside fleeing what's left of Ambar'ogúl. Who knows, you might just have a bigger part to play in liberating the O'gúleesh who chose to stay home. It's hard to predict everything."

"And *I* have to go put that thing on an altar?"

"You and no one else."

The halfling ran a hand through her black hair. "Any plan for how we're gonna pull off something like that?"

Corian smirked. "We're working on it."

"Fine!" Lumil spread her arms and thrust her head toward Byrd, who flinched away from her aggressive lunge. "I'll go get the damn traitor and knock his lights back on. But if he starts talking gibberish, that's on you."

The goblin woman stalked across the warehouse, shaking her head.

"Stop." L'zar's one-word command was soft, his eyes still closed, but it held enough power to make Lumil freeze on the other side of the couch. "Let him be for a little longer. Tell me what we got out of him so far."

"Right." Lumil cleared her throat and tugged down the bottom of her jacket. "That asshole's been smuggling O'gúl technology across the Border piece by piece. Best we can figure out, it's been over the last hundred years at least."

"And he's figured out how to make the machine parts work with Earthside tech," Byrd added. "Which is supposed to be, like, impossible."

"Obviously not." Persh'al stood from hunching over his keyboard and turned to face the group. "It's all old-school tech from more than two cycles ago, from looking at what we snagged from that new portal. We already know the new O'gúl tech doesn't make the crossing, so I'm trying to figure out what the exact components are that *do* make it across. I still don't have a clue how that scaly fucker got it all to sync with the dying breed of Earthside relics these humans call *cutting-edge*."

Cheyenne smirked. "Accurate description, honestly."

The blue troll shot her a skeptical look. "You think so?"

"I haven't found a system I can't crack into yet. I might be able to help you if I could read any of that." She pointed at the O'gúleesh code flashing across his screen in white, blue, and green.

Persh'al chuckled. "That's one more thing we don't have time for, kid. And I'll tell you what, I sure as shit don't have the qualifications or the patience to teach anyone how to read O'gúleesh."

"Yeah, I didn't think so."

"We'll figure it out. Just takes a little reverse-engineering and some thinking outside the box." Persh'al thumped his chest with his fist. "But I've been here a hell of a lot longer than that scaly bastard's been smuggling over tiny tech parts in his lizardy boxer shorts. I'm willing to bet my right hand that I know more about Earthside tech than he does."

Lumil snorted. "Aren't you right-handed?"

"Yeah. So?"

"I mean, don't you need that one?"

Byrd sniggered until he stepped back against the table being used as a desk.

Persh'al pointed at him. "Watch it, man."

"Yeah, yeah. My bad."

Cheyenne shook her head and looked at Corian. "So, what do we do now?"

The nightstalker scratched behind his tufted ear. "Well, the first step is to make sure the Crown doesn't find out about L'zar being out. For as long as possible, anyway. We can't keep it a secret forever, and when she *does* find out, she'll double her efforts to take you down however she can."

"Because he found a way around the prophecy, right?"

Corian squinted at her over a slow, knowing smile. "You put those pieces together fast, don't you?"

"When I *have* the pieces? Damn straight, I do."

His nose wrinkled for a split second when she said it, and Cheyenne looked away to give him a minute. *At least he didn't have to break his promise not to give me those pieces.* She glanced at Lumil and Byrd, who'd started bickering again over which one of them had eaten the most Crunchwrap Supremes from their last Taco Bell run. *We've got Thing One and Thing Two to thank for that.*

"And now that she's passed the trials," L'zar said from the couch as if he'd been part of their conversation the whole time, "the Heart of Midnight isn't going to work for shit. She needs protection. That's why I cut my sentence short."

"I still don't get why you thought that was necessary," Cheyenne muttered. "It feels like a bigger risk to have you running around wherever you want and almost tossing nice new cars off the road."

Corian shot her a confused look, and she shook her head.

"I made a call, Cheyenne." L'zar still hadn't opened his eyes, his hands folded behind his head over the armrest. "You passed your trials. That means every O'gúl loyalist will know by the end of the day if they don't already. The Crown wants you, one way or another. Option A is she brings you across and offers you a place in her ranks. Option B is she sends someone to slit your throat and ship your head to her throne in a fancy gift-wrapped box."

"Jesus." The halfling grimaced.

"She's done it before." The drow didn't move. "And she hasn't even sent her worst after you. I need to be here to keep you safe when she does because she will, eventually."

"Well," Cheyenne said, "I mean, I guess I appreciate you wanting to step in and defend me, or whatever. But I don't see how you can protect me all the time when you're supposed to be hidden. And trust me, I get attacked pretty much everywhere these days. Someone's bound to recognize you sooner or later."

"Corian?"

"Yeah."

"Where's the *nalís*?"

"With everything else I own." The nightstalker shot Cheyenne an amused glance and rolled his eyes. "I'll get it."

"Do." L'zar sat up in one swift, fluid movement, his long legs sweeping onto the warehouse floor with an ease that should have been impossible under the circumstances. He leaned forward, propped his forearms on his thighs, and met his daughter's gaze. Then he blew a lock of straight bone-white hair out of his face and wiggled his eyebrows once.

I can't figure it out. He either doesn't give a shit about anything but his next private joke, or he cares about everything so much that it's all the same thing.

She folded her arms and turned away from him to watch Corian. The nightstalker's fingers finished their swift, efficient gestures before a portal opened into the single room of the basement labeled Apartment D. The portal stayed open even after Corian had stepped through, and the magicals in the warehouse watched him rummaging through metal shelving filled with all kinds of junk.

L'zar chuckled. "You've really been living in style, haven't you?"

Corian tossed aside a rolled-up piece of cloth and slid away a box of candles, then reached into a worn boot behind it and pulled out a small, lidded tin. The portal closed swiftly behind him after he stepped back through, and he shot L'zar a cursory glance. "It's a hell of a lot better than a prison cell. I'll tell you that much."

The drow's smile returned, and he lifted his chin, staring at the tin in the nightstalker's hand. "I know magicals who would sell their souls to get into your stash."

"Many have tried." With a raised eyebrow, Corian pulled the lid off the tin and drew out a small pin in the shape of a smooth, round leaf. It was half the size of a dime and glinted under the warehouse's dusty lighting. "This should work."

"Yes, it should." L'zar pushed himself to his feet and approached his daughter and the nightstalker, holding out his palm. Corian dropped the pin neatly into the purple-gray hand, and the drow closed his fingers around whatever it was with a nod. "How are you with spell-work, Cheyenne?"

The seriousness of his question and the fancy air he put on while holding that tiny pin made her burst out laughing. L'zar glanced at Corian, who shook his head with a small shrug.

"What's so funny?"

"Ask Corian." Cheyenne doubled over again, snorting with laughter, and stuck her thumb out toward the nightstalker. "He'll give you a more accurate answer."

Corian clicked his tongue and stared at her until she'd pulled herself back together. Another snicker escaped her and she turned away from him, pressing her fist against her mouth. *I'll lose it if I see his face when he answers that one.*

"Well?" L'zar raised an eyebrow.

The nightstalker tilted his head, turning down the corners of his mouth to keep from chuckling too. "Cheyenne's incredibly proficient with her innate abilities."

"Of course she is. She passed the trials. That's not what I asked."

Corian cleared his throat. "I wouldn't advise her to cast spells if she has a choice." He shook his head.

Cheyenne barked another laugh and stumbled backward, doubling over once more in silent, breathless laughter. Corian snorted, then his low, rumbling chuckle filled the warehouse as he watched her fall into hysterics. He looked back up at the scowling L'zar and shrugged. "Her spellwork's shit."

The drow raised an eyebrow at Cheyenne, who howled again and walked across the warehouse to get away from the conversation. "Then it looks like I finally get to teach her something."

CHAPTER SIX

Cheyenne stared at the leaf-shaped pin in L'zar's open palm. He raised an eyebrow and tossed his head toward his side of the couch. "You can sit a little closer, Cheyenne. I don't bite."

"No, I'm good." She clasped her hands together, unaware that she'd mimicked her father's casual position, forearms propped on her thighs, head sunken a little between her shoulders. "What's that do?"

"This will allow me to get to you quickly no matter where you are if you find yourself in a situation where a little backup would come in useful."

"Assuming I can cast a spell when I need to, right?"

L'zar shook his head. "No. The only spellwork this needs will happen right here. The *nalis* will do the rest."

"So, what? It lights the Drow Signal, and you come racing to my side with your super-speed?"

"It opens a portal on command."

She frowned. "How's that?"

L'zar studied the tiny pin in his palm. "Nightstalker blood in this little trinket, kid. Corian doesn't like it, but it's an old drow trick."

A paper wrapper crinkled loudly in the warehouse, and Cheyenne looked up to see Corian sitting at the corner of Persh'al's table, another of his damn sandwiches raised toward his open mouth. He paused to give her a shrug, then buried his teeth in his mid-morning lunch.

"Nightstalkers are the only magicals who can open portals like he does, aren't they?"

"Inherently, yes." L'zar extended his open palm toward her. "But not for someone who has one of these."

I bet that's how all those skaxen loyalists summoned the portals they thought they could drag me through.

"Okay, so what do I have to do?"

L'zar's thin smile twitched. "The same thing I'm about to do." He switched the *nalís* into his opposite fist, then held his other palm toward her. "Hold my hand."

"Seriously?"

"Don't be a child."

"But hold your hand like a child?"

The drow took a deep breath through his nose, his nostrils flaring as he stared Cheyenne down. "I'll wait."

She glanced at the ceiling and slapped her hand into L'zar's. A flare of the warm, tingling magic she'd felt when he'd healed the black-magic sores in her shoulder raced up her arm and across her back. The halfling stared at her pale hand, clenched in his slate-gray fingers.

L'zar's eyes widened. "There it is." After another deep breath, he closed his other hand around the *nalís* and muttered, "*Abdur orzj.*"

The tingling warmth of their magic buzzed between them again, and he turned toward her to offer the *nalís*. His grip on her fingers didn't budge.

Cheyenne opened her hand to accept the cold, surprisingly heavy metal of the *nalís* pin. She swallowed and stared at the thing. *He's gonna cut off my circulation with that grip.*

"Your turn."

She shot him a playful grimace. "Sorry. What am I supposed to do?"

"Say the incantation."

"Um."

At Persh'al's table, Corian snorted and shook his head, chewing fervently.

"Can you say that one more time?"

L'zar closed his eyes, fighting to maintain his composure. The pressure of his fingers around her hand increased slightly, and the halfling almost laughed through the pain. *Good.* Something *needs to get under his skin.*

"*Abdur orzj,*" he muttered.

"Right. Got it." She curled her fingers around the *nalis* and blew air out through loose lips. "*Abdur orzj.*"

Though he tried to hide it, she caught the quick, precise movements of his free right hand casting some other spell beside his thigh.

"Should I be doing that too?" she asked. "Because, to be honest, the hand gestures pretty much elude me."

L'zar looked at her in surprise. Corian chuckled and bit into his sandwich again. Persh'al spun around in his office chair and folded his arms to watch the show.

With a grunt, the drow released his daughter's hand, his jaw working beneath his slate-gray skin. "Do you enjoy being this irritating?"

Cheyenne grinned. "That's a family trait, isn't it?"

"Ha!" Persh'al's chair lurched forward with the force of his laughter, then he quickly spun back around and started furiously typing on his keyboard.

Corian licked his lips and set the second half of his sandwich back on the wrapper with a crinkling thump. When he wiped his mouth with a hand, Cheyenne was sure it was also meant to wipe off a smile.

"That'll work now." L'zar stood from the couch and headed quickly across the warehouse toward the private office at the opposite end.

"So, no finger spells?"

"No." Before he got halfway across the room, Cheyenne's phone buzzed again in her pocket.

She took it out and closed her eyes when she recognized Sir's number. *Again?*

"Are you going to answer that?" L'zar drawled.

"I don't want to." The halfling declined the call and shoved the phone back into her pocket. "Not while I'm in the same room with any of you, honestly."

"Not offended at all," Persh'al added with a chuckle.

"Who was it?"

Cheyenne looked at L'zar, all traces of his irritation wiped away by insatiable curiosity. "The FRoE official who's gonna give himself an aneurism yelling at me about why *you* left Chateau D'rahl."

"Well." The corner of the drow's mouth twitched upward. "Don't keep him waiting too long. You can keep playing the clueless token half-drow for a bit longer with those idiots. We don't want them getting in the way of what we're trying to do. Just don't tell them where I am." He winked at her, then spun again and marched toward one of the back offices before disappearing inside.

"Yeah. 'Cause I needed a friendly reminder about that one." Cheyenne shook her head and stood from the couch, holding the apparently activated *nalís* in her open palm. "How does this thing work?"

"You've seen *Star Trek*, right?" The nightstalker laughed when she answered with a deadpan stare. "Stick it on your jacket or shirt or wherever. If you need him, just tap it and say his name. Thinking it will work too. The *nalís* won't keep you hidden like the pendant did, so expect a little more action. Only use it if you really have to."

"Great advice." Cheyenne pinned the *nalís* to the hem of her maroon shirt and shrugged. "Here I was, thinking how great it would be to summon L'zar through a portal just for fun."

"All right." Corian slid the open *Cuil Aní* with the *marandúr* into her backpack and handed it to her by the straps. "Go do what you have to do. We'll reach out when we've come up with the next steps, yeah?"

"Sure. Assuming the FRoE doesn't lock me up first, just for being his kid."

"They won't." Corian smiled as she took the pack from him, then cast a new portal behind her. "They need you too much."

"True. Honestly, I'm amazed they realize that." Cheyenne turned halfway toward the portal and nodded at Persh'al. "See ya."

"Later, drow." The blue troll lifted a hand in farewell before turning back to his computer.

"Are the goblins still outside?"

Corian glanced at the warehouse's back door and shrugged. "We made a new rule. If they bitch at each other for longer than a minute, they gotta take it outside."

"Good rule. See ya."

The nightstalker nodded, and Cheyenne stepped through his portal. In the split second it took her to realize he'd ported her right back into the elevator of her apartment building, the portal had closed behind her. "Portal jokes. Awesome."

Her back pocket buzzed again, and as she took it out to glare at Sir's number one more time, the elevator doors opened.

"Oh. Hey, Cheyenne." Matthew Thomas smiled at her from the other side of the doors, his hands thrust deep into the pockets of his navy slacks. "How's it goin'?"

"Swell."

"Do you need to get out?"

"No." She pressed her lips together and lifted her phone, giving it a little shake. "Thought I left my phone until I found it, so we're good. Going down?"

"Yeah." Her neighbor chuckled and stepped into the elevator with her.

Cheyenne leaned against the wall and punched the button for the lobby. The doors closed, and the elevator descended.

"You headed to class?"

She looked at him for a second before staring at the wall over the button panel. "Not today."

"Oh, okay. I just thought, you know, with the backpack?"

"Yeah, it's just a big purse. On my back."

Matthew nodded slowly and stared at the elevator wall on his side. "How's Ember?"

Of course. "She's fine, I guess. You haven't stopped by to ask her yourself?"

"No. Had a full morning of conference calls, and now I'm needed in person for more meetings, apparently."

"About dabbling, right?"

He chuckled again. "Something like that."

The elevator reached the ground floor with a little ding and opened onto the huge lobby of the Pellerville Gables Apartments. Cheyenne gestured for the guy to step out first, and he gave her a crooked smile.

"See ya, neighbor."

She forced herself not to roll her eyes. "Have a good one."

Matthew shot her the winning smile that apparently worked very well on Ember. Not so much on the half-drow.

That guy's got way more going on than he's told either of us. Welcome to the club, I guess.

Cheyenne waited for the elevator doors to close, then her phone buzzed again. With an irritated jerk, she snatched it out of her pocket and accepted Sir's call. "Is somebody dying?"

"Keep ignoring my calls and it might be you, halfling. You need to get down here."

Stepping slowly out of the elevator, Cheyenne glanced around the empty lobby. "What happened?"

"What happened? Are you kidding me right now? L'zar Verdys is on the loose, running around doing only Eleanor Roosevelt knows what, and you're the only goddamn person I know who can make sense of the steaming pile of rhino shit spewing from that bastard's mouth. You're coming in for questioning, and I mean now. If your ass isn't down here in an hour, I'll be knocking on your front door."

"Fine, but you really need to stop with all the yelling."

"If I feel like yelling, Cheyenne, I'll goddamn yell as much as I want to! I've got a fucking drow thorn in my ass, and you're gonna come pull it out for me. Go sob to someone else about your sensitive little halfling ears. I don't have time for that shit." The receiver slammed down and ended the call.

Cheyenne fought the urge to throw her phone across the parking lot the second she stepped out of the lobby and shoved it back into her pocket instead. *Great. I get to go be interrogated by the FRoE's finest raging lunatic. This'll be fun.*

CHAPTER SEVEN

Forty minutes later, Cheyenne parked the Panamera beside the long line of black FRoE Jeeps and vans and utility vehicles at the base. Despite her reasons for having been called here, when she pressed the automatic lock button on the key fob and her car let out that soft, high-pitched chirp, the halfling smirked. *It's the little things.*

She stalked up to the front doors and wasn't surprised to find the lobby empty. When she headed right toward the short hall leading into the common room, someone cleared their throat on her left and made her stop.

Sheila stood there in her full six-foot-ten ogre glory, her mop of yellow hair hanging down between her eyes until she tossed it aside. "This way."

"Right." Cheyenne shot a final glance at the empty hall and the disturbingly quiet common room, then crossed the lobby full of empty cubicles to join her apparent chaperone through the base. "We're not having this meeting in the training room, are we?"

Sheila cast her a sidelong glance and smirked. "He wouldn't last ten seconds in a padded room with you."

"That's what I thought." They headed quickly down the hall, and Cheyenne squinted at the closed doors of the training room when they passed it. *I don't want to get shut up in there again anyway.*

41

The ogre woman led her down more corridors in the huge FRoE compound and past a long row of smaller offices until they stopped at double doors at the end of the hall. "It'll be faster if you just tell them what they want to know."

Cheyenne spread her arms. "I'm an open book."

Sheila glanced at the ceiling before opening both doors at once. She stepped inside and held one door open for Cheyenne to step through while the other one swung closed again beside her. Then the ogre woman took two sharp steps sideways and stood against the wall, her hands clasped behind her back in a way that looked eerily like Rhynehart's go-to stance.

The halfling gazed at the huge conference table that took up most of the room. In it sat four FRoE officials she hadn't met yet, and of course, Sir was there too. He glared up at her, swiping his hand across his salt-and-pepper mustache before sitting back in his chair and folding his arms. "Sit down already so we can get this over with."

The other door closed softly behind her, and she glanced at Sheila. The ogre woman stared straight ahead and didn't move. Without a word, Cheyenne took the empty chair at the head of the table and scanned the faces and hands of the four other officials. *No rings. No masks. They're all human and at the top of the FRoE chain. Here we go.*

A middle-aged woman with long auburn hair pulled back in a tight bun nodded at the halfling. "Thank you for coming, Cheyenne."

Cheyenne glanced at Sir, whose scowl hadn't softened one bit. "No problem."

The woman didn't offer her name or the names of the other officials sitting with them before she grabbed a recording device in the center of the table and slid it toward her. She made a big show of making sure Cheyenne saw the thing, then she pressed a button and folded her hands in her lap.

"Are you aware that this conversation is being recorded?"

The halfling frowned at the device. "Yeah."

"Do you consent to the recording of the conversation we're about to have?"

Glancing at Sir, Cheyenne bit her bottom lip and got comfy in the desk chair. *He's playing everything by the book 'cause it's his ass on the line this time.* "Yeah."

"Thank you. Please state your name."

"Cheyenne Summerlin."

"Tell us what you know about L'zar Verdys."

The halfling smirked but quickly got rid of it. "You're gonna have to be a little more specific."

Sir's fist thumped on the table, garnering disapproving glances from the other officials. He cleared his throat and leaned forward. "You know damn well what we wanna hear."

Cheyenne met his gaze and stared the man down. "I know he's my father, and I know he's been a prisoner at Chateau D'rahl for the last, I don't know, fifty years?"

The woman questioning her looked slowly from Sir to Cheyenne. "Seventy-five, to be exact. His sentence was for one hundred years on Cell Block Alpha. Are you aware that L'zar Verdys, also identified as Inmate 4872, disappeared from his cell at that same high-security facility?"

"You mean, he escaped?"

The other officials shifted uncomfortably in their chairs. Sir clenched his fist even tighter on the table, and Cheyenne's drow hearing picked up the otherwise inaudible creak of his knuckles.

"Are you aware of the situation, Ms. Summerlin?"

"Yeah, I'm aware. Major Carson called me this morning to tell me."

The officials' eyes widened at both the use of Sir's real name and the fact that he'd called an unaffiliated third party about such classified information.

Looks like someone else is keeping secrets.

Sir's face bloomed a dark shade of red, his mustache twitching and his beady eyes never leaving the half-drow's face.

The woman with the auburn bun cleared her throat. "Do you know where L'zar Verdys is at this moment?"

He could be anywhere. Cheyenne met the woman's gaze and shook her head. "No."

"Bullshit," Sir hissed.

"Major." All it took was one glance from the woman, and Sir flung himself back into his chair again.

Sir's got his own Sir. Look at that.

"Ms. Summerlin, have you had any contact with L'zar Verdys

outside of your approved visits to Chateau D'rahl in the last few weeks?"

"Yeah."

More shifting in seats. The three officials exchanged excited glances and Sir's eyes narrowed even farther, making him look like he was about to sneeze.

"Where and when were these instances?"

Cheyenne wrinkled her nose and spread her arms. "This might come as a surprise, seeing as none of you have stepped into the whole drow experience, I'm guessing. One of L'zar's many endearing qualities is his ability to show up in my head. That's where I've seen him."

Sir lurched from his chair. "We're not fucking around, halfling!"

"Neither am I," Cheyenne muttered.

"I swear to Abe goddamn Lincoln, Cheyenne, if you don't cut this shit out—"

"Major Carson." The woman barely raised her voice, and Sir turned his wide-eyed stare on her instead.

"She just told us the drow talks to her in her head. Are you seriously putting stock in that?"

The woman glanced at Cheyenne, tilted her head, then slid one finger toward the recording device and paused it. "I've spent my entire career questioning witnesses and suspects, Major, both human and magical. I've gotten pretty damn good at spotting a lie even before it's finished being told."

Sir scowled, his mustache bristling against his nostrils. Cheyenne had to scratch her nose, just looking at it.

"There's no way that's possible," he muttered.

"Really?" The woman blinked slowly and lifted her chin toward him. "Until 1999, it wasn't possible for an incarcerated inmate to break out of Chateau D'rahl. Until yesterday, it wasn't possible for a new Border portal to erupt in the middle of Henry County, or anywhere else in the world, for that matter. And for the majority of people in *this* world, magic and other realms are not and will never be possible. Unless you have any evidence to directly disprove Ms. Summerlin's claims, Major, I strongly suggest you take your seat and keep your mouth shut. Understood?"

The man swallowed thickly, sniffed, and gave the woman a stiff nod.

"Sir." Then he sat, his fingers clawing the armrests of the chair. The protesting groan of the wood in his grip was loud enough for everyone to hear.

Cheyenne stared at the center of the table so she wouldn't end up provoking him even more with the laugh threatening to burst out of her. *Looks like everyone's getting a taste of their own medicine today. And I get to be right in the middle of it.*

"Now, may we continue?"

The halfling felt the woman's gaze on her and nodded once. "Sure."

The recording resumed. "Ms. Summerlin, are you currently harboring the magical fugitive L'zar Verdys in your home at the Pellerville Gables Apartments?"

Cheyenne glanced at her and raised an eyebrow. "Absolutely not."

"Were you in any way involved in L'zar Verdys' escape from Chateau D'rahl?"

"No."

"Thank you. For the purposes of whatever future use this recording may serve, please state that everything you've told us this morning is, to the best of your knowledge, accurate and true."

"It is."

The woman folded her hands on the table and readjusted in her seat. "I'm inclined to believe you, Ms. Summerlin. Now, I'd like to move on to a slightly different subject. Tell us about that new portal on the Summerlin estate. That's where you grew up if I'm not mistaken."

"Yeah." *This'll be easy.* "I was visiting my mom last night, and the portal just shot out of the ground."

Sir snorted and folded his arms but didn't say a word.

"Was there any type of warning preceding this event?"

"An earthquake. And a bunch of flashing lights."

"And was there any form of magic being cast before the new portal appeared?" The woman shook her head, searching for the words. "Any spells or incantations? Something that might have gone wrong?"

The halfling frowned. "I'm guessing you know this just like everything else, but I have to bring it up. You know who my mom is, right?"

"Yes, Ms. Summerlin. I'm aware of your familial connections."

Cheyenne's laugh was humorless and wry. "Bianca Summerlin would put her elbows on the table before she'd let someone get away with even saying the *word* 'magic.' There were no spells or incantations. We were in the middle of dinner, there was an earthquake, and then the huge black spikes of rock shot up out of the ground. As far as I know, it was random."

"Of course." The woman dipped her head and gestured toward Sir. "Major Carson has informed us that he's sent a team of his top agents to your mother's house in Henry County to monitor this new portal, which is, in essence, why this organization was founded. Did you see any individuals cross through that portal between the time it appeared and when our agents arrived on the property?"

"No." Cheyenne licked her lips and met every pair of eyes staring right back at her. "But something else came through."

Sir sat a little straighter in his chair.

"Such as?"

"I have no idea what to call them." The halfling shrugged. "Just a bunch of dark shapes, really. Trying to come through and lashing out at anything that moved, I think. If you asked some of the O'gúleesh on the reservations, they'll all tell you that those things only exist between the portals. That's part of the crossing, I guess—getting past them."

"Have you made the crossing yourself?"

"No." *Better leave it at that if she can smell a lie like she says.* "But I fought one of those things coming out of the portal in my mom's back-yard last night. It shouldn't be able to do that."

"No, it should not." The woman eyed the three nameless men at the table, and they seemed to come to some sort of unspoken decision by wiggling their eyebrows. "I think we have everything we need from you, Ms. Summerlin. I'm sure it goes without saying, but if you come across any more of those portals, please reach out to Major Carson to inform him. We need to keep a lid on this for as long as possible while we look into what's happening."

"Sure. I'll keep him updated."

The four officials stood from their chairs, and the woman grabbed the recorder to slip it into her pocket. "Thank you for your time, Ms. Summerlin. Major."

Sir stood as well, pressing his fingertips on the table and nodding as he watched his superiors remove themselves quickly and calmly from the room. As soon as the doors closed behind them, he turned a blazing glare on Cheyenne. "You'll keep me updated, huh?"

"Unless you don't want me to." The halfling didn't bother to stand. "Were you trying to prove something with that?"

"Were *you*?" He took a sharp breath through his nose, his head quivering as he forced himself back under control. "I don't buy any of your drow-telepathy bullshit for a second. But you see or hear or smell anything about another one of those portals, halfling, and I better be the first name in your head. Then we'll all agree to keep pretending you're not hiding L'zar in some halfling shoebox somewhere."

Cheyenne frowned and dropped her head back against the chair. "Okay."

He hissed and kicked the rolling desk chair. Then he had to pull it out of his way in order to get to the doors. "Get off my base."

The man slammed his hand against one of the double doors and shoved it open before disappearing into the hall.

The halfling swiveled back and forth in the chair, then spun fully around to look at Sheila. "I think that went pretty well."

The ogre woman blinked at the far wall, then flicked her gaze toward the half-drow slouching in the chair. A small smile lifted one corner of her mouth. "You've got some bargaining chip, halfling."

"I know, right? It's amazing I haven't used it up yet." Cheyenne pushed herself out of the chair and stuck her hands in her back pockets. "I can show myself out if you have somewhere else you need to be."

"This was it," Sheila replied, smirking. "I'll hang out here for a few more minutes until Hurricane Sir blows over."

With a snort, Cheyenne nodded and headed across the room. "Good idea. See ya."

"Yep."

The halfling pushed the doors open and slipped into the hall. It was just as quiet as when Sheila had led her down here, but two seconds later, something crashed against the wall in an office on her right, followed by Sir's furious roar of, "Goddammit!"

Yep. Perfect time to get outta here.

CHAPTER EIGHT

W hen she made her way back through the pseudo-maze of the FRoE compound's hallways and entered the lobby, Yurik was leaning against the short hall into the common room, his arms folded. "How'd it go?"

Cheyenne stopped and glanced at the front doors, then turned to look at the intensely muscular goblin with a shrug. "Better than I expected."

"Where's Sir?"

"Rampaging in his office, I think."

Yurik looked over his shoulder and let out a sharp whistle. Bhandi and Tate appeared at the end of the hall behind him, their eyes showing a mix of amusement and caution.

"The Goth drow lives," Bhandi said with a chuckle. "Unbelievable."

"I didn't even try, honestly. Haven't seen you guys in a while. What's up?"

Tate rubbed his bald purple head covered in dark, swirling tattoos. "Just trying to stay outta the shitstorm." He glanced over his shoulder, then leaned forward and lowered his voice. "We've been hearing stuff about a new Border portal poppin' outta nowhere. Is that for real?"

Cheyenne wrinkled her nose. "Yeah, it's for real. I saw one up close and personal last night." *They don't need to know about the one before that. Not yet.*

"Man." Bhandi jerked her head back in disbelief. "How does something like that even happen?"

"I have no idea."

From the hallway behind Cheyenne came the echoing slam of a door, followed by another string of curses from Sir and what sounded a lot like a shiny leather shoe hitting a wall.

"We're still on duty. Technically." Yurik leaned forward to glance across the empty lobby. "Wanna meet up tonight and tell us all about it? Peridosh at like six or something?"

"Sure." Cheyenne walked backward toward the front doors of the compound and shot her FRoE-agent friends a thumbs-up. "Good luck gettin' outta here alive."

"Nah." Tate waved her off. "Plenty of room to hide in this place."

Bhandi raised her eyebrows at him and looked him up and down. "Speak for yourself."

The troll man rolled his eyes and turned back toward the common room. Bhandi chuckled as she followed him, and Yurik jerked his chin up at the halfling. "Meet you at the elevator."

"Sounds good."

Sir's stomping footsteps came down the hall faster, and Cheyenne playfully hunched over to mime creeping out the door. Yurik laughed, stole another wary glance across the lobby, then made himself scarce.

The halfling hurried across the parking lot toward her shiny new car, hitting the unlock button for that little chirp that made her smile. *I passed that test with flying colors. I seriously hope those guys can handle more than one new portal if they keep showing up, but I guess it's out of my hands.*

She slipped into the driver's seat and started the engine. "Okay, twelve o'clock, and I have nothing to do."

Strapping herself in, the halfling drove across the huge FRoE parking lot and ran through her mental list of things to check. *I'd call Maleshi if I had her number. Her office hours are at one.*

The thought made her laugh as she sped between the gate towers on either side of the road onto the base. "There's an image. Ambar'ogúl's greatest war general sitting behind a desk at VCU. Guess there's only one way to test that theory."

. . .

Cheyenne slung her backpack over her shoulder and locked the Panamera, then headed quickly out of the student parking lot at Virginia Commonwealth University and made her way toward the Computer Sciences building. Near 1:00 p.m., the campus was buzzing with students either just finishing or just starting their lunch breaks.

The halfling picked up the pace across the huge lawn of the quad, ignoring the noise from so many college kids running around during their free time. *It's a lot weirder to be here on a Tuesday with no classes. Now I'm the one teaching them, and none of these people can tell.*

The Computer Sciences building was thankfully fairly empty at this time of day, and Cheyenne approached the office of Professor Matilda Bergmann with a skeptical wariness. When she reached her old professor's office, she found the door wide open, like it usually was when she stopped by for office hours.

Double lives is right. She went right back to her regular human-looking life after everything we saw the other day.

The halfling stopped outside the open door and knocked gently.

Maleshi—Cheyenne couldn't unsee what she'd seen or forget what she knew about the nightstalker woman now—glanced up from her desk. She looked like Mattie all right, black wavy hair, shining green eyes, some weird wardrobe combination of black gaucho pants, a black shawl with tiny, multicolored flowers crocheted all over it, and a hot-pink shirt underneath that matched the hot-pink laces of her running shoes. The nightstalker grinned when she saw the half-drow in her doorway. "Just like old times, right?"

Cheyenne snorted and stepped inside, closing the door behind her. "Kinda. I honestly wasn't sure you'd be here today."

Maleshi sat back in her chair and shrugged. "Even when shit hits the fan, kid, you gotta keep going the best way you can. A little bit of normal is all it takes to keep from losing what's left of your sanity. Which, by the way, I fully expect you to keep a tight grip on after this too. You've got classes to teach."

"How could I forget?" When she reached the desk of the O'gúl-war-general-turned-low-key-IT-professor, Cheyenne slipped her backpack off her shoulders and set it gently on the edge. Maleshi raised an eyebrow. "Thought I'd update you on the good news."

"*Good* news?" The nightstalker laughed wryly. "Who are you, and what have you done with the halfling?"

"Minor good news, I guess. What happens after this, well, it's probably more bad news wrapped up with a stupid bow of destiny or something like that, but I'm trying to look on the bright side." Cheyenne pulled out the still-open *Cuil Ani* with the *marandúr* coin inside and set it down beside her backpack.

Maleshi's gaze settled on the open drow legacy box and her eyes widened. Then that fierce grin lit her features, and the inhuman light Cheyenne had seen so many times behind the woman's green eyes flashed again. "You did it."

"Yeah. I did it." The halfling pointed at the box. "There's my great drow legacy—a coin I can't spend on this side. Apparently, it took almost dying at a newly erupted portal ridge to activate the rest of my magic and get this thing open. Who knew?"

Those green eyes flickered up toward Cheyenne's face. "You haven't lost your flair for the dramatic."

"That's the least dramatic I could be about it."

"What?" Maleshi pressed her fingers on the surface of her desk and slowly stood, leaning forward to get a closer look at the open box and Cheyenne's unassuming prize inside. "There's a new portal?"

"*That's* what caught your attention?" The halfling folded her arms and took a step back from the desk. "I was more focused on the 'almost dying' part, but hey, I guess that only applies to me."

Still hunched over the *Cuil Ani*, Maleshi shot her former student an amused glance. "Did you really almost die?"

"Yeah. New Border portal opened, new crazy-ass in-between monster tried to squeeze out, and the thing almost squeezed the life out of *me*. I fried it into a pile of ashes and sent it back where it came from."

"With what?"

"Black fire."

Maleshi stared at the halfling with calculated intensity. The corners of her mouth twitched, and she let out a short, harsh laugh of disbelief. "Yeah, I'd say that'd just about do it. Looks like you made it out of that little skirmish well enough."

Cheyenne shrugged. "I'm chalking that up to lots of practice getting my ass kicked, plus a huge jar of darktongue salve."

The nightstalker grinned. "Stings like a bitch, doesn't it?"

"In the best way."

They shared a laugh, and Maleshi tucked the long black waves of her human-illusion hair behind one ear. "So, you almost died, but you didn't. Then you opened your legacy box and put a whole new level of detailed plans in action. Get used to it, kid. With what we've got comin' down the pipeline, I'd say that's gonna be your new normal."

"Yeah, I figured." Cheyenne picked up the box and stuffed it back into the bottom of her bag.

"Where did you find yourself fighting in-between monsters that almost squeezed the life out of you?"

Zipping up her backpack, the halfling shook her head. "In my mom's backyard."

"No shit?"

"Yeah, and I was the only one around who knew how to handle it. I almost got my ass handed to me, but it could've been a lot worse."

Maleshi folded her arms, then lifted one hand to rub her lips. "A new portal on Bianca Summerlin's property with only a drow halfling to see it happen. That's pretty big."

"Big enough to make L'zar break out of prison again to come find me."

The nightstalker froze. "Say that again."

"He's out, Mal—" Cheyenne glanced over her shoulder at the closed office door. *I can't call her that here.* "Saw him up close and personal this morning. He almost ran me off the road."

A bark of surprised laughter escaped the professor, and she slapped her hand over her mouth. "Why the hell would he risk everything to do that *now?*"

Slinging the backpack over her shoulder again, the halfling could only shake her head. "He said he's here to protect me now that I passed the trials, which I guess means he thinks he's in the clear."

"Since his dead-child prophecy is a moot point these days." Maleshi's eyes widened. "He could protect you, sure, but if the wrong people find out he flipped that prison the bird and is out walking around, it's gonna take a lot more than one drow's protection to stop the Crown."

"I know. We went over all that this morning." Cheyenne paused, studying the war general's face. "Can you give me an honest answer about something?"

"Hmm?" Maleshi shook herself out of her thoughts. "Honest answer? I'll try, Cheyenne, but I've been out of this game for so long, there's a whole lot I can't even pretend to know."

"You're back in it, though, right?"

The nightstalker smirked. "Was that your question?"

"No. That was a bonus."

"I'm back in it. What we saw the other day at that new portal? What we *did*?" Maleshi tapped the edge of her desk and cocked her head. "I never thought I'd say it, especially Earthside, but I've lost the option of staying neatly hidden away in a fake human life to avoid the whole thing. And if L'zar's out for good this time, I don't have a choice anymore."

"Lucky for us, right?"

The nightstalker laughed. "For you, maybe, and those other goons who'd follow L'zar into their own undoing without a second thought. What's your question?"

Cheyenne tightened her grip on the straps of her backpack and scanned the bookshelf behind Maleshi's head. "Has he always been this crazy?"

"You're not talking about eccentricities, right?"

The halfling shot her former professor an exasperated look. "You know I'm not."

"Yeah, I know you're not." Maleshi smoothed her hair away from her face with both hands and tilted her head from side to side. "The short answer is yes. He's always been at the top of the drow-lunatic list."

"What's the long answer?"

"Ha. That covers centuries of O'gúl history, kid."

Cheyenne smirked. "We have a few hours."

"Uh-huh." Maleshi tried not to smile, but it didn't work.

CHAPTER NINE

"I can tell you this much, at least. Everyone in Ambar'ogúl knows that drow father of yours as a charlatan and a prankster, one of the greatest O'gúl thieves to make a name for himself like that *before* he lost his head for his crimes. That prophecy he tried for so long to disprove wasn't the first he paid for. I'm sure it won't be the last, and as far as I know, all the others have been just as dark and just as disappointing." Maleshi frowned, closing her eyes briefly as the memories came slowly to the surface. "If he wasn't a *little* crazy before trying to undo this last prophecy, he sure as hell is now after breaking it with you. How does anyone spend hundreds of years trying to create and groom an heir promised never to live through their trials and hold onto their sanity?"

"Yeah, it doesn't sound possible." *Watching dozens of his kids die when he already knew they would. Definitely a recipe for crazy.*

"Well." Maleshi chuckled. "On the other hand, this isn't his first time making the impossible possible. You're his heir, Cheyenne, whether you like it or not. You passed your trials, and you're still alive and kickin'."

The halfling scowled at her backpack and the legacy box inside. "L'zar didn't have anything to do with that. *I* made it possible."

"That's my point. L'zar's prophecy was unraveled because he did nothing. If I had to guess, I'd say he had a hunch about that, and that's why he let himself be locked up in that prison for so long." Maleshi spread her arms. "I just hope he learned his lesson with that one."

"He doesn't seem like the teachable type."

The nightstalker raised her eyebrows. "He's not, which is why he should've stayed behind bars until we get this other portal business under control."

"We're getting there, I think." Cheyenne studied Maleshi's shimmering green eyes, which narrowed in interest now. "L'zar's lying low at the warehouse for now. I think."

"He better be."

The halfling chuckled. "Who knows, right? I was there this morning. Apparently, they found the guy who's been meshing O'gúl and Earth technology, so at the very least, it should keep them all busy."

"They found him." Maleshi broke into another grin. "You know, I'm ninety-nine-percent sure L'zar doesn't give a rat's ass about that little piece of our puzzle. He's focused on you. I, on the other hand, would *really* love to hear what they told you."

"Not much." Cheyenne shook her head, trying not to laugh at the crestfallen look eating away the nightstalker's eagerness. "They had some scaly dude tied to a chair when I showed up. They shoved him in a closet and told me they'd figure out the rest."

"Well, that's frustrating."

"Yeah. So is being dismissed by all the magicals following the crazy drow to their own ends. Whatever they figure out, I'm not sure they'll tell *me*."

"They'll tell you, Cheyenne." Maleshi nodded slowly, the cold, hard intensity of General Hi'et returning to her features. "You deserve to know as much as everyone else, if not more. And if they don't know that by now, you'll just have to make them tell you."

Cheyenne leaned away from her old professor and raised an eyebrow. *She's got battle-lust written all over her, even with that illusion spell.* "I'm not gonna start interrogating the people who are trying to help me."

"What?" Maleshi laughed. "Who said anything about interrogating? Just a few good pops with your magic, kid, and they'll get the message."

"Jeeze. If you'd talked to me like that when I first starting coming by here for *your* help, I wouldn't have come back."

"Well, it's a good thing I know how to play my hand, isn't it?" The nightstalker winked. "Thanks for stopping by to show me that special drow trinket you finally got open, but don't worry about dropping by on your days off to fill me in. I'm thinking about popping into that warehouse for a little visit."

"To interrogate the scaly dude?"

"Ha. Wouldn't that be fun?" Smirking, Maleshi slowly lowered herself into her chair again. "I wouldn't turn down the offer to be perfectly honest, but I've got a prophecy or two to sort out. I've come to the realization that I might need a little help with that."

"You don't look happy about that part."

"I've been sucked back into a war I left behind me centuries ago, Cheyenne. On purpose. If I don't look happy about that, it's because I'm not."

The halfling narrowed her eyes and looked the nightstalker up and down. "Because you're going to Corian for help, right?"

Maleshi stared right back at her. "That's one of the reasons, sure."

"What happened between you two, anyway?"

"Enough. Nothing that needs to be dug up right now in Mattie Bergman's office, thank you very much."

Cheyenne raised her hands in surrender. "I'm just curious."

"You can be as curious as you wanna be. I'm not strolling down that particular memory lane with you today."

"No problem." Cheyenne took another step back and grabbed the straps of her backpack again. *I could hold my own in here if I pushed too far. Wrong place and wrong time, though.* "Can you at least tell me what you found out about that weird-ass prophecy you bought from Gúrdu?"

Maleshi's eyes narrowed even more, then she laughed. "Yeah, you're just curious."

"I can't help it." The halfling chuckled. "It was creepy."

"Yes, it was." Taking a deep breath, the general-turned-professor sat back in her chair again. "I've figured out most of it on my own. That prophecy was talking about the new portals in a roundabout way. I'm pretty sure the Crown's involved, but not intentionally. She sent those shipments through the new portal we found, but my bet is, that was a happy coincidence. She found it and used it."

"Well, it's been there for a while."

Maleshi frowned. "What makes you say that?"

Shit. I can't make promises to keep secrets and let something like that slip. "Heard mention of it somewhere."

"Uh-huh. Well, however long it's been there doesn't matter if we've got new ones popping up in reclusive socialites' backyards, does it?" Maleshi leaned sideways into the armrest of her chair. "At a basic level, it looks like the Crown's spreading madness is running out of space in Ambar'ogúl and starting to seep through Earthside. I don't think the Crown knows how directly the two are connected. Not yet, anyway."

"If she does, she doesn't care."

"Hmm." Maleshi gave the halfling a tight-lipped smile. "You're starting to talk like an O'gúleesh who's seen what's happening on the other side."

Cheyenne spread her arms. "Camouflage."

"Very funny."

"What about the rest of the prophecy?"

"What about it?"

Cocking her head, Cheyenne twirled a hand in the air. "That part about cutting out the heart and the rot. Destiny or chains. 'Blood binds to blood' was in there too, and I've heard that part before."

"You don't let too much slip through your head, do you?"

The halfling smiled. "I have a pretty decent memory. I'm choosing to credit my mom for that one."

With a snort, the nightstalker nodded. "That's a little deeper than I can go."

"But you *think* you know what it means, don't you?"

"Maybe. That's why I need an extra nightstalker brain to help me figure it out."

Cheyenne frowned. "I might be able to help. Before I had that pendant, I was getting a lot of crazy dreams with all kinds of prophecy pieces screamed at me."

"Which I noticed you aren't wearing anymore."

"It stopped working, mostly. And you're changing the subject."

"I'm entitled to change the subjects I don't want to talk about." Maleshi leaned forward with a sarcastic shake of her head. "Are you gonna take the hint, or do I need to use stronger tactics?"

Casting the woman a sideways glance, Cheyenne pursed her lips. "You won't fight me in your cute little office as a college professor."

"Of course not, but I can find you pretty much anywhere else, and I've been brushing up on my portal-casting."

"Right." The women stared each other down, and when the corner of Maleshi's mouth twitched into a smirk, Cheyenne choked back a laugh. "Okay, fine. Go talk to your nightstalker buddy from a past life about it first, but I want to know what you guys come up with. Don't make me make you tell me."

Maleshi chuckled. "My own advice coming back to bite me in the ass. That's been happening a lot lately."

"Hey, good to know I'm not the only one." With a final glance around the office, Cheyenne took a deep breath. "Anything else?"

A soft, timid knock came at the door. They both quickly glanced that way, and Maleshi cleared her throat. "It's open."

A kid in a button-up plaid shirt with insanely thick glasses and a real live pocket protector with two glinting pens peered through the door when he opened it. His eyes widened when he saw Cheyenne, and his shoulders hunched as he reconsidered opening the door any farther. "Um, Professor Bergmann?"

"Yes?" Maleshi grinned and batted her eyes.

"Am I interrupting something?"

"Nope." Cheyenne nodded. "I was on my way out. She's all yours."

The kid cowered against the cracked door when the Goth girl with a backpack headed across the office toward him.

"Cheyenne, hold on a minute." Maleshi grabbed a pen from the jar and a pad of sticky notes from the desk drawer, then scribbled something on the top note and peeled it off. She stood quickly and crossed the room, shooting the other student a reassuring smile as she handed the note to the halfling. "Just in case."

"Sure." Cheyenne took it without looking, then stopped in front of the door and waited for the kid to open it so they could trade places. His eyes were huge behind the thick lenses. "I'm not gonna bite."

"What?"

"The door, Mr. Thomas." Maleshi gave him a pert smile.

"Oh. Um, yeah. Um, sorry?" He pushed the door open, pressing his back against it like he wanted to melt into the wood as Cheyenne stepped into the hallway.

"Good luck." The halfling raised her eyebrows and brushed past him. Maleshi's soft chuckle and muttered reassurances that her startled student shouldn't rely on luck followed Cheyenne through the hall.

CHAPTER TEN

Cheyenne tried the handle of her apartment door before bothering to pull out her keys. *Of course it's unlocked.*

She stepped inside and found Ember sitting in her chair at the far end of the coffee table, watching something on their fancy TV. The halfling shut the door with a smirk. "Good to see you're keeping busy."

The fae's eyes remained glued to the TV screen. "Just trying to turn off my brain with something that has nothing to do with the last twenty-four hours."

"And that would be?"

"*Stranger Things.*"

Cheyenne blinked. "That was *not* what I expected you to say."

"Hey, it's better to watch someone else live through something that's guaranteed not to be real." Ember finally looked away from the screen, met Cheyenne's gaze, and chuckled, lifting one shoulder in a half-hearted shrug. "Even if it's, like, weirdly close to what I just found out *is* real."

"You do you, I guess." The halfling set her backpack on the floor beside the couch and headed toward the wrought-iron staircase leading to the mini-loft over the bathroom that served as her private office.

"How did the meeting with the deranged escaped convict go?"

Cheyenne snorted as her black Vans echoed with a metallic clang up the stairs. "Pretty much the way I expected. The only real thing I learned is that drow use nightstalker blood for instant portal-casting."

"Say what?"

"Yeah, I don't know how that works, but it's a thing."

Ember returned her attention to the TV. "I'm zoning out again."

"Have fun." The halfling reached the top of the stairs and paused, gazing at Glen's hastily rewired setup and the boxes of miscellaneous cords, cables, and spare parts against the wall. *At least I had time to put together the most important components.*

She stepped toward the desk and powered on her custom tower, then turned on the monitor and sat in the rolling office chair. Her forearms thunked on the plastic armrests as she swiveled back and forth. Cheyenne grimaced. *Couldn't find a decent office chair as part of their show apartment, huh? Last upgrade on the list, I guess.*

Her personal server blinked from its temporary place on a small table against the wall on her left, and as Glen powered up to full working order, Cheyenne glanced through the thin metal rail around the mini-loft to see Ember fully engaged in her zone-out time with the TV.

It still feels like someone's watching me. Guess that's what I get for having an open office anyone can look into.

That thought made her pause, and she squinted at the wall on her left as if she could see through it and into the apartment across the hall. *Matthew Thomas and his cybersecurity firms. That's not dabbling. But Ember would've told me if he'd even asked about snooping around up here.*

The login screen popped up on her monitor, but she pulled her phone from her back pocket instead and initiated a quick Google search on their friendly neighbor.

"Of course he's on Wikipedia."

"What's that?" Ember tilted her face up toward the mini-loft but didn't take her eyes off the TV.

Cheyenne shook her head. "FYI, Em. If I'm talking when I'm up here, it's to myself."

"Uh-huh." The fae slid her hands off the armrests of her chair and into her lap but didn't say anything else.

She's not even listening.

The halfling turned back to the long list of accolades and accomplishments on their neighbor's Wikipedia page and shook her head. *Should've checked him out sooner. This guy's got his fingers in everything. Cybersecurity. Market trading. Prosthetics technology? All he's missing is advanced weapons technology and military contracts, and I'd say he's trying to take over the world.*

Scoffing at her phone, she set it beside her keyboard on the flimsy office desk and shook her head. *I can look into that later. As long as he stays out of my business, I'll stay out of his.*

Rolling back her shoulders, she logged into her desktop and went through the process of running her VPN and rerouting her entries several times before diving into the dark web. "Not like he could find me even if he did have something sniffing through the building."

"Huh?"

"Thinking out loud, Em." Cheyenne scooted closer to the desk and shook her head. *Gotta quit that habit, apparently.*

It felt like forever since she'd poked around on the Borderlands forum in the guise of "Third Quarter Projections," but when she landed on the forum's main page, a smile crept across her lips. *Feels a lot more like home than waking up in my old bed this morning.*

Fortunately, the pinned thread about the missing magical kids and the status of their return home had been pulled from the top of the page. *Great. Corian's on top of running the forum, but he can't send me a warning text before portaling into my mom's house.*

The halfling took a quick scroll through the most recently posted topics, looking for anything about new Border portals or creepy shapeshifting monsters on the loose. The last thing she needed right now was to get an earful from Corian about the magical community freaking out over new unregulated portals. *The FRoE will lose their shit if this gets out of hand. More than usual, anyway.*

The posted topics were on the same subdued, relatively boring themes as the first time she'd scoured through the forum.

Cheap Ways to Hex Customers Who Won't Pay Their Tabs?
Sale on Used Summoning Candles. Read thread for full details
Can't find dragonroot for simple transparency spell. Help.

Cheyenne sat back in her chair and smirked. No more missing kids and black-market trading. The Borderlands had turned into a magical Craigslist.

She scrolled down the page and stopped at the one topic title that stood out over all the rest.

Anyone Heard from Our D-Class Resource Lately?

"For real?" The halfling glanced down at Ember again, but the fae either hadn't heard her or decided to ignore Cheyenne's muttered self-talk.

I've been off the Borderlands grid for less than a week, and people are already calling a halfling out for not making any noise.

She shook her head and clicked on the thread.

Fists4Daze: Just thought I'd put this out there in case anyone has seen or heard anything. One of my neighbors mentioned seeing someone in Peridosh who might've been our friend. Something about a basket full of ingredients from the potionmaster.

holdmyGrog911: @Fists4Daze If we're talking about the same D-class, I'm having a pretty hard time imagining them going all-out for a bunch of spells. We've all heard the stories at this point, and spells weren't part of this friend's equation.

CrownUndone21: I'm with @holdmyGrog911. It's not like we have a registry for all D-class Earthside. But potions and spells don't fit our friend's MO.

hideORdie: Seriously, @Fists4Daze? Things have finally settled down around here, at least where I am, and you're trying to spread more rumors? What about the kids, man? What about all the black magic that, as far as I've heard, hasn't been seized yet? My nephews just got home after being locked up like a bunch of radan in a freakin' cult mansion, and it's gonna take them a long time to put all that shit behind them. If you're so worried about finding something to worry about, go back home. There's plenty there for you to get your fell-damn fix for deadly crap. The rest of us came here to get away from it. Just let things be calm for a minute!

sharpst8kbringzalldavamps: Somebody's getting touchy ^^

Fists4Daze: @hideORdie I wasn't trying to stir anything up. Just curious. If this D-class friend had a hand in fixing any of the craziness in the last few weeks, it'd be good to know they're still around. Just in case, you know? Looking for a little reassurance.

hideORdie: @Fists4Daze Nothing's crazy right now, which should be reassurance enough.

TrollonaRoll818: @hideORdie I totally get where you're coming from. Why should we be looking for trouble when we finally have a little peace from explosions and missing kids and black magic being sold like candy? (Sorry to hear about your nephews, btw. Those kids are strong. They'll be okay.) But I have to agree with @Fists4Daze on this one too. There's no harm in checking in about where our friends are and what they're up to. It's not like this D-class friend owes us anything, but I know I sleep a little easier at night, thinking somebody is out there who doesn't have a problem standing up for the little guy. Whether that's helping us where F-Force failed or stepping in where scumbags from back home are trying to sink their teeth into our new lives Earthside. Everybody's shaken up by what happened. It's not too much to ask for a little reassurance now and then, especially for those of us with family on this side.

FellwineThis44: This is the most useless thread I've ever seen. I can't even believe I just wasted my time reading these comments. @TrollonaRoll818 Grow some balls. This isn't your therapist's office. @hideORdie Your nephews shouldn't have been running around town getting into that nasty shit in the first place. What kind of parent lets that happen? I'd blame your brother instead. And spells are for pussies.

sharpst8kbringzalldavamps: @FellwineThis44 Dude. Get a life.

sharpst8kbringzalldavamps: @FellwineThis44 Also, my grandma could whip your ass back to the other side with her simplest spell. I would know. I've got the scars to prove it.

Cheyenne rolled back in her chair. *There's always something to argue about. Not sure how I feel about people waiting for me to come save them.*

She glanced at her phone again and thought about the first new portal ridge and all the O'gúl loyalists trying to smuggle in weapons of magical mass destruction. "I guess that's what I'm doing anyway."

After logging out of the Borderlands forum, she dipped into the Y2Kickass server just to check. No new messages from Todd or the master-hacker-wannabe who'd decrypted Corian's stupid map for her in record time. Cheyenne smirked. *I'd know who to ask for help if we needed more of that for these O'gúl war machines using human tech. But if I can't read Persh'al's code, Mini-Me sure as hell can't either.*

Below her, the credits rolled at the end of Ember's show. The fae girl ran a hand through her hair and glanced up at the mini-loft. "You hungry?"

"Got your appetite back, huh?"

"Well, you know, wheeling into the kitchen is pretty much all the exercise I'm gonna get today."

Cheyenne chuckled. "Yeah, I could eat."

Ember clicked the remote in her hand, and the TV sank back down into its hidden slot in the entry table beside the door. Then she tossed the remote on the coffee table and pushed back to head to the kitchen. "I'm really glad you didn't inherit your mom's culinary tastes. I mean, our kitchen's not as big, but no way in hell am I cooking for you like Eleanor does."

The halfling practically skipped down the metal stairs, the chains on her wrists clinking as her hand squeaked on the iron railing. "I'd have to pay you for that."

CHAPTER ELEVEN

"So wait." Ember grabbed both empty containers from the frozen dinners they'd turned into a late lunch and set them in her lap. "You went in to get interrogated by the FRoE, and that asshole without a name is the one who got in trouble?"

She wheeled herself across the kitchen and tossed the containers in the trash as Cheyenne took their forks to the dishwasher. "Yep. I was mostly telling the truth, too. At least, I didn't have to straight-out *lie* about anything."

Ember hissed out a disbelieving laugh. "That guy really hates you."

"Oh, yeah. I'm not his biggest fan, either."

"How did you get away with not telling them where L'zar is?"

Cheyenne shrugged. "Probably because I honestly believe he could be anywhere. He *might* still be at the warehouse. Or he could be running around DC in broad daylight, sending cars off the road and giving people heart attacks. Something tells me that's more his style."

"Jeeze."

The halfling turned and grinned. "But *that* drow's not my responsibility. It was his choice to break out of prison and apparently mess up whatever he's been planning with Corian and the others. They're the ones dedicating their long-ass lives to this guy. I'm just his kid."

Ember barked out a laugh. "That normally wouldn't mean much, but I think the circumstances change that a little, don't they?"

"Nope." The halfling leaned against the wide marble island and folded her arms. "I've got more than enough to worry about without trying to keep tabs on L'zar Verdys and whatever crap he gets himself into. Maleshi called him one of the greatest O'gúl thieves with his head still on his shoulders. If that's true, it means he's good enough at whatever he does not to get caught."

"Cheyenne, I don't know if you realize this, but a person has to get caught first before breaking out of prison."

Cheyenne shot her friend an exasperated glance before a small laugh slipped out. "I meant, he doesn't get caught unless he wants to. What I don't get is what he was planning on doing for the last twenty-five years of his sentence that didn't really mean anything. Wait to be released so he could meet me for the first time when I'm forty-six?"

"Maybe he was always planning to break out early."

"Yeah, I thought about that." The halfling glanced around their massive kitchen. "But Corian and Maleshi seemed really surprised and a little pissed-off when I told them the drow let himself out of the prison-bag."

"It's still weird to hear you call her that."

"I know, right? I almost called her that to her face when I stopped by her office earlier. And yeah, she went back to work." Ember shook her head, and Cheyenne shrugged. "But I think you're right about the breakout plan. My guess is, it's a mix of both. Like they were already supposed to have something in motion before L'zar left Chateau D'rahl, and he was too wrapped up in his victory to wait any longer for whatever plan to unfold."

"*His* victory?"

"I'm convinced that's what he thinks this is. I passed the drow trials, I obliterated that thing at my mom's house, and apparently, I unraveled a centuries-old prophecy about L'zar Verdys' kids never living long enough to see what any of that's like. And yeah, he looked awfully proud of *himself.*"

Ember frowned and wheeled herself into their sweeping living room, glancing out the long wall of windows at their view over north

Richmond. "The only things he can take credit for is seducing your mom and staying behind bars for so long."

"Yeah, well, good luck telling *him* that." The halfling joined her friend in the living room and flopped into one of their new black leather recliners. "I think me being frenemies with the FRoE and all these new Border portals popping up put a wrench in everyone's plans. Kinda hard to cover all the bases centuries in advance, though."

With a snort, the fae stopped between the coffee table and the occupied recliner and folded her arms. "A lot can happen in a few centuries."

"True. Feels like it's all happening right now, though."

"Screw him." Ember shrugged. "He let you spend twenty-one years trying to figure all this shit out on your own. The guy deserves massive wrenches in his plans."

"Thank you." The halfling yanked up the handle on the side of the recliner until the footrest came all the way up and she was lying as close to horizontal as one could get in a chair like this. Then she stuck both hands behind her head and stared at the high ceiling of their apartment. "Normally, I'd let him crawl into whatever plan-machine he built to pull out those wrenches himself, but there's a portal ridge and a team of pissed-off FRoE agents at my mom's house and a bunch of old O'gúl parts for war machines sitting in Persh'al's warehouse, plus the inevitable attacks I know are still headed my way. If the Crown was already halfway to finding me before Corian gave me that pendant, there's no way in hell she doesn't know I passed the trials. You know what? Maybe *that's* why L'zar had to find his heir so badly."

The living room fell silent, and Ember cocked her head. "You lost me on that last one."

"What?" Cheyenne sat up enough to still spread out in the recliner and look at her fae friend at the same time. "Oh. Breaking news, Em. The drow puzzle box opened right up. And I found out what my legacy really is."

"For real?" The fae's eyes widened over a slow, excited smile. "What was it?"

"A giant, useless coin."

"Aw, seriously?"

"Yep."

Ember blinked, then a startled laugh burst out of her. "He really didn't think *that* one through. One coin. He had no idea who your mom was when he found her for one night of Cheyenne-making, did he?"

A low chuckle made its way up the halfling's throat, growing into a laugh until they were both too breathless to say anything.

"Oh, man." Cheyenne wiped the tears off her cheeks and cranked the recliner all the way back again. "I think the drow insanity is contagious."

"Nothing insane about a good sense of humor." Ember chuckled and wiped her eyes. "That can't be it, though, right? Your legacy being just one coin a crazy thief gave you?" She laughed again.

"Apparently not." Folding her arms, the halfling stared up at the ceiling again. "I found out this morning that the *real* legacy, if we're still calling it that, is on the other side."

"In Ambar'ogúl?"

"Yep. And I'm the only one who can go get it."

"No. No way." Ember shook her head and tried to wheel closer to Cheyenne's armchair. The chair caught on the edge of the coffee table, and she grunted, backing up and inching forward in an irritated three-point turn before finally pushing herself alongside the extended recliner to loom right above the halfling's face. "You're not crossing over because some lunatic who happens to be your father told you that's what you need to do."

Cheyenne swallowed. "He's not the only one who said it, Em."

"Who the fuck cares what anybody else said? These people have been watching you and waiting for you to break some stupid prophecy all by yourself. They could've stepped in at any point in your life to help you, and they didn't. This sounds like they're putting you on the front lines because they don't have the balls to do it themselves."

"Uh-huh. That's what I meant. I'm pretty sure that's all I am to L'zar anyway."

Ember's brows drew together as she studied her friend's apathetic expression. "You're not going, are you?"

With a deep breath, Cheyenne slowly turned her head toward her friend and met Ember's gaze. "If there wasn't all this other stuff going on, no, I wouldn't go."

"Jesus. Are you serious?"

"I *have* to. Whatever dark shit that's going on over there is seeping out of the portals and making new ones because there isn't any more room. This world, the only one *we* know, is just the overflow tank now."

"And you're trusting the magicals who left you high and dry to deal with all this by yourself." Ember's lips pressed tightly together, then she ripped her gaze away from Cheyenne and pushed herself across the living room. "You're just gonna take their word for it and make that crossing because they said *your legacy* is waiting for you on the other side?"

"Not *just* because of that, no." Cheyenne looked back at the ceiling, but now the recliner didn't feel nearly as comfortable. "Nobody's come right out and said it, but I'm pretty sure they all think that if I can put that stupid coin on the O'gúl altar, I'll be able to stop what's starting to happen over here. You know, giant portals ripping out of the ground and causing earthquakes and unleashing monsters that aren't supposed to exist."

"Well, halflings weren't supposed to exist either, Cheyenne. Should we just throw you off a cliff somewhere and dust off our hands?"

Cheyenne snorted. "That *would* solve a lot of my problems."

"I'm serious!"

Slowly, the halfling sat up in the recliner, pushing the handle back down so her feet touched the floor. When she raised an eyebrow at her friend, Ember's face reddened and she couldn't hold back a nervous laugh.

"I mean, yeah. That would solve your problems. Not anyone else's."

"I'm not trying to fix anyone else's problems, just my own. And I definitely count those things coming out of the portals and the Crown's thugs bringing *war machines* Earthside as my problems. I'm not just gonna sit around and let that happen if I can do something about it."

Ember folded her arms. "I would."

"Well, it's a good fucking thing you're not L'zar's kid, then. Or we'd all be screwed."

They stared at each other, then Ember laughed and leaned over her lap, burying her face in her hands. "That was a total lie." Her voice was muffled through her fingers. "If I could walk, if I could do anything beyond levitating in this stupid wheelchair, I'd come with you."

Cheyenne bit her lip. "I know, Em. I wouldn't let you, but I'd appreciate it."

"If I had real fae magic, halfling, you wouldn't be able to stop me."

"You sound really sure about that."

Ember dropped her hands in her lap before sitting back up again to look at her friend. "You haven't seen a full-blooded fae in action, have you?"

"Nope. Looking forward to the day, though."

"This plan is insane. You know that, right?"

"Well, yeah. It's L'zar's plan."

The fae shook her head. "How are you gonna do it, then?"

"I have no idea. That's what I'm waiting for the *rebels* to figure out and tell me."

"And that's why you came back to the apartment? To sit around and wait for a phone call?"

Cheyenne rolled her eyes. "Yeah, that's exactly why I'm here. 'Cause I have nothing better to do. No classes to teach, no training with a nightstalker, no FRoE operations where everybody hates my guts but still needs me around. I *don't* have anything better to do."

"We need to fix that." Ember nodded at the remote on the coffee table, and the halfling laughed.

"Shopping therapy lost its thrill?"

"Binge-watching therapy is totally a thing, you know."

A sharp buzz came from Cheyenne's backpack on the other side of the couch. Frowning, she stood and patted her back pocket. *Nope. Left my phone on the desk.* She walked around the couch and sighed when she pulled the burner flip-phone from the front pocket of her backpack. "Maybe I spoke too soon."

"I thought those guys called you over and over."

"Yeah, normally." Cheyenne flipped open the phone and saw a message from the only number that had been saved in it. Yurik. "Huh."

She opened the text and cocked her head.

Still on for froyo at 6. Be there or be square.

Cheyenne snorted. "That guy is stuck in the wrong decade."

"That definitely needs an explanation."

"Oh." The halfling glanced at her friend and shrugged. "A couple FRoE agents wanted to meet up later tonight. I might call them friends in a parallel universe."

"What? Cheyenne, the drow halfling, has more than one friend?"

"You're hilarious." Cheyenne typed a reply on the awkward, sticky buttons of the flip phone.

I'll be there. You keep being square.

Then she tossed the phone back into the backpack's front pocket and ran a hand through her hair.

"So, what does 'meet up' mean when we're talking about FRoE agents who normally would've shipped any halfling they found back across the Border?"

Cheyenne shrugged. "These are the same guys who took me to Peridosh the first time."

"*Oh!*"

"Hey." A mischievous grin crept across the halfling's mouth as she looked at her fae friend. "Wanna come?"

CHAPTER TWELVE

E mber squinted and turned her head to shoot Cheyenne a skeptical sidelong glance. "Are you serious?"

"Yeah. It'll be fun. And you've never been, right? I get to hand over the marketplace-rookie mantle to you."

"Um, hello?" The fae gestured at herself. "There's a reason I've never been, and now there are two reasons I shouldn't go."

"Oh, come on. Don't tell me fae aren't supposed to get injured either."

"Not if they have *magic* to keep themselves from getting injured. And I'm way less worried about the wheelchair than I am about *looking like a human.*"

"Okay." Cheyenne rubbed her hands together and nodded. "Good thing I have something to take care of that part too."

Ember's eyes practically popped out of her head. "You what?"

"I'll be right back." The halfling chuckled and hurried across the living room before throwing open her bedroom door. The silver ring she'd cast as her illusion charm was right where she'd left it on top of the black dresser. She grabbed it, held it up to the thin light coming from the upside-down chandelier lamp on the other side of her bed, and grinned.

When she reached the living room again, Ember had grabbed the remote and was waiting for their TV to finish lifting up out of the entryway table. "Seriously? I tell you I have this great way for you to finally take a trip to Peridosh, and the first thing you do is turn the TV back on?"

"My skills in having no expectations whatsoever have been honed over a lifetime," Ember said blankly, staring at the black screen.

"Wow. Even with me? Thanks."

The fae turned toward her and smirked. "Doesn't mean I can't still get excited. What's this awesome new way?"

Cheyenne lifted the ring between her thumb and finger and shook it. "Surprise."

"I'm still waiting."

"What, you can't tell what this is?" The halfling chuckled. "I made you your very own fae disguise."

"Um..."

"Okay, so technically, I cast a personal illusion charm on this ring and was planning on using it for myself. You know, when I had to look like a drow and wear that magic-killing necklace at the same time. But now the pendant's useless, so those days are over for me."

"*You* cast an illusion charm?"

The halfling moved across the living room to sit on the armrest of the recliner beside her friend. "It took me hours. Corian almost ripped me to shreds. Don't let it go to waste."

Squinting at the ring, Ember slowly held out her hand. "If you charmed this for yourself, Cheyenne, I don't think it's gonna work for me."

"I mean, I didn't make it *personal* with blood or anything. The charm is made for showing the magical side, if you will." She dropped the ring into her friend's open palm and shrugged. "And full disclosure, when I managed to do this one the right way, I was planning on making one for you too. Then I got busy."

"Hey, it's the afterthought that counts."

"Don't make this weird. Just try it. If my old troll neighbors could lend me an illusion charm they didn't make for a drow halfling, I don't see why this won't work for you. That's the point of a generic charm, right? Covers a wide range of uses?"

"I don't even *have* a magical-looking side. I never have."

Cheyenne scoffed and waved off her friend's hesitation. "Just shut up and put on the ring. I wanna see what happens."

"Fine, but don't blow holes in the wall when this doesn't work."

"Maybe I should've left you with my mom. You fit right in with the skeptics and pessimists there."

Ember shot her an exasperated glance, then slipped the ring onto her middle finger in one smooth, swift motion. A soft white glow flashed around the human-looking fae, then Ember's features shifted. At first, it was almost impossible to tell the difference, but then the girl's skin lightened to a shade a lot more like Cheyenne's human coloring. Her eyes gave off an unsettling violet light, and her brown hair took on a darker shade with more red in it. The blonde highlights were distinctly lavender now, and her body gave off a shimmering pink glow in a thin halo, especially over her bare skin. The halfling couldn't see it if she looked directly at it, but the minute she shifted her gaze, there was that pink glow again in her peripheral vision.

The fae didn't notice a thing. "There. See? You made an illusion charm for yourself, and if I don't end up looking like a drow, I look—" Ember glanced down at her hands and frowned. "What the hell?"

"Yeah, go look in a mirror."

Ember wrinkled her nose at the halfling and wheeled herself back to turn toward the kitchen. "Don't tell me what to do. I'm gonna look in a mirror."

Cheyenne chuckled as her friend moved swiftly across the living room and disappeared through her open bedroom door. The chair bumped against a wall or two, then the bathroom light flicked on.

"What the *hell?*"

"Told you," Cheyenne called.

"What did you do to my eyes? Why am I pink and purple?"

"Must be the real you, Em."

"This is insane!" Ember cackled in her bathroom, then bumped around a bit. When she reappeared in the doorway, she'd centered herself enough to wheel the chair back into the kitchen without making a dent. "You did this?"

"Yeah, I know it's hard to believe."

"You *did* this!"

Cheyenne cocked her head. "You okay?"

75

Ember let out another wild laugh and looked at her hands again as her chair rolled slowly forward, turning them over in amazement. "I have no idea. Is this what I'd look like right now if I was born looking like this?"

"Have *you* never seen a full-blooded fae in action?"

"It's a hell of a lot different when it's *me*." The fae slipped the silver ring off her finger, and the pink glow and the violet light vanished.

This time, Cheyenne saw her friend's cheeks fill out the slightest bit and the almost imperceptible shift in her eyes when they faded to their normal brown color.

"You saw my eyes, right?" Ember pointed to her face. "They got all big and weird-looking."

"Not *that* weird."

"It's pretty fucking weird, Cheyenne. And you just slip in and out of drow and human like changing your underwear or something."

The halfling snorted. "That's a weird comparison, but okay."

The ring went back on Ember's middle finger and her fae appearance returned, full glow and everything. "Look at this!"

Stepping toward her friend, Cheyenne fought back a laugh and pointed at Ember's hand. "Hold up your hand for a second."

"Why? What's wrong?"

"Nothing's *wrong*." Cheyenne grabbed Ember's hand and pressed their palms together with a frown. "Weird."

"Hey, I'm already freaked out about looking like a fae with an illusion charm. You're not helping."

"I couldn't get that ring on anything but my pinky. Corian said fae have small fingers, but yours aren't *that* much smaller than mine."

Ember took her hand back and laughed. "Seriously? It's *magic*, Cheyenne. Why is that not enough of an explanation for you?"

The halfling cocked her head and chuckled. "Huh. I guess that's the only answer I need."

Glancing at her legs, Ember turned down the corners of her mouth and shrugged. "The only thing that would make this better is if my legs started working again."

"Aw, my bad. I should've started with something even *I* know is seriously advanced magic."

The fae smirked. "I don't think a spell for that exists, but I saw myself in the mirror and couldn't help wondering." Ember shook her head. "Doesn't matter. I've only had one physical therapy session so far."

"Which Dr. Boseley said went really well, right?"

"Yeah. But admittedly, *looking* like a fae in a wheelchair is a lot better than not looking like one." Ember blinked quickly, sniffed, and met her friend's gaze. "Thank you."

"Just something I had lying around. You know."

"Uh-huh."

"So." Cheyenne sat back down on the recliner's armrest and wiggled her eyebrows. "Is that enough to get you to come to Peridosh with me and some FRoE boneheads or what?"

"Damn straight, it is." Ember grinned. "Let's get the hell out of here."

The halfling glanced at the clock over the stove and choked back a laugh. "We're gonna have to wait a little longer. Yurik said six."

"Whatever." The fae stared at her hands and shook her head. Her grin stayed put. "That's just more time for me to get used to seeing myself like this. Otherwise, your FRoE friends are gonna think *I'm* the crazy one."

"Worst-case scenario."

Shooting her friend a quick glance, Ember studied her arms and patted her face a few times. Then she grabbed the remote from where she'd propped it between her legs and handed it to the halfling. "Pick whatever you wanna watch. Maybe it'll distract me."

Cheyenne stared at the remote but didn't touch it. "I wouldn't even know where to start."

"What? You just scroll through the shows and pick something. Do I need to show you which buttons to press?"

"I don't watch TV."

"It's not TV, Cheyenne. It's Netflix."

"Same thing."

Ember dropped her hand and the remote into her lap with a thump. "Are you kidding me? Now you're gonna tell me you didn't watch anything as a kid, either."

Cheyenne shrugged. "Did you see a TV at my mom's house?"

The fae's luminous, violet-glowing eyes narrowed, then she stared at their blank TV against the wall. "You grew up in that big fancy house without TV."

"No movies, either. I mean, I had the internet, but I dare you to imagine Bianca Summerlin sitting down for movie night with a bowl of popcorn."

"Ha." Ember blinked and shook her head. "That's pretty much impossible. Okay, fine. *I'll* pick something, and you can pretend to enjoy it for three hours while I pretend to ignore that *I look like a freakin' fae.*"

The halfling bit her lip to keep back a laugh as her friend jerked the remote toward the TV every time she pressed a button, her eyes comically wide. "Is that how you get the buttons to work?"

"Shut up and sit down." Ember kept clicking through the selection on their smart TV, but she lowered her hand into her lap.

CHAPTER THIRTEEN

"Okay, that's it." Cheyenne leaned forward in the armchair and snatched the remote off the table. "If I have to watch one more episode about whiney people trying to break out of prison, I'm gonna break the TV."

"Too much?" With a short laugh, Ember gestured toward the screen. "I promise it gets better after the first few episodes."

"I've already wasted three hours on the first few episodes." The halfling turned off the show and sent the TV sliding back down into its hidden spot in the table. "I can feel my brain melting."

"Right. Well, we can't all be insanely smart hackers who teach their professors' classes and kick criminal ass on the side for fun. The rest of us need hobbies too."

Laughing, Cheyenne tossed the remote on the coffee table and stood from the chair. The chains on her wrists jingled when she stretched her arms high above her head. "You can have your hobbies, Em. I'm done with watching weird shows for the next month—at least."

"What time is it?"

"Almost five-thirty." Glancing at her friend, Cheyenne raised an eyebrow and spread her arms. "Ready for your first trip into Richmond's very own underground marketplace? Literally."

"That's still a dumb question. Of course I'm ready."

"I thought so. Let me just grab my stuff." The halfling went up to the iron staircase to the mini-loft to get her phone off the desk. As soon as she slid it into her back pocket, someone knocked on the door.

"It's open," Ember called.

"Em!" Cheyenne pointed at her over the railing as the doorknob turned. "The ring."

"Shit." Ember struggled with the illusion charm on her finger as the door swung inward. She managed to pull it off a second before Matthew poked his head through the door, and his gaze settled on her as the flashing light of the broken charm receded. "Hey, Matthew."

"Hey. You said it was open."

Cheyenne stomped extra-loud down the metal staircase.

He glanced up at her and chuckled. "I thought it'd be okay to just come on in."

"Yeah, it's fine." Ember's hand clenched tightly around the ring, which she buried in her lap like she was trying to hide something.

"What are you guys up to tonight?"

"We've got plans." Cheyenne stepped past him to open the coat closet between the front door and the kitchen. "Jeeze, Em. Have enough jackets?"

"Grab the purple one." Saying the word "purple" made her snort, and she glanced into her lap as if the illusion charm would slip right out from within her tightly clenched fist.

"Sure." The halfling held back a chuckle and grabbed the purple jacket off its hanger before shutting the door.

Matthew glanced between them with a confused smile and opened the front door a little wider. "What kinda plans?"

Cheyenne lifted Ember's jacket hooked over one finger and nodded at their nosy neighbor. "The going-out kind."

The fae took her jacket and shot Cheyenne a warning look.

"On a Tuesday?" Matthew cocked his head.

"Why not?" Cheyenne grabbed her baggy hoodie with the white hand flipping the middle finger on the back and tugged it on.

"I need to get out," Ember added with a shrug. Then she patted the armrests of her chair. "Can't drive myself anywhere unless it's in this thing."

"Oh." Matthew's smile faded a little. "Well, I'm having some friends over a little later. If you guys wanna drop by when you get back, you're welcome to."

Ember sat straighter in her chair and smiled. "Thanks. That sounds fun."

"If we have time." Cheyenne stopped beside her friend and stuck her hands in the front pocket of her hoodie. "Who knows how long we'll be out?"

"Right. Sure." Matthew's gaze dropped quickly to Ember's fist in her lap, which she tried to hide by folding her arms. "You know where I live, so just knock."

Ember laughed and smiled at their tall, weirdly intrusive neighbor from across the hall.

The halfling glanced from her friend to Matthew Thomas, neither of whom seemed capable of pulling out of their shared gaze. *What is up with these two?*

"Okay, well." Cheyenne stepped behind her friend's chair and grabbed the handlebars. "Time to go. Have fun at your house party."

"Yeah, I will." Matthew stepped back into the hall as Cheyenne pushed Ember out of their apartment. "You will too, if you decide to come by."

"We might." Ember stared up at him with a goofy smile, her puffy purple jacket folded in her lap while Cheyenne pulled her keys out to lock up.

"If we have time."

Their neighbor chuckled. "You mentioned that part already."

"Oh, good." Grabbing the chair's handles again, Cheyenne nodded at the guy and pushed Ember down the hall. "See ya."

"Have fun."

"Thanks." Ember looked at him over her shoulder one last time. She laughed when she saw the halfling's skeptical frown and whispered, "What? It was nice of him to invite us."

Cheyenne waited until Matthew's front door closed again with their neighbor on the other side of it. "How much do you wanna bet he wouldn't have invited me if I wasn't standing right there next to you?"

"Huh. I wonder why."

Shaking her head, the halfling punched the elevator's call button and folded her arms. "I'm a lot nicer to him than I am to the people I really don't like."

"But you don't *like* him, either."

"I don't know." Cheyenne squinted down the hall at Matthew's front door. "There's something weird about that guy. Beyond his ridiculously obvious crush on you."

"Why is *that* weird?"

"It's not. He just makes it creepy when he walks right into the apartment and stares at you." The elevator doors opened, and Cheyenne pushed her friend inside before hitting the button for the lobby. "If I didn't have all this other stuff going on, I might do more than Google the guy."

"You Googled him."

"Yeah. That's a thing."

"Cheyenne." Ember tipped her head all the way back and looked exasperated. "Why is it so weird that somebody's nice and helpful and happens to have a thing for your housemate in a wheelchair?"

"I'm not talking about that last one, Em. The weird part is that nobody's that nice all the time on the outside unless they're secretly trying to get something out of it. He hasn't once snapped back at me. That's a red flag."

"Does it ever occur to you that nobody wants to snap back at a Goth chick who looks like she's ready to punch someone's lights out at any given second?"

Cheyenne laughed. "Of course it does. And the people who have a problem with the way I look are the people who don't want anything to do with me, including a little round of stinging banter. I don't care about that. But that Matthew guy didn't react once to the way I look *or* what I say. Nothing. It's like he's just…"

"Nice?"

The elevator doors opened again on the ground floor, and Cheyenne pulled Ember backward into the lobby. "*Too* nice, Em. Too nice to be genuine."

"You know what?" The fae leaned forward to slip into her jacket as they headed toward the front doors. "I think you've spent way too much time studying your mom."

"What's that supposed to mean?"

"It means you're a lot more cynical than you wanna admit. Or that you've been taught to expect the worst from people."

Cheyenne hit the handicap button beside the front doors and waited for them to slowly open. "I'm pretty sure I heard you say something about perfecting the art of having no expectations."

"Okay, well, no expectations and expecting the worst are two different things."

"The outcome's the same, though, right? You're never disappointed, even if you're wrong."

Ember looked at the halfling over her shoulder and wrinkled her nose. "That's not how *you* think about the world."

"Maybe. Maybe not." Cheyenne shrugged it off and wheeled her friend toward where she'd parked the Panamera in the apartment complex's huge parking lot. *That doesn't make Mom's motto any less accurate. Everything comes with a price.* "Assuming he is genuinely a *nice* person, I still say he's trying to get something out of it."

"Oh, yeah? Like what?"

They reached the car, and Cheyenne locked the chair's wheels before unlocking the car with that perfect little chirp and opening the passenger side door. "I mean, to get in your pants, for one thing."

"Oh, my God." Ember rolled her eyes and braced herself against the chair. "Stop talking and help me get in the car."

"What? Don't tell me you haven't caught onto that by now."

Ember laughed. "We're not having this conversation. Not right now."

"Uh-huh. Because then you'd tell me that you're totally into it."

"Do I have to make this transfer myself?"

Cheyenne snorted and bent down to assist her best friend into the car.

She pulled into the parking lot on Union Hill ten minutes before 6:00 p.m. As she unfolded the wheelchair and locked it up beside Ember's door, Cheyenne found herself glancing around for a car that looked like it could have come straight out of a time machine from the '50s.

Ember laughed when they got her settled in the chair. "Who are *you* looking for?"

"I told you about that old guy who does custom work on cars, right?"

"This is where you met him?"

"Yeah." The halfling chuckled. "He was cool. I should call him."

"What the hell would you have him do to a brand-new Porsche?"

Shrugging, Cheyenne shut the door and turned toward the street off the parking lot. "Whatever he wanted, I guess. It'd just be a cool thing to do."

"I don't get it."

"Hey, you had your moment to go crazy with putting the apartment together. Which, by the way, is totally awesome. This guy does it with cars." Cheyenne had to help Ember get the chair over the bumps in the parking lot's entrance, then again when they reached the ramp up onto the sidewalk beside the rows of shops lining the street.

"You know, I never stopped to think about how crappy these ramps are before I tried pushing myself up onto one." Ember jerked down on the wheels as Cheyenne pushed the back of her chair. "All about perspective, right?"

"That's a good way to put it."

They didn't pass many other pedestrians on the street, given the mid-October chill in the air and that it was Tuesday. Ember glanced in the windows of every single shop they passed, grinning at her reflection. "So, how do we get down there?"

Cheyenne pointed at the marque above the froyo shop two stores ahead of them. "Gotta hit the frozen yogurt place first."

"Hey, I like dessert before dinner as much as the next girl, but I'm not in the mood for froyo."

The halfling laughed as she stopped beside the door and pulled it open. "Neither am I."

"Oh. It's *this* place?"

"Yeah. And it's nowhere near the best part."

CHAPTER FOURTEEN

"You're late, Cheyenne." Yurik stepped away from the counter at the back of the froyo shop with a smirk.

"By like three minutes. Relax." The halfling shot Ember a crooked smile as they made their way past the tables and chairs and the stations of cookies and candy pieces.

"Who's your friend?" Tate stuck his hands in his pockets and eyed the two magicals they'd been waiting for.

"This is Ember." Cheyenne gestured toward the FRoE agents wearing their temporary human masks. "Yurik, Tate, and Bhandi."

"Hey." Bhandi jerked her chin at Ember and folded her arms. "You been here before?"

Ember shook her head, wrinkling her nose with an unsure laugh. "First time."

"All right. Another newbie." Yurik turned toward the man behind the counter and held out his fist for a bump. The man shoveled a heaping spoonful of lime-green frozen yogurt into his mouth and stared at the disguised goblin. "Okay. Good to see ya, Joe."

Tate snorted and headed toward the back of the empty store. "Come on."

The group followed him toward the door marked Employees Only.

Ember's eyes widened when he opened it and gestured for everyone to step inside.

"Do any of you work here?"

Bhandi sniggered. "No way. Our job is about as far away as you can get from serving ice cream to kids."

Joe shook his head as he glared after them. "I shouldn't have to keep tellin' you it ain't ice cream."

"Yeah, yeah." The troll woman waved him off and stepped into the tiny room.

Yurik followed, and Tate waited for Ember and Cheyenne to enter before he stepped inside and pulled the door shut behind him. The lights flickered on to illuminate the stainless steel walls of the elevator to the magical marketplace under Richmond, Virginia.

Ember pressed her lips together and scanned the small, cramped space as they started to move down. "We just walked into an elevator."

Bhandi snorted. "Good one."

Tate shot her a frown and shook his head.

"What? She said, 'We walked into an elevator.' Oh." The troll woman looked at Ember and grimaced. "That wasn't a joke?"

"Uh, not really. The chair's pretty new for me. Still adjusting to my word choice, I guess." The fae's smile was tight and a little uncomfortable.

Bhandi shook her head. "Man, I'm sorry. I thought that was on purpose."

"Don't worry about it."

Cheyenne leaned against the wall of the elevator and watched the whole thing play out, her eyebrows raised. Perfect ice-breaker right there.

"Half the shit that comes flying out of Bhandi's mouth is just that." Tate shrugged at Ember with a quick glance at the troll woman. "The other half is, like, only half-serious."

"Yeah, okay." Bhandi scowled at him. "I can be serious."

"Not where we're goin'."

Yurik cleared his throat. "So. Ember. What made you decide to come with the halfling for your first time down here?"

The fae looked up at Cheyenne and chuckled. "She convinced me it would be worth my time, I guess."

"You guess." Tate nodded and slipped the thick black ring off his finger before shoving it into his pocket. "Have you *seen* Cheyenne fight somebody? 'Cause that's when she gets real convincing."

"Right." Cheyenne rolled her eyes.

"Yeah, I have." Ember shrugged. "She didn't have to fight me, though. It just took some stories about you guys, and I figured I'd come watch the show."

"*Oh!*" Yurik put a hand to his mouth and stared at Bhandi. "Was that a burn from the new girl?"

Bhandi lifted her chin and glanced from Ember to Cheyenne and back again. "What stories?"

"All of them."

The troll woman hung her head as Tate and Yurik burst out laughing. "A troll can't make *one* mistake."

"Yeah, right." Yurik pulled off his ring, and his topknot faded into the yellow strip down the center of his head, his skin changing quickly from human-pale to washed-out-goblin-green in an instant. The bullring through his septum stayed where it was. "Like you've only ever made one mistake."

"All right." Bhandi glared at him. "Should we talk about all the shit you pulled at Rez 17 last year? 'Cause I sure as shit could come up with some stories of my own." The troll woman raised an eyebrow at Ember and slipped off her "mask," sticking the black ring in her pocket. "I've got plenty of stories too. And I *know* you haven't heard those."

Tate sniffed at the air and leaned against the wall of the elevator as Bhandi's auburn-haired illusion faded, revealing her purple skin and thick, braided scarlet hair that matched the color of her eyes. "Smells like fae in here."

"Seriously?" Ember looked up at Cheyenne. "That's three times in one day."

The halfling smirked at her friend and slipped into her drow form to match everyone else's magical appearance. "Guess I'm the only one who doesn't pick up on it."

"Wait, that's *you*?" Tate grinned. "We get to show a real fucking fae around Peridosh for the first time. There's a lot more to celebrate than I expected."

Cheyenne nodded subtly at Ember, who didn't miss a beat and stuck her hand into her jacket pocket to slip on the illusion-charm ring. With her other hand beside her thigh, Ember finished the trick by moving her fingers in a quick series of gestures. Cheyenne pressed her lips together.

She really thought that one through. No one's gonna know she wasn't wearing an illusion.

Ember's light-brown hair deepened with a purple tint, the blonde highlights taking on the same violet color as her luminous, slightly larger eyes, and the fae glowed with internal pink light.

"No shit." Bhandi pointed at Ember as she shot Yurik a surprised glance. "Did you know what she was?"

The muscular goblin shrugged.

"Man, I haven't seen a fae in decades!" Clapping her hands, Bhandi nodded repeatedly. "This is just the kinda thing I needed today."

Ember spread her arms. "Well, here I am."

"Hell, yeah, here you are." The troll woman folded her arms and briefly eyed the wheelchair. "How long are you stuck in that thing?"

"Dude." Tate shot her another disgusted glance and shook his head. "Not the kinda question you ask someone you just met."

"Hey, I'm just curious. I didn't know fae rolled around with their own set of wheels."

Yurik snorted. "Shoulda known your head would still be up your ass."

"Hey, screw you!"

"No, it's okay." Ember lifted a hand, trying to stop the tense reactions before they got even worse. "It's a lot better to be asked about it than have you pretend I'm on my feet like everyone else."

"See?" Bhandi flipped Tate the bird. The troll man snorted and shook his head.

"Honestly, I have no idea how long I'm gonna be in this thing. It hasn't even been a week." Ember patted the armrests with another shrug. "But it's proof that fae can get messed up just like anyone else."

"Nah." Yurik waved her off. "You'll be outta that thing in no time. I heard fae are expert healers."

Bhandi snorted. "Who told you that, huh? The same gremlin who tried to sell you a tonic for hair growth?"

"I *have* hair, man. Tate's the bald one."

"By choice." Tate rubbed his bald, tattooed head, then gave it a sharp smack.

"Nice." Bhandi reached out to do the same, but Tate blocked her and batted her hand aside.

"Don't touch my head."

"Oh, *now* you have a problem with personal space, huh?"

"What, you want me to start playing with your hair too?"

Cheyenne and Ember shared confused glances, then the halfling looked at Yurik. The goblin's arms were folded, and he raised his eyebrows with a little shrug.

Everybody's tense tonight. We'll fix that.

The elevator ground to a slow, shuddering halt when it reached the bottom of its long descent into the underground marketplace. Bhandi and Tate stopped bickering, and the troll woman's eyes lit up.

"This is why we're here, fae." The elevator doors opened the second Bhandi pointed at them. "I don't care what anyone else does, but I'm gettin' hammered."

"Hasn't changed since the last time we were here," Tate muttered as he followed her out of the elevator. "Or the time before that. Or before that."

"You know what? Just quit yacking at me until I get at least a whole pitcher of grog down my throat, huh? Think you can do that?"

"Maybe."

Yurik rolled his eyes and pushed himself away from the wall to step into the wide, sweeping entrance of the underground marketplace for magicals only. Cheyenne left next and waited for Ember to wheel herself out onto the relatively smooth stone floor. The fae's luminous violet eyes widened even more when she saw the wide, sweeping arc of the massive tunnel stretching farther than they could see. "Holy shit."

"Welcome to Peridosh, Em." Cheyenne nudged her friend's shoulder and nodded after the FRoE agents disappearing into the throng of hundreds of magicals conducting their business down here. "I'm sure your first time will be less eventful than mine."

"We can only hope, right?" Ember laughed. "I'm not much good in a bar fight right now."

"Don't worry. I've got your back."

"Yeah, I bet you do."

CHAPTER FIFTEEN

"Woven rugs over here! With thread straight from back home, people! Stained with pure O'gúl radan dye and everything."

"Hey, you. Fae! Yeah, you. You need a Vrexes Scrubber for your potions? Don't even bother with the shop down there. That goblin's on his way out. I got what you need at much lower prices."

Ember spun away from the orc as he reached toward her over his table, a sludge-covered thing that looked like a squid dangling from his hands. "I'm good."

"Oh, come on. Fae like you needs to keep up her supplies, yeah?" Spit flew from the orc's mouth between his jutting tusks as he spoke. When Ember moved past his wares, the guy walked around the table and tried to follow her.

Cheyenne stepped between them and glared up at the vendor, who had a good six feet on her. "She said she's good."

The orc's eyes widened when he took in the drow standing in front of him. "Sure, sure. I'm just tryin' to make a living, you know? Gotta do what we gotta do."

"Well, do it from behind your table."

"Uh-huh." He looked after Ember one more time with a grimace of disappointment, then returned to his post behind his spread of nasty-looking wares. The squid-thing dropped onto the table with a splat, sending dark, muddy sludge splattering onto a tall, gangly goblin walking by at the right time.

Cheyenne left those two to argue and caught up with Ember. "People can get a little pushy down here."

"People?" Ember looked up at her with a smirk. "Every magical I've met is a *little* pushy, Cheyenne. I'm pretty sure that comes with the territory. You know, living in this world where we're not supposed to be."

She's not talking about the FRoE agents or us. We were all born here.

The halfling nodded. "Makes sense. Just don't be afraid to push back."

"Oh, I can push if I have to. Don't worry about that."

Cheyenne snorted. "I'd like to see that."

"Careful what you wish for, ha—" Ember stopped herself and wrinkled her nose. "I'm guessing that's not gonna fly down here, huh?"

"No. We can keep that part to ourselves." *Let the rest of these magicals keep thinking I'm a full-blooded drow. Just like they think those FRoE agents are in the same boat as everyone else.*

They pushed their way through the moving, bustling crowd. Cheyenne hadn't noticed how uneven the stone floor in the massive tunnel was until Ember slowed down. The halfling turned to ask if she needed help, but a soft violet light lifted the fae's wheelchair for two seconds before lowering her again on the other side of a rough patch of protruding stone.

Ember wiggled her eyebrows. "At least I can do *this* much for myself."

"Looks like you're gettin' the hang of it."

"That's what happens when I can only do one thing with my magic."

Cheyenne shook her head as she stared at a knobby, twisted-looking magical with skin that looked like tree bark. He hunched over a long walking stick and sneered at Ember, but when he glanced up at Cheyenne's narrowed golden eyes, he quickly looked away and thumped his cane faster against the stone floor.

A piercing whistle cut through the din of magicals shouting out their wares and shoppers shouting their annoyance over each other.

"Hey, Goth drow!" With one hand clutching the large handle of the Empty Barrel's front door as she held it open, Bhandi leaned back over the throng and waved at the tavern. "I thought you knew the drill by now. Hurry the hell up!"

Ember laughed. "She calls you 'Goth drow?'"

"It's better than 'rookie.' Doesn't mean she has to shout it out every chance she gets." Cheyenne stared right back at the magicals walking past her, most of whom noticed her for the first time once she'd been called out by her race for everyone to hear. Other vendors peered over their tables to get a better look at the drow in their midst, and the halfling nodded toward the tavern. Bhandi had already slipped inside, and the door shut again with a muted thump. "Come on. If you want an O'gúleesh drink, Em, we better get in there before she drinks that place dry."

"O'gúleesh drinks, huh?" Ember followed her friend through the crowd toward the tavern. "You sound like you fit right in down here."

"I'm trying." They stopped at the two steps leading up to the huge, thick wooden door beneath the rotting wooden sign with the tavern's name painted sloppily across the boards. "You want some help up these?"

Ember frowned at the stairs and cocked her head. "Just open the door, maybe?"

"You sure?"

"Hey, if you can run around the state testing your magic on every idiot who pisses you off, I'm allowed a little trial and error too, don't you think?"

"I'll open the door, then." Trying not to laugh, Cheyenne quickly climbed the stairs and pulled on the massive iron handle. Raucous laughter and a few angry shouts spilled out of the Empty Barrel, but she was focused on her friend.

Ember rolled backward three inches, then grabbed the wheels and gave them a fierce tug to launch the chair forward. The small front wheels hit the side of the first step with a thud and almost threw the fae forward, but her hands and all four wheels lit up with strobing purple light, and the chair soared over the steps and right through the door. It landed on the sticky wood of the tavern floor with a squeak, knocking into the closest table. Frothy grog sloshed over the sides of the tankards on the table while their owners leaped away from the sudden interruption.

"Hey, watch it!"

"Sorry. Sorry." Ember backed the chair up and aimed it at the center aisle running the length of the tavern. She looked over her shoulder and grinned at the orc shaking spilled grog off his hands. "Still learning how to drive this thing."

"Well, drive it somewhere else, huh?"

"Yep." She glanced at the orange-skinned, rat-faced skaxen woman sitting on the other side of the table and nodded. The skaxen slammed her palms on the table and hissed. Ember's grin disappeared, and she hissed back before quickly wheeling herself down the wide aisle between the dented, sticky bar and the rows of tables.

Watching with a mix of amusement and caution, Cheyenne stepped into the tavern and let the door swing shut behind her. The orc and skaxen at the closest table glared at her too, but they quickly looked away and leaned over their dripping tankards when she jerked her chin at them.

Either I look scarier than normal today, or the magical gossip train has made its way around Peridosh. I wonder who they think I am?

"All right! That's what I'm talkin' about." At the end of the bar toward the back of the tavern, Bhandi pounded both fists on the dented wood as Ogsa set two frothing pitchers of grog down in front of her.

"I'm assuming this is going on your beefy friend's tab too," the tavern owner grumbled. The intricate gold designs encircling her tusks glinted in the low light as she stuck her hands on her hips.

"Nothing changes that much in a few days, Ogsa." Bhandi grabbed the pitchers and raised them in a double-fisted salute. "It's always on Yurik's tab."

Yurik had been leaning against the bar, watching Ember's entrance with a crooked smile. When he heard Bhandi say his name, he blinked, straightened, and turned to face her. "Wait a minute."

The troll woman had already whirled away from the bar and was headed toward their regular table in the back corner, where Tate waited with three empty tankards.

With a grunt, Yurik turned back toward Ogsa and shrugged. "Yeah. I guess it's on my tab."

"And when, exactly, are you going to pay that tab, huh?" The orc woman leaned away from the bar and folded her arms. "It's been open for at least two months."

"Yeah, I know." He scratched his head. "I'll bring you your money next time. How's that?"

"Hardly convincing is what it is." Ogsa's yellow eyes darted toward Ember and Cheyenne making their way toward the bar. When she recognized the halfling, a low, deep chuckle burst out of her. "Back for more, huh?"

"Hey, Ogsa." Cheyenne stopped at the bar beside Yurik and gave the tavern owner a fleeting, tight-lipped smile. "I'd promise not to redecorate your tavern this time, but it's not up to me if some idiot decides they want to fight me again."

"Ha!" Ogsa slapped her side of the bar. "I don't think anyone's gonna mess with you after last time, drow. You made a name for yourself when you splattered that ogre's hand all over my walls."

Cheyenne glanced down at Ember, who pressed her lips together and pointed at the table in the corner. "I'm just gonna go to the table."

"Sure."

"Would you look at that!" Ogsa leaned over the bar to peer down at Ember. Her green-gray lips parted in a wide grin around her tusks. "I haven't had a fae in here since the year I opened this place. You don't want that grog swill I serve the rest of these brain-addled misfits, do ya?"

Ember chuckled. "Not if it's as bad as you say it is."

The orc woman barked a laugh. Sitting three stools down at the bar, the shriveled old troll and the white-skinned magical with glowing red eyes beside him jumped and shot her disapproving glances. "It's worse than that, fae. I'll whip you up a little something better suited for your people. Haven't pulled this out of the back in decades, but the stuff sure as shit never goes bad. You'll like it, I promise. You *can* drink in that chair, can't you?"

The fae's large, violet-glowing eyes narrowed at the tavern owner, and she smiled in an unspoken challenge. "I can do a lot more than drink in this chair."

"Ha! I bet you can. Never met a fae who couldn't do everything they wanted."

Ember glanced up at Cheyenne again, raising her eyebrows. "I'll be at the table."

"Sure."

"Wait, what are you making her?" Yurik asked, scanning the shelves of magical booze behind Ogsa.

"That's for me to know and her to drink, goblin."

"How much is it gonna run up my tab?" The agent spread his arms. "I'm not going to go broke just because you made something fancy that costs more than the rest of us are drinkin'."

Ogsa scowled at him. "You're already broke."

Yurik flashed the orc woman a mischievous grin and cocked his head. "Now you're hittin' below the belt."

"Don't worry about it," Cheyenne cut in. "I'll cover Ember's drink."

"Oh, yeah?" Ogsa studied her with a crooked smile. "She's with you, huh?"

"Yeah."

"And what does the *Aranél* want, huh?"

Cheyenne felt Yurik's confused gaze settle on her. "I'll just stick with the grog swill for now."

"Huh." Ogsa chuckled again. The rag she picked up from behind the bar was so dirty, it couldn't have done more than spread the stickiness around as she wiped the slab of wood in front of her. "Okay. I'll getcha what you want."

"How much do I owe you for the two, then?"

"You? Nothin', *Aranél*. Your drinks are covered."

Cheyenne shot Yurik a sidelong glance, the corners of her mouth turning down in surprise. "My drinks are covered."

The huge metal ring through the goblin's septum flapped against his upper lip when he shook his head. "That's bullshit."

"And before you ask, goblin," Ogsa said, turning halfway toward the shelves of unlabeled, multicolored O'gúleesh liquor bottles lining the wall behind her, "the answer's no. She can't just take over your tab, and she won't be gettin' half a dozen rounds for free so you and your buddies can go crazy in here at no charge."

"Of course not." Yurik chuckled and spread his arms. "That would be outrageous."

The orc woman raised a thick eyebrow at him and grunted.

"Might as well add a glass of fellwine to my order, then," Cheyenne added. When Yurik barked a laugh and Ogsa grinned around her tusks again, she added, "It's my friend's first time here."

"Hey, if you can get that fae to drink fellwine, I'll wipe this idiot's tab clean and call it an even trade." Chuckling, the orc woman turned to make the rest of their drinks.

"Well, now I've *really* got something to look forward to." Yurik brushed off the front of his navy and neon-yellow striped sweater with an obnoxiously large collar and looked up at Cheyenne with a grin. "If we have to force that green shit down your friend's throat, I'd be okay with it."

The halfling snorted. "Good luck with that."

With a quick glance over his shoulder at their table in the corner, Yurik cleared his throat and slid along the bar until his forearm almost touched Cheyenne's. She eyed his arm and raised an eyebrow.

"Right. Sorry." He sidestepped away from her but leaned toward her again to mutter, "What's the deal with your friend, anyway?"

"I have no idea what that means."

Yurik shrugged. "We came down here to pick your brain about the portals and whatever else got Sir's panties in a bunch. Didn't expect you to bring a friend."

Cheyenne turned to face him squarely, leaning sideways against the bar. "I didn't think I had to ask permission."

"No, you don't. I just wanna know how much we can trust her. You know, because of what we do for a living."

"Right." Cheyenne's gaze flickered toward the table in the corner, where Ember talked animatedly with her hands while Tate chuckled and Bhandi nearly sprayed a mouthful of grog everywhere when she laughed. The halfling shot Yurik a crooked half-smile. "I'll put it this way. I trust her a lot more than I trust the three of you."

He snorted. "That's not saying much."

"Not really, no. But she wasn't exaggerating when she said she's heard *all* the stories." Cheyenne nodded toward the table. "Ember knows who you guys are and what you do, and it looks like she doesn't give a shit."

"What about keepin' what she knows to herself?"

"If she had a problem doing that, I'd be in a *lot* of trouble."

Yurik laughed and tapped his knuckles on the bar. "I guess I'll take your word for it."

"You better. She needs this as much as I did the first time."

"Huh. So, if some asshole decides to pick a fight with *her* this time, should I stay in my seat again and let her handle it?"

Cheyenne scoffed. "No. You'll stay in your seat and let *me* handle it."

"Deal." The goblin drummed his hands on the bar as Ogsa returned with two tankards of grog, a copper cup of fizzing, green-glowing fell-wine, and a shimmering silver drink letting off sparkling bursts from the top of what was supposed to look like a fancy crystal chalice.

"You tell your friend there's plenty more where that came from if she wants it." The orc woman slid the drinks across the bar.

"What is it?"

"You get a few perks around here, drow." Ogsa nodded at the weird crystal chalice. "But getting your hands on my secret recipe ain't one of 'em."

"Ogsa!" A hulking figure covered with a long black cloak and hood smacked a black-gloved hand on the bar. "I've been standing here for hours!"

The orc woman pounded a fist on the bar and pointed at the disgruntled patron. "Unless you and your two heads are payin' double for every drink, Ogden, keep your forked tongues in your fell-damn mouths." Then she walked down the bar toward him, ignoring everyone else until the next eager magical stole her attention.

Yurik nodded at the chalice of sparkling silver alcohol as he grabbed his tankard of grog and the copper cup of fellwine. "I'm not touchin' that."

"Sounds like someone's scared of a little fae liquor."

Turning away from the bar, the goblin glanced from the chalice in Cheyenne's hand to her face and cocked his head. "Maybe. Good thing you're not afraid of shit, right?"

He headed toward their table before she had a chance to reply.

I'm pretty sure that's what got me into this FRoE-friend mess in the first place.

Cheyenne took a tentative sniff of the mystery drink and wrinkled her nose before walking after him.

CHAPTER SIXTEEN

"Here you go, Ember." Yurik slid the fellwine across the table toward her, trying to keep a straight face. Tate snickered. Bhandi lowered the tankard she'd nearly turned upside down over her face, belched, and slammed it on the table before reaching for one of the pitchers. She paused when she saw the copper cup, then chuckled and refilled her drink.

Ember glanced into the cup in front of her, then sat back in her wheelchair and smirked up at the goblin. "Let me guess. You're gonna tell me fellwine goes down best when it's knocked back in one go, right?"

The amusement faded from Yurik's face, and he looked between the fae and the copper cup. "Shit."

"Did I tell you about that?" Cheyenne took the empty chair beside Ember and set both drinks on the table.

"Maybe. But I've seen a few shots of that stuff start a riot at family reunions." The fae shook her head and laughed. "I know better."

Tate chuckled into his tankard.

"Come on." Yurik gestured toward the fellwine. "Just a little sip, then, huh?"

"Not my thing."

He glanced at the bar and leaned over the table, lowering his voice.

"If you drink that, Ogsa's gonna wipe out my tab. I'd owe you one for sure."

"Well, then she knows what she's talking about." Ember chuckled. "Sorry."

"Gonna drink that? Right on." Bhandi across the table and snatched up the copper cup. She lifted her tankard in the other hand, guzzled half of it, and poured the fellwine in with the rest of her grog before lifting her tankard for a toast. "To the fae. Not as naïve as she looks."

"For real? There wasn't a time limit on getting her to drink the stuff." Yurik stared at the troll woman, and no one else raised a glass to join in on the toast.

"Right. Like you had any chance of Ogsa knocking out what you owe her." Bhandi took a long sip of her fellwine bomb, practically slammed the tankard down on the table, and shook her head with a whoop of surprise. Her scarlet braids flew in every direction. "Holy shit! I just invented the magical Irish Car Bomb."

Cheyenne and Ember exchanged amused glances. *At least Bhandi never had to deal with real car bombs. I can keep that to myself.*

Tate leaned forward in his chair, chuckling. "There's no way you're the first magical to mix suicide in a tankard."

"I don't care what anyone else did with it." Bhandi took another swig and grimaced, clenching her eyes shut. "But damn. I think I've got a new favorite."

Yurik snorted. "I'm not paying for your pitchers of grog *and* more fellwine than anyone should drink in one night."

"Well, you're not paying for anything, are you? Not yet."

"You've lost your damn mind, haven't you?"

Bhandi pointed at the muscular goblin and opened her mouth to reply, then took another gulp of fellwine-grog before sucking in a sharp breath. "You've known that since the first time we geared up and shipped out on assignment. Don't pretend you're surprised *now*."

"No, I'm just surprised you're still breathing."

"Ha!" The troll woman slammed both fists on the table and leaned forward, leering at her fellow agent. "This troll doesn't go down that easily. We've all been through some shit, man. If that hasn't killed us by now, a Fellwine Car Bomb sure as shit isn't gonna do the job."

"Yep." Tate shifted in his chair and lifted his tankard for another toast. "Here's to going through shit and not dying."

"I guess that's good enough." Yurik lifted his tankard, waiting for Bhandi to finish glugging down more of her O'gúleesh concoction.

"Hell, I can drink to that." Cheyenne lifted her frothing tankard, and the FRoE agents laughed.

"Yeah, Goth drow's seen the ugly side of the coin enough times too," Bhandi shouted, leaning toward the halfling with a wry smile.

Ember picked up her chalice of fae-inspired whatever and clinked it lightly against the raised tankards over the center of the table. "To not dying."

All cups were lowered and tapped on the table before the magicals raised their drinks to their lips and finished the toast. Bhandi downed the rest of hers, belched again, and emptied the pitcher into her tankard before pouring from the other. "And how'd *you* almost die, fae girl?"

Tate slapped his palm to his forehead.

"What? Honest question. She's the only one I haven't seen in action."

Ember took another sip of her glowing silver drink, smiling at the warm rush of magical alcohol blooming quickly in her cheeks. "I wouldn't call it being in action, necessarily." When she glanced at Cheyenne, the half-drow raised an eyebrow and shrugged. "I was shot in the spinal cord."

This time, Bhandi did spray her next mouthful of grog and fellwine all over the place, but she had the presence of mind to duck away from the table and aim it at the already sticky floor of the tavern. The patrons sitting closest to their corner table eyed the troll woman in disgust. She ignored them and wiped her dripping chin with the back of a hand as she sat up again and stared at Ember. "Shit."

"Something like that, yeah." The fae smirked over the rim of the chalice as she drank again.

"Well, you look good for taking a bullet in the back," Yurik added with a shrug.

"More like *through* the back. The asshole shot me here." Ember gently touched her lower abdomen. "And now I'm in this chair. Temporarily."

Tate let out a low whistle. "If you're still runnin' around with

Cheyenne after something like that, man, I have no doubt you'll be back on your feet. I heard fae are pretty good at that."

"What happened to the other guy?" Yurik asked.

Ember smiled at Cheyenne, the pink glow around her body pulsing with the magical booze in her system. "Cheyenne paid him a visit."

"Fuck." Bhandi's eyes widened, and she glanced around the table to meet her fellow operatives' gazes. "I'm pretty sure we all know what *that* means."

Cheyenne forced herself not to say anything and smiled grimly instead. *I didn't get to tell her what really happened with Durg and now's not the right time.*

Ember took another sip of her fae drink. "But my story's not nearly as interesting as hers."

Yurik barked a laugh and sat back in his chair. "Oh, yeah. We know all about Cheyenne's interesting story."

"I doubt that." Ember's eyes flashed violet.

"Now, *this* is getting good." Bhandi propped her forearms on the table and stared expectantly at Cheyenne. "I have a feeling that if you don't tell us what's up, Goth drow, your friend's gonna spill the beans for you."

Cheyenne laughed it off but eyed Ember with a raised eyebrow. "You feelin' okay?"

"I feel fucking great!" The fae grinned at her, then eyed the chalice in her hand. "Shit. That orc got me drunk on four sips."

The FRoE agents burst out laughing.

"That's her job, man." Tate's laughter settled into a chuckle as he scratched the back of his bald head. "Enjoy it."

"Yeah, especially 'cause it's free," Yurik added, feigning insult.

"You know what, greenface? We're all tired of hearing you bitch about the tab you haven't even paid yet. Quit changing the subject." Bhandi pointed at Yurik, who flipped her the middle finger before the troll woman returned her gaze to Cheyenne. "I wanna hear this interesting story Ember's so sure we don't know."

"You *don't* know it." Ember tossed a hand in the air and laughed. "It happened last night."

"So, what the hell is it?" Bhandi's wide eyes didn't leave Cheyenne's face. Tate and Yurik reflected the troll woman's intense fascination as they leaned forward over their tankards.

Cheyenne shot Ember a sidelong glance. "Remind me not to take you out for drinks if I wanna bring up any subject on my own."

"Oh, come on." Ember snorted. "You were gonna tell them anyway."

"Tell us what?" Yurik sniffed and slid his finger beneath the giant bullring in his septum to scratch his upper lip.

The halfling smirked and slowly raised her tankard to her lips for her second sip of the night. *I guess now's as good a time as any.*

"Quit fuckin' around, Goth drow," Bhandi muttered. "What the hell happened?"

Cheyenne lowered her tankard and glanced at the ceiling. "I had another one of those almost-dying moments last night."

Tate hissed out a laugh. "Is *that* all?"

"Not even close." *This is so weird to talk about. L'zar and Corian were right, though. Keep the FRoE on a tight leash as long as I can.* "A new portal opened at my mom's house."

"What the fuck?" Bhandi's amused smile disappeared, replaced by a deepening frown.

"Like, *at* her house?" Tate asked.

"Yeah. Right outside in the backyard."

"Damn." Yurik let go of his tankard and sat back, stroking his chin. "So, it's really happening."

"Seems like it. Whatever *it* is."

"Man, I was seriously hoping Sir was full of shit." Bhandi tried to laugh, but it didn't have any of her usual gruff lightheartedness.

Cheyenne shrugged. "I mean, he is."

The agents chuckled, shaking their heads.

"I'll drink to that." Bhandi lifted her tankard to do just that.

"You'll drink to anything."

"Damn straight." The troll woman knocked back another gulp, set her tankard down, and raised an eyebrow at Tate. "And you're about to get your face bashed in if you keep acting like you're not as bothered by all this portal shit as the rest of us."

"Yeah, I'm bothered by it." Tate folded his arms again, the dark-blue and black tattoos rippling on his biceps. "Mostly 'cause I don't know what the hell it is."

"Neither do I," Cheyenne added. *Mostly.* "But what I do know is that the new Border portals popping up don't act like they're supposed to."

"Well, that's obvious." Bhandi leaned forward. "Those things aren't supposed to exist."

"Right. They're doing a lot more than existing, though." The halfling took another sip of her grog and watched the agents' reactions. *I don't know how much I can tell them, but they might know something I don't.*

"Wait." Yurik frowned. "There's more than one?"

"Probably." Cheyenne gestured toward herself and Ember. "The only one we've seen up close and personal is the one that sent an earthquake through my mom's house and opened in her backyard."

Ember blinked quickly and shot her friend a confused look.

Please just roll with it, Em. The FRoE can't know I'm hiding a second portal with L'zar Verdys and his crew.

"And the earthquake almost killed you, or what?" Bhandi squinted and glanced between Cheyenne and Ember.

"Not the earthquake. The portal's leaking."

Yurik snorted. "Okay. Now it sounds like you're playing Sir's bullshit game."

"She's not." Ember shook her head. "I've never seen anything like what came out of that weird black rock last night."

"So it's *leaking.*" Tate cocked his head. "Leaking what?"

"You guys have heard O'gúleesh talk about the crossing, right?"

"Once or twice, sure." Yurik scratched his head. "Honestly, it sounds more like they all drank the Kool-Aid before coming Earthside."

"Crazy-ass stories," Bhandi added, waving the whole thing aside. "Shit about monsters made of smoke and octopuses coming up out of the ground or whatever."

Tate frowned at her. "It's *octopi.*"

"What? Are you shitfaced already?"

Ember shrugged. "They're both right."

The troll looked at the fae with surprise and confusion.

Yurik shook his head. "Who gives a shit? Cheyenne's trying to make a point, and I wanna hear it."

Cheyenne glanced around the crowded tavern, pleased to find that most of the other patrons were deliberately not looking at her. Then she leaned over the table toward her friends and lowered her voice.

"My point is that whatever those things are, that's what's leaking out of the portals."

"Bullshit," Bhandi muttered.

Ember pulled the chalice closer but didn't pick it up. "No bullshit. I saw it too. That's what Cheyenne had to fight off by herself last night."

The halfling shrugged. "That's what almost killed me last night."

Yurik swallowed. "Damn."

Tate vigorously rubbed his bald head, his scarlet eyes darting around the table before settling on the tavern's ceiling. "How the hell are our people supposed to keep things under wraps if new portals start popping up everywhere?"

"New portals that fight back," Bhandi added with a grimace.

Cheyenne cocked her head. "I'm pretty sure that's the question that launched Sir into his...whatever he's going through right now."

"Midlife crisis?"

"Mental break?"

"Tossing out his last goddamn marble?"

The operatives looked at each other and chuckled, but it was strained this time.

"All of the above, probably," Cheyenne added. "I called him last night after I *didn't* die and told him what happened and what I knew. That apparently wasn't enough to keep him from losing his shit."

"It never is." Bhandi cocked her head in another small solo toast and tipped back her tankard.

"Is that why he called you in this morning?" Yurik asked. "To get the drow's advice on how to handle a mess like that?"

"No." Cheyenne let out a humorless chuckle. "He sent Rhynehart out to my mom's with a whole team to keep an eye on the thing, no questions asked. Almost. They've been there since last night, and as far as I know, nothing else has tried to push through the portal. I seriously hope they're still there."

"So, he ordered you on base to talk about L'zar."

Cheyenne raised an eyebrow at Tate. "You know about that too, huh?"

"It's impossible not to hear the guy raving like a lunatic. He hasn't come to any of us about it, and he won't. But yeah. The whole base knows."

"Well, I can't say I'm surprised."

"You know where he is?"

The halfling turned her attention to Yurik and gave him the deadpan stare she'd perfected over a lifetime of using it. "I've gone on more than enough *missions* or whatever with you guys to figure we're cool. You showed me this place, and you've had my back more than once. So I'll tell you that I have no clue where L'zar Verdys is right now, and I'm dead serious when I tell you not to ask me again."

Yurik spread his arms and dipped his head. "Hear you loud and clear, Cheyenne. Didn't mean to push a button."

"Everything's pushing everyone's buttons right now." The halfling took a long drink of her grog to hide her face inside the metal tankard. *And I'm sick of people asking me about that damn drow.*

"Nobody pushes Goth drow and gets away with it, huh?" Bhandi's eyelids drooped over her scarlet eyes, and she swayed in her chair when she raised her tankard again. "That ogre figured that one out pretty damn quick."

"More than one ogre." Tate snorted into his tankard.

"That's *right*. Took the legs right off that one at the mansion, didn't ya?" Bhandi shook her head and belched again. "Those sick kidnapping fucks."

Ember looked at Cheyenne with a questioning frown, and the halfling shrugged. "Rough day for everyone."

"You can say that again." Yurik stared into his tankard. "And you were right about those bastards taking the kids for whatever black-magic shit they were tryin' to pull. At this point, I'll believe what you're telling us over anything spraying out of Sir's mouth."

"About the portals?"

The goblin nodded.

"What's he saying?"

"Nope! Pause. Time out," Bhandi shouted and slammed her tankard onto the table. "I can't listen to this shit on an empty stomach."

"You never have an empty stomach."

"You know what, Tate?" The troll woman lurched out of her chair, swaying again, and raised her hands in front of her, wiggling all ten purple fingers. "I used to think that whole thing about fellwine giving somebody berserker-rage strength was a load of bull too. But right now, I'm really feelin' like I could rip your head right off your shoulders."

Tate smirked. "You could try."

"Raincheck." Bhandi gestured drunkenly toward the bar. "I'm gonna get us some grub. Ogsa cooks like she's never done it before, but damn, it sure soaks up the booze."

Before anyone could stop her, the troll woman stumbled out from behind the table and staggered toward the bar. She knocked into a short, timid-looking troll woman also on her way to the bar. The other troll hissed at Bhandi and snarled something incomprehensible over the din of the many magical patrons filling the Empty Barrel. Bhandi hissed back and shoved the other woman away before slamming both fists on the bar and squinting at the long row of shelved liquor bottles.

"Is she always like that?" Ember asked, then hiccupped and blinked in surprise.

"Yep." Tate stared at the troll woman's back as she hunched over the bar. "Every single time. Nobody down here knows what she could do to them if they ever caught her out in the field. Crazy-ass troll is a helluva soldier."

Yurik chuckled. "But they know not to mess with Bareass Bhandi down here."

Ember burst out laughing. "People call her that?"

"Oh, yeah. I think it stuck."

The fae laughed and shook her head. "What does somebody have to do around here to pick up a name like that?"

Tate snickered. Yurik fought back his own laugh and picked up his tankard again. "It's pretty damn obvious, isn't it?"

CHAPTER SEVENTEEN

"That's more like it." Bhandi shoved a huge platter of O'gúleesh tavern grub that looked like dog food into the center of the table and belched. "Anyone want some?"

Tate jammed a handful of fried grasshoppers into his mouth and crunched loudly. "Not after you've been shoveling that into your face with both hands."

"That's how you're *supposed* to eat it." The troll woman gestured at the platter. "Didn't come with utensils, did it?"

Ember leaned forward to grab a piece of what she hoped was pita bread off the smaller plate beside the platter. "I think that's what these are for."

"Huh?" Bhandi glanced at the plate. "When did those get here?"

Tate and Yurik snickered and kept eating their bar snacks.

Cheyenne watched her friend take a huge bite of the bread. "How is it?"

"Better than I expected."

"Hey, she's catching on." Yurik wagged a finger at the fae. "Lower your expectations as far as possible in this place, and you'll have a great time."

Bhandi winced, thumped her chest, and shook her head. "Something's stuck."

"You can keep that kinda problem to yourself." Tate eyed the troll woman sideways and shook his head.

Cheyenne smirked. "Okay. So now that the starving troll's got her fix, let's get back to what *you* guys have heard about those portals."

"You know, watching a new one pop up right before fighting whatever crazy things came out of it would make most people run away screaming."

The halfling eyed Yurik with a raised eyebrow. "I'm not most people."

"Yeah, we've figured that out by now. Why are you so interested?"

Cheyenne leaned over the table again. "Listen. My mom lives out in the middle of nowhere, pretty much. It's just her and her housekeeper."

"She's got a housekeeper?" Bhandi scrunched her face again, finally belched, and sat back with a sigh.

"Yeah. You done?"

The troll woman gestured for the halfling to continue.

"They won't leave the house. As in, my mom refuses to leave, despite having seen everything that happened in her backyard last night. That was why I called Sir and asked for a team to go up and protect her from whatever else tries to sneak Earthside. I let him think I was turning the whole thing over to you guys, 'cause portals are half of what you people do, right?"

"You *let* him think." Yurik snorted. "Well-played."

"Well, I needed to keep my mom safe. That's why I'm interested. Sir's put me on portal duty, and if I see anything else, yeah, I'm gonna let him know. But if you guys have heard something I haven't, I wanna hear it too. Leaving my mom up there with Rhynehart and a bunch of your guys in gear was hard."

"Did you hear that? The Goth drow *does* have a heart." Bhandi dragged the second pitcher toward her and dumped it over her tankard. A mere splash fell into her cup, and she shook the pitcher before scowling at it. "I need more."

"Hold off on that for a minute, huh?" Yurik took the pitcher from her and set it on the opposite edge of the table. "Let the fellwine kick in."

"Since when did you become my mom, asshole?"

He smacked her on the shoulder with the back of a hand and

gestured toward Cheyenne. "Since we're trying to have a serious conversation here. That's the whole reason we met up."

Bhandi folded her arms and slumped back in her chair. She almost slid sideways out of it but managed to correct herself. "Twenty minutes. Then I'm fillin' up."

"Whatever."

Tate settled his forearms on the table and glanced at the full tavern around them. "We don't know much, honestly. I mean, yeah, everyone knows about L'zar, and we've heard a few things from the other side of closed doors about new portals. So far, it sounds like Sir's trying to pull active personnel off the reservations to form a scouting team. Kinda stupid, but that's what Karzen told me, anyway."

Yurik nodded. "It's not any of us. We go out in the field to pull off the kind of operations where you've tagged along with us. No point tying up a tactical team for a new portal that just showed up. They're gonna send the guys who handle rez regulation."

"That's a seriously stupid call."

"Care to elaborate on that one?"

Cheyenne ran a hand through her hair, the chains jingling on her wrist. "These new portals *need* a tactical team. I mean, correct me if I'm wrong, but I'm pretty sure rez regulation and registering new O'gúleesh once they make the crossing doesn't have shit to do with fighting shape-shifting things that aren't supposed to be able to come through the portals at all."

"Right." Bhandi snorted. "And someone who's spent their entire career stationed at a rez right next to those giant portal towers won't have any insight into how to handle the new ones."

The halfling cocked her head. "Sir didn't have a clue about the new portal until *I* called him. If the top guy is that blind to what's happening, you really think the Border patrol is gonna be prepared enough to handle something none of them have ever seen?" Cheyenne leaned closer and lowered her voice. "You guys said it yourselves. Everyone you work with was born Earthside. None of you made the crossing, so you have no idea what I'm talking about with those things spilling out onto this side. But a tactical team knows how to fight them off. Right?"

Yurik frowned at Tate, who stroked his hairless tattooed chin. "Sir's grasping at straws."

Cheyenne offered a small shrug. "I hate to break it to you guys, but Sir doesn't know nearly as much as he thinks he does."

"Ha!" Bhandi slapped a hand on the table. "Try saying that to his face."

"Oh, I already have."

The table fell silent as the three FRoE agents stared at Cheyenne in shock. Then they burst out laughing again. Bhandi thumped her fists on the table, sloshing around the dogfood-looking grub on the platter, and Tate nearly fell out of his chair when he doubled over and leaned too far sideways.

"Jesus." Yurik wiped his eyes and glanced at the tavern's ceiling. "You have a death wish, don't you?"

"Hey, I don't work for him." Cheyenne shrugged, grinning. "I don't work for anyone. Even if I did, that wouldn't stop me from tellin' it like it is."

"No wonder Sir's so pissed off all the time." Tate chuckled. "He can't control you, but he can't afford to cut you loose, either."

"He'll figure out how it works eventually." The halfling's statement sent them into another round of uncontrollable laughter.

Bhandi stomped her feet over and over until her knees thumped the underside of the table and almost sent it flying. Ember rolled backward in her chair just in case, but Tate and Cheyenne caught the table and settled it upright before any of the dishes could slide onto the floor.

"Hey!" Ogsa leaned over the bar and pointed at the group in the corner. "Don't make me throw you out!"

Bhandi spread her arms. "For laughing?"

"For acting like a bunch of lunatics and scaring off my customers." The orc woman nodded at the front door, where two tall magicals in long crimson robes headed quickly out of the tavern.

"Nah." Bhandi scoffed. "If they're scared of a good time, they don't belong here in the first place."

"Whatever you call it, cut it out." Ogsa chucked her dirty rag onto the bar and went to pour more drinks for her other patrons.

Smirking, Bhandi shot Ember a conspiratorial wink. "She really does love us."

Ember chuckled. "Why? You scare off her customers and don't even pay for your drinks."

Tate barked a laugh, his eyes bulging in his head. Bhandi glared at him.

"At this point, Cheyenne might be the only reason that orc lets us in here anymore." Yurik lifted his tankard and what was left of his grog toward the halfling. "And I'm okay with that."

Cheyenne returned the toast and drained the rest of her tankard. She studied the dark, empty metal bottom and turned toward Ember. "Moment of truth, Em. No more booze at the table."

"So fill 'er up!" Bhandi roared, garnering a fresh round of disgruntled looks from the magicals at the closest tables.

"Maybe another night." Ember blinked and widened her eyes when she realized she'd drained whatever fae drink had filled the chalice. "Drinking with your mom was one thing. This is like drinking for the first time all over again."

"Damn." Bhandi peered at the chalice. "I should've ordered one of those instead."

"Yeah, right." Tate snapped his fingers and pointed at her. "You couldn't handle anything made for a fae."

"You wanna bet? Buy me a drink in one of those fancy cups, troll breath. I'll knock you flat on your ass."

"Not from the floor, you won't."

Ember's head wobbled, and she shook her head. "I'm ready to go. I gotta build up a tolerance, apparently."

Cheyenne snorted and stood. "Fair enough."

Yurik pulled his phone from his pocket to check the time, and his eyes widened. "Shit, it's nine-thirty. How did we stay down here so long without anyone trying to pick a fight with the drow?"

"Very funny."

"All right. Come on." Pushing to his feet, Yurik nodded at his fellow agents. "We're gonna blow this joint too."

"At nine-thirty?" Bhandi stretched her legs out under the table and folded her arms. "Without a barfight?"

"Yeah. I gotta report to some damn eval at the ass-crack of dawn."

"I don't need you to drive me back." The troll woman's eyelids drooped.

"Sure. Good luck finding an Uber driver willing to deal with your ass. Good luck finding anyone who can drive you onto the base." Yurik cast the bar a sideways glance. "So, if you want a ride, better get up now. I'm tryin' to make it out of here before Ogsa starts badgering me for payment."

Tate stood and peered into all the empty tankards in disappointment. "She always badgers you."

"Yeah, but I told her I'd have her money next time. If she doesn't see us leave, maybe she'll forget."

"She's not gonna forget." With a groan, Bhandi stood and pointed at Cheyenne. "Especially not when we're walkin' outta here with a drow and her fae friend. Might as well shout about it instead." The troll cupped her hands around her mouth and leaned so far back, she should have fallen over. "Pay attention, chumps! We have friends!"

The garbled drone of dozens of conversations dipped at Bhandi's shout, and heads turned to eye the drunk troll woman screaming for attention. Yurik rolled his eyes and stepped away from the table. Tate had already made his way halfway across the bar, and Ember took her cue from them before wheeling down the center aisle.

"Hey!" Ogsa shouted.

Yurik spun with wide eyes, but when he realized the tavern owner wasn't talking to him, he snuck through the crowd and headed for the door.

"You like your drink?"

Ember shot Cheyenne a confused look, then waved at the orc woman behind the bar. "Yeah, it was strong. Thanks."

"Ha." Ogsa smacked the bar, a thin mist of spit flying from between her protruding tusks. "You come back any time. There's plenty more where that came from. Gets stronger, the more you let it sit."

"Awesome." Ember bobbed her head and pushed herself down what was left of the aisle now that the Empty Barrel had gotten so busy.

Cheyenne stuck her hands in her pockets and followed her friend, occasionally staring down the other patrons. *Doesn't look like anyone wants to test their luck tonight. Guess I left the right impression last time.*

Tate held the door open for them, his eyes widening when Ember didn't slow down as she approached the steps. "Hey, you need any help?"

The wheels and the fae's hands pulsed with a cloud of violet light as she raced out of the tavern door. Her magic hovered her over the steps and set her gently down on the uneven stone of the marketplace.

"Of course you don't need help." Tate chuckled as he kept the door open for Cheyenne. "Why would I even ask?"

Ember lifted her hands from the wheels and grinned over her shoulder at him. "Doesn't mean I don't appreciate it. I can't pull these tricks up there whenever I want."

They all glanced at the expansive tunnel ceiling yards above them. Tate shrugged. "True. Kinda nice to get out in public without wondering who's gonna piss their pants when they see your real face or a few flashing spells and shit, huh?"

"Definitely refreshing." Ember took a sharp breath and yawned. "We need to get going before I have to ask my trusty assistant for her expertise, namely pushing."

As Ember turned her wheelchair toward the elevator at the far end of Peridosh, Tate caught Cheyenne's gaze to mouth, "Trusty assistant?"

Chuckling, the halfling shrugged. *I guess tipsy Ember thinks I work for her too.*

The door to the Empty Barrel flew open with a bang, and Bhandi stumbled out into the crowded avenue. She turned and shot the middle finger at someone inside. "Screw you too, fishface! Yeah, take your fancy glass eye and shove it up your ass. You might like the view." With another belch, the troll woman jumped off the last step and spread her arms as the door swung shut behind her. "What gives, huh? None of you toolbags wanna hold the door open for *me*?"

Yurik reappeared from the crowd and stepped up beside the troll woman, his hands shoved into the pockets of his olive-green corduroys. "Nobody knows how long it's gonna take you to do anything. Who's the fishface?"

"Fuck if I know." Bhandi stumbled into him and slapped his hands away when he tried to push her off his shoulder.

"Did Ogsa ask about me?"

"What, you in love with her or something?" Bhandi scoffed and cut a zigzagging pattern across the stone floor. "Shit, man. I knew you had bad taste, but that's taking it to a whole different level."

Yurik gave Cheyenne an exasperated glance and gestured at his fellow agent, who was staggering after Tate and Ember. "This is why the fellwine isn't a regular thing."

Cheyenne snorted. "I thought she could handle herself?"

"Depends on your definition of handle. Can she drink three ogres under the table one right after the other, bash their heads in with drunken kung-fu, and wake up the next morning with a raging headache and a clear memory of the whole thing? Sure."

"Sounds like that's a regular thing."

"Uh-huh. But she can't *handle* herself. I'm surprised she didn't try to fight me for more grog."

Cheyenne shook her head, then her drow hearing picked up an odd, muted rumble. She frowned and paused in the center of the avenue. *What is that?*

Oblivious, Yurik kept walking. "Honestly, Cheyenne, before we brought you here the first time, I was sure no one else could make as much trouble down here as Bhandi does. She was pretty sure of that too, come to think of it."

Cheyenne stared at the ceiling, searching for the cause of that sound.

"You had one drink." Laughing, the beefy goblin doubled back to join her. "I already know you're not a lightweight. Don't tell me you're seeing faces in the walls."

"No faces." Slowly, Cheyenne lowered her head to meet Yurik's yellow gaze. "Does this place have earthquakes?"

He scoffed. "How should I know? I'm not the maintenance guy." His crooked smile disappeared, and he shot a quick glance at the ceiling too. "Why do you ask?"

"I hear something."

"Super drow ears. I get it." Yurik fell in step beside her as she started walking through the crowd again. "But after everything we were just talking about, you can't blame me for asking why your mind went immediately to an earthquake."

"It sounds like something's moving up there." When she saw the near-panic in his wide eyes, Cheyenne shook her head. "Don't freak out, all right? Could be an earthquake. Could be something shifting around. If we see a bunch of flashing lights and this whole place splits apart with giant black stones shooting up like twelve-foot knives, *then* I'll tell you it's a new portal."

"Shit, is that all?" Yurik tried to joke, but it wasn't as easy as he wanted. "What if it is?"

"Then we deal with it. But I really hope it's not."

CHAPTER EIGHTEEN

Cheyenne peered through the crowd and easily spotted Bhandi's weaving figure and her scarlet braids swinging left and right as she stumbled around. In front of the troll woman, Tate walked beside Ember, who didn't seem to have a problem navigating the bumps in the stone floor with her newfound fae magic.

The unknown rumble grew louder for a split second before slowly fading. *Sounds like it's moving.*

A pebble dropped in front of her, followed by a few chunks of stone and supportive concrete. Cheyenne stopped and looked up at the ceiling again, stepping aside to avoid the much slower rain of dust filtering down from above.

Yurik followed her gaze and grunted. "Haven't seen that happen before."

"I don't think it's supposed to do that."

The rumble grew into a roar, drowning out the shouts of vendors and customers weaving around each other. Then the entire tunnel shuddered. Stacked goods rattled and spilled off of tables and shelves onto the floor. Magicals shouted in surprise, and one of the storefronts on Cheyenne's left exploded away from the wall.

"Shit. Come on!" She took off toward the rest of their friends, who were approaching the other side of the tunnel.

"What the hell's going on?" Yurik shouted behind her.

Cheyenne ignored him, her hearing focused on that moving rumble now coming from beyond the wall of the marketplace tunnel. Another shop crashed down on itself without warning, spraying wooden beams and glass and chunks of stone into the avenue. Everyone was shouting now as magicals scrambled to gather their scattered wares or tried to get a closer look at what was happening.

"Get away from the wall!" Cheyenne waved for everyone to clear a space, but only a few magicals heard her.

The rumble increased, picking up speed toward the end of the tunnel as whatever made the sound smashed against the small shops lining the wall. A spray of shattered glass and a stone gargoyle erupted from the roof of an O'gúleesh shoe store and hurtled toward the halfling. She raised a shimmering black shield above her head and left it there as she darted beneath it. The glass peppered her drow shield with a sound like hail coming down on the roof of a car, followed by the startling bong of the gargoyle before it fell to the stone floor in pieces.

Yurik ducked under her shield seconds before it dropped away, unable to take his eyes off the rippling wall of the tunnel now that whatever moved on the other side had made it past the rows of storefronts.

"Ember, stop!" The second she shouted it, Cheyenne knew her friend couldn't hear her. Tate didn't even turn around, and Bhandi kept stumbling forward, talking to herself and flinging her hands in the air. The halfling grunted and slipped into drow speed, darting around the frozen magicals in her way until she grabbed the handlebars of Ember's wheelchair to make her stop.

As soon as she dropped back to normal speed, a collective shout of surprise and anger rose from the magicals pushed off their feet by the shockwave she'd left behind.

"What the hell?" Ember's hands clamped down on the armrests, and she looked quickly over her shoulder, expecting some kind of attack. "Cheyenne."

"Sorry. Just hold on." The halfling nodded toward the buckling stone wall and the thing picking up speed toward them. "Because that's happening."

Tate's mouth dropped open. "I didn't know the walls could do that."

A cracking boom echoed through Peridosh's wide miles-long chamber. Shouts of surprise followed as magicals ducked and tried to find the source. The ground trembled again, making everyone stumble into each other.

"What's happening?" Ember shouted.

"I don't know, but we need to stay away from the wall!" The rumbling stopped before the halfling finished yelling. Her last words echoed in the sudden silence, and everyone in the marketplace froze in anticipation.

"Wait." Cheyenne cocked her head. "Do you guys hear that?"

"No." Tate turned to study her. "But that doesn't mean shit, does it?"

"Shh." The halfling stared at the wall where the churning thing behind it had stopped moving. The rumble grew until it doubled in intensity. *It's coming from everywhere.*

"What the fuck are you morons doing?" Bhandi stumbled toward them, swinging her arms from side to side as she turned with each step. "I thought we were getting' outta this—"

"Christ, she went hard tonight." Yurik shook his head and pointed at the troll woman. "Hey, just stay right there."

"Don't tell me what to do." Bhandi staggered forward and finally noticed the devastation in the wall across the tunnel. "Did you do this?"

The rumbling grew louder, and Yurik nodded. "Yeah, I hear it now."

"You can't just go around blowing up walls like some wall-blowing Rambo party."

"Bhandi, get away from the wall."

"Bite me!"

Dislodged pebbles jumped around on the stone floor as the trembling picked up again. Ember wheeled toward the opposite wall, and Cheyenne rolled her eyes before leaping to grab Bhandi's arm. "Get away from the wall."

"That's *my* arm, Goth drow!" Bhandi whirled and wrenched herself out of Cheyenne's grip before lifting both fists in front of her. She squinted with one eye and couldn't keep her fists from swaying wildly in front of her face as she stepped toward the wall. "I'll fight you for it."

"The hell you will." Cheyenne leaned away from the troll woman's sloppy swing and snatched Bhandi's arm again. "You need to—"

The other side of the tunnel exploded behind them with a crack of stone and a thick plume of dust and pebbles. Cheyenne whirled and found the source of all the rumbling, clicking, and thin metallic squeaking. Two-thirds up the wall of the cavern, a cone-shaped piece of metal spun as it pierced through the last bit of the stone and cement that had been hiding it.

"What moron thought it was a good idea to dig their way down here?" a magical shouted gruffly from the crowd.

"That's probably one of Surgil's fucked-up inventions."

Low chuckles filtered across the crowd as the magicals realized the threat wasn't nearly as bad as they'd expected.

An ear-splitting screech of metal on metal came from the digging machine poking out of the wall. The corkscrew nose stopped spinning and split apart like a hatching egg. Six long, glistening black appendages like unfolding crowbars burst out of the wall beside the split face of the machine. The cavern filled with a desperate scrabbling sound before the contraption pulled itself free from the wall and dropped almost a dozen yards to the ground with a clang.

"That doesn't look like Surgil's work."

The black legs heaved the metallic body off the ground, and the machine creature hissed and clicked, gears grinding as silver lights blinked on and off behind the split digging nose.

Cheyenne stared at the thing that clacked warily against the stone floor, scuttling back and forth like a confused crab. *It's looking for something.*

An electric green light bloomed in the center of the split digging cone, then the machine launched a ball of churning green fire into the center of the crowd.

Screams went up from the gathered magicals, followed by rallying shouts of anger and surprise. Peridosh's wide avenue filled with flashing lights as the magicals unleashed attack spells in return. Blue flames and crackling red spheres and a barrage of metal shards blasted the black and silver carapace of the machine standing at the end of the tunnel.

A series of harsh, grating clicks rose from the contraption's split cone, then it rose on the six nimble metal legs and scrambled toward the gathered crowd.

"What the hell is it?"

"Bring it down!"

"Hey, watch out!"

The machine ignored all the attacks as it reached the first row of tables along the left side of the avenue. It skittered forward, lifting tables and booths and carts with its thin metal legs and flinging them aside.

"Ember!" Cheyenne darted toward her friend, whose chair was pinned between a broken table and a metal shelving unit that had fallen behind her.

The machine-creature raced toward the fae, flipping random items in all directions. It caught one of its legs beneath Ember's chair and tossed her aside before Cheyenne thought to slip into her drow speed. When she did, she wrapped her arms around her friend and took Ember to the other side of the avenue, setting her gently down beside a stack of crated supplies. Then she stepped back into the center of the wide walkway and hurtled black spheres at the creature.

Cheyenne's magic blasted into the side of the machine suspended within her drow speed. The sparks flared in real-time across the metallic surface, then a series of clicks and squeaks and whirring mechanisms rose from the contraption. Black and silver lights flashed within the black metal carapace, and the machine's sharp, flexible legs clacked against the stone floor in enhanced speed until the split-open digger-beak pointed directly at the halfling.

Her eyes widened. "Shit."

The machine leaped toward her, another round of green flames building from some mechanism within its inorganic core. Cheyenne sent the black tentacles of her magic lashing from her fingertips with one hand and curled them around two of the thing's glinting legs. She managed to jerk it out of its leap toward her but had to throw up another shield when the green fireball erupted from the split metal beak. Both the fire and one of the machine's flailing limbs hit the halfling's shield with enough force to send her flying out of drow speed.

Cheyenne sailed backward over the startled, confused crowd of Peridosh's magical shoppers. Some of them were so focused on getting off their own attack spells that they didn't notice the drow flying over their heads. Gritting her teeth, Cheyenne reached out with both hands and sent whipping black tendrils toward the beams of a storefront as she passed it. The tendrils curled around the high beams and held fast, jerking the halfling out of her trajectory and swinging her into the store's front window.

Glass shattered as she barreled through the side of the shop, skidded across tables covered in stacks of dusty old books, and finally stopped in a heap against a bookshelf on the far wall. A shower of books fell on her one by one until she shook her head and gathered her wits enough to stand.

The shopkeeper, an old troll woman with purple skin so dark it was almost the slate-purple of a drow, stood from behind her desk. The pipe she'd been smoking was forgotten in her loose hand, thin lines of gray smoke curling up in front of her face.

"Sorry." Cheyenne stepped carefully over the scattered books on the floor. "I'm just gonna go take care of that thing."

The machine outside in the main avenue skittered across the stone floor amidst the shouts of the underground magicals as they tried to fight it off.

The bookshelf beside Cheyenne groaned and started to tip forward. She braced her hand against it and shoved it back against the wall. But she misjudged the force of her drow strength, and the frame of the wooden bookshelf splintered against the stone wall. The shelves buckled, books toppled to the ground, and the halfling stepped quickly away before she could do any more damage. "Sorry. I'm just trying to help."

A skaxen and two goblins flew past the shattered window of the bookstore, screaming as they hurtled across the marketplace and crashed into someone else's shop.

Cheyenne pointed outside and glanced briefly at the old troll woman.

She hurried across the book-littered floor, trying not to slip on any of the volumes and break her neck in the process. The shopkeeper didn't say a word.

Once she made it into the wide avenue again, Cheyenne pushed her way through the crowd, darting around fleeing magicals as they rushed in a flowing tide toward the other end of Peridosh. The machine creature clicked and whirred, skittering across the stone and tossing aside everything in its path. It moved so quickly now that sparks flew from those hooked metallic legs scrabbling on the floor. Then it lurched forward with a shrieking scrape as it slid across the stone. Purple and orange sparks flew against its back, and the machine creature turned to aim its flashing black and silver lights at Tate, Yurik, and a screaming Bhandi.

All three FRoE agents pelted the thing with their magical attacks, and it didn't make a difference. The machine spat a volley of green fire at each of them, then leaped onto the wall and crawled upside-down along the tunnel like a spider—toward Cheyenne.

Magic isn't gonna bring that thing down, at least not that way.

The halfling watched the machine skitter toward her overhead and reached out with her earth manipulation. Her fingers hooked around that pressure in the air, and she pulled at the wall of the tunnel. Huge chunks of stone burst from the ceiling, but the mechanical creature kept coming.

Change of tactics, then.

Cheyenne glanced at the open stone floor in front of her and gauged the machine's speed. She waited until the last second, when it hung upside down right in front of her, ready to launch itself at her, then hooked her powers around the tension she felt in the earth beneath her instead and pulled it apart. The stone floor of Peridosh buckled and spread open in front of her as the insectoid machine dropped toward her.

Slipping into drow speed, Cheyenne stepped back and sent black tendrils whipping from both hands. They coiled around the mechanical creature, which struggled against the bonds of her magic in real-time but didn't have the means to save itself from its slow-motion fall.

With a shout of intense effort, she tugged the creature to the ground with all the force she could muster, falling on one knee to carry through with the momentum. The second the machine hit the stone and the foot-wide crack running through it, Cheyenne slipped out of her enhanced speed, released her tendrils, and pushed down with her magic.

The machine's hooked legs scratched at the floor as it tried to right itself, but it couldn't get to its feet again before the half-drow's magic curled around the crack in the earth and split it wider. With another grating screech, the metal beast braced its legs on either side of the chasm opening around it, sparing two of those metal claws to try to pull itself back to the surface.

A ball of green flame spewed from its beak and nearly caught the halfling square in the face. Cheyenne ducked and snarled, trying to squeeze the earth back into place around her inorganic attacker.

"Just fucking go down!" She brought her arm up in a wide, curving arc like she meant to strike the thing with a hammer. With her magic still tightly gripping the earth's energy, one side of the chasm lurched against the other when her fist hit the stone floor. Rocks and metal parts and tiny gears burst from the crack before both edges folded in on each other, crashing down and down, burying the metal beast in a puff of dust and a stream of thick black smoke.

The whirring gears and clicks slowed and fell silent within seconds.

Cheyenne paused, waiting for that rumbling sound to start up again. All she heard were a few pebbles clacking down the sides of the chasm as they fell and the heavy, tensely waiting breath of over a hundred magicals spending their Tuesday night in Peridosh.

CHAPTER NINETEEN

After catching her breath, Cheyenne slowly pushed herself up off her knee and stepped cautiously toward the chasm she'd created and mostly sealed again. She glanced at the closest magicals staring at her in awe and admiration and shrugged. "I wouldn't get too close to all this."

Someone barked a laugh and quickly covered it.

She walked around the jutting destruction in the middle of the marketplace's avenue and stopped to pick up a piece of one metallic black leg that had been pinched off. Then she grabbed one of the odd-looking gears that still flashed a muted silver light and stuck that in her pocket. *I know exactly who's gonna tell me what the hell this thing was and why it was here.*

Her black Vans whispered across the dust-covered stone as she skirted around the staring awestruck magicals lining the storefronts. They were still pressed against each other to get out the way, but now they were avoiding the halfling who looked like a full drow, not the inexplicable metal monster.

Cheyenne found Ember right where she'd left her and crouched beside her friend. "You okay?"

The fae blinked quickly and leaned forward to stare at the crumpled mess of earth down the tunnel. "I've just been sitting here. Are *you* okay?"

"I'm still alive, aren't I?" Smirking, Cheyenne turned and found Yurik. "Hey. Bring her chair, huh?"

The goblin dragged a palm across his forehead and glanced at the destruction over the buried machine, then darted toward the other side of the avenue to grab the wheelchair.

"What the hell did that thing want?" Ember stared at Yurik as he half-rolled, half-carried the wheelchair toward them.

"Mass destruction. A pile of bodies." Cheyenne shrugged and slipped one arm around Ember's back while the other hooked under her friend's knees. "I'm not trying to sound cocky or anything, but there's a good chance it was here for me."

"Yeah, that doesn't surprise me."

With a snort, Cheyenne lowered Ember into her chair and nodded. "At least you're not scattered all over the ground too."

"I'm pretty grateful for that." Ember grabbed the armrests and shifted into a more comfortable position. Without thinking about it, she kicked one heel against the footrest and shoved herself farther back into the chair. Then she froze. "Holy shit."

"Did you just straighten that leg by yourself?"

Ember's mouth opened and closed without any sound as she stared at her foot. "If you saw it, I'm not hallucinating."

"I hope not." Cheyenne grinned. "Somebody said something about fae being great healers, didn't they?"

The fae girl barked a laugh and gripped her wheels. "One step closer, I guess. Sort of."

"Hell yeah, you are. We can freak out about that later. Right now, I think we need to—"

A single hollow bang echoed through Peridosh. The halfling straightened and shot an exasperated glance at the orc with his fist hovering over a metal shop door. He pounded it again, then again, and the other O'gúleesh lined up along the avenue picked up the same rhythm. They hit and kicked and thumped their fists against anything metal they could find, throwing up an earsplitting ruckus.

"Woah." Ember stared at them. "What's happening?"

"No clue. Come on." Cheyenne turned toward the back end of the tunnel and the waiting elevator.

Ember and the FRoE agents followed, and the metallic banging rattled the air even faster.

"Okay, I get it!" Cheyenne whirled around and spread her arms, gazing over the eager faces of the magicals giving her an O'gúleesh standing ovation. "Woohoo. Yeah! Let's hit stuff!"

She snatched up a broad, shallow metal bowl that had somehow been left untouched on a skaxen's table and thumped her fist against it several times. When she dropped it back onto the table and rolled her eyes, the skaxen pressing himself against the wall of the shop behind him threw his head back and cackled. His fist kept thumping the metal door beside him anyway. The laughter was picked up by a handful of other magicals as they stomped and punched and smacked their approval.

Shaking her head, Cheyenne turned back toward the end of the tunnel and rolled her eyes. When she caught up with Ember, the fae laughed and shot her a sidelong glance. "You look like an insane person."

"Guess it runs in the drow side of the family." The halfling shot a skeptical glance over her shoulder. Even the O'gúleesh who stared at her with terrified eyes instead of flashing her eager grins kept pounding away on whatever metal they had at hand. "I'm sick of them doing this every single time, and I have no idea what it means."

"Sounds like applause."

"Well, clapping and whistling and maybe not looking at me like I'm a walking piece of meat would be a hell of a lot less creepy."

Tate jogged to catch up with them, and Yurik turned to follow the halfling and her friend. "Does this happen everywhere you go?"

"Only when there are a bunch of O'gúleesh around. You know, the ones who weren't born here."

"So weird." The troll man turned to frown at the magicals still pounding on steel and silver and iron. "Oh, shit. Bhandi! What the hell are you doing?"

Bhandi had found someone else's private tankard of whatever booze they preferred and was knocking it back. She chugged and pumped her fist in the air with the same rhythm, which also happened to match the loud rhythm of so many fists and boots hitting metal.

"Seriously?" Yurik raced toward her, snatched the tankard out of her hand, and set it down on the table. "Sorry."

The grinning orc didn't even look at the tankard. He didn't seem to notice Bhandi at all as he held his metal folding chair in one hand and smashed his fist into it over and over, enlarging the dent in the seat with each blow. And he stared at Cheyenne.

"They're not cheering for you, you damn drunk." Yurik spun Bhandi around by the shoulders and nudged her toward the end of the tunnel.

"Hey, I'm gonna do me. Those losers can cheer for any losers!" Her arm swung back behind her to point at the crowd. "Fuck 'em."

Rolling his eyes, Yurik grabbed a fistful of the back of her black leather jacket right below the collar and half-carried, half-dragged the inebriated troll woman with him toward the elevator. Tate, Cheyenne, and Ember were waiting for them.

"Hey." Bhandi reeled away from Ember and pointed at her. "You're a damn fae."

"And you're trashed."

"Nah." The troll woman blew a raspberry and staggered past all of them the second the elevator doors opened. "I'm Bhandi." Her fists slammed into the steel wall before her face had a chance to do the same.

Yurik glanced at Tate and raised his hand. "Not me."

"Me neither. If she can't walk when we get back to base, I'm pullin' her outta the car and leavin' her ass in the parking lot."

The rest of their group entered the elevator. Ember's wheels flashed purple as she glided over the bumpy metal strip, then the doors closed. When the elevator shuddered and lurched into its ascent, Bhandi's eyes bulged in her head. She leaned forward and puffed out her cheeks.

"Don't you fucking dare," Tate growled. "Not here."

A garbled moan escaped the troll woman, then she let out another belch with a few green fellwine bubbles. They floated around her face, popping quickly, and she watched them until she went cross-eyed. "This was the shittiest night we've ever had down here. I'm just sayin' right now while I can still..." Her eyelids and head drooped at the same time, then she jerked her head back up with a gasp. "Nothing happened."

"What?" Yurik laughed sharply. "Where were you the whole time that metal spider was tearing apart the market?"

"Spider? I didn't see a spuckin' fider."

Tate bowed his head and covered his eyes with one hand.

Cheyenne chuckled. "She didn't drink that much, either. I mean, for her. What the hell was in that fellwine?"

"Huh." Yurik stared at the opposite wall of the elevator and leaned back. He chuckled, and it grew into a full-blown belly laugh. Tate looked up from his palm and shot Cheyenne a confused glance. When the huge goblin finally settled enough to talk again, he smashed a fist into his other hand. "Shit. Ogsa knew this fae wasn't gonna touch that cup. I bet my entire Polaroid collection the orc spiked it for fun."

Tate's scarlet eyes flashed when the realization hit him, and he grinned. "Oh, shit. She slipped Bhandi a magical roofie."

"'Cause who the hell else would drink fellwine with two full pitchers of grog lying around?" Yurik punched Tate's shoulder. "We're both smart enough to leave that shit alone."

"Ha! And it was free!" The troll man nodded at Bhandi, who'd sagged against the elevator wall and now stared at her raised fists, squinting one eye and then the other over and over.

"Damn. No wonder that tavern's been down there since the very beginning. Ogsa knows how to play."

"I'll show *you*," Bhandi muttered, then brought one fist cracking against the other with full force. It knocked her elbow into the corner of the elevator with a loud bang, and the rest of her followed until her forehead smashed into the steel wall. "Fuck."

The guys cracked up again. Cheyenne pressed her lips together and tried not to laugh at the troll woman struggling to get her footing. Bhandi smacked her forehead, glanced down at her palm, and chuckled.

"She's gone, man."

"Might be some rope in the back of the SUV." Yurik shrugged. "We could tie her up and lead her into the building. Get her in her bunk, at least, and lock the door from the outside so she can't get out."

"Yeah, you do that." Tate shook his head. "And good luck not getting your throat slit when you're the one who has to let her out in the morning."

"Okay, fine. Maybe the parking lot's better."

Ember sat up from leaning over her lap and opened her eyes. "It wasn't a spider."

Yurik chuckled. "Oh, yeah."

"I mean, besides it being a machine." The fae shrugged. "It only had six legs."

"Five, now." Cheyenne lifted the broken metal leg, which looked a lot like a crowbar covered in black paint.

"Huh." Tate shook his head and stared at the glistening machine part. "It's creepy that you took that. You know that, right?"

The halfling turned the black rod this way and that, watching it catch the elevator's bright overhead lights. "That whole thing was creepy."

"But that's your whole deal, isn't it?" Yurik gestured at her. "Goth drow and everything. No wonder you knew how to smash that thing to pieces."

"Me being Goth doesn't mean I know what this is."

"So why'd you take it?" Tate folded his arms. When Bhandi's fist smashed into the wall inches from his head, he leaned out of the way and didn't break the halfling's gaze.

"I don't know. I'm good at figuring out how things work." Cheyenne lowered the leg to her side again and wiggled her eyebrows. "And I guess I just wanted a souvenir."

"You would." The troll man shook his head with a smirk. "And when you find out how *that* thing works, I'm guessing you're not gonna tell any of us about it."

"Probably not. I mean, not unless this thing turns out to be some kinda FRoE tracker hunting off-duty agents, then sure. Maybe I'll let you in on it."

"Yeah, thanks for lookin' out, halfling. You're a real part of the team." Yurik snorted and stared at the piece of metal dangling beside her thigh. "If that thing's supposed to hunt FRoE, it was broken. Didn't even notice us until we started flinging magic."

"It didn't seem to have a target, did it?" *Which doesn't make any sense. Neither does it waking up to fight back when I was in drow speed.*

CHAPTER TWENTY

The elevator shuddered to a stop, and the doors opened to reveal the Employees Only door on the other side.

"Oh, shit." Tate reached into his pocket and almost dropped his black illusion ring before jamming it onto his finger. His violet skin and scarlet eyes faded to tan and brown, though the tattoos remained. "Dude, we gotta get her mask."

"Her what?"

Cheyenne looked down at Ember and wiggled her fingers, then slipped back into her human form. "Illusion charm."

"Oh." The fae stuck her hand in the pocket of her jacket and slipped off her illusion charm.

The halfling watched the fingers of Ember's other hand move uselessly in her lap. *She's tipsy, but she's keeping up a good front.*

Ember's pink and violet coloring faded into her regular human-looking-fae form. While Yurik struggled to pull Bhandi away from the wall, Tate turned toward Cheyenne with a grimace. "Can you, like, make sure we don't get stuck in this elevator or something?"

"Yep." Cheyenne cracked the door open and peered around the froyo shop. "Hey, Joe."

The grumpy man behind the counter shot her an expressionless glare that rivaled the half-drow's. "What?"

"We're having a little trouble in here. Can you come here for a sec?"

Joe glanced blandly around the front of his store and blinked. "I don't leave this goddamn counter until this place closes, which is pretty much never. But there's no one here anyway. What's your problem this time?"

Cheyenne peered around the counter to take in the empty storefront. "Oh. Is there some kinda button to keep this thing from goin' back down before we get everyone out?"

Joe set his magazine down on the counter and scowled at the crack in the door above her head. "I swear, if that crazy troll puked in there again, I'm gonna make her mop it up with her face."

"Why the hell are you trying to kill me, you bastards?" Bhandi shouted, followed by some quick thumps. "I'll rip your arms off and shove 'em in your ears!"

"Hey, grab her arm, will ya?"

"What does it look like I'm tryin' to do? Woah, woah, wait! Hold the door."

Cheyenne slipped into her drow form long enough for her enhanced strength to pull the thick elevator doors apart again. They banged back into the wall with a shudder, then she opened the door again, met Joe's gaze, and shrugged.

"No button. Just pull her into the bathroom 'til someone gets her under control."

The halfling let her drow form fade and opened the door before turning back to the agents. "You hear that?"

"Yeah. I just don't know how to—ah! Fuck!" Yurik clamped both hands over his nose, and blood dripped from beneath his palms. "We're tryin' to *help* you, asshole."

Bhandi flailed around against the back of the elevator, her arms whipping in every direction.

"Was that her elbow?" Tate asked with a grimace.

"Yeah, and my face." Yurik stalked out of the elevator, turning sideways to slip past Cheyenne, and headed for the bathroom across the narrow hall.

"All right." Tate held up both hands in surrender and waited for Ember to wheel herself out of the elevator before he backed out of it too. "Bhandi."

"Nobody fucks with this." The troll woman tapped her chest and lurched toward him, her eyes flitting everywhere but his face. "I'll send all your ancestors to the grave!"

"Well, too bad they're already there. But hey, we got another pitcher. Waitin' for you right in that room across the hall." Tate gestured toward the bathroom, where Yurik leaned over the sink, cursing at his bloody nose in the mirror. "See? Your favorite goblin's already getting started."

"He's not my favorite." Bhandi blinked and dropped her hands against her thighs. "You say another pitcher?"

"Uh-huh."

"Well, shit. You shoulda strat...stratted...just say that next time, huh?" As Bhandi walked calmly out of the elevator, the doors rumbled shut behind her. She kicked the Employees Only door, and Cheyenne caught it before it could crack against the back wall.

"Hey, put your mask on, huh?"

The troll woman swung around to face Cheyenne and pointed in her general direction. "Like you?"

"Yeah."

"What the hell for?"

"It's a themed party." Cheyenne shrugged and glanced at Tate for reinforcement. His mouth dropped open, and he shook his head.

"Everybody's doing it," Ember added.

Bhandi tried to slip her hand into the front pocket of her tight burgundy pants, crouching sideways before she withdrew her illusion ring. She held it up in front of her face, and Tate had to grab her other hand and aim a finger into the ring for her. Her purple troll skin and scarlet braids melted into light-amber skin and long, straight brunette hair. Then she jerked her hand out of Tate's grip and headed toward the bathroom. "Now let's go."

Yurik stumbled out of the bathroom with his own human illusion returned and snarled over his shoulder, "Next time I see your ugly mug, asshole, I'm gonna make you eat it."

Ember snorted and choked back a laugh.

The goblin slammed the bathroom door shut behind him and thumped it with the side of his fist. "Can you believe that? Douchebag took our pitcher."

"Oh, hell, no." Bhandi rushed the bathroom door, but Yurik caught her in one arm and spun her toward the front of the froyo shop.

"I took care of it. Look." He gestured toward the blood smeared under his nose and nudged her forward. "He got in a good hit, but I laid him out. Time to go."

"Aw, man." Bhandi glanced over her shoulder at the bathroom but let herself be guided toward the front of the shop. "Hey, Joe." She stopped and blinked, trying to focus on the man's expressionless face. "What are *you* doing down here?"

The guardian of the elevator into Peridosh raised an eyebrow and said nothing.

"Keep moving." Yurik gave her another forceful nudge and Bhandi stumbled forward again, knocking into tables and chairs. Then he turned to glare at Tate. "Another pitcher in the bathroom? Really?"

"You ran with it. Kinda testin' our luck to say someone stole it, though, doncha think?"

"Yeah, sure. Next time, *you* can tell her it was just a trick to get her mask on. Deal with that shitstorm on your own."

Bhandi shoved the glass door open, rattling the bell dangling from the handle, and marched out onto the sidewalk.

"Shit." Yurik sped up to follow her outside. "Somebody's gonna run her over."

"Or get run over." Tate turned back to give Ember and Cheyenne an apologetic shrug. "Nice to meet you, Ember."

"Yeah, you too."

He pointed at the halfling. "Hit us up if you find anything else that would be remotely helpful. You know, for keeping our heads attached to our shoulders."

"Same." Cheyenne jerked her chin at him. "Yurik has my number."

"Uh-huh. Later." Tate slipped out the front door and stopped, clapping both hands to his bald head. "What are you *doing*?"

Ember leaned forward in her chair as she and Cheyenne headed toward the door, peering through the windows. "Should we, like, help them or something?"

"Nah. They'll figure it out." The halfling held the door open for her friend, and by the time they peered down the street, the FRoE agents had disappeared. "See?"

"So vanishing into thin air is 'figuring it out' in your world, huh?"

Cheyenne chuckled and headed in the opposite direction down the sidewalk toward the parking lot across the three-way intersection. "Really?"

"Yeah, it totally is." Ember laughed as she pushed herself quickly down the sidewalk. Brief flashes of purple light helped her navigate the cracked, bumpy pedestrian ramp before they crossed the street.

A jogger turned the corner in front of them, glanced at the glowing wheels, and nodded. "Nice lights."

The girls gave him ten seconds to jog down the street before they burst out laughing. "Oh, man. People see what they wanna see, don't they?"

"That's a lot easier when the lights are the only thing I can do." To prove her point, Ember wheeled up to the curb of the sidewalk lining the parking lot. Another pulse of violet light illuminated her hands and the wheels, lifting her up and setting her gently back down. "And I don't even have to think about it."

"I'm pretty sure that's how magic is supposed to work, Em." Cheyenne pulled her keys out of her pocket and pressed the unlock button. The Panamera chirped on the other side of the parking lot, headlights flashing. "Like moving your limbs, right? Hey, which is something else you can do now."

"Don't get my hopes up." Ember smirked up at her as they navigated the parked cars at Union Hill. "It was one little kick. Barely anything. I've been trying the whole time to do it again."

"You did it once. You'll do it again."

"You don't know that."

Cheyenne shrugged and opened the passenger side door. "Just a feeling, but when I have a feeling about something, I'm usually right."

"Ha." Ember locked the wheels and pushed herself up on the armrests so the halfling could help her transfer. "Now you *do* sound cocky."

"I'm cool with that." With Ember in the passenger seat, Cheyenne folded up the chair and took it to the back of the car, popping the trunk.

"I'll tell you this, though," Ember called through the open door. "I'd take cocky Cheyenne over chasing a wasted troll all over Union Hill any day of the week."

The halfling opened the driver's side door and slid behind the wheel. She tossed the machine-bug leg into the back seat and started the engine. "Thanks, Em. I'm flattered."

Laughing, the fae strapped herself in. "Yeah, you should be."

CHAPTER TWENTY-ONE

As soon as they got out of the elevator on the top floor of Pellerville Gables Apartments, Cheyenne glanced at the empty elevator. "This place has some serious soundproofing."

"What?" Ember laughed and gestured at the end of the hall and the only two apartments on it. "I heard that bass halfway up here."

"Huh. Guess I was really focused on not hearing it." *And way more focused on why a giant crawling machine dug its way into Peridosh. Especially when Corian and his little gang are supposed to be on top of that.*

"Sounds good though, right?" Ember bobbed her head as she wheeled down the hall.

"If you say so."

"I mean, I'm not normally a fan of dubstep, but this song could maybe grow on me."

Cheyenne shook her head and eyed their neighbor's front door with a raised eyebrow. "I think it just sounds better through thick walls and a closed door."

"It's not *that* bad."

"It's not my jam."

With a snort, Ember stopped in front of their apartment door and searched through her jacket pockets. "Crap. I never grabbed my keys."

"Good thing you take me with you." Cheyenne caught up with her and unlocked the front door. Just as she pushed it open into their apartment, Matthew Thomas's front door opened too. The heavy electronic music blasted into the hallway, and the halfling ducked at the sudden blaring volume. "Jeeze, that's annoying."

"Hey! Right on time." Matthew stood in the open doorway, his arms spread wide.

"For what?" Ember shouted across the hall.

"To join us. I know you guys just got back, but it's still early, right?" He grinned at them and tilted his head, arms still open and weirdly inviting. "I mean, if you're up for it. Of course."

Cheyenne felt Ember looking up at her and gauging her decision. The halfling ignored her and raised an eyebrow at their overly friendly neighbor. "You got a lotta people in there, huh?"

"A few, yeah." Matthew chuckled. "All good people."

"And everybody's making a lot of noise. Fun party gets pretty loud."

"I know." His crooked smile didn't waver as he glanced over his shoulder. Someone inside cheered, and the shouting swept across his apartment to enter the hall. "We're the only ones on this floor, so I figured I could get away with it."

"Okay, Matt. I'll make you a deal."

Ember's eyes widened, and Matthew perked up despite the halfling's use of his unapproved nickname. "Let's hear it."

"Ember can do whatever she wants, obviously. But I'll come to your party and do a little schmoozing if you can explain how you knew we were here without it sounding like total bullshit."

The fae girl choked and brought a fist to her mouth to hide a surprised cough. Matthew Thomas cocked his head. His smile remained, but this time, the side of his nose wrinkled so much that it made him squint.

Like he knows he's been caught.

He chuckled and shook his head. "I'm not following."

"Oh, yeah?" Cheyenne cast a suspicious glance through his open apartment door across from her own and lifted her chin. "Okay. Have a good night. Neighbor."

Without waiting for a reply, she turned to her front door and stalked inside, heading straight for the side of their apartment with her bedroom so Matthew couldn't watch her any longer. But her drow hearing picked up every word of the conversation in the hall.

"She having a rough night or something?" Matthew asked through another casual chuckle.

"You'd have to ask her." Ember's wheels rolled along the floor.

"What about you? I'd still love for you to come join us. You don't have to stay long, and from what I hear, your Uber ride home is pretty cheap."

The fae laughed, but it fell flat. "Maybe another night, Matthew. We came home early 'cause I was feeling really tired. I won't be doing myself any favors if I don't get to bed in the next five minutes."

"You sure? There are some people here I'd really love for you to meet."

"I'm sure. Thanks. Have fun." Ember wheeled quickly through the doorway and grabbed the door to throw it shut behind her. It didn't quite slam, but it wasn't quiet, either. Then she put both hands over her mouth and stared at their black and silver area rug. "Oh, my God."

"Yeah." Cheyenne tossed the broken machine-bug leg onto the couch and folded her arms.

"Oh, my *God*." Ember glanced at the door and grimaced in disgust. "Do you think he's watching us?"

"Depends on how you define that, Em."

"I don't mean with his eyes. Well, I do."

"I can see where you're going with this." Cheyenne slumped into the closest black leather recliner and dangled one leg over the armrest. "So I'm gonna take a wild guess and say yeah. I think our day-trading, cyber-security-CEO of a neighbor has cameras all over this floor. Maybe in other parts of the building. Who knows?"

Ember dropped her hands into her lap and stared at the halfling. "That's what I was thinking, but, I mean, we can't prove that, can we?"

"Not yet. Shouldn't be hard to do, though."

The apartment fell silent as they looked at the vaulted ceiling and the wide expanse of their shared loft. "You don't think he had them here?"

"Well, it *was* a show unit for a long time." Cheyenne ran her hands through her black hair, smoothing it away from her forehead as she dropped her head back against the recliner. "I'd be more creeped out about him running surveillance in here before we moved in than if he stuck something under our noses after we met."

"How the hell is *that* creepier?"

"If he bugged our apartment after falling madly in love with you at first sight, Em, that makes him a stalker. Which isn't ideal, sure, but it's focused. If he had stuff in here way before that, though, I'd say that ventures into psychopath territory."

Ember snorted. "That's funny, coming from you."

Cheyenne glanced quickly at her friend, and they burst out laughing. "Almost. But people who watch everyone constantly for no reason other than because they can have a lot more issues than one lonely dude with an obsessive crush."

"That's messed up."

"I didn't say it wasn't."

A chill raced down the back of Ember's neck, and she shuddered, shaking her head. "You think he can hear us right now?"

"If he can, serves him right." The halfling grinned at Ember and stuck her middle finger in the air, waving it back and forth at their apartment. "Just for fun."

"How can you be so calm about this?"

"Come on. No point in freaking out until I can prove something one way or the other."

With a deep breath through her nose, Ember grimaced and wrapped her arms around herself. "Just the idea is enough to convince me. I mean, all the pieces fit. He always shows up at the worst times."

"Or the best times. For him."

"Yeah, mostly when you're gone."

"I know."

"Oh, shit. If he's watching us in our apartment, he saw me with that illusion charm."

"Yeah. Hypothetically." Cheyenne stretched her arms above her head before sinking back into the recliner.

"But it makes sense!"

"Hypothetically, Em. Look, if he's got something in our apartment and he saw you put on that ring, he did a damn good job of acting like it never happened."

"Well, if he's like us, it wouldn't surprise him, would it?"

The halfling raised an eyebrow. "Do you honestly think he's like us?"

Ember opened her mouth, paused, then said, "No. No way. I can always tell."

"Yeah, me too. At least, now that I know what to look for."

"So, you're saying that he didn't freak and he's not a magical, so he didn't bug our apartment?"

"Or he's got an insane poker face, and now he's even more curious than he was in the beginning."

Ember slapped her hands on the armrests and gripped them tightly. "You're not helping."

Cheyenne couldn't hold back an unapologetic chuckle. "This wasn't supposed to be a *helpful* conversation. I knew there was a reason I had a weird feeling about that guy."

"Please don't say, 'I told you so.'"

"I'm not. I still don't know what's going on with him." The halfling nodded at the couch and the metal leg. "He didn't give that thing a second glance when we showed up."

"Oh, shit. You think he had something to do with that machine in the market?"

"I seriously doubt it. I mean, that thing right there does look a lot like a crowbar."

Ember snorted. "Yeah, I wouldn't think twice about you walking around with a crowbar, either. Fits your whole 'Back the fuck up and don't talk to me' vibe."

"Thanks." Still staring at the broken leg, Cheyenne pulled her phone out of her back pocket and frowned. "I don't think I'll be carrying that around with me for much longer. Probably not a good idea."

Ember swallowed. "Okay, I know you don't like loud noises and everything, but Cheyenne, I swear, if that thing starts moving on its own, I'm gonna scream."

"Really?" The halfling turned her frown on her friend. "Never pegged you as a screamer."

The fae cocked her head and narrowed her eyes. "I can't tell if you're serious or if that was a poorly timed innuendo."

Cheyenne shrugged and glanced at her phone. "Whatever."

"Who are you calling?"

"Corian." She pulled up his number and hovered her thumb over the call icon.

"You think he could help us with our creepy-neighbor problem?"

"Oh, *now* you think he's creepy."

Ember glanced at the door and lowered her voice despite the loud bass thumping from across the hall and the constant drone of voices and outbreaks of laughter. "Yeah. You finally got me to see things your way, and I don't think I can *unsee* them."

"Corian would help if I asked him."

"Great."

"But I'm not gonna ask him."

Ember groaned and buried her face in her hands.

"Hey, not until I look into what Matthew Thomas might or might not have done in here. If I can take care of it myself, I will. So for now, we'll just keep the door locked, and it's all good."

Blinking furiously, the fae wheeled herself toward the front door and turned the chair sideways so she could flip the knob lock and reach the deadbolt. "Honestly, Cheyenne, figuring out if someone bugged my apartment would be number one on my priority list."

"Well, we do have our differences." Cheyenne forced herself to make the call and lifted the phone to her ear. "This is a little more important right now."

"What is?"

"That damn leg." The halfling glanced at her friend and raised her eyebrows. "I've seen something like that before. I'm pretty sure I fought my first O'gúl war machine at Peridosh tonight."

"Your first *what?*"

"Yeah."

CHAPTER TWENTY-TWO

orian's low voice came in scratchier than normal over the phone. "What's up, kid?"

"Oh, you know, just a regular Tuesday night. Pretty chill. Having fun."

A long pause greeted her in response. "What happened?"

"Yeah. That's what I'm wondering."

The nightstalker said, "Look, we're in the middle of decoding some shit I can't pretend to understand."

"We?" Persh'al added in the background. "Uh-uh. I'm decoding, man. You're just breathing down my neck."

"Ain't that what supervisors are for?" Byrd shouted from the other side of the warehouse.

Corian's thick swallow and slow, irritated exhalation came through loud and clear. "Obviously, I don't have time for games, Cheyenne. And I'm not in the mood."

"Right. Because you caught the guy who figured out how to make the other-side tech work over here, and now you're diligently trying to keep that knowledge out of anyone else's hands. Does that sum it up?"

"Yeah, just about."

"Good. So maybe you can tell me why an assembled piece of that machinery tunneled all the way under Union Hill and crashed a pretty big underground party. If you catch my drift." Cheyenne pulled one leg up onto the recliner and rested her elbow on her knee, propping her phone against her ear.

Corian's pause was even longer this time. "What?"

"I know you heard me."

"That's impossible."

"Apparently not. I'm staring at a leftover piece of it lying on my couch right now. Took some parts with me. You know, in case it helps you guys figure out where you went wrong. Because this wasn't supposed to happen."

"No, it was not." Corian pulled the phone away from his mouth as he said it.

Oh, yeah. I can see him shooting Persh'al the evil eye.

"Tell me what happened."

Cheyenne said, "The thing came out of nowhere, man. Or it came from underground. Really loud digger, but I couldn't pin it down until it popped out in the middle of a fun little shopping center and started throwing things around."

"What did it want?"

"Seriously?" She couldn't help but laugh. "I really hope these machines don't *want* anything."

"You know what I mean."

"I have no idea why it was there, okay? But my best guess is it got a jump start on the others and came looking for me, seeing as all the living beings with brains and normal bodily functions have failed so far."

"That might be the case. You say you brought back some parts?"

Cheyenne eyed the black metal leg and nodded. "Yeah. After I buried that thing in the middle of the tunnel."

"What? You engaged it?"

"Hey, it engaged *me*. And everyone else down there. I wasn't about to let it tear the place apart."

"Cheyenne, did you attack it with your personal weapons?"

"We're still talking in code, right?"

"Answer the question!"

She pulled the phone away from her ear and frowned at it. "Yeah. That's pretty much my go-to reaction. Something drops out of the wall

143

and comes running at me, I'm gonna get it with fire first. I mean, not *that* fire."

"But you made direct contact."

"That's what I said. Then it turned on me, and I had to improvise."

"Shit." Corian's phone clattered against a hard surface, and Persh'al's voice came through closer than before.

"What's going on?"

"Put that thing on speaker, will you?"

"Uh, yep." There was a tap, then the blue troll's steady breathing came through loud and clear. "You're on speaker, kid."

Cheyenne frowned at the black metal leg on her couch. "What's going on?"

"If you'd buried that thing using nothing but earth, Cheyenne," Corian called from some distance away, "we wouldn't have this problem. But a direct attack means that thing's operating system, more or less, got a lock on your signature. That was the one thing they didn't have."

"Christ." The halfling rolled her eyes and glanced at Ember, who widened her eyes in a silent request for an explanation. Cheyenne shook her head and lifted a finger. "So, what do we do?"

"I'm coming to get you. Where are you?"

"At home. *My* apartment. Just don't show up in Ember's bedroom or anything, okay?"

"Is that where you're planning on being in the next few minutes?"

She grimaced. "Dude."

"I'll show up wherever you are, Cheyenne." Something clattered across the cement floor of the warehouse, followed by a hissing string of curses as Corian cleaned up whatever mess he'd made. "Just wait for me, all right? Don't go anywhere, and don't touch whatever parts you brought back with you."

"Well, one's in my pocket, and I carried the other one home with me like a baton."

The nightstalker growled in frustration. "Well, don't pick it up again, got it? I'll be there as soon as I can."

"Okay. Is this gonna be a long wait?

"Persh'al, turn that off."

"You sure?"

"End the fell-damn call, troll!"

"Well, fuck the Crown sideways, man. Chill out. I'm just trying to help."

The line disconnected, and Cheyenne stared at her phone, gritting her teeth.

"Not a good call, I take it?"

Looking up at Ember, the halfling shook her head. "No, not really. I might've stepped in it by taking down that fire-breathing machine-bug and saving hundreds of lives. But of course, none of that matters because I'm the *chosen one* who can't be left alone or trusted to take care of anything on my own. Which is pretty hard to do when not one goddamn person does what they say they're gonna do!"

The heat of her drow magic flared up her spine without being summoned, and a drow with purple-gray skin and bone-white hair now fumed on the black leather recliner.

Ember bit her bottom lip and folded her arms. "You might wanna take it easy on your phone, though. I mean, not like you couldn't afford a new one, but personally, I hate having to get new phones."

Cheyenne dropped her phone into her lap and made a noise that landed somewhere between a snort and a growl, then looked at her friend. Ember raised her eyebrows and slowly nodded. "Awesome. I just threw a tantrum."

"A minor tantrum, yeah." The fae's smile bloomed on her lips, and she shrugged. "I *will* say a full-drow tantrum is a lot cooler than you running away to hide what you can't keep down."

"At least I've got *that* behind me."

"No more covering your ears."

"No more crushing beer bottles with my bare hands." They smirked at each other, and Cheyenne had to pull her gaze away. *That was the night everything changed. That's how I got here, and the only part I regret is not stepping into who I am sooner.* She glanced briefly at Ember's wheelchair. "Okay, so Corian will be here in who knows how long. Don't feel like you have to wait around with me."

"Oh, trust me. I don't." The fae yawned and smacked her lips. "I wasn't kidding when I said I was tired. That orc's fae juice hit me hard, and now it's starting to fade. Just like me."

"I noticed."

145

Ember reached into her jacket pocket and pulled out the silver illusion-charm ring. Grinning, she wiggled it and raised an eyebrow. "I'm assuming I can keep this."

"It's all yours, Em. That pendant's magic dried out, and I don't have anything to hide anymore."

"Sounds very freeing."

Cheyenne snorted.

"Seriously, thanks for this. And for taking me out with your weird friends tonight."

"So weird. They were a lot less tense when they took *me* out, but I can't blame them. Lotta shit goin' on for everybody."

Ember leaned forward to peel off her purple jacket. "Still, I had fun. Something else we have in common, right? Took twenty-one years and a whole world of hurt for either of us to finally get out into the world of magicals as ourselves."

"Glad I could help you with that." Cheyenne took a deep breath and slipped back into her human form. "I think those agents liked you."

"As long as they know I won't be anyone's token fae friend." They shared a small, tired laugh. "Seriously, though. I'll take being a part of that whole world, even underground and with a giant machine-bug thing attacking everyone, over watching you almost die fighting portal monsters any day of the week."

"Don't get sappy on me, Em. It might ruin our friendship."

Scoffing, Ember tossed her jacket over the back of the couch and pointed at it. "Hang that up for me, will ya? I'm gonna go pass out."

"Night."

"I hope so."

Cheyenne couldn't help the hint of a smile as she watched her friend wheel quickly across their wide-open loft apartment. The fae didn't hit any doorways or corners on the way into her bedroom, and the door closed softly behind her.

The halfling blew out a long, slow sigh and scratched her head. Then she looked over her shoulder at the iron rail around her mini-loft office. *Looks like I have some digging to do and a few minutes to kill. Time to figure out what Mr. Nice Guy Neighbor is up to.*

CHAPTER TWENTY-THREE

Although she didn't hop on the dark web, at least not to start, Cheyenne ran a double-encryption through her regular server and then powered up her VPN as a bonus. *I'm not gonna let Glen run so much as a Google search on this guy without extra protection. Not that he could be better than me anyway. Dude probably has a whole team of cybern-erds working for him and never touched a piece of code in his life. Money'll do that. Just not to me.*

She did run another Google search on Matthew Thomas, and her browsing wasn't interrupted this time.

Cybersecurity, market trading, and advanced prosthetics were just the tip of the iceberg for their weirdly calm neighbor. As far as the rest of the world could see, Matthew was also on the board, if not the founder, of several international non-profits and global charities providing educational funding, support, and school supplies for grade-school kids in underprivileged communities.

This guy's reputation rivals Bianca Summerlin's, only he's not hiding a bastard halfling in that loft apartment.

Cheyenne wrinkled her nose.

Nobody's this altruistic just because. Cheap shot, trying to hide whatever else he's doing behind helping kids learn and sending them books they'll never have time to read.

She clicked into several of the non-profits and charities to poke around, but as far as she could tell, nothing was out of place. Matthew Thomas's name was right there on every board of directors and list of trustees. He'd even gotten a scholarship named after him, which apparently he funded personally for a hundred kids right out of high school based on financial need, scholastic merit, and what the site called "an exceptional understanding of personal growth and potential, combined with a fierce desire to improve, succeed, and better both themselves and their community."

"Okay."

She scrolled through the scholarship info page and found a snippet of an interview with the man himself.

"Yes, I read through every single submitted application. This is something I'm providing personally, not through one of my many other organizations. [laughter] So there's nobody else reading through these incredible essays that land on my desk. And let me tell you, selecting only a hundred of these a year is one of the hardest things I've ever had to do. So, how do I make that decision in the end? I'm looking for heart, dedication, and perseverance. I'm looking for someone who really wants this, and who, in a perfect world, is unlikely to squander the opportunity by partying all through college and letting everything else take a back seat to the present moment. It's an unrealistic expectation, I know, but I have high hopes for these kids. I want to see that they do and if they can dive deep into themselves and show me what they want to be seen instead of showing me what they think I want to see. That greatly raises their chances of receiving one of these scholarships."

"Oy." Cheyenne scrolled through the rest of the interview excerpt and shook her head. *Sounds like a genuinely good guy obsessed with helping others. Why does he rub me the wrong way?*

After scrolling through his Wikipedia page and clicking on several links to his various organizations and high-profile firms, she decided to start with the cyber-security pillar of all Matthew Thomas's dabbling, ThomasSafe.

"So humble and original." She snorted and waited half a second for the page to load.

A prickle of suspicion rose along the back of her neck, and she grabbed the monitor with both hands to angle it down toward the desk. *Can't have him snooping on me snooping on him, if that's what's happening here.*

Cheyenne rolled the office chair away from the desk and spun it lazily toward the back corner of the mini-loft. She scanned the crease between the wall and the ceiling and grinned. *If he's watching and doesn't freak out after this, I'm going with the psychopath option.*

The halfling slipped into her drow form and enhanced her speed a fraction of a second later. Then she stood and rolled the chair behind her toward the corner. The swiveling chair didn't move when she stepped onto it and peered up into the corner, running her hands along the walls and the ceiling, searching for a different kind of mechanical bug. *They'd be small, and this is a ridiculously obvious place to put a tiny spy camera.*

She spun the chair to face the rest of her elevated office and scanned the potential hiding spots. Reaching out toward the wall behind her, the halfling let off a small, controlled burst of telekinetic energy, and the rolling office chair lurched toward the center of the mini-loft.

"Woah." Her arms shot out to her sides for balance, and she chuckled. "Having this much control makes things way too easy. No wonder every drow wants to pass their trials."

The chair had stopped right where she wanted it, beneath the recessed light fixture in the ceiling. Cheyenne reached up and quickly unscrewed the spiral bulb. Then she ran her finger around the edge of the fixture before turning her attention to the lightbulb itself. *All this twisting glass makes for a lot of surface area. A camera could be stuck in just the right place.*

She turned the bulb over in her hand, running her fingers along every edge of the twisting glass. A soft pop sounded behind her, followed by, "What are you doing?"

The surprise made her slip out of drow speed as the lightbulb slipped from her fingers and smashed on the wooden floor beneath her. She turned too quickly to look over her shoulder and almost fell off the chair. *So much for looking for bugs faster than anyone could watch me.*

Corian stood between her and the far corner of the mini-loft, his arms folded and his head tilted comically far toward his shoulder.

"I'm changing a lightbulb."

"Like that? I didn't know it took enhanced drow speed to get non-essential repairs done."

"Well, maybe I was trying to buy myself a little extra time and finish everything before you got here."

"Right. Because that's a commonly asked question. 'How many drow halflings does it take to screw in a lightbulb?'"

Cheyenne glared at him and leaped off the chair, careful not to land in the shattered glass. "Well, now I have my answer. None. But the nightstalker has awful timing and broke the lightbulb."

"I didn't touch your lightbulb."

Rolling the chair back into place at her desk, Cheyenne shook her head. "This wins the Most Useless Conversation award by a landslide."

"I agree. Can we go on? I didn't spend a quarter of an hour doubling up on dampening wards to stand here and chat."

"Yeah, I know." After glancing around the mini-loft, she stooped to grab a sheet of paper from the printer on the floor and used it as a dustpan for as much glass as she could sweep onto it with her hand.

Corian frowned. "You want some real cleaning supplies? Gloves, at the very least."

She rolled her eyes. "Apparently, I'm immune to broken glass. And no, this isn't the first time I've tested that theory."

"That sounds like something I should be concerned about."

"You know what?" Cheyenne stood, carefully rolled the paper to keep its contents from spilling out, and tossed it in the black tin trashcan left over from Pellerville Gables Apartments' days of pretending the mini-loft was a working office. "If you had been around when I found out on my own why I don't get cuts, you'd realize that's the last thing you need to worry about. I broke a lot of things trying to rein in the drow when I didn't want it to come out. And now that I have a handle on my magic, I'm still breaking things because you like to whip up a little portal surprise when I'm focused on other things."

"Cheyenne."

"What?" She shifted her weight onto one hip and widened her eyes at him.

"Let's talk about this somewhere else. Where it's safe."

"Fine." Cheyenne gestured toward the couch in the living room. "The leg thing's over there."

Corian moved in a light-brown blur. The next second, Cheyenne's hair scattered away from her face. The folded paper in the trashcan fluttered in the breeze of the nightstalker's return. He lifted the black metal bar and nodded at the oval of black light hovering midair behind him. "Let's go."

"Yep." She brushed past him, stepped through his portal, and found herself for the second time today standing in front of Persh'al's open-ended square of computer tables. Glancing down at her feet, she frowned. "Did you run out of candles?"

"No, I ran out of warding stones." The portal closed behind Corian as he stopped beside her. "Candles are the next best thing, and that's all I had on me at the time. Apparently, Byrd's been growing quite the collection."

Leaning against the left end of the closest six-foot table, Byrd cocked his head with a little shrug. "They make me feel safe. Maybe we should've lined your pockets with them, huh?"

"I *was* safe," Cheyenne muttered. "Still am."

"You're safe *here* because we have the right tools at our disposal." Corian nodded at the ring of glistening stones of every color and rough, unsanded cut encircling them. "You were relatively safe before you gave that machine everything it needed to track you down and make the Crown's objective a hell of a lot easier to reach."

"Okay, first, how the hell was I supposed to know that trackers work with *magic*, too? Those canisters or whatever that you took from the smuggled crates worked with blood. Everything else works with blood. I haven't been doing this for centuries, which *you* know. If you want me to make sure I don't go handing out my personal calling card to every-thing that attacks me, you should've told me that was possible."

Sitting in his executive office chair in front of his monitors, Persh'al scratched his head beside the neon-orange mohawk. Then he spun in his chair and met Cheyenne's gaze. "We screwed up on that one, kid."

"Yeah, you did."

Corian frowned at her, clenching his jaw. "You're not the only one who's allowed to make mistakes."

The halfling folded her arms and met his gaze. "I'm fine with that as long as you guys stop acting like you don't ever make any."

"Until you came into the picture, we didn't."

"See, that's the opposite of what I just said."

Persh'al lifted a finger and waited for the half-drow and the night-stalker to turn their scathing glares on him. "I just wanna remind everybody that what's happening right now is new territory. L'zar's kid passed the trials. Portals are popping up like daisies in the fall, which isn't a thing anyway. And we've got O'gúl tech up and running and pursuing an objective before we can figure out how the hell that's possible or how to stop it. There's more than enough room for mistakes when we have no idea what we're doing, but a really big one would be to keep standing there blaming each other for what's already done. Right?"

Neither of them said a word.

"Oh, come on. *Right?*"

Cheyenne shot Corian a sidelong glance and slipped out of her drow form, feeling the heat of her magic drain slowly into the base of her spine. Then she pulled her gaze away to study the opposite side of the warehouse and shrugged. "Yeah. You're right."

"Corian."

The nightstalker stared at the open iron beams of the ceiling and raised his eyebrows. "Everybody makes mistakes."

"I'm gonna take that as consent, and I don't give a shit if you like it or not. So let's move on and quit treating this like it's the end of the world."

Byrd snorted. "It might be."

"You're not helping, goblin." Persh'al pointed at him and raised a warning eyebrow. "Bright side is now we know at least one of those machines was already up and running and looking for something, presumably Cheyenne. If that's the case, we need to figure out how the hell its programmer knew to send a piece of obsolete tech after her without using any kind of magical tracker first."

"Not obsolete anymore." Cheyenne stepped out of the ring of stones and gestured toward the war machine's broken leg dangling from Corian's hand. "I figured bringing something back that's been activated might help."

Persh'al's eyes widened. "From Peridosh?"

"I seriously hope I wasn't supposed to fight off another one of those things somewhere else." She reached into her pocket and pulled out the strange, almost S-shaped metal cog. "And this."

The blue troll caught it easily when she tossed it at him. Squinting at the metal piece, he sucked in a long, hissing breath. "I'm gonna need some time to pick these apart. If there's any stored memory, I should be able to find it. I can run it through a human system, but the O'gúl analysis will take some time."

"Complicated language, huh?"

Persh'al looked at Cheyenne, and his squint deepened when he grimaced. "Not really. I just have to do all the comparisons by hand."

"Ew."

"Tell me about it."

Corian stalked across the warehouse, dropping the black metal bar on the table with a clang as he passed it. "In the meantime, we'll dig around for our own information. Who knows? That might be faster."

"Sweet. Time for round three." Byrd straightened and rubbed his hands together.

"Of what?" Cheyenne watched the goblin move around to the other side of Persh'al's square before she followed him.

Persh'al cleared his throat and rolled his chair toward his monitor and keyboard. When the halfling shot him a curious glance, he shook his head and dove into his system.

Byrd stopped at the warehouse's thick steel door leading to the back of the property and shoved it open. "We're tryin' again!"

"Already?" Lumil shouted from outside. "Didn't think he had it in him."

"He might not." Byrd chuckled and opened the door wider as Lumil stepped inside. "But Cheyenne's here."

"Oh, hey." The goblin woman jerked her chin at the halfling, wiping slightly damp hands on her pant legs. "What's up, kid?"

"I'm waiting for someone to tell me."

Lumil ignored her and eyed Corian instead, who was busy opening another portal in the center of the warehouse. "How does L'zar's kid showing up make the lizard head more willing to talk?"

Byrd sniggered. "I mean, look at her!"

The goblin woman looked Cheyenne up and down and smirked. "Yeah, she's pretty terrifying. You've done this before, right? I thought I heard you mention something about that."

Glancing at the portal quickly opening in front of Corian, Cheyenne shrugged. "I need somebody to tell me what you're talking about before I can answer that."

"Persuasion, kid." Byrd smashed his fist into the other palm. "A direct and intentional line of questioning."

Lumil leaned away from her counterpart and shot him a mocking frown. "Interrogation. The physical kind."

"Yeah, I've been there once or twice." *Didn't take much to make Durg squeal. Good thing he did.* "You guys still have that scaly guy locked up somewhere?"

"Damn straight, we do." Byrd marched toward the center of the warehouse, where Corian's portal had now opened fully into whatever room lay beyond. "We spent twelve hours straight huntin' this asshole down. No way is he gettin' turned loose anytime soon."

"Has he said anything else?"

"Eh." Lumil wrinkled her nose and wiggled her hand back and forth. "He started mumbling two hours in last time. If he said anything, it was pretty fuckin' indecipherable."

Cheyenne slowly joined them behind Corian, peering around the edge of the open portal for a better look. "He didn't look so great this morning, either."

"Oh, he wasn't." Lumil chuckled. "Hey, let me know if he looks worse or the same, huh? It's hard for me to tell. You spend all day bashing a guy's face in, and everything tends to kinda run together."

Corian looked slowly over his shoulder and fixed the goblin woman with his glowing silver eyes. "I understand your particular brand of humor, Lumil, but I don't enjoy it. This isn't a game."

Lumil's lips curled in a tight, humorless smile. "Don't talk down to me, nightstalker. I know exactly what this is."

"I know you do. Just try not to look like you enjoy it so much."

Corian glanced at Cheyenne and gestured at the open portal. "This is where we try to figure out how tonight happened. You gonna have a problem with this?"

Pressing her lips together, the halfling shook her head. "Nope."

"Then let's wake him up." Corian stepped through the portal, followed quickly by Byrd, who rubbed his hands together vigorously and chuckled through his nose.

"After you, kid." Lumil nodded at the portal and flexed her hands. "I'm still warming up."

CHAPTER TWENTY-FOUR

The portal took them into some kind of basement with a cement floor, ceiling, and all four walls. The room was empty except for the blood-splattered office chair with an equally stained coil of rope hanging limply over the armrests, a bright and unfiltered lightbulb dangling overhead, and two sets of iron manacles attached to brackets in the cement walls by sturdy iron chains. Those manacles were closed around the silver-scaled magical's wrists and ankles. He sat relatively upright against the wall, though his arms dangled six inches above either side of his head, which slumped all the way forward so his chin touched his chest.

"Go ahead," Corian muttered, staring at their unconscious prisoner.

"Oh, yeah." Byrd stepped forward and squatted in front of the scaly magical, then reached into the inside pocket of his dark-brown vest and pulled out a handful of dried leaves. They crunched loudly when he squeezed the bundle in both fists. He slowly opened his hands again and waved them under the lizard-man's nose.

The prisoner gasped and reared back, thumping his head against the cement wall as his eyes flew open.

Byrd blew on his cupped hands, sending the leaves and dust into the other magical's face.

The lizard-man screamed and jerked against the manacles around his wrists. He was too weak to do more than lash out with his feet when the chains wouldn't let him go any farther. "You sadistic fuck!"

Spit flew from the lizard-man's mouth, his blood-red tongue flicking out between rows of tiny sharpened teeth.

Or maybe it's just a mouthful of blood. Cheyenne shoved her hands into her pockets and studied the O'gúleesh prisoner who was working Earthside for the Crown.

Byrd smirked and stood, dusting the rest of the crushed leaves off his hands as he stepped slowly backward. The lizard-man eyed the puff of dust with wary yellow-green eyes. "You think you're onto something with that shit? Go ahead, bring in a whole fucking pile and bury me. I'm not telling you shit."

"The thought did occur to me." Corian's voice was low, calm, and controlled, his hands clasped behind his back. The prisoner's eyes flickered up to settle on the nightstalker's face. "If I left it up to these two, that's exactly what they'd be doing right now. Or something equally painful for you, no doubt."

The magical sniggered. The glistening silver scales around his hooded eyes, thin lips, and flattened nose had taken on a sickly green hue. "Next you're gonna tell me I'm lucky you stopped them 'cause you're the one calling the shots around here. But you ain't."

Corian's nose wrinkled in response.

Cheyenne pressed her lips together. *He's more upset about the poor grammar.*

His prisoner couldn't tell the difference. "Yeah. I see right through you. Marchin' in here like you're the big feline in charge of how this is all gonna play out. Everybody in this dark little room knows it's bullshit. I saw him with my own eyes. L'zar's sittin' at the head of this table, and next to him, you're a fucking housecat."

Corian turned slowly to look at Lumil and Byrd. "Well, at least he's talking again."

"I guess." Lumil raised her clenched fists at her sides, and the bright-red spinning symbols of her magic flared to life around them. "Let's skip to the part where he tells us something we don't already know."

The lizard-man's bloody sneer faded as his reptilian eyes flickered between the goblin woman and the nightstalker. "Nothin' you can do to make me talk, bitch."

"Not when you're lucid." Lumil stepped toward him. "But hey, no one expects you to remember squealin' your head off like a little piggy when you're in that much pain."

His gaze dropped to the spinning, sparking symbols swirling like circular saws around her fists. "You're lying."

"There's only one way to find out, right?"

"And there's only one way to make this easier on yourself," Corian added.

Cheyenne glanced at him. *I wonder how long it's been since they had to play this good-magical, bad-magical crap. Seems a little rusty.*

The lizard-man snorted. A layer of pink foam had gathered at the corners of his mouth and around his nostrils. More of it sprayed out in front of him as his breath quickened. Despite his valid fear of Lumil's fists, his scaly upper lip lifted in a twitching snarl. "If you'd already made me talk, you wouldn't be back in here to try again."

"Under the previous circumstances, sure." Corian dipped his head. "You would have called our bluff. But circumstances have changed in the last few hours, Lex, and we're not bluffing."

Lex lifted his chin and thumped his head against the wall, glaring up at the nightstalker. "What circumstances?"

"We know about your personal cache of machine parts, and I imagine the team we sent out to collect your things will be returning from that little errand shortly. In the meantime, we've discovered another little problem we're *really* hoping you can clear up for us." Corian gestured at Cheyenne without taking his eyes off the scaly prisoner.

With a sputtering hiss, Lex looked her up and down and cocked his head. "A human. That's your problem?" He let out a weak laugh and smacked his lips. "Listen, I don't know what you heard about my expertise, but you're outta luck with this one. I can't fix ugly."

"Oh, man." Byrd shook his head with a low chuckle. For once, Lumil didn't try to smack him out of it.

Cheyenne blinked, wiping her face clean of any expression. *I can play this game, no problem.* "Wish I could say the same."

"Oh, yeah? You think your tiny white human hands are gonna do more damage than the goblin's whirly fists?"

"Nope." It only took a second's thought about the Nimlothar seed still connecting her to the root of drow power to pull all her magic up from the base of her spine to race through her body. Byrd and Lumil stepped nimbly away from her. When the purple light flashing behind Cheyenne's golden eyes reflected in the shimmering silver scales covering Lex's face, she knew it had the desired effect. She lifted both hands and summoned twin orbs of churning black magic hissing with purple sparks. "But these will."

The prisoner's yellow-green gaze darted from the drow halfling's purple-gray face to the devastating attack spells roiling in her palms. Then he glanced quickly at Byrd, Lumil, and Corian in turn. A thin, stuttering wheeze burst from between his thin lips.

He's laughing.

"You found the *mór úcare*. Sneaky fell-damn bastard."

"I barely had to lift a finger." Corian took a step forward, eliciting a subtle flinch from Lex. "She wants this as badly as the rest of us do, if not more. I'm sure you understand why."

"She's an idiot. So are you."

Corian's eyes narrowed.

Cheyenne started to step forward, but Lumil beat her to it. The goblin woman moved so quickly, Lex didn't see it coming. She dropped to one knee in a slide and landed a bone-crunching left hook to the underside of the prisoner's jaw. The perfect aim rocked him sideways instead of back against the wall, red sparks and dark blood flying in all directions. Lumil rode her momentum and gracefully swung her knee off the cement floor before marching toward the opposite side of the cramped room. She bounced once on her toes and circled back around to resume her place on the other side of Cheyenne.

The halfling met the goblin's gaze and raised her eyebrows. Lumil winked.

"Oh, shit. Look at that." Byrd pointed across the floor in front of them. Two shimmering silver flakes glinted on the cement. "I didn't know you could pluck a taratas like a bird."

Lumil barked a laugh. "Must be losing his integrity. Not like he had any to begin with."

Cheyenne stared at the thick rivulets of green-black blood running down the right side of Lex's chin. Where they started were two dark, glistening patches of flesh beneath his missing scales.

The prisoner's sides heaved as he fought to catch his breath after the blow. Then he pulled enough strength from somewhere to swing his head up and glare at his captors. Even then, his slitted eyes shivered in their sockets while his head wobbled.

"That was just to get your attention, Lex. Time for you to listen." Corian stepped across the room, casting his lengthening shadow over the bleeding, swaying prisoner. He dropped into a squat in one fluid movement and cocked his head, leaning close. "That drow behind me met one of your little toys tonight. Took her less than a minute to crush it to pieces, some of which she brought with her."

Cheyenne killed her sparking black orbs and folded her arms. *Okay, I'll let him get away with that little embellishment.*

"So we know you have at least one digger up and running. Or *had*, I should say. Now you're going to tell us how many others you've activated and what you used to track her down."

Lex let out a strangled choke and lurched against the restraints. Corian didn't react, having stopped less than an inch from the farthest their prisoner could lean away from the wall. The choking continued, and the scaled magical's eyes widened even as they rolled in lazy, unfocused circles. "You're fucked!"

"What did you *use?*"

The prisoner slumped back against the wall, his mouth hanging wide open as the strangled chokes became raw, grating laughter. "I didn't." His eyes rolled back in his head as he screeched, leaning sideways against the chains. He took sharp, gasping breaths before shrieking again.

Cheyenne leaned toward Lumil but couldn't look away from the taratas bucking on the floor. "I think you broke him."

"Nah. That's just a taratas laughing. You wanna hear the most annoying sound in the world, this is it."

The halfling frowned. "Looks like he's having a seizure."

"Yep."

Corian's ears twitched, but the rest of him remained perfectly still in his squat. "I can do this all night, Lex. So can Lumil. I promise you won't think this is very funny for long once she takes a few more scales off your face."

With a final raw, wheezing inhale, Lex dropped his head back

against the wall and aimed his constantly shifting eyes in the nightstalker's general direction. "I didn't have shit to track your precious *mór
úcare*." He fell into another round of choking, wheezing giggles. "That
digger set out on a hunch. And even my *hunches* get more done than
that goblin's fucking fists! I don't need to track the drow, you furball
piece of shit. No one else will have to either after this. She's too close!"
Lex shrieked again and leaned forward to slam back against the wall in
his lunatic mirth. "She's too *close!*"

Corian stood smoothly from his crouch and stalked past the gathered magicals into the center of the room. Cheyenne turned to watch
him and noticed the opposite wall didn't have a door. The nightstalker's
fingers moved quickly, and another portal opened in front of him.

"What are you doing?" Lumil asked, scowling at Corian's back.

"We're done here."

"Are you kidding me? He's spouting a load of bullshit just to get to
you. Give me five more minutes. I'll knock the crazy right out of him."

"*Not now!*" The growling shout echoed through the tiny cement
room, and Corian stepped through the portal as soon as it fully opened.

Lex's shrieking cackle had died down into guttural bursts of amusement, and he leaned his head back against the wall again, his eyes
closed. "You go on and try to figure *that* one out, *nilsch úcat*. They're all
coming for her now that they know. You think you can stop the O'gúl
Crown? I'll be slamming my tankard down on your dried skulls before
year's end!"

"You crazy shit." Lumil kicked the taratas' splayed legs. He jerked
away and cackled again, leaning sideways until his chained wrist grew
taut and stopped him from hitting the floor. "Come on."

Both goblins headed toward the portal, and Cheyenne spared a final
glance at the prisoner. He was too far gone to notice.

CHAPTER TWENTY-FIVE

Corian's portal shrank and disappeared with a soft pop as soon as Cheyenne stepped back into the warehouse. "What the hell was that?"

"Yes." Lumil pointed at the nightstalker. "That's what I was gonna ask. We went in there to get information."

"And we got it." Corian paced across the center of the warehouse, his silver eyes glowing fiercely. One tufted ear twitched, and he shook his head.

"That wasn't information, man." Byrd gestured toward the nonexistent portal. "That was him pissing all over us."

"Shut up." The nightstalker didn't look at any of them as he kept pacing, pivoting neatly on his heel each time he reached a wall.

"Don't tell *me* to shut up," Lumil muttered, scowling at him.

Cheyenne stared at the floor. "He's right, though."

"Oh, you too? We just met a few days ago, kid. You've got real balls, thinkin' you can tell me to shut up."

"We did get information." The halfling glanced briefly at Lumil. "That machine wasn't tracking me."

"No." Corian spun again and headed toward her without looking up from the floor. "He said he didn't have to."

"Because the digger was tracking on a hunch." Cheyenne tapped her fist against her mouth and closed her eyes.

"You both are crazy as that taratas." Lumil snorted and walked toward the couch at the other end of the warehouse.

"What hunch?" Corian muttered.

Byrd pointed at the empty space in the air where the portal had been. "You know we can just go back and ask him, right? Maybe not give him as much time to laugh about it and just beat him 'til it comes out. That worked last time."

Both nightstalker and halfling ignored him.

Byrd shot them both a suspicious glance, then hurried after Lumil. "You're right. It's all systems down with those two."

"Who was with you?"

Cheyenne opened her eyes and found Corian spinning away from the opposite wall again. "What?"

"Who was with you in Peridosh? If that thing was tracking a *hunch*, Cheyenne, it was tracking someone its programmer suspected would be with you. To get to you through them."

"That's impossible." The halfling shook her head and closed her eyes again.

"Just go through it again. All of it."

"I was with three FRoE agents, and I know for a fact that none of them has had contact with an O'gúl war machine. They don't even know those exist."

"I'm happy to agree with you on that one, but we can't overlook anything. Go deeper. Did the digger attack any of them?"

"No. It just dropped out of the wall and headed straight for—shit!"

"Straight for whom?"

Cheyenne's eyes flew open. "Ember."

"You brought your fae friend with you?"

"Yeah. We share an apartment, and I'm helping her adjust to a new lifestyle that's totally my fault. I've been bringing her with me a lot lately."

"And that might've been the hunch. But it still doesn't add up." Corian spun and paced toward her again. "Fae magic is impossible to trace."

"Really?"

"Yeah. That's why you never see one. Or at least, most of us don't."

"Well, she hasn't been fighting anyone recently. I'm positive of that."

"Fine. It wouldn't have been her magic anyway." The nightstalker stopped in front of her and met her gaze. "You haven't been drawing your friend's blood and using it for some kind of secret Peridosh trade, right?"

She blinked. "What the hell do you think I do in my spare time?"

"Not that, obviously. I still had to ask."

Cheyenne turned away from him and ruffled her fingers through her bone-white hair, her chains jingling. "If that thing couldn't track her magic, are you saying it could still track her blood?"

"Blood doesn't lie, kid." Corian swallowed thickly. When she shot him a curious glance, he avoided her gaze and kept walking. "And you're sure *she's* not selling her own blood down in the market? No judgment. I've known plenty of fae who've built their empires selling blood right from their veins."

"Yeah, I'm sure. She doesn't need to do that for money, and that was her first time down there anyway. It was supposed to be fun."

"Hmm." He scratched his jaw. "Bit of a shortage of that these days."

"Of fun? Yeah, remind me to tell you when I find some." Rolling her eyes, Cheyenne took some determined steps toward the back wall of the warehouse, then paused. "You know what there isn't a shortage of?"

"Cheyenne, I couldn't begin to guess."

She whirled around to face him, and the grim realization in her golden drow eyes made him step back. "Ember's blood."

"I thought we just went over that."

"Yeah, with your stupid ideas. Open a portal."

His nose wrinkled in irritation. "I'm the one who barks orders at you, kid."

"Open the goddamn portal, Corian!"

The door to one of the small, square offices behind him shot open and hit the wall with a bang. "Is it really too much to ask for a little peace and quiet? Ever?"

"Cheyenne." L'zar propped his hands on either side of the doorway and grinned. "For some reason, no one thought it was a good idea to tell me you were here."

Corian cocked his head when L'zar turned his discerning gaze on his nightstalker second in command. "It was on my to-do list."

"Tell him to open a portal to my apartment." Cheyenne jabbed a finger at Corian. "Otherwise, I'm running all the way back to Richmond, and I don't think I have the time for that."

L'zar's grin faded. "What's she talking about?"

"She hasn't gotten around to telling *me* yet, either."

"Jesus." Cheyenne smoothed her hair back from her forehead. "We were talking about blood, Corian. Ember spent two weeks in the hospital after she was shot. They took enough samples there to start a whole new blood bank and name it after her."

"Shit."

"Yeah."

"Your fae friend?" L'zar stepped out of the doorway slowly as if sudden movements would make his daughter explode.

"Ember." Cheyenne stared at him, fighting to keep herself under control. "That's her name." She took off after Corian, who was halfway across the warehouse and headed for the circle of ward stones.

L'zar grimaced and followed them. "I know her name, Cheyenne. I met her this morning. What did she do?"

"Apparently, all she had to do was be my friend. How long is this gonna take?"

Corian grunted, his fingers moving quickly as he muttered the portal spell. "It's a little more complicated than the regular 'toss up a hole through space' kind. We need to make sure no one can follow us back here."

L'zar cleared his throat. "I know you two have had the luxury of spending a lot of time together over the last few weeks, but I haven't, so I'd love to know what the fuck is happening right now."

Cheyenne growled in frustration, but Persh'al saved her from having to reply.

The troll rolled back in his chair and caught L'zar's attention. "One of the old machines was activated and found Cheyenne in Peridosh. She crushed it, but it caught her signature, and a fun little chat with Lex made them realize the thing was tracking *Ember* instead of Cheyenne. Programmers assumed they'd be together, they were, and now everyone who's behind this first wave of war machines knows how to find Cheyenne *and* how to hit her where it hurts."

L'zar raised an eyebrow at his friend and dipped his head. "Thank you."

"Because apparently someone stole a bunch of fae blood from a hospital, and that's how they've been tracking Ember."

"I heard them work that one out, Persh'al."

"Right." The troll nodded curtly, spun back around to face his desk, and got down to some serious typing again.

L'zar turned his gaze to Cheyenne, and a tiny frown flickered across his eyebrows. "Does she mean that much to you?"

I was gonna say that looked like empathy until he opened his stupid mouth. "She's my best friend. My *only* friend, for a while, so yeah, she means that much to me. I'll fight you with everything I have if you tell me I should just let her deal with it herself."

He eyed her, then looked at Corian.

The nightstalker nodded, and the rest of his portal bloomed into place within the circle of stones. "No one's leaving Ember to handle this on her own. That isn't an option."

"Good. I hope she doesn't need us." Without another word, Cheyenne stepped over the ring of stones and headed through the portal leading into her living room.

Corian and L'zar shared glances, which were cut off by the nightstalker disappearing through the portal behind the halfling.

The portal closed almost immediately. L'zar hissed, stalked the two yards toward the couch, and roared in frustration. He sent his foot crashing into the side of the sunken brown couch, and it flew across the warehouse with a screech and the sharp crack of snapping wood. The couch hit the back wall in a puff of dust. L'zar stayed where he was, his shoulders hunched and fists clenched so tightly, the veins stood out on his forearms. The only sound in the warehouse was the whirring of the fans in Persh'al's computer towers and the escaped drow's angry, heaving breaths.

"That couch has been here for a long time," Persh'al muttered.

Whirling to face him, L'zar ran a hand through his disheveled shoulder-length hair and inhaled deeply through his nose. "It was falling apart anyway."

The blue troll shrugged and spun back to his keyboard. "I guess it's better than you putting a fist through any of my tables."

Standing against the wall on either side of the door to the supply closet, Byrd and Lumil stared at L'zar with wide eyes. Lumil cleared her throat. "You good?"

Tilting his head from side to side to stretch his neck, L'zar clasped his hands behind his back and walked at a slow, deliberate pace across the warehouse. "*This* is the real prison."

Byrd snorted. "I didn't think we were *that* bad."

Persh'al turned to shoot him a warning glance. "You'd make a piss-poor guard anyway. He was talking about the fact that he can't do anything for her."

"I know what he was talking about." Byrd waved toward the computers behind Persh'al and rolled his eyes. "Get back to your nerdy coding shit. Nobody asked for an interpreter."

The goblin man stalked toward the couch and flung himself onto it. Another puff of dust erupted from beneath him before the couch creaked, shuddered, and collapsed in the center.

CHAPTER TWENTY-SIX

The only thing Cheyenne heard in her apartment was the soft pop of the portal closing behind Corian. "Em?"

"She's here, right?"

"Yeah. She went to bed right before you broke my lightbulb."

Corian ignored the comment as he spun in a slow circle, taking in the high ceilings and the wide wall of windows facing north. "So we keep an eye on the place."

"Shh. Hold on." Cheyenne cocked her head at the soft, rustling whir coming from the other side of the kitchen. It could've been the fridge or a fan in Ember's room until she heard the quick series of clicks and something metal tapping against glass. "Something's here."

She stormed across the kitchen, the nightstalker on her heels. "A digger's not going to show up quietly and try to sneak in while she's sleeping."

"What the fuck!"

Ember's shout spurred Cheyenne into action. If she'd bothered to try the doorknob, she would have found it locked, but she sent her fist through the door instead. The wood splintered and flew in every direction, and the halfling had enough time to take in at least three dozen tiny, glistening shapes swarming across the bedroom walls before two of them leaped at her.

"Ah!" She batted the flying black things away from her face. They hit the floor with a thud and instantly flipped onto their spindly legs again to face her. *"Tiny* bugs this time? Are you serious?"

The closest machine-beetle let out a metallic creak and launched a spray of bright-green pellets. The first few caught Cheyenne in the ribs before she dodged sideways to avoid the rest. She snarled in pain and brought her foot down on the two-inch mechanical bug before it could do anything else.

"Cheyenne!" Ember stared at the long lines of machines scrambling up the walls and across the ceiling, forming a canopy over the fae and her bed.

Cheyenne summoned a crackling black orb in one hand and took aim.

Corian gripped her wrist and held her back. "Don't give them anything else to use against you."

"Seriously?"

The nightstalker took off in a blur of brilliant silver light. The beetles gathering on the ceiling above Ember screeched as they were scraped off the ceiling and tossed across the room like a handful of pebbles.

"Oh, my God." Ember hunched over and jerked the comforter up to her chin.

The beetles hit the floor, dresser, and small desk with tinny thuds, then leaped back to their tiny clicking feet and scrambled toward the bed again.

Cheyenne stomped on as many of them as she could while Corian swiped handful after handful of the things off the walls in his enhanced speed. The mechanical creatures took about ten seconds to process what was happening. When they did, the change happened all at once.

The tiny crawling machines stopped skittering toward Ember and focused on their new targets. Cheyenne raised her foot to stomp on the next skittering beetle. The thing clicked at her, and one of its front legs whirled around on its hinge until it stuck straight up in the air.

Her foot came down before she could stop herself. "Fuck!"

She jerked backward and staggered against the wall. The machine-beetle dangled from the bottom of her shoe, its upturned appendage stuck through the soles of both the rubber tread and Cheyenne's foot.

The halfling blasted it with a churning ball of black energy and incinerated the thing on contact.

Corian slipped out of his enhanced speed right in front of her. "I told you not to do that!"

"It stabbed me in the foot! I'm not touching those things with my hands." Without giving him time to argue further, Cheyenne unleashed her black and purple sparking attacks on the metal beetles skittering across the wooden floor toward them.

Tiny gears and broken metal shards sprayed across Ember's room. The fae stared at the whole thing from behind her lifted comforter, the black and purple lights of Cheyenne's magic pulsing against her face and reflecting in her eyes.

When Cheyenne finished decimating the swarm of O'gúl insect machines, the room was filled with smoke and the bitter scent of hot metal. No one moved.

"None of those things made it through the first shot." She turned toward Corian and raised one finger. "Nothing to lock onto. Nothing to report back."

A high-pitched screech and metallic whir came from the top of the headboard before two larger green pellets of magical sludge spewed from the surviving metal beetle. The first splattered her lifted hand, sending searing pain racing through her fingers and up her wrist. The halfling screamed and launched a roiling black sphere of sparking energy right back. The second green-sludge attack missed her by inches and sailed past into the kitchen as the last spy machine disintegrated all over the back of Ember's bed.

The fae was almost hyperventilating as she stared blankly through the open doorway. Her hand lifted slowly to gently touch the side of her head in reassurance. "That was way too close."

"Come on, Em. I'd never hit you." Cheyenne sucked in a sharp breath and shook out her hand. "Ah! What *was* that stuff?"

Corian shot her hand a sidelong glance. "Something meant to stay with you for quite some time if I had to guess."

"You know, I had a black-magic potion tossed all over my shoulder and had to deal with those open wounds for days. This just feels like I put on a glove lined with broken glass."

"But it's not cutting you, right?"

Cheyenne glared at him and ignored the rhetorical question.

"You still have the darktongue salve, right?"

"Yeah, I still have it."

"I'd get it if I were you. For your foot, too."

"Shouldn't we be focusing on what just happened and how those things got in?"

Corian turned to face her and blinked slowly. "We'll focus on that as soon as you clean up. The longer we stand here arguing about it, the more time any potential side effects have to develop. The nasty kind."

Cheyenne looked at Ember and nodded. "Are you okay?"

"Uh, maybe?" The fae swept her gaze slowly across the metal fragments, the bits of ground steel bugs, and the charred spell dents littering every surface of her room. "I'm not convinced this isn't a super-messed-up dream."

"It'll sink in soon enough."

Cheyenne shot Corian a warning glance and shook her head. "That's not helping. I'll be right back, Em. Just gotta grab the magical first-aid kit."

As she left the bedroom, Corian nodded at Ember and turned toward the door. "I'll give you some privacy."

"No! Please don't." Ember shrank beneath her comforter and scanned the room again. "Just in case."

"All right." The nightstalker stayed awkwardly by the door, gazing everywhere in the room except at the fae girl in her pajama tank top, ducking like a kid hiding from the boogieman.

Cheyenne lifted her backpack off the floor beside the couch and grabbed the zipper. "Damnit!"

She jerked her burning hand away and shook it out, then unzipped the main pocket with her other hand. When she removed the brown glass jar of the darktongue salve from the bottom of her pack and tried to open it, the mere pressure of her agonized fingers against the jar made her snarl.

Okay. Maybe there are *nasty side effects that show up fast.*

She took the salve with her, limped to Ember's room, and held it out toward Corian. "I need some help."

He took it from her without a word, unscrewed the lid, and scooped out a giant glob of the sticky white substance.

Cheyenne's eyes grew wide. "Hey, that's expensive stuff, or so I've been told."

"Uh-huh." He crooked his goo-covered fingers at her, urging her toward him.

"You can put some back. It only takes a little."

"Not after an attack like that. This is for the whole hand."

"Aw, really?" Cheyenne eyed the large glob of salve on the night-stalker's fingers and grimaced. "Like, all at once?"

"Like, all at once." Corian smirked. "Don't worry. I'll make sure to massage it in."

"You're enjoying this."

"A little." He waved for her hand again, and she slowly extended it toward him. "Mostly because I told you not to use attack spells. I'll call this a fair trade."

"You know, I liked it better when we were punching each other in the face and calling it training." Cheyenne pulled back her hand before he could touch the salve to it. "Is my skin supposed to be doing that?"

"Give me one example where a drow lighting up like radioactive waste is a good thing."

"Fine." She stuck her hand out the rest of the way and looked at Ember. "Hey. You're pretty quiet."

"Ya think?" The fae snorted, but it pulled her out of her near-catatonic state, and she gazed at her friend. "I don't even know what's going on right now."

"Don't worry. We'll fill you in on all the—ah! Goddammit! You *asshole.*"

Corian clutched her injured hand in both of his now and smeared the healing salve all over it. "Can't be gentle with this one, kid. Go ahead, let it out. I'll try not to be offended."

Cheyenne's eyes twitched as tears spilled over and trailed down her cheeks. "I take it back. This is much worse than the holes in my shoulder."

Her mouth fell open and she gasped, staggering back against the wall and clutching her stomach in a silent scream. Corian's grip on her hand was as firm as ever, and he kept rubbing the salve in.

"I've seen way bigger guys than you pass out with much smaller surface areas covered in this stuff." Corian chuckled. "I guess I shouldn't be surprised."

The halfling grunted and said, "Apparently, it takes me having no clue what I'm doing and a bullet through my hip to make me pass out. And that one time I saved an entire FRoE team from being crushed to death. I think that's it."

"Well, it looks like you won't be adding blowing up O'gúl beetle spies to that very short list." He released her hand and raised both of his, stepping away to give her some space. "Give it a minute."

She blinked through her watering eyes and tentatively opened her hand. The green glow rising through her skin had disappeared. "Feels like my hand fell asleep."

"It almost fell off."

"What?"

Corian shrugged. "Probably. You didn't want to test that theory, did you?"

"You're full of stupid rhetorical questions today." Cheyenne shook out her hand and wiggled her fingers. "I can handle this."

"Wanna take off your shoe?"

"Hey, if you try rubbing that stuff on the giant needle hole in my foot, I promise you you'll end up getting kicked in the face."

"I'll let you handle it, then."

"Does that stuff heal everything?" Ember stared at the brown jar in Corian's hand before Cheyenne snatched it away.

"Short of a knife wound, yeah. I've had plenty of opportunities to test it." The halfling lowered into a squat and grimaced.

"Wait." Ember bunched the comforter under her chin and swallowed. "Can we get the hell out of my room first?"

Corian pointed toward the kitchen. "I'm still happy to step out and give you a minute."

"Don't. I just realized I like having a nightstalker around too. It's just, the mess in here gives a whole new meaning to 'don't let the bedbugs bite.' This is suddenly the last place I wanna be."

With a snort, Cheyenne stood from her crouch and nodded. "You need any help?"

"No, I can handle the chair." Ember tossed the comforter off her lap and pushed herself toward the edge of the bed. "Just stand watch."

"As reassuring as I'm sure that would be for you, Ember, we can't stay here all night on the off-chance that something else might show up in your bedroom."

She snarled in frustration and looked up at him, propping herself on her hands and pausing on the verge of transferring into the chair. "I'm pretty sure you can spare five goddamn minutes."

Cheyenne raised her eyebrows and glanced at the floor, trying to hide her smirk.

Corian hummed and shot the halfling a sidelong glance. "I'm starting to get why this fae is your best friend."

"Yeah, I might be rubbing off on her a little."

CHAPTER TWENTY-SEVEN

"This makes me want to kill someone." Cheyenne was stretched out on the couch, her leg out straight in front of her and all the muscles taut as she forced herself to breathe through the pain.

"That is so cool." Ember leaned forward to watch the wound in the bottom of Cheyenne's salve-covered foot seal itself from the inside out.

"Which part?"

"The instant healing part." Ember shook her head. "Please don't kill someone. I mean, unless you need to."

Corian lifted his phone to his ear and eyed the girls as he waited for Persh'al to pick up. "If we handle this correctly right now, that won't be a choice you have to make any time soon."

Cheyenne sucked another sharp breath through her teeth, then the unbearable sting flaring through her foot receded. "Handle it how?"

He lifted a finger for her to wait and turned away. "Hey. Yeah, we found something, all right. Nope. All good. We just need to double down around here for the time being. Yeah. What about Lumil? Does she know how to cast without blowing anything up first?"

Ember and Cheyenne exchanged wide-eyed glances, and the halfling whispered, "I have no idea."

"Fine," Corian continued. "No, it can't wait 'til tomorrow. If she doesn't get her ass through the next portal that shows up in that ware-

175

house, I'll pull her from interrogation duty. Yeah, that's what I thought. Just be ready." He hung up and slipped the phone back into his pocket.

"So, everyone's coming over to *my* place now, huh?"

"Not everyone." Corian scanned the apartment's high ceilings. "Obviously, one of us won't be leaving the warehouse to go anywhere. Well, for as long as his patience holds out."

"You mean, L'zar," Ember muttered.

He looked down at her and narrowed his glowing silver eyes. "Right. He mentioned meeting you."

She gave him a thin smile and spread her arms. "You don't have to talk circles around the fae girl. I know pretty much everything Cheyenne knows at this point."

"I see. We'll talk more about that in a minute." The nightstalker opened a portal and stepped into his basement apartment.

Ember stared at the dark circle of light and the magical disappearing through it. "That doesn't get old."

"You get used to it pretty fast." Cheyenne pulled her healed foot in to see for herself. "At least when there's a nightstalker around who just can't get enough of casting them. Speaking of which, why are Persh'al and Lumil coming here?"

Corian rummaged through the junk on his shelves. He pulled out an open cardboard box, dumped its contents on the floor, and used it to hold his more carefully selected items. "Because, Cheyenne, I can't build the kind of wards you and Ember need to protect you at home by myself. Persh'al might seem like he only has an eye for computer stuff, just like you."

The halfling snorted. "Yeah. I love computer stuff."

"But he has a wide range of spellcasting experience and practical application when he gets out of that chair to use it." More items clunked into the box tucked under his arm, and he stood back to scan the shelves for the next hidden thing he wanted. "And Lumil is, well, at the very least, she channels one hell of a support."

"So Byrd drew the short end of the stick and gets to stay behind to babysit L'zar?"

"Not really." Corian bent over to pull a thin square shape from beneath a pile of smaller items on the bottom shelf. "Byrd's skills with wards are right on par with your spellcasting ability."

"Oh."

Ember frowned through the portal. "Why do I get the feeling this guy's dissing your spellwork?"

"Probably because he is." Cheyenne crossed her legs beneath her on the couch and shrugged. "I guess the goblin and I are both useless in this arena."

"No, you're not. You made me that ring."

Corian stepped back through the portal, the half-full box tucked under one arm and the thin, square piece of hardened leather clenched in his other hand. "I thought you made that for yourself?"

"The Heart of Midnight's useless now, so it turned into a gift."

"And it works?"

"Oh, yeah." Ember grinned. "Perfectly."

"Huh."

Cheyenne shot Ember an exasperated glance and gestured at the nightstalker. "See that? That's the kind of reaction I get for pretty much everything."

"When we have the time for me to throw you a party, Cheyenne, I'll get right on it." Corian set the box on the coffee table and lifted the square of hard leather. "Remember this?"

"You mean, the O'gúl hornet's web I bought from the crotchety potionmaster who acted like I was trying to abuse a power I didn't know I had?" Cheyenne folded her arms. "Yeah, I think so."

"Well, tonight's the night we get to use it." He set the leather gently down on the table beside the box and stepped back. "Don't touch it."

"Do I at least get to learn how to put up wards?"

"We don't have time for that either." Corian shot her a sharp glance and dipped his head. "Before you call me out on it, I know I said I'd teach you, and you'd have to figure the rest of it out on your own."

"A lot's changed since then. Yeah, I get it."

"I thought so." The nightstalker opened another portal between the recliners and the northern wall of windows. When it grew to its full oval height, he nodded and stepped aside.

Persh'al came through first, a massive black duffel bag in one hand and an energy drink in the other. He nodded slowly and scanned the apartment. "Nice digs, kid."

"Thanks."

Lumil stomped after him with a scowl, but it faded quickly when she took in her new surroundings, and she let out a low whistle. "Not too shabby, halfling. Not as many rooms as I expected, but I'm sure you'll find something bigger eventually."

Cheyenne sat back on the couch. "Excellent backhanded compliment."

"You're welcome."

"Okay." Persh'al dropped the heavy duffel bag with a thump and took a huge gulp of his energy drink. "What are we lookin' at?"

"Bedroom on the other side of the kitchen." Corian nodded that way, and the blue troll took off toward the open door.

"Now, *this* is what you guys need in the warehouse." Lumil slumped into the closest recliner, stacked both booted feet on the coffee table beside Corian's box, and jerked the lever up so fast, the chair rocked backward when the footrest snapped up. "Oh, yeah. I mean, how hard is it to buy new furniture in a place with almost no furniture? That couch lasted, what? Thirty years?"

Corian frowned at her as he crossed in front of the recliners to take the other one. "What's up with the couch?"

"L'zar smashed it right after you left."

Ember's bedroom light switched on. "Deathflame on a fucking cracker."

Lumil craned her neck to peer over Ember's head. "That sounds fun."

"You said it was taken care of, Corian," Persh'al called from the bedroom. "Not obliterated."

Cheyenne looked over the back of the couch. "I thought that was the same thing."

Shaking his head, the troll rejoined them in the living room and unzipped the duffel bag. "I'm gonna need a second to find the entry point and whatever extra little tricks they used to get in. How big were these things?"

Corian held up his forefinger and thumb with two inches of space between.

Persh'al wrinkled his nose. "Too big for holes in the insulation. Small enough to tunnel in."

"Oh, great." Ember sat upright in her chair and gripped the armrests, nodding slowly. "Tiny *digging* beetles that came to kill me in my sleep."

Persh'al leaned forward to catch her attention. "Who are you?"

She slowly turned her head to shoot him a blank, shocked stare. "Ember."

"Huh." He sniffed and nodded. "Yeah, I thought I smelled fae. Nice to meet you. Glad you weren't killed in your sleep."

Ember let out a hesitant chuckle as the troll took a small black drawstring bag and something that looked like a telescope with him to her room.

"You sure he knows what he's doing in there?" Cheyenne asked.

Corian crossed one leg over the other and sat back in the recliner. "I'm sure. I'll join him when he's figured out what kind of wards will be the most effective. Until then, we need to talk about something else. All three of us." He gazed between Cheyenne and Ember with raised eyebrows.

They stared right back.

Ember leaned toward the couch but didn't bother to lower her voice. "Does this feel like getting called into the principal's office to you?"

"I never got called to the principal's office, Em. Never had a principal." Cheyenne squinted at the nightstalker. "But hypothetically, yeah. It kinda does." Then she laughed. "How many times did *you* get called in?"

Ember shrugged. "I'll tell you about it later. I'm more interested in why that nightstalker's giving us a creepy stare."

"Uh-huh." Cheyenne folded her arms. "I hope you're gonna try to make this interesting."

Corian blinked slowly. "Well, this is about how the two of you are gonna have to navigate things from here on out if you want to make it out of this nightmare alive. That interesting enough for you?"

Cheyenne waved her hand in a slow, sweeping motion, perfectly mimicking Bianca Summerlin's hospitable gesture of granting permission. "By all means. Continue."

CHAPTER TWENTY-EIGHT

"Yeesh." Rolling her eyes, Lumil grunted and heaved herself out of the recliner. "You guys go ahead and get all serious. I gotta hit the can."

Cheyenne jerked her thumb over her shoulder. "Right under the loft. Which is off-limits."

The goblin scoffed and headed that way. "You nerds and your fancy private systems. Don't worry, kid. I'm not even a little interested."

Corian stared after her as she sidled between him and the coffee table before heading straight for the door beneath the mini-loft. Once it closed behind her, he returned his attention to Cheyenne and Ember. "Have either of you heard the term *Nós Aní?*"

Ember cocked her head. "I'm a third-generation Earthside fae. All I heard was gibberish, and anyone in my family who might know what that means wouldn't tell *me* if you held a knife to their throat."

The nightstalker glanced at her legs and nodded. "Because they think you're useless."

"Pretty much. But that was true a long time before this chair came along."

"They're wrong."

Ember glanced at Cheyenne and pointed at Corian. "Did you tell him?"

"Nope."

"I'll take a wild guess and assume that for the first time in your life, you can finally tap into your magic."

Ember cleared her throat. "You're really creepy, you know that?"

"Must be my nature." Corian's tight smile bristled into a grimace. "And I saw the little stunt you pulled getting into that chair ten minutes ago."

"Well, I wasn't trying to hide it."

"I didn't think so."

Ember spread her arms and shrugged. "What does it mean, then? *Nós Annie.*"

"*Nós Aní,*" Cheyenne muttered. "That's what *he* is."

Corian and Ember looked at her in surprise, and the nightstalker frowned. "Who told you that?"

"No one. I put two and two together all on my own like a big kid." Cheyenne leaned back against the corner of the armrest and the couch cushion. "And yeah, I've heard the term before."

"I hope it didn't come with any unnecessary embellishments I'll have to teach you to unlearn. Or stories about me that might not be true."

"It didn't have anything to do with you, Corian." Cheyenne tipped her head toward Ember. "The guy who brought it up was talking about her."

"Interesting."

"Okay, but what does it *mean?*" Ember asked, leaning forward to better insert herself into the conversation.

"It's like a captain's first mate, Em. Or a second in command."

"A what?"

Corian scratched the side of his fur-covered face. "That's oversimplifying it quite a bit. But in a nutshell, sure, I suppose it's fairly accurate."

"You know what?" Ember rolled away from the coffee table and wheeled around the back of the couch. She stopped on the other side of the coffee table, the chair's front wheels rolling silently onto the black and silver area rug, and slapped her hands down on the armrests. "If I'm suddenly the topic of another cryptic conversation, I'm not listening to it from the other side of the room."

Corian nodded. "That's fair. It's a drow term for essentially what

Cheyenne described. Something of a best friend. The rest of it's a little more complicated."

"I can handle complicated." Ember gestured around their living room. "Obviously."

"It's interesting that someone else named Ember your *Nós Ani* before we did. Officially, at least." Corian glanced from one girl to the other and raised his eyebrows. "Who was it?"

"One of the staff at Ember's PT clinic."

"Wait a minute."

"No, really, Em." Cheyenne nodded at her friend. "It was before either of us knew your magic was coming back or that any of this craziness was about to come down on us. The guy was all coy about it, too. Said I'd made a good choice and that they'd take care of you while you're recovering."

Ember blinked, opened her mouth, and tried a second time to get words out. "You're telling me there are magicals working at that clinic, and I didn't pick up on it."

"Yeah. Your doctor's one of them. I don't know what she is, but I bet that's part of what makes her so good at her job."

"Why didn't you tell me?"

Cheyenne shook her head. "There wasn't a lot of time. Then everything else happened, and it got pushed into the corner."

"Well, I'm seriously glad I know now before I go back in tomorrow."

"No. You can't go back in there."

Ember's mouth dropped open. "You don't get to make that decision for me."

"I do if I'm the one taking you."

"I'll pay someone else to do it!"

Cheyenne lurched forward on the couch, leaning toward her friend's face. "That asshole at the clinic was the one who brought up the *Nós Ani* thing, and I wouldn't be surprised if he had something to do with stealing your blood from the hospital so all those damn machine-bugs could hunt you down."

"My *blood*?"

"We think that's how the digger found you in Peridosh," Corian clarified calmly. His gaze flickered toward Cheyenne when she pushed herself off the couch and started pacing behind it. "Someone got the word out about your connection to Cheyenne. They didn't have a better way to lock onto her directly, so they picked the next best magical."

"That's insane. I can't even *do* anything." Ember watched her friend's agitated pacing and shook her head. "I'm the least threatening person involved in this."

"But you *are* involved, and as Cheyenne's *Nos Aní*, you're a lot more threatening than you might think."

"I can't believe I didn't see it." Cheyenne pounded her fist on the back of the couch. "I *knew* something was up in that clinic, but the minute he started talking about taking care of you, I let myself ignore it."

"Did you get his name?"

"Marsil. He told me to pass along some kind of sworn-fealty message to L'zar from House Keldryk."

Corian rubbed his chin. "That doesn't sound like one of the Crown's zealots."

"Well, he sure as shit didn't look like a magical, but he's fooling the rest of the world about that too. I handed him what he wanted to hear on a silver platter."

"We don't have any proof that this Marsil of House Keldryk was the one who exposed Ember."

"I don't *need* proof. Who the hell else could know?"

"That information could've gotten out anywhere, just like word of you passing your trials. Just like the Crown's Earthside loyalists knowing she's looking for you and wants you taken out of the picture. She's got eyes and ears everywhere, Cheyenne. You can't jump to conclusions and assume everyone's lying to you."

"That's the only way to survive!" The halfling swung an open hand at the back of the couch and sent it scooting across the floor until the area rug bunched up beneath the coffee table. With a growl, she kept pacing along the same track, purple sparks flaring at her fingertips. *Do I really believe that?*

"You know that's not the only way," Corian muttered. "Things are complicated, kid, and they're only going to get more complicated for both of you from here on out. I promise I'll help you find whoever's responsible for putting Ember's name out there and setting those trackers on her. I give you my word on that."

Cheyenne took a deep breath and killed the purple sparks. "I'll hold you to it. I wanna start with that Marsil guy."

"Sure. Gently." Corian nodded. "Tomorrow. Tonight, neither of you are leaving this apartment, which might just be the safest place for either of you once we're finished."

"Yeah." Cheyenne nodded, slowed her pacing, and set her hands on the back of the couch. "Yeah, okay. That's the most important thing right now."

"Yes, it is."

"All right." Persh'al clapped his hands and headed toward them from Ember's room. "Definitely diggers, so we'll have to build the base around structural reinforcements and add extra repulsion layers on top of that. Maybe throw up a few good system-wide shocks just for fun. You know, *boom*." He mimed an explosion with his empty hand as he dropped the drawstring bag back into the duffel bag.

"You're still talking about wards, right?"

Persh'al winked at Cheyenne and grinned. "You'd be surprised how much wards and firewalls have in common, kid."

A loud, tuneless humming came from the other side of the bathroom door. All heads turned in that direction.

Persh'al grimaced. "How long has she been in there?"

"Pretty much the whole time." Cheyenne closed her eyes and walked around the side of the couch to slump down onto it again.

"Hmm. That's not gonna be fun." The troll nodded at Corian. "We can get started whenever you're ready."

"Great." The nightstalker pushed out of the recliner, casting a final wary glance at the bathroom door.

"Hold on." Ember reached toward him. "I wanna know what you meant by 'more complicated.'"

"And you will. We'll make time for that conversation later, Ember. Just not right now." Corian grabbed his box of supplies off the coffee table as Persh'al squatted in front of the duffel bag and took out handfuls of whatever he needed to cast their multi-layered wards.

The fae shot Cheyenne an irritated glance and shook her head. "So, what? We're just supposed to sit here and watch them reinforce the structural whatever?"

"I guess so. I'm kinda hoping I learn something."

"Then you better pay attention, kid." Persh'al placed different-colored stones two feet apart along the wall of windows. "We work fast."

Almost an hour later, Persh'al withdrew the O'gúl hornet's web from the hardened leather case and held it up to the light. "Man, I've always wanted to use one of these."

"Well, you know, I've been saving it for a special occasion." Cheyenne smirked when he glanced at her.

"I'm sure that special occasion had nothing to do with finding someone who knows what to do with it," Corian added.

She stared at him and blinked slowly. "Of course not."

"All right, here we go. Ready to amp up the power grid, goblin?"

Lumil scowled at Persh'al and raised her hands. In one, she held the telescope-looking thing, and a bundle of twisted wires flashing a multitude of different colors dangled from the other. "I feel like a circus clown."

"Not too far off." Persh'al chuckled and returned his attention to the hornet's web. The rare ingredient turned slowly at the end of the twine he held, the red and black threads of the web glinting in the light. "You're just grounding the power."

"I *know* what I'm doing."

"Okay, so come on. Up."

Rolling her eyes, Lumil raised her nameless items until they hung on either side of her face.

"Perfect." Persh'al looked at Cheyenne and wiggled his neon-orange eyebrows. "The finishing touch, kid, then we'll be outta your hair. For tonight, anyway."

Corian pulled his phone from his pocket to check the time.

Squinting at the Ogúl hornet's web, Persh'al lifted it until it spun in front of his face and muttered an incantation under his breath. Then he flicked his finger against the center of the web. A bright red light flashed from the dangling circle of woven threads, followed by a loud crack. The wards they'd placed around the apartment showed as layers of shimmering light, wavering one on top of the other along every wall, doorframe, and window.

When the light died seconds later, Persh'al chuckled. "Exactly how I imagined it. Now we just gotta find a good place to—oh. That'll work." He hooked the top of looped twine over an extending curl of the wrought-iron rail surrounding the mini-loft, then stepped back to take in the finished product. "I like it."

"Not conspicuous at all," Cheyenne muttered.

"It doesn't matter. No one's stepping into this apartment unless either of you explicitly invites them in." Corian wagged his finger back and forth between Cheyenne and Ember. "And I highly recommend that you don't hand out invitations for a while."

"What about you guys?"

"We built the wards, kid." Persh'al spread his arms as he headed toward his duffel bag on the other side of the room. "That's an extended membership. Plus, none of us is driving all the way out here from DC to knock on your front door. Why do you think we keep a nightstalker around? Hey, give me those things, will ya? You look like someone's failed sculpture attempt."

Lumil glared at him and tossed both items at his chest. Persh'al caught them and stuffed his tools gently into the duffel bag. "As long as that web's hanging in one piece right there, these wards'll hold forever, theoretically."

"Let's hope we don't need them forever." Cheyenne handed Corian his re-packed cardboard box as he passed her to join Lumil and Persh'al.

"I don't think you will. But this is a good start, and the wards will hold." He nodded at her and tucked the box under his arm.

"Hey, before you go," Cheyenne rubbed the back of her neck and scanned the top of the wall of windows behind them. "Is there any kinda spell that checks for hidden tech like cameras or tiny microphones?"

Corian's silver eyes narrowed.

"The paranoia's finally gettin' to you, huh?" Persh'al smirked.

"No." She raised her eyebrows at him and offered a tight, sarcastic smile. "This apartment was a demo before we moved in. I just wanna make sure no one's watching the old-fashioned way, either."

Ember shot her a questioning glance, and the halfling shrugged.

"Yeah, okay." Persh'al sniffed and stood behind his duffel bag. He closed his eyes, lifted his hand in front of him like he was about to throw an invisible frisbee, and twisted his fingers in quick succession. Then he snapped his wrist and made a throwing motion before opening his hand.

The energy behind his spell washed over Cheyenne like a chilly breeze, making her skin tingle.

The troll slowly scanned the living room and shrugged. "Looks clean to me. But if there *is* anything in here, it'll show up purple."

"Okay." Cheyenne nodded slowly, gazing around the room to check for herself. "Thanks."

"No problem." He hefted the duffel bag.

"Get some sleep," Corian said. "That's all you need to focus on for now. And tomorrow, we'll get our answers."

"Right."

Ember raised her hand in a brief wave. "Thanks for showing up when you did. And beefing up security."

The corners of Corian's mouth twitched. "It's the least we could do."

Lumil snorted. "Don't lie to her, man."

The nightstalker ignored her and focused on opening a portal into the warehouse. Then he waited for Persh'al and Lumil to step through before he nodded one last time at Cheyenne and disappeared. The portal closed, and Cheyenne sank back into the couch.

"This has to have been the longest day of my life."

Ember ran a hand through her hair. "He just told us to get some sleep."

They looked at each other and chuckled wryly. "No way in hell am I gonna be able to fall asleep right now."

"I'm gonna have to take the couch. I think they skipped the cleanup in my room."

"Sorry, Em."

"Hey, having to pick up shattered machine bits is a lot better than someone else having to clean up scattered fae parts. I'll get to it eventually, but I am *not* sleeping in there tonight." Ember snatched the remote off the coffee table, aimed it at the entryway table to lift the TV out of its slot, and dropped it in her lap. "I don't care how long it takes. I'm falling asleep with the TV on."

As she wheeled around the couch again toward her usual show-streaming spot, Cheyenne slapped her thighs. "We still have ice cream, right?"

"At least two more pints."

The halfling stood and headed for the kitchen. "I'm on it."

CHAPTER TWENTY-NINE

T he next morning, Cheyenne managed to slip out of her bedroom, hop into the shower, and get halfway through drawing on another layer of thick black eyeliner before Ember stirred on the couch.

"What time is it?" The fae groaned and pushed herself up against the armrest.

"Nine-fifty." Cheyenne leaned closer to the mirror and smudged her eye makeup around a little before nodding. *Won't find* this *on a makeup tutorial. Smokey-eye in five seconds, 'cause I couldn't care less.* When she stepped out of the bathroom, Ember blinked.

"Woah. You look fancy."

"Yeah, right." Her hair was almost dry, so she pulled it away from her face and started on a loose braid. "This is my 'just got attacked by O'gúl war machines and had wards put up around my apartment before going to teach an undergrad class' look."

Ember snorted. "You make it seem so effortless."

"Well, I try." Tying off her finished braid, the halfling grabbed her black Vans from where she'd kicked them off by the couch the night before and jammed her feet into them. "You know, yesterday, I couldn't figure out why Maleshi would go back to campus and pretend to be a professor with everything that's going on right now."

"She *is* a professor."

"Sure, but not really. I get it now, though. The normal things are all that's left when everything else turns to shit."

Ember folded her arms and sat back against the armrest. "Not everything."

"Okay, fine. Slight exaggeration. But if I didn't have something to do right now, I have a feeling I'd go looking for trouble. I've recognized a pattern with that."

"I thought it was more like trouble finding *you*."

Cheyenne slung her backpack over her shoulder and cocked her head. "We can call it a fifty-fifty split. You need anything?"

"Nope." Ember grabbed the edge of her chair and pulled herself off the couch. The purple light of her magic engulfed her body, and two seconds later, she was sitting comfortably in the wheelchair with a smirk. "I think I'm gettin' the hang of this."

"Guess I'm obsolete, then."

"Oh, come on." Ember clicked her tongue and wheeled between the couch and the coffee table. "I'm sure you'll find *some* way to be useful."

"Ha-ha." Cheyenne headed toward the front door. "I'll be back in a few hours. Then we'll head to the clinic, and I'll figure out how to handle things from there."

"While I'm at my PT session." It wasn't a question.

"I think we should cover that when we get there. Gotta play it by ear, you know?"

"Uh-huh."

"Hey, if that Marsil guy running around with George on his nametag has anything to do with—"

"We'll figure that out later." Ember gestured toward the door. "You have a room full of eager young minds to expand."

Cheyenne wrinkled her nose. "Ew. I can't believe I'm grateful for that right now."

"Like you said, even the normal things count."

Grabbing the doorknob, the halfling paused and looked over her shoulder again. "Don't open the door for anyone while I'm gone."

"Aw, bummer. I was planning on leaving it open all day for anyone who wanted to stop by for a chat."

"Not even Matthew, okay? Until we figure out who knows what and where they heard it, we can't risk it."

"I *know*, Cheyenne." Ember spread her arms and shook her head. "I was here last night too, remember?"

The halfling gave her friend a knowing smile. "Yeah."

"But I will say, I feel a lot better knowing our apartment isn't bugged."

"As far as we know. If you see any purple dots, cover them and text me."

Ember gazed slowly around their apartment and grimaced. "Just when I was starting to feel comfortable in my own living room."

"Don't let it get to you, Em. If *I* haven't found any by now, they probably don't exist."

"I'm trying to believe that." With a disbelieving chuckle, Ember tossed her hand toward the front door. "I know the drill, halfling. Go teach your class."

"Yeah. See you in a bit." As soon as she opened the door, Cheyenne turned the lock on the doorknob, then doubled down with the deadbolt before sticking her keys in her pockets. Walking down the hall, she glanced up at the ceiling and the corners, not bothering to be discreet about it. *Should've asked Persh'al to throw that spell up out here, too. Whatever. As long as Matthew Thomas can't see inside our apartment, he can watch the damn hallway as much as he wants.*

When she reached the elevator and punched the call button, she swept her gaze across the hallway, grinned, and stuck up her middle finger. *Just in case.*

Cheyenne stopped in front of the small classroom where Maleshi's Advanced Programming class was held and pulled out her phone. *Wow. I don't think I've been ten minutes early for anything.*

The classroom was unlocked, so she stepped inside and figured she'd use the extra time wisely. When her undergrad students filtered into their seats ten minutes later, they found their Goth instructor slouched in her chair with her arms folded, one foot stacked on top of the other on the narrow desk, eyes closed.

When she figured it was time for class, Cheyenne jerked her feet down off the desk and leaped from the chair, clapping her hands. "Ready to get started?"

The undergrad students jerked to attention and shifted in their seats. Some of them gasped in surprise, and one kid folded his arms on his desk and buried his face in them.

"Oh, come on. Don't look so surprised. You guys came here to pay attention." She gazed at less than a dozen faces of students not much younger than her and stopped when she got to the girl with one side of her head shaved. The student slouched in her chair just like Cheyenne, her arms folded and an amused smirk barely creasing her lips. Cheyenne pointed at her. "Yeah, like that."

Man. I'm even starting to sound *like Maleshi.*

"All right, listen up." The halfling clapped her hands, and two students flinched. "That was better. We'll keep trying. Since you guys seemed to grasp the general concept of Monday's class, we're moving on."

A kid with ridiculously thick glasses and a fresh acne breakout raised his hand and didn't bother waiting to be called on. "But we'll go back to that when we're studying for finals, right?"

Cheyenne squinted at him. *No pocket protector today. He doesn't look nearly as terrified of me, either.*

"Look, you can go back to it if you want. I don't know what Professor Bergman told you about how this semester was gonna play out, but you can pretty much forget all of it. You'll do assignments, if I give you any, hopefully you'll ask me questions if you seriously don't get something, and you'll play around with what we've covered on your own time. Tests and quizzes and finals are a waste of time, so if something in this class doesn't interest you, drop it and find something that does. You'll be writing your own code and building an application or program or whatever for your final. Whatever you want, as long as it's not something a first-grader could do with their eyes closed. Make it something you actually like, huh? That's where the cool stuff happens, and there's nothing worse than being forced to work on something that bores you into another dimension. Well, almost nothing."

When she finished her diatribe, she spread her hands and gazed around the room. Most of the students just shot her blank, vapid stares.

Guess I didn't have a problem coming up with a half-assed syllabus on the fly. Good to know.

She closed her hands into fists and nodded. "Any more questions before I start and you shut up and listen?"

The thick-glasses kid raised his hand and leaned forward. "So, we don't need to remember everything from the semester for the final?"

Jeeze, he's really got a thing for finals.

A cold, itching tingle raced across the back of her shoulders. Cheyenne straightened and scanned the room again. *Pay attention to the warning buzz. I'm learning too.*

"Ms. Summerlin?"

"Uh-uh." She shook her head but didn't look at him. "It's Cheyenne. I already told you that."

"But you didn't answer my question."

The tingling buzz flared up at the top of her spine again and made her want to shiver. Then a low, droning hum caught her attention. *That almost sounds like a fly.*

"Um, hello?" The kid with his heart set on finals raised his hand with a weak wave.

"I didn't answer your question. I heard you. Pretty sure I answered it in that rare speech you just got, but I guess you need a recap." Cheyenne frowned and narrowed her eyes, glancing at the closed door at the back of the room, the corners of the back wall, and the empty aisle covered in old, slightly stained university carpet. *Where is it?*

The kid cleared his throat, and she shot him a fierce warning look. "No. You don't need to remember anything for a final unless you think it'll help you build something you can be proud of. No tests. No multiple-choice or fill in the blanks. Anything else not explicitly included in writing code for something you think is cool isn't gonna happen. Is that clear enough?"

"Well, what about a sample scoring card, then? You know, like, a list of what you'll be looking for at the end of the semester, so we can pass."

"Dude, it's not even the last week of October." Cheyenne shook her head. The slouching girl in the front row snorted. "I'll get you what you need to have when you need it, okay? It's okay to chill out and enjoy the next seven weeks of not having tests."

Finals Boy sank in his chair, his gaze racing back and forth across the surface of his desk as his cheeks reddened. "I just want to be prepared."

"I get it. Totally admirable. And there's a balance between—"

A dark shape the size of a housefly darted in front of the scowling kid's face. It caught the light just right and briefly glinted with copper and shiny black. The low hum returned, and Cheyenne watched the thing cut a straight line toward the right-hand wall. It landed there, the humming stopped, and the almost-fly spun smoothly on the wall, then it didn't move again.

No housefly moves that straight, just like real beetles don't stab people in the foot and spew radioactive magic.

"Between what?" A girl sitting dead center in the rows of desks cocked her head.

"What?" Cheyenne glanced at the student, but her gaze whipped automatically back to the dark speck on the wall.

"You said there's a balance. Between what?"

"Being prepared and giving yourself room to breathe." The halfling squinted at the not-fly and forced herself to look at her students instead. "Which is what we're about to do right now. Take some room to breathe."

"Huh?"

I need to grab that thing before it gets back to whoever's playing fly on the wall, without blowing this "not an actual instructor" act.

"You heard me." Cheyenne forced herself to smile, eliciting weird looks from her very confused students, and nodded. *Time to break out improv skills.* "This might surprise you, but I've learned a lot from the simple art of meditation."

The shaved-head girl in the front pushed up in her seat and looked over her shoulder to gauge her classmates' reactions.

"This isn't a meditation class."

"Hey, good for you." Cheyenne cocked her head. "You get a gold star for that one. I'm serious. Meditation, visualizing stuff. Whatever. Here's what's up. Everybody close your eyes. Take a deep breath." The kid in the second-to-last row with spiked hair and the hemp necklace from Monday frowned so deeply, it looked painful. "Yep, you're included in the general *everybody*. I promise I won't disappear or anything. You can do the exercise, or you can leave the room and find a different ten o'clock class three days a week."

Rolling his eyes, the student thumped back in his chair and closed his eyes.

Cheyenne immediately looked at the wall, where the dark speck of not-fly hadn't moved from its landing. "Okay. Since we've had such an illuminating conversation about the *end* of the semester, you guys are gonna meditate on what you want your final in this class to be."

"But you said—"

"Uh-uh. Eyes closed. We're in here for an hour and a half. You can spare a few minutes to realign your undergraduate intentions." *I sound like a lunatic. Not the first time.*

With another quick glance around the room to make sure every student had jumped aboard her excuse, Cheyenne stared at the spy machine on the wall. "Make it whatever you like. You picked this class for a reason, I hope, so find the thing you really like about Advanced Programming and dive deep. Imagine yourself sitting down, getting ready to write that code or program or stylesheet." Someone else snorted. "And you're totally in the zone."

This needs to be fast.

"Unaware of everything else around you."

And timed perfectly.

Cheyenne slowly raised her hand over the desk, aiming her finger at the back wall and watching the fly in her peripheral vision. "The only thing that matters is the end result, and it's gonna be exactly what you want."

Now.

The heat of her drow magic burst up her spine as she whipped her hand toward the wall on her right. A quick burst of bright purple sparks shot from her fingertip and hit the spy machine dead-center. The thing let out a surprisingly loud screech as its tiny mechanisms sputtered and sparked. *Shit.*

Before the metal bug fell two inches off the wall, Cheyenne hooked her telekinetic magic around the machine's energy and tugged it toward her. The round glinting body whizzed across the room as the students started in their chairs, distracted by the snap and crunch from the wall.

The halfling snatched the spy fly from the air and slipped back into human form half a second before her students opened their eyes and searched for the source of the sound.

"What was that?"

Cheyenne widened her eyes and gave them a tight-lipped smile as she slipped the fried machine into her front pocket. "What?"

"Sounded like somebody got shocked."

"Woah. Check it out." One guy sitting by the right-hand wall pointed at the quarter-sized char-mark on the wall, where a thin trail of pale smoke wafted toward the ceiling.

"Huh." Cheyenne pressed her palms on the top of the desk and leaned toward the burnt wall. "Probably some kind of electrical short or something."

Half the students who had turned to stare at her again looked mortified. The other half wrinkled their noses at the scent of burnt plaster and hot metal and looked dangerously confused.

"Good thing you're not teaching an electrical engineering class." The kid who'd pointed out the smoking dent in the wall slid out of his chair, opened his water bottle, and poured a stream of water onto the wall. It hissed briefly, and the smoke disappeared. "I hope the smoke alarm doesn't go off."

"We'll be fine." Cheyenne looked at the ceiling and brushed her fingers toward it like she was swatting away a fly. The feeling of her magic barreling toward the ceiling with a forceful breeze convinced her she was right. "So. Anybody get anything useful out of that brief, interrupted moment of internal focus?"

The students shifted warily in their seats to face her again, but no one had a thing to share.

"Then we'll move on. Feel free to try that again on your own time."

Rushing through the random choices for a topic she hadn't had the time to plan, Cheyenne nodded and stared at the table. *That was close. How the hell does Maleshi keep it together with crap like this?*

Walking out of that classroom and closing the door behind her at 11:31 a.m. made Cheyenne take a deep, relieved breath. *I'm glad that's out of the way. I get to do it all over again on Friday.*

She gripped the straps of her backpack and headed down the hall toward the main entrance. When her back pocket vibrated, she almost slipped into her drow form to fight the resurrected spy-fly. But she patted her front pocket instead, felt the bump of cold, deactivated metal against her thigh, and pulled out her buzzing phone.

"Hey, Mom."

"When can I expect these men to get off my property?"

Cheyenne slipped out the door and hurried across the lawn toward the closest student parking lot. *Yes, hello. I'm fine. Thanks for asking. Yeah, I'm never getting that from her.*

"As soon as we're sure nothing else is coming out of that thing in the backyard."

"Cheyenne, I would very much appreciate an estimated timeline."

The halfling sighed after pulling the phone away from her mouth so she didn't give Bianca Summerlin something else to be upset about. "I know. So would I. When I have one, the first thing I'll do is give you a call."

There was a long pause on the other end of the line. "If that's the best you can do."

"If it wasn't, we'd be having a different conversation."

"Yes. I suppose we would."

Cheyenne skirted around a group of laughing, shouting students tossing a frisbee and trying to tackle each other at the same time. She turned to glare at a lanky guy who was at least six-foot-four who'd almost knocked her over, but he shrugged and took off across the field. "I'm guessing nothing weird's happened since I left."

"This entire situation is weird." Bianca's disdain for the word came through loud and clear. "But if you're asking about any new developments, no. Nothing beyond my growing irritation and this *team's* obnoxious display of the tactical skill known as sitting around and waiting. Specifically on my lawn."

Forcing down a laugh, Cheyenne picked up the pace when the parking lot came into view. "They're there to keep you and Eleanor safe, Mom. I can't always be there to engage those things, and I'm not leaving you unprotected until I figure out how to get that whole thing off the property and out of your hair."

"Yes." The clink of ice against glass punctured the silence. "Just so you're aware, Cheyenne, I'm not unprotected. I went to the shooting range every Saturday at eleven when I lived in the city."

Then she hasn't fired a weapon in twenty-one years. Totally reassuring.

"I bet you hit ten out of ten in that red circle every time."

"Nine out of ten," Bianca muttered. "But I'm satisfied with ninety-percent accuracy."

"Believe me, I wish this was something we could take care of with bullets."

A blonde girl in yoga pants, a cream turtleneck sweater, and tan Ugg boots stared at Cheyenne and stepped sideways to put six feet between them as they passed each other. The halfling rolled her eyes and headed for her Porsche. *Right. Can't mention magic or bullets in public.*

"I know." Bianca took another quick, demure sip of whatever drink she'd made herself, probably a bruncheon cocktail, and hummed into the phone. "I know you're busy. Call me when you're able to move this process along."

"I will." The line went dead, and Cheyenne stuffed her phone back into her pocket. *I'd like to think she'd stop hanging up on me when all this is over. Pretty sure a magical portal and an impending war across the border aren't enough to change her habits.*

CHAPTER THIRTY

When Cheyenne stepped into her apartment at just after 11:50 a.m., the complete silence made her pause. "Em?"

"Hey."

Shutting the door and immediately turning the deadbolt again, the halfling stepped into the living room and peered around the corner into the bathroom beneath the mini-loft. "Everything okay?"

"It is *now*." Wet rubber smacked on marble, and Ember wheeled out of the bathroom with a grimace. "You think we can revoke those *invitations* Corian mentioned last night? 'Cause I kinda wanna tell that goblin chick she's not allowed to come over anymore."

Cheyenne chuckled. "Uh-oh."

"Yeah. Big uh-oh." Ember wiped her forehead with the back of her hand and shook her head. "I just spent the last hour cleaning that toilet. An *hour*. I think I've lost all sense of smell."

"Well, I can tell you used a lot of bleach."

"More than I've ever had to use on anything." The fae shuddered and rubbed her sweaty, slightly pruney hands on her pants. "Who *does* that in someone else's house? Not to mention that she'd never been here before, and they put up wards to keep everything *out*. Should've added something to the bathroom."

Laughing, Cheyenne folded her arms and shot her friend a sympathetic frown. "I could've done that."

"Hey, just because I can't walk, it doesn't mean I can't clean. Doesn't mean I *want* to, either, but I couldn't let that go on any longer."

"I'll make sure to say something about it."

Ember looked at her friend with wide eyes. "Don't. I was joking about the invitation. Mostly."

"Nah, don't worry about it." Cheyenne scanned the living room. "I'll make it sound like it came straight from me. Worst-case scenario, she gets all butthurt and doesn't want to come over again. Honestly, I just think she'll laugh and say, 'Welcome to the rebellion, halfling.' Or something equally stupid. But I'm right there with you. Not cool. You ready to head out?"

"It's already time to go?" Ember blinked and patted her pocket, then nodded at the coffee table. "Grab my purse, and we're outta here."

"Yep."

Once Ember had her purse nestled in her lap, Cheyenne unlocked the front door and held it open for the fae to wheel into the hall. She couldn't help but glance at Matthew Thomas' front door across the hall before she locked up behind them. Ember was already halfway to the elevator.

"Find any purple specks in the bathroom?"

The fae leaned forward to punch the call button and shifted in her chair. "Nope. I'd say it's a little creepy that tiny cameras in the bathroom even crossed your mind, but I gotta admit it was the first thing I thought of too."

"It's fine. We can both be creepy. Kinda necessary to deal with all this other stuff."

Ember shot her friend a sidelong glance. "You're way creepier than I am."

"Only on the outside."

"Ha. Nope."

"At least we have more proof that the apartment's clean, so there's less reason to worry about our resident Peeping Matthew."

"Shh." Ember glanced down the hall at their neighbor's front door and shook her head. "Didn't our suspicions start in the hall anyway?"

"Hey, if he doesn't like what he sees and hears, assuming he's watching and listening, that's his problem." The doors opened, and Cheyenne waited for her friend to roll inside first. A flash of purple light helped Ember across the ribbed strip of metal and the space between the hallway and the elevator. The halfling stepped in behind her. "He shouldn't be surprised by anyone who has an issue with being watched."

Ember pressed her lips together and didn't say anything until the elevator started its descent. "Maybe he's just trying to keep *his* apartment safe, you know?"

"What?" Cheyenne laughed. "Are you really trying to come up with excuses for a guy who seems to be keeping tabs on when we leave and come home?"

Shrugging, Ember scrunched her face and smiled sheepishly. "He's just so *nice*."

"Oh, man."

"It's true. You know it's true."

"Yeah, and *that's* creepy."

"Why? Because nobody can be completely nice at their core?"

"Most people aren't."

Ember snorted. "I didn't know you were that jaded about everyone in general."

"I don't care about 'everyone in general' or if they're one-hundred-percent nice. I just think it's pretty suspicious that this super-*nice* guy who's obsessed with you happens to own a bunch of companies in industries not known for being *nice*."

Ember frowned. "How much did you dig into him?"

"Enough to know it'll be pretty hard to prove he's not just a nice guy."

The fae threw her head back and filled the elevator with an unabashed cackle. Cheyenne smirked and stared at the black space between the doors. "We'll keep looking, I guess. Either we find a purple speck or you find some kinda dirt on him, and then I'll buy into your theory. But until then, I feel a lot better about my life when I'm not assuming the worst of everyone."

"You were pretty creeped out last night."

"I'd just spent my first night out in a magical marketplace with some nutjob friends of yours and got attacked by a giant digging-machine thing that isn't supposed to exist. My head wasn't in the right place."

"Okay, Em." The elevator doors opened, and Cheyenne gestured for her friend to exit first. "I'll play along and go with innocent until proven guilty, but I have a feeling I'm gonna end up proving him guilty."

"Then I'll change my stance." They moved through the empty, sprawling lobby of their building. "I gotta say, though, I didn't expect you to be so gung-ho about law and order."

"Only when it messes with my personal life."

When they were settled in the Porsche with Ember's chair tucked in the trunk, Cheyenne started the engine and paused. "Crap. I didn't call Corian."

"He's coming with us, right?"

"He'd better be. That was the plan." Cheyenne pulled out her phone to call him. He answered almost immediately.

"Ready?"

"Wow. Was your hand just hovering over the phone, or what?"

"I assumed you'd still be taking Ember to the clinic for her twelve-thirty appointment. It's twelve-ten, so yes, I was expecting your call."

Cheyenne fought back a smile. "Yeah, we're ready. We're already in my car, though."

"That's fine. Hard to trace a portal when the remnants are driving around the city. I'll be right there."

"Wait, can't you just meet us at the—"

He hung up before she could finish, and Cheyenne tossed her phone into the cubby under the dashboard.

"He *is* still coming, right?"

"Yeah, Em." Cheyenne twisted partially around and eyed the back seat. "Apparently he's just gonna—"

The black light of Corian's portal ballooned over the black leather seats in the back, and the nightstalker stepped through, ducking before sliding over to the other side. "Hey."

"Oh!" Ember jumped and spun around to glare at him over her shoulder.

"Open a portal in my car." Cheyenne raised her eyebrows.

"What the hell?" Ember scowled at him. "You should *really* warn people before you do that."

With his illusion charm in full effect, Corian looked like the average, upstanding Richmond resident with his light-brown hair, blue eyes, and open smile.

At least he's not still wearing that stupid red hat.

The nightstalker glanced at the magicals in the front. "I told Cheyenne I was coming."

"I didn't have enough time to explain that part before you popped into my car."

"Which is very nice, by the way." Corian spread his hands on the leather seats and sat back, adjusting comfortably. "I could get used to this."

Cheyenne shot him a quick glance in the rearview mirror. "Taking up my back seat, or just riding in a car, period?"

"Just because I don't have a car, it doesn't mean I've never been in one."

"I know. That fun little road trip out to the first new portal wasn't that long ago."

He strapped on his seatbelt and dipped his chin, staring at her reflection in the mirror. "You're just being a smartass, then."

"Right now? Yeah."

As she pulled out of the parking lot, Corian stared out the back window and nodded slowly. "When we get there, kid, Ember and I will stay in the car."

"And I'll go have a little chat with Marsil 'George' Keldryk." Cheyenne's grip on the wheel tightened with a creak of leather.

"*Only* a chat," Corian warned. "We have to be careful with how we approach this. If this Marsil is who he says he is, Ember can go in for her appointment, and nothing's changed. Then we'll shift our focus and look for another lead. But if he's only pretending?"

"I know exactly what to do with him if that's the case."

"Easy."

"It will be, yeah." Cheyenne rolled her shoulders back as she turned onto the next side street to head toward the physical therapy building.

"Don't go in there with magic blazing, kid. That's the most important part of this whole thing."

"Really? I thought the most important part was finding the assholes who stole Ember's blood to get to me and who keep sending their creepy war bugs after us."

Corian looked away from the window and stared at the rearview mirror, waiting for her to meet his gaze. "Were there more?"

"Yep." She reached into her pocket, pulled out the short-circuited spy-fly, and handed it to him over her shoulder. "*That* one found me in my classroom today."

"Another one?" Ember turned to peer at the tiny black metal shell of the bug-shaped machine in Corian's palm.

"So apparently, whoever's sending these things now knows exactly where to look. We can't let more of those things fly onto the campus and sit in on my class."

"Your class."

"Didn't I tell you I'm teaching now?"

Corian stared at the fly-machine and cocked his head. "Doesn't surprise me."

"Did your students see it?" Ember turned back around and stared through the windshield.

"I don't think so. They definitely didn't see me shoot it off the wall."

Corian glanced up at the rear-view mirror and chuckled. "How'd you pull *that* off?"

"Told them to close their eyes and meditate on what they wanted to do at the end of the semester." With a snort, Cheyenne shook her head and looked briefly at his reflection. "Only took me two seconds to hit that thing and stick it in my pocket."

"Unconventional distraction." Corian licked his lips in amusement. "But the speed is certainly impressive."

"Not to mention my aim."

Ember blinked slowly. "You guys are talking about this like it's funny."

"It is. A little." Corian studied the fried metal bug again. "The machines they're sending out are smaller every time, which makes me think that either the loyalists programming these things are changing their tactics with every failure, or they're running out of metal soldiers."

"Do you think that one was able to send anything back before I squashed it?"

"I don't think so. Something this small and mobile doesn't have the capacity to relay information remotely, as far as I know. These were built under the assumption that they wouldn't be seen and would return to base to make a report, so to speak. Can I keep this?"

"*I* sure as hell don't want it."

"Excellent." Corian slipped the tiny machine into his pocket and folded his arms. "After we check things out at the clinic, we'll know more about who we have to track down to keep these things away from you."

"Yeah. And if it's Marsil, we won't have to look very far."

Ember slowly turned her head to look at Cheyenne, but her friend stared intently at the road, oblivious to the fae's concerned glance. When Ember turned a little farther and frowned at Corian, she only got a shrug and a slow shake of the head in response.

CHAPTER THIRTY-ONE

The Panamera rolled to a smooth stop in the parking lot of the physical therapy clinic. Cheyenne shifted into park and punched the automatic start button. The purring engine faded, and she took a deep breath. "Ten minutes 'til you're supposed to be in there, Em. I'll be back out in five."

She unbuckled her seatbelt and opened the door.

"Cheyenne." Corian raised his eyebrows when she paused to look at him. "Easy."

"I got it." She slid out of the car and forced herself not to slam the door before stalking onto the sidewalk toward the entrance.

Corian sat back in the seat and watched her disappear through the glass front doors. "I've seen that kind of anger get magicals into a lot of trouble in my time."

Ember frowned at the clinic entrance, even after Cheyenne entered the lobby and vanished from view. "It gets humans into trouble too, I'm pretty sure."

"Yes. But if it's used the right way, it's very powerful."

The fae frowned. "I've already seen what she can do, so you don't have to keep talking in mysterious sentences. Just say it."

"Okay. There's another reason you and I are waiting here while Cheyenne has her chat."

"Right. Let me guess. You're about to tell me that I'm a liability because now these crazy people siccing their machines on us know they can get to her through me. Sure, I'm her best friend, but I can only use five percent of my magic, and I'm in a wheelchair. Basically dead weight, right?" When the nightstalker didn't reply, she turned and frowned at him. "Why are you smirking at me like that?"

"Because everything you just said couldn't be farther from the truth." Corian tilted his head and graced her with a warm smile. "Honestly, I'm more inclined to believe that having you in her life is exactly what Cheyenne needs to find her strength and keep her on track. Even if you haven't acknowledged it, I think you know."

She blinked quickly and turned back around, rubbing her wrist. "Maybe. So, what? You wanted to have a private chat to tell me not to give up?"

He chuckled. "You're not quite as good at guessing games as she is."

Ember glanced at the ceiling and let out a wry laugh. "She's better at a lot of things."

"But not everything. Ember, I'm not trying to tell you what to do one way or the other. The choice is yours. But since nothing's been officially sealed, I wanted to give you more information than you have right now so you can make the best choice."

"Okay."

"We touched on it last night. About the *Nós Aní*."

Ember frowned at the dashboard and bit the inside of her bottom lip. "Kinda hard to forget."

"Cheyenne figured it out. I am the *Nós Aní* to L'zar Verdys. I have been for almost two thousand years, and I will be until one of us meets our end in this life."

"Huh."

Corian glanced at his lap and smiled. "It's a lifelong position. No benefits, no paid vacation or sick leave. There's the occasional bonus, but really, it's one of those things you do because your heart's in it. And once you accept, there's no backing out."

"I thought I already accepted. Last night." Ember squeezed the fingers of her other hand to hold them still in her lap. "If being that for Cheyenne helps her, I'm all about it."

"I heard you, and I'm glad you feel that way before having all the facts."

"But there are downsides, right?"

"It depends on how you look at it. A *Nós Aní's* responsibilities are as unpredictable and complicated as the drow they serve. And no, I don't mean I'm L'zar's servant. If that offer were on the table, I'd run away screaming."

Ember laughed softly. "Me too."

"If you choose this, Ember, know that it's for the rest of your life. I supposed there's a certain truth to what Cheyenne said, that it's like a best friend or a second in command, and it's so much more. You could be her friend forever, and that wouldn't change anything. But a drow, and apparently even a drow halfling, is much more powerful with a *Nós Aní* at their side. Or in my case, an hour away from Chateau D'rahl for the last seventy-five years or so."

"So, I won't have to live with her forever, then?"

The nightstalker snorted. "Was that a serious question?"

"Not really."

"Good." He scratched his forehead and inhaled deeply. "There's a ceremony for this. Nothing grotesque or painful. You won't have to cut yourself or make any sacrifices. It *is* a drow ceremony, which can make things rather odd, with a tendency to throw in surprises just for fun. After that, though, you and Cheyenne would be bound together by magic and a bloodline that goes farther back than even L'zar and I do."

"And there's no turning back."

"Right. I believe I said that already."

Ember ran a hand through her hair and turned to look into the blue eyes she knew were silver underneath. "What's in it for the *Nós Aní?*"

Beneath his human illusion, the nightstalker's grin bordered on terrifying. "A strengthening of your inherent magic. Which, by the way, I believe you possess much more of than you've seen so far."

"Go on."

His soft chuckle sounded more like a growl. "When it comes to L'zar Verdys, and of course, his daughter, a chosen *Nós Aní* is essentially untouchable."

"Really?" Her eyes widened. "Like, I can't get hurt?"

"I didn't say invincible. We can still get hurt, and I have more times than I can count. But most magicals on both sides of the Border are smart enough to back down from any drow's *Nós Aní*. The consequences of picking a fight with the wrong one are quite severe."

Ember squinted at the human-looking nightstalker and cocked her head. "Anything else?"

"Hmm. Lifelong position, magically bound to a drow, more or less elevated status, stronger magic, and unwavering dedication. I suppose it goes without saying that it's important to like the drow."

"You like L'zar?"

Smirking, Corian shrugged. "Most of the time. Don't get me wrong, I'd like to wring his neck on occasion. Someday I might try it. That's about it. Now that you know, is it something you're willing to take on?"

Ember turned in her seat again and stared at the entrance to the clinic. A small smile lifted the corner of her mouth. "Of course it is."

"Good. We'll set something up in a day or two to make it official. Of course, Cheyenne will have to agree to it, though I have a feeling she already has."

"She won't if we tell her this is a one-way street for me with no way out."

"Probably." Corian folded his arms and gazed out the window at the half-full parking lot. "I'll leave it up to you as to how much you want to tell her before the ceremony."

"Why is that up to me?"

"Because that's what a *Nós Aní* does."

"All right. I'll figure it out."

"I know you will. And I'm happy to hear this is your choice. Cheyenne's going to need as much support as she can get for what she's about to do."

Cheyenne stood in the lobby of the physical therapy clinic with her arms folded, shooting challenging glares at anyone who dared to look the Goth chick in the eyes. *If he's not out here by the time I count to thirty, I'll rip through this place and go after him. One, two...*

An unmarked door opened on the other side of the lobby, and a short woman in scrubs nodded toward Cheyenne. "Right over there."

Beside her stood Marsil Keldryk, AKA George Gardener. Despite the woman's nervous frown, Marsil's eyes lit up when he saw Cheyenne, and he nodded at her before stepping into the lobby. "Thanks, Cheryl."

Cheryl cast the angry-looking Goth chick a fleeting glance, then disappeared on the other side of the door and pulled it shut behind her.

"I gotta admit, I was a little confused when I heard someone was out here asking for me personally. That doesn't happen. I'm still a little confused, though." The muscular assistant glanced around the lobby, his smile wavering uncertainly. "Where's Ember?"

"We need to talk." The halfling's low voice bordered on a growl, and she slowly unfolded her arms. *Calm and cool until he gives me a reason not to be. That's it.*

"Sure. Is everything okay?"

"In private."

Marsil looked around again. "Yeah, okay. Come on." He nodded toward the hallway wrapping around this side of the glass room the clinic called the gym.

Cheyenne stalked after him, focusing the intensity of her gaze on the back of his head and the short dark curls that weren't technically his. When the assistant stopped at another closed door at the end of the hall, he peered around the corner to be sure no one was watching and opened the door.

"The only room in this place I know nobody's gonna come barging in on a private talk. Hey!"

The halfling shoved him through the open door and followed close on his heels, using all her willpower not to slam the door when she shut it behind her.

"Careful." Marsil moved around, and something plastic fell and bounced across the floor. "Let me just find the light."

As soon as the overhead bulb switched on, Cheyenne grabbed the man by the front of his scrub shirt and pushed him against the wall, only the wall was a shelving unit in the supply closet. Rolls of stacked toilet paper bounced off Marsil's head and onto the floor, which he didn't seem to notice as he stared at the chick with her face inches from his. "Okay, this was not what I expected."

"You're gonna answer every single question I ask, got it?"

Frowning, he looked her up and down as much as he could, as close as she was, and shook his head. "You handle all your complaints like this, or do I give off some kinda vibe?"

Cheyenne let the heat of her drow magic flare through her and made the transformation in an instant.

Marsil's hands banged against the shelves behind him in surrender. "Woah, woah. Okay. You don't have to go that far. I'll tell you whatever you wanna know."

"The truth." She shoved him against the shelf again, and a box of latex gloves glanced off his shoulder. "Don't fuck with me. I'll know if you're lying."

He swallowed. "Sure."

"You said Ember Gaderow was my *Nós Ání*. That I'd made the right choice. Who else knows?"

"That you and I had a conversation two days ago?"

"That that's what you think she is to me." Cheyenne shoved him back again and leaned her fists on his collarbones.

"Just me!" Marsil breathed heavily and stared at her glowing golden eyes. "Okay, and Dr. Boseley, but you already knew she was one of us. That's it. I didn't have a chance to tell anyone else."

"How many other magicals work in this clinic?"

The man's eyelids fluttered rapidly as he tried to think. "F-five. Total."

Cheyenne sneered and leaned in until their noses almost touched. "How many of you are loyal to the Ogúl Crown?"

"What?"

"Answer me!"

He jerked away from her and slipped on the scattered supplies. Cheyenne dragged him back up and pinned him in place against the shelf again. As he searched her fiery gaze, his eyes darting back and forth between each of hers, his startled fear slipped away. "None of us. That's why I came to talk to you. If I was one of those nutjob loyalists, you really think I'd just walk up to the one drow the Crown wants dead more than anyone in both worlds for a little chat? And then let her *leave*?"

Cheyenne leaned away from him. "You know about that?"

"Well, yeah. Anyone who wants to see O'gúl monarch's head fly knows about that. You, the Crown's bounty on your head, your father—"

"You know L'zar?"

"I mean, not personally."

Cheyenne slowly released Marsil's uniform and took one small step backward. "Prove it."

"That I know who L'zar Verdys is?"

"That you're not one of those nutjob loyalists."

The man sputtered and gazed around the cramped supply closet. Then he grabbed a fistful of his shirt and pulled it down to expose his neck. "I don't wear jewelry anyway, but you don't see a bull's head, do you?"

"No." Cheyenne looked him over and shook her head. "But that doesn't mean anything if you've been waiting at this clinic for the right time to make your move. Or to use your job to steal blood samples from VCU Medical Center."

Marsil shook out the front of his shirt and shrugged to rearrange it. "Now you've lost me."

"*Ember's* blood. For tracking her to get to me. Know anything about that?"

He met her gaze. "Only that whoever *did* take fae blood to track your *Nós Aní* either has a serious set of *cajones* or a single brain cell. She's okay, right?"

"She's fine." Stepping back across the closet, Cheyenne folded her arms and nodded. *Nobody trying to collect a bounty on my head is gonna ask about Ember, or stand here and let me shove them against a shelf without fighting back.* "I need to know who broke into the hospital so I can wipe out what they have on her, at the very least."

"I'm sorry, Cheyenne." Marsil slowly shook his head. "I can't tell you anything about that. But I swear on my life and on House Keldryk that I've been loyal to the *Cu'ón* since I was old enough to make the choice. And I'll do it again."

"Okay. Maybe I made a rushed assumption."

Marsil thumped a fist against his chest and raised his eyebrows. "Right now. Marsil Keldryk. By the blood of my house, I swear fealty to Cheyenne, uh…"

She forced a tight smile. "Summerlin."

"Cheyenne Summerlin." His lips parted in a crooked, determined smile. "On my life, I'll follow you. I swear fealty to L'zar Verdys, the *Cu'ón*, and the four-pointed star rising against the O'gúl Crown. Everything I have. All of it's yours."

Cheyenne took a deep breath and slipped back into her human form. Then she rubbed the back of her neck and nodded. "Okay, I gotta admit, that part was pretty convincing."

"It better be." He lowered his fist and chuckled. "You've never heard that before, have you?"

"No, but I understand what's behind it."

"Good. You'll be hearing a lot more of that pretty soon, I'm sure."

They stared at each other in the cramped, disheveled supply closet. The halfling shrugged and cocked her head. "Sorry I slammed you against the shelves."

"Don't worry about it. I can take a hit. Sorry I gave you a reason to think you couldn't trust me, or that I'd do anything to hurt Ember. That's not what this is about."

"Yeah, I realize that now."

"Okay. Then we're good." With a quick glance at the door, he sidled along the shelf and paused with his hand around the doorknob. "Where is she, by the way? She's got a session now, right?"

"She's out in the car."

"Ah. Waiting for you to tell her whether House Keldryk turned traitor, huh? Well, twice, I guess. According to O'gúl law, we're all traitors, aren't we?"

Cheyenne smirked. "I guess so."

He nodded, looked her over one more time, then opened the door. "I gotta go pull some charts. Should I tell Dr. Boseley Ember's still coming in?"

"Yeah, thanks. I'll go get her."

"Okay." Marsil held the door open for her as she left the supply closet, chuckling when the halfling kicked a loose piece of plastic packaging someone had apparently forgotten to throw away. "I'll get that later. And feel free to have an open conversation with me in the hall from here on out, right?"

She turned and let out a wry laugh. "Got it. Hey. Thanks for telling me what I wanted to hear."

213

"The truth? Sure. Wouldn't be doing either of us any favors if I didn't hold onto what I know." With a final quick smile, Marsil nodded and turned down the hall away from the lobby. He picked at the front of his scrubs and snorted, shaking his head.

Cheyenne made her way toward the clinic's front doors. *At least I know this is a safe place, and that L'zar's "rebels" have a lot longer fuse than I do.*

CHAPTER THIRTY-TWO

Two hours later, Cheyenne slipped behind the wheel and closed the door behind her. "How'd it go?"

"Fine, I guess." Ember stared at her legs and shrugged. "Still couldn't get these things to move again. I'm guessing it's one of those 'activate your paralyzed limbs under duress' kinda things."

"But you've done it once." Cheyenne buckled up, turned on the engine, and pulled out of the clinic's parking lot. "It'll happen again, Em. And until it does, you've got one of the best physical therapists in Virginia working on getting you there the old-fashioned way."

"You mean, the *human* way." The fae chuckled. "Somehow, I can't see a bunch of O'gúleesh on the other side lining up to get their Western-medicine fix."

"Yeah. There's probably a lot more magic involved."

"Probably."

They rode in silence for the first half of the drive back to the apartment, then Cheyenne shot her friend a quick glance. "So, what did you and Corian talk about while you guys were waiting for me to stick my foot in my mouth and realize not everyone's lying to me?"

"A few things." Ember clenched her fists in her lap and slowly opened them again. "Which I kinda want to talk to you about too."

"Sure. Corian told me to give him a call when we get home, which

215

probably means he's got some other weird mission for me to try not to screw up. And he asked if I had the rest of the day free, so whatever it is, I'm guessing it'll take a while. When I get back, though?"

"Actually," Ember said, "I don't think you wanna wait for this."

Cheyenne did a double-take and frowned. "What did he do?"

"What?"

"I mean, he's a total asshole sometimes, but I didn't think he'd screw with *your* head."

"He didn't. He was totally normal and polite. I guess. Made some jokes."

"Okay, so what happened?"

"He told me a little more about this whole *Nós Aní* thing."

"Oh." Cheyenne sat back in the driver's seat and loosened her grip on the steering wheel as they rolled up to a red light. "What, like how he's been L'zar's for forever? And that should be enough to convince you that the most wanted drow on both sides of the Border isn't a bad guy, just misunderstood?"

Ember barked out a laugh. "Sort of. He said he might wring L'zar's neck someday."

The halfling grinned. "I bet that was cool to hear."

"I mean, I get it, and I've only met the guy once."

"There's more, though, isn't there? Come on, Em. Spit it out."

"Fine. Okay." Ember stared at her lap. "Basically, I'm *almost* your *Nós Aní*, and he wanted me to know it's a lifelong thing where we're bonded to each other by some drow ceremony so we both get superpowered magic, and if I choose to do this, I can't back out of it somewhere down the road unless one of us dies."

"What the fuck?"

Ember glanced at the traffic light and pointed. "Light's green."

"What did you say to him after that?"

A car honked twice behind them. "Cheyenne, the light!"

"If I keep driving right now, I'm gonna crash this brand-new car." Cheyenne shifted into park and turned to face her friend. "Did he try to make you agree to this?"

"No, he didn't try to make me do anything. He said it was totally my choice."

Two more cars honked and really laid on their horns this time.

"Maybe you should just pull over up at the next street."

Without looking away from her friend, Cheyenne rolled down the passenger-side window and stuck her hand out to flip the bird at all the drivers losing their minds behind them. Then she punched the emergency lights and raised her eyebrows. "Please tell me you didn't give him an answer before telling me about this."

"Well, nothing's *official* until whatever ceremony thing happens."

"Ember."

"Yes, I gave him an answer. Which was, of course, I'm ready to be your *Nós Aní*, so let's do it."

"No. No way."

Ember turned to look at the halfling with minor irritation. "See? I knew before I brought this up that you'd be against it if I told you everything. That makes me perfect for it."

"I didn't want you dragged into all this." Cheyenne ran her hand down her cheeks and closed her eyes. "That is why we did the whole thing with the apartment, Em. To keep you safe, not to put you front and center in this whole O'gúl rebellion thing."

"You didn't put me anywhere, Cheyenne." Ember leaned forward and tried to catch her friend's gaze. "I'm *choosing* this."

"I can't let you do that." Cheyenne shook her head and chewed the inside of her cheek, unable to look the other girl in the eye. "I let you down once by not standing up when it counted, and I won't let that happen again."

"Oh, my God. Come *on*." Ember slapped her thigh. "This happened because I got shot by an asshole orc, not because you failed. But if you're worried about *letting me down*, I can tell you right now that not stepping up to let me be this for you when it's what I want is just another form of running away. Maybe worse. You can't do all this on your own, halfling. I can help you better than anyone else. I mean, yeah, that's what Corian said, but I know it's true. I can feel it."

Cheyenne stared blankly through the windshield as the irritated drivers veered out of the lane behind her and passed through the intersection, honking and flipping her the bird in return. "That's a huge decision to make, and it apparently lasts forever."

"Yep. Bring it."

Slowly, the halfling turned to look at her best friend and swallowed. "Are you sure? I mean like, really, *really* sure?"

"You've done more for me than anyone's done in my entire life." Ember nodded. "I'm behind you one hundred percent. I'm doing this."

Cheyenne ran her hand through her hair and studied the intersection again. "Shit."

"Yeah, tough break when someone else is just as stubborn as you are, huh?"

"Which means *I* don't have a choice."

"Sure, you do." Ember sat back against the seat and smirked. "You can go on a flying halfling rampage and make an ass of yourself, or you can suck it up and stop pretending you don't think this is awesome."

"Okay, Em. I'll suck it up."

"Great." The fae pointed across the intersection and froze. "Oh. You meant, 'Shit, the light's red again,' didn't you?"

"It was dual-purpose, for sure." Cheyenne tried to keep a straight face until she shot Ember a sidelong glance. They both snorted and waited for the light to turn green again before Cheyenne remembered to turn off the emergency lights.

When they got back to their apartment, Cheyenne called Corian to tell him she was home.

"Great. Give me two minutes."

"Sure. And then you can give me two minutes for a quick chat about some other stuff before we do whatever it is you're planning." She glanced at Ember, who rolled her eyes and wheeled into the kitchen toward the fridge.

"You wanna just tell me now?"

"No, that's okay. It's better in person."

"All right. I'll be there soon."

Cheyenne stuck her phone in her pocket and turned to the kitchen, folding her arms. "Did he say anything about what this whole *Nós Aní* ceremony entails?"

Rummaging through the fridge, Ember paused to peer at a jar of pickles and stuck it in her lap. "Just that I won't have to cut myself or make any sacrifices. 'Nothing grotesque or painful,' I think is what he said."

"Great. That in no way means that it's gonna be fun. Or even safe."

"Yeah, because Corian and L'zar aren't even remotely concerned about your safety."

Cheyenne cocked her head. "Okay, fair point."

"We'll be fine. Whatever it is, we'll do it, get it over with, then start kickin' ass. Figuratively for me. I'm sure you've done that literally many times."

Chuckling, the halfling took a deep breath and jumped when Corian stepped through his portal into her living room. "Jeeze. Does that ever stop being a surprise?"

"I thought you said you got used to it?" Ember called from the kitchen.

"Yeah, I guess I'm still working on that."

Corian dipped his head toward her and kept one foot on the other side of the portal. "Time to go. And bring the salve."

She frowned. "Okay."

The nightstalker nodded at Ember as Cheyenne grabbed her backpack and slung it over her shoulder. Ember jerked her chin at him and unscrewed the lid of the pickle jar with a pop.

Cheyenne stepped toward the portal and raised an eyebrow. "Any specific reason I need to bring the whole jar?"

"Just good to be prepared. Come on."

"Later, Em."

"Bye. Have fun." The fae crunched a pickle spear and watched Cheyenne and Corian disappear through the portal, her smile widening.

They stepped into Persh'al's warehouse, and Cheyenne grabbed the nightstalker's arm to keep him from storming off. "Hold on. I get two minutes, remember?"

He glanced across the warehouse before begrudgingly meeting her gaze. "Okay. What's up?"

"You should've come to me first about the *Nós Aní* thing."

Corian shifted his weight. "That wasn't meant to come across as going behind your back."

"That's what it feels like. She told me all about what it is and what she'll have to do, at least in the general sense. Did you not think it was important for me to know?"

He squinted, bit his bottom lip, and lifted his chin. "That was a conversation between two *Nós Aní*, kid, and those are rare enough as it is. The important thing is that she didn't waste a second before telling you everything you needed to hear, which is exactly why she's the one you want stepping up to this."

"I already knew that. Just don't pull that crap again, all right?" Cheyenne followed his gaze across the warehouse and shook her head. "If we're gonna be fighting a war and saving at least one of these worlds, I have to be able to trust you."

"You can." The nightstalker's silver eyes settled on her face and softened. "It won't happen again."

"Okay. Thanks." She couldn't help but frown as she watched him walk past Persh'al's empty workstation tables toward the center of the warehouse. *That was surprisingly easy.*

"We ready to do this or what?" Already standing in the center of the warehouse, Persh'al rubbed his hands together and shifted from one foot to the other.

"Ask him." Corian nodded at L'zar, who sat cross-legged on the cement floor, his eyes closed and his hands raised in front of him to form an open circle.

"Yeah, I already tried that. He's in deep." When Persh'al blinked, it looked a lot like a facial tick.

Maybe all those energy drinks finally caught up to him.

"Well, Cheyenne's here." Corian waved her forward. "So we're just waiting for this last part, and then you guys can head out."

"Shit." The blue troll vigorously rubbed his bald head, his orange mohawk quivering, and paced in a short line beside the meditating L'zar. "It's the wait that's killing me. I think."

"You'll be fine." Corian stuck his hands in his pockets and briefly glanced at L'zar again. "You know what you're doing."

"It's been a long time, man." Persh'al noticed Cheyenne had joined them and looked away before spinning around to pace again. "*Long* time."

The nightstalker smirked. "Just like riding a bike, as I remember it."

"Your jokes aren't funny, you know that?"

Cheyenne leaned sideways to get a better look at L'zar's profile. "What's going on?"

"Just a little preparation."

"For what?"

Corian nodded at the cross-legged drow.

A purple light flashed and grew brighter in the space between L'zar's curved palms. The flashes sped up into a violet strobe, and when the light disappeared the next second, something round and silver appeared in its place. It dropped to the floor with a clink, then L'zar's golden eyes flew open and he gave a sharp, raw gasp.

Corian stepped back. "Is that it?"

L'zar looked down at the thick silver wrist cuff in front of his crossed legs. "Yeah. That's it."

"Crazy, man." Persh'al shook his head and picked up his pacing again. "I don't know how you last that long and don't lose your mind."

Picking up the cuff, L'zar smirked. "Maybe I lost my mind a long time ago. You ever think of that?"

Persh'al stopped and shot the drow an unamused glance. "So I've heard. Everything's a rumor these days, isn't it?"

"Not everything." L'zar rose fluidly to his feet and noticed his daughter standing slightly behind him. He turned toward her with a wide smile, though his golden eyes narrowed. "Good. You're already here."

"Sure am." Cheyenne spread her arms and glanced at the magicals standing around her. "Still wondering why, though."

"Here." L'zar handed her the metal cuff and nodded. "This is for you."

"Not my style, but I appreciate the gesture. I think."

"It's not a fashion statement, Cheyenne. Take it."

Frowning, the halfling accepted the cold, heavy band of metal and turned it over in her hands. "What is this?"

"Put it on and keep it on." L'zar stared at the cuff. "Right now. I want to watch you do it, so I know it's working."

Corian nodded. "Go ahead."

"As a drow, if you would," L'zar added without meeting her gaze.

Cheyenne pulled up her drow magic and transformed in a split second, then slipped the metal cuff onto her wrist next to the wrapped silver chains. A wave of icy energy tingled up her arm, and that was it.

Pursing his lips, L'zar looked her over intently and nodded. "That'll do."

"Awesome." Persh'al rubbed his head again. "Good to know you didn't waste all that energy conjuring a dud."

Corian shot him a warning look, and the troll hissed in irritation before turning away to walk in a tight circle between L'zar and the back door.

"What does it do?" Cheyenne turned her wrist over and studied the plain silver band.

"I've made improvements on that one." L'zar clasped his hands behind his back. "This will make your halfling identity almost impossible to detect. They won't be able to see what you really are."

"I've already got a handle on my magic. I don't need a charm for that."

"I'm not talking about hiding your drow face from humans who wouldn't recognize what they saw." With a deep inhale, L'zar raised his eyebrows and gave her a thin smile. "And this is not a charm. I'd call it a shield. Now there's nothing on the outside to hint that half of you is human."

"What?" Cheyenne looked at Corian for an explanation. "Why would I need help to hide being a halfling?"

"Because it's a lot harder to do on your own where you're going."

"Where am I going?" Her eyes widened as she glanced from the nightstalker to L'zar.

Persh'al clapped his hands again, then shook them out as he rejoined the loose circle. "Then I guess we're all good, and I'm startin' to get twitchy."

"One moment." L'zar lifted a finger toward his troll friend but kept staring at Cheyenne. "When the time is right, you and I will be doing this together. Unfortunately, I can't be the first one to take you, because the Crown has been keeping tabs on me, more or less, for a very long time. I've managed to stay under her radar so far, and we don't want to blow that wide open." He looked at Corian and pressed his lips together, nodding once. "Corian and I are working on a little something to help in that respect, but it will take time. Until then, you need to know what you're getting into."

"Yep." She couldn't pull herself away from those golden eyes boring into hers. *This isn't gonna be good.* "I'd love to know what that is."

"Yes." L'zar's lips twitched into a vanishing smile. "Before you take your *marandúr* to Ambar'ogúl to claim your legacy and all your rights as a drow who's passed her trials, you need to know what to expect. Scope out the lay of the land, as it were."

Cheyenne tried to ignore Persh'al's continued nervous pacing and glanced at Corian. "I don't get it." *There's no way he's serious about this.*

"Yeah, you do." Corian nodded at her while L'zar stepped away, hands still clasped behind his back. "You're taking your first trip across the Border, Cheyenne, and Persh'al's going with you as your guide."

A laugh burst out of her, and she glanced at the millennia-old magicals staring at her. "Good one. I can't go across the Border. I don't belong there. What's really going on?"

"You can, and you will." L'zar pointed at the silver cuff on her wrist. "And as far as anyone else is concerned, while you're wearing that, you belong in Ambar'ogúl just as much as the rest of them."

"You guys are serious."

"Completely." Corian nodded at Persh'al, who cleared his throat and took off across the warehouse to his computer tables. "This is important, Cheyenne. Things are coming together quickly now, and we all agreed this is what needed to happen next. To be prepared."

"What about the war machines?" She shook her head, feeling the smile on her face and somehow unable to rip it off. *This has to be a joke.* "We still don't know where they're coming from."

"We got a tip about an hour ago. Byrd and Lumil are on it as we speak. Ember's safe for now, with the wards around your apartment. I'm happy to check on her if you want me to."

"No, it's okay. I'll go home and tell her what to expect."

"You don't have time for that," L'zar countered, standing stock-still two yards away. "Corian will make sure she knows what's happening. Right now, you should leave."

"What? How much time *do* I have?" Cheyenne frowned at her stoic drow father, but he didn't answer.

Persh'al joined them again in the center of the warehouse with a grunt, hiking up the stuffed-full trekking pack over his shoulders. "None. Time to go."

"Right now?"

"Come on, kid. I'm not carrying this thing just for fun. My car's out front."

Cheyenne swallowed and looked at Corian, still hoping he'd crack a smile and tell her to relax. He raised an eyebrow instead and flicked one finger toward the front door as Persh'al opened it.

"Shit." A small, dry laugh of disbelief escaped her, and she spread her arms. "I'm going to Ambar'ogúl."

CHAPTER THIRTY-THREE

Cheyenne Summerlin closed the door of Persh'al's SUV on the frontage road and tightened her grip on the straps of her backpack.

"Don't just stand there, kid." The blue troll nodded across the dirt road toward the tree line. A strong breeze sent the first fallen leaves of autumn skittering across the ground. His neon-orange mohawk fluttered slightly, and he gazed up and down the road with a grimace of distaste. "We've already been waiting long enough."

"*Please.*" Cheyenne followed him into the thick woods, her black Vans crunching over sticks and underbrush. "You guys whipped this plan up after I told you about the war machine in Peridosh."

Persh'al threw his hands in the air, and his stuffed trekking pack swung against low-hanging branches when he turned to look at her. "*Now* you have something to say, huh? Two-hour drive, and the first thing you say to me is that I'm wrong."

"I didn't say that." Cheyenne kept her voice low, glancing around the forest. *Apparently, we don't need to be quiet this time. I'd be able to hear us from five miles away.*

"Not in so many words. But that's what I'll tell *you*, Cheyenne. You're wrong."

"About the half-cocked planning method you guys rely on so much?"

"No, not that." He stepped over a fallen tree and sniffed, taking a moment to scan the trees. "Fine. This wasn't the original outline, sure, but there's been a Border crossing in your future since the minute you passed the drow trials."

She squinted at the back of his bulging pack. "Which happened less than forty-eight hours ago. You're not building a strong argument."

"You know what?" Irritation built in the troll's voice, then he chuckled. "You're good at that—picking apart all the details until the other person talks themselves into a corner."

"I've been doing it for a while." *And I have a master of manipulative negotiation for a mom.*

"Yeah, I bet. Reminds me of someone else I know."

Cheyenne rolled her eyes.

"I'm gonna try again because I don't like not finishing a thought." Persh'al ducked when a raven swooped down from the treetops on their right, then snorted when the bird hopped off into the bushes. "*You* haven't been waiting that long for this next big step in claiming who you are. And yeah, technically, the rest of us have only been waiting twenty years to see if the kid L'zar was so sure about would make it through the trials without—well, you know. That kid's you, all right?"

"That part's been covered already."

"Thing is, though, kid, before you came along—and I mean before you were conceived, not only before you were aware of all this shit going on now—the rest of us have been walking a tightrope of waiting and trying to live something like a normal life for centuries."

Cheyenne frowned and walked a little faster through the underbrush to catch up with him. "Why would some other kid of L'zar's have to make the crossing? I thought they were all drow."

The troll let out a sharp, bitter laugh. "They were all at least *half*-drow, I can tell you that much. L'zar's half of the DNA."

"What?"

He turned again to shoot her a confused glance, and his eyebrows twitched. "Sorry, kid. If you thought you were the only halfling who sprang forth from L'zar Verdys' overactive loins, you're wrong."

"Dude. I don't wanna hear about his loins."

"Oh, *you* don't wanna hear about 'em? Try spending centuries with

Ambar'ogúl's most wanted while he tries to break through his damn prophecy over and over with those loins. In the beginning, I tell you what, man, that drow was fellfire-bent on proving that old crone wrong, and talking about his plans and his deeds and his *seeds* was pretty much all he did. I almost slit his throat myself once, just to get him to shut up about it."

Cheyenne stopped when the troll pushed through the scraping branches of a thorny bush without bothering to hold them aside for her. They swung back into place, then she lifted them again so she could follow without being smacked in the face. "No, you didn't."

"Ha. True. But I thought about it more than once. But believe me, kid, that drow father of yours has made this crossing more times than even he can count. Fathered plenty of full-blooded O'gúleesh drow who would've grown into fine dark elves on their own. You know, if they'd made it. And I know of at least three others who were Earthside halflings like you."

She grimaced at the thought. *So Bianca Summerlin wasn't the first woman to get her pants charmed off by a mystery drow in a human mask. Not sure that'd change her opinion of it.*

"And none of them made it either," she muttered.

"Nope. Not a one." Persh'al shrugged and tightened the straps of his pack. "Of course, I think some of the earlier casualties were a product of the times. One of these kids made it right up to the Great Depression."

"All right. Stop." Cheyenne opened her clenched fists to let some blood into her fingers. "I don't wanna hear about his other kids."

"Yeah, yeah, I get it." Persh'al cleared his throat and kept trudging through the woods. "It's sad, man. It sucks, but you had nothing to do with it. So don't start blaming yourself for what happened to them, huh?"

"No, I'll blame L'zar."

He wheezed out a laugh and shook his head. "Everybody does. But his endless search for an heir stops with you, kid. If I were you, I'd think of it that way. No more lost hope for the next heir."

"I said I don't wanna hear about it," Cheyenne snapped. Two birds took off from their nest yards away, startled by her shout.

Persh'al stopped and turned all the way around to look at her. His mohawk fluttered at the tips when he nodded. "Okay, this is me taking the hint."

"Okay." She took a deep breath and shoved her hands into the front pocket of her hoodie. The cold, heavy silver wrist cuff sliding against her fingers reminded her of what she was about to do. *Head in the game, halfling. Leave the rest of it in the past where it belongs.*

They walked for another five minutes until they breached the tree line again and entered the wide clearing of the six-month-old portal ridge. The fists of stone shot toward the sky in a long line of glistening black stone cutting across the clearing and into the woods for at least another mile. The thin wall of light rising from the center of the ridge still shimmered with the soft pink light of Maleshi's shield.

Persh'al pressed his lips together and nodded. "At least it's still holding. That's a plus."

"So, how are we supposed to get through?"

"Why do you think *I'm* here?" Maleshi stepped out from behind the closest end of the portal ridge, where Cheyenne had decimated the black columns to send those writhing creatures back to the in-between. The rubble lay untouched, but the nightstalker woman walked a wide path around it anyway, careful not to get too close to even the smaller fragmented chunks.

Persh'al cocked his head. "How long you been waiting for us?"

"Long enough," Maleshi said, her illusion spell gone to reveal the dark fur around her face and on her tufted ears. Her glowing silver eyes narrowed slightly. "I almost called Corian, but he'd panic and send out a search party."

The troll snorted.

"So, I spent my time taking a walk up and down this thing." Maleshi shot the portal ridge a disapproving glance. "Still no clue how it got here, but it feels pretty established to me. I guess six months will do that."

Cheyenne walked toward the center of the clearing, staring at the ridge and the tall wall of shimmering pink light. "What about all the bodies and the crates of old tech? Any clue what happened to those?"

Persh'al whirled to frown at her, then the halfling gestured toward the front of the ridge. The troll took a look for himself and raised his eyebrows. "Well, shit. I'd forgotten all about those assholes. Now I'd like to know where the hell they are."

Maleshi chuckled darkly and joined them in the center of the clearing. "I know they didn't just get up and walk away."

Persh'al hissed in agreement, and the magicals shared a glance Cheyenne couldn't quite read. She didn't like it.

"That's not funny."

Both the troll and the nightstalker turned to look at her. A surprised frown flickered across Maleshi's brows. "You're still having a hard time swallowing the wartime lump."

"No, I have a hard time swallowing jokes about the loyalist prisoners who died right here. If it had to happen, fine. But we said—"

"We'd leave it behind us. I hear you." With a slow, understanding nod, Maleshi turned back toward the portal ridge and stuck her hands on her hips. "And now they're all gone. Not a scrap left behind. Which is a little weird even for bodies left out in the middle of the woods. Carrion eaters usually leave mementos."

The halfling folded her arms. "So, those loyalists had people on this side to come for the bodies."

"Maybe. Maybe not. We could say the same thing for all the war-machine contraband, too."

Persh'al shook his head. "They'd take the crates, sure. Not the bodies. Haven't known a Crown-bowing scumbag to bury their own Earthside, and I've seen plenty of them pass up the opportunity."

"Then, what?" Cheyenne shrugged. "They just disappeared into thin air?"

Maleshi shook long dark hair the color of her fur out of her face and scanned the length of the portal ridge. "The way things are right now, Cheyenne, it wouldn't be impossible that the portal swallowed the whole mess all on its own, even with my shield up there. Bodies *and* boxes."

"Do portals generally do that?"

"No. Not at all." The nightstalker shot her a thin smile before stepping forward to approach the ridge. "We're seeing this for the first time together, aren't we?"

Persh'al gripped the straps of his pack and started pacing along the line of stone. "Just take it down already."

Maleshi looked slowly over her shoulder and watched his short, nervous turns. "If I didn't know better, I'd say you're itching to get across."

"Yeah, *back* across when we're done." He shot her an irritated glance before looking at the sky. "And you do know better."

"I like to think I do." Maleshi took two more steps toward the portal ridge and raised her hands. The spell she muttered under her breath was a lot shorter than the one she'd cast to put up that shield, which sputtered with pink light, flashed once, and disappeared. Now the shimmering wall of light extending into the sky returned to its original black intensity. She dropped her arms against her sides and stepped back, studying the change. "Always easier to tear something down, isn't it?"

Cheyenne shook her head. "Building something's easy if you're doing it right."

The nightstalker looked at her sidelong and let out a soft chuckle. "Can't argue with you there, kid."

"Oh, boy. Okay." Persh'al stopped beside Cheyenne, rubbing his hands together. "This is it. We're going through."

Cheyenne raised an eyebrow and studied the black columns of stone. "You need me to hold your hand?"

"Shut up. I'm *your* guide."

"Just wanted to make sure you hadn't forgotten."

He scoffed. "Like you're not nervous."

"Not really." Cheyenne fought back a smile when Maleshi chuckled on the other side of her. Then she pulled the heavy silver cuff from her hoodie pocket, let her drow magic wash over her, and slipped it onto her wrist. She twisted her arm to study the thick bracelet and tried to drop into her human form just to check. Her hand and arm below her pushed-up sleeve remained the same purple-gray as the rest of her, and she reached up reflexively to touch the tip of one pointed ear poking through her stark white hair. *Here's hoping this thing works the way L'zar said.* "Right now, I'm just curious. We'll see what happens."

Maleshi set a hand on the halfling's shoulder, removing it when Cheyenne looked into her glowing silver eyes. "You're in for a hell of a ride, kid. I'm looking forward to hearing all about it."

"Yeah. We'll all sit down for story time later."

With a snort, the nightstalker nodded toward the portal ridge and clasped her hands behind her back.

"Now or never." Persh'al cocked his head and walked forward like he was about to break into a run, but he didn't.

Cheyenne caught up to him. "Anything I should know before we do this?"

"Yeah. Keep moving."

They stepped between the closest pillars of stone and disappeared from the clearing.

CHAPTER THIRTY-FOUR

Cheyenne's lungs felt like they'd been set on fire. Two seconds later, she was breathing again, gasping for air.

Beside her, Persh'al doubled over in a fit of coughing and nudged her arm with the back of a hand. "I said, keep moving."

Blinking with watering eyes, Cheyenne nodded and slowly stepped forward with him.

The last of his coughing fit faded, and the troll thumped his chest. "Whew. I haven't missed that part a bit. You know what they say, though. Better out than in. We'll pop out on the other side in no time."

"Really?" Cheyenne finally cleared her vision enough to focus on their new surroundings. The realm of the in-between was a haze of gray light and black smoke, which wafted up from the ground she couldn't even see. When she looked up, she couldn't find the sun or the moon or any source of light, and a thin wind moaned across a nonexistent landscape. "Something tells me it takes a lot less time to get lost in here than to make it to the other side."

"Oh, it does." Persh'al cleared his throat. "If you're trying to find anything. That's why we're moving, kid. And moving and moving and, well, eventually we'll get to where we need to be."

A mound of cracked gray-washed dirt on their left let out a choking sound and spewed a geyser of black smoke straight into the air. Cheyenne grimaced. "Smells like manure."

"Yeah?" He gazed slowly around the indiscriminate landscape and shrugged. "I always get patchouli. Can't stand patchouli."

"How long is this gonna take?"

Persh'al let out an indecisive hum and waved aside another cloud of black smoke snaking toward them. "Time isn't a thing here. I mean, it's not like Earth and Ambar'ogúl run on the same clock anyway, but I'm pretty sure if we could time it from the outside, we'd be stepping out of this thing two seconds after we stepped into it, no matter how long we're stuck in here."

"Stuck?"

"I don't mean *stuck*-stuck." He shot her a nervous glance. "I mean walking-stuck. Until we get through."

"Great."

The moaning wind kicked up with a loud whistle, buffeting away the smoke and the thick screen of black fog covering the ground. Something skittered toward them in the breeze, and Cheyenne looked down to see dead black leaves rolling across what looked like the surface of a marsh beneath them. But her feet weren't wet, and the glistening water or whatever it was didn't move around her when she took another step. One of the dead leaves caught against the inside of her shoe, and she bent down for a closer look.

"Are these bones?"

"Well, don't touch them." Persh'al shook his head. "Seriously. I have no idea what those things are, and I don't care. Let it go."

She picked up her foot, and the bone-leaf thing fluttered away with the others. When she looked up again, they were heading toward a lone tree growing from the smoky haze, its branches bare and twisted like gnarled claws. "That wasn't here ten seconds ago."

"Nope." Persh'al wrinkled his nose and kept walking forward. "And it won't be here ten seconds from now, either. This place isn't exactly a place."

"Obviously."

"Whatever you think you see in here, kid, don't pay any attention to it. That's how you get *stuck*-stuck in here."

"What about those creatures? I'm sure we should pay attention to those."

Persh'al shrugged. "Yeah. If they notice us. Might depend on the mood they're in."

"Their mood?"

"Sometimes they don't even show up. Not everyone has to fight a bunch of slithery, spikey, whatever-else creatures when they're crossing. As long as we don't run toward or away from anything but go exactly where we wanna go, we'll be fine." He chopped his hand through the air in a straight line ahead of them and nodded.

The wind died, and in seconds, the black smoke spewing from a larger collection of liquid-less geysers blotted everything from view.

"Ah, shit."

"Keep moving?" Cheyenne asked, gauging where he was by the sound of the troll's heavy breathing.

"That hasn't changed. Slide your foot out to make sure you're not gonna knock yourself out cold on a—" His foot thumped something solid, and he grunted. "Whatever this is. Just move around it and find how to keep going. What was that?"

"My arm."

"Huh." Persh'al gave her forearm a little squeeze, then nudged her sideways as he tried to step around whatever was in his way. "I hate this."

Another gust of wind broke the wall of thick, blinding smoke in front of them, and when it cleared, they were standing in front of a huge black boulder.

"What the hell!" Persh'al's grip tightened on her arm as he scowled at the rock. "See what I mean, kid? No tree, and now we're rock-climbing."

Cheyenne pointed slightly to their right, where a narrow passage cut through the rock. "That's wide enough for us to get through, right?"

"Should be. One at a time, anyway. Cross your fingers that it doesn't move while we're in there. Keep going." They moved toward the passage, shoes crunching on whatever the black fog was hiding beneath them. Persh'al slipped between the boulders first, the sides of his bulging pack scraping the walls. "Didn't look so tight from the outside."

The wind dropped in the passage, but the smoke hadn't found its way in with them. Cheyenne looked again at the eerie gray sky with no source of light and kept moving. Pebbles toppled down the side of the boulder, bouncing off the rough wall beside her before hitting the ground without a sound. She looked at the wall and jerked away, nearly bashing her shoulder into the opposite side of the cleft stone. "Ugh."

"Huh?"

A face was etched in the stone wall, mouth open as if it had been caught inside the boulder halfway through a scream. Like someone was trying to push their way out of it.

"Face in the wall," she muttered.

"Oh, yeah. That happens sometimes."

She skirted around the face, which thankfully didn't move when she passed it. "Is that what happens to magicals who get lost?"

Persh'al said, "No idea. Maybe. Or maybe it's the place's idea of a good practical joke. Scare the pants right off ya and make you run until you *get* lost. Like I said, kid, ignore what you see."

Before they'd made it remotely close to the end of the passage, the rock walls on either side of them disappeared. Blinking quickly, Cheyenne lifted her elbow to test the air, but there was nothing there anymore. "This is nuts."

"Yep. That's the abridged version." The troll looked around them in every direction and shrugged. "Nothing now. Just smoke and more smoke. And that'll change again soon, I'm sure."

"So, how do we know when we're getting close?" Cheyenne glanced quickly to the right when something skittered across the unseen ground.

"Looks kinda like a door. Or a doorway. Not one of these shifting illusions, either." Persh'al waited for her to catch up so they could walk side by side again. "When you see it, you'll know. As far as I can tell, the doorways are the only constants in here. And you won't find yourself stepping through one only to find that it's a fake. I think."

"Wonderful."

The skittering and rustling sound rose again, and Cheyenne paused. "Something's moving."

"Uh-huh. And we need to keep moving too. Just don't—"

"Hey!" Something heavy and cold slithered across the top of Cheyenne's shoe. She kicked it off and gritted her teeth. "Something just ran over my *foot*."

"Time to pick up the pace." Persh'al grabbed the sleeve of her hoodie and tugged her along beside him. "Eyes open, yeah?"

"Like I could see anything anyway." They walked quickly over nothing and through wisps of black smoke.

About four yards ahead, more smoke ballooned into a dark, solid shape that didn't disappear again when the wind kicked up. The dark shape glinted in the pale gray light, and when it turned sideways, Cheyenne hissed. "That looks like a tentacle."

"Sure does." Persh'al flicked his wrist, and a bright-green whip of crackling magic materialized in his hand. "Get ready and don't fall back. That's about it."

"Right." Cheyenne summoned two sparking, hissing black orbs and stayed close to his side.

The next thing she knew, the tentacle wasn't yards away but right in front of them. It whipped toward them and crashed into the ground at their feet. The halfling launched her sparking attack at the thick section and severed it. A shrieking cry rose from every direction, sounding close and far away at the same time.

"I'm guessing they're in a bad mood today."

Persh'al scowled at the flopping severed tentacle as they stepped over it. "Funny. Keep going."

They made it four feet before another shape rose from the ground in front of them, reared back, and opened into a gigantic mouth with rows of sharp teeth dripping with something green and noxious. Cheyenne reeled away from the stench blasting out of that mouth before she hit it with two more black spheres. Her magic scattered shards of monster and green goo in every direction, but the pieces disappeared before they hit the ground.

Persh'al snorted. "You gonna let me get a shot in or what?"

The halfling grinned. "Sorry. Next one's all yours."

"You know, you're a lot more fun when you play nice. I'm sure it wouldn't—"

Two more tentacles darted toward them through the smoke-thick air. Cheyenne and Persh'al leaped away from each other to avoid the lashing strike, then the troll's sparking green whip cracked against the tentacles and coiled tightly around them. Something screamed, and the glistening appendages shattered.

"Not as satisfying as I thought, but fine."

That skittering sound returned again, this time magnified by a hundred. Cheyenne peered through the fog around them as they kept walking. "Sounds like those creepy bugs."

"Could be anything, really."

A massive shadow blocked the grim light overhead, then something dropped from the sky and landed with a wet smack beside them on the left. A hairy, spike-studded body rose from the ground, eight eyes shifting in all directions as the spider-thing leaped toward them. Persh'al lashed out with his whip and the spider screamed, then the skittering grew louder on the right.

"Whoa." Cheyenne blinked at the swarm of fist-sized black crabs scrambling toward them. She let off round after round of her black orbs, which smashed into the creatures and scattered them like bowling pins until the things changed tactics. Hundreds of them leaped on top of each other to form a new shape, and Persh'al grunted beside her, cracking his whip against the huge spider while it danced back and forth in front of him.

"You got those things?" he asked, ducking beneath the swipe of a hairy leg.

"I'm pretty sure, yeah." Cheyenne kept blasting, but no matter how many scuttling black crabs she knocked off the newly forming creature, more took their places.

Persh'al sent a ball of blue flames at the spider with one hand and coiled his green whip around two of its legs with the other. A sick, wet crunch filled the air, and the spider thing toppled to the ground before disappearing in the black fog.

"Well, that was—" He turned and saw the crab creature building itself larger while Cheyenne unleashed her attack spells all over it. "*What?*"

"I don't know!" The halfling stepped forward and pushed with both hands outstretched. A wave of telekinetic force burst from her palms and sent the growing mountain of scrambling crabs flying.

"Hey, that's a good one." Persh'al nudged her with his elbow. "Kinda makes me think of—"

"Get down!" She clapped a hand on his shoulder and shoved him onto one knee as she dropped.

The scattered crabs had pulled themselves together in midair and now swooped toward the crossing magicals as a giant pair of wings and nothing else. The thing shrieked and sprouted two sets of talons as it dove, and one of them snagged the strap of Persh'al's huge trekking pack and jerked him backward. "Shit!"

Cheyenne spun on one knee and fired another black sphere into the flying creature's underbelly. It exploded and dropped the troll, who was already two feet off the ground. He landed on his ass and groaned.

"You okay?"

"Uh-huh." He accepted her hand up and held his whip out to the side. "Keep moving."

They hurried forward in no particular direction. Cheyenne glanced over her shoulder, but nothing followed them. *Yet.*

"These things are a lot easier to tear apart than last time."

The troll snorted. "Last time, they'd made it into the real world, where things are solid. They're easy now, sure, but I've never seen so many quite like this."

"Think that's why they're leaking out Earthside?"

"Maybe. I don't have the focus to try to figure that one out right now." He leaped sideways and knocked into her when another geyser spewed black smoke. "And now I'm all jumpy. Sorry."

"We're good." Cheyenne pointed ahead and nodded. "That kinda looks like a doorway."

Persh'al squinted up ahead, and a grin broke across his blue face. "Yes, it does. Let's get the hell through it."

They broke into a run toward the dark, shimmering outline that was a relatively rectangular shape—a door without any walls or support.

I bet it doesn't even touch the ground.

The light coming through the doorway was less gray than the rest of this place, and it only grew brighter as they approached.

"We have to run forever too?" Cheyenne panted.

"Time and distance, kid. Not really things here. Just like that tree, we'll be there before we—"

The ground exploded in front of them and sent them both flying back through the smoke. A grating shriek shook the air, and the thick black smoke poured from a new fissure in a billowing wave.

"Dammit!" Persh'al pounded his thigh and pushed himself to his feet. He cracked his green whip and snarled at the creature coalescing from the smoke. "This better be the last one."

"We can take it." Cheyenne summoned two more black spheres and launched them at the glowing red eyes in the center of the smoke creature.

The thing darted straight up at the last second, avoiding her attacks, then dove in a roaring column toward Persh'al. The troll cracked his whip at it, but his magical weapon went right through the new monster without any effect. His eyes widened just before the barreling stream of smoke hit him square in the chest, and the rest of the monstrous shape coalesced around him.

"Fuck!"

"Persh'al!" Cheyenne sent another attack at the top of the smoke monster swirling around the troll. *Shit. Goes right through it.*

"Get this thing off me," the troll shouted. "It's— Ow!" A flash of green light burst from within the smoke, and the bodiless creature roared.

"I'm trying." Cheyenne sent another telekinetic wave toward the cyclone wrapped around Persh'al, which was growing tighter by the second. It blew the smoke away for a mere two seconds, long enough for her to catch a glimpse of the troll clawing at two thick, glistening tentacles coiled around his neck. He snarled and gasped for air, then the smoke drew in on itself again and hid him.

I'll go through the list, then.

Cheyenne darted toward the smoke creature and sent black tendrils of whipping magic through the smoke, feeling for Persh'al. She felt the tug when her magic caught something, and she pulled.

The black cloud roared and tossed her aside, and she lost hold on what she hoped was Persh'al and flew sideways. Before she reached the ground, a stream of black darted out of the funnel around the troll and wrapped around her upper arm before jerking her forward. Cheyenne growled at the slicing pain tearing through her bicep and somehow managed to dig her feet into the ground. The creature pulled her closer anyway, and she grabbed the now-hardened tentacle with her other hand. "Fuck you."

She didn't have to think about which ability to use next, and she barely thought about the Nimlothar seed bound to her body before her hand erupted in black flames. The tentacled smoke-creature screamed, and Persh'al screamed with it. Cheyenne dug her fingers into the in-between monster's flesh and sent the black fire racing across the appendage. The vortex of black smoke materialized into a snarling mass of tentacles and glistening black flesh before the fire consumed it.

In two seconds, the entire thing was in flames. The creature let out another piercing screech before it shattered into fragments that blew away in the next gust of wind.

Persh'al was on his knees, his fists pressed into the ground as he fought to draw in the air he hadn't been breathing.

"Hey. Come on." Cheyenne offered him a hand up again, and his grip slipped from hers. She grabbed his arm instead and hauled him to his feet. "Persh'al. Hey, you okay? Look at me."

The troll's eyelids fluttered, but he finally focused on her face and blinked slowly. Then he nodded and reached up to touch his throat. "I'm good. Shit, man. That was new."

"Yeah." The halfling glanced at the doorway, which was now six feet in front of them, and pulled him with her. "Come on."

He stumbled forward and croaked out a chuckle. "That was the black fire, huh?"

"That was the black fire. Guess I'll start with that one next time."

"Did you know you weren't gonna burn me up too?"

"I had a hunch."

Persh'al choked out another laugh, which cut off when another small, hand-sized tentacle snaked around the corner of the doorway. He blasted it with a ball of green flames and grabbed Cheyenne's hand, jerking her quickly behind him as he darted through the doorway.

CHAPTER THIRTY-FIVE

The return of things like gravity and visible ground beneath them made them stumble when they burst through the portal. Persh'al let go of Cheyenne's hand when he tripped on a loose stone, but he caught himself and straightened. "Fuck that place, man. Gets worse every time."

"Wasn't as bad as fighting those things on the other side, though."

"Yeah, easy for you to say. You weren't one being choked by a whatever-the-hell-that-was."

"True." Cheyenne smiled innocently when he shot her an exasperated glance.

With a wry chuckle, he stepped toward her and extended a hand. "But you *were* the one who fried that thing. Thanks."

"Hey, if I don't have a guide over here, I'm screwed." She shook his hand, and when he released her grip, the troll stood beside her and looked out over the expanse of land where they'd crossed over.

"Oh, man." He scratched his head and frowned. "Looks like this place is screwed too."

"Ambar'ogúl has deserts too, huh?"

"Not like this. At least, not naturally."

The ground stretched flat and barren in front of them, the earth split and cracked as far as they could see. Two trees emerged from the dead landscape to their left, dry and gnarled. One of them had cracked and fallen halfway against the other, which looked like it was about to crumble anyway. All of it was a charred, dusty black.

Cheyenne blew strands of her white hair out of her face and scanned the open ground. "You sure we made it out?"

"Very funny." Persh'al turned and pointed to the blackened, partially split boulder behind him. "That's not moving. If we were coming back the same way when we cross over again, that rock would still be here."

"Right. No smoke, either."

"Well done on your first crossing, kid. Welcome to Ambar'ogúl." He smacked her arm with the back of his hand, and Cheyenne flinched away from him with a hiss. "Whoa. That's a nasty one."

She glanced down at her arm where the smoke-tentacle had grabbed her and grimaced "Shit."

The thing had burned a hole in the sleeve of her hoodie and through some layers of skin. Her purple-gray flesh glistened in the bright sunlight streaming down on them, the edges of the burn charred black like the dead land around them. Kneeling, she shrugged off her back-pack, careful not to knock the other strap against the fresh wound. Then she unzipped the bag and pulled out the jar of darktongue salve. When she unscrewed the lid, the scent of rotting strawberries over-whelmed them both.

Persh'al stared at the brown jar and scratched his chin. "Smells like darktongue."

"It is."

"You, uh, you ever use that stuff before?"

She looked at him and raised an eyebrow. "Unfortunately, yeah."

He chuckled. "Want some help?"

"Thanks, but that might get you a drow hand around your throat instead of a tentacle."

The troll raised his hands and took a step back. "Fair enough."

Cheyenne dug her fingers into the jar and twirled the thick, stretchy white goo around her hand. "You mind ripping that hole open a little more, though?"

"Sure." He leaned forward and gently peeled the singed fabric off her arm. Cheyenne gritted her teeth as he yanked once and widened the shredded hole. "Sorry."

"Don't be. That's just a warmup, right?" Her smile was tight and forced as she stared at the open wound, then she blew out a quick breath and went for it. Her arm burned worse than the tentacle when she smeared the salve across it. A growl escaped her, and she choked it back.

"It's cool, kid." Persh'al glanced around. "Nobody out here to hear you—"

"Fuck!" She hunched over her knees and clenched her eyes shut as the salve did its work patching up her arm. Tears squeezed out of her eyes, and she sucked in slow breath after slow breath through her nose. "This is taking forever."

"Nah. You'll be all right." She didn't fight him when he reached down to take the jar from her and screwed on the lid. "Just to keep this in one piece."

"Yep." The pain slowly died, and she took another deep breath before looking at the bluish-green sky. "The sun over here kinda looks the same."

"Two moons, though." He handed her the jar, which she shoved back into her pack before running a hand across her newly healed flesh. "We got a long way to go before we can stop again. You ready?"

"Yeah. Thanks." Cheyenne pushed to her feet and shrugged her backpack on again. Then she turned to take another look at the portal disguised as a cracked boulder. The scarred black earth stretched around them for miles, but a tall mountain range rose in the distance. "You sure this wasn't a desert?"

"Used to be a lake." Persh'al nodded, and she turned to follow him across the dry, shriveled ground. "Not much of anything left here now."

"This is the rot."

"What?"

Cheyenne shook her head. "Heard it in a prophecy. Something about cutting out the rot."

"Huh. Makes sense. I mean, either the lake caught fire, dried up instantly, and the flames ate away the bottom, or the life was taken right out of this place by something else."

"Something else like the Crown?"

"I wish I knew the answer to that one, kid. I'd say that's a pretty safe bet."

. . .

They walked across the charred lakebed for an hour before they reached the edge of the basin. After a steep climb up crumbling dirt and rock that broke away beneath their fingers, Persh'al dusted off his hands. "Been a while since I've hiked like that."

Cheyenne snorted. "That was pretty easy."

"Uh-huh. Your face says somethin' else."

She wiped at her forehead and flicked beads of sweat off her hand. "It's the middle of the day in what's basically a desert. And I'm wearing all black."

"You did that to yourself." With a crooked smile, he turned away from her and pointed down the other side of the elevated basin. A round dirty-brown dome rose from the sea of short, scrubby brown grass below them, with two smaller rectangular outbuildings on either side. "That's where we're headed first. Should be able to get something a little faster than our own two feet."

Cheyenne cocked her head. "I doubt that."

"Okay, faster than *my* two feet, halfling. Unless you wanna pick me up and run superspeed in no particular direction."

"I'm good."

"Then let's go."

The climb down the other side of the dry basin was a lot gentler and easier, though Cheyenne had to stop halfway to the bottom to take off her hoodie and stuff it in her backpack. The sound of metal banging on metal and magicals shouting at each other greeted them when they reached flat ground. When they got closer, half a dozen square huts came into view on the other side of the huge domed building. "You know what this place is?"

"It says it right there on the wall—oh." Persh'al chuckled and dropped his hand. "I keep forgetting you can't read this stuff. It's a waystation, more or less. And a small village, looks like."

"But you haven't been here before."

"When that desert was still a lake, kid, this valley down here was all farmland. I've been here before, but not like this."

The rectangular outbuildings were open at one end, and Cheyenne caught a glimpse of a huge ogre standing inside, smacking a huge wrench against a piece of machinery that looked like a small fishing boat hovering two feet off the ground. When he saw the drow and the blue troll approaching, he chucked the wrench into the machine and stared at them.

Two dirt-smeared goblins walked quickly between the dome and the second outbuilding on that side, dragging a rope net with a pile of metal boxes and machine parts behind them. They slowed down when they saw the two, and the goblin woman on the right frowned.

"Doesn't look like they're happy to see visitors," Cheyenne muttered.

"They probably aren't, but they'll do business." Persh'al pointed toward the door cut into the side of the dome. A short, grizzled orc with a long black braid spilling down his back shoved out the door just before they reached it and paused at the sight of them. His lips curled in a snarl before he stalked away, not bothering to hold the door. "Okay, hopefully they'll do business. Let me do the talking, and I'll take care of it."

"No problem."

Persh'al grabbed the handle and opened the door for them again, gesturing for Cheyenne to enter first. It was much darker and cooler inside, lit by small fist-sized lamps floating at different heights beneath the rounded ceiling. They passed a few crooked tables and wobbly chairs as they headed toward the horseshoe bar toward the back. Two of the tables were inhabited by other magicals, all of them dirt-stained, sweaty, and glaring at the unannounced visitors.

The goblin woman behind the bar was too busy polishing a metal canister with a dirty rag to look up at the newcomers. She squinted at the thing, rubbed it again, and nodded toward the array of items spread out on the bar beside her. "Look through all that first. New shipment just arrived, but I promise you it ain't fancy."

"We don't need anything fancy," Persh'al said. "Just looking for a working zip and some water. If you have any."

The goblin thunked the canister on the bar and looked up. Her eyes widened when she saw Cheyenne, and she set both hands down on the bar and leaned forward. "You sure about that?"

Persh'al asked, "Which part?"

"Any of it."

"Yeah, I'm sure." He removed his pack and set it at the edge of the bar. "We got a long way to go. Could use a little help."

"Help don't come cheap, troll." The goblin woman scratched her head, wiggling the ratted, dusty coils of yellow hair piled on it. She watched him dig into the front pocket of his pack, then glanced at Cheyenne. "But I bet both of yous know that already, doncha?"

Cheyenne stared right back at the goblin until the other magical sniffed and looked away. *What's that about?*

"Oh, sure." Persh'al pulled out a thick black case the size of Cheyenne's cell phone and popped it open. "Not fancy and not cheap. We're not picky, either."

The goblin's eyes widened when Persh'al flicked out a thin piece of blue-tinted plastic the same dimensions as the case and set it down on the bar. She licked her chapped lips and glanced at Persh'al, then leaned sideways and barked, "Cork! You got one of them skiffs up and runnin' yet?"

An orc sitting at one of the tables scratched his chin, flaking off a layer of dust crusted on his face. "Maybe."

The goblin woman raised her eyebrows at Persh'al and shrugged.

He swiped another thin card of blue plastic off the top of the stack in his black case and set it down on the first. "How 'bout now?"

"Yeah." She chuckled and slid both thin cards across the bar. "We got somethin' for yous. Still want that water?"

"As long as it won't kill us."

A wheezing laugh escaped her, exposing yellow-stained teeth. "You're in the Outers, *lugahw'o*. Anything could kill ya."

Persh'al rapped his knuckles on the bar and nodded after her. "Better make it two."

Cheyenne shot him a confused frown. "You're paying for water?"

He shrugged. "It's a start."

CHAPTER THIRTY-SIX

Cheyenne drained the last of what this place called water and dropped the copper cup on the table with a grimace. She swiped at her lips and pulled out grainy bits of sand and a blade of brown grass. "This is the best your plastic money could buy, huh?"

"It's a skyvein alloy, kid, not plastic. And I'm fairly sure this *is* the good water." Persh'al swirled the rest of his around in the cup and smacked his lips. "At least she didn't try to sell us grog instead."

"I guess." She glanced around the domed building, feeling the other magicals' eyes on her even before she met their gaze with a deadpan stare. "Feels *off* in here."

"Yep." He sat back in his chair and eyed the table of orcs across the room. "That's because you're here. Nothing personal."

"What?"

A dented metal chair scooted back across the floor, and an orc with a long, webbed scar covering one massive bicep lumbered toward them. He pulled out a chair at their table with one hand and guzzled sloppily from a cup in his other hand, then took a seat with the strangers. "Cork'll be out there fixin' yous up with that skiffer for a while yet. Don't get twitchy, nah."

Persh'al nodded. "We'll wait."

"Uh-huh. I see you do." The orc fixed his yellow eyes on Cheyenne and leaned forward over the table. "I ain't seen a *mór edhil* since I was a crawler, yeh. What you doin' all the way out the Outers?"

Cheyenne eyed his slowly growing sneer. *At least I understood most of that.*

Persh'al slapped the table and gestured toward the halfling. "This *mór edhil* wanted to see what was up is all. Help doesn't come cheap, isn't that it?"

The orc's eyes flickered toward him. "You take the *veréle* to rope this one all over no-land?"

"I'm not an idiot. I can buy enough sparking tech to last two lifetimes with what I'm making on this job."

Cheyenne folded her arms and stared at him. "It was that much, was it?"

He spread his arms with a crooked smile, and the orc burst out laughing.

"Oh, sure! This one knows empty holes 'bout how much is what, yeh." He pointed at Cheyenne with a grubby finger, the yellow nail chipped in two different places. "You ain't gettin' what's worth out here, nah. Nothin' but ground slop, life wets, and us *outernóre*. Payin' all the *veréle* for that. You won't be coughin' that out again."

I have no idea what that means.

The halfling cocked her head and shrugged. "Just something I wanted to try."

Persh'al smirked.

"Ha!" The orc let out a wheezing laugh before snatching up his copper mug and draining the last of whatever spilled out the sides of his mouth. "And then you skuttin' all back into big lights and power switches. Yeh. Cork'll have that skiffer ready real quick." He clicked his tongue, stood, and went right back to his table, shaking his bald head and chuckling.

Cheyenne leaned toward Persh'al and tried not to laugh. "I paid you a lot of money to be my guide out here, huh?"

"It makes sense, all right." He set his forearms on the table and leaned toward her too, lowering his voice. "Drow don't show up in the Outers as a general rule."

"Outers being way out in the middle of nowhere, I'm guessing."

"Yeah. This place, though," He glanced around the domed building and shook his head. "Last time I was here, this wasn't nearly so far out as it is now. I mean, farming was a decent way to keep a family and a village going. Plenty of business, plenty of travelers coming through. These magicals are scrappers. Scavenging most of their supplies, too, if I had to guess. Looks like the Outers have moved *inward*."

"Toward the Crown."

Persh'al nodded. "At the capital, yep. Which is where most drow pretty much converged at the turn of the new Cycle. New monarch, new dictatorship, new ruling class if we're talking about it in the simplest terms. So, you're playing the well-cultured city girl with a flair for the dramatic." He chuckled. "It's kind of a low blow for these guys, but it's the only story we have that makes sense."

Cheyenne glanced at the table of orcs, who burst into raucous laughter. "They think I paid you to show me around to look down at them from my high horse."

The troll scratched his chin, twisting his puckered lips to the side. "Pretty much."

"That sucks."

"It's what we're sticking with until we get into the bigger cities, all right? You won't be such a rare sight at that point, and then you can be whoever you wanna."

She sat back in her chair and nodded. "Sure. I mean, I know how to act like someone who's got a lot of money to toss around."

He hummed in amusement and shook his head. "You know how, but you don't walk that walk. Not Earthside, and I'm pretty sure you won't put that hat on even for an act."

"Is that a challenge, troll?" Cheyenne snorted.

"Hey, I've already been tossed around enough for one day, okay? Keep sittin' there looking slightly disdainful and aloof, and I think that'll work just fine."

The domed building's only door jerked open, spilling bright sunlight in a thick beam across the floor before a hulking shadow blocked it. "Oyup, Muhaya. Skiff's all buzz."

The goblin woman behind the bar nodded and pointed at Persh'al and Cheyenne. "Yous hear that, travelers? Cork's got your ride. Best get outta here before he breaks it down again."

They stood from the table, slinging their bags over their shoulders, and Persh'al nodded. "'Preciate it."

"And I appreciate your *veréle*, troll. You come back any time for bad water."

The orcs at the table chuckled as the strangers walked past them toward the open door. The one who'd asked about Cheyenne raised a hand and wiggled his thick fingers. "Race away, yeh, *mór edhil*. Have a good smile at the scrappy."

She jerked her chin up at him with a small smile, and the table exploded in rough laughter again.

The orc named Cork did hold the door open for them, then he grunted and nodded toward the outbuilding on their left. They followed him quickly, catching curious, wary glances from the other magicals living and working at the waystation, but no one else spoke to them.

When they passed the first open garage, the huge ogre inside snarled and shook his head before getting back to pounding on his project. Cork led them to the second outbuilding on that side and flicked his hand toward the closest wall. It crackled with a sputtering blue light and rolled up like a garage door before they all stepped inside the long, dark, rectangular space.

"This one." He smacked his hand on the side of a boat-looking vehicle with a metallic clang. The thing's hull was patched with different-colored sheets of metal, and it rested on a raised platform just inside the open door. "You know how to spark?"

Cheyenne glanced at Persh'al, who nodded slowly, the corners of his mouth turned down. "Oh, yeah. I'm not gonna turn that thing on in your shop, though."

Cork grunted out a laugh, exposing missing teeth. "You got more know than you show. Get out. I'll bring it."

Persh'al nodded for Cheyenne to follow him out of the garage, and they stood off to the side while Cork rubbed his hands vigorously. When he clapped them together, blue sparks shot out between his palms. He climbed over the side of the skiff, setting the whole thing wobbling on the platform as he sat. Then he set both glowing blue hands on the control panel at the front, and the vehicle flared to life with a low hum. It lifted a foot off the platform and jerked forward, bouncing out of the garage but still hovering a foot off the ground.

When the orc jumped out again, he was grinning. "Good enough."

Persh'al chuckled. "Good enough, *outernóre.*"

They shook hands briefly and Cork sniffed, swiping under his nose with a meaty gray-green forearm.

Cheyenne looked away from the hovering machine and nodded at him. "Thanks."

His yellow eyes narrowed and he cocked his head, looking her up and down. Then he snorted and waved her off. "You ain't pullin' that out here. Don't roll, nah."

"We won't." Persh'al stepped toward the hovering skiff as the orc walked away. Cork glanced at them over his shoulder and scoffed, muttering under his breath on his way back to the domed building.

Cheyenne gestured after him. "He didn't think I meant that, did he?"

"Not a lotta drow say thank you, kid." Persh'al shrugged out of his pack and tossed it into the back of the skiff. "Out here, manners are pretty much a joke."

"Fine. I'll just be an asshole, then."

"Yeah, that might be the best way to keep anyone from getting too suspicious. Hop in."

She slung her backpack into the back beside his, then climbed over the rounded lip of the hull and stared down at the bench crossing the front of the skiff. "Does it matter where I sit?"

"Nope. No driver's seats, no roads, no wrong side of the lane. Just sit."

Cheyenne sat where she was on the right-hand side, and Persh'al crossed the front of the skiff, chuckling.

"You look like you're about to jump out and run away, kid."

She snorted. "I do not."

He hopped over the side, settled down next to her on the bench, and scooted two inches away from her when she stared at the pant legs almost touching hers. "First taste of O'gúl tech for ya. Keep in mind, this humming beast we're sittin' in isn't even halfway to state-of-the-art, but she's purring, all right."

"And hovering."

"Yeah." Persh'al studied the control panel covered in O'gúl symbols, half of which had either faded from the metal surface or been scrubbed off.

"Is that the magic part or the tech part?" Cheyenne squinted and peered at the controls, which didn't include a steering wheel, a lever, or even a joystick.

The troll grinned at her and nodded. "Both. I'd say buckle up, but our friend Cork apparently isn't too concerned with safety. So brace yourself."

She gripped the side of the hull and shoved her feet against the front wall of the skiff beneath the dash. "If you throw me out of this thing—"

"If I throw you out, I'm throwing myself out too." Persh'al laughed and lifted his hand over the dash. "Damn, it's been a long time."

Green light flared across his palms and pulsed around his fingers. He lowered them both onto the dash and stared straight ahead. The skiff rose another six inches from the ground and added a high-pitched whine to the low hum of its magical generator, but that was it.

"Huh. These *outernóre* don't know shit about steering." The troll shifted one hand a quarter of an inch to the left and let off another pulse of green light. The skiff turned slowly to the left, aiming away from the garage and the other buildings of the waystation to face the hill they'd descended from the dry basin. "Now we're talking. It's like riding a bike, kid. Just takes a bit of—"

The skiff lurched forward and raced toward the hillside. Cheyenne grabbed the underside of the control panel to keep from flying backward, and Persh'al let out an excited whoop, then started laughing again.

"How the hell do you steer this thing?" she shouted over the rumbling drone of the engine. Or generator? Power source?

"Like puttin' one foot in front of the other!" He slid a finger down the panel's smooth metal surface, then swiped it to the right. The skiff banked away from the hill, spewing up a spray of dirt and sand and dry grass ripped from the ground. Then they were tearing across the flat expanse of dead ground past the waystation, heading away from the blackened, dried-up lakebed and toward O'gúleesh civilization.

Cheyenne squinted against the wind buffeting her face. Her white hair streamed behind her, and she turned to look at Persh'al when she felt him staring at her.

"You look as insane as L'zar right now."

"Ha." The troll grinned. "Maybe I am, kid. Feels damn good to be back behind the wheel of something I understand."

She grinned and gazed out over the brown grassland as they zipped across it through the Outers of Ambar'ogúl. "There *is* no wheel."

"I know!"

CHAPTER THIRTY-SEVEN

They raced across the flat, lifeless plain for another hour before the landscape changed. A huge mountain range curved toward them from the left, then another from the right until they were funneled into a pass twenty feet wide carved between the rocky ledges. Persh'al slowed the skiff to a safer speed once they reached the pass, and Cheyenne studied the high, jagged cliffs on either side of them.

At least there aren't any faces trying to break through these.

Persh'al stared straight ahead, his eyes narrowed in determination as his mohawk fluttered in the air. "Once we get through this, we'll be in the Oronti Valley. We'll see things start to change once we get there. The rest of this? This isn't the real Ambar'ogúl, not the way I know it. Trust me."

Cheyenne frowned. "Oronti Valley?"

"Yeah." He looked at her and raised his eyebrows. "You've heard of it, huh?"

"Yeah. I'm not sure it's like you remember it."

"What makes you say that?"

She shook her head and watched the end of the pass growing steadily closer. "Some old neighbors of mine used to live there. A troll family with a young kid."

"Oh, nice. Represent." Persh'al thumped a fist against his chest and chuckled.

"They made the crossing, obviously. Because of what happened to the valley."

His smile faded, and he looked away from her for two seconds before quickly returning his gaze. "Were they farmers?"

"I think so. Maybe *radan* herders?"

"Oh, I see." The troll shot her a crooked smile and shrugged, his confidence restored as he returned his attention to the end of the pass. "I wouldn't put too much stock in stories from the Oronti Valley villagers, kid. The *outernóre* like to make fun of everybody right to our faces. Farmers and herders? They embellish stuff. Like, a lot. We have a saying where I come from: 'The Crown takes a shit, and the farmers saw her fly off on a dragon.'" He burst out laughing and slapped a hand down on the control panel. The skiff skittered sideways, and he instantly readjusted with a muttered curse.

"Who's 'we' in that scenario?"

"Huh?"

"You said 'we' and 'where you come from.'" Cheyenne fought back a laugh when she looked at his startled, confused expression. "Who else uses that saying?"

"Shit, kid." Persh'al rubbed his head and slumped his shoulders. "Okay, maybe it's only been passed around as a joke. An inside joke."

"Yeah?"

"Okay, between me and myself. Are you happy now?" He shot her a sidelong glance. "How do you *do* that?"

"I just asked some questions, man. The rest was all you." The smile broke free on her lips. "You probably don't hold up very well under interrogation, do you?"

"Depends on what kind." Leaning away from her, Persh'al stared down the quickly shortening pass in front of them. "Apparently, I'm a sucker under drow questioning. But let me tell you, I can take a beating and keep my mouth shut. I've done it before, and I've still got it. If that's what you're worried about, you shouldn't be."

Taking a deep breath, Cheyenne readjusted her position on the hard bench beneath her and glanced up at the cliff walls racing past them. *If I'd forgotten why we're here, he just handed me a fucked-up reminder.* "That won't be something we have to worry about. That's why we came here, right? So I can see what I need to see before L'zar crosses with me next time and we put an end to all this? The war. The rot coming through the portals. Having to take a beating and keep our mouths shut."

The troll wrinkled his nose. "That's the goal, sure. No guarantees in this game, though, kid. L'zar knew that when he started this whole thing. Damn drow acts like he has all the answers to the universe, but he's always filtering what he can't control into the equation. Sometimes, shit goes bad."

"Yeah, I've noticed." Cheyenne lifted one shoulder in a half-hearted shrug. "I guess what matters is how often it goes bad, right?"

"Sure. That's a good way of looking at it."

"So." She rested her forearms on her thighs and leaned forward. "How often does shit go bad for L'zar Verdys and his band of rebel O'gúleesh?"

Persh'al snorted. "You need to trademark that."

"I'm serious."

His smile disappeared as he shot her a quick look. "Yeah, you got your serious face on and everything. Honestly, kid, the last seventy-five years have been the quietest. Still some bumps in the road, but nothing we couldn't handle as soon as we hit 'em."

"So you're saying it's pretty smooth sailing as long as he's behind bars."

"I didn't—" The troll shook his head and stared straight ahead. "You and your questions."

"That's what I thought."

"Okay, look. He's a crazy dude. I'll give you that. Maybe not clinically insane, but he's got his moments. For as much of a pain in the ass as your father is, the rest of us wouldn't have walked through fellfire and back for him if we didn't believe in what he's doing."

Cheyenne straightened and rubbed her thighs. "I heard L'zar doesn't care about anything or anyone unless there's something in it for him."

"Who told you that?"

"Corian."

Persh'al hissed out a breath in a mix of surprise and amusement. "Straight from the nightstalker's mouth. I wouldn't call Corian a liar, but I wouldn't call L'zar a tyrant gorging himself on the subjects he's supposed to be protecting either."

"Kinda hard to do when he doesn't have any subjects."

Persh'al shot her a quick glance and jerked his head forward again. "No, he doesn't. But that's what the Crown is doing, and those of us who are fed up with her bullshit and want to see something better for all O'gúleesh are willing to put up with L'zar's less than perfect qualities. There's no doubt in my mind that he'll get us to where we wanna be, especially now that you're in the picture."

"Well, I don't have any subjects, either."

"You're somethin', kid. I tell you what." The troll snorted and shook his head. His face lit up as they reached the end of the pass. "Now, *this* is what you want to…"

The skiff dropped softly down the incline when they emerged from the pass, carrying them swiftly over the rock-strewn hill at the base of the mountains. The Oronti Valley stretched out in front of them in gently rolling hills.

That's the only gentle part of this whole place.

The travelers stared at the wasteland studded with dilapidated or ruined buildings. On their left, a dead forest reached toward them from the curving mountain range, the trees bare and gnarled. Most of them had fallen over or broken in bent, twisted fragments. Some patches still had their leaves, but they were few and colored a grotesque black-tinged yellow. Some of the trunks oozed a thick, noxious yellow substance that made Cheyenne think of an infected sore. Some of the grass had returned to the valley, but it was brown—white in some places—and untouched by working hands for a long time.

"No." Persh'al blinked and scanned the destroyed land. "This too?"

"If farmers are known for embellishing stories, I'm guessing it wasn't this bad a year ago."

"A year?" The troll gave her a blank look, reeling from the realization that he'd been wrong about what they'd find here.

"That troll family." Cheyenne frowned at the devastation. "They said they were driven out of their home and made the crossing a year ago.

The *radan* disappeared, and things got bleak. They didn't give me specifics, but I'm sure they would have mentioned something like this."

Persh'al muttered something and shook his head. "In just a year Earthside."

"Is time different over here?"

"Not that different, kid."

The skiff skimmed above the broken land, sending small, unseen creatures skittering through the long white-brown grass in their wake. Persh'al took them to the right and toward a thicker forest that didn't look nearly as bad as the first. However, the closer they got, the more wrong everything felt.

The trees still had their leaves, but they pulsed with dark light like a heartbeat. So did the trunks and the roots that had pulled up out of the ground, as if they were trying to remove themselves from the source of the sickness. Persh'al slowed the skiff to a crawl, and the air around them filled with a wet, slurping sound, almost in perfect sync with the sickly pulsing of the trees.

"That's a river, right?" Cheyenne pointed through the forest at the slowly moving surface of shimmering black liquid. Where the river broke over protruding rocks, green foam built up around the obstacles, some of it trailing downstream.

"Not anymore." Persh'al pressed his lips together and took them along the edge of the forest—close enough to see what it had become, but not too close. "I can't believe this. Things have been bad enough to send refugees across the Border, but I haven't heard anything about whatever this is."

"It's happening too fast." The halfling's nostrils flared when the scent of rotting meat wafted toward them on a cool, slightly humid breeze. *That's the opposite of refreshing.*

"Must be. I've never seen a change like this happen so quickly."

A huge dark shape lumbered away from the riverbank ahead of them. Persh'al moved the skiff out of the way to avoid the thing, groaning when they got close enough to see what it was.

The animal looked like a cross between a cow and a buffalo, with a gigantic rack of black antlers growing from its skull. The antlers were twisted and misshapen, ballooning into clubs in the middle and at the end, and they weighed the creature's head down on one side so that it moved with its head perpetually twisted. The thing snorted when they passed, staring at them with three glassy black eyes and a fourth as disgustingly yellow as the sludge oozing from the other forest across the valley. A fifth limb protruded from its chest, dangling there without muscle or bone to give it purpose.

"Shit." Persh'al ran a hand down his cheek and turned the skiff away from the tree line and back out into the valley's open brown grass.

Cheyenne couldn't help but look over her shoulder at the mutated creature. Two smaller beasts with blood-red snouts and what looked like claws instead of antlers sprouting from their heads stepped up behind the huge male. "Please tell me those aren't the *radan* my neighbors were so nostalgic about."

"Those aren't *radan*." Swallowing thickly, Persh'al clenched his jaw and dropped both hands in his lap, letting the skiff take them where it would across the abandoned valley. "Mutated, sure, but I'd go so far as to say they don't even have half of the original makeup anymore."

"Nothing mutates that quickly."

"Nope. Not even in a world where magic is the norm, kid. Fuck with genetic code in nature, and you're way outside the realm of magic the way it's meant to be used."

Cheyenne nodded. "So, things are bad."

"Right now, I'm okay with that understatement."

They approached a group of buildings barely hanging on to their frames. The roofs had crumbled in, doors broken, rubble strewn all over the place. The fence posts of what had once been livestock pens and stables were splintered and hanging sideways as if the animals had known what was happening and tried to outrun it.

Persh'al slowed the skiff again when they got closer, and they saw the bodies—four of them tossed against each other, purple skin and scarlet hair fluttering in the reeking wind. "Shit. These magicals were still living out here."

"Until not that long ago." Cheyenne scanned the wreckage of the half-dozen buildings forming a semi-circle beside them. "Looks like somebody came through and tore everything apart."

"Yep. So, this is the new normal out here, huh? The Oronti Valley reduced to this farm and the other four we saw?"

"Didn't get close enough to see what was left."

Persh'al returned his hands to the control panel and scowled. "Yeah. I think we've seen enough of this one too."

The skiff's low hum stopped, let out a metallic screech, and sputtered out.

"What?" The troll ran his hand over the panel, bringing that green light to his fingers again, but the controls didn't respond. The skiff slowed to a stop and came in for a smooth landing on the long grass three yards from the last outbuilding and fell silent. "Dammit. That orc took my *veréle* and gave us half of what we paid for."

"What's wrong?"

"That's what I gotta check?" With a growl of frustration, Persh'al leaped over the side of the skiff and stepped around the hull toward the back. He pressed a button on the side panel, which clicked in protest and didn't budge until he kicked it open and got to work.

CHAPTER THIRTY-EIGHT

C heyenne stood and got out of the skiff, gazing around the empty valley. "The thing picked a great place to break down."

"Nah, we're all right." The troll squatted, grunted, and rummaged around inside the open panel. "I mean, yeah, I wanna get out of here ASAP, but we're on our own. Don't worry, kid. I just need to tighten this—"

A piece of metal snapped, wires sputtered, and pieces clanged around in the mechanical opening.

"Tighten it, huh?"

Persh'al chucked the broken piece onto the grass. "Too tight for these useless pieces. That's what I get for buying from a bunch of scrappers. I'm honestly amazed it got us this far, and it's crap without that part. So..." He stood, dusted off his pants, and spread his arms. "You can hike, right?"

"Across an open valley? Sure."

"Great." The troll bent over the back of the dead skiff and pulled on his bulging pack. The strap caught on something underneath, and he fought to free it.

A crunch of broken wood and the rustle of dry grass reached Cheyenne's ears, and she turned slowly toward the outbuildings. *That's not just the wind.*

"Hey, kid. Wanna take a look in here and see what I'm missing? I can't get this—"

"Shh." She hushed him so softly, she thought he might not have heard. Another soft rustle of grass pressing against the earth reached her, and she scanned the space between the buildings, searching for movement.

Persh'al glanced at her and slowly straightened. "Not all alone, are we?" he whispered.

Cheyenne slowly shook her head and leaned sideways, waiting for the next slow footstep.

The wall of the building in front of her shattered when a sizzling yellow ball of magic crashed through the rotting slats. She ducked and caught a glimpse of two narrowed yellow eyes through the hole in the wall before a bolt of bright orange whizzed over Persh'al's head. He leaped aside and whirled, flicking his wrist to summon the sparking green whip.

Someone let out a raw, warbling battle roar, and four magicals barreled toward Cheyenne and Persh'al from between the buildings—two orcs, a troll who barely looked old enough to call himself full-grown, and a skinny yellow-green magical barely four feet tall with pointed ears and yellow fangs.

The yellow guy screamed and slashed his hand through the air as he darted toward Cheyenne. She lashed out with her black tendrils, curling them around his arm to toss him away from her. A bright yellow dart shot down at her from the sky and barely missed her hand. "What the—"

A rusty, dirt-coated orb bobbed in the air six feet above her, its multiple layers spinning in opposite directions. The gangly yellow magical slid across the dirt where she'd tossed him and motioned again with a flick of his wrist. The floating orb darted behind Cheyenne and blasted her with another dart as the magical shot yellow sparks at her head.

The halfling raised a shield in front of her and turned to launch her purple sparks at the floating orb. They crackled against the metal ball, which let out a shrieking whine and dropped to the ground, covered in purple light.

The yellow magical screamed again and leaped to his feet. "Get your own, *mór edhil!*"

"What?"

One of the orcs crashed into the side of the building in front of Persh'al with a grunt, then pushed away and kicked at nothing but air. The ground erupted in front of Persh'al, and a steel plate rose and jerked toward him. The troll leaped aside and cracked his whip at the flying saucer-thing, sending it right back at its owner like a frisbee.

The troll kid whipped around the buildings, tossing disks of light and riding another sheet of metal that clicked and squeaked.

Cheyenne spun and watched him sail past her. *Kid's got a hoverboard. What is this?*

The disks of blue light sailed over her head when she ducked and buried themselves in the wood of the shed. The kid veered back around to head toward her and pulled more disks out of a pouch to get in more target practice. His first projectiles pulled themselves out of the wood to join the others, and eight flashing disks sailed toward Cheyenne, spinning and whirring.

She raised a shield at the last second, and the slicing metal pinged against the black surface. Then she leaped aside and sent two churning black orbs into the disks, catching six of them at once. They split in half, while the other two changed course to head for Persh'al, and Cheyenne heard the hum of the kid's hoverboard behind her seconds before he leaped from the thing and knocked her to the ground.

With a shout, she pushed the kid off and wrapped him in her black tendrils. He struggled violently, kicking and bucking on the ground as she held him in place. "Cut it out, kid! What are you doing?"

"Go feed off the Mother's tit, yeh," he spat. "She got lots more for her *mór edhil* spawn!"

"Cheyenne!" Persh'al blasted the second orc back with a bolt of green light, then sent his whip after the two disks racing toward him. He only got one, and Cheyenne slipped into drow speed.

The second disk slowed inches from his nose, spinning in suspension and pulsing with blue sparks shooting from the center out to the razor-sharp edge. She released one handful of her tendrils from around the tied-up troll and reached out to grab the disk. It buzzed briefly between her fingers and shuddered.

When she slipped back into normal time, the troll was expecting to see her forehead split by his metal weapon. Instead, he saw her raise the disk in one hand and crush it. Metal shards and hair-thin wires flew out around them, peppering the kid's face. "Bitch!"

"Hold that thought." Cheyenne kept him there, wrapped in her tendrils, and launched a volley of purple sparks at the weird yellow guy leaping at her on all fours. Her attack caught him in the shoulder, and he spun out of the air. Screaming, the yellow magical shot both hands toward her, and a spray of metal darts burst not from his hands but from somewhere up his tattered, dirt-crusted sleeves.

She leaped aside and released the kid from her coiled black whips. He spun into the air and raced toward her at the wrong moment. The dozen metal darts from his yellow-skinned friend pierced his back and sent him to the ground, his scarlet eyes wide with pain and disbelief.

"Urae!" The yellow magical snarled and focused on Cheyenne again. "Always *takin'*. We'll take back!"

He lunged at her, and Cheyenne lifted a shield. The yellow magical smacked into the shimmering black surface with a clang, his long, dirt-smeared face smashing against it at the same moment that Persh'al's next attack hit him square in the back. The sandwiched magical slid down Cheyenne's shield before dropping to the ground, and she stepped back to search for the next attack.

None came.

"Damn." Persh'al opened his hand. The green whip disappeared, and he took a step back to eye the two orcs he'd taken down. One of them had gotten his own flying metal plate stuck in his neck, and the other had been tossed head-first into the next building over, everything below the waist dangling out of the hole made by his head and shoulders. He grunted, kicked once to find the ground too far beneath him, and passed out.

"Oh, man." Cheyenne stepped toward the troll kid lying on his side, scarlet eyes still open in surprise and a dozen points of steel protruding from his chest. "I threw him out of the way, and he just kept coming."

"Not your fault, Cheyenne."

She grimaced and shook her head. "Yeah, but I was part of it."

"Sure. Attacked by a tiny group of desperate raiders who relied way too much on broken tech and had no idea how to fight together."

Persh'al rolled the short-circuited metal ball beneath his shoe. "Junk. That's what they're puttin' their faith in these days."

Cheyenne pulled herself away from the troll kid's dead eyes and turned. "Fighting with machines. So, that's a thing for everyone on this side, not just the loyalists and their shipped crates?"

"Oh, yeah. This is newer tech, but it worked like shit 'cause they treated it like shit. Looks cobbled together, too. They'd be better off if they learned how to fight without it. Come on. We'll leave the other two to wake up on their own, but we should hurry." He stopped by their failed skiff and grabbed his pack, snorting when it lifted freely this time.

Cheyenne grabbed hers and headed past the small farm but stopped when he whistled. "I thought we were going that way."

"We are. With that much gear on them, I seriously doubt these guys walked all the way out here on their own. If they have a skiff or a shuttle or hell, even extra hoverboards, we could use 'em."

The halfling followed him around the outside of the buildings arranged in a horseshoe. The four raiders had built a camp here after going through everything the troll family had and chucking it into piles. Two skiffs were pulled up along one side of the farthest building, and Persh'al turned away from the closest one with another low whistle. "They've been out here a while."

Rubbing his hands together, he summoned the green light between his palms and cautiously set them down on the dented skiff's control panel. The thing popped and let out a growling cough, then hummed to life and lifted two feet off the ground.

"Excellent." Persh'al heaved a massive burlap sack out of the back of the skiff and threw it as far as he could. The top burst open with a puff of black dust and what might have been carrion flies.

"Jeeze." Cheyenne scowled and breathed through her mouth. "They've been riding around with a dead body in the back seat?"

"Not a dead magical. Definitely at least one rotting corpse of *something* in there." With a grimace, he slung his pack into the back and climbed in. "Come on, kid. We've got places to see. I honestly don't know who we'll find. We'll play that by ear."

The halfling turned toward the last two breathing raiders and shook her head. "We can't steal their skiff and leave them out here."

"*Oh*, yes, we can." Persh'al patted the bench beside him, glanced at his hand, and wiped it off on his pants. "*They* attacked *us*, and they wouldn't hesitate to steal all our stuff and leave us here if the roles were reversed. Only difference is, they'd slit our throats while we were unconscious just for fun, and who knows what else. I've seen raiders and scrappers do nasty shit to anyone who gets in their way."

She shrugged. "Still."

"Hey, two of them got taken out, one by the skinny-ass gremlin and the other by his own gear. That leaves two raiders and one skiff. They'll be fine. Let's go."

Cheyenne eyed the last skiff and pressed her lips together. *Valid points. Fine.*

She dropped her backpack beside his and climbed over the edge. Persh'al studied the control panel, which had even fewer symbols to help him steer. He hummed in indecision, then pressed both hands down on the metal, and they took off at a slow but steady pace toward the other side of the Oronti Valley.

"What is that, anyway?" Cheyenne nodded at the control panel.

"There are many possible answers for that, kid."

"I mean, what you did with your hands? What those guys back there did. All the gestures and whatever. Are those spells that work with the tech or what?"

"Uh, sometimes." Persh'al chuckled and lifted his hands to peer at the mostly unmarked panel. "If you know your gear, you don't need any help. It melds with your magic and is basically like a projection of yourself. Most magicals don't get that far, especially out here. No training and no time to improve when you're desperate for an extra boost to take whatever you can get. I'm sure our little surprise party had a few other pieces strapped on 'em somewhere. Personally synced, right?"

"So, anyone can do it."

"Sure! Anyone with magic." He turned to see the halfling studying the control panel and the soft glow emanating from between the poorly welded seams. "Think you found a new hobby?"

Cheyenne shot him a blank stare before returning her attention to the edge of the valley. "I just wanna know how this works."

"Uh-huh. I know the feeling. Kinda itches, doesn't it?" The troll chuckled and stuck his hands in his lap as the skiff soared across the dry grass. "I'll tell you what. When we get to the city, I'll find you some toys."

The corner of her mouth twitched. "You can stop trying to turn this into a kiddie field trip. I'm fairly sure we're past that point."

"Very funny. We can call it gear or tech or whatever, but I'm talkin' about the good stuff. The finely tuned artistry of cutting-edge O'gúleesh tech. My fingers are tingling just thinking about it." Persh'al wiggled his fingers at her, and she swatted them away with a snort.

"Well, keep your tingly fingers to yourself. Just so we're clear, this hovering fishing boat isn't considered cutting-edge, right?"

He shot her a sly smile. "Not even close."

CHAPTER THIRTY-NINE

The farther they traveled away from the Border portal in the Outers and, "In toward civilization," as Persh'al called it, the healthier the land became. On the other side of the Oronti Valley and through another gently sloping mountain pass was another thin forest. Most of its trees were dead or dying, but there was new growth underneath, and what little wildlife they saw looked less affected by the blight than that mutated creature.

"That troll kid," Cheyenne said as the skiff took them around a village with living, breathing, working magicals going about their business. "He called me the same thing: *mór edhil.*"

"An old word for drow, kid. Spit in your face in some circles, muttered while groveling at your feet in others."

"Okay." *Neither of those things seems like a fun way to have a conversation.* "He said some weird stuff when I had him pinned down. That I just keep taking."

"He wasn't talking about you specifically. He doesn't even know you." Persh'al gave her a reassuring smile, and she rolled her eyes.

"Trust me, I knew it was an insult. I've got thicker skin than that. But everyone out here thinks the same thing about the drow— that they just keep taking."

The troll scratched the back of his head. His mohawk, having lost most of its rigidity, was now flopping down the back of his neck. "Well, yeah. Didn't used to be that way."

"New Cycle. New Crown."

"You said it, kid. What else did he say?"

She wanted to laugh, but the image of the troll kid's vacant eyes staring at the grass by his head made that impossible. "Something about sucking on my mother's tit or whatever."

Persh'al barked out a laugh. "Not *your* mother. *The* Mother. Capital M. It's an old word for the Crown, who clearly weren't always such heartless, bloodthirsty assholes. I mean, there's a certain level of it that comes with being a drow. That's just how it goes. But the old Cycles produced saints compared to this bitch on the throne. No, this one *eats* her children."

"Not literally."

He shrugged. "I wouldn't put it past her. That troll kid was just spittin' venom 'cause that's all he knows. The Crown's been fucking up Ambar'ogúl for centuries, obviously, but she still favors the other drow over the rest of them."

"Doesn't sound like it when she cut down all the Nimlothar and forced everybody to pass their trials in her own private arena."

"I said she favors them, not that she's nice to them."

Cheyenne shook her head and watched the rolling landscape around them. They passed a paddock with a herd of what looked like fluffy miniature giraffes, and Persh'al steered the skiff around a copse of trees beside a much smaller river. "Looks like the water's getting better too."

A round creature on three spindly legs stood like a stork at the edge of the river. The minute its elephantine trunk touched the surface, a red flash of light raced up its snout and across its back. The thing shrieked and ran down the riverbank before disappearing around tall, thorny bushes with tiny orange flowers.

Persh'al blinked. "Mostly, yeah. Drinking that goo in the Oronti Valley would've killed that thing."

"It didn't kill the mutant *radan*."

"No, that furball on stilts wasn't a mutant. *Carako*. They're a real pain in the ass if you're trying to keep wildlife out of your sheds and stables. They can change the length of their legs pretty much at will."

Cheyenne couldn't help but laugh at the image. "The water's gotta be clean somewhere if that thing's still running around like normal. And the villages look like they're keeping things going."

"I know." The troll stroked his hairless chin and looked over his shoulder at the last circle of gathered huts they'd passed. "That's the interesting part."

"You think that's on purpose?"

He gave her an appraising look and slid his finger slowly across the panel to take the skiff around a tall outcropping of moss-covered rock. "Do *you?*"

"Kind of." Cheyenne folded her arms and couldn't help but look at the thick silver cuff around her wrist next to her wrapped chains. "If everything looked like the Oronti Valley, or even all black and dead like the lake, I wouldn't think twice about it. The plague or whatever seeping out of this world and trying to break out through the portals."

Persh'al nodded, watching her with a crooked smile. "Keep going."

"The Crown's the one fucking things up. Usually the source of infection starts at one point and spreads." She spread her fingers and held them out in front of her, trying to find the piece she was missing. "But the part that's spreading here didn't start out at the lake. Everything looks less sick and more normal the closer we get to the drow who's supposed to be doing all the damage."

"There it is." Persh'al thumped a fist on his thigh. "That's the interesting part. And I'm willing to bet that's what most O'gúleesh haven't wrapped their heads around yet. Either that or they're not willing to look at it."

Cheyenne shrugged and stared at a passing herd of ostrich-looking birds with antlers growing out of their backs instead of wings. "You sound like you have a theory about why that's happening."

"That's because I do. I've had a feeling about it for a while. I've heard so many stories from Earthside magicals who made the crossing for the same reason. Just like your neighbor friends, yeah? This inner ring of normalcy is part of the Crown's game, that's what I think. Whatever she's cooking up on her damn pedestal is eating away at everything, and she's tapping into more energy than she should be to keep the little pocket around her sparkly clean. To keep the O'gúleesh close and fat and happy so they don't go wandering around and stumble over what she's causing."

"Like an illusion spell?" Cheyenne frowned at the field they crossed, which was green this time and dotted with purple and yellow flowers pulsing with soft light. "That's a huge illusion."

"Not nearly as big as the one she's casting up here." Persh'al tapped his temple. "My guess is she's feeding on energy that doesn't belong to her. Taking it from Ambar'ogúl itself, starting with the Nimlothar, most likely, then everything else. Hell, I wouldn't be surprised if she was taking it from magicals. And where's it all going? To her. Most of it. The rest is filtered back into some very strategic places. Keep this little belt around her city well enough to convince anyone who comes this far out that there's nothing to worry about, and keep the inner city too good to leave, so no one comes this far out."

The halfling frowned. "That sounds like way too much work."

The troll's chuckle was devoid of humor. "Never underestimate what a drow will do to get what they want. Especially this one."

"She's already ruling the entire world, isn't she? What else *could* she want?"

Persh'al shrugged. "More power. More control. To live forever and hold onto those things forever. What else is worth doing all this? Man, it would be hard enough having to run Ambar'ogúl. I mean, sure, there are other rulers, but they're spread out trying to take care of their own little piece of the pie. She's trying to take the whole thing."

Cheyenne ran a hand through her hair. "That's the most anybody's told me about what's going on over here."

"Well, hey. You're here, I'm here, and Corian and L'zar stayed the hell back from this one. Personally, I've never been a big fan of keeping things all hush-hush and super-secretive, tiptoeing everywhere."

"No, you just sit behind a monitor and dig into people's lives."

Persh'al laughed. "So do you."

"Got me." Cheyenne glanced at the silver cuff again and frowned. "If this is what we're up against, I'm not sure half a dozen rebels are gonna do much to change anything."

"Yeah, take that doubt and shove it up your ass, kid."

She chuckled.

"It's not just half a dozen of us. There are way more than you think, Earthside *and* right here in the place that's too messed up for us to call it home anymore. And I already told you." He shot her a sidelong glance and raised his eyebrows. "Never underestimate what a drow's willing to do to get what they want. There's a reason the Crown didn't want you to pass your trials and a damn good reason why she wants L'zar out of the picture."

"Because he's a crazy, selfish, buzzing fly in her ear?"

"Something like that."

An hour later, they stopped at the first real town. Low steel buildings extended in two long rows, with a wide avenue between them. Magicals moved between the buildings, stopping to talk or fight, going about their business. Persh'al slowed the skiff down at the edge of a four-foot steel wall around the two-mile perimeter of the town and hopped out. "You hungry?"

"Oh, yeah. Totally." Cheyenne stared at him. "All the mutant animals and the dead bodies really worked up my appetite."

"Yeah, I bet. When was the last time you ate?"

She squinted at the metal wall. "Okay, fine, but I don't want any of that glowing blue veggie-fruit stuff."

He chuckled. "What?"

"With the tentacles. It was in a salad."

"Okay, kid. Whatever you think you've had from here isn't what you're gonna find in a place with more tech than magic."

"And that's here, huh?"

"Eh. I'd call this half and half." He kicked the side panel of the deactivated skiff and bent over to unscrew something from inside. Waving the thin black tube at her, he nodded, then stuck the piece in his pocket. "Junker like this doesn't come with owner recognition, so we take the keys."

"Great."

"I'm serious. We're getting closer to a hell of a lot more magicals all squashed into one place. The only time I wanna walk after this is once we reach the capital. Come on."

After they grabbed their packs, Cheyenne followed him toward the gate in the metal wall. A blue light blinked in the center of the gate, then a round hole opened in the metal and launched a ball of blue fire at them.

Cheyenne stepped back, and Persh'al chuckled. "They're checkin' for warrants, kid. You don't have an APB out on you in Groulco or Kur Vróst, do ya?"

She raised an eyebrow and stared at his goofy smile. "Several. I'm surprised you haven't heard."

He ignored the sarcasm and stepped toward the stream of blue flames. "Look, swipe your hand through it like this. It won't burn ya. And then we'll be all in the clear to—"

The blue flames switched to orange in an instant, and the gate let out a high-pitched whoop. The top of the wall opened, and two levers unfolded to extend long rods down toward the startled troll before small round beads gathered at the tips like flower petals.

"Are you kidding me?" The beads flashed orange, and Persh'al raised both hands in surrender. "All right. Stand down, man. Damn. I'm walkin'."

A slow, rumbling chuckle came from the other side of the wall, and the troll shook his head as he returned to the skiff.

"What just happened?" Cheyenne followed him, glancing back at the extended rods and the orange beads that seemed to be following them.

"Warrants." Persh'al slammed his hands down on the skiff's panel, which lit up and rose again before he jumped over the side.

"Oh, *you* have warrants." The halfling climbed onto the bench beside him and dropped her pack in the back. "Was it Groulco or Kur Vróst?"

He glanced at her but had to look away again as he muttered, "Both."

Cheyenne barked a laugh and turned to look at the levers hanging over the wall. "And you just set off the alarm."

"It'll be a lot more than that if we don't get outta here. Dammit. I didn't even think to look for those."

"Hey, don't beat yourself up. I'm sure it's easy to forget you're a wanted troll somewhere."

"Damn right, it's easy to forget." He flicked the control panel, and they lurched away from the metal wall to keep heading inward. "It's been almost two thousand years, and I even checked the system before we…oh."

"Let me guess. Warrants stuck in the old system."

Persh'al slowly turned his head to look at her, his orange eyes widening. "You unlock mind-reading before you opened that puzzle box?"

"That would've been helpful, but no. I did the same thing a few years ago too. Made changes in someone else's system and failed to look for the old backups from before the updates. Barely got outta that one alive."

"Well, trust me, I'll be fixing that little issue." He turned and flipped the bird at the metal levers, which folded back in on themselves as the skiff sped away from the wall. "Shitty town anyway."

CHAPTER FORTY

They passed half a dozen other towns that were clustered together and larger the closer they got to the capital. Other hovering vehicles raced past them in both directions without roads or signs or any form of directing traffic.

The hills became steeper, dotted with patches of trees and late-blooming wildflowers. The skiff struggled up the next hill, and Persh'al gave it another little jolt of magic fuel to get up the rest of the incline. When they reached the top, Cheyenne's jaw dropped.

The city stretching below them looked remarkably like the New York skyline built three times as high—rising skyscrapers and towers, most of them connected by open walkways at every level. Hovering crafts darted around the lower levels, and smaller, faster vehicles whizzed through the air around the towers. *No planes, though. No landing pads. So nobody's flying in or out overhead.*

Stone, metal, and glass had been used to craft the metropolis, which looked like it had been added on to forever without the previous structures giving way to time. A tall translucent wall of light encompassed the expanse of the vast city, outside of which more buildings were scattered.

"You're gonna get something caught in there if you don't close your mouth." Persh'al snorted and moved the skiff down over the other side of the hill.

"That's the capital?"

"Oh, yeah. Hangivol in all its messed-up glory. Doesn't look any different than I remember."

"Seriously?"

"When we get down there and start walking the streets, kid, we'll find out how close to the mark I was about what's going on here. Then we'll know how to handle things when we get back Earthside."

The ground rumbled as they glided down the hill, sending huge clods of dirt tumbling after them. Cheyenne turned and saw the top of a massive metal tank crest the hill, the whole thing hovering off the ground by less than a foot. "They didn't send anyone after you, did they?"

"Huh?" Persh'al looked over his shoulder and grunted. "Not for me. That's an army tank, all right."

"It's as big as a house."

"Yep. Can you picture Maleshi sittin' at the helm of that thing?"

Cheyenne wrinkled her nose. "Kinda, yeah."

He laughed wryly. "Happened a lot."

"Watch out."

"What?" He turned again as the house-sized tank spilled over the top of the hill and raced toward them at top speeds. "Those morons!"

Persh'al swiped both hands across the control panel, and the skiff bounced sideways across the slope, narrowly escaping being run over or knocked aside by the metallic beast racing toward the city. Their skiff wobbled from side to side, and he brought them down slowly with an aggravated snort.

"Nobody cares about the little guy anymore." He leaned over the console and shouted at the war tank, "What happened to keeping the peace, huh?"

Cheyenne pressed her lips together and watched the speeding contraption. "Is there an army stationed down here?"

"Of course there is. I don't know what it looks like after Maleshi up and left since she was the last piece of decent glue holding the whole thing together. But yeah, there's an army."

"Great."

It took them another half-hour to reach the tightly packed buildings in the outer ring of Hangivol's shimmering wall of light. More magicals than even Peridosh could hold bustled between these buildings, barking orders and questions at each other, moving around pits bursting with green flames, and working with machines to apparently build more machines.

"Industrial sector," Persh'al muttered, moving the skiff slowly through the intense heat coming from the pits. "Not inside the city walls because who wants all this noise and heat and stink crammed right up against...well, okay, a different kind of noise and heat and stink."

"What do they make out here?" Cheyenne stared at a metal claw on a ten-foot crane pulling a huge sheet of metal with a snarling wolf's head forged on the side.

"Everything. Anything. The big stuff, right? Some of it's craftsman-ship, but it's the old-school kind. Metal is metal, though, huh? We're still working with it like we always have."

An empty pit filled with green flames sputtered out when a ten-foot-tall magical stepped through it, the ground trembling beneath his lumbering footsteps. *Those aren't feet, those are hooves.*

The big guy caught her staring and spread two enormous, black-crusted wings out on either side of him, blocking out the light from both the green fire and the sun behind him. A low growl rumbled out of him before he grabbed a sheet of metal bigger than he was and stepped back through the flames.

"As long as we keep moving and don't try to talk to any of these guys, we'll be in the city before you can say, 'Fuck, that's some hot fell-fire.'" Persh'al steered the skiff toward a steel tunnel angling upward, and a tingling buzz of warm energy washed over them when they passed through. He shuddered. "I never liked that."

"What was it?"

"Uh, a decontamination chamber. Sort of."

Cheyenne stared at him as the tunnel leveled out, then dropped gently back down again. "So, we just drove through a contaminated industrial sector."

"More or less. I mean, not with sickness or anything. Don't freak out. The city's been running some kinda filtration system forever.

Working with fellfire has its downsides, namely one of the worst smells I've ever smelled."

"I didn't smell anything."

"Right. Well, you don't until the fumes have had a good day or two to settle in." They exited the tunnel, and Persh'al turned the skiff to the right, navigating through all the other vehicles swarming in through the open corridor lining the city wall. "I took the fastest route, kid. We won't stink, and we saved a bunch of time by not having to go all the way around the city to the *front.*"

"I'm guessing not many magicals come in through the back."

"Yeah, most try to avoid the fellfire."

Cheyenne glanced over the metal rim of the curving lane filled only with other hovering crafts. On their left, the shimmering translucent wall rose almost straight up before it curved inward toward the highest towers miles away at the city's center. Two larger crafts whizzed passed them, darting between the other milling vehicles and eliciting shouts of outrage from other drivers.

"All right, here we go." Persh'al banked to the right, cutting off another driver behind him. The skiff dipped into another tunnel on the side of the corridor, and they entered an underground parking lot. When they slowed to a stop, the metal wall beside them flashed yellow. "Suck it. I'm not wasting any more *veréle* on junk."

Cheyenne gazed around the low parking lot underground. "This is not what I expected."

"This is Hangivol, kid. I wouldn't expect anything if I were you." He grabbed his pack and waited for the halfling to grab hers before he led her across the empty lot toward a raised round platform against the far wall. The metal beside the skiff flashed yellow again and made a chirping, clicking sound. Before Cheyenne could ask, Persh'al waved dismissively and stepped up onto the platform. "Yeah, yeah. Sound the alarm. I don't give a shit. Watch this, though."

She frowned at the skiff as the wall flashed again. Something whirred and clicked, and a silver light bloomed around the skiff before the entire thing crunched in on itself. The metal squealed and popped until a tightly packed ball of metal hovered inside the silver bubble. "So, no more skiff."

"Nah, we don't need it. That's O'gúleesh towing for ya." Persh'al winked at her as the round platform jerked and slowly lifted away from the floor. "Let me tell ya, I was terrified the first time I got a parking ticket in DC."

"Not as bad in comparison."

"Right? It's good to have a positive outlook."

The platform lifted them up through a circular chute in the metal ceiling above them and stopped to let them off. Cheyenne stared up at the city's shimmering outer wall in front of them. "How many things do we have to go through to get inside?"

"It's overkill, I know. Almost there."

Other magicals lugging their things with them moved down a narrow walkway twenty feet above the whirring traffic lane encircling the city toward a huge orc standing guard at one of the entrance points. Cheyenne and Persh'al fell in line with the rest of them and waited for their turn.

She leaned toward the troll and muttered, "You sure you won't set off any outstanding warrants with *that* guy?"

"Of course I'm sure." He cleared his throat. "No way are they looking through a two-thousand-year-old database."

"Very convincing."

"All right, keep all that to yourself for five more minutes, kid. Let me do the talking. You just stand next to me looking fed-up and pissed-off."

Cheyenne snorted. "Easy."

"Yeah, I thought so."

They reached their turn in line and stopped in front of the giant orc. He towered at least a foot over them and growled, "Hands."

Persh'al extended both of his, trying to look like he was going through the motions just like the next magical.

The orc raised his hand over Persh'al's open palms and made a fist. A drop of purple light descended from his glove like a spider on silk and bloomed across the troll's blue fingers. Then it disappeared, and the orc glanced at Cheyenne. "What're you doin' with this one?"

Cheyenne couldn't take her eyes off the dime-sized bull's-head on the shoulder of the orc's black vest. *Don't blow this. Nobody knows you're here.* "I took a tour through the Outers. The troll was my driver."

The orc's yellow eyes narrowed, and he shot Persh'al a quick, disapproving glance. "What were you doin' all the way out there?"

Pull the drow attitude card, right? She blinked slowly. "I was bored."

"Huh. I can't imagine that changed much out there."

Finally, she made herself look up at him and raised an eyebrow. "It didn't. I'm still bored."

The orc snorted and waved them through the doorway cut into the metal wall. "Go on."

"Yep." Persh'al practically jogged through the narrow doorway.

Cheyenne followed him, gazing at solid metal walls six feet thick before they stepped out on the other side. She followed the troll to the right down the platform inside the wall, and when she looked up, there was the curving dome of light stretching so high and so far toward the center of the city, she lost sight of it.

"Can you believe that?" Persh'al pointed at a staircase on their left, which they took down to the city's lower level. He glanced up once at the entry point they'd just passed and shook his head. "Didn't even bother to check *your* record."

"I don't have one."

"Yeah, yeah. Rub it in. Looks like drow are getting more special treatment than usual these days."

"I don't think you should be disappointed about that." Cheyenne gazed up at the high buildings built along the city wall. *How many walls does this place have?*

"I'm not disappointed. If I was worried, it was for nothing." Persh'al nudged her arm and nodded at an alley between the two buildings in front of them. "Come on. The sooner we get away from all this traffic and security bullshit, the sooner you get to see the real Hangivol."

Cheyenne followed him through the alley and ignored the first gurgling hunger pain in her stomach. *This feels like I stepped into a sci-fi movie instead of a world full of magic.*

"Trust me, kid." Persh'al looked over his shoulder and nodded at her. "This is a whole new world in here."

CHAPTER FORTY-ONE

The alleys twisted and turned in a maze of identical metal walls. Some of them had O'gúleesh symbols etched into them, and a random selection of those pulsed with different colored lights. Just when Cheyenne thought she should ask if Persh'al knew where they were going, the alley ended, and they stepped into a courtyard the size of a football field.

"Okay." Persh'al grinned. "This is a lot like I remember."

The courtyard put Peridosh to shame. Shops and steel carts and fluttering tents lined the rows of steel buildings stretching into the sky. Holographic lights and magically suspended lanterns of every color floated in all directions. Buzzing energy and crackling magic and whirring mechanisms were a constant undercurrent to the noise of hundreds of magicals, and it made Cheyenne clench her eyes shut. *I'm not gonna last very long in this noise.*

"Okay." Persh'al rubbed his hands together. "Oh, hey, a sparksetter. I promised you toys, didn't I? Come on."

The second they stepped out to cross the courtyard, a rumbling blur raced around the corner from a different passageway.

"Whoa. Watch it." Persh'al stepped quickly back and tugged Cheyenne with him.

A mound of shifting, tumbling rocks in a generally humanoid shape crunched past them. Magicals dodged out of its way before filling the gap the creature left behind it, then it disappeared down another side street, taking the rumble with it.

"Stone-eaters." Persh'al snorted. "You know, sometimes I think they're blind. You okay?"

"Yeah." Cheyenne waved off his hand when he reached for her shoulder. "Really loud in here."

"That's one of the tradeoffs, but we can find plenty of things to distract you. Stay close, huh?" He stepped into the fast-flowing crowd of magicals on foot and hoof and fluttering through the air.

She snorted and took off after him, narrowly avoiding being clipped by something that looked like a dog-sized gerbil with wings. An ogre growled at her when she almost bumped into him, and she growled back before darting around him to follow Persh'al's bulging backpack.

He stopped outside a storefront with a bunch of O'gúleesh runes scrolling across the metal wall in flashing colors. "This is gonna blow your mind, kid. As long as it doesn't *actually* blow your mind, but we'll see."

Frowning, she followed him through the open door into a shop lined with shelves brimming with metal boxes and gadgets, curling wires, and tiny shiny squares of who-knew-what. Cheyenne ducked beneath a dangling string of silver chains, and she realized they were individually moving links folding over and over against each other and slithering through the air like flying metal serpents.

Persh'al turned toward the counter on the far right and wiggled his eyebrows. When he reached it, he drummed his fingers on the metal surface and nodded at the skaxen behind it. The other magical held a small metal box in one hand, the other raised above the box and shooting a buzzing orange light onto it from his long-nailed finger. Sparks flew as the metal heated and reacted to his spell. Persh'al cleared his throat.

"What?" The skaxen lowered his hand and shot the troll a scathing glance.

"Looking for an activator, a basic model. Whatever you have."

The skaxen rolled his eyes and glanced across his shop. The same orange-sparking finger flicked across the room, and a spinning tray with undulating metal arms zipped through the air toward a tangled mess of wires hanging on the opposite wall. When it buzzed back toward the counter, it carried a thin metal tube in its pincer-like grasp. This dropped into the skaxen's open hand, and the orange-skinned magical stared at the open door of his shop like he'd rather be anywhere else. "Full head for this one."

"What?" Persh'al thumped his pack on the counter, rattling the small metal pieces, and pulled the black case from the front pocket. "Full head for *that*? Come on, man. That's only worth half."

Cocking his head, the skaxen lifted the metal tube beside his face, and the spinning tray with arms hovered down above it, ready to snatch the thing away on command. "Full head."

Persh'al spread his arms. "I'll go two-thirds, huh? Don't cheat me out of a bad deal."

"The newer models go for triple. I sell 'em for double, and you'll cough up a full head or you can keep walkin'."

"All right, all right. Cool it."

Cheyenne folded her arms and watched the transaction. *He's as bad at bartering as he is at lying.*

Slipping three of the hair-thin plastic cards from the top of the case, Persh'al stared at the skaxen before laying the payment slowly down on the counter. "You got any of the newer models?"

"Nope." The skaxen set the metal tube on the table, then returned his attention to the box in his hand. The orange sparks flared to life on his other finger as he pointed toward the door. "None of that trickles down from Uppertech."

"You know what? Never mind." Persh'al snatched up the metal tube, tucked his money case back into his pack, and slung the thing over his shoulder. A stand with dangling strings of glowing metal leaned sideways on its own to avoid the giant piece of luggage as the troll headed toward Cheyenne in the center of the shop. "Okay, the skaxen's a thieving liar, but I got you something."

"That looks like a metal shotgun shell."

"Ha. Think again, kid. This is a basic-model activator, like a remote control for your magic. All this crazy gear." He wiggled his head, gazing around the stuffy shop, then handed over the metal tube. "This feels like buying a teenager her first cell phone."

Cheyenne stared at him until he shrugged, then she took the metal tube and turned it over in her hands. "My first time in the city, and you brought me to a magical Radio Shack."

He snorted. "It's nothing fancy, but you might get a taste of how things hook up around here. If it'll even work for you with the whole mixed ancestry thing. You don't read O'gúleesh, do you?"

When she glanced at him in disgust, Persh'al nodded toward the skaxen, who was busy ignoring them. "No."

"Well, it's worth a shot. If it doesn't work, I'll sell it and make a little profit."

"No, you won't," the skaxen murmured.

Persh'al scowled at him. "Nobody's talking to you, ratface." The shop owner didn't respond, focusing intently on welding that little box with his spell-gun finger.

"I don't know what I'm supposed to do with this." Cheyenne rolled the tube between her fingers.

"Oh, yeah. Little button on the bottom. You might feel a slight—"

Cheyenne's pressed on the bottom of the tube, and the thing sprang open in a blur of moving parts that unfolded and raced across her hand, clamping down on her skin in half a second. "Shit."

"Pinch." Persh'al cleared his throat. "That's about it."

She shook her hand, and her eyes widened when the thin lines of metal netting didn't budge. "It's a glove."

"Not quite. Give it a few seconds."

"To do what?"

"Huh." He peered at her hand as she turned it back and forth. "Hey, you sold me a dud activator?"

The skaxen didn't look up. "You tryin' to be a pain in my ass?"

"Yeah, 'cause this thing's not—"

The metal net on Cheyenne's hand flashed, and she sucked in a sharp breath at the flood of buzzing energy that coursed up her arm and into her shoulder. Her eyelids fluttered, and she shut them to help focus on the sensation. *Not the best-feeling power surge. Not the worst, either.*

Persh'al watched her and shrugged. "Okay. Never mind."

The tingle of tech-magic pulsed one more time up her shoulder and the side of her neck before fizzling out in the back of her brain. Then it died, and Cheyenne took a deep breath. "That was weird."

The troll chuckled. "Oh, yeah. Maybe it *will* work for ya. Wait 'til you open your eyes."

Her eyelids fluttered open, and she blinked away the blue and green flashes of light in her vision. But instead of disappearing, the fuzzy lights solidified into crisp, clear letters around the perimeter of her vision, blinking and recalibrating when she focused on different pieces of gear around the shop. "Holy shit."

"Yeah." Persh'al grinned.

"Viewscreen in my *head*." The halfling's eyes darted around the shop, and when she stopped at the metal box in the skaxen's hand, her vision filled with scrolling lines of code in a programming language she recognized. "Looks like the basic model comes with language options."

With a snort, Persh'al shook his head. "All right, quit screwin' around."

"I'm not." When she looked at him, the flashing lights dimmed and faded into the background. *So, I'll be able to tell a magical from a robot, I guess.* "I can read this." She pointed at the rack behind the troll and scanned the description that appeared. "This is a ward-sniffer, right?"

"No shit." He chuckled. "I know for a fact no activator system runs in any human language, but you can read that?"

"Yep. I guess I *can* read O'gúleesh now. Makes sense, since the written language is half-magical." A slow grin spread across her face, and she laughed. The lines of code and the readjusting letters from O'gúleesh runes into words and numbers she understood flashed across the surface with otherworld tech running through it. "This is so cool. Kinda makes me think of *The Matrix*."

"Ha. Cool movies. *This* is real."

"Uh-huh." Cheyenne moved slowly through the shop with a crooked, amazed smile. *I bet I could figure out how every piece in this place works if I picked it up and spent two minutes looking at it.* She made a full circle around the small room, then stopped in front of the counter and the skaxen still working on his private project.

The scrolling code blinked an error message when she focused on the line of his magic soldering through the box. She leaned closer and pointed at it. "I'd move a centimeter to the right. You're gonna cut through something important in there."

The orange light bursting from the skaxen's finger sputtered out, and he lowered his hand with the box to the counter before glaring at her in disgust. "Piss off."

"Yeah." Cheyenne laughed and lifted her hands. "Yeah, I'll do that."

She turned in a daze and headed toward the open door. Persh'al hurried after her and grabbed her arm as they stepped outside. "If that thing's gonna make you walk around all day like you ate a bunch of magic mushrooms, the psychedelic kind, I'm gonna tell you to take it off."

Cheyenne gently brushed his fingers off her arm and nodded. The courtyard lit up in a whole new way now, streaming all the information she could possibly want to know about every gadget, system, and magically synced piece of gear on each passing magical and built into the metal walls. "I'm good."

"You sure? I'm not gonna lie, kid. You look like you're trippin' balls."

The halfling pulled her gaze away from the wealth of O'gúleesh information and smiled at him. "Come on, Persh'al. Don't tell me the first time you used one of these, it wasn't a total trip for you."

He tried to stare her down, but the humor in her glowing golden eyes was infectious. The troll chuckled and scratched the wind-blown fluff his mohawk had become. "All right, you got me there. But get used to it quick, huh? A blissed-out drow drooling all over the streets is gonna bring the kind of attention we don't want."

"I'm not drooling."

"If you say so." He grinned and nodded for her to follow him into the throng of magicals going about their business in the lower marketplace of Hangivol. "And don't get too attached to having that around. It's only temporary. This is the kinda tech that doesn't make it across the Border, so as soon as we go Earthside again, you're back to being illiterate."

"Fine. But I'm keeping it on 'til we go back."

CHAPTER FORTY-TWO

I n the first five minutes of their trek through the crowded streets of the lower marketplace, Cheyenne figured out how to turn down the background noise with the activator so her enhanced drow hearing didn't give her an enhanced drow headache.

Durg's niece was right; an activator does all the heavy lifting. No spells and no studying. No wonder magicals don't wanna leave the city.

Now it was a lot easier to follow Persh'al without being distracted by every unknown sound. He led her through a second series of alleys and passages until they came to another market courtyard, more or less. This one sold food, clothing, potions, and one scrappy yellow magical had a stack of cages full of squawking birds—striped chickens with two heads and lionlike tails instead of tailfeathers.

"Okay, what are those?" Cheyenne asked, staring at the yellow-skinned magical hawking caged birds.

"Hmm?" Persh'al followed her gaze and wrinkled his nose. "O'gúleesh chickens, basically. They taste like shit in comparison, honestly."

"No, I meant the guy selling them."

"Oh." Persh'al chuckled and pulled her away when the magical caught sight of her staring and gave her a cold sneer in response. "That's a gremlin, kid. A tamer one than the raider, for sure. They're pretty harmless for the most part, until you cross their arbitrary line in the sand and flip their switch into total nutjob. I stay away from them if I can. Ticking timebomb of rage, those guys."

"Uh-huh." Cheyenne sneered back at the gremlin, whose attention was quickly diverted by a new potential customer.

Persh'al leaned toward her and lowered his voice. "I'd cut it out with the staring from now on, yeah? Maybe you've noticed an odd reaction or two in Peridosh when magicals see a drow down there schmoozing with the rest of us. Same holds true in Hangivol but magnified."

"I thought this was drow city." Cheyenne glanced into an open storefront and thought immediately of Gúrdu the raug Oracle. The setup inside was exactly the same, low tables and heaps of cushions scattered around the floor, hookahs on every table, flickering lanterns in every color, suspended magically below the low ceiling. But this room was full, littered with magicals sprawling across the cushions and taking huge pulls from the hoses, staring at each other with vapid eyes and dull, washed-out smiles.

"It *is* drow city. Hey, I said, quit staring." Persh'al grabbed her upper arm and pulled her forward. "You keep standing in front of the wrong places like that, and someone's gonna draw you in. L'zar will rip my head off if I let you stop for a magical ride in a nectar barn."

She shot him a questioning frown, and he released her arm before nodding in the direction they were headed.

"Think Earthside opium den, kid. That shit'll drug you up until you're nothing but drow-headed goo. Got it?"

Cheyenne raised an eyebrow and skirted around a group of old troll women huddled around an outdoor stove controlled by magical tech to maintain the perfect heat, their scarlet braids a washed-out pink and their violet skin nearly gray. "As long as you get it that you're not *letting* me do anything."

"Fine, Cheyenne. I'm not gonna argue semantics with you, because the outcome's the same. All I can do is strongly advise against something, yeah? And it's my ass on the line if you decide to do the complete opposite."

Fighting back a laugh, she nodded slowly and forced herself not to stare at the pair of huge orange eyes peering out of the pitch-black alleyway beside them. "I trust you, troll, so advise away."

He snorted. "Yeah, okay."

The streets grew narrower and darker the closer they got to the center of the city. Her activator-enhanced vision picked up less technology now, most of which was a quick scroll of code when she glanced at a doorway or a holographic sign flitting in bright colors across metal walls.

"All right, time to move on up, huh?" Persh'al cast brief glances at the few dozen magicals milling down the side street before he stepped into another alley. At the end of that was a broad staircase, the steps made of metal grates. The entire thing lit up in her vision with quickly scrolling symbols rearranging themselves from O'gúleesh to English in a blur of color. "Shit. Should've bought two of those things."

He waved her forward to climb the first few steps, then tapped the metal rail with the back of his hand. "You're gonna have to get us up this one, kid."

"I'm pretty sure you just have to keep walking up."

"Ha. You'd think so, wouldn't you? Not that simple. Since you're all synced up with that fancy piece of machinery on your hand, be a useful incognito drow and find the switch."

Cheyenne stared at him, ignoring the blue and green updates flashing at the edges of her vision. "You lost me."

Persh'al scanned the metal railing. "You're looking for Uppertech. District 5, I'm pretty sure, or whatever district we're not in right now. Things don't look the same since the last time I was here."

"Yeah, I imagine a couple hundred years will do that." Cheyenne looked down at the metal rail of the staircase leading up toward what looked like another walking level cut into the metal buildings between the alleys. A dozen words scrolled across the railing's surface—Halter's Deck, Ritfarrin, Qi'woc. Then she found the words Uppertech District 5: Open and pointed at it. "One more step above you."

Grinning, Persh'al stepped up the stairs and gripped the rail where she pointed. "This one?"

The words flickered before disappearing beneath his hand. "I guess. Your hand's right on the words."

"Perfect." He gripped the metal rung beneath the rail and gave it a sharp twist. The staircase clicked and squeaked, shuddering beneath them as more grated stairs unfolded from the top at a ninety-degree angle and built a brand-new walkway above them. The new stairs hit the roof of a tall building on their left with a clang, and that was it. "Gotta know where you're going in this place. One wrong twist and you end up in Desire's Pit covered in tiny…you know what? We don't have to go there."

Cheyenne cocked her head and followed him up the stairs. *I'm down with the activator. Not so sure I'm into a city with a place called Desire's Pit.*

The newly unfolded staircase on their right was as sturdy as the first when they reached the landing and turned left to head toward the opposite rooftop. She peered over the rail at the fifty-foot drop and took a deep breath. "These stairs don't move on their own, do they?"

"Come on, kid. This is Ambar'ogúl, not Hogwarts."

Cheyenne gave a surprised laugh. "Sounds like those books are a huge hit with Earthside O'gúleesh."

"Oh, yeah? I only read the first one. Couldn't get over the massively inaccurate description of trolls, but whatever."

They reached the end of the staircase and stepped onto the roof. On the other side, another metal wall rose at least another thirty feet in front of them, and the shape of a doorway in the blank steel wall swam in Cheyenne's vision, with scrolling code and more commands than she could follow before they reached it.

"You see the door with that thing?" Persh'al gestured toward the wall.

"I see something." When he pointed at the lit rectangle of metal, she nodded.

"You know what? Maybe you should be *my* guide." He placed his hand on the glowing section of metal. It pulsed with green light and the wall disappeared, opening another doorway through the thick sheet of steel.

"Whoa." Cheyenne peered into the newest tunnel, blazing with more scrolling code on every wall.

"Yeah, whoa is right. Glad you're enjoying yourself."

Fast-paced warbling music wafted toward them through the tunnel, and after a short walk, dazzling white light spilled into the darkness between the metal walls. Then they were out, and Cheyenne squinted against the brightness and the ramped-up code and identifying labels scrolling across every surface. "Jeeze."

Persh'al chuckled. "Yeah, it takes some getting used to. Feel free to take that thing off if it's too much."

"Not too much." Cheyenne focused on the flashing words in the upper right-hand corner: Darken Analysis. *There's a prompt for everything.* She waved her hand toward the flashing command, which responded instantly. The layers of code filtered away from her vision and left only two things behind: an option to turn super-scan back on and a smaller, more focused strand of data hovering over the shiny steel building on her right where she'd been staring. "Can this thing read my mind?"

"Kinda. More like it reads your magic, but these days, one could argue they're the same thing. Lose control of one, and the other's not far behind, am I right?" Persh'al laughed so hard he snorted, nudging her with the back of his hand again before gesturing around. "This is Uppertech, kid. Formerly known as Uppershim, with serious upgrades."

"No kidding." Cheyenne gazed around the courtyard, taking in the bright, polished steel flashing a blinding silver where Ambar'ogúl's sun glinted off the shiny surfaces. "This is different."

"The upper echelon." The troll spread his arms to encompass the entire area. "Five districts. As I'm sure you've noticed, this one's for entertainment of the culinary variety. Mostly. Don't ask me about the others because that's not where we need to be right now."

She grinned at him. "District 5, 'cause you're still hungry."

"Caught me red-handed, kid. Keep up." He marched away from the tunnel, pumping his arms at his sides and looking even more ridiculous with the bulging pack swinging behind him every time he turned to take in a new sight. "Smell that? Ah, That's real O'gúleesh cooking for you. Clean, delicate, better than a Michelin-star restaurant. You'll see."

Eleanor would have a thing or two to say about that.

CHAPTER FORTY-THREE

The courtyard of Uppertech's District 5 was filled with as many magicals as down below, though these citizens were obviously wealthier. Their oddly styled hair and flowing, shimmering garments made the garb of the O'gúleesh on the lower level look like rags in comparison. A tall, lithe fae draped in silk and bathed in a daisy-yellow aura drifted past them, her feet barely touching the ground, if at all. An ogre woman with silver-painted lips and kohl around her eyes moved with a haughty, condescending grace most of her species didn't have. Two tall goblins, one of them with a monocle that clicked, turned, and flashed blue light wherever he looked, strolled slowly across the metal floor, muttering to each other. The other had thick chains of gold and silver draped around his neck and down both the front and back of his shirt. They jingled with each step, and Persh'al leaned toward Cheyenne when she stared after the goblins.

"Looks like your personal style made an appearance in high-society fashion on this side." He nodded at the silver chains wrapped around her wrists, and she shot him an unamused look. "Or not."

They walked past a steel fountain in the center of the square, which emitted a thin stream of violet mist that hovered over the basin in an illuminated cloud. The scent of cherry blossoms, damp earth, and an underlying taint of raw meat was overwhelming. Cheyenne wrinkled her nose and had to turn away. "What's with the community perfume?"

"I said loud and smelly, didn't I? It's supposed to cleanse the palate from the lower levels. They've bumped it up a notch since last time I was here."

"It's not an improvement."

"I'm with you there." Persh'al pointed at a glistening marquee above a narrow doorway. The building was the same bright metal as everything else, with tall, thin windows reaching floor to ceiling on either side of the door. Each window reflected a different holographic scene in motion: fancy parties, laughing magicals, and the thin plastic cards of O'gúleesh currency exchanging hands. "That's our first stop, kid. I think better on a full stomach, and short of the bathhouse, a bar is the best place to listen in on what everyone's too buzzed to keep to themselves."

"There's a bathhouse?"

Persh'al glanced at the purple cloud of mist over the fountain and grimaced. "Not remotely on the sightseeing list."

Cheyenne looked at the thin metal sign with a thick etching of O'gúleesh symbols. Her activator flashed the translation right beneath it: Wildhaven.

They headed toward the entrance, and a burst of tinkling laughter rose from the front of another store. A group of magicals had gathered in a circle, watching a video hovering in the air between them.

"Can you imagine?" A troll with oiled crimson hair gestured toward the image. Gem-encrusted rings glinted on every one of his fingers. "Having to drag an entire shipment like that. On *foot*."

"There's misfortune, and then there's sheer laziness." The orc woman's high nasal voice grated on Cheyenne's nerves. "Honestly, I don't see why they are still let into the city."

A tall figure dressed in a flowing gray shirt and trousers emerged from the storefront. Cheyenne froze mere feet from the front door of Wildhaven when she saw the purple-gray skin and bone-white hair of her heritage. *Another drow.*

"The same might be said for any of you," he muttered as he passed the tittering circle of magicals. The smiles disappeared from their faces and they stared after him, looking nervous. The drow forgot them immediately and crossed the plaza on his own business. His golden eyes flickered toward Cheyenne and looked her briefly up and down before he disappeared between two brightly polished steel buildings.

"Cheyenne." Persh'al paused with his hand on the iron handle of the bar's front door. "We're trying to blend in, remember?"

"Yeah." She looked one more time at the alley where the drow had disappeared, then followed the troll through the open door. "If this is supposed to be drow city, how come that's the only one I've seen?"

The door closed softly behind them, inaudible beneath the lilting music coming from all directions inside the bar.

Persh'al cleared his throat and brushed off the front of his shirt before gazing around the brightly lit room. "They've migrated to the inner sanctum, for lack of a better term. In and up." He shot her a quick glance and shrugged. "Compared to where the Crown's been putting up all the drow she wants to keep at her side, Uppertech might as well be another farming village."

"I don't see how that's possible." Cheyenne blinked, scanning the glass and metal surfaces glinting around them. Everywhere she looked, information scrawled across her vision. *Like we stepped into a machine that happens to serve booze.*

"Yeah, well, maybe one day you'll see it. Who knows, right?" Stepping out of the small vestibule inside the door, Persh'al nodded for her to follow.

Wildhaven was filled with a low buzz of polite conversation and delicate laughter. Glasses and silverware clinked, voices mingled at a poised volume, and the music drifted softly over all of it. Cheyenne couldn't pinpoint where it was coming from and gave up trying. *Sounds like Rachmaninoff underwater.*

A shiny silver orb the size of a softball bobbed toward them from the other side of the broad dining room. It stopped in front of the newest guests and blinked with pink light. "Welcome to Wildhaven. Please sit wherever you like. May I take your luggage?"

Cheyenne fought back a laugh. *That floating metal hostess sounds like Betty White.*

"No, thanks." Persh'al nodded curtly, shooting the hovering orb a thin smile. "The luggage stays with us."

When the orb didn't budge, the troll nudged Cheyenne in the ribs and cocked his head, still staring at the blinking pink light.

So it's all politeness and etiquette coming from a robot. This is weird.

She lifted her chin and stared at the blinking light as if it were an eye. "I prefer to keep my belongings on my person, thank you."

With a final blink, the silver orb darted away from them and left the restaurant's newest patrons to find seats.

The dining room was studded with round tables surrounded by curving booths draped in white fabric. The backs of the booths rose five feet higher than the tables, forming individual pockets of privacy. "Looks like we won't be hearing much drunken gossip from those tables."

"Nah." Persh'al waved her off. "We'll sit. Gorge ourselves on the kind of meal I haven't had in a few centuries, and *then* we'll start listening in. This is just the front room, kid. The back room is where all the action happens."

He slid off his pack beside an empty circular booth and shoved it toward the center before sliding in after it. Cheyenne did the same, slipping quickly onto the smooth seat of a woven material that felt like fur, and frowned. "By *action*, you mean what?"

"Relax. We won't be fighting anybody. To tell you the truth, I'd get my ass kicked in two seconds without an activator. Of course, I've had way more practice fighting with bare magic than any of these yuppies, but nobody here would be caught dead without their tech. So no, we play it safe, we listen, do some schmoozing, see what we can dig up. Don't make any waves, and don't get caught with your pants down. And try to have fun while you're at it, huh? You look like L'zar when he gets woken up from a nap."

She sat back in the booth and shook her head. "No, I don't."

Persh'al shrugged and scanned the clear surface of the metal table, projecting an illusion of glass.

"I did notice one thing that might be important."

He looked at her quickly and raised his eyebrows. "Already? I haven't even ordered yet."

Ignoring his attempt at a joke, Cheyenne leaned toward him over the table and glanced through the opening in the booth. "That floating hostess that wanted to take our stuff. I stared right at it, and the activator didn't pull up anything."

Persh'al frowned. "Doesn't work that way. Every piece of tech in this city has a signature."

"Not that piece."

"You sure you didn't just tone down the images? Or maybe you're getting used to activator eyes and don't remember seeing something."

Cheyenne stared at him and raised her eyebrows. "I've been paying attention, Persh'al. That round little robot and its blinking eye didn't bring up a single line of code. Not even a name."

"Shit." The troll narrowed his orange eyes and gazed through the opening in the booth. A troll in something like a ballgown passed their table, giggling delicately into her hand as a magical with red-and-black mottled skin and a dozen tiny horns protruding from his skull muttered some stuck-up joke. Then Persh'al glanced quickly at the ceiling and sat back against the booth. "Yeah, I'd say that's pretty important. Sounds like there's a lot more going on here than the assholes in charge want anyone to see."

"So, we're gonna go after that orb and pick it apart, right?"

"Nope." Summoning a pale green light at the tip of his finger, Persh'al stroked the glass-looking tabletop, which lit up with a long list of menu items in a soft yellow. "We're gonna eat. Then I'm gonna play nice and get some conversation going. *You're* gonna keep an eye out for more tech you should be able to read like an open book but can't."

"Great," Cheyenne muttered and dropped her gaze to the table.

"See anything that gets your mouth watering?"

She scanned the menu items illuminated in front of her and cocked her head. "I can read the words, but they mean nothing to me."

"All right, how 'bout this? You just sit back, look like you're enjoying yourself, and I'll order for both of us. You'll love it." Persh'al busied himself with the interactive menu, and Cheyenne stared through the booth's opening.

The floating metal orb, or maybe a different one, slowly passed their table, also lacking any signature. *Kinda hard to enjoy a weird meal when we have no idea what's going on.*

CHAPTER FORTY-FOUR

"I've never been more disappointed." Persh'al slipped five blue plastic cards from his money case and set them on the table. The cards and table flashed together, then his payment disappeared. "This was a total joke, man. Coughing up that much *veréle* for a tiny little pile of roasted *angarfat* and a few crumbs of crushed *grylyf* for what? *Presentation?* They need to change the name of that dish to Most Expensive Snack Ever That Doesn't Even Taste Like *Grylyf*."

Cheyenne aimed the two-pronged fork at the tower of mint-green jelly on the side of her plate and gave it another tentative poke. Hundreds of tiny bubbles appeared on the surface when the jelly wobbled and opened one at a time to reveal milky-white eyes that stared back at her. "This stuff has eyes."

"Well, yeah. That's what gives it the crunch. You're not gonna eat it?"

She cocked her head and set the fork down on the plate. "I'm not into being stared at by my food."

"Huh. Then can I have it?"

Cheyenne slid the plate across the table toward him, and the troll grinned. She couldn't watch him devour the ogling jelly in three huge bites, then the fork clattered to the plate, and Persh'al took a long gulp of the slightly sweetened complimentary water.

"Okay. That's a little better. You liked the rest of it, though, right?"

"The bread that kept growing back until I finally shoved the whole thing in my mouth?" She scrunched her nose and shook her head. "Feels like it's still growing in my stomach."

"But it tasted good. And it'll stick with you for the rest of the day, won't it?" He chuckled and scooted out of the booth, lugging his pack behind him. "Oh, yeah. I can operate on a half-full tank. Let's get to work."

Cheyenne shouldered her pack and gazed around the restaurant. Most of the dining magicals ignored them as Persh'al led her toward the center of the far wall. Those who looked up to catch a glimpse of a blue troll and a scowling young drow traipsing around with their luggage scowled and rolled their eyes.

Wouldn't be the first time I've broken the dress code. They can deal.

On the far wall was a tall, arching doorway decorated with swirling silver vines and metal leaves that fluttered on their own. Persh'al knocked lightly on the solid metal wall inside the arch and turned to wiggle his eyebrows at her. "The real party's always in the back room, you know?"

"Totally." *Not that I go to parties, but I have a feeling this one's gonna be a lot more like Bianca Summerlin's soirees than anything else.*

The doorway shimmered and the wall disappeared, emitting a foggy blue light that somehow didn't make it out into the pristine cleanliness of the dining room. Persh'al nodded at her. "You know what you're lookin' for."

"Yep." She followed him through yet another short tunnel, her skin tingling when the wall solidified behind them again. "Back doors into Hangivol's citywide mainframe. The closed ones."

"Just don't open them. The last thing we need on this trip is to set off any alarms."

"You mean, besides the one you tripped at whatever town that was?"

Persh'al snorted. "I'll owe you one if we can agree that never happened."

"Fine by me." Cheyenne laughed when his floppy orange hair bounced against his neck as he shook his head.

The music in the back room intensified before they exited the tunnel. *Seriously? Now it's O'gúleesh dubstep, and this is not a soiree.*

The massive room beyond was dark and thick with odorless smog lighting up in shapes and symbols in bursts of different-colored lights. Suspended lanterns hovering below the ceiling flickered with green and purple flames, casting thin spotlights on the magicals moving back and forth below them. A circular bar glinting with dangling metallic strands that shuddered with the beat of the pounding music sat in the center of the room, where a snake-eyed magical with translucent skin and four arms poured drinks. A stage took up the left wall, though the flying magical doing cartwheels under a purple spotlight obviously didn't need it. The dance floor was covered by a dark, bobbing mass of heads and hair and flailing limbs, and the rest of the room was lined with more tables and chairs, these open for everyone to see everyone else.

Persh'al bobbed his head to the music and turned to shoot Cheyenne a huge grin. "Better, right?"

"Than the front room, yeah?" She caught up with him and had to raise her voice over the music. "Are people not supposed to know this is back here?"

"No, everyone knows, but a hoity-toity little troll living in Uppertech isn't gonna go clubbing where everyone else can see. The other magicals in here all pretend they're not trying to hide something too."

"What happens in the club stays in the club, huh?"

"You said it. Want a drink?"

Cheyenne snorted and turned to watch the eight-foot guy who could've been a tree if he wasn't shaking all over the place to the music. "Sure. Like, grog or something."

"Not an option up here, kid. I'm not goin' strong, either."

They reached the bar, and the translucent bartender nodded as she set down three black bowls in front of her other customers, their surfaces rippling with pink flames. The magicals dressed for a night out at the opera grabbed the bowls, laughing hysterically, and drained them.

Couldn't pay me to dress like something I'm not so I could be myself in secret.

"Whatcha want?" The bartender set two four-fingered hands on the bar, her snakelike eyes flickering between Persh'al and Cheyenne.

"Two mudshines."

The bartender frowned and opened her mouth to spit some

scathing remark, then a flock of small silver orbs swooped down from the ceiling, blinking multicolored lights. They stopped over Persh'al and Cheyenne's heads and hovered slowly around the circular bar.

Cheyenne glanced at one from the corner of her eye. *No info on those things, either.*

Eyeing the spinning orbs, the bartender scratched her hairless translucent head with a third hand. Her mouth snapped shut, and she forced a smile at her new customers. "I'll have to bring something out from the back. If you don't mind waiting, of course."

Persh'al shrugged. "No problem."

Casting him another tight-lipped smile, the bartender reached up with a fourth hand to swipe at something on the ring lining the bar overhead. Her other hands lifted two short glasses from beneath the counter, and the fourth reached into the pocket of her sleeveless black jumpsuit. Then she turned to help two more customers.

Persh'al and Cheyenne exchanged glances, and when he raised an eyebrow and nodded at the still-hovering orbs, the halfling shook her head. He leaned against the bar. "It'll be easier to talk with some drinks in us. You know, get things loosened up."

"How loose?" She eyed him sidelong and forced a smile.

The troll twirled his finger around the room. "Loose enough to have as much fun as the rest of these lucky bastards. That's what I'm aiming for." He held her gaze and slightly dipped his head.

That's what I thought. Somebody's watching us, just like they're watching the bartender and everyone else. If that was code for "we need to act drunk," I can only go so far.

Cheyenne leaned back against the bar, propping up her forearms behind her and bobbing her head to the music she'd turned way down with her temporary activator. *I can't remember the last time I tried to fake my way through enjoying something.*

A group of orcs standing beside one of the tables against the wall roared with laughter and raised their drinks. The next second, one of them lashed out and socked his neighbor square in the jaw. The sucker-punched magical bellowed in rage as his glass fell and shattered, splashing sparkling liquid all over the floor. "You've stepped *way* out of line, Forul. Try that again, and I'll—"

"You'll what? Throw more *veréle* at me? Your payment's useless. I want what I came for."

"Well, you'll leave disappointed, then."

The orcs snarled at each other, standing toe to toe and growling through their protruding tusks. The others in their group stepped away and looked elsewhere, knocking back their drinks and pretending they had nothing to do with their arguing friends.

Cheyenne narrowed her eyes. *An orc-fight with only one punch? Why are they holding back?*

A quick glance at the other tables showed that the other magicals who'd clearly noticed the fight were very obviously trying to forget it had happened. The two orcs still glared at each other, grunting and trying to make the other one back down. A show of green sparks spat from the fingers of the guy who'd thrown the punch, then another orc walked quickly from where he'd been standing at the corner of the club and approached them.

Cheyenne nudged Persh'al's arm and nodded as subtly as she could toward the altercation.

"That's enough," the third orc growled. This one wore a well-tailored black suit, the sleeves cut to three-quarter length, and two silver stripes crossing diagonally on his chest.

A bouncer in the latest fashion. The halfling tried not to make a face.

The bouncer stood close to the enraged orcs, stuck his face right into the middle of their fight, and muttered something only they could hear. Then he snapped his fingers, and a floating silver tray raced across the room to stop by his outstretched hand. He pulled two inch-long vials from the tray and handed one to each of them.

The angry orcs glanced at what they'd been given, then flipped open the caps of the vials and raised the containers to their huge nostrils for a quick, harsh snort. Opening his hand again, the bouncer waited for the vials to be returned before he stepped away. The brawlers shook their heads, then their yellow eyes widened as they stared at each other. The one who'd hit first let out a wild burst of laughter and clapped his recent enemy on the shoulder, then they fell all over each other, snorting and guffawing and shoving each other around like best friends.

The bouncer walked slowly across the club, his hands shoved into his pockets as he eyed the other magicals living it up around him. When he passed Cheyenne, he caught her gaze, raised an eyebrow, and dipped his head. A curving silver earpiece wrapped around the back of his dark-green ear, and she focused her attention on that before the orc disappeared in the crowd.

Shit. That's not a bouncer. That's a drug dealer keeping the peace.

She stepped away from the bar to find him again, but Persh'al turned toward her and shrugged. "How long does it take to get a decent glass of mudshine around here, huh?"

Cheyenne turned back toward the bar. *Right. I'm here to watch. That's it.*

As if the troll's layered question made it happen, a thin slat in the surface of the bar slid aside, and a tall, wide dark-blue glass bottle rose slowly from the opening. The bartender snatched it and cracked open the top with her bare hands before pouring the dark-brown liquid into two short glasses. When she slid the drinks toward Cheyenne and Persh'al, her snakelike eyes flickered toward the small metal orbs still moving in slow circles around the bar. Her smile looked more forced than the words hissing out of her mouth. "On the house."

"Really?" Persh'al glanced at the bubbling brown mudshine and cocked his head.

"For the wait."

Cheyenne grabbed one glass and lifted it with a nod at the strained-looking bartender. "Excellent."

As soon as the halfling accepted the offer, the floating orbs darted away, slipping into the dark ceiling again to watch and wait. The bartender shook her head and didn't look at either of them before she slid around the bar to take someone else's order.

Persh'al clinked his glass against Cheyenne's and nodded toward the tables lining the walls. "If we're quiet enough and smile for the floating cameras, we can talk about what just happened."

Cheyenne plastered a cheesy grin on her face.

The troll took a huge swig of his drink and shook his head. "Never mind. You focus on not looking like a lunatic, and I'll look happy enough for both of us."

The pert smile he shot her in return looked real. Cheyenne put on her most convincing air of bored superiority and raised the glass to her lips. The mudshine fizzed in her mouth and almost made her cough. "This is the next best thing when there's no grog?"

Persh'al nodded at her glass and chuckled. "I bet there hasn't been a single bottle of this stuff cracked open in Peridosh. Too expensive. It's swill in Uppertech."

CHAPTER FORTY-FIVE

They sat with a chair between them at the table in the corner, watching the club and the magicals letting down their high-society hair for a night. Three more potential fights were broken up before they started, either by free drinks delivered just in time by more flying trays sent from the bar or by a drug-dealing bouncer's open hand while everyone else pretended not to see.

"I'll tell you this much." Persh'al sipped at his drink and scanned the club. "This shit wasn't part of the deal last time I was here. Bar fights were a thing, and if they didn't end in a good laugh, you were tossed out onto your ass and headed to the next bar over."

"What about the drugs?"

"Man, there's always *something* to make you think you're feeling good. Not handed out by the employees, though."

"The bouncer had a scrubbed earpiece."

"Then the bouncer and those flying cameras are playing the same game." Persh'al leaned over the table, smiling at a group of passing trolls with their hair molded into giant red pillars who didn't spare him a second glance. "And I'm not convinced the security stops with whoever owns this place."

"The bartender." Cheyenne looked at him and took a tiny sip of the weird bubbly liquor. *Nothing more suspicious than a drow at a club who doesn't touch her drink.*

"That's what I'm thinking. She was terrified of those things watching her."

"I'm fairly sure she was about to tell us to screw off. "

Persh'al nodded. "Absolutely, and that's when the peacekeeping robots swooped in to remind her of her job. Which isn't necessarily pouring drinks."

Cheyenne stuck her elbow on the table and rubbed her lips, searching the club for whatever else might break loose. "It's to keep people happy."

"Stoned and drunk and enjoying themselves, no matter what. What we need to figure out is if it's happening everywhere else. High security at a club is one thing."

Taking another sip of the weird drink, Cheyenne centered her attention on a skaxen in a glittering cape who abruptly stood two tables down. "Something else altogether if it's happening everywhere in the city. That would pretty much prove your theory about what the Crown's trying to do here, wouldn't it?"

"With a lot of missing pieces left to fill in until we can call it proof, but yeah." Persh'al frowned at the skaxen, who leaned over his table and thrust a finger into a tensely smiling goblin woman's face and hissed something unintelligible. "I want to burn that cape."

"Skaxens and glitter don't mix well, that's for sure."

The skaxen slapped a hand on the metal table and whirled away to storm across the club, the awful cape whipping out behind him. The goblin woman's smile faded as she watched him leave, her brows drawing together in wary concern.

Two orc bouncers stared the skaxen down, but before the rat-faced magical could get to the exit, a spinning tray with a shot of something neon-yellow swerved in front of him.

"I could find better piss in the Outers!" His orange hand shot out and smacked the tray and the shot glass aside, spilling the drink all over a gremlin woman in a puffy dress with a weird, spiked collar rising up the back of her neck. She flapped her arms and hissed at him, but her anger filtered away when a new tray came to deliver her a neon-yellow shot as well. She smiled grimly and took it while the skaxen stormed toward the door. The two orc bouncers stopped him, muttering something too quiet for anyone else to hear.

Cheyenne glanced around the club. The dance floor was still full and in full swing, but the magicals who weren't dancing or hadn't drunk themselves into oblivion were silent, looking everywhere but at the skaxen arguing vehemently with the bouncers.

I wonder if this thing turns the volume up too.

Without needing to be prompted, the activator responded. Her eyelids fluttered as a river of electric energy climbed up her hand and arm and into the back of her head. Then the conversation she'd wanted to hear came in loud and clear.

"You good?" Persh'al leaned forward to catch her attention.

Cheyenne nodded and shot a second-long glance at the skaxen before tapping her finger on her lips and looking away. *We need to work on our secret signs, apparently.*

The troll said something else, laughed sharply, and drank more mudshine, but she wasn't listening.

"This is the last time we'll offer you a way out, Bergo," one of the orcs grumbled. "Take the goldsmile and enjoy yourself. Forget about whatever happened and think about how good you have it here right where you are."

"Lotta bastards would sell their kids to get moved into Uppertech, man. You know that. Hell, even just to get inside the city walls. You know what's gonna happen if you start causing problems."

The skaxen snarled and jabbed a clawed orange finger toward the second orc's face. "Don't talk down to me, Rinter. We came up the same, and you've sold your life for a fell-damn piece of junk."

"It's a job, and I'll be around a lot longer than you if you don't get smart and take the fucking vial."

"I'm not touching that filth. You can't drug me into complacency, not like she's drugged you, apparently."

The first orc, who Bergo the skaxen obviously didn't know as well, glanced at the two silver orbs creeping quietly down from the ceiling toward the altercation. He nodded at the skaxen, and the orbs disappeared again.

"It'll wear off in a few hours," Rinter muttered. "Take it. Sleep it off, and screw your head on right, huh?"

"You can take the deathflame torch you're holding so fell-damn tightly," the skaxen sneered, shaking his fist, "and shove it up your ass. This is all wrong. All of it!"

"Shut up!"

"You've all lost your fell-damn minds," Bergo screamed so everyone could hear. He jabbed a finger at the other club patrons, who wouldn't meet his gaze. Cheyenne winced at the squeal in her head, and the volume dampened immediately. "It's poison, you idiots. All of it!"

Rinter slammed his fist into his old friend's jaw and sent the skaxen staggering sideways. Two seconds later, a panel opened in the metal wall behind him, and half a dozen snaking silver whips snatched him around the middle. Bergo screamed, the mechanical arms jerked him into the wall, and the panel slid back into place. The skaxen's cries cut off abruptly, and the conversation in the club picked back up below the pounding bass of the weird music as if nothing had happened.

What the fuck? Cheyenne's activator turned up the volume as she focused on the disappearing panel, which didn't bring up a hint of a visual. She picked up the bouncers' conversation instead.

"You gave him way too many chances," the first orc growled. "We're here to stop things *before* they turn into a shitshow like that."

"Come on, man." Rinter shrugged under his co-worker's yellow glare. "I know the guy."

"You *knew* the guy. Not our responsibility to keep friends or make new ones, got it?"

"You didn't have to call in the—"

"Do I need to put in a request to transfer you, *dae'bruj*? Or you think you can handle yourself and keep following direct orders from the top?"

Rinter grunted and rolled his shoulders back. "No, sir. I got it."

"Good. Keep your eyes open." When the orc in charge scanned the room and found Cheyenne watching him, she pulled back the volume on her activator and shot him a winning smile she hadn't pulled out since Bianca's congratulatory party six years ago for the newly elected governor. She raised her glass of dark-brown Uppertech swill toward him before taking a sip.

The orc looked her up and down, then dipped his head and kept moving through the club.

"Fuck." Cheyenne thunked her glass on the table and scowled. "What the hell was that?"

Persh'al glanced around the room with a thin smile, though his hand around his drink trembled with the effort to keep from chucking it across the room. "Something that shouldn't be possible here. This isn't Hangivol anymore. This is the Crown's prison."

"Hey, keep it down." Cheyenne forced a soft chuckle and nodded. "If I could tune in on that whole conversation, anyone else in this place could be listening to us."

"Remind me to ask you what they were talking about when we're not on the verge of stepping through the deathflame, okay?"

"What does that mean?"

The flickering smile he gave her was mostly genuine. "The root of all death and life, kid. Carries the same versatility as the human f-bomb, but with a richer historical context."

She snorted. "Whatever."

"We're stuck here a little longer than I wanna be, but anyone who gets up to head out after that brilliant demonstration is asking to be sucked up into the walls next." Persh'al drained the last of his mudshine and slammed the glass on the table. "I'm gonna do some schmoozing. See what I can dig out of somebody."

"You sure that's a good idea right now, with everybody this tense?"

"Better now than never, and I'm an excellent conversationalist. Watch and learn, Cheyenne." His lighthearted words were weighted by the quivering anger beneath his voice and his rigid posture as he stood from their table and made his way toward the goblin woman who'd upset the vanished skaxen.

Cheyenne sat back in her chair and swept her gaze across the other tables and what little of the dance floor she could see on the other side of the round bar. *Really? He goes right for the magical involved in that whole thing?*

CHAPTER FORTY-SIX

Persh'al stopped at the goblin woman's table, which was empty now except for her, and nodded. "Enjoying yourself?"

The goblin woman turned her glass inward, as if she thought he would try to take it from her, and met his gaze without blinking. "Always."

"That's good to hear. But isn't it always?"

She gave him a thin-lipped smile and swallowed. "Without fail. I come here quite a bit to reassure myself about how much I enjoy all this."

Leaning over the table toward her, Persh'al said, "You know what would make me enjoy the rest of my evening?"

Her scarlet eyes narrowed as she tried to figure out if he was flirting with her or trying to send some other type of message. "I have no idea."

"That was a first for me." He set a hand on the table and barely jerked his head toward the club's entrance, where the skaxen had vanished into the walls. "I would *love* to hear more about what happens next."

The woman's eyelids fluttered, and she swallowed thickly again despite the small, thin smile. All put together and viewed from a distance, it might have looked like she was flirting right back. Cheyenne saw the goblin woman's fist clench around a handful of her skirt by her thigh. *She's trying not to lose her shit.*

"You can keep walking." The goblin woman met Persh'al's orange gaze and lifted her chin. "I'm here to have a good time, not to tell you stories. That one doesn't have a happy ending."

"Right. I won't keep you from the party, then." He nodded, and the woman turned away from him in her chair to watch the dancing on the other side of the club. Her hand shook as she raised her drink to her lips, then the tremor disappeared.

Persh'al turned toward Cheyenne and spread his arms, then made his way through the laughing, drinking magicals to schmooze with someone else.

The halfling spun her half-full cup in a slow circle on the table, watching intently. *Nobody's having a good time in here unless they're hammered or hyped up on whatever is in vials.*

Loud, startling laughter came from somewhere closer to the dance-floor. There was Persh'al, spreading his arms and grinning from ear to ear while he fake-laughed it up with a group of magicals in fine evening clothes. He pointed to his head, then at a puff of purple-gray hair rising two feet above the circle of magicals. More laughter followed, then Persh'al's eyes widened, and he barked genuine laughter this time. "That's the most ridiculous thing I've ever heard! I mean, who told you that was a good idea?"

The laughter faded, and the blue troll spun in a small circle and scratched his head. "Oh, sure. We'll walk right up to the fightmaster and say, 'Hey, why don't we bring back mercy killings? Wouldn't that be a trip?'"

Cheyenne clenched her jaw. *What the hell is he doing?*

Persh'al stumbled backward with a giggle, then widened his eyes. "No offense, you puffy-haired whatever-*you*-are. But you're an idiot."

The circle of partygoers who'd just been laughing right along with him quickly disbursed, leaving him alone with a short, pink-faced woman with two long rabbit-like ears dangling past her shoulders. The puff of purple hair belonged to her, and her eerily glowing green eyes darted back and forth as she searched for an escape.

"You know what I'm saying, though, right?" Persh'al practically shouted, waving his hand around.

So we're going with the public-drunkenness plan. That would've been nice to know. Cheyenne stood and grabbed both their packs. Persh'al's nearly pulled her over as she struggled to free it from the corner table without smacking anyone in the back of the head.

"Well, lemme lay it out for you," Persh'al continued, swaying back and then dangerously forward until he loomed over the rabbit-eared magical. "There's tradition, and then there's a useless show of weakness. It's pathetic. If we wanted *mercy*, we'd be somewhere else, wouldn't we? Mercy didn't build this mighty empire. Mercy didn't open up this club. I mean, *look* at this place. It's fantastic!"

Another orc bouncer with a silver charm dangling from one bleached-white tusk rounded the other side of the bar. He walked with his hands behind his back, not ready to step in yet.

But Persh'al sure as hell got his attention. Guess we're improvising now.

"Of course, you already know *that*, don't you?" Persh'al laughed and jabbed a finger at the magical woman, who looked like a startled rabbit. Her indecision and the pressure of being noticed but not exactly watched made her freeze.

"You...you..." Persh'al wagged his finger at her and squinted with one eye. "What are you, anyway?"

"I-I'm..." The short magical lifted her chin and tried to collect her dignity. "I'm finished with this conversation."

Before she could walk off in a huff, the bouncer had made it to the wide circle everyone else had given Persh'al and his unintended victim. The orc dipped his head. "How are we this evening?"

"Thirsty." The rabbit-eared woman squeaked and bustled toward the bar.

"Aw, come on!" Persh'al turned and reached after her. His gaze paused briefly on Cheyenne with their packs, and his wink could also have been a drunken eye roll. "We were having such a good time. Don't go and ruin it now. I can't help it if I haven't seen a...a..." He pouted and turned back toward the bouncer, his face contorted in disappointment. "I don't even know what she is."

"I see." The orc reached into his pocket. "I might have a little some-thing to cheer you up, *lugahw'o*. Make you forget about *all* the things you don't know."

Cheyenne paused in front of a recessed niche in the wall and caught a glimpse of huge, clawed gray hands covered in a patch of wiry red fur wrap tighter around a glass. She ignored the urge to peer around the corner to see what kind of magical sat in the hidden cubby in the wall and watched Persh'al's over-the-top acting. *I'll give him credit for that, at least. Might be the only way to get our hands on one of those vials.*

"I've been abandoned," Persh'al whined, throwing his hands up. "Rejected. Spurned, man. You hear me?" He clapped a hand on the bouncer's shoulder and leaned toward the other magical's ear. The orc bore it with surprising dignity and raised an eyebrow. "Nothing's gonna help this mood."

"Trust me. This will." The orc pulled another small metal vial from his pocket and turned to block the transaction from everyone else's view. No one was looking, anyway. "And it's on the house, *lugahw'o.* Make you right as the old fighting pits."

Persh'al's shoulders sagged, and he let out another nostalgic whine. "The fighting pits."

"I miss 'em too. Here."

Cheyenne took one step toward the scene playing out, then leaped back again when the magical sitting in the alcove beside her stirred. The table bumped, and a huge shadow emerged from the recessed wall, blocking all the flashing lights and flickering candles from Cheyenne's view.

Whatever the hulking magical was, it took two slow, thudding steps toward Persh'al and the bouncer and loomed over them. Two massive, hooked wings tipped with thin lines of red fur stirred against the magical's back, and Cheyenne nearly dropped Persh'al's pack.

"I've been looking for you." A low, female voice cut in above the pounding music coming from everywhere.

Persh'al looked into the face Cheyenne couldn't see and broke out in a wide grin. "*Hey!*"

"You need a little boost too?" the bouncer asked, craning his neck to look up at the newcomer to the conversation.

"No, *hidna.* But thank you. I've got to take this naughty little troll out to District 3 to help him pay some of his debts. You know how strict Melsaria is with making payments on time, don't you?"

The orc chuckled and stuffed the vial back into his pocket. "You better go with the *golra*, brother. I've seen the Matron's bad side. And no doubt she can help you perk right back up again."

Persh'al groaned and held his hand out toward the orc. "I don't want to go to District 3 moping like a *carandyll* before Brightforge Day."

"You won't." The hulking magical nudged him toward the front of the club. "I brought you something myself."

"Oh, *lovely*." Persh'al clapped his hands, then leaned around the giant creature in front of him and waved at Cheyenne. "Come on. You have to come with us! My friends are your friends."

He shot her another flashing grin, but the beast with wings nudged him forward again with her clawed hand.

The bouncer stepped toward Cheyenne and glanced over his shoulder. "You're friends with *that* sniveling troll?"

She lifted her gaze and let it linger on the charm dangling from the loop around his tusk. *I've channeled Mom before. Feels like a good time.* When she looked at the orc's yellow eyes flashing with amusement, she raised an eyebrow and gave him a tight smile. "I don't think it's any of your business who my friends are. And I'll thank you not to ask me that type of prying question again."

In an instant, the orc's smile disappeared. He blinked and dipped his head before stepping around her to take up some other post around the club.

Cheyenne headed toward the club's entrance. *Lucky for me this is drow city. And apparently, drow rule the world.*

CHAPTER FORTY-SEVEN

Cheyenne's new activator showed her exactly where to knock on the solid metal wall beneath the arched doorway inside the club. The metal in front of her disappeared, and she hurried down the short tunnel. *I'm screwed if he doesn't stall that thing before I lose him.*

When she stepped back into the fancy dining room of the Wildhaven, she caught a fleeting glimpse of Persh'al's blue head and fallen orange mohawk before the giant winged thing blocking her flew through the front door. The windows lining the front wall were useless for seeing through. *They're probably not even glass. Everything in this messed-up city is metal.*

She hurried toward the front door and shoved it open, not paying a second thought to the pair of magicals in their party finery who leaped away from her, hissing and sneering until they realized she was a drow. Then they shut up and averted their gazes while she stormed out into the bright, glistening plaza of District 5. The halfling turned and scanned the brilliantly shining buildings. *Come on, Persh'al. I'm out of my element here.*

When she'd almost turned a full circle with no sign of her troll guide, a green light flashed in an alley three buildings down. Her activator-enhanced vision lit up with a bright-yellow circle at the same alley,

314

which flashed again. Gritting her teeth, Cheyenne took off past the rows of bars and meticulously clean storefronts. Every magical who saw her heading their way moved aside to let the drow pass, and none of them looked her in the eye.

These guys make everyone in Peridosh look like bold warriors. Or maybe just incredibly stupid.

She had two more yards to go until the flashing yellow light in her vision and the alley met each other. Then a hand stuck out of the alley, making her flinch until she realized Persh'al was the only magical she'd seen with blue hands like that. She picked up the pace and slipped into the alley just as Persh'al withdrew his hand.

"Don't ever leave me stranded like that again." She shoved his bulging pack against his chest, cutting off his low chuckle as the force of her swing slammed him back against the metal wall. "And what the hell was that back there, huh?"

"I told you I was a great conversationalist." Persh'al caught his breath and fumbled with his pack before slinging it over his shoulders again with a grunt. "And you did fine back there, kid. Talked your way outta something else, from the looks of it."

"Yeah, well, I have experience with people expecting me to talk down to them." Cheyenne looked slowly up from the chuckling troll and met the burning-red gaze of the winged magical who'd whisked Persh'al out of the club faster than she could follow. "That's a literal thing for you, though."

The magical loomed at least seven feet over her, her dark-gray face framed by a mane of red hair punctured by two curling black horns sprouting from her temples. Her wings hugged her back tightly as she folded her arms and raised a thin eyebrow at the drow halfling. Then her black lips curled in a smile. "You get used to it."

"Yeah, I bet."

"Oh. Yeah. Cheyenne, Nu'ek. Nu'ek, Cheyenne. Introductions aren't really my thing.

"Well, we don't have time for them anyway." Nu'ek glanced into the dazzling plaza and frowned. "Let's go."

Cheyenne pointed after her as Nu'ek turned and headed down an alley almost too narrow for her broad shoulders. "She's your friend."

"Yep. Always add a little truth to your lies, kid. That's what makes 'em good." He took off after his giant friend, whose clawed feet clacked on the ground with every trembling step.

The halfling shot another glance at the mouth of the alley and hurried after them. "Apparently, you can only lie to complete strangers."

"I'll take my win where I can get it. I just wish the scary *golra* had waited another fifteen seconds. I was *this close* to snatching that vial out of that orc's fat fingers."

Nu'ek tossed a hand in the air, flashing the patch of red fur on the back of it. "You didn't want that poison, Persh'al, trust me."

"Oh yes, I did."

The *golra* disappeared around another corner, forcing Persh'al and Cheyenne to pick up the pace. "I never pegged you as a goldsmile-head. Does your master know you've got a nose for it?"

Cheyenne looked at the troll with wide eyes. "Your master?"

"He's not my master. And no, he doesn't know because there's nothing *to* know. Honestly, you giant, hairy mountain, I'm a little insulted that you'd even think that's why I wanted it."

Nu'ek stopped at the end of the next alley, placed her huge gray hand against the wall, and turned to look down at him. "Then what did you want with it?"

"Well, I wanted to know what the hell it was since nobody's talking. Like at all." Persh'al rubbed his head. "But now that I know it's goldsmile, it's a moot point. Have any ideas why bouncers at an Uppertech club are handing the stuff out like Jell-O shots?"

"Like what?" The wall flashed beneath Nu'ek's hand, and thin panels of metal ejected and folded in on each other, opening into a doorway with plenty of room for the large *golra* to pass.

"Never mind." Persh'al shook his head. "I'm stuck in centuries of Earthside gabble."

"There's a reason nobody's talking up here." Nu'ek glanced up the wall, scanning it for something, then stepped through the open doorway. "So you should stop until we get to where we're going. Then you can run your mouth all night if you have to."

Persh'al sniggered. "I missed you."

The *golra* grunted. "Sure."

Cheyenne and Persh'al walked through the doorway side by side, staying a good six feet behind Nu'ek as she stomped ahead. The scrolling analysis lines in her vision were few and far between now, even when she turned up the activator. "Do you know where we're going?"

"Not really." He nodded at Nu'ek's back. "But she does. Right now, that's good enough for me."

"I see you haven't raised your personal expectations since you made your great escape." The *golra's* low voice echoed around them, then she stepped into an alcove off the tunnel and waited for them to join her.

"If I had any expectations coming into this, they'd all be disappoint-ed." Persh'al and Cheyenne stepped onto another round platform. The halfling ducked and stared up at the huge magical when the tip of the golra's black wing twitched beside her head. The platform lit up and lowered like an elevator down another metal tunnel. "And even without them, I'm *still* disappointed. You're not just luring me away from the good stuff so you can chuck me out the door like you did when your brooding foreman said he didn't like the way I laugh, are you?"

Nu'ek glanced down at him. "I'd forgotten about that."

"Uh-huh. I bet you have."

"You've come back, troll, and I can only think of one reason why. Is this her?"

Persh'al raised his eyebrows at Cheyenne and shrugged. "Yeah, this is her."

"Good. Now shut up until I tell you it's safe."

"Yep." He gripped the straps of his pack and looked at the top of the vertical tunnel moving slowly away from them. "One more question, though. How'd you know we'd be in Wildhaven?"

Nu'ek grunted. "I didn't. That was an amusing coincidence."

"Really?" Chuckling, Persh'al rubbed his forehead and studied what he could see of his friend's face from so far below her. "You just hang out there by yourself on random nights to lighten the mood?"

One of the thick black talons arching from the *golra's* feet tapped the metal platform beneath them. "I like the music."

"Huh."

The platform settled gently at the bottom of the tunnel, then Nu'ek led them down another series of alleys and passages between metal walls not nearly as clean and bright as in Uppertech. Cheyenne gazed between the high walls at the narrow strip of sky. It shimmered above the translucent dome around Hangivol, less bright now than when they'd arrived at what she guessed was the middle of the afternoon. "We're back on the lowest level, right?"

"This is the level we came in on," Persh'al muttered as they turned another quick corner after Nu'ek's trailing wings. "Not the lowest."

"For real?"

"Oh, yeah. And now I'm gonna shut my mouth because I *know* this is something better said elsewhere, yeah?" He gave her a reassuring nod, then they pulled up behind the giant *golra*, who'd stopped at another unmarked wall.

It opened the same way beneath her touch, panels folding out to reveal another doorway. Nu'ek grunted and ducked, nearly doubling over as she squeezed her massive body into the much smaller entrance. "If you say a fell-damn word about this, I'll pull you through and throw you like a spear down these stairs."

Persh'al snickered but didn't open his mouth.

The staircase was steep and narrow and just kept going down. Cheyenne studied the walls, seeing an occasional flicker of blue text scroll by as they passed. *Losing technology underground. Big surprise.*

They climbed steadily down for what felt like at least half an hour. The halfling instinctively pulled her cell phone out of her back pocket, then immediately shoved it back in when she saw nothing but a black screen. *Of course it doesn't work here.*

With another grunt and a screech of talons on stone instead of metal this time, Nu'ek squeezed herself out of the narrow staircase and straightened up in the large, open room at the bottom. Her black and red wings shot out to their full span for a much-needed stretch.

"Whoa." Cheyenne stepped back to keep from clotheslining herself on the barb-tipped ends of those wings, her hair billowing around her face in the kicked-up gust of air.

Nu'ek tucked her wings against her back again, stretching her muscular gray arms straight up over her head. "District 5 isn't built for *golra*."

"Makes sense. Nobody wants to serve a bunch of you in one place. They'd run out of fellwine in five minutes."

The *golra* ignored him and interlaced her fingers for a good knuckle-crack. Then she extended one hand toward the blank stone wall at the base of the staircase and cast the first pure magic spell Cheyenne had seen in Ambar'ogúl.

A buzzing tingle of magical energy washed across the halfling's skin, and she let out a slow breath through pursed lips. *Feels more like the Nimlothar power boost. Makes sense when I'm standing in the only world where magic was supposed to exist.*

The stone wall lit up with hundreds of thin glowing purple strands, all of them drawing inward and converging in front of Nu'ek's outstretched hand. A whirlpool of spinning purple light grew on the door, then the *golra* flicked her fingers, and the circle flashed.

Cheyenne blinked quickly and had to look away, but when she gazed at the wall again, she found the spell slowly fading. Now at the center was the four-pointed star, which pulsed once before fizzling out in a puff of violet-colored smoke. "I've seen that before."

Nu'ek let out a thoughtful hum. "That's not surprising."

"Oh, yeah." Persh'al chuckled. "I forgot you used the front door of the warehouse a few times in the beginning."

The *golra* shoved her hand against the stone wall with a grunt, and the entire section of it drew back into the wall before shifting to the side and opening another room beyond. The ground shuddered beneath them, and the growling rumble of stone scraping across stone made Cheyenne wince.

"Right." She gave Persh'al a questioning look. "On your wards." *And other places.*

"Not my wards, kid. Our favorite drow built those around the warehouse. They've got some serious juice behind 'em, lemme tell ya."

Cheyenne blinked at the opening in the wall, which Nu'ek could pass through at her full height. "And who put the wards up here?"

Persh'al snorted. "Who do you think?" Then he darted after the *golra* and into the darkness of the next room.

For being a wanted drow on two different worlds, L'zar really gets around.

Taking a deep breath, Cheyenne stepped through the stone wall after her guides. The minute she passed through, the huge slab of stone slid back into place behind her with a resounding boom. Another wave of magical energy burst through her with her next step, and she felt a small, tight pinch somewhere in the back of her head. Then even the activator's blinking blue Active light in her vision winked out, and she stood in complete darkness.

CHAPTER FORTY-EIGHT

A ball of normal-looking flame burst to life in Nu'ek's palm, and she nodded for Cheyenne and Persh'al to follow her down another passage to the left.

Cheyenne leaned toward the troll and whispered, "My activator went dead."

"Oh, yeah?"

"Just turned off. Kinda hurt a little."

He chuckled, and Nu'ek turned over her shoulder with a knowing smile, her dark face lit by the dancing shadows of the flames across the walls. "The wards beyond these walls have stood for centuries. We've had to add extra layers on the inside to cover our tracks."

"You know, I felt something," Persh'al said, readjusting his pack. "Guess that's what cut the switch on your gear, kid."

"It keeps the Crown out of our heads," the *golra* added. "When we go dark, she goes blind."

"Well, you sure took that one literally." Persh'al snorted and gestured toward the light in Nu'ek's hand.

She ignored the joke and led them around a curve in the passage before they stopped at another door, which was carved of thick black wood and had steel bolts down either side. The door was at least two feet taller and that much wider than their winged guide, and Nu'ek grabbed the iron ring on the side of the door before jerking it open.

How many doors do we have to go through in this place?

Soft, warm light spilled through the open door, followed by the sound of a dozen low voices. The *golra* disappeared into the room beyond, and Persh'al turned to wiggle his eyebrows at Cheyenne. "Try to keep an open mind, huh?"

"What?"

He didn't reply before slipping through the massive doorway. Cheyenne pursed her lips and followed. *What am I walking into?*

It was a chamber nearly three times the size of Persh'al's warehouse in DC. The place was lit by floating torches and orbs of light bobbing against the stone walls. A huge table of glittering black metal took up the center of the space, though the twenty chairs around it were empty. On the other side of the cavern was a stone well that dove even deeper into the earth of Ambar'ogúl, and dark, shimmering light hovered over the lip like the wall of light between the pillars of the new portal ridges. High-backed armchairs dotted the chamber, clustered in groups of three or four, and spaced along the walls were at least two dozen tunnel entrances of various sizes. Each of these was marked with an O'gúleesh symbol illuminated in different colors, but without a working activator, Cheyenne had no idea what they meant.

"By the blood of Op'paro," someone shouted, cutting off the easy conversation inside the room. "Persh'al Tenishi. You're still breathing."

Persh'al spread his arms. "I've gotten pretty good at that, yeah."

Cheyenne took a quick count of the magicals staring at her, most of them trolls, orcs, and goblins. She couldn't begin to guess what the others were; two of them were covered in sharp, green-tipped quills and one could have passed for a nightstalker if it weren't for the orange flames flickering in her eyes and the five bushy tails flitting behind her. The other magical had blood-red skin covered in spiderwebs of black and small buds of horns sprouting from his head.

One of the magicals draped in a thick black cloak that concealed everything except two burning red eyes stepped forward. The next second, the figure dispersed into millions of swarming, swirling black specks that darted across the room and rematerialized a foot in front of Persh'al, the cloak whipping around its ankles without exposing an inch of the magical's body. "You think you can just step through that door, and we would welcome you back with open arms?"

Frowning, Persh'al eyed the magical, then shrugged. "I did expect it. Just not from you, Berloth."

The figure lifted a four-fingered hand gloved in black leather from beneath its cloak and slowly reached out toward Persh'al's neck.

Cheyenne clenched her fists, watching intently. *If this goes south, I have no problem blasting our way out of here.*

Then a low chuckle emerged from the black hole beneath the figure's hood, and the hand clamped down on Persh'al's shoulder to give it a tight squeeze. The leather glove creaked. "Took you long enough."

The blue troll smiled. "You've waited longer."

The handful of the staring magicals chuckled and approached the newcomers. Nu'ek stood aside and folded her arms, watching the reunion from at least two feet over anyone else. The cloaked figure released Persh'al's shoulder and stepped back. "And how much longer must we wait for the rest?"

Persh'al dipped his head. "We're almost there."

"Except you brought the wrong drow." One of the magicals with green-tipped quills cocked her head, a green-gray tongue poking out between dark lips.

The red-and-black-skinned magical narrowed all-black eyes at Cheyenne. "We're not picking up strays."

Cheyenne dipped her head and glared at him. "You did *not* just call me a stray."

"Look at that." The magical sneered at her, his black eyes glinting. "It talks."

"What the hell is this?" Cheyenne turned her gaze onto Persh'al now.

The troll slowly shook his head and folded his arms, gazing at the group of magicals hidden below the city. They gathered slowly in front of their old friend and the drow halfling, emanating suspicion and a distrust Cheyenne could almost taste.

He better know what he's doing.

Persh'al lifted his chin and scanned the faces of his alleged friends. "Who's got a problem with the drow standing next to me?"

"All of us," hissed a goblin with a burned, blackened patch of mottled scars across her forehead. "We don't know this one, and a drow we don't know is a drow who'll bring this whole thing down on our heads."

"Take another look." Persh'al gestured at Cheyenne without looking away from the sneering faces. "Notice anything familiar?"

Someone hissed, and for an unbearably long ten seconds, Cheyenne's skin tingled under fifteen scrutinizing gazes.

She turned to Persh'al. "I'm not doing this."

"Just wait."

"Hey, I know when I'm not wanted, and I didn't come here to be stared at like some freak in a circus." She spun around and headed toward the open door into the dark passageway beyond.

"Cheyenne."

The second she reached the huge wooden door, it swung shut on its own with a resounding boom. She whirled and glared at the back of Persh'al's head and his limp mohawk. "Tell me what's going on, or I'll blast my way through this!"

"Blood bonds with blood." The deep voice echoed from the other side of the massive chamber, and a hulking dark shape appeared from one of the open tunnels beneath a glowing red O'gúleesh rune. When the hulking raug stepped into the light, and everyone turned to look at him, the chamber fell deathly silent.

How the hell did Gúrdu get here before we did?

But it wasn't Gúrdu. This raug was much older, his gray skin wrinkled and lined with age. He shuffled forward, thumping a gnarled cane on the ground with every step. Persh'al turned to meet Cheyenne's gaze and dipped his head.

"You've heard that before, haven't you?" the raug growled as he limped toward the front of the chamber.

Cheyenne gritted her teeth and forced herself to reply. "More than once."

The raug stepped onto the widening path the other magicals made for him, passing Persh'al without a second glance. He stopped in front of Cheyenne, towering over her by at least a foot. He took a long, whistling sniff of the air, then snorted in her face.

She jerked her head away from the hot breath rustling through her hair but didn't look away from the glowing orange-brown eyes studying her. "Step back."

Persh'al sucked in a sharp breath.

The raug's eyes narrowed, then he stepped aside, thumping his cane on the stone floor with a crack before addressing everyone else. "This is not the drow we hoped to see in our midst, but she is not the *wrong* drow."

The other magicals shuffled their feet and exchanged wary glances.

"You can't know that." An orc missing half an ear grimaced, his thick lower lip curling around two thick tusks painted black.

"Persh'al said to look closer." The raug snorted and waved a red-clawed hand at Cheyenne. "And you idiots closed your eyes. Open them and see who stands before you."

The old one left Cheyenne's side and headed back through the wide-eyed magicals. His thumping cane stopped in front of the massive black table, where he lowered himself into a chair and closed his eyes with a long, growling sigh.

The catlike woman with five tails cocked her head and pointed at Cheyenne. "Tell us who you are."

The halfling lifted her chin. "Cheyenne Summerlin."

Persh'al cast a wary glance at the suspicious crowd, then hurried over and stopped beside her with his back to the others. He leaned slightly toward her and whispered, "I know you don't like the way it tastes, kid, but you gotta tell them what they wanna hear. *Your* name doesn't mean anything in this room, but you know the name that does."

She shot him a sidelong glance. "Are you kidding me?"

He met her gaze and raised his eyebrows.

This is my coming-out party, huh? Guess it had to happen sooner or later.

With flaring nostrils, Cheyenne looked away from the blue troll beside her and folded her arms. It was a lot easier to say the words she hated when she was staring at the far wall of the chamber instead of the hungry eyes of suspicious magicals.

"My name is Cheyenne Summerlin. And my—" She swallowed and grimaced. *Just fucking say it.* "My father is L'zar Verdys."

Her words echoed through the chamber, and no one moved.

Persh'al nudged her with his elbow as a slow, triumphant smile spread across his lips. "Nicely done."

Cheyenne shook her head and kept staring at the back wall.

"Persh'al," the black-and-red magical growled. "What is it?"

The blue troll stepped forward, gesturing at the scowling halfling. "You heard the drow. This is what happens next."

"He did it?" A troll with rings of jagged black tattoos encircling his arms glanced at Persh'al and Cheyenne. "He broke through?"

"Endaru's balls, man. Come on. You've got Foltr's seal of approval and heard it straight from Cheyenne's mouth. This is L'zar's kid standing here. How much more proof do you need?"

The magical hidden within the black cloak reared back and bellowed with laughter. The startling sound seemed to break the others out of their shocked silence, and everyone started yelling.

"That fell-damn drow should have come himself!"

"Why'd you bring her *here*?"

"We need to move now!"

Glancing slowly away from the back wall of the chamber, Cheyenne cocked her head and looked at Nu'ek. The *golra* stood like a hulking statue at the side of the chamber, her red-furred arms folded. Then she met Cheyenne's gaze and gave a small, barely imperceptible shake of her head.

L'zar left them all here and expected everyone to sit tight and wait for his signal. He should've expected chaos.

"All right, hold on." Persh'al raised his hands to quiet the others down, but it was useless.

"Right here in the city, Persh'al? Have you lost your mind?"

"Not the last time I checked."

"If she's spotted here, we lose everything!"

"She won't be."

"We need L'zar. Does his daughter know the first thing about what's required of her?"

Persh'al clenched his fists. "You know what? If you'll just shut up and listen to me, I'll tell you."

"We've been waiting quietly for centuries! If L'zar's not here to tell us himself, what the hell are we supposed to do?"

The shouting continued, and Persh'al dropped his hands. He looked at Nu'ek, and the *golra* rolled her eyes. Then she stomped her clawed foot, her talons shrieking on the stone floor and sending up a spray of sparks, and roared. The chamber shook, knocking dust loose from the ceiling, and everyone stopped.

"Shut your useless mouths and sit down!" Nu'ek growled, her wings stretched to their full span as she glared at the magicals who said they were loyal to L'zar's cause. "If you want your fell-damned answers, now is the time to listen. You know who we serve."

One by one, the magicals shot her scathing glances and turned to take their seats around the massive black table. Foltr the raug sat motionless in his chair, clawed hands folded over the top of his gnarled cane, his eyes still closed. No one said another word, and Persh'al returned to Cheyenne's side, lowering his voice. "That didn't go quite like I expected, but I think they got the message."

Cheyenne frowned at him. "What are we doing here? They want L'zar, not me."

"Just hang in there with me, kid. All right? I'll take care of the rest." He nudged her arm. "Some entrance, though, huh?"

She snorted. "Honestly, I thought we were gonna have to fight our way out of here."

Persh'al shrugged and gestured for her to follow him to the massive black table with the others. "We still might. But at least we'll get a chance to fill them in on what's happening first, right?"

"Oh, sure. I feel so much better." Her deadpan glare had the opposite effect and made him chuckle.

CHAPTER FORTY-NINE

"So, L'zar's spawn finally lived to tell the tale." The second quill-covered magical folded his arms and sat back in his chair, staring at Cheyenne. "Did she pass her trials yet?"

Foltr cracked his cane on the floor and leaned forward. "She wouldn't be here if she hadn't."

Cheyenne snorted. "*She* can speak for herself. If you have a question, why don't you look me in the eye and ask?"

The aging raug let out a soft grunt of amusement, and the other magicals around the table shot the halfling fleeting glances.

Even these guys don't want to look at me.

"I still don't understand why you brought her here." The horned magical with the red and black flesh stuck his black tongue between his teeth and bit down in disgust. "Right under the Crown's nose, Persh'al. I think you've spent too much time letting your brain rot in that other realm."

"Hey, it's the last place the Crown will look for her." Persh'al opened his pack on his lap, paused, and scanned the faces around the table. "And we needed to see what's been going on before all the other pieces get put into play."

"Things have changed since the last time you were at this table." The cloaked figure spread his gloved hand on the black wood in front of him and hissed softly. "Not for the better."

"Yeah, we picked up on that pretty quickly." Persh'al pulled two large metal lockboxes from his pack and slid them toward the center of the table. "These are straight from L'zar. Do whatever you want with them once Cheyenne and I leave."

"That's why you're here?" the black-tusked orc asked. "To bring us cheap gifts?"

Persh'al glared at him with narrowed eyes. "Not so cheap when I tell you L'zar's putting everything in motion. The next time you see him, he'll be standing right next to his daughter. Maybe before she claims the last rite, maybe after, but he's coming."

"What is he waiting for?"

"We hit a roadblock, all right?" Persh'al glanced at Cheyenne and rolled his eyes. "It's probably hard to get real-time updates down here in this fancy dark cave, but in case you haven't heard, there are new portals opening, maybe as we speak. Who knows?"

A nervous murmur passed around the table, and the old raug shifted in his seat to face the blue troll, leaning over the top of his cane. "Explain that."

"I can't."

"It's the Crown," Cheyenne said. All eyes focused on her, and Persh'al cleared his throat. "At least, that's what we think."

When she looked at him for clarification, he gestured for her to continue and sat back in his chair. "You take this one, kid. I'm tired of talkin'."

"Continue," Foltr growled, his orange-brown gaze flicking across her face.

Guess I'm stepping into this role, whether I like it or not.

Cheyenne took a deep breath. "When we crossed over today, everything had been destroyed—the land, the wildlife, all of it. Pretty nasty stuff."

"Where was this?"

Persh'al thumped a fist on the table. "In the Outers, Jara'ak. Where do you think?"

"Let the *Aranél* speak!" Foltr thumped his cane again and glared around the table. "The next *dae'bruj* to open their mouth out of turn will spend the rest of the evening rubbing valdishwort all over an old raug's aching joints. Are we clear?"

Cheyenne glanced at the raug's gnarled hands sprouting white-gray hairs and the layers of orange-tinted dirt beneath his clawed nails. *I wouldn't wanna rub anything into that cracked skin.*

When the aged magical looked at her again and nodded slowly, she returned the gesture and frowned. "What does that mean? '*Aranél.*'"

Foltr chuckled and shot Persh'al a knowing smile. The blue troll leaned toward her and muttered, "A term of endearment. Mostly."

"Uh-huh." She scanned the amused expressions around the table and cocked her head. "We weren't sure what was happening in the Outers until we got closer to Hangivol. Whatever the Crown's doing here, it's spilling death and decay everywhere beyond the city, and it's starting to leak out of Ambar'ogúl. Making new portals. Spilling things onto Earth that aren't supposed to be anywhere but between worlds."

A muscular goblin with gold rings piercing the elongated backs of both ears narrowed his eyes. "None of this sounds like anything that would concern L'zar."

"Well, it does when the Crown's using those new portals to smuggle war machines across the Border," Persh'al snapped. "The bitch already has a bounty on Cheyenne's head. She hasn't found L'zar's kid, and she won't until Cheyenne and L'zar are standing right in front of her at the Rahalma. That'll be a lot harder to do if the Crown consumes the resources we have on Earth first."

"Leave Earth to itself," the quilled woman shouted. "We have enough here to deal with."

"Leave Earth to itself?" Cheyenne leaned forward over the table. "That's not an option."

"You might be L'zar's daughter, *Aranél*, but no one here has sworn fealty to *you*. That other realm is useless and weak. If the Crown takes it before we finish what we started, it hardly makes a difference."

"There are billions of people in that other realm!" Cheyenne slapped her hands on the table and lurched to her feet, snarling. "We're not leaving them unprotected."

"What has Earth done for us?" Another orc jabbed a meaty finger at Cheyenne and grunted. "Taken the one drow who can make a difference on this side while we try to hold together the last crumbling pieces of an old Cycle that didn't sow terror and death."

Cheyenne gritted her teeth, itching to unleash her magic, which burned hotter than ever through her blood. "It's done a lot more than that. Without 'that other realm,' I wouldn't be here. You'd have one more nameless child of L'zar Verdys lying dead at his feet. Or maybe none."

"You've got a weakness for the humans, *Aranél*." The black-and-red magical sneered at her. "That didn't come from L'zar. Was it your fool mother, then?"

"Watch it."

"Raised you as an Earthside-born drow, taught you to defend the weak because she's forgotten what blood runs through her veins?"

Fury boiled through Cheyenne's body, and she didn't even try to stop the purple sparks flaring from her fingertips. The magicals sitting closest to her leaned away, except for Persh'al and the old raug. "Earth is my home, asshole. You have a seriously fucked-up misconception about what humans are worth, *and* what they're capable of."

"See? You've grown too attached."

"I'm attached because I'm one of them!" A flare of black flames burst from within the drow halfling's eyes, her purple sparks crackling across her skin like an electric current before quickly disappearing.

The sixteen other magicals gathered around the table stared at her with wide eyes.

"Is this true?" a goblin man asked, lowering his hand. He'd been picking his teeth.

Persh'al sighed. "It's—"

"No, I got this," Cheyenne snapped, jerking her hand out toward him and gesturing for him to wait. "I'm not full human, but my mother is. And I'll tell you right now, if I had to choose between her and anyone else in this room, I'd choose her every time. Not because she's my mother, but because that *human* could take down entire armies with a few well-placed words and a little leverage. I don't give a shit who's sworn loyalty to L'zar or to me. We're not sacrificing Earth just to make you feel like L'zar hasn't wasted your time."

The cloaked magical with the glowing red eyes started laughing again, his form flitting between a humanoid shape and a swarm of black specks swirling above his chair. The black-and-red magical with the small horns studding his scalp hissed at the halfling but didn't argue again.

"Well." Foltr leaned back in his chair and lifted his cane to set it across his lap. "There's no denying who fathered this one, is there?"

A round of low, tense chuckles rose from the gathered magicals.

"You can sit down, kid." Persh'al nodded when she glared down at him. "You made your point."

Cheyenne sank into her chair and folded her arms. *I lost my shit. Apparently, that's what it takes for them to smarten the hell up.*

"You're not wrong about the portals." Nu'ek, too large for any of the chairs around the table, took a slow step forward from where she'd been at the side of the chamber. "If they're opening on the other side on their own, things are worse here than any of us knew."

"It's bad enough already," the quilled woman added.

"We figured as much." Persh'al nodded and gazed around the table. "We were at Wildhaven when Nu'ek found us. The peacekeepers aren't contained to high-end restaurants and Uppertech nightclubs, are they?"

"No." The black-tusked orc grimaced with distaste. "It's everywhere. The Crown's lost her mind, and she's taking the whole fell-damned city with her."

"We hear about the *outernóre* making the crossing in droves," the cloaked magical added, fully materialized for the conversation. "That's been causing enough problems, but what other choice do they have? They're starving. Terrified. And of course, she won't lift a finger against the raiders now taking everything that's left in the Outers. They don't even have the means to buy their way into the city where everyone else thinks it's safe."

"And those with any *veréle* are moving as close to Hangivol as they can get, if not right into it." A troll woman with a thin silver chain dangling between a stud in either ear shook her head. "The fell-damned Mother's drawing her blinded children ever closer under the guise of luxury and safety, but this place is a madhouse, and the Crown's made it impossible to leave."

"I'm guessing it gets worse above Uppertech," Persh'al muttered.

"Of course. The lower levels don't have it as bad as the inner circles."

"What about once you're inside the city?" The blue troll scanned the faces gathered around the table. "We watched a guy get eaten by a wall just for calling out truths. Granted, he was louder about it than he should've been, but if most magicals are too afraid to be that loud, I'm trying to figure out why the Hangivol Exodus hasn't happened yet."

"Oh, we can all come and go as we please," Nu'ek replied. "If you've got business outside the city, sure. As long as you bring it right back."

Persh'al's eyes narrowed. "And nobody has much business outside a city doing all the business with itself."

"The Crown abandoned the Outers." Foltr grunted. "From Simmara all the way to Teridól would be seeing the same by now if it weren't for their stewards. They walk as tight a rope as we do, trying to placate her while keeping their wards safe within the territories."

"But here," the troll woman added, "O'gúleesh can do whatever they want whenever they want. Tech runs most of the grunt work these days, and the fortunate Hangivol-dwellers are living it up on every level outside the Edhilór."

"What's her reasoning for handing everything over to the pawns?" Persh'al asked. "I know fell-damned well it isn't to keep up her dazzling reputation."

"Total control disguised as complete freedom." Nu'ek folded her arms. "And access to an entire metropolis of magic she can draw from at will."

"Right. And that's causing the blight."

"Causing it. Perpetuating it. Maybe even trying to hide it. But as long as the tainted river of pleasure flows through Hangivol, those living here have fewer reasons to look any farther than the next poison they all call privilege," the black-tusked orc growled as he swept his hand across the table. "Unless you let the act slip. Even a whiff of dissatisfaction brings the Night and Circle down on your head."

Persh'al's eyes widened. "The Night and Circle?"

"No honor left in serving the Crown, *lugahw'o.*" The raug dipped his head toward the blue troll and closed his eyes.

The table fell silent, then Persh'al chuckled and shook his head. "I wonder if they'll change their tune when General Hi'et lights the death-flame under their asses."

"General Hi'et abandoned her post," the quilled man muttered.

Cheyenne frowned at him. "Well, she picked up a new one Earthside."

"What?"

"She would never!"

"General Hi'et is gone."

The surprise and uncertainty buzzed around the table, and Cheyenne glanced at Persh'al. "When was the last time you sent updates over here?"

He shook his head and waved her off. "Longer than it should've been. We've been busy, kid. You know that."

"Sounds like we should've dropped that little nugget of information at the beginning of this stupid meeting." When Persh'al only shrugged in response, Cheyenne closed her eyes and took a deep breath. *L'zar left a shitstorm behind him to start a new one Earthside. They need to smooth out the kinks in this process.*

CHAPTER FIFTY

"How much do you know about General Hi'et?" the black-and-red magical shouted over the din.

"Not as much as I thought until a few days ago." Cheyenne shook her head. "But enough to know that you're following the path she started before she left. Maleshi's fighting for Earth *and* Ambar'ogúl from the other side. If anyone still thinks Earth isn't worth saving after that, you shouldn't be here."

Foltr let out a harsh, croaking laugh that made everyone quiet down again.

Cheyenne leaned away from him in her chair and eyed him. "That wasn't supposed to be funny."

The raug gurgled out more laughter and wheezed, wiping spittle from the underside of his quivering gray chin. "Maleshi, is it?"

"Yeah. We've been on a first-name basis for a while." *With me mostly calling her Mattie, but they don't need to know that.*

"It would seem so." The old raug chuckled again and pointed at her with a crooked orange-clawed finger. "Forget what these fools think they know about what we've been waiting to see, *Aranél.* You've brought a new future to this aged raug at the end of his days."

"Nah." Persh'al waved off the comment. "You've got at least another thousand years left in you."

Nu'ek snorted. "By the Veil, I hope not."

The gathered party broke into unrestrained laughter, this time without the weight of doubt and wary indecision. The raug chuckled with them and closed his eyes.

When the noise died down again, the magicals returned their attention to Cheyenne. Some of them smiled. The rest looked less tense.

If the old raug approves, the rest of them follow. Good to know.

"So, the pieces are in play on both sides." The troll woman with the chain dangling across her face gestured at Persh'al. "If the Crown is taking the war to Earth, she won't stop even if he and his daughter make it to the Rahalma."

"Not if," Cheyenne added quickly. "When."

Persh'al shot her a wide-eyed glance, and she shrugged. *Yeah, I've already committed this far. Might as well go the whole mile.*

"Of course." The troll woman dipped her head with a small, secretive smile. "*When* you stand at the Rahalma. But how much will that truly change?"

Persh'al scratched his head. "L'zar seems to think that's the endgame. I have to agree with him."

"So, he will bring the war back to the blackened heart of Ambar'ogúl," Foltr muttered. "With a daughter who defied the mysteries of prophecy."

"Something like that, yeah."

Cheyenne couldn't look away from the old raug's glowing orange eyes. *Why do I feel like I'm not getting the whole picture?*

"Then we'll fight." The black-tusked orc pounded his fist on the table again and nodded. "Right where we are. I've been sitting on this fell-damned oath for centuries, and I mean to see it through."

"Good choice." Persh'al pointed at him and grinned. "Go through those cases, huh? We have things to wrap up Earthside, but L'zar will be here as soon as he's finished working out the kinks. Then you'll know what to do. We still have the territories on our side?"

"Last we heard, Simmara and Teridól still wait for us to send word. Ki'uali is harder to reach, but we have no reason to think they'd turn back now."

"Right." The blue troll slapped his hands on the table and stood. "I think we covered pretty much everything." He nodded at Cheyenne and added, "Get ready for the long ride home, kid."

"You're leaving already?" the troll woman asked, raising an eyebrow.

A pained frown flickered across Persh'al's brows when he looked at her. "As much as I'd love to stay, Elarit, this was only supposed to be a day trip."

She shot him a brief, unamused smile. "Pity."

"Hmm." He forced himself to look away from her before plastering another smile on his face and aiming it at Nu'ek. "I'm assuming you can get us back out without too much trouble?"

The *golra* folded her arms and raised an eyebrow. "I'm assuming you haven't forgotten who built these tunnels."

"Me? Nah. Long memory, *golra*. Doesn't mean I memorized the map, though."

Nu'ek snorted and turned away from the table to head across the massive chamber.

Cheyenne stood as multiple conversations picked up again, the impromptu meeting apparently over. A rough, leathery-feeling hand wrapped around her wrist, and she looked quickly down at the old raug sitting beside her.

"You *will* be prepared, *Aranél*," he muttered. "L'zar has always been a thorn in the Crown's side, but you, I think, will be the blade."

Gúrdu's voice came back to her. *"Cut out the heart, cut out the rot. The shackles of the old laws rise. For the last scion, it is destiny or chains."*

Taking a deep breath, Cheyenne nodded. "I hope so."

"Oh, yes." Foltr chuckled and released her arm. "Yes, we all do."

He closed his eyes and said nothing more, which Cheyenne took as a sign that she'd been dismissed. She slung her pack over her shoulder and headed around the table as the magicals stood. Some of them nodded at her before returning to their conversations. The halfling felt their eyes on her when she wasn't looking, but no one blatantly watched her anymore.

Yeah, take a good long look at L'zar's halfling kid who wasn't supposed to exist.

She found Persh'al on the other side of the chamber, locked in an intense but quiet conversation with the troll woman with the silver chain across her face. He kept leaning closer, trying to convince her of something, but Elarit wasn't having any of it. When she caught sight of Cheyenne, she pressed her hand against Persh'al's chest, and he immediately stopped. "Your time's up, *ma gairín*."

"What?" Persh'al followed her glance and saw Cheyenne standing there, watching him with a blank expression. "Oh. Yeah. You ready?"

"Yep."

"Sorry." He chuckled and stepped back. "This is—"

"Elarit Masharun." The troll woman's lips twitched into a smile as she studied Cheyenne with scarlet eyes. "I don't expect you to remember the name once you leave, *Aranél*. It wouldn't be the first time."

Persh'al made a choking sound and leaned toward Elarit. "Come on. That's not fair."

She ignored him.

"Nice to meet you." Out of pure habit, Cheyenne extended her hand. The troll woman stared at it blankly.

"It's an Earth thing," Persh'al muttered and waved Cheyenne's hand aside.

"That activator isn't," Elarit said and slowly lifted her gaze from the web of metal strands around Cheyenne's hand to the halfling's face. "Did Persh'al buy you that toy?"

Cheyenne bit back a laugh. "Yeah."

"Hmm. That's what I thought. He's always been cheap when it comes to gifts."

Persh'al snorted. "Wait a minute!"

Elarit shot him a knowing glance and pulled a small coil of silver from the pocket of her flowing skirts. She nodded and offered it to Cheyenne. "You'll have a lot more fun with this."

"What is it?" The halfling took it, turning the coil over in her fingers.

"An upgrade. When you're out of our mandatory dark zone down here, put it behind your ear." The troll woman winked.

"Thanks."

"We're going right back to the Border," Persh'al said quickly. "She won't be able to use it."

"I can build another with my eyes closed, Persh'al." Elarit cut her gaze toward him and tilted her head. "She'll want to see what these can do, and the way you're headed will give her plenty of time."

He grunted and rubbed the back of his neck, then finally nodded at Cheyenne. "All right. You can keep it."

The halfling snorted. "I don't need your permission for that."

Elarit laughed and folded her arms. "You certainly don't."

"Okay, everybody laugh at the troll trying to make things right. Very helpful." When Elarit's smile disappeared, he pointed at Nu'ek, who was standing by one of the only two tunnels cut into the chamber walls that were big enough for a *golra* to pass through. "Go tell her I'll be right there, huh? I need another minute.'

Cheyenne glanced at the trolls and gently slipped Elarit's activator into her pocket. "Sure. Just don't take too long."

"I'll take as long as I need, kid. Go mind your own business."

With a curt nod and a barely hidden smile, Cheyenne gave Elarit a silent goodbye and turned to join Nu'ek at the other end of the chamber. *Looks like I crashed a private troll party.*

The *golra* snorted when Cheyenne stopped a few feet away, and they both watched Persh'al plead with Elarit in hushed tones for something she wouldn't give him.

"Is that what it looks like?"

Nu'ek glanced down at the halfling and raised an eyebrow. "I have no idea what it looks like to *you*."

"It looks like that troll expected somebody to wait a couple hundred years for him, and he came back a couple hundred years too late."

"Then it's exactly what it looks like." Nu'ek chuckled, her folded arms bouncing against her stomach. She scratched a bicep covered in a strip of wiry red fur, which sounded like dry leaves being raked across dead grass. "Those two have been playing that game for so long, we're all sick of watching it, even with the relatively long breaks in between. She'll give in eventually, and when she does, I'll be the first to lift a tankard and tell them both to piss off and make it official already."

Cheyenne swallowed a laugh. "What do you call that on this side?"

"Putting Persh'al out of his misery." They shared a short chuckle.

"I meant, the 'making it official' part."

"I know." Nu'ek rolled her shoulders back and looked at the vaulted ceiling of the cavern, stretching out her muscular gray neck. "It's called a *myrein*. When all this is finished, we'll need something to celebrate. Take our minds off what's been done."

339

Cheyenne frowned. "I'd think stopping the Crown would be enough to celebrate."

The *golra* folded her arms again and shook her head, the smile gone from her steely features. "After so much loss, *Aranél*, even a definitive win starts to feel like just one more struggle to overcome. There's little to rejoice about when you're the last ones standing in a battlefield. But a *myrein*? A *myrein* focuses on the future."

"Right." Cheyenne glanced up at the huge winged magical beside her, but Nu'ek had turned her attention to the others still gathered in small groups around the table. *That's why they're here. Focusing on the future and forgetting everything they had to give up to get there. This thing is a lot bigger than I thought.*

Persh'al grabbed Elarit's hand and held it in both of his as she turned away from him. The troll woman's small smile betrayed the apathy she tried so hard to project. When Persh'al raised her hand to his lips, she looked down at him over the shimmering silver chain across her face and closed her eyes. Her scarlet fingers lightly brushed his cheek, then she turned without another word and slipped away from him to join someone else's conversation.

Staring after her, Persh'al took a full ten seconds before he spun and stalked toward Cheyenne and Nu'ek. "Let's get the hell out of here."

The *golra* nodded and took off down the tunnel, summoning another handful of fire to light their way. Cheyenne fell in beside Persh'al and cleared her throat. "So, Elarit, huh?"

Persh'al shot her a wide-eyed stare, then shook his head. "Should've known you'd pick up on that."

"I think everyone's picked up on it."

"Yeah, well, everyone can mind their own damn business, can't they?" His raised voice echoed down the tunnel, though Nu'ek acted like she hadn't heard. Persh'al scratched the back of his head and muttered, "You can keep what you saw to yourself, kid. The crew Earthside doesn't know anything about it."

"Are you sure?"

"Oh, yeah. I'm sure." He snorted. "If they knew, they wouldn't have sent me across with you."

Cheyenne's eyes widened, but he wouldn't look at her. "That's a shitty reason to make you stay behind."

"Not when they think I'm over here following orders."

"*What?* He ordered you to—"

"Drop it, all right?" Persh'al looked at her with a creased brow, his jaw clenching in the flickering light of Nu'ek's fire in front of them. "Now's not the time."

Cheyenne swallowed and stared straight ahead. *So, L'zar sticks his fancy drow nose in everyone else's business too. Okay. That's one more thing to set straight when the time is right. Whenever the hell that is.*

CHAPTER FIFTY-ONE

Nu'ek led them down the tunnel for another hour at least before luminescent panels lit up overhead. The *golra* snuffed out her flames and turned to nod at Cheyenne and Persh'al. "We're getting close."

"Close to what?" Cheyenne gazed at the flickering lights and couldn't tell if they were powered by magic or the return of working technology down here.

"A transport station." Nu'ek pointed down the dark tunnel, which slowly illuminated as their presence activated the overhead lights. "The Crown's blocked most of the portals around the city. Fortunately, she's got about as much control over the portals as she does over us. But the ones she either can't touch or doesn't care about are at least as far out as Oronti Valley, if not farther."

The halfling grimaced. "So we have another, what? Four hours or more to go?"

Persh'al grunted. "Nah, kid. We'll be moving a lot faster on the way back."

Five minutes later, the tunnel opened into a wide rectangular room. Directly across from them was a heavy metal door with a circular window, and the entire wall curved away from the room's entrance.

Cheyenne studied the corners of the room and frowned. "That's not a wall, is it?"

"Good work." Persh'al strode across the room and gave the curving metal wall a quick slap. "More like taking the subway, kid, without the crowded seats and the smell."

Nu'ek raised an eyebrow. "I don't understand half of what you say anymore."

"It's another Earthside thing, *golra*. I'd say you should visit sometime, but there's even less room for you there than there is here. Unless you've been brushing up on your transformation spells."

"That would be a waste of my time."

"Right. Well, good thing you're staying here while we light this baby up and get the hell out of the city." Persh'al pressed the door of the O'gúleesh shuttle, but nothing happened. "Oh, come on."

He pressed a few more times, ran his hand over the metal from side to side and top to bottom, then pounded it with a fist. "Nu'ek!"

The *golra*'s thick jaw clenched and unclenched as she stared at the agitated troll. "It was fully functional the last time I was here."

"Which was when? Right after I left?"

Her apologetic shrug was even more awkward coming from a magical her size.

"Shit." He scowled at the door and tossed his arms in the air. "Now what, huh? L'zar's expecting us to report back before dawn over there, and we're not taking another fell-damn skiff to the Outers. That's not gonna happen."

"Tell him the station went dead."

"Oh, sure. I'll just pop back into the wanted drow's hiding place hours late and hand him excuses. The guy freaks out when you bring him the wrong beef jerky flavor. How do you think he's gonna react when his kid goes missing for hours and he can't find her?"

"I'm not missing," Cheyenne muttered.

"Yeah, and he won't know that 'til we get back to tell him, will he?"

"I'm sorry." Nu'ek dipped her head toward him and spread her arms. "We can try another station."

"And risk that one being dead too? Don't screw with me, *golra*. If this one's dead, the others are dead too. Damn. And here I was, thinking these things had a few hundred years left until they cut us off."

The troll ranted on, but Cheyenne tuned him out when her fingers closed around the coil of Elarit's activator in her pocket. She pulled it out, frowned at the metal lines of the first device spreading across her hand, and peeled that one off. The minute she slipped the chains off her fingers, they withdrew with a metallic clink until the pieces had folded themselves back into the metal tube of the activator's original shape. She stuck it in her other pocket and studied the Elarit's coil. *Worth a shot, right?*

"Hey, are we still inside the wards? The ones for all the tech?"

Persh'al stopped mid-sentence and shot her a quick glance before scowling up at Nu'ek again. "You'd better hope you have a useful answer to *that* question."

The golra let out a low growl and stomped toward the entrance to the station. Her claws screeched on the stone floor, and she swiped a hand across the open air leading into the tunnel they'd just exited. Pale light shimmered over the doorway, which filled with a thin metal panel that slid into place to block them off.

"Huh." Persh'al glanced around the long room and nodded at Cheyenne. "Yeah, maybe the wards were interfering with the controls. Good thinking, kid." He pointed at her and hurried back to the door of the underground train to try opening it again.

"That wasn't where I was going with that," Cheyenne muttered.

He snarled at the unresponsive door and smacked it again. "You sure you know how to dampen the wards the right way?"

Nu'ek folded her arms and scowled at him. "I know what I'm doing."

"Yeah, looks like it."

Cheyenne turned slightly away from him and slipped the coil behind her ear. The thing pinched her skin and sent a vibrating burst of energy crackling through her head. She clenched her eyes shut tight and bowed her head, gritting her teeth through the discomfort.

"You know what?" Persh'al spread his arms and crossed the room again to the metal door sealing them off. "Get this damn thing open and take us up to the lower levels. If I have to rewire someone's skiff, fine. It's breaking about five laws and two different promises, but what the hell? It's better than getting my head ripped off."

"Hold on a minute." Cheyenne took a deep breath and slowly

opened her eyes. She staggered sideways at the barrage of information flooding through not just her vision but her entire mind.

"Cheyenne." Persh'al stomped toward her. "You good?"

"Oh, yeah." She blinked, and the second she thought about tuning out all the extra data, the new activator responded. Turning slowly, she met the blue troll's concerned gaze and grinned. "I'm excellent."

"You look stoned. Are you...shit." His shoulders slumped as he looked her up and down. "Did you put that coil behind your ear?"

"Yes, I did."

Nu'ek chuckled. "Now we're even."

Persh'al whirled to face the golra and spread his arms. "What's that supposed to mean?"

"We might have forgotten to run a systems check on the stations." The winged magical chuckled. "But you forgot about the activators."

"I didn't forget." The troll's mouth opened and closed soundlessly, then he turned and pointed at Cheyenne as she approached the shuttle's door. "All right, fine. Just be careful with that thing, kid. You hear me? Better yet, take it off and hand it over. That thing could just as easily fry your brain if you don't know what you're doing."

"Persh'al." The halfling stopped with her face inches away from the metal door, passing her hand over the surface and watching the streams of data flow around it.

He sighed. "What?"

"Shut up."

Nu'ek's rumbling laughter echoed in the transport station's single room. The troll scratched the back of his head, growling wordlessly as he paced in front of the shuttle.

Unable to wipe away the crazed grin, Cheyenne studied the scrolling data that was translated almost instantly for her convenience. *What am I looking for? An on-switch? A command for...oh.*

She pressed the blinking dot on the door and lines of information splayed out in different directions, telling her exactly what to do and in which order. By the time she finished following the activator's command, she'd drawn a four-pointed star on the shuttle's outer door. With a quick laugh of disbelief, she stepped back and watched the illuminated blue light fade from the rusty metal surface.

As soon as it did, a low hum rose from the other side of the door, followed by pale blue light glowing through the round window from the inside. Some kind of engine powered up and a high whine filled the station.

"Well, shit." Persh'al snorted and glanced quickly at Nu'ek before staring at the activated shuttle again. "You guys send someone down here to revamp security or what?"

The golra slowly shook her head. "I'm not the one with the long memory."

"Yeah, throw that one right back in my face, why doncha?"

"This is so cool." Cheyenne leaned away from the shuttle and scanned the full length of the craft pressed up against the edge of the station's apparent platform. "You weren't kidding when you said that first one was basic. That's like DSL versus wi-fi."

"Uh-huh. And you're riding high-speed internet now, kid. Okay. Turn it down a second so we can bid this giant bat on two legs *adieu*."

Nu'ek frowned. "I don't understand."

Cheyenne turned down the scrolling data with a ghost of a thought and faced the *golra*, still grinning. "It means goodbye."

Persh'al scoffed. "I swear, we need some kind of Earthside translator for you guys. If we're gonna be fighting this war from both sides of the Border, we all need to be on the same page."

"That'll never happen." Nu'ek stepped forward and thumped her chest with a huge, clawed fist. "But you can try."

"Sure, I'll get right on it in my spare time. No problem." With a snort, the troll returned the gesture and nodded curtly at the *golra*. "I'm glad you found us. Saved me some time trying to remember where the hell you built all those tunnels."

"Saved him from making a total fake-drunk ass of himself too," Cheyenne added. She pressed her fist against her chest too and nodded at Nu'ek. The *golra*'s glowing red eyes widened, but she kept her fist just below her breastbone over the weird-looking vest. *Yeah, okay. Maybe I did it wrong, but at least I'm trying.*

"I look forward to seeing you again, *Aranél*. Preferably after you've claimed what's yours and before the rest of us step into battle behind you."

Persh'al shot Cheyenne a quick glance, then cleared his throat and headed for the shuttle door.

"When I toss a drow coin on the Crown's altar, yeah." Cheyenne shrugged. "I get it. I'm kinda hoping that changes the whole imminent-battle thing, but we'll see."

"Yes." Nu'ek glanced at the shuttle when Persh'al finally managed to activate the sliding door. "We shall see."

"Come on, kid." Persh'al waved the halfling toward the open door-way. "We gotta get moving. L'zar's pretty attached to us making this timeline, and I'm pretty attached to my head."

With a last nod at the *golra*, Cheyenne turned and stepped into the shuttle. The door slid closed behind her with a hiss, and the blue lights flickered overhead.

"Okay." Persh'al tossed his much lighter pack on the second row of seats behind him and rubbed his hands together. "The rest of this needs a manual boost. Take a seat, and I'll get us moving."

"No way." Cheyenne chuckled and waved him away from the controls in front of the door. "If I have to say goodbye to this thing when we make the crossing again, I'm gonna use it as much as possible first."

"Great." Persh'al eyed her warily, then gave in and slumped down in the first row of decidedly uncomfortable metal seats. "Try not to break anything, huh? Including yourself."

"You need to relax, man. I got this."

"You know who else said that? Every idiot who got their hands on high-level spells and tried to cast them alone without any training. I had a friend like that once. Blew up his entire house and the top half of his body."

Cheyenne stared at the data scrolling across the control panels, reading it with eager awareness as quickly as it showed up. "We've already established that I suck at spells. But this, I'm good at this."

"How do you know?"

Her fingers moved in a blur across the controls as she activated the commands she wanted. The high whine of the shuttle's power source stopped, and the vessel shuddered in place before slowly moving forward.

347

Cheyenne looked over her shoulder and raised an eyebrow. "You were saying?"

Persh'al laughed and shook his head. "Nothing, kid. I'm keepin' my mouth shut from here on out."

CHAPTER FIFTY-TWO

"Okay, but seriously. I remember these things being a lot faster."

Cheyenne glanced down at the controls and shrugged. "It's only been ten minutes. Whatever kind of engine this thing has needs to fully power up."

Persh'al cocked his head. "Did a fancy activator tell you that, or you making an educated guess?"

She stepped away from the control panel without buttons, levers, or instructional symbols of any kind and leaned against the wall of the shuttle's cabin. "Do you even know what this thing can do?"

"Yeah. It can take us from A to B really fast." He snorted. "When it hasn't been docked for who knows how long without powering up. I knew we made the crossing Earthside without covering all our bases. Should've drawn out a plan for keeping everything in top shape."

"Oh, this thing's still in top shape." Cheyenne pointed at the control panel. "We've got about thirty seconds left 'til it is warmed up. After that, this can do a lot more than just moving *really fast*."

"Quit screwing around, kid." Persh'al folded his arms and sat back in the chair. "I've dismantled and rebuilt machines a hell of a lot more complicated than this tunnel train. I know what it's capable of just by looking at it."

She grinned. "Wanna bet?"

"Ha. Sure. Why not? You'll lose."

Cheyenne looked back at the timer displayed on the control panel through her upgraded activator and waited for the countdown to reach zero. When it did, she pulled up the drive for kicking the generator into gear, and with quick swipes on the panel lighting up with a blue glow beneath her finger, the shuttle lurched and doubled its speed.

Persh'al sucked in a breath, pressed back against his chair. Cheyenne leaned forward against the acceleration and drummed her fingers on the control panel.

"Jeeze, kid. Okay. You proved your point."

"Not yet. I'm just getting started."

He peeled himself off the back of the metal chair, adjusting to the newest speed, and shook his head. "You think this old wreck of a machine can go faster than this?"

Cheyenne chuckled and folded her arms. "You haven't spent a lot of time on this thing."

"This one specifically? You know, I can't say that I have. They all look and act the same. How fast are we going?"

"About eighty miles an hour. And that's at fifty-percent, it looks like."

Persh'al scratched his head. "For real?"

"Just wait 'til we get out of the city."

"How does that even matter? We're underground."

"Yeah, and then we won't be."

The blue troll sat forward in the metal chair, braced his hands on his knees, and stared at the control panel. "We won't be? This is the shuttle out to Charibor, right?"

Cheyenne glanced at the scrolling control panel. "No. Grimmer."

"What? Oh, that giant bat with horns is gonna get it."

"Sounds like you're not a fan of Grimmer."

"Not a fan?" Persh'al lurched from the chair and spread his arms. "Last time I saw Grimmer, it made the Oronti Valley look like a paradise."

"So it was dead with this blight or whatever since before you went Earthside. I thought all that happened after you guys followed L'zar across the Border. The last time, anyway."

"No, Grimmer isn't blighted, kid. Might as well be, though. It's a den of thieves if you will."

Cheyenne cocked her head with a smile playing on her lips. "Really?"

"Kinda, yeah. L'zar has a creepy fondness for the place, but they don't like me over there."

"Let me guess. It's 'cause you keep tricking them with your foolproof lying skills."

Persh'al glared at her. "Funny. I'm laughing on the inside."

"Then what happened?" She couldn't hold back a wry laugh at the thought. "I'm guessing any place L'zar 'has a fondness for' isn't number one on most people's sightseeing list. You must've really screwed something up."

The blue troll stared at the control panel, his nose twitching. "First of all, Grimmer is a territory, not a city. Like, an entire country."

"Oh, even better."

"They have no problem with thieves and fire-starters. L'zar spent a lot of time there, blending in. Until he didn't anymore."

Cheyenne glanced at the next speed level powering up on the control panel. "Nice deflection, but we're not talking about L'zar. What did *you* do?"

"Fine. L'zar steals physical things. Sometimes living things. And I steal information."

"Oh, so you hacked into the territory's system and did some damage." She wrinkled her nose. "That's a disappointing reveal."

"Uh-huh. They were really disappointed when I sold their security codes to the highest bidder. And the second- and third-highest. Then Grimmer contracted L'zar before they found out that we—you know what? I don't need to tell you this."

"Don't stop now." Cheyenne grinned. "It was just getting interesting."

Persh'al stared at her with widening eyes, then he wagged a finger in her direction and went back to his metal seat. "You're dangerously like your father, you know that?"

The amusement drained from the halfling's face, and she turned to face the control panel. "No, I'm not."

"You don't like that. I get it. If you did, I'd say there's something seriously wrong with your moral compass. And your brain, probably."

She snorted.

"But it's true. I've seen that look before, kid, and it wasn't on your face."

"There wasn't a *look*."

"There was a look, Cheyenne. It's the same look L'zar gets when he's put together some complicated little puzzle in his head and can't wait to move the rest of the pawns into position."

Cheyenne's fist clenched at her side while her other hand hovered over the scrolling data glowing above the controls. "I don't use people like he does."

"Not yet, maybe. Not on purpose!"

The shuttle sped up again, pressing the troll back against his seat with a metallic thump. Cheyenne's shoes squeaked across the floor at the burst of momentum, and she steadied herself with a hand against the wall. Then she looked over her shoulder to raise an eyebrow at the startled troll. "You were saying?"

"Too much, apparently. Crown be damned, kid. How fast are we going now?"

"One-twenty." She shrugged. "Might be a good idea to keep it here. We don't wanna have another mode of transportation break down on us or anything."

"Hey, I paid for a working skiff. Never trust an *outernóre* junker handing over a machine with a smile on his face. I learned my lesson on that one, okay? Again."

Cheyenne's lips twitched into a smile, and she pushed herself toward the front of the shuttle again. "Whatever."

"What are you doing now?" Persh'al glanced down at his hands, which were still gripping the edges of the metal chair, and forced himself to let go.

"Just checking things."

"Well, don't check *too* much, huh? Some of this stuff, even *I* don't know what every command does. You were joking about a breakdown, but that's still a possibility."

"Okay, Persh'al." She scanned the controls and the scrolling data commands, biting back a laugh.

"Don't, 'Okay, Persh'al,' *me*. What's that even mean, huh?"

"It means I'm starting to figure you out."

He swallowed.

"Hey, *this* is cool." Cheyenne's finger swiped across the smooth metal panel, and a series of blue lights illuminated in strips on either side of the shuttle's ceiling. They pulsed twice, then a slow, steady beat rose inside the cabin. "Eh, the music in that club was better."

"That music sucked."

"Yes, it did. But this works for now."

Persh'al squinted at her. "I'm not sure I like the way that sounds, kid."

"Why? You still afraid I'm gonna break something?"

"Kinda."

"You need a distraction." With a low chuckle, she swiped at the four different commands that had nothing to do with each other, then glanced up at the metal ceiling. *Just like writing programs, only this works physically. I think.*

"What did you do?" Persh'al glanced nervously around the shuttle, shifting in his seat.

"Seriously, man. Chill out." Cheyenne added more commands and nodded. "This should do it."

"Hey, I'm not taking orders or advice from a...whoa!"

The metal walls around them disappeared, rendered transparent by Cheyenne's newly constructed command. The ceiling and floor disappeared next, leaving only the three rows of metal chairs and the control panel up front. Now, the drow halfling and the blue troll sailed through the darkening light of dusk, across an open field of brown grass dotted with glowing purple wildflowers, at a hundred and twenty miles per hour.

"What the hell!" Persh'al gripped the sides of his chair even tighter and pulled his feet up from the ground hurtling beneath them. "This is...you can't just... *Shit!*"

Cheyenne laughed and gazed at the sprawling field and the thick forest coming up quickly on their left. "Ready to chill out now?"

"Not when I'm in a flying chair!"

"We're still in the shuttle."

"I *know* that!" His voice broke, and he swung his legs up to set his boots down on the chair beside him. "I'm still about to piss myself."

"Hmm." Cheyenne activated another panel on the wall in front of

Persh'al's seat, and a metal drawer unfolded from what looked like thin air before shooting out in front of him. A soft yellow light blinked as a tray lifted from the hovering drawer to present the troll with two tin bottles. "Refreshments. You think that'll help?"

Persh'al peered at the bottles, frowned, and glanced at Cheyenne. Watching the landscape whir past them behind her head made him dizzy, and he clenched his eyes shut. "You didn't program this shuttle to make us a drink. I know you didn't just do that."

"No. This thing is fully stocked, or at least it's supposed to be. I don't know if that stuff's still any good."

Eyeing the tin bottles like one of them might bite him, the troll reached out and snatched one from the tray to inspect the thin label. He cracked the lid, took a tentative sniff, and barked a laugh. "Mudshine."

"Hey, our favorite swill."

"I'll tell ya, this stuff never goes bad." He took a small sip and wrinkled his nose at the sharp sting of bubbles climbing up his face. "Okay. Okay, yeah. I'm chill."

Cheyenne watched him guzzle half the thing down in one breath and raised her eyebrows.

When he looked at her now, it was a lot easier to forget the unnerving sensation of racing across open ground without walls or a floor beneath them. He grabbed the other bottle and raised it toward her. "Want one?"

She glanced at the map blinking at the corner of the controls and shrugged. "We got another half hour. Sure." With a final swipe at the panel, she sent the drawer back into the unseen wall again.

Persh'al cringed when she stepped across the invisible floor toward him, but he swung his legs down off the second seat so she could settle beside him. Then she took the tin bottle of mudshine and cracked it open. "You know what, kid?"

"What?" Cheyenne sniffed the bottle and rubbed her nose.

"When you next make the crossing to this side and get your hands on another activator, remind me not to freak out about it, huh?" He chuckled and shook his head, lifting his bottle toward her in a toast. "I guess you *do* know what the hell you're doing."

"You mean, with all this? Please. This was just for fun." She tapped her tin bottle against his and took a long, fizzy drink.

"Just for fun." Persh'al stared blankly at the field and the approaching forest in front of them, then downed the rest of his mudshine. "I should've kept that second bottle for myself."

CHAPTER FIFTY-THREE

The shuttle's system took over when they approached the closest Grimmer city, an expanse of nearly black ramshackle buildings rising haphazardly from the field fronting the forest on their left. The sun had set now, and Cheyenne stared up at the glittering dome of stars in Ambar'ogúl's night sky. Then the walls regained their opaque solidity, and the stars were replaced by the smooth metal ceiling. The music cut off, and the shuttle slowed considerably.

"Guess that means we're getting close." She stood and walked slowly toward the controls with a steadying hand against the wall.

"Yep. That's a relatively safe assumption. Probably the only one we'll have out here."

"That mudshine was supposed to lighten your mood, Persh'al. Not turn you into a pessimist."

"This *is* me in my lightened mood, kid."

Cheyenne studied the data moving swiftly across the console and cocked her head. "If you say so. We're five minutes out from the Grimmer transport station."

"Excellent." The troll belched and folded his arms.

"How come there aren't any other stops on the route?" She turned to face him, leaning against the edge of the console. "We passed other towns back there. None of them had a station."

Persh'al let out a noncommittal hum and closed his eyes. "These things were built to unite the territories. You know, 'cause they're all so spread out. I'm pretty sure the shuttles were just for show. Dignitaries could travel back and forth on a straight line to the capital to show the rest of the world that they supported the Crown by zipping across Ambar'ogúl instead of casting portals in secret or whatever."

"Huh. And Grimmer sent dignitaries."

"Well, I mean, back before this place was known as a happy hub of theft, violence, and debauchery, yeah. I'm sure they sent someone."

Cheyenne's fingers drummed on the edge of the console. "When did they turn to the Dark Side?"

He looked at her. "Ha. Right around the time L'zar Verdys decided he was fed up with his life the way it was going and had to make a change. He calls it 'an inspired improvement.' Most people wouldn't agree with that."

"So, he wasn't always a manipulative asshole trying to overthrow the Crown, huh?"

"Oh, he's always been a manipulative asshole."

They both chuckled, and Cheyenne ran a hand through her hair. The chains around her wrist clinked against the thick silver cuff keeping her tethered to her drow form and made her pause. "What did he do before that inspiration struck?"

Persh'al stared at her, then quickly looked away and shrugged. "Not sure. That was a long time ago."

"Huh. Too long ago for you to remember?"

"Yeah. We live a long time on this side, kid. At least, we used to before the new Cycle brought us to where we are now. A lot happens, and most of it isn't worth remembering."

Cheyenne narrowed her eyes and studied the blue troll's jaw clenching and unclenching as he stared blankly at the front of the shuttle. *I call bullshit.* "But you have such a *long* memory, right?"

"What?"

"I heard you say that twice today. And everyone else in L'zar's secret little Hangivol hideout didn't call you out on it, so it's gotta be mostly true."

Persh'al's orange eyes flickered. "I didn't know L'zar before he became what he is now."

"But you followed him once he took up this whole rebellion thing after Maleshi left."

"Like I said, kid. Some things aren't worth remembering."

She was about to keep pressing, but the shuttle slowed, shuddered, and jerked to a grating halt beneath them, knocking her hip against the control panel.

Persh'al nearly spilled out of his seat, but his hand clamped on the back of it, and he pulled himself up again. "Not much of a smooth landing with these things."

"Yeah, time will do that, won't it?" Cheyenne stared at him and pursed her lips. *What is he not telling me?*

"Sure will." Clearing his throat, the troll stood and reached behind the row of seats for both their packs. He tossed the backpack to Cheyenne, then strapped his much lighter pack over his shoulders and turned toward the shuttle door. "Back on our feet, right? We get to take a nighttime hike through the woods. Woohoo."

He passed his hand over the door, his palm glowing with green light, and it slid open. Cheyenne followed him out, pausing in the doorway to gaze at the cabin and the blinking data flashing across every surface in her vision. She gave the metal wall a little pat and jumped the two feet onto the soft grass. *I'll be back. Can't stop that from happening now. This won't be the last time I get to play around with O'gúl tech.*

The door slid shut again with a stuttering hiss, and she glanced around the open land in front of them. The transport station in Grimmer was apparently just a raised platform at the base of a small hill, the forest running alongside them on the left. Cheyenne and Persh'al turned when the shuttle's high whine returned, then the thing accelerated back the way they'd come.

"Looks like someone programmed an immediate return," she muttered.

"Smart. Nobody wants to give Grimmer an open invitation to the capital, or they didn't, anyway. Any of these people set foot in Hangivol, it'd be like open season for the Crown to snatch 'em into the walls and bag 'em for whatever she's doing." Persh'al shook his head and turned toward the woods. "Not our problem right now."

"But it will be." Cheyenne cast a final glance over her shoulder at the quickly receding blue glow of the shuttle. "When I come back with L'zar and his coin."

"*Your* coin, kid. But yeah, then it'll be our problem."

They trudged through the forest, which fortunately hadn't been touched by the poison that had taken the far half of the Outers. Leaves rustled in the breeze, and twigs crunched underfoot. Something small and dark flitted from the branches and swooped toward the ground, followed by a squeak that cut off abruptly.

Cheyenne stared at the deflated pack thumping against Persh'al's back. "What did you smuggle across the Border in that thing?"

"In what thing?"

"Your pack."

He snorted. "Oh. Basic plans, kid. Personal messages from L'zar. Schematics, I think."

"Of what?"

"Uh, the center of Hangivol." An unsure chuckle escaped him as he ducked beneath a low-hanging branch in their path.

"He has schematics of the Crown's palace." Cheyenne scowled at the thick vegetation growing wild through the trees. "How does L'zar—"

"We already told you, the drow have been passing their trials in the Crown's Nimlothar court for a long time."

"You were around when the new Cycle turned, weren't you?"

Persh'al nodded. "Oh, yeah. Spent half my life in the old Cycle that should've lasted a hell of a lot longer than it did and the other half darting around under this bitch of a Crown's new reign."

"L'zar's not that much older than you."

"Ha. Drow live a long-ass time, kid. He doesn't look it, good for him and everything, but he's got a few thousand years on me."

Bingo.

"Then there's no way in hell L'zar had to pass his trials in front of the Crown. Not the one who's sitting on the throne now."

Persh'al paused, his boots crunching on fallen twigs, and glanced up into the treetops. "You're right."

"Then how does he have schematics of her—you called it something else earlier."

"The *Edhilór*. The center, basically."

"Sure. That. If he wasn't *summoned* or whatever to pass his trials at the last Nimlothar in front of her, he had to get blueprints of that place some other way. I seriously doubt you can just Google 'blueprints of the Crown's *Edhilór* in Hangivol.'"

"Well, Google doesn't exist over here, so you're right again."

"So how did he get them?"

Persh'al glanced at her over his shoulder, then picked up the pace through the woods. "Jeeze, you're pushing this, aren't you?"

"When I wanna know something, I push. When I still don't get answers, I get pissed off. That's not easy information to come by, so how the hell did he get it?"

"I didn't say the schematics came from L'zar, kid. You put those pieces together on your own."

Cheyenne stopped and glared at the back of the troll's mostly shaved head, his limp mohawk fluttering. "Because they fit."

Persh'al walked a few more paces before realizing she wasn't behind him. He turned and cocked his head. "Just because a thing makes sense, it doesn't mean it's the truth. That works the opposite way too, you know. Things you can't logically fit together aren't automatically impossible, which I'm sure you've figured out by now."

She folded her arms. "You're deflecting again. Cut it out."

"I'm trying to make a point. Most of the time, you're right on target. Maybe even ninety-nine percent, which is creepy and makes me feel weird. But don't let it go to your head. If you get all cocky and start jumping to conclusions, that opens a big-ass door to seriously screwing up. People get hurt that way. People die for assumptions."

He's still hiding something. "I've figured that out too. Why won't you just give me a straight answer?"

"I will. Guess who else spent centuries inside the *Edhilór*, memorizing it from the inside out?"

Cheyenne bit her lower lip and held the troll's orange gaze. *Damn. Maybe he's right.* "Maleshi Hi'et."

"Tada!" Persh'al spread his arms and gave her an exaggerated bow before spinning around and tromping back through the trees. "She finds another piece, and it fits too, doesn't it?"

Scowling, Cheyenne grabbed the straps of her backpack and trudged after him. *I don't jump to conclusions, not when I can feel something's off. But it makes sense.*

The ground angled upward in a shallow incline, and they kept climbing. The halfling studied the forest around them, listening for the rustle of branches or the sharp snap of twigs that didn't come from Persh'al's loud stomping. *He really doesn't know how to be quiet.*

Then it hit her. "Wait. You said, 'Guess who else.'"

"What?"

"As in, Maleshi isn't the only one who knows their way through the Crown's *Edhilór*. L'zar does too, doesn't he? I was right."

"Endaru's balls, Cheyenne." Persh'al craned his neck and slumped his shoulders, grunting at the thin slivers of starlight falling through the branches. "You're still goin' on about that?"

"Yeah, because you said—"

"I know what I said, and it's a figure of speech, okay? Just drop it already. You have your answer."

"Shh." Cheyenne reached out toward the troll and froze.

"Don't shush at me like I just stopped wearing diapers."

"No, I'm serious, Persh'al. Stop."

"Seriously?"

"*Yeah*, seriously," she spat in a harsh whisper. "Shut up."

The troll stopped moving and scanned the trees around them.

Cheyenne cocked her head and let her enhanced drow hearing find the sound she'd heard. *What is that? Whispering? Crying?*

She blinked and nodded toward the top of the hill. Persh'al cringed when she moved swiftly toward him, making almost no sound in the underbrush. He stared at her feet with wide eyes and whispered, "How do you *do* that?"

"Practice. Be quiet." Leaning toward him, she pointed up the incline through the trees. "Someone's up there. It sounds like a lot of someones, but I don't know how many."

The blue troll swallowed thickly. "How 'bout a ballpark?"

"A dozen, maybe."

Persh'al glanced up the hill and squinted. "We're coming up on a Border portal the Crown hasn't squeezed to dust in her grip. It's not one of hers."

"How do you know that?"

"Her thugs are louder than I am, and we would've been stopped at the bottom of the hill."

Cheyenne took a deep breath, watching for movement. "So, these are magicals trying to cross Earthside too."

"Refugees? Probably, yeah. Unless the Crown has a bunch of silent-footed drow waiting to pounce on anyone who thinks it's safe." The troll glanced at her feet again and scowled. "Is it the shoes?"

"I'm quieter barefoot." She paused to listen again. "That's someone crying, or trying not to."

"Yep. My bet's on refugees, then. Just in case, though…"

A miniature orb of her black energy materialized in her palm, sputtering black and purple sparks. Cheyenne put her hand behind her and nodded. "Yeah, I'm ready."

CHAPTER FIFTY-FOUR

P ersh'al moved a lot more silently as they crested the hill. The trees thinned out, and Ambar'ogúl's two crescent moons spilled silver-blue light on a group of magicals huddling around a large black boulder on the hilltop. Three more climbed toward the boulder from the opposite side of the hill, whispering to each other and trying to be as silent as possible.

"Maji." A small orc boy tugged on his mother's sleeve.

"Quiet."

Across the clearing, two orc women clung to each other and stared with fearful eyes at moving shadows in the dark forest around them. The younger one whimpered, and her companion wiped at the tears on her cheeks before drawing her closer.

"Maji, look. Someone else came too." The orc boy pointed at Cheyenne and Persh'al at the edge of the woods. His mother turned slowly, saw the newcomers watching them from between the trees, and shrieked.

"Shit." Cheyenne dissolved her energy sphere and raised her hands.

The orc men who'd brought their families to the portal out here in Grimmer turned toward the supposed threat. One of them rushed toward the mother and her young child with a shout, summoning a huge ball of green flames in both hands. The others took up the cry of alarm. The orc women screamed and huddled behind each other, and Cheyenne and Persh'al found themselves staring at a line of five orc men with magical attacks raised and at the ready.

"Whoa, whoa. Hold on." The halfling kept her hands raised and stepped slowly from the trees.

"Cheyenne," Persh'al whispered fiercely.

"Everything's okay." She said it loud enough for everyone to hear. "See? I'm not here to cause any problems."

The orcs' eyes widened when Cheyenne stepped fully into the moonlight, and they shifted on uncertain feet. One of them snarled at her and raised the crackling glow of his green attack even higher. "You can't stop us!"

"Zilder, no!"

"Stay behind me!" The orc men moved closer together, blocking Cheyenne from the women and children.

Jesus. Everybody hates a drow. "I'm not trying to stop you," Cheyenne muttered, looking each of them in the eye and nodding. "I promise."

A skinny orc with one arm in a sling of dirty rags growled, shifting back and forth in anticipation. "Your promise means nothing to us, *mór edhil.*"

"Okay. That's fair."

"Cheyenne," Persh'al whispered. "I'm not fighting these magicals."

She stopped walking forward and said through clenched teeth, "Neither am I. Get over here."

"What are you doing?" Another orc's green-fire attack flared to twice its starting brilliance, making the others beside him blink and lean away from the blaze.

"Just trying to show you what's going on. You don't have to take my word for it, but a drow traveling with a troll might change your mind." Cheyenne nodded slowly, watching the orcs scan the dark forest they couldn't see with their bright magic flaring in their faces. "A *troll…* Dammit, Persh'al. Come on."

He groaned behind her. "All right, all right. I'm coming out!"

The underbrush rustled and snapped as he stormed through the tree line and trudged up to stand beside Cheyenne, both hands raised too. She shot him a sidelong glance, and he shrugged.

The skinny orc's attack spell sputtered out, and he leaned forward, squinting at them. "He's blue."

Persh'al rolled his eyes. "And you look like you couldn't lift your own shoe."

Another orc chuckled. His neighbor shot him a warning glance, and he shut up immediately.

"Why are you traveling with a blue troll?"

Cheyenne met the gaze of the largest orc man who'd spoken and gestured toward the black boulder behind their families. "Same reason you brought everything you could fit into a few bags to take with you."

"You want to make the crossing?"

She nodded and slowly lowered her hands. *At least they're asking first and saving the fight for later. Hopefully never.* "Yep. This blue troll and I are stepping right through that portal too."

"She's lying." The orc who'd thrown his wife and child behind him snarled. "The Crown has spies everywhere. This one's no different."

"Ha!" Persh'al dropped his hands and gestured at the huddled magicals around the black boulder, all of them in threadbare clothes and looking haggard and worn-out. "If the Crown wanted to stop you, you wouldn't have made it out here. And we can all admit you're flattering yourselves with that thinking, right? You think she'll spend the resources she has to stop a few small families and this starving wannabe?" He gestured at the skinny orc, who stared blankly at the ground and shrugged.

"She stopped my cousin," one of the orc women added softly. "Sent guards to the portal and had everyone rounded up and carried away in chains."

Persh'al cocked his head. "Was it at *this* portal?"

"No. It was in Simmara."

"Well, see? There you go. No guards here. No Crown spies. We're just trying to get across to the other side like everyone else here."

"But she's a drow."

Cheyenne sighed as Persh'al stomped toward the line of orc men. Confused and wary, they stepped away and let him pass. Then they turned their gazes on the halfling again, and their suspicion quickly returned. *What's it gonna take to convince these guys?*

"Look, the Crown can suck it for all I care."

"Suck what?"

She clenched her eyes shut and shook her head. *O'gúleesh talk, halfling.*

"She can eat the deathflame torch, all right?" The orcs' eyes widened, and one of the women behind them gasped. "Honestly, I'm really looking forward to the day somebody takes her down and buries her for good. Or mounts her head on a spike. Who knows?"

Two orc mothers covered their children's ears with both hands and glared at the halfling.

"Whoever does that has my full support."

Persh'al grimaced and rubbed the side of his shaved, orange-speckled head.

"Time to turn a new Cycle, right? Which I'm guessing all of you are trying to do on your own by packing up your lives and taking it all with you through the crossing. Good call right now if you ask me. It would also be a pretty good call to let my friend and me through so we can get where we're trying to go. And if you keep up, we'll help you get to the other side in one piece."

The orc men exchanged surprised looks, and one by one, their attack spells petered out. "You've made the crossing?"

"Sure, once or twice." *Almost.*

The skinny orc readjusted his huge bag over his shoulder and nodded, stalking across the line of his friends until he stood in front of Cheyenne. "I'll go with you."

"Cabrus, we don't know a thing about her!"

Cabrus cut off the doubting orc with a flying hand gesture from chin to groin. The orc mothers covered their children's eyes now, and Cheyenne thought, *they've got their own middle finger over here. Not surprising.*

"I know all I need to know," Cabrus said with a grunt. "The Crown's loyalists are too scared to talk about her the way this drow just did. The rest of us are too. I believe her, and if I have to choose between walking beside a drow through the crossing and walking alone, I'll take my chances with the drow." He nodded at Cheyenne, then stalked through the group of staring orcs until he joined Persh'al beside the portal boulder with a snigger. "And a blue troll, I guess."

Persh'al snorted. "What a fantastic team."

The refugees fell silent, apparently waiting for someone else to make the decision for them. Cheyenne stepped through the small crowd, counting three young children and an old, frail-looking orc woman who scowled at her. She stopped beside Persh'al and the skinny Cabrus, then gazed at the weary refugees and shrugged. "That was a serious offer, by the way. We can help you get across safely. All of you."

"And what does the *mór edhil* want in return?" the old orc asked, pointing at Cheyenne with a gnarled green finger.

Cheyenne studied the aged magical and shook her head. "Nothing."

The wizened orc threw her head back and cackled. "Done. Can't go back on your word now."

"Fegri, wait!"

"No. I've come this far. The rest of you can stand around like dullards trying to figure this one out, but I'm taking the leap. I've got a drow bodyguard. Can you believe *that*?" The old woman cackled again and hobbled quickly toward Cheyenne and Persh'al. "Wouldn't mind giving this here blue troll a personal thank you, though."

Persh'al frowned as the elder pursed her wrinkled lips and eyed him. Then he chuckled and glanced at Cheyenne. "The old one's got a dirty mind."

The halfling smiled at him. "At least she's grateful."

"All right, listen up." Persh'al waved the unsure group of orcs closer. "We're going through. Anyone who wants to come along is welcome, but I'll tell you right now, we're not turning back for anyone. Once you go through, it's dead ahead or plain dead, got it?"

The crying orc woman whimpered again but stepped forward in her older friend's arms.

Cheyenne leaned toward Persh'al and muttered, "Was that necessary."

"Yeah, it was. They need to know the risks, kid."

"Just by looking at them, I'd say they already know."

He dipped his head and frowned. "Well, now no one can say we didn't warn 'em. Let's move."

Persh'al slapped Cabrus' arm with the back of his hand and nodded for the skinny orc to step up to the boulder beside him. "How's your aim with those fireballs?"

"Uh, decent."

"Decent. We can work with that."

Persh'al leaped onto the boulder and disappeared. Cabrus quickly followed him, and Cheyenne offered her hand to the old orc woman.

"I don't need that." Fegri clapped a wrinkled, gnarled hand to Cheyenne's cheek and grinned, exposing worn-down yellow teeth between her stunted tusks. "I got more jump in me yet, *mór edhil*. You make sure I don't have to use it."

Grunting, Fegri pushed herself up onto the boulder and vanished.

Cheyenne dipped her chin at the other waiting orcs and nodded. "Time to go."

No one moved, so she slowly turned and climbed onto the black stone. *I can't make them come with us, but I hope they do.*

She took one more step toward the top of the boulder and slipped through the portal opening. The pressure of entering the in-between burned in her legs and brought an instant, pounding headache. Then she drew a long, gasping breath and staggered forward.

Persh'al and Cabrus were still coughing, trying to clear away the stark pressure of crossing from one world to the non-world between. Fegri chortled, her gnarled hands clasped in front of her as she watched the others catching their breath. "Look at that. Pays to be an old crone some days, don't it?"

Cheyenne cleared her throat and approached her. "That didn't bother you?"

"That little pinch? Bah. I've been smoking bilweed since I was a pup. Who knew I'd be grateful for the fell-damn stuff?" Fegri patted a small purse strapped to the belt at the top of her skirt and chortled again. "And I'm taking it Earthside."

I'm gonna pretend that's O'gúleesh tobacco and not ask any questions.

"Can't stop for too long," Persh'al wheezed, clapping Cabrus on the shoulder. The skinny orc grunted and stepped forward.

A round of gasps and startled, choked coughing rose behind them.

"Ah." Fegri peered at the line of orcs stumbling through the portal into the in-between. "They're not as dumb as they look. Keep moving, children! We're following the blue one."

Tittering, she hobbled off behind Persh'al and Cabrus, eyeing the black smoke spewing from geysers in the nonexistent wasteland between worlds.

Cheyenne turned to wave the others forward, and the thin line of orcs became a frightened, trembling group of them on the other side of the boulder. "Gotta keep moving. Stay close."

The orcs supported each other through coughing fits and wheezing breaths, but the sight of the dead nothingness around them and the black fog creeping across the in-between in thick tendrils got them all moving quickly.

Yeah, that'd light a fire under anyone's ass.

CHAPTER FIFTY-FIVE

Cheyenne and the rest of the refugees caught up with Persh'al, Cabrus, and Fegri fairly quickly. The two orc women jumped at everything that moved, but Cheyenne forced herself not to snap at them about it. *Anything I say right now is only gonna terrify them even more.*

She hurried to the other side of Persh'al and glanced at Cabrus, who stared at the shifted non-landscape with wide eyes. Behind them, Fegri muttered to herself, squinting at everything and letting out the occasional sharp bark of laughter.

Leaning toward the troll, she muttered, "You know, I think we might've overlooked one important detail in all this?"

"Oh, yeah?" Persh'al warily scanned the twisting fog around them. "What's that?"

"We're not going back the way we came."

"Uh-huh."

"Going through that portal in Grimmer is gonna spit us out at a reservation." A tree half a dozen yards on their right groaned in the eerie silence. The sound cut off abruptly when a puff of black smoke wafted in front of it and took the dead thing somewhere else in the in-between. "Isn't it?"

"Probably."

"Persh'al, I cannot show up at a Border rez. The FRoE's gonna recognize me and start asking way more questions than I can reasonably refuse to answer."

"Relax, kid. We covered that part." Persh'al slipped a small vial out of his pocket and wiggled it beside his hip before secreting it away again. "Not as fancy as the *nalís* L'zar gave you, but it's powered by the same thing."

Cheyenne frowned. *Nightstalker blood in a vial. Cute.* "From Corian?"

"Yeah." The troll darted a quick glance at Cabrus, who might or might not have been listening as he staggered forward and tried to look in every direction at once. "The second we're out of this place, I'll use it, and we'll pop right back into the warehouse. Only room for two, though, yeah?"

"Right." *Can't let any first-time Earthsiders slip into a nightstalker portal cast by a blue troll. Nobody wants to deal with that fallout.*

"We've been walking for a long time," Cabrus croaked.

"I heard there was supposed to be monsters." Fegri cackled behind them, making the skinny orc jump.

"Nothing's *supposed* to happen here," Persh'al replied, "as long as we keep moving."

"It does seem a little less eventful," Cheyenne muttered.

"Nah, that's because you've done this. Recently." Persh'al turned and raised a hand toward the clustered refugees shuffling along behind them. "How we doing back there?"

Every orc making the crossing looked at him with glowing yellow eyes, but no one said a thing.

"Good enough for me." The troll cleared his throat and peered through the fog. "Maybe Nu'ek had it right the whole time, shippin' us to Grimmer for a crossing with a lot less action."

"Huh." Cheyenne frowned at a sickening wet, slithering sound coming from the right. "Might be a good time to knock on wood."

"Oh, sure. Let me just go find some real quick." Persh'al snorted. When he glanced ahead again, he broke out in a grin and pointed. "Hey. Doorway."

"That's it?" Cabrus gulped. "That's the other side?"

"Sure is, Toothpick."

"What?"

Persh'al nudged the skinny orc's shoulder and shook his head. "Term of endearment. Hopefully, you'll learn something about it when you pop out on the rez. Check it out, everybody! This is our stop coming up."

A chorus of whispered voices rose from the terrified refugees, and one of them started crying softly.

Cheyenne frowned at the doorway. *They don't know what's waiting for them after this. It's gotta be better than what they're leaving behind, but a Border rez isn't worth tears of joy.*

"Just keep moving," Persh'al added.

A clicking growl echoed through the nothingness, rising mere yards in front of the crossing party. The black, gelatinous shape gyrated in the air, and Persh'al halted the line.

"Shit."

Some of the orc women screamed. One of them darted away from the group, but Cheyenne grasped the orc woman's wrist and yanked her back in. "Stay together! That's the only way we're gettin' outta this."

She summoned crackling black orbs in both hands, but before she had a chance to let loose, Cabrus blasted the growling black shape with a thick column of green fire. The in-between beast shrieked and wobbled like a mountain of Jell-O, then burst into a million fragments and blew away on the next gust of source-less wind.

"Decent aim." Persh'al nudged the skinny orc with his elbow. "You weren't kidding."

Cabrus grinned until he remembered what they were doing here and why. "We keep going, right?"

"Yep. Everyone to the doorway. That big ol' rectangle of light in the middle of nowhere. Come on. Hurry it up."

The terrified refugees pushed forward in a single mass. Cheyenne turned and scanned the streaks of black smoke drifting across her vision. *I know there's more where that came from.*

"Hey, kid." Persh'al waved her forward as the group passed him and booked it to the doorway. "Any particular reason you're standing there wasting more time?"

"It can't be just one." She turned and headed toward him.

"Sometimes one is all you need. Don't be ungrateful." He nodded at the doorway. "We're lucky this time."

The orc women screamed again, the men shouted, and Cheyenne and Persh'al turned to see the two black, glistening tentacles whipping out from behind the suspended doorway.

"Or not."

They raced forward to join the fight. The orc men hurled flashing green attack spells at the waving tentacles, missing most of the shots. The monster hiding behind the doorway skittered into view. It looked like a giant crab, with four more grotesque tentacles sprouting from its back. It clicked and shrieked at them, freezing the refugees in their tracks.

Cheyenne hurled two black orbs of sparking magic at the crab thing's center and split it cleanly in half. One giant claw twitched and clicked on the ground before melting. The other rose on its own and drew the rest of the shattered crab-thing with it. It let out another grating screech, and the beast rose on thousands of tiny legs like a giant, morphing centipede.

"Get through the doorway!" Persh'al waved the frightened orcs forward, then flicked his wrist and brought up his trusty green magic whip.

The women and children broke into a run. The orc men ushered them forward and turned to launch their own attacks at the grotesque, scrambling new form the monster had taken. Each hit sent clouds of black smoke and shattered fragments through the air, but the creature kept racing toward them.

Persh'al lashed out with his whip, glancing over his shoulder to watch the fleeing refugees' progress toward the door. "Just need to give them time!"

"Yep." Cheyenne blasted the clacking, squealing centipede-thing with more churning balls of black energy and lifted a shield in front of two orc men staring down the wrong end of the monster's spitting acid. The green slime pinged off the shimmering wall of her shield and disappeared beneath the black fog covering the ground. "Go!"

The orcs took off toward the doorway, tossing a few more attacks before they disappeared. Only three of their crossing party were left, and Cheyenne waved them away before darting toward the other side of the portal after them. Wind howled through the in-between, and

Persh'al threw crackling darts of blue light at the monster between lashing out with his whip.

A screech ripped through the air, and the wind kicked up again, buffeting them. Cheyenne looked up and saw another massive bird-like creature, though its face and what could have been its beak opened in its belly to let out another piercing shriek. She flung her black tendrils at the creature's amorphous legs, and they yanked the creature's limbs from its body. The thing swooped down from the sky as Persh'al battled the centipede, and the last three orcs raced through the glowing doorway.

"Time to go, kid!" Persh'al stepped back, putting himself between the snapping, spitting monster on thousands of legs and their exit.

"Couldn't agree more." Cheyenne darted away from the flying monster as it landed in front of her with a shuddering boom. A column of glistening black burst from its headless shoulders like a newly grown neck and a huge red mouth opened wide to snap at her. She sent another black energy sphere blasting through the back of that mouth, and the creature reared back.

She froze when she saw something moving inside the creature beneath the surface of its shifting skin. Racing, pulsing lights of muted silver darted up the creature's sides like LED lights, interspersed with symbols she didn't recognize. "What the hell is that?"

"Cheyenne!"

The halfling whipped her head toward Persh'al, her hand lifting toward the activator she hadn't removed. *That wasn't supposed to still be there.*

A slimy tentacle wrapped around her ankle, so cold it burned her through her pants. Snarling, Cheyenne summoned another energy sphere and threw it at the bird-creature that had now become another thing on sharp, spearing legs. Then it jerked her off her feet and bashed her against the ground.

"Shit. Hold on!" Persh'al attacked the centipede again, which kept sprouting new legs and growing back whenever he blasted it apart. Then the centipede froze, let out a series of ominous clicks, and turned away from him before scuttling toward Cheyenne. "What?"

The troll cracked his green whip around the centipede's pincer-tipped head and jerked back. The creature's body severed beneath his magic with a wet slurp. The head burst before it hit the fog-covered ground, and by the time a new one grew in its place, the centipede had forgotten Persh'al.

"Dammit!" Cheyenne flew through the air again by her ankle as the new monster flung her around. Two more hits with her black orbs severed the tentacle around her leg, but another reached out and caught her arm before she hit the ground. Searing heat blazed through her bicep, and she screamed before clamping her other hand down on the tentacle. That hurt just as much, but she clenched her teeth through the pain and held on. "Should've started with this!"

The black fire flared across her skin, sending a blazing wave of drow heat through her body before she pushed it out along the in-between creature's flesh. The thing shrieked as the flames consumed it, and Cheyenne dropped five feet with a thud.

"Cheyenne! Look out!"

She turned just in time to see the centipede's razor-sharp pincers glinting with some foul substance before the thing was on her.

"Hold on!" Persh'al shouted.

The ground lurched away from her as the centipede's thousands of legs stabbed into her skin over and over. It tried to scramble across her body, but they were both whisked into nothingness. She couldn't even hear Persh'al shouting for her as she punched the sharp-tipped legs and kicked away from the writhing monster.

She fell hard against something at her back and cried out. The centipede tumbled away, rolling over and over until it righted itself and turned to face her. This one had the flashing silver lights inside it too, pulsing up and down its long body and illuminating it from inside. *This is seriously weird.*

The creature lunged at her again, and Cheyenne waited until the last second before falling to her knees and grabbing the underside of the monster's head with both hands. Tiny barbs pierced her palms, but she ignored them and unleashed another full, devastating blast of her black drow fire. The thing writhed and shrieked, hissing and spitting as the flames shot down its entire body. With a loud pop, the creature burst and lurched away from her, tumbling into a dozen pieces on the unseen ground.

Groaning, Cheyenne pushed herself to her feet and looked around. "Persh'al?"

Only the wind replied, howling through the nothingness of the in-between. Her foot scraped against a large, slanted rock jutting from the black fog, and she frowned. *Well, that's where I landed. And where the hell's the doorway?*

She spun quickly around, searching the thick smog for any sign of Persh'al and the doorway out of this place. "Hey! Where are you?"

Something slithered behind her, and she whirled around again to see nothing but thick, drifting black, smoke. *No fucking way did I just get stranded in here.*

She stepped forward, looking for the way out, and another stiff wind blew out of nowhere. The black smoke moved aside, and a new doorway appeared not ten feet in front of her. Beside it was another crumbled bit of stone. Cheyenne glanced behind her and took another slow step forward. *Doesn't matter what portal. Get the hell out.*

The second she took off toward the new doorway, the in-between filled with earsplitting roars and grating shrieks. A shadow built to the right of the doorway, and Cheyenne darted around it before launching herself through the opening and out onto the other side.

The strobing flash of purple and green lights momentarily blinded her. She stumbled forward through two black pillars of stone jutting from the earth and nearly fell on top of a black tactical bag lying there in the grass. Then her vision adjusted to the darkness, and she found herself staring at the back end of Bianca Summerlin's house in Henry County, the bright lights over the dining room table shining through the entire back wall of windows.

Holy shit.

Someone shouted in front of her, and figures scrambled in the dark. The flashing light of the Border portal lit up FRoE agents in various stages of surprise as they readied their weapons to attack what they couldn't see in the middle of the night.

Cheyenne spun toward the house and was about to slip into drow speed before she locked eyes with Rhynehart. He had a fell rifle trained on her, his eyes wide behind the screen of his FRoE-issue helmet. The other agents stationed at the new portal ridge shouted, Cheyenne paused, and a blinking yellow light lit up in the top left corner of her vision: Sleep.

Without thinking, she waved her hand toward Rhynehart and the one blinking word, trying to get all the flashing lights out of her eyes. A bright-yellow spark burst from her hand and pelted Rhynehart. He grew rigid, his eyes rolled back in his head, and he toppled backward like a felled tree.

What the hell was that?

"Hands up, magical!"

Fell weapons powered up with high-pitched whines, glowing with green fell ammunition, and Cheyenne burst into drow speed. She hurtled across her mom's backyard and only looked back once to see the FRoE agents still training their weapons at the unknown magical they couldn't see. The bright lights of the newest portal shimmered, illuminating the tip of a glistening black tentacle reaching through from the in-between.

They can handle it. I need to get out of here.

CHAPTER FIFTY-SIX

Cheyenne ran at drow speed for ten minutes and stopped at the edge of the Henry County line. Trees groaned and branches snapped in the shockwave of her passing when she finally stopped just off the main road. Chest heaving, she looked around the empty road, the forest around her silent but for the last crickets holding out until autumn's first cold snap in the middle of the night.

"Shit." She stomped off the road and into the trees, then pulled out her cell phone and had to wait to turn it on. When it did, the screen lit up not only with her home screen but now with the quickly scrolling lines of data picked up by Elarit's activator. "What?"

The halfling practically ripped the activator off the sensitive skin behind her ear, hissing at the sharp pinch. Her eyelids fluttered, and she blinked away the pain before sticking the metal coil in her pocket. *So many things that aren't supposed to happen just happened. Somebody better have an explanation.*

It was a lot easier to focus on her phone now, and she pulled up Corian's number before jamming the phone against her ear. He picked up after the first ring.

"Where the hell are you?"

"Henry County."

"*What?*"

Cheyenne licked her lips and blew out a long, slow breath, trying to calm down. "I don't know what happened. I was with Persh'al and everyone else, then the whole place just... Did he make it back? Is he there?"

"He's here. Cheyenne, are *you* okay?"

She spun again, searching the darkened trees in the starlight. "Yeah, I'm fine, I think. Just really fucking confused."

"Listen, pin yourself on a map and text it to me. I'll come get you."

"How did it *do* that, Corian? It just picked me up and—"

"Cheyenne. Hey."

"Yeah."

"Your location. Got it?"

"Right." She hung up on him without a second thought and pulled up her GPS before sending him the link. Thirty seconds later, a dark, shimmering circle opened in the air above the middle of the road. Corian stepped halfway through, searching for her, and Cheyenne jogged out of the trees to meet him.

"Come on." He reached out for her, guiding her with a hand against her backpack and scanning the road before they both stepped back through.

"Oh, shit." Persh'al was pacing in the center of the warehouse. He stopped when Cheyenne and Corian stepped through the portal, which closed behind them with a soft pop. "Fuck!"

He raced toward her and grabbed her by the shoulders. Cheyenne winced and pulled away from him, then got a good look at her arms. Her sleeves were shredded to ribbons, the skin beneath slashed and bleeding enough to make Persh'al release her immediately and clap his blood-smeared hands to his bald head.

"I'm fine." Cheyenne stretched out her arms and grimaced. "It's not as bad as it looks. Probably."

"It's bad, kid." Corian nodded, and Lumil ran toward them from the other side of the warehouse, pushing a wheeled office chair ahead of her.

Shrugging out of her backpack, Cheyenne eyed the chair and the dark bloodstains covering the upholstery.

Lumil slowed down, glanced at the chair, and shrugged. "I disinfected it."

"Great." The halfling slumped into the chair and clenched her eyes shut. *At least they're not tying me down for an interrogation like they did with the last guy in this chair.*

She shivered, her teeth chattering as a wave of chills washed over her.

Corian stood beside the chair and gently guided her to lean forward. "Take off the shirt, Cheyenne."

"What?"

"Whatever that was got you everywhere. Take it off."

Persh'al swallowed and turned away. Gritting her teeth, Cheyenne lifted as much as she could of her shredded shirt over her head, and Corian quickly helped her with the rest of it.

She looked down at her bare chest and stomach, smeared with blood above hundreds of tiny puncture wounds. Her teeth chattered again, and Corian looked her over carefully before pointing at her backpack. "Salve in there?"

"Yeah."

"Persh'al, get it."

The troll stepped sideways, trying not to look at the shirtless Cheyenne while reaching for her pack.

Cheyenne rolled her eyes and laughed despite how quickly the rest of her was going numb. "Dude, I'm sure you've seen worse than a drow in a bra. Just get the damn jar."

He glanced at her with a frown, snorted, and moved a lot faster when he wasn't trying not to look at her. The jar of darktongue salve came out, her backpack thumped to the floor, and then Corian held the large brown glass container and unscrewed the lid.

Cheyenne rocked forward in the office chair, her eyelids fluttering again as another wave of chills washed over her and made her shiver.

"Here." Byrd appeared out of nowhere with a handful of towels, but Corian brushed him aside.

"We don't have time. Persh'al, I need extra hands."

"Mine?"

"Now!"

Persh'al leaped toward them, and the last thing Cheyenne saw were four hands reaching toward her, two of them covered in tawny fur, two of them light blue, covered in globs of the sticky white healing salve. A second later, her arms were pulled gently forward by someone she couldn't see. Then the darktongue salve did its work.

The flesh on her arms felt like it was on fire, raging all the way up her neck and spreading into her cheeks. Cheyenne screamed and lurched back in the chair.

"Keep going," Corian muttered.

"Seriously?"

"If she loses any more blood, we're in trouble. Keep going."

Cheyenne's teeth chattered again, despite how hard she clenched her jaw against the agony in her arms. *If I don't bleed out in this warehouse, this damn salve's gonna kill me anyway.*

Corian grabbed her by her blazing shoulders, his tawny brow creasing in concern. "Sorry, kid."

Even if she'd been able to speak, she wouldn't have had the time to ask what he was doing. The nightstalker pressed down on her shoulders, and Cheyenne couldn't help but lean over her lap. Then his hands covered the puncture wounds bleeding freely on her back, and a new wave of searing agony washed over her. The pain pulsed up her spine and neck like her drow magic, bursting into her head.

"Damn."

Persh'al's whisper registered somewhere in the back of her mind, but that seemed to be disconnected from her body. *I'm screaming. I have to be screaming right now.*

The rest of the darktongue salve was quickly applied, but Cheyenne could no longer tell where that was or how much more was needed. She slumped over her lap again, gasping and blinking away tears of pain. Finally, the burning racing across every inch of her skin died as the healing salve finished its job. The in-between monster's puncture wounds healed from the inside out, and the only proof of their existence were the smears of blood on her arms, chest, and back.

Cheyenne drew a long, shuddering breath and ran her hands through her white hair, then propped her elbows up on her knees and held her head, not quite ready to open her eyes yet.

"There." Corian nodded and stepped back, studying her. "Good work, Cheyenne."

She blew out a breath and shook her head.

"You okay, kid?" Persh'al stepped toward her chair, and she looked at him with glazed eyes.

"Sure. As long as I don't have to do that again."

Corian's mouth twitched into a grim smile. "I don't think we missed anything."

Lumil returned with a bottle of water and cracked it open before handing it to the halfling, her yellow-orange eyes wide with caution.

"Thanks." Cheyenne guzzled half the water and ignored the streams of it spilling out of her mouth when her hand started shaking. She wiped off her chin and sat up in the chair. "Now what?"

"Now you get to tell us what happened." Corian folded his arms and studied her.

"I don't know what happened." Cheyenne met Persh'al's gaze. The blue troll shook his head. *Nobody knows.*

Corian watched their exchange and cleared his throat. "Start with when you got separated."

"That's pretty much it. We got the orcs through the doorway to whatever rez is on the other side."

"Rez 17."

"Okay. Then those things attacked Persh'al and me again. And I saw —" Her eyes widened, and she reached into her pocket to pull out the silver coil of Elarit's activator. "I was still wearing this, and I saw something inside those monsters. It wasn't like code, just a bunch of flashing lights and symbols. This thing wouldn't translate them for me, but I think the creature I was fighting knew I had it. That I could see *inside* its skin." She looked at Corian and shook her head. "I think it wanted to make sure I couldn't bring this with me Earthside."

The nightstalker's eyes narrowed when his gaze fell on the coil between her fingers. "Where did you get that?"

"From one of your friends hiding under the city." Cheyenne forced herself not to look at Persh'al, though she could feel him staring at her. *If anyone's gonna talk about Elarit, it should be him.* "It was supposed to be a temporary gift, right? 'Cause this tech doesn't make it across."

"No, it doesn't." Corian wrinkled his nose and nodded. "Keep going."

"I mean, that was it. The monsters knew I was wearing this, and the other one ignored Persh'al to attack me instead. That's how I got all torn up." Cheyenne gestured to her blood-smeared body and shrugged.

"Then we weren't at the portal doorway anymore. The in-between dropped me somewhere else, I blew that fucking centipede to pieces, and another doorway just appeared out of nowhere."

"And it took you to the portal on your mother's property."

"Yeah."

Corian rubbed his mouth, frowning at the coil in her hand. "Did anyone see you?"

"I mean, the whole FRoE team saw *someone* run out of that portal. I'm pretty sure they're busy fighting off the asshole things that tried to push through after me. Rhynehart saw me." At the blank looks both Corian and Persh'al shot her, Cheyenne added, "The team leader. He's the guy I've been working with the most, I guess. But I took care of it."

"You took care of it." The nightstalker groaned. "Cheyenne—"

"No, I mean, I knocked him out. That's it. The activator gave me the option, and I took it. He dropped, I got outta there, and then I called you."

Persh'al's mouth fell open, and he took two disbelieving steps backward.

"You *used* the activator?" Corian's question came out barely louder than a whisper. "On *this* side?"

"Yeah." Cheyenne stared into his glowing silver eyes and shrugged. "I know."

A low chuckle rose from the far end of the warehouse. Corian and Persh'al stepped away from each other and turned, giving Cheyenne a full view of L'zar standing in the open doorway of the square office turned guestroom. They all stared at the drow, who stared at the activator coil in Cheyenne's hand. L'zar's chuckles grew, then he threw his head back and let out a harsh, uncontrolled cackle. He lurched forward, holding himself up with a hand on either side of the doorframe.

"Shit." Persh'al rubbed his head and shot Cheyenne a quick glance. "L'zar?"

The drow just kept laughing, his glowing golden eyes wide and crazed with some private inside joke.

Cheyenne lifted her chin and glared at him from the office chair covered in her blood. "You think this is funny?"

Her father kept laughing, doubling over with his first step out of the doorway.

383

"Is he for real?" Cheyenne stared at Corian, but the nightstalker merely scratched behind his twitching tufted ear and averted his gaze. She leaped out of the chair, stumbling forward as it rolled across the floor away from her. "I almost didn't make it out of there, I just had my body turned inside-out by that salve, and all you can do is laugh?"

L'zar shook his head and leaned back against the doorframe again, wiping tears from his eyes as his laughter died down into bursts of chuckling again.

He's been standing there since I got here and didn't even try to help.

"Cut it out." She glared at him, and the drow pointed at her with another chuckle.

"Cheyenne." Another sharp laugh burst out of him as he pushed himself away from the doorframe again.

"You know what? Fuck you." Cheyenne flipped her insane father the bird and snatched her tattered, bloody shirt off the floor. She shoved it in her backpack, pulled out the bulky hoodie, and slung the pack over her bare shoulder. "I'm not gonna sit here so you can laugh at me. I'm done."

Corian stepped toward her. "Wait a minute."

"No. That asshole's insane. He doesn't give a shit about what happens to me, and I'm not gonna put everything I have on the line for a magical who does *that* when things get screwed up." She snarled at Corian and thrust a finger toward L'zar. "He's gonna get us all killed. Forget it."

She snatched the brown glass jar of salve out of Corian's hand and stormed across the warehouse toward the front door. *I need to get out of here.*

"Cheyenne." L'zar chuckled again, but she didn't turn around. "Stop."

"Eat shit."

A loud crack filled the far end of the warehouse, and a blur of gray and white raced past her with another crack. L'zar dropped out of enhanced speed in front of her, blowing her hair away from her face with the shockwave. He'd stopped laughing but grinned down at her instead, his golden eyes roaming over her face. His hand reached toward her cheek as if he were about to tuck her hair behind her ear. "You're not leaving."

"Watch me." Cheyenne slapped his hand away and stepped around him.

"That wasn't a request."

"I don't take orders from anyone, especially you." Just as she reached the door, a bolt of dark light caught her in the shoulder and spun her sideways. Cheyenne snarled and whirled to face him.

L'zar's smile had vanished, and he dipped his head in warning. "We're not finished."

"Oh, yeah, we are." She dropped her hoodie when she saw him slip into drow speed and met him there a second before his hand came down on her shoulder. Slapping it aside, she leaned away from him and hissed, "Don't touch me."

"I won't let you leave."

"You don't get to choose!"

L'zar reached for her, trying to pull her away from the door. Cheyenne ducked aside and threw a right hook at his face. His long, slender gray fingers clenched around her wrist to stop her and squeezed as he leered at her. "Until you place your *marandúr* on the Rahalma, I'm still the one calling the shots, *Aranél*."

Her golden eyes widened at the last word she didn't understand and the growing pressure around her wrist. Purple and black flames blazed behind them. "Don't touch me!"

Black fire burst to life across her skin. She ripped her wrist out of L'zar's grasp and sent her fist into his gut instead. The flames consumed him and sent him flying across the warehouse, jolting them both out of enhanced speed.

Persh'al ducked and leaped aside. Corian watched L'zar sail toward the back wall, then the black-fire-engulfed drow stopped in midair and hovered. Cheyenne's flames whipped around him, casting dark shadows in the dimly lit room. Another chuckle rose from his throat. The black fire receded to reveal an unharmed L'zar Verdys floating slowly back to the floor.

Persh'al slowly rose from his crouch. Lumil and Byrd pressed themselves against the far wall and stared at the drow halfling in utter shock.

As L'zar's feet touched the ground, he took a deep breath through his nose, let it out again, and grinned. "That was exquisite, Cheyenne."

She stared at him, glancing quickly at Corian before returning her glare to her father. "You're insane."

"Probably." A dark light flashed behind his glowing golden eyes. "And you're much more than I ever expected."

Cheyenne snorted and shook her head. "Looks like you need to raise your expectations."

She turned back toward the door.

"I wasn't laughing at you," he called after her.

The door handle sparked and sent a blaze of orange magic up her arm when she touched it. Hissing, Cheyenne jerked her hand back, shook it out, and gritted her teeth. "Let me out."

"You can leave when we've finished our conversation. I'm sorry for what you've had to experience in the last hour, Cheyenne, and I would very much like to discuss that piece of technology you brought with you from the other side."

"You can have it." She chucked the silver coil across the room, and L'zar caught it deftly.

Without looking at it, he handed it to Persh'al and waited.

The blue troll turned the coil over in his hands. "Unbelievable."

"Quite." L'zar clasped his hands behind his back and grinned at Cheyenne.

Corian frowned at the drow and took off toward the front door, skirting around Persh'al's tables. He stopped in front of Cheyenne and lowered his voice. "You okay?"

"Not while I'm trapped in here with that asshole."

He glanced over his shoulder, then leaned toward her, staring past her at the blank wall. "We need to know what happened to you between the portals. How you managed to make the crossing with that activator intact. This is huge for all of us, Cheyenne. Whatever's happening between you and L'zar—"

"There's nothing between us," she hissed.

"All right. But hear me out, okay? I'm sure what you saw in Ambar'ogúl was more than enough to show you what we're facing here. What everyone's facing here. We still need your help, and you need to put aside your anger so we can accomplish what we need to do."

Cheyenne turned her head to glare at him, and the nightstalker finally met her gaze. "He didn't lift a finger to help *me*, so why the hell would he keep fighting to protect everyone else on this side?"

Corian raised his eyebrows. "If he didn't care, Cheyenne, he would have let you leave."

She took a deep breath and stared him down. *Yeah, I've heard that before, only Mom's reasoning was a hell of a lot more convincing.* "I'm not sticking around to play games with him."

The nightstalker dipped his head in acknowledgment with a small, thin smile. "After that little display, I don't think he's interested in playing that kind of game with you, either."

Cheyenne looked across the warehouse at L'zar, who stood stock-still with his hands still clasped behind his back. His eyes were closed now, and a small frown creased his brow. "Did I hurt him?"

"Enough to make him want to hide it, yeah."

"Good." She shrugged her backpack off and dropped it by the front door, then snatched up her hoodie and tugged it on. "Let's go hear the mad drow's theory. Then I wanna go home."

CHAPTER FIFTY-SEVEN

L'zar had taken two folding metal chairs from Persh'al's tables and now sat in one of them. He gestured for Cheyenne to sit in the other, but she stopped six feet in front of him and folded her arms. A small smile creased his mouth, and he dipped his head. "As a general rule, Cheyenne, halflings don't cross to Ambar'ogúl, and if they do, they don't last long enough to even try to make a return trip. But you did."

"We covered that part." She glanced at the metal cuff around her wrist and slipped it off before shoving it into the front pocket of her hoodie.

"Yes. What we didn't cover is what happens when a halfling makes that crossing a second time to return to this world." He slowly looked at her and raised his eyebrows. "Because as far as I know, it hasn't been done."

With a quick glance at the activator coil Persh'al was turning over and over in his hands, Cheyenne frowned. "So, you're saying I could bring a piece of seriously advanced O'gúl tech through the portal with me because I'm a *halfling*?"

"That's what I suspect, yes."

"It could be a fluke, too," Corian added.

"She *used* it." L'zar folded his arms in the chair and studied his daughter. "With perfect accuracy, I'm assuming."

"Yeah." *Rhynehart was pretty accurately knocked on his ass, that's for sure.*

He let out another low chuckle, then stopped, raising a hand for her to wait. "I find the irony amusing, nothing more."

"What irony?"

"That taratas Lex and his peons figured out how to mesh old-world machines with human tech, and now we've gone one step farther, just by stumbling around in the dark." L'zar's dark, crazed smile bloomed on his face. "You, Cheyenne, *are* the mesh."

"You lost me on that last part."

Corian stroked his chin and cleared his throat. "Two worlds, kid."

"And I'm part of both. I know." The halfling took a deep breath and let her drow magic fade to return her to her black-haired, pale-skinned human form. "Just so we're clear, I'm not turning into a mule for ferrying advanced tech over here from the other side."

"Well, we still have to prove the theory." L'zar shifted uncomfortably in his chair.

Maybe I really did hurt him. Cheyenne studied her father, waiting for him to continue that thought.

"If we can replicate it, we'll have our answer."

"I'm not making that trip again just so you can prove yourself right."

"No." He looked at her and narrowed his eyes above a thin smile. "The next time you make the crossing, I'll make it with you. There's plenty we can do here until then to help us learn more about this discovery."

"Like using this baby to find the rest of Lex's damn machines." Persh'al waved the activator around before sticking it behind his ear.

Cheyenne turned to Corian. "I thought you guys had already rounded everything up?"

The nightstalker shrugged. "Byrd and Lumil did find his base of operations, more or less."

Lumil snorted. "That lizard's got some nasty-ass habits, that's for sure."

Corian ignored her. "But I'm not convinced they found everything. Especially after your apartment was attacked last night."

"Great. So we have more fun bug machines to look forward to."

"What the hell?" Persh'al slapped the side of his head and scowled at the floor. "Come on!"

Everyone else stared at him until he finally ripped the silver coil off the back of his ear and stormed toward Cheyenne. "Try it again."

"What?"

"Just put the damn thing on and tell me what happens, kid."

She took the activator from him and stuck it tentatively behind her own ear. It gave her a little pinch and a buzz, but that was it. "Nothing's happening."

"Well, you certainly don't look like a drow who just crossed over," L'zar muttered.

"Huh." Cheyenne pulled up her drow magic and made the transformation again. The instant her skin settled into its purple-gray tone, a burst of magic flared behind her eyes. The wards around the warehouse lit up in brilliant, shimmering lines, and she blinked quickly against the glare in her vision. A single thought toned down the brilliance. "Yeah, that did it."

"Are you kidding me?" Persh'al snarled.

Corian chuckled. Lumil stepped toward the blue troll and clapped a hand on his shoulder. "You drew the short stick on this one, bud."

Persh'al shrugged away from her and shook his head. "I could rig us all up for life with that thing, and the kid's the only one who gets to use it."

"I don't mind helping you out."

He glanced at Cheyenne and narrowed his eyes. "Yeah, figures." Then he stomped across the warehouse and slumped into his office chair, scooting toward his monitor to start working on much less advanced technology he could use.

Byrd snorted. "Who'd have thought, right? L'zar's halfling kid is the only magical Earthside who gets the best of both worlds—magic *and* serious new tech. Shit, that might just make you the most powerful being on this side of the Border."

Lumil punched him in the arm and shook her head.

"What? It's true."

L'zar waved the goblins aside with a small laugh of his own. "Don't get ahead of yourself. I'm not ready to hand over the reins just yet." Byrd laughed nervously, and L'zar looked to meet Cheyenne's gaze, his smile a lot more concerned now. "So don't get any ideas."

That's what he thinks he is, huh? The most powerful being in this world. Not after I lit him on fire and threw him across the room.

"You can take it off now, kid," Corian said.

Cheyenne spun and eyed Persh'al's complicated setup. The activator lit up in her vision with the scrolling lines of data she could now read, even without looking at any of his monitors. "I was serious about helping. Honestly, with this thing, I'd love to get my hands on what Persh'al's got goin' on in that system."

"Don't even think about it," the troll shouted at her. "My rig, my rules."

Lumil burst out laughing.

"Give him some time," Corian added. "He'll get over his resentment, and then I'm sure he'd appreciate whatever help you could give him."

"Which he'll accept either way." L'zar said it loud enough for Persh'al to hear, and the implication was perfectly clear.

Cheyenne turned back to her father, who'd closed his eyes again with a distracted smile. *Meaning, Persh'al won't keep me away from his system if L'zar orders him to let me have a go. Why do these guys put up with his shit?*

"But not tonight." L'zar's golden eyes glowed when he opened them again and settled his gaze on the halfling.

"Is there anything else you can tell us about your trip that Persh'al can't?" Corian asked.

"Not really."

"All right, then we'll let him go over everything on his own. You need to get some rest."

Cheyenne snorted. "You have no idea."

"We'll let you know when we're ready to move forward." L'zar nodded at Corian, and the nightstalker took a few steps back before summoning another portal.

"Take that damn thing off, kid," Persh'al called from behind his center monitor. "Keep it around for emergencies, but don't go around Virginia, trying to see everything at once with your fancy new gear. You'd light up magical frequencies like a detonated bomb, you hear me?"

"Yeah, I got it." She plucked the activator from behind her ear and grimaced at the sparking tingle she felt in her teeth as it disconnected.

Then she shoved the silver coil into her pocket and turned toward Corian's open portal.

Byrd approached her with her backpack dangling from his fingers and nodded. "Glad you made it back in one piece, halfling. You had us wondering for a minute."

"I'm not going down that easy. Thanks." She took the pack from him and nodded.

Corian gestured toward his portal, and she shot L'zar another fleeting look before joining the nightstalker at the shimmering oval of dark light.

"He's fine," Corian muttered. "You did well, kid. Don't let the other bullshit cover that up, huh?"

"Yeah, okay." *What do I say to that?* Cheyenne nodded, stepped through the portal, and stood in the center of her living room. The portal closed behind her.

Ember was asleep on the couch, lying under one of her throw blankets with a hand draped over the side so her fingers almost brushed the area rug.

At least she's safe and has no idea what just happened. And I need a shower.

Once Cheyenne had washed the day in Ambar'ogúl off her body and temporarily out of her mind, she threw on an oversized Van Halen t-shirt and a pair of loose gray pajama bottoms and sat on the purple velvet comforter on her bed. She glanced at the throw pillows and snorted at the black one throwing her a white middle finger in the soft light of her chandelier-shaped lamp. "I need rest, huh? That's not happening right now."

She stood and scooped up her bloodied, torn pants to dig the silver coil out of the front pocket. Turning it over in her hands, she paced across her room. *My whole apartment's covered in wards. If nobody's getting in, magical frequencies sure as shit aren't getting out.*

With a quick nod, she slipped into her drow form and stuck the activator behind her ear under her slightly damp hair. The pinch and tingling buzz burst through her, and her eyelids fluttered as the device synced with her magic and her brain. Then she gazed around her room and chuckled. "Holy shit. The wards in here make the warehouse look like a joke."

Thick, shimmering lines of orange and red outlined the edges of her room. Cheyenne stepped quietly into the living room, gazing at the north-facing wall of windows and the blinking magic illuminated in her vision. The O'gúleesh hornet's web dangling from the edge of the mini-loft pulsed with red and black light like a beacon.

A command for taking down the wards lit up in her vision, and she choked back a laugh. *That's the only recommendation this thing has, huh? Nope.*

She moved slowly through the rest of the apartment, catching thin, spaced-out lines of tech data from the TV hidden in the long black table by the door and in the clock over the kitchen stove. Then she glanced at Ember's room, where green light pulsed through the crack beneath the door. Cheyenne peered at the couch to make sure Ember was still asleep, then headed to her friend's bedroom.

Time to check out what I can do with this thing Earthside.

The green light blazed in her vision when she opened Ember's bedroom door, but it quickly dimmed. The shattered fragments of the destroyed beetle-machines were still strewn all over the room, untouched from the night before. Every shard and metal speck glowed green.

The least I can do is clean this place up a little.

The minute she thought it, the commands flashed in her vision one right after the other, giving her access to spells she would have spent a lot of time trying to learn and probably failing to cast. Cheyenne grinned. "If I played videogames, I'd say this is as close as it gets to VR but better."

She waved a hand toward the activator's first suggested command, and the pile of crushed war-machine at her feet lifted from the ground, swirled into a pillar of tiny pieces, and hovered there, waiting. "Oh, yeah."

The trashcan beside Ember's bed shot toward her after another wave of her hand, and she directed the spinning column of O'gúl metal parts into it. The pieces pinged against the metal can, and Cheyenne grimaced at the sound. *Easy and quiet. Just let it happen.*

She pointed at the scattered shards on the bed, and they raced across the room at her activator-synced command before dropping lightly into the trash.

It took her fifteen minutes to magically shove all the broken bits into the trash and thoroughly scour Ember's bedroom for any remaining green glows. When she was satisfied with the cleanup, she set the trashcan against the wall beside the door and pointed at the bed. The unmade sheets and rumpled comforter jerked into place, followed by the huge pillows and the second gray throw blanket folding itself at the foot.

"There we go." Still grinning, Cheyenne nodded and left the room, leaving the door open behind her. *She's gonna flip when she sees this. Look at me, using the most advanced magic-enhancing tech in two worlds to do good deeds.*

She laughed softly as she crossed the living room. Ember let out a startlingly loud snore and smacked her lips. Cheyenne crept back into her own room and softly closed the door behind her.

The activator came off with another pinch before the halfling set it on her black dresser. She eyed the silver coil for a moment, then climbed into her ridiculously soft bed. *I haven't felt this right about something in a long time.*

CHAPTER FIFTY-EIGHT

Cheyenne had no idea what time it was when she woke up the next morning. She blinked slowly and took the time for a long stretch in bed. *Doesn't even matter. I have nothing to do today.*

The low drone of the TV filtered into her room, and she snorted. "Way to veg out first thing in the morning, Em."

She threw the comforter off, pushed out of bed, and drew the covers back up in a semblance of order before snatching the activator off her dresser.

Ember was still on the couch when Cheyenne entered the living room, the remote lying in her lap as she stared at the TV.

"Morning." Cheyenne tousled her hair, which had dried into a tangled mess of loose black curls.

"Hey, you're up." Ember turned off the TV and pointed at the bathroom. "I've come up with at least six different scenarios for how you got blood all over your backpack, and, I mean, that used to be a shirt, right?"

The halfling glanced at the rag of shredded shirt spilling out of her open pack beside the bathroom door. "Yeah. The blood's mine too. Sorry."

She snatched up the tattered rag and took it to the kitchen trash.

"You know, when Corian stopped by yesterday to tell me you'd left to make the crossing—jeez, just saying it still blows my mind—he forgot to mention the part where you'd come back covered in blood in the middle of the night."

Cheyenne snorted as she returned to the living room and slumped into one of the leather recliners. "That part can't surprise you much."

"No, not really." Ember shrugged and pushed herself farther up the couch's armrest. "I'm more surprised that you agreed to go over there. I mean, I know you have to eventually for that coin or whatever, but this came out of the blue."

"I know." Running a hand through her hair, Cheyenne glanced at the ceiling. "It was nuts."

"You okay?"

"Yeah, I'm fine now. Almost didn't make it back."

"*What?*"

"But I did. And I'm totally fine, Em. Promise. And I need to send some kind of thank you basket to Yadje for that darktongue salve."

Ember stared at her friend, then a grin broke out on her face. "Tell me everything."

Cheyenne laughed. "In a nutshell, Ambar'ogúl's fucked. Magicals who can afford living in the capital are being held prisoner in one giant, endless party. And halflings can apparently bring advanced O'gúl tech across the Border." She leaned forward and wiggled the silver coil at the fae. "Like this."

"A metal spring. Nice."

The halfling stood and walked toward the couch. Ember gestured to the wheelchair beside her, and Cheyenne shrugged before sitting down in it. "Doesn't look like much, right?"

Ember stared at the coil and bit her lip. "Nope."

"It's an activator, Em."

The fae's eyes widened. "For real?"

"Yeah. I'm pretty sure this is what got me in trouble last night on our way back, but it's real. And it works."

"You're screwing with me."

"No, really. I used it last night."

Ember reached for the silver coil and studied it intently. "I bet it doesn't work for anyone else."

"I mean, Persh'al's the only other magical who tried to use it. Didn't work for him, and he was pretty pissed about it."

"I bet." Biting her lip, the fae lifted the coil with a questioning glance. "You think maybe?"

"Go for it." Cheyenne sat back in the wheelchair and folded her arms. "If it works for you, it blows a hole right through L'zar's theory, but it might ramp up *your* magic."

"Right."

"Behind your ear."

Ember swiped her hair around over her other shoulder and lifted the activator to her head. She grimaced at the sharp pinch and waited. "Now what?"

"You see anything different?"

"No."

"Yeah, it's an instant on-switch." Cheyenne shrugged. "Guess that proves the halfling theory."

"Damn." Ember removed the coil and handed it back. "I mean, good for you. That part's awesome. Just got my hopes up a little, I guess."

"Don't worry, Em. We've already seen your magic. You keep going the way you're going, and you'll be walking again too."

The fae snorted. "You mean, go into underground magical market-places and almost get ripped apart by war machines sniffing my blood? Yeah. A few more weeks of that, and we can throw the chair out altogether."

"Very funny." Cheyenne stuck the activator back in her pocket. "That's not gonna happen again. I promise. We'll figure out how to jumpstart your magic too."

"Maybe."

A loud, urgent pounding came from the front door. The girls shared a curious glance, then Cheyenne stood from the chair. "What time is it?"

"I don't know. Eight-thirty, maybe."

"That's too early for a surprise visit. I don't even know anyone who'd drop by the old-fashioned way anymore."

Ember snorted and turned the TV back on as Cheyenne approached the front door. She stood on her tiptoes to peer through the round peephole and reared back. "What the hell?"

"Who is it?"

Cheyenne blinked and shot Ember a furious scowl over her shoulder. "It's Rhynehart."

The fae grimaced. "Uh-oh."

"Yeah, uh-oh for *him*." The halfling unlocked the deadbolt and the lock on the doorknob, then jerked the door open a few inches to glare at him in the hall. "What are you doing?"

Rhynehart grimaced. "We need to talk."

With an irritated growl, Cheyenne slipped through the door and yanked it closed behind her. She shoved him away from her apartment and shook her head. "You can't just show up where I *live*, Rhynehart. This is crossing a serious line."

He glanced down the hall at the elevators. "You sure you wanna have this conversation out here in the hall?"

"I don't wanna have this conversation at all," she hissed. "And *you* should be up at my mom's house with your team. You know, guarding that rock and keeping her safe."

"My guys are still up there, Cheyenne." He folded his arms. "And apparently, they did what they were up there to do last night. It went active, and they had to fight off a bunch of nasty black things spilling out of an invisible space between those rocks. Huge things. Two tentacles and a giant claw." Rhynehart mimed pincers with his hands and raised an eyebrow. "But they took care of it."

Cheyenne frowned. "Yeah, sounds like that was just a baby. And you could have told me all that over the phone, man! You didn't have to show up at my door. No, you *shouldn't* show up at my door."

"Well, I had to come see for myself."

"What are you talking about?"

"I wanted to make sure you were here instead of running all over who knows where gettin' into more trouble than I can imagine."

The halfling folded her arms and glared at him. "If I was, that's none of your damn business. Also, I'm fairly sure we all agreed that me working with you people had conditions, like staying the hell out of my personal life and especially out of my apartment."

Rhynehart glanced down the hall again and shook his head. It took him longer than usual to lift his gaze to Cheyenne's. "I saw something else come out of those rocks last night."

Shit. I should've knocked him out harder. She pressed her lips together and didn't say a word.

"I know what I saw, Cheyenne. My guys briefed me on the things spilling out of that opening because I missed the whole thing. Now, I know I can't prove shit about seeing you appear out of thin air before my team took action on those weird-ass whatever-they-ares, but I know it was you. This was the first stop I made after waking up."

Cheyenne studied his deep frown. "Who else knows?"

"Just me. I didn't come here to bark more of Sir's orders at you." Rhynehart snorted. "Frankly, after hearing what my team went up against last night, I don't think any of my people have a goddamn clue what's happening or how to handle it on a wider scale, even Sir. But whatever you're doing, kid, don't let it get in the way of me doing *my* job. Got it?"

She stepped back and raised an eyebrow. "You're not gonna try to pry answers out of me?"

He shook his head and raised both hands. "I don't even *want* answers at this point. Look, you obviously know more about what's happening than we do. It sucks, but I'm not gonna endanger my guys to try playing at your level. Shit just got weird. I mean, weirder than I've seen in my entire career of doing pretty weird shit. We don't have the resources or the leverage anymore to force you into anything. L'zar's out. You gave us that new opening on your mom's property, which we now know isn't just a pile of rocks. It's not ideal, but I have no problem with the idea that we'll have to work next to each other from now on, if not together."

"Huh." Cheyenne looked him up and down and shrugged. "Gotta say I didn't expect that."

"Yeah, well, I've been doing this long enough to know when to throw in the towel and switch to a different tack." He rubbed his chin and glanced behind her at her front door, looking for the right words. "If anything else comes up that you think we should know, I hope you'll keep making those calls."

"I will. Just like I told you about that thing on my mom's property." She snorted. "As much as I'd love to, I can't be everywhere at once."

"You get pretty damn close, though, don't you?" The man's lips twitched into a tight smile. He started to turn away from her but paused, lowering his voice. "You were right about that portal, Cheyenne, so I'm taking a risk and trusting that you're right about whatever else you think you're doing. Don't make me look like an asshole."

"No problem. You're good at doing that all on your own."

They stared at each other for a moment longer, then the FRoE agent grunted a humorless laugh and pointed at her. "Maybe. Is that why you won't let me inside?"

"Maybe." *No way am I giving him an open invitation to step through those wards just for a talk like this.*

He eyed the door again. "You're not keeping an escaped convict in there, are you?"

"Please. I want him in my apartment even less than I want you in there. And no, I still can't tell you where he is."

Rhynehart shrugged. "Worth a shot."

He shrugged and headed down the hallway toward the elevators.

Cheyenne watched him until he disappeared through the elevator doors. At the same moment, Matthew's front door opened across the hall, and his face lit up with a cheerful smile when he saw her.

Not now, neighbor.

She jerked the door open again, slipped inside, and leaned against the door to close it. "Shit. That was close."

"What the hell happened to my room?" Ember shouted.

"Oh." Cheyenne slid the deadbolt into place and nodded before hurrying across the kitchen toward her friend. "That was me."

"What?" Ember wheeled backward and stared at the halfling. "It was a mess in here. I mean, I know I'm a heavy sleeper, but I would've heard the vacuum. Wait, you didn't vacuum up tiny crushed pieces of magical spy-bugs, did you?"

Fighting back a laugh, Cheyenne shook her head and leaned through the doorway to grab the trashcan. "No vacuum. An O'gúleesh activator that isn't supposed to exist over here."

The fae peered at the pile of metallic dust in the trashcan and swallowed. "Oh. Like, a cleaning spell or something?"

"Or something. I don't even know what it was. The gear did it all for me."

"Jesus." Ember spun her chair around to watch Cheyenne dump the smaller trashcan into the kitchen's much larger bin. "That thing's gonna make you unstoppable."

"You're not the first person to say that." Cheyenne returned Ember's trash can and stopped outside the bedroom door, folding her arms. "Can't use it all the time, though. Apparently, it's got some crazy magical frequency that would be way too easy for the wrong people to pick up on over here."

"Well, yeah, if that's the only one that exists." A surprised laugh burst from Ember's mouth when she looked through her open bedroom door again. "And you made the bed."

"It felt right."

"Thanks. I might be able to get into my closet for a change of clothes without freaking out now." The fae smoothed her hair away from her face. "So, what did your FRoE friend want?"

"To make sure he wasn't losing his mind, I think."

"Ha. I'm having a hard time believing you're the person he'd go to for that kind of reassurance."

Cheyenne said, "Yeah, me too. But I might've had a part in him questioning his sanity."

Ember turned her chair around and shot her friend a sidelong glance through narrowed eyes. "Well, now you *have* to tell me the whole story."

"That's a given." Stepping toward the fridge, Cheyenne opened the top freezer door and peered inside. "I need something to eat first. The last meal I had was way too small and tasted weirdly like raw tuna. I couldn't even eat most of it."

"The food's not that great over there, then, huh?"

Cheyenne shrugged. "It had eyes."

CHAPTER FIFTY-NINE

After relaying her entire trip into Ambar'ogúl, Cheyenne set the empty container of her microwavable stir-fry-for-breakfast on the coffee table and sat back in the recliner. "So now everyone's waiting on whatever L'zar's next step in the plan is. Which of course, nobody wants to tell me."

Ember stared at the halfling, her mouth slack. "Oh, man. I can't believe you're going back there. Sounds like a shitshow."

"Yeah, pretty much. But I have to, Em. Whatever putting that giant drow coin on some monarch's altar is supposed to do for me, that's what has to happen next—assuming L'zar and Corian know what they're talking about and the whole thing won't be a huge waste of time and energy. Not to mention putting a lot more magicals in danger."

"They have to know what they're doing." Ember rubbed her palms down her thighs and shook her head. "There's a lot at stake in this."

"I know, and it's only gonna get worse until we can stop the Crown's poison from spreading all the way across the Border. I still don't see how me dropping a coin on some table is gonna make that easier for us."

"Maybe it's the halfling thing." Ember shrugged. "If you can bring something like an activator across and get it to work on this side, there's probably something you're bringing over there with that coin, right? Something connected to the human side of you, or whatever."

"That might be part of it, sure." Cheyenne sat back in the recliner and frowned at the empty frozen-dinner container. "L'zar knew he'd have another halfling kid the night he left my mom that puzzle box, but he didn't know about me being able to bring advanced tech into this world until after I did it."

"So the coin-on-the-altar thing is just a hunch."

"No. They told me about that part of the plan the minute I opened the box. Apparently, that's the last step, but I still feel like I'm missing something, like why it's so important."

Ember tucked her hair behind her ear and gazed around the living room in thought. "Is taking that coin over there supposed to give you more powers?"

"I don't know. That's the way they made it sound. Claiming *the rest* of my legacy." With another shrug, Cheyenne stood from the chair and looked at the mini-loft. "Now I'm supposed to wait for someone to call me and fill me in on what happens next."

Ember chuckled. "I bet you hate that."

"Yeah, I don't like sitting around and waiting." She pulled the activator from the pocket of her sweatpants and grinned. "Which is why I'm gonna go introduce this thing to Glen and see what happens."

"Uh-huh." Ember grabbed the remote off the coffee table and aimed it at the TV. "Have fun."

Cheyenne was already halfway up the metal staircase by the time the background noise of Ember's newest show filled the apartment. She brought up her drow magic, her skin and hair making the transformation instantly, and stuck the activator behind her ear. Once the initial pinching sync-up faded, she stood in front of her computer and rubbed her hands together.

"Okay, Glen. Time to see how well you handle a little boost in teamwork."

"What?"

The halfling snorted. "Talkin' to myself, Em."

"Right."

Cheyenne sat in the cheap office chair and powered up her computer. The minute Glen's fans started whirring and the whole system turned on, everything lit up in her vision with more scrolling lines of code and flashing lights. *This is gonna be fun.*

The data streams were filled with basic processes she already knew and understood, so she pulled up her VPN and dove into the dark web headfirst. She went straight to the Borderlands forum and stopped when the home page filled her monitor. *Holy shit.*

The data streamed across her vision, the excess spilling outside the physical confines of the monitor screen to scroll across the desk. Hundreds of back-channel entry points and strings of encrypted data unraveled in front of her. Cheyenne grinned and focused her attention on the most recently posted topic threads. The second she zeroed in on the poster's username, a flashing line of data rolled out, showing the coded makeup of the user's VPN, their most recent dark-web browser history, and two different IP addresses used to hop onto the forum. After that came the magical's name, which she hadn't seen before, and a physical address labeled Most Recently Confirmed Location.

A surprised laugh burst from the halfling's lips, and she scrolled down the forum's home page. Every single username brought up the same personal data no one else was supposed to see. Grinning, Cheyenne took it all in and had to sit back in her chair at the realization. Her hand went up to the activator behind her ear.

This thing breaks human tech wide open. I could hack into anything with this. Not like I couldn't before, but now it's too easy.

She glanced at the wall on her right and brought up the image of their friendly neighbor's huge smile when he'd stepped out of his front door that morning.

I could hack into Matthew Thomas' database too, and I'd bet my entire rig that it'd be as easy and untraceable as—"

The buzzing of her phone on silent caught her enhanced hearing and ripped her right out of that train of thought. "Crap."

She lurched to her feet and ran down the stairs.

"You okay?" Ember called after her.

"Phone's ringing." It was still shoved into the back pocket of her blood-stained pants from last night, but she pulled it out and quickly answered Corian's call. "Hey."

"Why do you sound out of breath?"

Cheyenne forced herself to breathe slowly. "I'm not. I ran down the stairs to get my phone. What's up?"

"We've moved up the timeline a little." Corian paused, presumably to step away from Lumil and Byrd, who were bickering about something in the background. "We're holding the *Nós Ani* ceremony today."

"Wait, what?" Cheyenne turned to look through her open bedroom door at Ember, who was thoroughly engrossed in her show.

"After what Persh'al told us about your quick trip over, we've all decided that is the next thing on the list. It'll help you and Ember both, as I'm sure she already told you."

"Yeah, she did."

"Good. I'll be at your apartment at two o'clock. Make sure you're both ready for this. And wear something nice, huh?"

Cheyenne snorted. "Something nice. I'll see what I can do."

"I'm sure you'll come up with something appropriately off the mark," Corian said, chuckling. "This is a big deal, Cheyenne. For both of you. Oh, and don't eat lunch."

"Lunch?"

The line went dead, and she stared at the home screen of her phone. "Seriously, that's all I get?"

She looked up and found Ember staring at her. "You're gonna disappear for some other crazy mission now, aren't you?"

Cheyenne snorted and paused in the door of her room. "Kinda. You've been invited too."

"What?" The fae turned off the TV and tossed the remote on the coffee table. "Those guys have lost their minds."

"According to the crazy rebels, we're doing that ceremony today."

"No shit?"

"Yeah. We can expect a nightstalker portal at two."

Ember laughed. "I don't even know what to say to that, except to remind you that you can't even try to back out of this now."

"I'm not gonna try, Em. You made your point about the whole *Nós Ani* thing. And from what I hear, I'd be stupid to fight a fae when she's made up her mind."

"Yeah, right."

Cheyenne glanced at her phone again. "I'm gonna put on some real clothes, then you up for a quick shopping trip?"

Ember cocked her head. "For you or for me?"

"Sure." The halfling slipped back into her room to find something to wear that wasn't bloody, ripped, or pajamas.

An hour later, Cheyenne and Ember moved slowly down the formal-wear aisle at a consignment store outside Jackson Ward, browsing the racks for something that would pass for nice. Ember ran a thin, sparkly black dress through her fingers and shook her head. "I don't get why we're dressing up for this. It's weird, right? Like, putting on a show for five other magicals inside a warehouse?"

"Yeah." Cheyenne pulled a black shirt off the rack and wrinkled her nose at the flowered pattern on the sleeves before putting it back. "But it's an excuse to get out. Pretend we're two normal people about to dress up for something that's totally not normal."

"That makes just as much sense." Ember held a hot-pink minidress against her chest and looked at her friend. "You think they'd approve of this one?"

"I don't give a shit what *they'd* think. I'd tell you to burn it."

Ember laughed and put the dress back, both her fingers and the hanger flashing with pale violet light as the hook rose from her fingers and returned to the rack. "What do you think the ceremony entails, huh? Obviously, sacrifices and bloodletting are out."

"Unless Corian was lying to you to get you to say yes."

"Guess we'll have to see. Just putting it out there, though—I didn't write a speech or anything."

"Nah, they probably have a script." The girls snickered and kept searching through the racks. "Or it's one of those repeat-after-me deals."

Ember tilted her head and pulled the corners of her mouth down in a haughty impersonation of pompous dignity. "'Do you, Ember Gaderow, profess your undying loyalty to the halfling child of the world's most-wanted drow criminal?'"

"Ugh." Cheyenne shot her friend a sidelong glance and chuckled. "You do a pretty good job of looking just like my mom, though."

"Hey, you think they invited her too?"

They burst out laughing, ignoring the skeptical glances of the other women milling through the boutique who preferred a less giddy shopping experience.

"Wait a minute." Cheyenne pulled a heavy black romper from the rack, complete with pockets, a silver zipper up the front, and black satin along the collar and on the cuff of each long sleeve. "I like this."

"Looks like a mechanic's jumpsuit in fancy black."

"I'm goin' with it."

Ember shook her head with a small smile and kept moving down the rack. "I'm not gonna find anything in here. I don't even know what I'd— Whoa." She looked over her shoulder to make sure no one was watching, then pointed at a hanger. Everything flashed purple, and the simple, slate-gray dress with short sleeves sailed into her hand. "Yeah, this is it."

"Yeah?"

"Oh, yeah. I'm not into jumpsuits."

Cheyenne snorted and took the dress from her friend, pinning its hanger in one hand with her own outfit. "Fair enough. Let's get outta here."

They moved through the aisle and headed toward the checkout counter along the far wall. The halfling stopped when she looked at the mannequin in front of them and cocked her head.

"I need that too."

"The jacket?" Ember wrinkled her nose. "You're going all out, aren't you?"

"Hey, it works. Semi-formal meets trench coat with a hood, and it's my color." Cheyenne sorted through the jackets behind the mannequin before she pulled out the last one in her size and grinned at it. "I needed a new jacket anyway."

Laughing, Ember wheeled herself toward the checkout counter. "At least you know what you like."

"Hey, I've got an extremely specific style. Pretty hard to replicate too."

"I bet your mom and Eleanor loved shopping for Christmas presents, huh?" They reached the desk, and Ember's smile faded when she saw her friend's hesitant frown. "What?"

Cheyenne placed the items on the counter as the short, smiling clerk came toward them to get started on the purchase. "Would it surprise you if I said Bianca doesn't believe in Christmas?"

Ember blinked. "No, not really. I probably should've guessed that."

"Eleanor snuck past the barricade a few times, but it was more like books and then parts when I started building computers." Cheyenne chuckled. "You know, performance-based gifts."

"Jeeze."

"Did you find everything you were looking for today?" the clerk asked, smiling sweetly at her newest customers.

"Yeah, thanks." Cheyenne pulled her wallet out of her back pocket and slipped out her card.

"Excellent. Would you like me to box these for you?"

"Oh, no. Just in the bag is fine." Cheyenne flipped her credit card against her fingers and nodded.

"Sure." The woman removed the clothes from the hangers before folding them gently and placing them in a large brown paper bag with handles. "There you are. Enjoy."

Cheyenne and Ember glanced at each other, and the halfling cleared her throat. "I think you forgot to ring me up."

"No, I did not." The woman glanced around the shop and leaned forward with a conspiratorial smile. "Your purchase is covered today, ma'am. No questions asked. I wish I could be there to see it, but I gotta keep things running around here if you know what I mean." She winked at Cheyenne, and a flash of green light flared briefly behind her large brown eyes.

Now I'm getting expensive clothes for free from a magical at a consignment store.

Cheyenne tried to smile back as she put away her card and her wallet. "Well, thanks."

"Think nothing of it, *Aranél*." The woman grinned at Ember next, nodding as Cheyenne took the bag.

"Okay." Ember gave the human-looking magical a weak wave before wheeling herself toward the front doors. "Have a good one."

"You too. Good luck."

An electronic bell dinged when the girls stepped outside. Cheyenne glanced over her shoulder at the woman behind the counter, who raised a hand in farewell and wouldn't stop smiling.

"What was that?" Ember asked, heading to Cheyenne's shiny black Panamera parked in front of the store.

The halfling gritted her teeth and unlocked the car, ignoring the chirp that usually brightened her mood. "Marsil told me he hadn't said anything to anyone about you."

"But she knows who *you* are, apparently." Ember moved away from the passenger side door and flicked a finger at it. The handle flashed purple, and the door swung open in front of her.

Cheyenne tossed the bag into the back and helped her friend transfer into the passenger seat, aided by the fae's boost of magic lifting her out of the chair. "And it sounded like she knew about the ceremony. What else could she be talking about?"

"Marsil couldn't have told her about that. We only just found out."

"I know." Cheyenne popped the trunk, folded up the wheelchair, and stored it before slipping behind the wheel. Both front doors closed at the same time, and she and Ember exchanged dubious glances. "Somebody's been spreading the word. Really damn fast, too."

"That doesn't make sense." Ember strapped herself in and stared at the front of the consignment store. "Who would openly put that information out there? Especially when everyone on this side following L'zar knows the Crown's still looking for you."

Cheyenne punched the engine's start button and buckled her seatbelt. "An idiot, that's who. At least they keep the wards up around the warehouse, 'cause if the wrong people find out about this, we're gonna have a different kind of party."

CHAPTER SIXTY

Back at their apartment, Cheyenne finished putting on the extra layers of thick black eyeliner and nodded at herself in the mirror. She'd pinned her hair into something resembling a fancy up-do, the slight curl left in her black locks spilling down to frame her face. She smoothed down the front of her new romper, looked herself up and down, and then stepped out of the bathroom as Ember wheeled out of the kitchen.

"Whoa." The fae grinned. "Okay, the jumpsuit works. Especially with the black lipstick."

"See? Told you. Nice dress."

Ember glanced down at the gray dress, which fell just below her knees. "Thanks. Admittedly, I wish I had more magic tricks to work with, but putting on these leggings would've been a bitch without them."

Cheyenne chuckled. "You did okay."

"Yeah. Pretty soon, I'll snap my fingers and voila! Instant wardrobe change." Ember snapped her fingers, and a soft pop came from the center of the living room as Corian's portal appeared beside the coffee table. The fae's eyes widened as the nightstalker stepped out of thin air in black dress slacks and a dark-gray button-up shirt. He gazed around the apartment until he found Ember staring at him. "That was creepily punctual."

"Ember." He nodded at her, then turned toward Cheyenne. "Are you ready?"

"Yep." Cheyenne grabbed her new coat off the back of the couch, reaching into the deep pockets to double-check that her phone and the activator were still where she'd put them. "Let's do this."

Ember nodded and headed toward the portal. Cheyenne joined her, and Corian gestured for them both to step through the shimmering, opaque wall of black light.

"Why isn't this one see-through?"

He smiled at the halfling and dipped his head. "It's a surprise."

"Oh, boy." Ember pushed herself through the portal.

"I'm not a big fan of surprises," Cheyenne muttered.

"I know. Try to make an exception for this one." Corian gestured toward the portal again and nodded.

Trying not to roll her eyes, she turned toward the wall of light and took a deep breath. *It better be a good one.*

When she stepped through, she almost toppled into the back of Ember's wheelchair. She stopped herself with a hand on the handles and moved to the left, her eyes widening at the scene before her.

"Sorry," Ember muttered blankly. Her chair flashed violet and moved two feet to the right.

"No problem." Cheyenne's mouth dropped open as Corian arrived behind them and the portal disappeared. "What's going on?"

"Surprise." Corian chuckled and stepped past them and strode toward the center of the huge clearing in front of them.

At the center was a massive tree, its trunk twisted and angling to the side as gigantic branches snaked out in every direction. Each bough was large and thick enough to walk comfortably across, some of them dipping down to skim across the dark, dew-studded grass, and every bit of the tree pulsed with an internal light that changed from black to purple to black again.

Ember gazed at the pitch-black sky studded with stars. "It's not supposed to be dark out right now."

"Trees aren't supposed to glow, either," Cheyenne muttered.

At the base of the massive trunk stood L'zar, Byrd, Lumil, and Persh'al, each of them wearing some variation of a formal suit. Lumil had tied a crimson scarf around her neck to hide the scar encircling her flesh, and the combination of that and an outfit that weirdly matched Byrd's made her look like a green-skinned pirate with yellow hair.

L'zar chuckled, his hands clasped behind his back. His well-tailored suit shimmered bright-silver when he reached out to gesture at the clearing around them. "The *Nós Ani* have always been bound at night beneath a Nimlothar, but we don't have time to wait for dark or find one of these trees which don't exist Earthside. Still, tradition's important, isn't it?"

"I guess." Cheyenne slipped into her jacket and glanced at each of the magicals waiting for them beneath the tree. Corian took his place beside L'zar, waving for her and Ember to join them. "So, all this is a giant illusion?"

L'zar dipped his head. "In a manner of speaking. Mostly."

Ember easily wheeled herself across the cold, wet grass, her eyes lighting up with the pulsing glow within the illusion of the Nimlothar tree. "I can't believe this."

"Right there with you, Em."

They stopped in front of a glowing silver line drawn in the grass, separating them from L'zar and the others. On the other side of that line were a silver pitcher, two silver goblets, and a wickedly sharp ceremonial dagger glinting in the artificial starlight.

Cheyenne grinned. "Hey, you guys promised no sacrifices."

Ember snorted.

"Well, no." L'zar studied the dagger at his feet. "That's not for either of you."

A new portal appeared on the halfling's right and Maleshi stepped through, wearing a cocktail dress in a bright, startling shade of pink.

Cheyenne nudged Ember's shoulder and nodded at the general. The fae glanced that way and laughed. "Yeah, see? *She* can pull it off."

Maleshi grinned at them and stepped forward as her portal disappeared. Then she stopped in front of Ember and extended her hand. "I'm thrilled to finally meet you, Ember. Maleshi Hi'et."

"Yeah, I know." The fae stared at her but took the nightstalker's hand, which was covered with fine dark fur.

"I didn't think you knew about this," Cheyenne said as Maleshi's glowing silver eyes met hers.

"Oh, I wouldn't miss this for the world, kid." The general nodded and put a hand on Cheyenne's shoulder. "Good timing, right?"

"Sure." The halfling laughed in disbelief and stared at the glowing trunk of the Nimlothar. "So, what now?"

Corian stepped toward the silver line in the grass.

Another portal opened across the clearing behind them. Corian's gaze flickered that way, and his frown made Cheyenne turn around. Marsil Keldryk stepped through the oval of shimmering light, finally revealing his true form as a goblin, also in formal attire. Right behind him came Dr. Boseley, her red hair a mass of scarlet curls on top of her head.

"My physical therapist is a troll," Ember muttered.

"Looks like it, yeah."

Two more portals opened, then two more, and a stream of other magicals Cheyenne didn't recognize stepped solemnly into the ceremonial clearing. She stared at each of them. All were dressed for the special occasion, and every face gazed at her with a broad, eager smile.

Marsil and Dr. Boseley had moved around the clearing to make room for the others. Cheyenne glanced at Ember, then went toward the goblin assistant. "I thought you and I reached an understanding yesterday. That included not telling people about any of this."

"We did, Cheyenne." Marsil smiled politely at her, though a small frown flickered across his brows. "I was invited."

"You *what?*"

L'zar laughed and stepped forward as another half-dozen magicals appeared in the clearing. "We do have to keep this quiet. Mostly. But I couldn't let you go through this without something of an audience. That's the best part."

"An audience." Cheyenne stepped away from Marsil and stared at the quickly growing crowd lining the edge of the clearing. Those in front had to step forward to make room for the newcomers. "I don't know any of these magicals." She squinted at the newest people emerging from the portals. *What's happening?*

R'mahr, Yadje, and their daughter Bryl grinned when they saw Cheyenne beneath the huge tree. Bryl bounced on her toes and waved. The halfling smiled and waved back, then scanned the other faces. *That has to be Tony, and he's an orc.*

Scowling, Corian stepped toward L'zar and lowered his voice. "You sent invitations."

"Yes, Corian." The drow smiled at all the newcomers and didn't bother to look his friend in the eye. "Relax. I only sent a few."

"Really? Because they keep showing up, and I'm counting close to eighty right now."

A large portal opened behind Marsil, and Gúrdu's hulking gray form stepped through. Maleshi laughed when she saw him. "You too, huh?"

The raug Oracle's orange-brown eyes narrowed at the nightstalker general. "I'm not here for you," he growled, but a low rumble of laughter escaped him as he walked away from the Nimlothar tree to take his place among the other witnesses.

The clearing buzzed with hushed voices and eager conversation, everyone staring at the Nimlothar tree and the drow halfling standing beside her awed fae friend in the wheelchair.

L'zar cocked his head and shrugged. "Oops."

Corian hissed. "That's not an answer."

"They're excited. Word spreads quickly around here." The drow turned toward his *Nós Aní* and raised an eyebrow. "They could use something to look forward to, don't you think?"

"You should've been more selective." Corian folded his arms and took a deep breath, scanning the crowd. "This many of them in one place is asking for trouble."

"We can handle trouble, brother. Let it go and enjoy yourself."

The nightstalker grumbled something unintelligible, and when he caught Cheyenne listening to the conversation, he shook his head and turned away.

She kept watching him and didn't miss the exasperated glance he shot Maleshi. The war general grinned at him and spread her arms.

"So much for feeling ridiculous in front of five other magicals in a warehouse," Ember muttered.

"Sorry, Em. I had no idea it was happening like this."

The fae glanced up at her friend with an unsure smile. "But it's happening."

"Yeah. Whatever *it* is."

L'zar glanced at Cheyenne. "You'll do the rest of this as a drow."

Nodding quickly, Cheyenne summoned the flare of her magic up the base of her spine, and she made the transformation in front of everyone.

Her father spread his arms wide and cocked his head. "Let's begin."

CHAPTER SIXTY-ONE

"Seeing as things are a little different for this binding, I hope nobody holds it against me if I ditch the old tongue for one that's more realm-appropriate." L'zar grinned as the crowd of magicals chuckled politely.

Corian stood behind him and to the side, his arms folded and his scowl ceaseless as he kept a wary eye on every dark shadow within the clearing.

"Today, we bind a drow and her *Nós Aní*, chosen in friendship and full awareness of what this binding entails. The fae Ember Gaderow, and the drow Cheyenne Summerlin, *my* daughter." L'zar gestured to each in turn and chuckled. "The only thing I'd change is the last name in that announcement, but I suppose I can't win 'em all, right?"

Another round of soft laughter came in response, though it was tense and unsure. Cheyenne glanced at Maleshi, who closed her eyes and shook her head.

L'zar smiled at his daughter, then lifted his chin. His voice was like a cracking whip across the clearing. "The old laws still stand, even in this world. Blood from the heart of Ambar'ogúl draws like to like. The *mór edhil* still stand as they were meant to be, and the *Nós Aní* stand beside them."

Without needing a cue from L'zar, Corian knelt in front of the silver

416

pitcher and poured a dark, shimmering liquid into each of the goblets. The clearing was so silent, even those standing at the farthest edges could hear the drink trickling into the cups.

L'zar sank to his knees in front of the goblets and picked up the dagger.

"By the power running through my veins and yours, Cheyenne, I give my blessing." Staring up at his daughter, he wrapped his other hand around the blade and pulled, slicing his palm open. Blood poured from his clenched fist, which he held over one goblet and then the other, adding a few drops to each. The dagger fell to the damp grass, and he passed his hand over the cut in his other palm. Cheyenne saw the wound heal quickly beneath the golden light glowing behind his hands. Then L'zar grabbed the silver goblets and set one foot forward in the grass, his other knee planted firmly while he leaned toward Cheyenne and Ember. "Drink."

This is so creepy.

The halfling stared at her father's wide, eager eyes above his knowing grin. She and Ember glanced at each other, then Ember reached out to take the goblet in front of her. Cheyenne did the same, gazing into the shimmering black liquid within the cup. "All of it?"

"As much as you can stand," L'zar muttered. "Do it."

The girls lifted the goblets to their lips at the same time. Cheyenne's nose tingled with the scent of blueberries, eucalyptus, and the undertone of blood rising from other odors she couldn't distinguish. The drink was overly sweet and bitter at the same time, and she got down two swallows before she couldn't handle any more.

Ember gulped and sounded like she was choking before she pulled away from the goblet and grimaced.

L'zar nodded and reached for the cups again. Then he set them on the ground and rose to his feet. "You'll repeat after me. Together."

The fae snorted and immediately covered her mouth to hide a smile.

Cheyenne shot her a sidelong glance. *We called this part.*

L'zar raised an eyebrow and decided to ignore their inside joke. "By the old laws and the heartblood of Ambar'ogúl, we are bound."

Cheyenne and Ember took deep breaths and repeated his words in unison. "By the old laws and the heartblood of Ambar'ogúl, we are bound."

An explosion of brilliant silver light burst from Cheyenne's and Ember's chests the second the last word left their lips. It lit the clearing like a flare, and Cheyenne heard her friend's startled gasp and realized she'd made a similar sound. The light crackled and burst away from them, twirling up in a long column before it darted into the illusion of the darkly glowing Nimlothar tree. The tree's bark pulsed brighter, let out a blinding flash, and then darkened again.

L'zar stared at the tree and cocked his head, his voice ringing out in the stunned silence that had overtaken the gathered magicals in the clearing. "Huh."

"Cheyenne." Ember leaned forward in her chair. "I feel weird."

"Yeah, that whole thing was weird." The halfling stared at the tree, then glanced down at her drow father, who was still craning his neck toward the branches.

L'zar finally turned and shrugged. "I didn't expect *that* to happen."

"*What?*"

"It's fine." He waved her off and shot the tree another confused look. "Some Nimlothar somewhere responded to this ceremony and accepted your *Nós Aní* like it would have in the old days, so we have that going for us."

Corian shook his head and scowled. "There's only one left, L'zar."

Cheyenne swallowed. "It's with the Crown, right?"

Her father pursed his lips and tilted his head from side to side. "Yep."

"So now she knows what we just did."

"Probably." He clicked his tongue with a remarkably high level of casual apathy. "An unforeseen consequence. But congratulations. You and your *Nós Aní* are bound."

Cheyenne gritted her teeth and glanced at Corian, who stared at L'zar and looked like he wanted to stab the drow in the back. *I'm feeling the same thing right now.*

Ember rubbed her temple. "What's going on?"

The Nimlothar that was supposed to have been nothing more than an illusion flashed again, its sputtering light blinking brighter and faster until the entire thing disappeared. The illusion around the clearing cut off abruptly, and everyone was dazzled with the sudden intensity of real sunlight instead of the dome of fake night overhead. The crowd of magicals shifted uneasily and looked around, talking to each other in low voices.

Cheyenne glared at L'zar. "What did you do?"

"What did *I* do? That was *your* power, Cheyenne, and it was very impressive."

Someone shouted a warning, and they all turned to see a dark portal crackling open inside the tree line of the clearing. Three more burst into existence, then a dozen dark ovals of light ringed the clearing. The air around them wavered like heat rising from hot cement, then more magicals poured through the portals.

Screams broke out as the first of the Crown's loyalists launched attack spells. Cheyenne saw a bull's head sewn onto the shoulder of the closest orc's shirt as he hurled a ball of searing green flames into the crowd. "Shit."

She reached into her jacket pocket, pulled out the activator, and slapped it on behind her ear. By the time she'd refocused her vision with the advanced technology's extra kick, Persh'al, Byrd, and Lumil had jumped into action. They ran toward the loyalists spilling through the open portals, tossing attack spells at them.

Maleshi vanished in a flash of silver light and darted across the clearing. Loyalists choked and cried out, dropping left and right as she took out those closest to the crowd of innocent magicals too terrified to fight back.

A whirring buzz filled the air and dozens of small, black metal orbs whizzed through the portals, unleashing yellow sparks on the crowd. They lit up in Cheyenne's vision like flares, and the activator locked onto one after the other as she shot rounds of purple sparks at the flying machines, blasting them from the air.

"Over here!" Corian gestured toward the huge portal he'd summoned where the Nimlothar illusion had stood. "Into the portal!"

He lunged forward and slashed his elongated claws into the throat of a snarling skaxen leaping at him.

Lumil and Byrd took up the cry, waving for the crowd to run toward Corian's portal as they fought the loyalists tearing after them. The red, spiraling magic around Lumil's fists buried itself in chests and heads, sending snarling loyalists flying.

Magicals ran in every direction, screaming and shouting and trying not to get hit in the crossfire. Cheyenne focused on the flying machines, launching attack after attack at them as fast as she could.

One of them darted away from her magic at the last second and swooped toward Ember. The halfling spun around and saw her friend leaning forward, oblivious. Cheyenne blasted the machine, sending shattered fragments all over Ember's back and the top of her head. "Em, what's—"

A huge body slammed into her from the side and knocked her to the ground. Grunting, Cheyenne rolled onto her back as the stumbling orc loyalist sneered at her and raised two hands filled with black light dripping some foul sludge into the grass. She reached out with both hands, and her black lashing tendrils whipped toward him. They coiled around his wrists before she jerked her arms sideways and sent him reeling into Byrd's back. The goblin turned with a roar and pummeled the orc with fists and flaring bursts of orange light.

Scrambling to her feet, Cheyenne scanned the clearing for more of the flying machines. Only one more remained, and she hurled a hissing arc of purple sparks at it. Green flames streaked in front of her toward the terrified magicals darting across the clearing, and she raised two shields between the innocent bystanders and the barrage of crackling attacks. She recognized Marsil, who glanced at her with wide eyes before ushering Dr. Boseley toward Corian's open portal.

Gúrdu bellowed on the other side of the clearing, pummeling through attacking loyalists with his fists and sending them flying like startled birds. Persh'al's green whip crackled and sparked, and Maleshi streaked back and forth across the clearing in a silver-and-black blur.

A low, ominous rumble came from Cheyenne's right. She spun that way and scanned the open loyalist portals. The ground rumbled with an oncoming war machine seconds before her activator located the thing coming from the farthest portal. It was as tall as she was, covered in thick metal spikes as it rolled through the portal like a miniature tank. Flashing blue lights blinked around the perimeter of what looked like a swiveling head. A window opened and unleashed a red burst of magic into the center of the clearing that tore into the ground, scattering grass and clods of dirt and magicals from both sides.

Cheyenne scanned the data scrolling across her vision. The machine's swiveling head turned its blinking lights toward her and fired again. She threw up a shield with both hands, and the red attack blasted it, shoving her back across the ground as it roared against the dark light of her shield.

"Take it down!" Persh'al shouted, dodging a snarling skaxen before lashing the creature in the back with his whip.

Lumil and Byrd ran toward the war machine, but it opened fire with smaller windows on its sides and sprayed crackling red light like bullets.

Weak points. Find the weak points.

Cheyenne stared at the war machine rumbling across the grass, immune to the magical attacks her friends unleashed. A blinking yellow light lit up at the base of the machine, and she summoned a sphere of her crackling black energy. An ogre lumbered toward her, letting out a fierce battle cry, and she sent the orb into his face instead. Her other hand launched another sphere at the machine, which lit up with purple and black sparks before fading again, to no effect.

That's not gonna work.

The halfling sent snaking black tendrils at a grotesquely scarred goblin racing after the last of the innocent onlookers hobbling toward Corian's portal. They wound around his throat and jerked him back, and the goblin croaked and slammed into the ground as the last terrified troll woman ran past Corian and through his portal to safety. The nightstalker closed the portal, nodded at Cheyenne, and darted across the clearing in a flash of silver light.

The O'gúl war tank fired again, hitting more loyalists than Cheyenne's friends. She focused her activator-enhanced vision on the scrolling data and the machine's moving parts. Another command blinked at her, and she cocked her head. *Or I could just take it apart.*

Without having to think about it, the halfling swiped the command in her vision, and a welded piece of the machine's siding squealed, rippling until it ripped free and hurtled into the trees. Cheyenne stepped toward the thing, searching for the next command that would let her pull the tank apart piece by piece. More red explosions burst from the window between the tank's blinking lights and she dodged what she could, occasionally throwing up shields to protect the others between ripping off more parts.

Behind her and four yards away from where Ember sat in her

wheelchair, the sky darkened. Ember turned away from the battle to look at the crackling, hissing black portal ten times the size of the others opening where the Nimlothar illusion had been. The fae's eyes widened as a rolling crack like thunder emerged from the portal, blasting Ember's hair away from her face with a numbing cold wind. "Cheyenne!"

"Little busy, Em." The halfling launched two spheres of black energy at two goblins scrambling toward her, knocking them off their feet before they crashed into the trees at the edge of the clearing.

"Yeah, I know, but this looks bad."

CHAPTER SIXTY-TWO

Cheyenne turned away from the war machine and froze when she saw the hissing, sparking outline of the massive portal in the air. *Like the first time I trained with Corian. That one's coming straight from the other side.*

"Shouldn't you do something?" Ember shouted, trying to get the attention of the other rebel magicals. They were all busy fighting the loyalists, and Cheyenne took a few steps closer to her friend before having to throw up another wide shield beneath the war machine's next artillery blast.

"Yeah, probably. Corian!"

The nightstalker dropped out of his enhanced speed at her shout and looked at the massive portal. His silver eyes widened, then he raced toward the ogre he was fighting and threw a spray of magical spikes at him. The ogre bellowed and crashed to the ground but somehow managed to snag the nightstalker by the ankle. Corian growled and turned to fight the hulking loyalist off.

The war machine angled toward Cheyenne, and the activator helped her rip two more handfuls of its inner parts through the gaping hole in its side. A chorus of dark, wailing voices came through the growing portal from Ambar'ogúl, and Cheyenne blinked beneath the wave of déjà vu washing over her. *I've heard that before.*

A skaxen leaped at her, shrieking with laughter as his long claws slashed toward her face. She blasted him back with telekinetic force and focused on the war machine, which launched another red magical bomb across the clearing. *Take that thing down first, then I can deal with the rest.*

Ember glanced at the crackling portal, which was still emitting the dark chant in a chorus of otherworldly voices. *Does no one get that this thing is the biggest issue right now?*

The surface of the portal rippled like a giant pool of black sludge. Sparks flew in every direction, and a dark hand emerged from the other side.

"Cheyenne! Something's coming through!"

The halfling tore another chunk out of the war machine, making it shudder and momentarily pause in its rumbling advance across the clearing. "In a second."

"I think now's probably better." Ember jumped in her chair when the tank's next blast hit Cheyenne's large shield and sent her sailing through the air. The halfling landed on her back four feet from Ember and skidded across the grass with a snarl.

The hand coming out of the chanting portal reached out farther, dark nails glinting against slate-gray skin. The chanting intensified until it almost drowned out the sound of the battle. The rest of the arm followed, then came the tip of a dark boot poking out from beneath the hem of a black robe rippling like water. A figure cloaked from head to toe in swirling black emerged from the portal, leaning forward against the force of magical laws that should have made this impossible between two worlds.

"Cheyenne!" Ember glanced at her friend, who was too busy blasting black energy spheres into another ogre barreling toward her to pay attention to the warning. The figure stepped fully out of the shimmering portal and turned its head. Ember gaped at the two glowing golden eyes within the hood's black pool and thought she felt her heart stop.

The figure turned away from her and headed toward Cheyenne, stepping slowly forward as it hovered an inch above the grass. The dark hand that had emerged through the portal now reached for the drow halfling as the chaos of battle raged.

She won't make it.

A rush of fierce energy bloomed in the center of Ember's chest and she shouted something unintelligible beneath the noise, awed by the words flowing out of her as if her voice had taken on a life of its own. Purple and pink light burst around the fae, surrounding her in a halo of shimmering magic as she reached out with both hands.

That light hurtled toward the dark figure approaching Cheyenne. The glowing golden eyes within the hood locked onto Ember a second before the fae's magic pummeled the black cloak enshrouding the stranger. A shriek of rage and pain filled the clearing, and the figure hurtled back into the massive portal, hissing and twisting within the billowing folds of the whipping black robe. The chanting voices screamed, and the shuddering dark portal from Ambar'ogúl snapped shut with a resounding boom. For a brief moment, the battle in the clearing paused at the startling sounds and the hideous tremble shaking the ground.

Cheyenne sent a wave of earth and jagged shards of stone at the orc bearing down on her. He slid across the ground and roared when the ground opened and swallowed him beneath her manipulation, burying him in two seconds. Then she whirled to face the portal that was no longer there and saw Ember.

"Holy shit."

The fae stood two feet in front of her wheelchair, surrounded in pulsing violet light that whipped her violet-streaked hair away from her pink-tinged face. Then her arms dropped by her sides, and her legs gave out beneath her before she crumpled to the grass.

"Go on," Persh'al shouted, nodding toward Ember as his whip cracked around an orc loyalist's leg and brought the magical crashing to the ground. "We're almost done here."

Cheyenne darted toward her friend and slid to her knees in the grass. "Ember. Hey. You okay?"

Ember blinked her large, luminous violet eyes and shook her head. "Yeah, I'm just...fuck."

"Uh-huh." The halfling let out a wry chuckle despite the situation and studied her friend, who was now in full-on fae mode. "You were standing."

"And now I'm not." A small, unsure smile spread across Ember's lips.

The rolling O'gúl tank let out another fiery red burst of magic that hit the ground a foot behind Ember's wheelchair. The chair went sailing, and Cheyenne threw a shield up behind her friend to keep off most of the dirt chunks and small rocks rocketing toward them.

"I'll be right back." The halfling lurched to her feet and ran toward the war machine. The activator identified three more weak spots, and Cheyenne swiped her hands through one after the other. Fragments of black metal and blue chips and panels of thin steel mesh ripped away from the machine and flew across the clearing. A piece that looked like one of the floating spy orbs in Wildhaven burst from the machine's side, and Cheyenne sent it into the head of a skaxen loyalist about to throw himself on her. The orb cracked against his skull with a hollow metallic ring, the loyalist dropped, and the activator lit up with the final attack directive.

Cheyenne focused on the pulsing blue light emanating from the machine's torn side and opened fire with her crackling black energy spheres. They penetrated the metal hull one after the other as the machine's forward-facing windows opened and sprayed the ground with more pellets of red magic. The halfling stepped forward and pushed against the pressure she felt in the earth. Another rippling wave of dirt and buried stone hurtled away from her foot and hit the war machine, toppling it and exposing the undercarriage. The activator went haywire, blaring an alarm in Cheyenne's vision and zeroing in on the final target beneath the O'gúl tank.

She roared with effort, and instead of sparking black orbs flying from her hands, she sent a column of black energy in an endless stream at the exposed heart of the war machine. The contraption sparked and let out a low whine that grew to a shriek before it exploded mid-air. Blue light and metal shards sprayed in every direction, peppering the clearing and burying themselves in the ground, the trees, and any magical not quick enough to get out of the way.

Cheyenne fell to her knees and summoned a shield in front of her. Persh'al screamed as a shard of metal ripped through his side and sent him spinning to the ground. Somehow, when the halfling tossed a hand toward her friends and L'zar's loyal followers, she pulled enough shields into place to protect the rest of them from the shrapnel. Metal pinged off walls of dark light as the Crown loyalists cried out, unprotected from the barrage.

Breathing heavily, Cheyenne gave herself a moment to collect her thoughts before looking at the smoking, sputtering remains of the war machine. Nothing but the spinning top remained, its blue lights blinking in random bursts before they died.

Then she got to her feet and faced the others. Her shields dropped, Byrd rushed to Persh'al's side, and low groans of pain and disorientation rose from the last of the O'gúl loyalists taken down by their own malfunctioning machine.

A bolt of silver raced across the clearing and stopped in front of the dismantled tech. Corian gazed down at the wreckage, then met Cheyenne's gaze and nodded.

The halfling turned, stumbled, and righted herself before hurrying to Ember's side again. She knelt in the grass. "Sorry."

Ember barked a laugh. "For *what?*"

"That last distraction." Cheyenne gave her a crooked smile, then glanced up at where the looming portal from Ambar'ogúl had opened beside them. "You got rid of the other big one, didn't you?"

"I guess." Ember shrugged and stared at her unmoving legs. "I have no idea what happened. I just did it."

"That's a start. Thanks, Em."

The fae blinked at her friend and let out a disbelieving laugh. "Yeah. Anytime."

"I'm still a little lost with the whole fae-Ember look. You decide at the last minute to slip that ring on for the magical fight?"

Slowly lifting both hands, Ember turned them toward Cheyenne and shook her head. "No ring."

"No ring! Whoa." The halfling gave her friend another once-over. "Was that on purpose?"

"I don't think so, and I don't know how to turn it off."

"Well, maybe the ceremony turned it on. For good."

Ember swallowed and stared at her glowing pink hands. "Guess we need to find me a different illusion charm, then."

Cheyenne snorted, then Maleshi's sharp order cut through the clearing. "Line them up!"

She turned to see General Hi'et, silver eyes blazing and no less terrifying in the ripped pink cocktail dress, shoving a bound goblin loyalist to his knees. *Shit.*

"I'll be right back, Em."

"Yeah."

"You sure you're okay?"

"I'm fine. I just need to sit for a minute." The fae snorted at the unintended irony, and Cheyenne pushed to her feet again and headed toward Maleshi.

CHAPTER SIXTY-THREE

Byrd, Lumil, and Corian had gotten busy rounding up the surviving loyalists bound with flickering ropes of crackling silver magic. Over two dozen magicals with the bull's head emblem on them somewhere, either pendants or patches, had survived the battle they'd brought to the *Nós Aní* ceremony. They snarled and struggled against their bonds, but Lumil was ready with her supercharged magic of spinning red symbols around her fists. One blow with those was enough to keep the prisoners quiet. Most of them, though, shot vengeful looks at Gúrdu, who was standing guard over the line of loyalists on their knees. The raug grunted and sneered at them, crunching on something that looked an awful lot like a tiny dry-aged hand before Cheyenne looked away.

She stopped next to Maleshi. *I hate to assume what she's thinking, but I can't let this happen again.*

"So, what now?"

Maleshi shot her a brief glance before snarling at the last loyalist Lumil shoved onto the grass. "Are you injured?"

"No."

"Good. You can stand down, Cheyenne. We'll handle this."

Cheyenne glanced at Corian as he marched across the clearing to join the general. "No one made it out of the clearing."

Maleshi nodded curtly. "And no one will." Her silver claws slid out of her fingers with an ominous whisper, glinting in the afternoon sunlight.

"Wait a minute." Cheyenne stepped in front of the nightstalker war general, forcing Maleshi to look at her. "You can't do this."

"This isn't your decision to make, Cheyenne." The general's dark upper lip twitched into a sneer. "I'll only ask you to step aside once."

"Ask all you want." The halfling clenched her fists and held the woman's glowing silver gaze. "I'm not moving."

"These magicals are prisoners of war," Maleshi snarled. "If we don't deal with this threat right now, directly, we might as well paint a target on our chests and tell them to go ahead and open fire."

"They can't do anything right now." Cheyenne gestured behind her at the bound magicals on their knees, most of them spitting and hissing curses. "Which makes them much less of a threat than when they were trying to kill us."

Maleshi let out a low growl and leaned toward the halfling. "Cheyenne."

"You gave me your word that we'd leave the past behind us as long as what happened at the first portal ridge didn't repeat itself. If you give the order to kill these loyalists *on their knees*, I *will* stop you, and then you and I are done." Cheyenne clenched her fists and leaned toward the general in turn, staring her down. "I really don't want that to happen."

The nightstalker woman scowled and took a long, deep breath through her flaring nostrils. "What else do you suggest we do with them? We don't have our own Chateau D'rahl."

"No, but I know the people who do." Cheyenne turned to shoot the lined-up prisoners a fleeting glance. "And I'm willing to bet that none of these assholes are gonna show up in a certain system on this side."

Maleshi snarled. "You want me to hand our enemies over to a bunch of Earthside-born playing with fell weapons?"

"We all have the same enemy at this point. Right?" Cheyenne cocked her head. "*Right?*"

The general studied the halfling and hissed. She lifted a hand between their faces, her eyes narrowing as she made sure Cheyenne saw the glinting, razor-sharp points at her disposal. Cheyenne hissed right back and shot a burst of purple sparks from the fingertips of both hands.

I can play her game. And she'll cool off. She'd better.

A low chuckle devoid of humor rose from Maleshi's throat. Her deadly claws retracted, and she leaned forward until their noses almost touched. "Make the call, Cheyenne. If your other friends fail to contain this as effectively as I would have, whatever happens afterward is on your hands."

"At least it's not more blood."

"No. Not today." With a snarl, Maleshi spun away from her and stalked across the clearing. Her fingers moved quickly, and a new portal opened yards in front of her.

Corian shot Cheyenne a wary glance, then took off after the general. "Maleshi, wait."

She whirled on him and slashed her hand toward his face. A burst of silver light flared between them with a screech like blades meeting. When the light faded, Corian's claws were locked with Maleshi's. She snarled at him. "Not now."

"We might not have another chance," he muttered.

Cheyenne looked away from them and tried to focus on the line of kneeling loyalists in front of her instead. *I'm not supposed to be hearing this.*

Her activator flashed a command for lowering the volume, and she flicked her finger to accept it. Corian's voice traveled to her as a muffled, muted drone. *Look at me. I'm choosing not to eavesdrop 'cause I can help it.*

The nightstalkers' tense conversation continued, then Maleshi jerked her hand away from him, sparks flaring between their claws, and disappeared through her portal. After it closed, Corian stood perfectly still, his back rigid.

"I heard about those two," an orc growled. "Looks like they're still—"

Lumil's blazing red fist cracked into his face and dropped him. A broken piece of tusk flew over three prisoners and bounced in the grass. "Anyone else need help keeping their fell-damned opinions to themselves?"

"That doesn't count for me, right?" Persh'al wheezed out a laugh and grimaced. He sat halfway between the line of prisoners and Ember, who was holding his side as Byrd knelt and propped him up in the grass. "'Cause this shit really hurts, man."

"Corian," Cheyenne shouted.

The nightstalker spun, saw Persh'al covered in blood, and headed toward the blue troll.

A black burst of light enshrouded the line of bound, kneeling prisoners. Every one of them erupted in screams of agony, doubling over and shaking their heads, then staring blankly at the sky without blinking.

Cheyenne spun to face them. "What's happening?"

Corian joined her, his jaw clenching and unclenching beneath the tufts of tawny fur lining his cheeks. He stared at the screaming magicals and swallowed. "I'll let him explain that to you."

L'zar stepped out from between the trees beside Ember. "I don't remember you complaining this much about flesh wounds, Persh'al."

Persh'al twisted around as far as he could and snorted when he saw the drow stepping toward him. "It's not complaining if it's the truth, man."

"Oh, sure. You're squawking like that to get my attention." L'zar knelt beside his friend. "What's the magic word?"

The troll chuckled. "Bastard."

"Hmm." L'zar ripped the last piece of shrapnel from Persh'al's side and tossed it to the grass as the troll roared in pain. "Seems fitting, doesn't it?"

Persh'al glared at the drow's grinning face. "Just fucking do it."

L'zar slapped his palm against the wound, the blue troll screamed, and gold light flared beneath the drow's hand. When the healing finished, L'zar jerked his hand away and stood. Byrd slipped out from behind Persh'al and got to his feet. The troll fell onto his back in the grass, gasping, and blinked at the clear blue sky.

Byrd stared at him.

"Just leave me here, man. I need a second to bask in not dying."

The goblin shook his head and went to join Lumil, who was pacing in front of the line of prisoners.

"Did I hear you say something about calling in a special cleanup team?"

Cheyenne glared at her father as he moved casually toward her, his hands clasped behind his back. The kneeling prisoners had given up screaming in lieu of whimpering and moaning, hanging their heads as they sagged where they'd been left in the clearing. "What did you do to them?"

"No one can know I'm with you, Cheyenne." He shot her a sidelong glance before his gaze flickered back toward the prisoners. "Not until it's time."

"Don't even think about it."

"About what?"

"Murdering these prisoners after they've been captured." Cheyenne's anger burned through her veins alongside her drow magic. "I just made a promise to Maleshi I seriously hope I won't have to keep."

L'zar chuckled softly and closed his eyes. "I'm not killing anyone. Not right now, at any rate."

"So, what did you do?"

He turned to his daughter and gestured at the prisoners. "We now have a few dozen deaf, mute, and blind loyalists to hand over to your friends in black. I sincerely hope they're more competent than they've proven to be so far."

"What?" Cheyenne stared at the moaning loyalists kneeling in a neat, submissive line.

"It might have been better for them if you'd let General Hi'et do things her way, but you made your choice."

"This isn't okay." The halfling shook her head, clenching her fists as she ran through all the possibilities of what was in store for the loyalists. "You might have killed them anyway, just on a longer timeline."

"Not at all. They'll regain what they've lost once they set foot in their homeland again."

"How are they gonna make the crossing if they can't see, huh?"

"Well, that's something someone else will have to deal with, isn't it?" L'zar met her gaze again. "You took responsibility for these magicals when you stayed Maleshi's hand. The general has thousands of years of experience in weighing the pros and cons, Cheyenne, and there's a singular truth in all of this that she's come to understand very well. And she's not the only one."

"Oh, yeah?" The halfling gave him a tight-lipped smile of disapproval. "What's that?"

"Everything comes with a price."

A cold wave of disbelief washed over her body. *No fucking way have L'zar and Bianca been comparing notes.* "What did you say?"

"You heard me. It's time for you to learn how that applies to the way we do things from here on out. The way we handle this war and hopefully stop it in its tracks before the real cost must be paid."

"And what about the cost of you disappearing when we got attacked? You went off and hid in the woods while the rest of us put our necks out there to protect the others *you* invited here." When her father didn't reply or even acknowledge her, Cheyenne leaned toward him and muttered, "How many of your loyal rebels know they're following a coward?"

"Like I said, no one can know I'm with you." L'zar raised a thin bone-white eyebrow, then nodded toward Ember. "Right now, I'm much more interested in what happened with your *Nós Ani.* That portal she closed was a direct line to Ambar'ogúl."

Cheyenne glared after him as he walked across the clearing. Tuning out the low moans of the prisoners behind her, she headed stiffly toward Ember and the rest of their group, who had gathered around her. When Ember saw her coming, a burst of violet light lifted her from the grass and deposited her in the wheelchair Persh'al pushed quickly toward her.

The clearing was thick with a tense silence. Then Ember gazed at the faces of those staring at her and shrugged. "Anyone wanna tell me what the hell just happened?"

"You had your first taste of what's possible as Cheyenne's *Nós Ani,*" Corian said with a small nod. "And that awakened what looks like a large portion of your magic, if not most of it."

"Yeah, I figured that part out on my own. I'm talking about the portal, or rather the big one. Who was that?"

L'zar glanced at Cheyenne and cocked his head. "That portal opened straight from the other side, Ember."

"What?" The fae looked at Cheyenne for answers, but the halfling could only shrug and shake her head. "How is that even possible?"

"With a lot of magic the Crown shouldn't be able to use." L'zar lifted his chin and looked first at Corian, then at Persh'al. "Looks like we were on the right track. The Crown's now siphoning magic from the land *and* her subjects, which means we have even less time than I thought."

Cheyenne swallowed. "Because now she knows about Ember."

"Now she knows." Corian nodded. "A child of L'zar's who's passed the trials *and* been bound to a *Nós Aní* is more of a threat than she imagined possible. The Crown will redouble her efforts to stop you, and she'll be expecting you to take the next step."

Cheyenne snorted. "That stupid coin."

"What she won't expect is to find me at your side, Cheyenne." L'zar dipped his head in concession. "*If* we can contain things long enough for Corian and me to finish what we started."

The halfling waited for either of them to offer more information on that little nugget. When they didn't, she spread her arms. "Care to share what that is?"

"We need to get L'zar across the Border without alerting the Crown," Corian muttered. "She's had hundreds of years to perfect her methods for keeping him out of Ambar'ogúl."

"That's one hell of a security system."

L'zar snickered and turned toward his daughter. "When you know the right locks to pick, none of it matters. We're just waiting for the tumblers to turn."

"Right. Because you're the best O'gúleesh thief either world has ever known."

"Something like that."

"We should go," Corian added. "Ember bought us plenty of time before the Crown will make another attempt like this, but I'd rather not push it. The sooner we leave, the harder it'll be for her people to trace us again."

"By all means." L'zar dipped his head and waited for Corian to cast another portal in the clearing. The whole time, he stared at Ember, studying her like someone else would study a piece of chocolate cake.

The fae met his gaze and leaned away. "Whatever you're thinking, cut it out."

He chuckled and closed his eyes.

Corian's portal glistened with dark light as it opened, and he gestured for the others to head through into Persh'al's warehouse. Before anyone else moved, Ember wheeled herself over the grass toward the opening. "I don't know about the rest of you, but I'm ready to get out of here."

"Right behind you, Em." Cheyenne nodded when her friend gave her a thin smile before she rolled across the warehouse's concrete floors.

Byrd and Lumil went next. The goblin woman shot another look at the lined-up prisoners and snorted. Then L'zar stepped through, his chin lifted and his golden eyes focused on something only he could see. Persh'al scooped up one of the round flying machines Cheyenne had shot from the sky, tossed it once in his hand, and nodded as he followed the others.

Corian caught Cheyenne's gaze, and she turned away from the portal toward the prisoners immobilized in the center of the clearing. "I have to deal with this first."

"I understand." With the flick of his wrist, the portal closed. "I'll wait."

"Thanks." She dug into the pocket of her fancy new trench coat and pulled out her phone. *This is gonna be one of my weirder phone calls, for sure.* "Hey, where are we right now?"

Corian raised an eyebrow.

"I mean, geographically."

The nightstalker pressed his lips together and turned away to hide a smile. "Savage River State Forest."

"Shit. That's hours from them." Cheyenne rolled her eyes and pulled up Rhynehart's number. "This is not gonna be pretty."

"It doesn't have to be pretty, kid, as long as it gets done."

"Yeah, I've noticed that's how you guys operate with most things, but there are different levels to that. Getting something done doesn't always have to be a shitstorm."

A slow grin broke out on Corian's feline face. "I've always agreed with that sentiment, Cheyenne. That's something L'zar still hasn't managed to wrap his head around."

She snorted. "Well, I'm not here to clean up L'zar's messes. Just my own."

The phone rang twice before Rhynehart picked up her call. "I didn't expect to hear from you again for a while."

"It's not like I ever *plan* to call you." With a quick glance at Corian,

Cheyenne stepped away from him and pretended like that made a difference.

"So, what made you pick up the phone?"

"First, I should probably tell you that I can't say anything about the how or the why. Like, at all."

"Uh-huh."

"That's part of working next to each other, right? This has to be something you tell me you can handle without any questions since I can't answer them."

Rhynehart paused on the other end of the line and cleared his throat. "Well, what *can* you tell me?"

"I've got two dozen magicals tied up in front of me."

"You what?"

"Are you gonna hear me out, or should I call someone else?"

Rhynehart sighed. "Sorry. Keep talkin'."

"I'm ninety-nine-percent positive none of them are in your system. At all. And even if they are, you won't be able to get their names out of them."

"What did you do?"

"Jesus, I didn't do anything! I'm trying to clean this up the best way I know how, and right now, that's calling the one guy who said he trusts that I know what I'm doing. Don't tell me I made the wrong choice."

"Sounds like there's more to this situation."

Cheyenne let out a slow breath and forced her anger back down where it belonged. *There's a time and a place. This isn't it.* "Yeah, there's a lot more, but I'm hoping you've got some special FRoE tricks up your sleeve for this one. These magicals aren't registered, and they've been causing a lot of problems over here."

"Which falls right into my jurisdiction."

"I know. It's just a little more delicate. They're pretty much useless for anything but taking up space right now, and the only way to change that is to take them back across the Border. I mean, by the hand."

"Uh, you know my guys don't make that crossing."

"Yeah, but you send some of the bad eggs back through the rez portals. Give someone a free pass in exchange for ferrying these ones across. Worst-case scenario, no one steps up to the plate, and you push these ones through anyway."

"Best case, we're getting rid of two dozen jerkoffs who somehow slipped in right under our noses, plus whoever takes our offer as a guide."

Cheyenne nodded. "Exactly."

"Sounds like a win-win for the FRoE. What's in it for you?"

Closing her eyes, the halfling bowed her head. *I can use it as a bargaining chip. That's it.* "I won't have to kill them."

Rhynehart cleared his throat again. "All right, that's a reason I can accept. If I send a team out to take these guys off your hands, are they gonna find themselves stepping into something they didn't sign up for?"

"Not if they're quick about it."

"Hmm. Looks like we have a deal. Where are you?"

"Savage River State Park."

"No shit. I've got a transport team making a rez delivery about an hour away from there. I'll send 'em over. You hang tight until they get there."

"Sorry. I have somewhere else to be, but these guys aren't goin' anywhere."

"What, you got 'em chained up in a basement or something?"

"No. Just make sure your team knows they're coming to pick up magicals who can't see, hear, or talk, all right?"

"Useless. You weren't kidding."

Cheyenne glanced at the line of prisoners and cocked her head. "I know. I'll send you the location."

"Yeah, that'll help."

"And thanks. For, you know, not trying to dig too deep."

Rhynehart chuckled over the phone. "You're not goin' soft on me already, are you?"

"Not even close." She hung up to solidify her point and imagined the guy laughing when he realized the line had gone dead. After that, she texted the agent a pin on a GPS map and slipped the phone back into her jacket pocket. When she turned again, she found Corian standing there with his arms folded. "What?"

"You know, I've spent a long time watching you get yourself into varying degrees of trouble and blasting your way out of it again."

"You realize how creepy that sounds, right?"

Corian snorted. "I'll own it. But I gotta say, kid, that was the first time I've seen you deal with a mess without spreading it around any farther. That was clean."

"Not completely." She glanced at the prisoners again as she approached him. "These guys are crossing the Border no matter what. They'll either make it and get all their senses back, or they'll end up as monster food, and I won't ever know which one it was."

"True. I won't lie to you and say you'll forget about it in no time, but they have a chance. That's more than they would have if you hadn't taken this on."

"Yeah. Doesn't feel like it." Cheyenne watched him cast his spell to summon another portal into the warehouse, then blinked and looked into the trees. "Where's Gúrdu?"

Corian grinned as the portal bloomed in front of them. "Hard to keep track of a raug. Even harder to keep track of an Oracle."

"He can't open a portal, right?"

"Nope. I wouldn't worry about him, though."

"No, I'm just worried about whoever runs into him before he shuts himself back up in his creepy throne room."

Chuckling, the nightstalker gestured for her to step into the warehouse. "I stopped trying to figure him out centuries ago."

CHAPTER SIXTY-FOUR

Persh'al's warehouse was as quiet as the clearing when the portal closed behind Cheyenne and Corian. Ember spun her wheelchair around to face them and broke out in a grin. "You know, when someone says they're right behind you..."

"Sorry, Em. I had to take care of a few dozen prisoners first." Cheyenne felt L'zar's eyes on her and glanced briefly across the room to see them narrow. She shook her head and turned back to her friend.

Ember frowned. "I'm guessing you'll tell me about that later."

"Good guess."

"Ember." Corian pulled a thin metal band from his pocket and handed it to her. "Use this until you figure out how to cast an illusion spell for yourself. I'm sure Cheyenne has a whole book for you to dive right into."

The fae studied the bracelet and slipped it over her glowing pink wrist, and her newly awakened fae form melted into the human form she'd inhabited her entire life. Ember chuckled. "Thanks. I still don't even know if I'll be able to cast spells."

"After what you did with that portal, I have a feeling it'll come quite easily to you."

"A hell of a lot easier than it is for me," Cheyenne added.

"Well, that's not hard."

She shot Corian a sidelong glance and pursed her lips. Then her activator flashed in the corner of her vision, and she turned that way to see Persh'al staring at the small metal orb in his hands. "What are you planning to do with that thing?"

The troll didn't look up at her. "Take it apart and poke around a little."

"Can I see it?"

Persh'al blinked, then rolled his eyes and handed it over. "Knock yourself out, kid. It's dead."

Cheyenne studied the round attack machine, with its scrolling lines of data and flashing lights. Soft blue light pulsed weakly in the center of the orb like a fading heartbeat. "Not entirely."

The blue troll looked at her and scoffed. "Because you're wearing that fancy headpiece that tells you everything you wanna know about everything, huh? No, I get it. Use what you got, right? And you've got halfling superpowers that let you do the impossible with tech that doesn't do shit for the rest of us over here."

Meeting Persh'al's gaze, Cheyenne offered him a small smile. "You're a little cranky."

"Am I?" He folded his arms and glared at her, but his resolve broke and he gave a wry chuckle. "Shit, kid. Do your thing. I won't stop you."

"Like you could." She returned her attention to the orb. *Those are some kind of tracking codes underneath a little puzzle.* "Can I take this with me?"

"What? No. Get your own leftovers."

Cheyenne wiggled the metal orb at him. "Give me a day with this thing, and I'll find out where all the machines that attacked us in that clearing were supposed to report afterward. Then we can go take out whoever's been sending them at us."

"A *day*." Persh'al snorted and rubbed his head. "Kid, I've been working on tracing signatures back to the source for weeks. Yeah, that's right. *Before* we found that damn shipment at the new portal."

"I'm sure you'd get there eventually." Cheyenne pointed at the activator behind her ear. "But I can do it faster."

"Please. You've had one of those things for two days."

"And you didn't know half of what a transport shuttle could do before I showed you. How many times did you ride in one of those things?"

Persh'al's mouth dropped open. Leaning against the wall of the warehouse, Byrd snickered.

"The sooner we find the rest of the tech Lex's goons are hiding, the sooner we can cross one more thing off our list." Corian nodded at the blue troll, who rolled his eyes again and stalked toward his computer.

"I'll give it back when I'm done," Cheyenne called after him.

"Whatever. Have fun."

She watched him until he sat behind his huge center monitor and all but disappeared. *He'll get over it.*

She slipped the metal orb into her jacket pocket, and Corian stepped toward her. "If a day's all you need, take it. We'll wipe out the machines on this side, and that frees us up for the rest."

"What about the new portals? If we're going back to the other side, the Crown's gonna send more shipments across, and we won't be here to stop them."

Corian nodded. "That's something General Hi'et and I have been working on—a temporary freeze of as many of the portal ridges as we can get our hands on. Once L'zar finishes the spell he's been working on to keep the Crown from seeing him on the other side, we'll have a short window, and we should use it."

"I thought you were helping him with that."

The nightstalker's eyebrows flicked together, and they glanced at the office in the back of the warehouse when L'zar pulled the door closed behind him and disappeared. "What he's trying to do has to be done all on his own. I'm just facilitating, more or less."

"Huh." Cheyenne studied the office door. "What kinda spell takes days for someone like L'zar to cast?"

Corian gave her a warning glance. "The kind that only someone like L'zar is mad enough to attempt."

That means, don't ask any more questions because he won't answer.

"Okay. I'll leave him to his madness, then."

"Smart move." Corian smiled at Ember. "Despite our little party being crashed, you both did well today. Things are gonna get a lot more interesting after the *Nós Aní* binding."

"Really?" Ember raised her eyebrows and flashed him a fierce grin. "I hadn't noticed."

Shaking his head, Corian cast another portal from the warehouse into the girls' apartment and stepped back. "Try to lay low, huh? Call me if anything happens, but I'm expecting you to pull through and have that machine figured out by tomorrow."

Cheyenne patted her jacket pocket as Ember wheeled through the portal. "Come on. Hacking into things someone doesn't want me to see is one of my skills."

"Among many." The nightstalker smiled and nodded at the portal. "So get to work."

Snorting, Cheyenne stepped through the portal and disappeared. The oval of dark light closed with a pop, and Corian let out a heavy sigh. Byrd and Lumil stared after him and turned away to handle their own business when they realized he was headed for L'zar's makeshift bedroom.

Corian knocked lightly on the door, and a flash of black light spilled through the crack above the floor before L'zar growled. "What?"

Slowly, the nightstalker opened the door and slipped inside. "Any progress?"

L'zar sat cross-legged on the floor facing the far wall, his hands resting in his lap. "It's rather hard to tell when I have you breathing down my neck every time I try to work."

Corian clasped his hands behind his back. "I'll take that as a yes."

The drow dropped his shoulders, and his unbound white hair spilled around his face. "Progress, sure. But I have no idea if this will be ready tomorrow or a month from now."

"We don't have a month."

L'zar hissed and spun to face his friend. "I know what we *don't* have, Corian. We almost lost her at that damn ceremony."

"No one forced you to stand back while we fought."

"No." The drow pushed himself across the floor until he pressed his back against the wall. His head followed with a thud. "Just my own shortcomings. I wasted too much time in that prison."

"Hmm. Maybe you should just tell her."

"Absolutely not." L'zar shook his head, propping his forearms on his bent knees. "She'd never agree to do this if she knew."

"You think Cheyenne will agree to keep going when she finds out on her own instead of hearing it from you? Because she will find out, one way or another. When you two set foot in that chamber and she takes what's hers to take, there's no way to keep that secret anymore."

L'zar closed his eyes and let out another long, slow exhale. "She'll be fine. She's strong."

Corian tilted his head and studied the drow he'd called his friend for thousands of years. "She also knows when to admit she's wrong and ask for help. She might not like it, but I wouldn't expect her to."

"I'm not wrong."

"No. Not so far. Age and wisdom aren't synonymous, brother. There's a lot you could learn from her, probably even more because of who she is to you."

L'zar waved a dismissive hand and sagged in exhaustion against the wall where no one but Corian could see. "You know how it goes. Can't teach an old drow new tricks and all that bullshit."

Folding his arms, Corian frowned above a small, barely discernible smile. "Are you sure about that?"

The drow's golden eyes flew open. He stared at the nightstalker and shook his head a fraction of an inch. "Not at all."

"Good." Corian pulled the door open again.

With a snort, L'zar watched his friend step out of the room. "That's a shitty way of trying to make me feel better."

"No, that was for me. The day you tell me you know everything is the day I'll know you've lost your mind for good." Without waiting for a response, the nightstalker stepped back into the main room of the warehouse and pulled the door shut behind him.

L'zar's laughter followed him.

CHAPTER SIXTY-FIVE

Cheyenne Summerlin sat in the black leather recliner in her living room with the thin silver coil of the O'gúl activator attached behind her ear and studied the broken piece of the old-school war machine straight from the other side of the portal. "If I didn't know better, I'd say this thing is still active."

"But you know better, don't you?" Ember Gaderow sat in her wheelchair between the coffee table and the couch, scanning the loose pieces of paper she'd laid out on every surface she could reach.

"Well, yeah. Of course I do." Cheyenne turned the dead-looking orb of O'gúl metal over and over in her hands. "I brought most of these down, plus the tank."

"While the rest of us were fighting off those scumbags who crashed our super-official ceremonial party," Ember said and reached for the closest piece of paper, a page from the middle of the copied spellbook Maleshi Hi'et had given Cheyenne.

The drow halfling looked at her fae roommate and raised an eyebrow. "Finally."

Ember laughed. "Finally, what?"

"It's been, what? Three hours. I wondered when you'd start talking about it like a badass fae *Nós Ani*."

"Oh, you mean the badass who stood on two legs that don't work and blasted that creepy whatever-it-was back through the portal before it could kill you?"

Cheyenne glanced back down at the O'gúl tech in her hands and wiped a tiny smile off her lips. "Yeah. That one."

"You're welcome." Ember returned her attention to the pages of Maleshi's handwritten and printer-copied spellbook. "How have you not gone through all these spells yet? I mean, seriously. Anything I can think of, she wrote down in more detail than I thought was possible."

Cheyenne cleared her throat. "I *have* gone through them."

"For real?" The fae looked at her best friend with a playful frown. "Okay, I meant trying to cast any of these spells. Charms. Wards."

"For the record, Em, I've tried a ridiculous number of those spells and screwed up every single one."

"Oh, come on." Ember grinned and swiped her light-brown hair, which was now streaked with fae-violet, away from her forehead. "What about the low-level ones, huh? Those are all in the front. Easy stuff."

"Not for me." Cheyenne pulled her legs up onto the recliner and crossed them beneath her, hunching over her lap and studying the dark orb of O'gúl metal. "I'm not kidding. I spent a few hours with those 'low-level' spells and almost blew up my old apartment."

Ember snorted. "To match your old car, huh?"

"Ha-ha."

The fae lifted a piece of the laid-out spellbook and fluttered it in the air. "The easy ones are *really* easy, Cheyenne. I mean, look at this. Maleshi wrote down everything from start to finish, including the different hand gestures, and there are only, like, three for this one."

"Hey, if you think they're super easy, awesome. You're one up on me, 'cause apparently, I just can't nail down how to work a spell that isn't, you know, part of the whole drow-halfling thing."

"That's ridiculous. You just need some extra practice."

"Ember." Cheyenne met her friend's shimmering violet gaze. Ember's eyes were now larger and much more luminous than before the fae's magic had fully manifested just a few hours before. "Ask Corian."

"I'm not gonna ask *Corian*!"

"He told L'zar my spellwork's shit." The halfling cracked a smile, and the young magicals cracked up. "It took me *hours* to make that illusion ring for you, which you don't need anymore."

"Nope. I got an upgrade." Ember tossed her hand toward the thin silver bracelet Corian had charmed to provide a human-looking illusion now that she was running around in full fae mode all the time. "Really, though? You couldn't even nail the beginner spells?"

"What part of 'almost blew up my old apartment' is confusing you?" Cheyenne laughed. "Everybody has their skillset, Em. As far as I'm concerned, mine doesn't even include *beginner* spells. I'm more of a 'run in with drow magic blazing and fight my way through the issue' kind of chick."

"Well, thank God."

Bent over her crossed legs, Cheyenne propped her elbow on her knee to swing the cold metal orb out to the side and shot her friend a wide-eyed look of mock insult. "I'd love to hear your explanation for that one."

Ember shrugged and pursed her lips, trying not to smile as she pretended to be focused on absorbing Maleshi's low-level spell instructions. "All I'm saying is, if you added these seriously powerful spells to your 'drow magic blazing,' we'd all be in deep shit."

"Ha. Thanks for the vote of confidence, Em."

"Think about it. If you could do *everything*, you'd be just like…" Ember's luminous eyes widened as she glanced at her friend. "Oh."

Cheyenne's nostrils flared. "Just like L'zar?"

"Hey, you said it, not me." Ember replaced the loose page and got back to studying the spellbook.

"I'm nothing like him, Em."

"Not where it counts." The fae girl tapped her lips, then leaned forward in her chair to rearrange some of the pages on the coffee table and the couch. "That's the only part that matters, and for the rest of it, you can blame genetics."

"Fuck genetics. I blame L'zar for all of it."

"Well, he *did* lead us through that ceremony, so maybe give him one exception, huh?" Ember glanced at her pink-tinged forearm and the now-visible glow of her fae aura. Then she looked at Cheyenne and gestured to her new permanent appearance. "I wouldn't trade this for anything."

"Fair point, but don't give him all the credit for that one, Em. L'zar Verdys didn't make you fae, and he sure as hell didn't make you my *Nós Aní*. We chose that."

Ember looked at her friend for half a second, then returned to the pages with a small smile. "More like I chose it and you couldn't stop me, but okay."

"Yeah, don't let it go to your head."

"You too, halfling."

With another snort, Cheyenne returned her attention to the seemingly lifeless orb of O'gúl metal in her hand. *Lifeless except for the never-ending data stream. I seriously hope it's just the activator and not this thing relaying some kind of message to the asshole loyalist in charge of it.*

The activator behind her ear fed her line after line of O'gúleesh code, translating it instantly into English now that it had fully synced to Cheyenne's halfling brain. Her vision filled with the scrolling blue commands, then she found something she recognized. "Wait a minute."

Responding instantly to her voiced thought, the activator paused the data stream on the bit of code that had caught her attention.

"What's up?" Ember kept staring at the closest page of Maleshi's spellbook, only half paying attention.

"I've seen this encryption before." Cheyenne blinked, and the section of code flashed in her vision before zipping into the top right corner with an alert that it had been saved. "Whoa. This thing comes with screenshot capabilities."

"Cool," Ember muttered.

The halfling looked at her and frowned. *She didn't even hear me.*

Unfolding her legs from the recliner, Cheyenne stood and tossed the metal sphere a few times in her hand before palming it and heading for the iron stairs up to the mini-loft.

Ember leaned forward in her wheelchair, muttered the incantation laid out on the page, and twisted her right hand in the same patterns diagrammed in Maleshi's precise drawing. The leather recliner rocked on its legs before lifting a foot in the air.

Cheyenne stopped halfway up the short staircase. "Whoa."

The recliner thumped back down, ruffling the pages at the edge of the coffee table.

Ember looked at the halfling and grinned. "See? Easy. Good thing you've got a best friend who can pick up the slack for you, huh?"

Cheyenne narrowed her eyes. "Were you just waiting for me to get up so you could try that?"

"I was going for levitating you and the chair at the same time. Didn't notice that you got up." Ember spread her arms, her face lit up with excitement, and started studying the next spell. "This is awesome. I'll be done with these spells in three days."

"I'm pretty sure they're only useful if you can remember how to cast them after the fact," Cheyenne said, laughing as she dropped into the hard office chair in front of the wobbly desk. *I need new furniture up here.*

"That's the thing, though." Ember pulled another printed sheet of paper toward her, replacing the previous spell. "First time for a levitating spell, and I feel like I could do it again in my sleep."

"I'm just gonna chalk that up to intrinsic fae skills and remind you to keep your door closed if that's your plan."

The fae let out a short laugh but was already submerged in studying the next spell in the book.

Cheyenne set the metal sphere on her desk and stared at it. The activator resumed with the next layer of scrolling data winding around the O'gúl machine part, and she leaned down to power up her computer rig before punching the power button on the monitor. Glen whirred to life, and the halfling shifted around in the chair with a grimace. *Or at least bring a pillow up here or something.*

She drummed her fingers on the plastic armrests, and when her rig was ready to go, she pulled up her VPN access and set up to do some more dark-web diving. The activator fed her mashups of data lines everywhere she looked. Even a glance at her computer tower on the floor beside the desk brought up scrolling lines in flashing blue light. *Still gotta sift through all the useless stuff, huh?*

Cheyenne flicked her fingers away from her and the activator responded, shutting down the data stream showing her the inner workings of the hard drive and half the system she'd built herself. Then she pulled up access to the dark web and got to work.

I know I've seen that encryption before. Would've been nice to have this activator's screenshots back then.

Without typing a site address or a command in her system, the halfling found herself led down the rabbit hole she wanted almost faster than she could follow.

Her activator responded to her thoughts, pulling up the saved bit of encryption she'd inadvertently filed away and searching for the routes to the same data on the dark web. The piece of tech nestled behind her ear didn't do any of the actual work for her, which she figured out pretty damn quickly.

Enter command.

The words flashed in her vision, and Cheyenne opened the command program she'd rewritten five years ago to make life as a teenager half-drow hacker a hell of a lot easier. She copied the code the activator had sent her and pressed Enter.

"Holy shit."

Without the activator, she wouldn't have been able to see the pages' worth of addresses, user history, encryption banks, and fairly useless firewalls that one simple command had taken her through in an instant. Then she got a prompt to input a new command she didn't recognize. *I can't go wrong by following step-by-step instructions, right?*

Four more times, Cheyenne input what the O'gúl tech behind her ear prompted her to type, and the results took her through the dark web without stopping. *This is like warp speed through space. This is like... Okay, I already used* The Matrix, *but still.*

When she added the final command, which was only a third the size of the others, her screen pulled up the back end of a seriously enhanced firewall and dozens of securely encrypted files. Each of them would take her a few days to parse out in the Bunker, but Cheyenne wasn't trying to decrypt access files. She scanned the information on her monitor, every line bringing up a new burst of code from the activator until that line of encryption she'd filed in the headpiece's database lit up in bright yellow at the center of the screen.

"There you are."

She highlighted the line enmeshed in jumbled data on her monitor, then typed in the new command the activator prompted. The second she activated the command, she knew what she'd found even before she had the chance to read through all of it.

File updated: 09-30-2021
Next update: 10-30-2021
Registered Source: Combined Reality, Inc.
Source Owner: ThomasSafe

Below that were three different IP addresses, most likely for the physical server banks owned and operated by ThomasSafe, but Cheyenne didn't need a physical location anymore.

"That sneaky sonofabitch."

A bright flash of purple light came from the living room below the mini-loft. A muted thunderclap filled the apartment, followed by the patter of water on leather upholstery, the area rug, and the hardwood floors.

"Yes!" Ember pumped a fist in the air and stared at the tiny thunderstorm she'd conjured above the second leather recliner. "Wait, what sonofabitch are you talking about? Seems like you know a few."

Cheyenne leaned sideways in the office chair and swiveled toward the metal rail around the mini-loft. Ember's fingers twisted in a quick gesture before she tossed her hand aside like batting away a fly, and the two-foot storm cloud disappeared, leaving behind a pool of magical rainwater in the recliner and a sopping mess on the corner of the area rug.

The fae grinned up at her best friend, but her smile died when she saw the fury growing in Cheyenne's eyes. "Whoa, okay. Sorry about the chair."

"I don't give a shit about the chair, Em. You'll never guess what I just found."

"Well, you're usually right about that, so I'm not even gonna try." Ember folded her arms and sat back in the wheelchair. "Go ahead. Spit it out."

"I traced a piece of that war machine's data back to one of its programming sources."

"Okay. Why are you wearing your seriously pissed face?"

"Because that *source* is registered under ThomasSafe."

Ember laughed and dusted off her hands. "Good one. Try again."

"I'm dead serious." Cheyenne pointed slowly toward the far wall of the mini-loft and the hallway of the apartment building's top floor on the other side of it. "Our *dabbling* neighbor is powering O'gúl tech for the Crown's goddamn loyalists."

CHAPTER SIXTY-SIX

"*W*hat?" Ember whipped her head toward their front door and blinked. "No. Uh-uh. No way."

"I'm sitting here staring at the information." Cheyenne lurched from her chair and thrust her hand toward the monitor. "I knew it. I *knew* there was one thing that asshole was missing in his little private conglomerate. When I checked, he had everything covered except for weapons. He's obviously got that one under his belt too."

"That's insane."

"I *know!*"

"Wait a minute. Just hold on." Ember pinched the bridge of her nose, blinking furiously. "I don't even see how that's possible. He's so *nice.*"

"You need to get over that, Em." Cheyenne snatched the metal sphere on her desk and leaned over the rail, thrusting the broken war machine toward her friend. "Because *nice* guys don't write the programming that lets shit like *this* work in our world. *Nice* guys don't get involved in powering up technology controlled by magicals from Ambar'ogúl who keep sending war machines to kill us while the Crown's getting ready for an Earth invasion via the same goddamn tech."

She chucked the metal sphere over the rail, where it landed in the puddle of Ember's conjured rainwater nestled in the corner of the recliner. A few drops splashed on Ember's bare arms, but she hardly felt them. She took a deep breath. "There's no way he'd do that on purpose."

"Stop trying to defend him." Cheyenne ran a hand through her bone-white hair, her drow magic fueled further by her anger, and turned to stare at the information on her screen. "So you guys spent some time together while he unpacked all our crap in this place and hung artwork on the walls for you. That's not enough to clear him, Em. Matthew Thomas knows exactly what he's doing. A guy like that with his fingers in so many industry pies doesn't do stuff by accident."

"But we didn't find any cameras," Ember protested. "No purple dots, remember?"

Cheyenne shook her head in frustration. "That only proves he's not spying on *us*. You and me specifically. But he's shit. The guy who figured out how to meld O'gúl tech with Earth technology is our fucking *neighbor*. Right there. Right next door. I don't care if he knows who we are or what these machines are used for, he's the reason these things work!"

"Stop yelling at me, Cheyenne."

"I'm not yelling!" A burst of purple light flared behind the halfling's eyes. Ember tilted her head and raised an eyebrow. "At you. I'm not yelling at you." Cheyenne tossed her hair out of her face and folded her arms. The silver chains around her wrists dug into her arms and her ribs, the small pain pulling her back to the present. "Sorry."

"It's fine. We just need to think this through."

Cheyenne sat at her desk again and scanned the new data. "I shouldn't be this surprised. I knew there was something weird about the guy, like perfume trying to cover the smell of rotting meat."

"Okay, you can break out the 'I told you so' after we're a hundred percent sure this is real."

"Oh, I'm a hundred percent sure. Here. I'll show you." Cheyenne copied all the information she could find and sent it to her printer. As the apartment filled with the drone of the laser-jet printer buzzing across sheet after sheet of blank paper, she dove a little deeper into the update history for the first encrypted file with Matthew Thomas' company name all over it. "You won't be able to deny any of this when you see it. Neither will he."

Ember waited for the printer to stop. When it was still going five minutes later, she rolled her eyes and wheeled across the living room before heading into the kitchen. Cheyenne sat in her desk chair, arms folded as she glared at the printer pumping out pages and pages of incriminating evidence against their neighbor. *I got you now, asshole.*

By the time Cheyenne had gathered all the printed data and stacked it into something as close to a neat pile as she was going to get, she had almost fifty pages in her hands. Pulling off the activator, she ignored the sharp pinch and shoved the silver coil into her pocket before heading down the stairs.

Ember sat at the far end of the coffee table, calmly sipping a half-empty glass of water. "Think you went a little overboard?"

"No." Cheyenne glanced at the stack of papers and snorted. "This is just the beginning. I pulled this all up without having to crack into a single thing. I mean, relatively speaking."

"You mean, *your* version of cracking."

"Yeah." The halfling handed over the stack of papers still warm from the printer and jabbed a finger at them. "He's got no excuse, Em."

The fae rifled through the pages, shaking her head. "This means nothing to me. I'd ask you to go back up there and break it down a little more so someone with a *normal* above-average understanding could actually... Whoa."

Ember stopped flipping through the pages and scanned the dates of the file updates on the top of the stack now.

"Yeah, whoa." Cheyenne folded her arms. "It keeps going."

"These go back almost five years." The pages rustled as Ember flipped through them faster and faster.

"Once a month for the last five years at least, yeah. ThomasSafe has been actively updating these programming files. And I bet you literally my entire inheritance that if I took the time to dive into these, I'd find constantly updated patches, bug fixes, new update alerts, the whole deal. Matthew Thomas wrote a fucking *app* for remote-controlled war machines."

"His *company* wrote the app."

"Em, he's been pretty vocal about how much he likes to be 'hands-on' with his projects. He went on and on in an interview about how he reads every single scholarship application kids send him for his stupid college fund every year. Matthew isn't the kind of guy who lets other people take over a complicated project like this while he sits back and waits for the money to roll into his accounts."

"You think the Crown's *paying* him for this?"

"Well, he's not doing it out of the kindness of his heart." Cheyenne gave a heavy sigh as Ember shot her a warning glance. "Again, sorry."

"Don't apologize. Just quit talking to me like I'm an idiot. I'm trying to look at this from all angles."

That made Cheyenne pause. *From all angles. That's something I need serious practice with.* She took a deep breath and dropped her head back to stare at their vaulted ceiling. "Okay, then let's talk hypothetically."

"I thought we were."

"Proof isn't hypothetical, Em."

Ember flicked the stack of papers in her lap. "This proves what his company's been doing for at least five years. What it doesn't say is how involved Matthew is in this *or* what he thinks his company's been accomplishing for that long. And it doesn't tell us why he agreed to do it or what his intentions were."

"His intentions don't matter."

"For real?" Ember dropped the printed pages in her lap and spread her arms. "You're gonna stand next to me in this chair and tell me that when somebody makes a mistake, we should just throw their intentions out the window because they don't matter?" She slapped her hands down on the armrests.

"Oh, come on. Those are two totally different things."

"No, they're not. What if Matthew doesn't have a clue what his company's programs are being used for? Or if he got into this whole Ogúl-tech-app thing, thinking he was doing his part to help magicals who made the crossing come over here, huh? Tell me how that's different from you thinking your best option was to follow me to the skatepark that night instead of walking head-on into that meeting *with* me."

Cheyenne blinked a few times in surprise and swallowed. *No wonder my mom likes her so much.* "I can't."

"Thank you. So there you go." Ember picked up the stack of papers again and tapped them against her thighs to tidy the pile. "And just so we're clear, no, I still don't blame you for what happened that night. I mean, if I'm being painfully honest, getting shot might've been the best thing that ever happened to me."

"Yeah, that's definitely painful." Cheyenne grimaced. "And weird. What do you mean?"

"Without the whole hospital thing, maybe you wouldn't have had the time to step in every other day and tell me about whatever wild goose chase you were on that day. I wouldn't have needed any help. No PT. No new apartment." Ember snorted. "Okay, maybe you would've gotten a place like this anyway, 'cause your last apartment was shit."

"Thanks."

"Don't even try to pretend you're insulted by that." The fae girl studied the pink hue of her hand and forearm, now glowing with a fae's natural aura, then held her hand up toward Cheyenne. "Plus, I'm starting to think a spinal injury was what forced my magic into showing up. You know, all that crap about fae being natural healers or whatever. Even for myself."

"Okay." The halfling nodded. "I get your point. Just as long as you don't thank me for letting you get shot."

"Are you fucking kidding me?" Ember raised an eyebrow and shook her head. "Durg's the only one who gets credit for that, and he can suck it. But I *can* thank you for saving my life and hanging in there with me. I mean, you were the only person who cared that I couldn't just walk out of that hospital bed and keep doing things the way I've been doing them."

"Yeah, Em. You've already thanked me for that."

"For real, though. Now I have a personal chauffeur in a pretty sweet car, you're paying for *this* cushy place, and I look like an actual fae all the time now because some psycho in a different world wants you dead."

"Okay, okay." Cheyenne clenched her eyes shut. "Just stop."

Ember laughed. "Good, we're on the same page. The *real* question is how we deal with this new information about our surprisingly enmeshed neighbor."

The halfling nodded and turned to pace across the wide section of open floor between the sitting area and the north-facing window wall.

A wry laugh escaped her. "I was all pumped and ready to break down his door. You just burst my bubble, and it's all fizzling away again. Happy now?"

"Yes." Ember gave her a goofy salute. "*Someone* needs to talk you out of unnecessary chaos. Looks like I have the job."

"Well, you're the only person who hasn't tried to lie to me, manipulate me for some secret bullshit, or fight me, so there's that." The friends stared at each other with deadpan expressions before Cheyenne snorted and paced away from Ember again. The fae girl smiled and sat back in her chair. "You're right, though. I found all this stuff, and somebody's gotta do something with it."

"Just don't call Corian yet, okay?"

"What?" Cheyenne spun and paced back toward her friend. "You say that like it's my go-to solution."

"I just mean not yet."

The halfling rolled her eyes. "You know what? I only call him when I know I'm up against something I can't handle on my own, or when *not* calling him would be worse for me than having the kinds of conversations I don't enjoy. If it seems like a lot, that's because there's a lotta crap coming down the pipeline, and most of it has to do with L'zar in one way or another. And therefore Corian."

Ember raised her hands in surrender. "I didn't say anything."

"You didn't have to." Taking a deep breath, Cheyenne stopped beside her friend's chair and nodded at the papers in Ember's lap. "I'll just go talk to Matthew. Show him what I found."

"Ask questions *before* you start blowing holes in his apartment. All right?"

"Sure, whatever. Good thing my *Nós Aní* handles talking me out of unnecessary chaos like a pro."

"What? *Oh*, no." Ember waved her hands in front of her, shaking her head. "I'm not storming in there with you to start accusing our neighbor of fighting on the wrong side."

"Again, it's a little more than accusing if we have proof."

"You don't need me to call him out on any of it. I'll stay right here."

Cheyenne cocked her head. "The dude has an obvious soft spot for you, Em. We're gonna use it."

Ember grimaced. "Don't say it like that. It sounds so…"

"Smart? Prepared?"

"Heartless."

"Not compared to what could happen if the Crown gets more war machines over here and the magicals Matthew's been writing programs for succeed in activating an entire army of those things to wipe out whoever the hell they want. One tank was hard enough."

"Please," Ember replied. "Just because you had to spend a little more time figuring out how to take it apart doesn't mean it was *hard* for you."

"Still. And you're changing the subject."

"Okay, *fine*. I'll come with you, but don't expect me to start pointing a finger and making threats."

Cheyenne said, "That's my job."

"I'm serious."

"Sure." The halfling raised her hands in the same gesture of surrender and dipped her head. "We'll go in there, lay it all out, and give him a chance to explain himself."

"Thank you."

"*Then* I'll start blasting holes in his apartment."

CHAPTER SIXTY-SEVEN

"He's not home, is he?" Cheyenne pulled her hand away from the front door, and her drow vision that let her see through walls and physical objects stopped when she opened her eyes. "Nope. Not a single body in that apartment, so I'm guessing he's at one of those mysterious *meetings* he's always talking about."

Ember frowned. "I haven't heard him say anything about meetings."

"That's because he's always way more focused on sweet-talking you when you guys are hanging out doing whatever."

"Talking, Cheyenne. And sometimes making homemade pizza."

Cheyenne rolled her eyes. "See? Even that just feels forced. He's trying way too hard to hide his shady side."

"Right. We don't know *anyone* else who does that."

The halfling ignored her friend's jab and stepped away from the door. "We just need to keep an eye out for him and wait 'til he gets back."

"And what? You're just gonna stand there at the door, watching the hallway with your third eye or whatever?"

"It's not a third eye. And no. I'm not about to waste the rest of my night standing at our front door." Cheyenne's gaze fell onto the scattered pages of Maleshi's spellbook. "You see any spells in there for spying on people?"

"No." Ember snorted and wheeled between the couch and the coffee table again. "But there *is* something like a magical tripwire."

"I hope it makes him trip."

"Stop." Ember scanned the pages, then reached for the rest of the unbound spellbook nestled against the couch's armrest. She flipped through the different spells, then pulled out the page she wanted and paused. "You didn't wanna keep these in order or anything, right?"

"Seeing as I'm not the one who can cast spells with any degree of accuracy, I couldn't care less about organizing those things." Cheyenne cocked her head with a small smile. "Maleshi might have something to say about it."

"Maleshi handed you a magical bomb if the wrong person got their hands on this, and she didn't even bother to string it together. How hard is that? Most copy machines have hole punches anyway."

The halfling snorted. "Feel free to tell her that next time we see her."

"You think I'm afraid of an ex-general parading around Richmond posing as an IT professor? Please. Neither of those nightstalkers scares me."

"Listen to *you*. You're starting to sound like me, Em."

"With one major difference, halfling." Ember dropped the rest of the scattered spellbook back on the couch and skimmed the instructions. "*I* know the difference between not being afraid of someone and pushing their buttons until their head explodes."

Frowning, Cheyenne shook out her hands and set the chains on her wrists jingling. "I'll just let you do your thing, then."

"Uh-huh." Without looking up from the magical tripwire spell, Ember grabbed the stack of their proof against Matthew Thomas and dropped it on the coffee table.

The halfling picked up the papers, and almost sat in the recliner full of water. With a grunt, she picked up the war-machine orb, wiped it off on her pants, and slumped into the other armchair while Ember got to work.

Ten minutes later, a sputtering yellow light blinking around the perimeter of their apartment ripped Cheyenne out of her concentrated reading. "What was that?"

"That was a fae casting spells the right way." Ember blew on her fingertips and shook out her hand. "On the first try."

"At least we know your bragging skills are up to par."

"Hey, don't act like you're not impressed."

"I'm impressed, Em." Cheyenne gazed around their apartment and raised her eyebrows. "And the spell was?"

"I told you. A tripwire. Sort of." Ember read over the spell instructions one more time to double-check herself, then nodded. "Yeah. Around the whole apartment, but it's not like I could just step out into the hall and cast this thing there. Especially if he's got cameras on the hall."

"Which he probably does. Lemme see that." Ember handed over the spell in Maleshi's handwriting, and Cheyenne's eyes widened. "We don't have any of these ingredients, Em."

"I know."

"Then why the hell are you sure this worked?"

Ember waved for the halfling to hand the spell sheet back, and she snatched it up again before setting it aside in a new pile of spells she'd tried and successfully cast. "I built it on top of the wards your super-fun friends put up."

"Huh." Cheyenne squinted at the walls and craned her neck to look at the O'gúl hornet's web dangling over the side of the mini-loft. "That was a good call."

"Again, I know." Folding her arms, Ember basked in the halfling's surprise and couldn't hold back a laugh. "Look, I can't say if this spell would've worked without ingredients *or* using the wards as a giant battery, but I know it worked the way I did it. I can feel it."

"Okay. We've gone off nothing but *my* feelings before."

"Exactly. Basically, anything that moves around the outside of our apartment is gonna set off an alarm. Seeing as the wards are actively holding off digging machine beetles and flying spy-whatevers, the only kind of movement we should get will be out there in the hall."

"And then what?"

Ember shrugged. "And then some kind of alarm goes off. I'm guessing a few bright, flashing lights, maybe a warning pop or two. Couldn't figure out how to make it send alerts to my phone."

"Very funny. It's not like we have anywhere to go until he gets back, right?"

"Seriously? We were out in the woods just a few hours ago. Forget the whole ceremony part. We were also ambushed."

Cheyenne lifted a finger toward her friend. "Unsuccessfully."

"Doesn't mean it didn't happen. If you hadn't given me this spell-book, I'd be binge-watching some new show like nobody's business right now."

"Glad I was able to provide you with a constructive distraction."

Ember chuckled and snatched the remote off the coffee table. "Yeah, well, now I'm too distracted thinking about our impending chat with Matthew. He really does seem like such a—"

"If you call him a nice guy again today, I'll end up blasting holes first and asking questions later." Cheyenne slowly turned her head to shoot her friend a deadpan stare.

"A friendly person." Ember wrinkled her nose at the halfling and raised the remote toward the entry table beside the front door. The mechanism exposed their giant flatscreen TV with a soft hum. "So now I need a distraction from that distraction. You have any preferences?"

"Dinner." Cheyenne pushed herself out of the recliner and headed toward the kitchen.

Ember laughed and stared intently at the TV, flicking through her bingeing options. "I think we might be running a *little* low on groceries."

"We haven't even been here a week."

"And no one would *believe* the amount of food a drow halfling puts away just by looking at her."

Opening the fridge, Cheyenne said, "We have pickles."

"Have at it."

"*Or* delivery."

Ember grinned and snatched her water glass to down the rest of it. "Now you're talking my language."

Forty minutes later, in the middle of an *Orphan Black* episode Ember swore up and down Cheyenne would be really into, a bright yellow light flashed to the right of the front door. Cheyenne stared at the wall. "Did you see that?"

"See what?"

"A light."

A shrieking wail blasted through their apartment. Cheyenne reacted and slipped immediately into drow form, her black hair changing instantly into stark white as her skin went from Goth-girl pale to drow-halfling gray.

Ember jumped in her chair and clamped both hands over her ears. "What the hell *is* that?"

"You're the one who cast the *alarm spell!*"

"Shit." Ember leaned far over the side of her chair and rifled through the pages of spells until she found the one she wanted. She scanned the page as the wailing grew even louder.

Cheyenne scrunched up her face. "Turn it off, Em!"

"I'm trying. Shut up." Ember's fingers moved in the laid out pattern for deactivating the alarm, which cut off abruptly.

Breathing heavily in the sudden silence, the halfling looked at her friend and cocked her head. "Looks like the middle finger means something else altogether to the O'gúleesh who wrote these spells, huh?"

"No, this is just for you." Ember blinked. "Quit yelling at me."

Cheyenne rolled her eyes, trying not to laugh. "There was no other way for you to *hear* me."

A sharp knock came at the front door, and the halfling leaped to her feet.

"You think he heard the alarm?" Ember asked, forgetting all about flipping the bird as Cheyenne headed for the door. She slid the thin silver bracelet onto her wrist and looked like just another regular human in seconds.

"The whole building probably heard it. But why the hell would he knock on our door?" Cheyenne peered through the peephole into the hallway and groaned, slipping right back out of her drow form again. "Because it's not Matthew."

"*What?*" Ember sat back in her chair. "Who the hell is it?"

Unlocking the deadbolt and the lock in the doorknob, the halfling turned over her shoulder and muttered, "Pizza guy."

"Jesus Christ." The fae deflated in her chair and cracked up laughing as Cheyenne slowly opened the door.

"Right on time."

The kid standing in the hallway in front of their apartment stared at the maniacally laughing Ember. "Delivery for Cheyenne."

"Yep. Hold on." She lunged for her backpack sitting on the floor beside the couch and pulled a ten-dollar bill out of her wallet, handing it to the kid.

He stared at it. "You already paid."

"And that's your tip." Cheyenne held her hands out for the pizza, and Ember cracked up all over again. "Come on, man. Don't hold my dinner hostage."

"Sorry. Right. Sorry." The kid slid the steaming pizza box out of the sleeve in his arms and handed it over. "Thanks for the tip."

"Thanks for the pizza." Cheyenne shut the door before he'd had the chance to step away and turned around to stare at Ember. "The pizza guy."

"The *pizza* guy!" The fae howled with laughter, slapping her thigh. "And we were...you were so..."

"Yeah, you too." Laughing, Cheyenne took the box to the coffee table and cleared away the scattered papers with one hand. "Guy probably thought I'm in here as your caretaker, the way you're losing it right now."

"It wouldn't be the first time." Ember barked another laugh, clapped both hands over her mouth, and snorted back her laughter while the halfling opened their dinner.

"Wanna work on lowering the volume a little?"

"On the TV? It's not that loud."

"On the *alarm*."

Ember whipped her head up to meet Cheyenne's gaze. "The alarm!" She burst out laughing all over again.

Chuckling, Cheyenne slid the pizza box two inches away from her friend and shook her head. "This is worse than you drinking that fae whatever-it-was at the Empty Barrel."

"What?" Ember let out a mocking gasp. "We haven't opened a bottle of *anything* since we moved in."

"No, you were too busy opening all those boxes." The halfling pulled

465

out a slice of drooping pizza and nudged the box toward Ember now that the fae seemed to have pulled herself together again.

"We haven't officially moved in without opening a bottle and toasting to the place."

"Please. We've already eaten everything but the pickles, you were attacked in your sleep, and a band of O'gúleesh rebels built wards around the place. I'd say it's official."

Smacking her lips, Ember reached for a slice. "Now you're splitting hairs. And there's no way this is worse than me drinking in Peridosh, whatever you're trying to imply with that one."

"I'm *implying* that maybe fae get drunk off their magic. Ever think of that?"

Ember froze with a bulging mouthful of pizza and frowned. Then she shrugged, grabbed the remote out of her lap, and turned up the volume.

CHAPTER SIXTY-EIGHT

B y the second time Ember's tripwire spell went off, she'd adjusted the noise level to match the volume of the action sequence playing out on the TV. When the flashing yellow light raced across the wall and the front door again, both magicals sat up straighter, anticipating the blaring shriek that came next.

"Good work." Cheyenne gazed around the living room and slowly rose from her chair. "Sounds like another siren in this car chase that's been going on way too long."

Ember deactivated the alarm with a quick flick of her wrist and swallowed her last bite of pizza. "That's the point of a car chase in every movie. They go on way too long."

The halfling reached the front door and peered through the peephole again. "It's him."

"Matthew?"

"Yep. Just closed his door."

Ember snatched the wadded-up paper towel off the couch and wiped her hands, then brushed the pizza crumbs off her lap and from around her mouth. "Crap."

"You missed a spot."

"What?" Ember wiped the corner of her mouth with the back of her hand, sucked off the extra red sauce, then looked down and groaned. "Great. Grease stains all over my pants."

"I seriously doubt Matthew's gonna be focused on your grease stains, Em."

"But I can go change really fast."

"Hey, I *will* grab that wheelchair and push you all the way to his apartment if I have to."

"You could try." Rolling her eyes, Ember ignored the mess on her clothes and wheeled away from the coffee table to head toward the door after grabbing her new bracelet. "Don't forget, halfling, I have magic too now."

"Uh-huh." Cheyenne quickly gathered the printed stack of Matthew Thomas' dirty little secrets, then grabbed the remnant of the war machine from the recliner and headed for the door. She glanced at the clock over the stove and frowned. "Who stays in meetings 'til nine o'clock at night?"

"You don't know he was in a meeting." Ember opened the front door as much as she could before having to wheel herself out of the way for the rest of it. "You stay out *way* past nine some nights."

"Seriously, don't make a habit out of comparing me to the wrong people." Cheyenne pulled the door shut behind her as she followed Ember into the hall.

"I'm just saying."

"Yeah, I know. I get it. We have no idea what he's been up to, and that's the *point*. That's why we're doing this, right?"

Ember scanned the hall's ceiling and shrugged.

"Oh, nice. Make it super-obvious that we're on to his hidden-camera trick."

"Cheyenne, we're at his front door." Ember stopped and knocked on said door. "He's gonna find out what we know anyway."

"I *know* he's gonna find out," the halfling hissed. "But it'll work better for us if he's surprised."

The door opened quickly, and their tall, broad-shouldered neighbor grinned down at them. "Hey, Ember."

The fae girl cleared her throat and forced herself to smile back up at him. "Hi."

"And Cheyenne. You're both standing outside my front door."

Matthew chuckled, the corners of his eyes crinkling in amusement. "Everything okay?"

"We're fine," Ember replied quickly. "All good. How are you?"

He glanced from Ember to Cheyenne's scowling face and back again. "I'm a little surprised, honestly."

Ember raised her eyebrows at the halfling, and Cheyenne pretended not to notice. "We were hoping you had a few minutes to talk about some stuff."

"Oh. Well, yeah. You sure everything's okay?" Matthew glanced at his shiny wristwatch and raised his eyebrows. "It's kinda late."

"Thought we'd run a few things by the security expert," Cheyenne muttered, staring him down. "You know. For safety reasons."

"Uh-oh." Matthew leaned against the doorframe. "You get yourself into some kinda trouble?"

"Did I get myself in trouble?" Cheyenne gestured past him into his living room. "No. I'm not in trouble. But if I was, I wouldn't wanna stand here in the middle of the hallway talking to you about it."

"We're the only people who live on this floor."

"Can we come in, or what?"

Ember batted Cheyenne's arm, while the halfling made a poor attempt at hiding the stack of papers and the piece of O'gúl war machine behind her back. "We just wanted to talk to an expert. Just to see what we're dealing with here and whether this is something we should be concerned about."

Cheyenne cocked her head and narrowed her eyes at their neighbor. *Okay, she's nailing it right on the head with that one.*

Matthew's smile softened, and he shot Cheyenne one more quick glance before spinning away from the door and gesturing with a wide sweep of his arm. "Come on in. I stay up pretty late anyway. You guys want coffee? This espresso machine is better than anything you can get downtown."

"Sounds great."

Cheyenne cleared her throat. "No, we're good, thanks. Just here to talk."

"Okay. I'm just gonna make myself a latte. Ember? You want one?"

"Yes. Thanks."

"Cheyenne?" The halfling stared expressionlessly at him until he shrugged and turned slowly toward the kitchen. "Have a seat if you want. Won't even take me five minutes."

As he disappeared around the corner of his oddly shaped apartment, which was built into the corner wedge of the building, Cheyenne looked at Ember and raised her eyebrows. "Yes, thanks?"

"He has an *espresso* machine."

"I heard what he said."

"If nothing else, I'm gonna get a good cup of coffee out of this. He let us inside. Just chill."

Pressing her lips together and shaking her head, Cheyenne stepped out of their neighbor's entryway and entered the living room. The place was decorated in clean lines of dark and light gray with splashes of yellow, royal blue, and bright red in artwork, pillows, and even a streak of red running down the center of a dark-gray coffee table. *Like a kindergarten classroom for tech moguls.*

The roar and harsh rush of the espresso machine came from the other side of the apartment, and Cheyenne studied Matthew Thomas' home like it was just another abandoned warehouse with boobytraps.

"You're looking suspicious right now," Ember muttered as she wheeled past the halfling.

"Oh, really? Can't *imagine* why."

"You're not a big believer in 'innocent until proven guilty,' are you?"

"We already covered that this is the proof, Em." Cheyenne waved the stack of papers in front of her before shoving them behind her back again. A quick glance toward the kitchen didn't show her any sign of Matthew. *At least if he's watching us, he won't be able to hear a thing.*

"We went over this. *That* doesn't prove what we wanna know." Ember nodded at the kitchen and made her way toward the gray leather sectional taking up the corner inside the door. "Do I need to do all the talking on this one?"

Cheyenne joined her friend, casting a wary glance at the red stripe running through the coffee table, and plopped down on the couch. "If that's our tactic, we'll be here all night."

"What, you think you're the only one who can play magical sleuth with any level of efficiency?"

"Not when he's smiling at you."

Ember rolled her eyes. "Please."

"Seriously, you couldn't even turn down a latte."

"I'm trying to act *normal*, Cheyenne. When obviously none of this *is* normal."

The espresso machine cut off, followed by a few metallic taps and the hiss of the milk frother.

The fae sighed. "I know it's hard for you, but just sit still and let this play out, okay? I do *not* want this hanging over us the whole time we live here if we're wrong."

"We're not wrong." The halfling stuffed the stack of printed paper under her thigh and peered around the living room. "He knows exactly what he's doing. Look, it's been five minutes already."

"Okay. Here we go." Matthew appeared around the corner, carrying a huge gray mug in each hand. "Sorry that took so long. I'm gonna have to take that machine apart and clean it soon. I mean, yeah, it's amazing to be able to make my own cup of coffee like *this* whenever I want, but the maintenance part throws me off. I keep forgetting I'm the one who has to take care of it."

Ember grinned at him as he handed her one mug. "I bet you could find someone to do that for you."

Cheyenne closed her eyes in a long and exaggerated blink.

He chuckled. "Probably. But I try not to shuck a job off on other people if it's something I can do myself, you know?"

"Huh." Cheyenne leaned forward, propping her elbow on her thigh as she turned and raised her eyebrows at Ember. "Makes sense."

The fae ignored her friend's remark and took a sip of her latte. Her eyelids fluttered. "Oh, my God. This is amazing."

"Hey, thanks." Matthew lifted his mug toward her and lowered himself onto the puffy, insanely comfortable-looking suede loveseat on the other side of the coffee table. "Nothing like a great cup of coffee, right?"

"You sure you're not a secret barista?" Ember chuckled and offered her mug to Cheyenne. The halfling blinked, which was all the refusal she needed to make.

"Not as far as I know."

"Not even in a past life, maybe?"

Matthew took a long drink of his coffee, swallowed, and sat back in the loveseat. "It's all the espresso machine, I promise. I just push a few buttons."

"Well, it's working." Ember dove into her latte again.

Cheyenne stared at her friend and waited for the fae girl to get a move on. Ember smacked her lips and closed her eyes in appreciation. *Okay, enough bullshit.* "What's Combined Reality, Inc.?"

Matthew leaned forward as he swallowed his next sip and laughed in surprise. "Combined Reality, Inc.?"

"Yeah, you heard me."

Ember glanced at them, frowning.

"It's one of my smaller firms." Matthew crossed one ankle over his opposite knee and grinned. "Not a lot of people know the name, honestly."

"Because you're trying to keep it hidden?"

Ember closed her eyes and whispered, "Seriously?"

"No, actually." Their neighbor took another sip of his latte before setting the mug down on the tall side table next to the loveseat. "Because it's a private company and doesn't come up much in the public sector. How'd you hear about it?"

"I found it." Cheyenne hefted the metal sphere in her hand and tossed it across the living room. Matthew caught it swiftly and frowned at the broken war machine. "When I was trying to figure out how that thing works."

He turned the sphere over in his hands and shrugged. "I don't know what this is. Sorry."

"I'm talking about the programming inside it, Matthew." Cheyenne leaned forward and raised her eyebrows. "The access design. You know, activating new programs and relaying simple commands. Gathering information and sending it back to a control center. And I'm not talking about syncing up with the cloud, either."

With a self-conscious smile, he studied the metal sphere again and shook his head. "Well, unless you're going with a private radio frequency or jacking into a server somewhere else, I don't know how else that's possible. I don't see anything in here that would support plugging in directly." He scratched his cheek and tossed the metal sphere back at Cheyenne, who batted it aside like a fly.

The metal ball thumped onto the couch cushion beside her. "Don't insult me."

Matthew chuckled. "Seriously, Cheyenne, I have no idea what you're talking about. And insulting you is the last thing I wanna do."

"Because you're trying to keep up the nice-guy act? Not buying it."

"Would you buy it if I said I'm honestly a little scared of what you'd do to me if I got on your bad side?"

"You're already on my bad side, Matthew."

"Okay." Ember set her mug down on the coffee table and raised a hand to head off Cheyenne's impending outburst. "Can we backtrack a little and start at the beginning?"

"What does Combined Reality, Inc. do?" Cheyenne sat up and folded her arms.

"Cheyenne."

"I'm giving him the chance to lay it all out there, Em." The halfling gestured toward their sincerely confused-looking neighbor. *He's got a good poker face, I'll give him that.* "Now's your chance to start talking about what this other *private company* does, man."

Ember rolled her eyes. "You're being an asshole."

"No, it's okay." Matthew uncrossed his legs and settled both feet on the area rug beneath them. "I'm flattered that you're so interested. Like I said, Combined Reality, Inc. doesn't operate in the public sector."

"Neither do I."

He pulled back with a laugh. "What?"

Ember drew her hands down her cheeks and glanced at the ceiling. "Oh, my God."

"We're not talking in a public capacity, Matthew." Cheyenne glanced around his apartment and shrugged. "We're sitting in your living room. Are you the expert on your own businesses, or do I have to go hunt somebody else down?"

"Whoa. Hold on." Their neighbor spread his arms and blinked. "I have no problem talking about it, but I thought you guys had some kind of cybersecurity issue you wanted to talk about. Right?"

"So it's not cybersecurity, then. Okay." Cheyenne nodded and gestured toward the metal sphere beside her. "Does Combined Reality, Inc. write all the programming for stuff like this? Or are you just housing data storage? I didn't go too deep, but I'm having a hard time imagining that it's one without the other."

Matthew took a deep breath and smiled at the halfling. "You don't have a problem you want my advice on, do you?"

"Oh, yeah. We have a problem. It's you." Cheyenne stood up from the couch with a crinkle of paper as she gathered the printed sheets from beneath her legs.

"Whoa, whoa. Wait a minute." Ember lurched forward in her chair, thinking her friend was about to go straight for the jugular.

Instead, Cheyenne stormed around the coffee table and slapped the stack of papers down on Matthew's knee. "You can skirt around answering my questions all you want, but now you know what I know. Or at least some of it."

Matthew frowned at her without looking at the printed sheets. "What is this?"

"I asked first."

He gazed down at the papers and shuffled through them one at a time, his eyes scanning quickly before he moved on to the next page. Then he flipped through the rest and blinked. "Wow. This is insanely thorough."

"I'm still waiting for a thorough explanation." Cheyenne stepped away from him and folded her arms. "Go ahead. Go through as much of it as you want. I know you know what you're looking at."

"Of course I do." Matthew chuckled and stroked his chin. "I don't say this to a lot of people, Cheyenne. Again, the last thing I wanna do is insult you, so I hope you can take this as a compliment when I say I'm seriously impressed that you found any of this."

"Great. Now tell me what the hell you're doing with those programs."

He laughed in disbelief, shaking his head as he flipped through the rest of the stack. "I built one of the country's leading cybersecurity firms from the ground up. I wrote all our processes myself, so I know how strong my own data security is. Seriously, how did you get this?"

"That's none of your business." Cheyenne pointed at the papers. "But obviously, you're all up in mine."

"I wasn't aware this had anything to do with you."

"Cut the shit, man!" She clenched her fists and breathed slowly through her nose, fighting the urge to burst into full drow fury and light a fire under the guy's ass in a different way. *Sparking ball of black energy right under his nose would get him talking. Just keep breathing.* "I found what you're hiding, okay? Game's up. You're coding programs and syncing capabilities into those machines, and you need to start talking before I—"

"Cheyenne!" Ember's barked command sounded so much like Bianca Summerlin, it pulled the halfling right out of her rage.

She spun to face her friend. *"What?"*

"Can we talk in private for a second? Maybe out in the hall?"

"No, no. Stay here." Matthew waved the papers in his hand, staring at them as he stood from the loveseat. "I'm happy to give you guys some space. I should probably go draft a few emails anyway." He looked at Cheyenne with a confused smile.

"Go write your emails." She folded her arms and glared after him as he headed around the corner into the rest of his apartment, chuckling to himself. *This isn't going the way I wanted.*

CHAPTER SIXTY-NINE

"Okay, listen." Ember wheeled toward her, lowering her voice. "If you think I'm not all about figuring out how to stop the bastards who sent those spy-beetle things after me, you're nuts."

"He's just laughing it off."

"And you need to cool it." Ember leaned forward and tried to peer around the corner. The sound of fingers typing on light-resistance laptop keys came from the other side of the weird wall dividing the living room from the rest of Matthew's apartment. "He's way more interested in figuring out how you got past his defenses."

"His defenses?"

The fae rolled her eyes. "Or whatever stupid hacker lingo you guys use. I seriously don't think Matthew has a clue about what's going on, at least not about who his *clients* are." Ember nodded at the metal sphere on the couch.

"Or maybe he's just a good liar."

"Yeah, okay. Maybe. But instead of jumping from talking around this whole thing in infuriatingly vague terms to *threatening* him with physical violence, it might be a good idea to cross some middle ground first."

Cheyenne met her friend's gaze and pursed her lips. "Now who's being infuriatingly vague?"

Ember groaned in frustration. "Seriously, for how smart you are, you can be ridiculously thickheaded sometimes."

"Sure. *You* try rolling around in my head for a day."

"I'll take a hard pass on that, Cheyenne." Ember lowered her voice even more and cocked her head. "We haven't brought up anything about where that war machine is *from*. Nothing about magicals, the portals, the other side, any of it."

The halfling narrowed her eyes and looked toward the kitchen, half-expecting to find Matthew spying on them from around the corner. "You think he knows about all that?"

"Hey, I'm taking your opinion into account here. If he knows everything about his companies and what they're up to, he'd know about that part too, right?"

Cheyenne rubbed her mouth. "Probably. He's all over trying to fix the hole in his security he's not gonna be able to find. If he's that involved in what Combined Reality, Inc. does, he'd at least know about the tech he's writing programs for."

"Finally." Ember glanced at the ceiling.

"Hey, I would've come to this conclusion on my own...eventually."

"Yeah, only after you realized hitting him with deadly magic wasn't gonna get you anywhere." The fae shook her brown hair out of her eyes and gripped the armrests of her chair. "We'll bring that up too. Mention something about magicals or technology not from Earth, right? Then we can gauge his reaction."

"Before doing what, Em?"

"Before we show him we're part of that whole world."

"Are you insane?" Cheyenne hunched her shoulders when she realized how loud she'd said it. "We can't just show up at our neighbor's apartment going, 'Hey, look at us. We're magicals from another world most people will never know exists. Feel like telling us all your secrets now?'"

"If he's been doing business with magicals, what's the big deal?"

"The big *deal*." Cheyenne wrinkled her nose. "Shit, Em. You're making me feel pretty stupid right now because I can't come up with an answer for that."

"You're not stupid, you're pissed." Ember shrugged. "Sometimes that makes you stupid, but it's temporary."

A surprised laugh burst out of the halfling, and she ran a hand through her hair as she took a deep breath. "Okay, we'll do this your way."

"But for real this time, huh? You didn't stick to that plan."

Cheyenne headed back to the couch and dropped onto the leather cushion again. "Your way was taking way too long. I'm not a fan of small talk and drooling over homemade lattes."

"No shit." Ember followed and parked her wheelchair beside the end of the couch. "So, when he doesn't start freaking out about magic and different worlds, we'll show him what's up with us."

"Yeah. Sure."

"I'll say something about this bracelet, okay?"

Cheyenne shot her a quick frown. "Why?"

"Why? So you know I'm about to take it off."

"I'm pretty sure I'll know what you're doing the minute you do it."

"You don't plan anything ahead of time, do you?"

The halfling grinned and folded her arms. "Not to your level of detail."

Rolling her eyes, Ember sat back in her chair and slowly shook her head. "You should try it sometime. Maybe then you wouldn't have to use so much of that healing salve."

"And ruin all the fun? Come on." When they looked at each other, both girls snorted. "But hey, that's why I have you, right? To handle all the detailed planning for me."

"Don't push it."

Cheyenne glanced at the ceiling and shrugged. "I mean, you *do* have a private chauffeur."

"I can't believe we're having this conversation now." Ember clenched her eyes shut. "Okay. If you can keep the lid on the drow through the rest of this conversation, sure. I'll plan stuff for you."

"Deal."

"I'll believe it when I see it."

Thirty seconds later, Matthew reappeared from around the corner, the stack of papers still clutched in his hand as he scratched the back of his head. He stopped in the living room and looked at his guests like he'd forgotten they were there. "Sorry. Do you guys need another minute?"

"Nope." Ember smiled. "We're good, thanks. Perfect timing, actually."

"Mmhmm." He sat in the loveseat again. "So, now that you've blasted through what I thought was an impenetrable virtual wall, you wanna tell me what you're looking for?"

There it is. Open invitation. "Yeah. How'd you start making deals with O'gúleesh magicals?"

Matthew finally looked up from the printed details of his company's work and blinked. "The what?"

"Come on. Maybe you haven't seen anything that looks like that before." Cheyenne pointed at the metal sphere. "But you don't let other people handle things for you if you can do it yourself, right?"

"Right." He bit his lip and frowned.

Ember took a deep breath. "So you know that whatever parts Combined Reality, Inc.'s working with aren't from here."

"If you're talking about foreign materials, then yeah." Matthew's frown deepened. "You know foreign trade is part of the technology industry."

Cheyenne rolled her eyes. "We're talking *way* foreign. Like, *not-Earth* foreign."

Their neighbor blinked rapidly and shifted in the loveseat. "I don't know where you're trying to go with this."

"Yeah, you do." The halfling narrowed her eyes. "You know, it always creeped me out that you never had a problem looking me in the eye until now, but it's a pretty dead giveaway that you're hiding something."

"Also a dead giveaway that he *wasn't* hiding anything before," Ember added, turning to give her friend another pointed stare.

Cheyenne ignored her and focused on Matthew. "You know about magicals, Matthew. Don't you? The O'gúleesh refugees coming across the portal from that other world. The weird tech they're bringing with them. And you're the one who helped them figure out how to get that tech to work over here when it's not supposed to."

He laughed and tilted his head, opening his mouth but unable to find anything to say.

Turning to look at Ember, Cheyenne shrugged. "I'd say that looks like an admission of guilt, wouldn't you?"

"It's an admission of something."

"Okay, just take a step back for a second and listen to what you're saying." Matthew leaned forward in the loveseat and propped his fore-arms on his thighs, clapping his hands together. "You're trying to convince me that there are people from some other world who can use magic. That magic's even real. I know you're smart enough to get into my files, but all this makes you sound like crazy."

"Or crazy smart." Cheyenne grinned. "I never said anything about magic."

"What?"

"O'gúleesh magicals, man. That's as far as I went. You pulled out the 'magic is real' thing all on your own, so can we finally agree to be on the same page for two minutes? That's about as much patience as I have left."

Ember cleared her throat and fiddled with the silver band on her wrist. "What do you guys think of my bracelet?"

Cheyenne snorted. "For real?"

"*What?*" Matthew scrunched up his face and shook his head. "Are you guys on something right now?"

He stopped when Ember slipped the illusion charm off her wrist and wiggled it in front of her. Her human appearance faded, revealing her fae-pink skin, violet-streaked hair, and luminous purple eyes as the air around her glowed with that faint pink aura. The small pointed tips of her ears poked out from beneath her straight hair, and she raised her eyebrows at Cheyenne.

The halfling spread her arms and slipped into drow form. "So either we're all crazy, *you're* on something, or we can quit fucking around and start talking to each other like adults. Up to you."

Matthew's jaw dropped as he took in the revealed magicals sitting in his living room. "You?" Then he threw his head back and bellowed with laughter.

Cheyenne and Ember exchanged glances, and the fae set the thin silver band in her lap. "Not the reaction I was expecting."

"Yeah, kinda hard to gauge." The halfling folded her arms and stared at their neighbor as he fought for breath in the loveseat.

"I can't believe it!" Matthew pointed at them and barked another laugh. "You. *Both* of you!" His laughter dwindled into nonstop chuck-ling, and he dipped his head to wipe the tears from the corners of his eyes, sniffing as he tried to get control of himself again.

"You know, there's a fourth option I didn't think I had to mention," Cheyenne muttered, her golden eyes narrowing. "Wanna guess what that is?"

"Cheyenne." Ember frowned at her and shook her head. "Last resort."

The halfling's nostrils flared. *Good first resort too. But she's right.*

"Wow. I'm sorry." Matthew cleared his throat and blinked back the last of his tears. "That was just the last thing I expected. And I'm not laughing *at* you, to be clear."

"Do enlighten us," Cheyenne said flatly, raising an eyebrow.

"It's ironic." He took a quick drink of his latte. "That's all it is."

"That's not even close to a good enough answer."

"Okay, okay." Lifting a hand to gesture for them to wait, Matthew ran his other hand through his hair with another chuckle. "Honestly, this whole week, I thought I was neighbors with a couple of VCU grad students doing their thing. I mean, you guys aren't *normal* grad students."

"Clearly." Ember's face wore a surprising copy of Cheyenne's scowl now.

"No, I'm trying to explain how weird this is." Matthew blinked quickly and shrugged. "I didn't think to look past what you guys show the rest of the world. And this whole time, two magicals are living next door to me. Hell, I've spent plenty of time in the elevator with Cheyenne."

"What?" Ember's eyes widened.

Cheyenne grimaced and shook her head. "Just...standing in the elevator."

"And I had no idea that either of you is this." He grinned at them and took another long drink of his latte.

The halfling stared at him and fought to bring her annoyance levels down to bearable. *Either he's about to attack us, or we just broke our neighbor.*

"Em."

"Yeah?"

"How do you feel bout continuing this conversation my way now?"

Ember folded her arms and wasn't at all amused when Matthew fell into another fit of awed laughter. "Well, I won't stop you."

CHAPTER SEVENTY

Cheyenne summoned a burst of crackling purple sparks in her palm and stared at their war-machine-dabbling neighbor.

"Whoa, whoa." Matthew leaned back in the loveseat, lifting both hands and eyeing her warning magic. "What are you doing?"

"Something I've been wanting to do since you showed up at our apartment to introduce yourself." She shrugged. "Trust me, this is on a small scale."

Ember shot her a sidelong glance and shook her head a fraction of an inch.

"Okay." Matthew squinted at the purple sparks bouncing between Cheyenne's fingers. "I'm not sure why you're threatening me with that stuff."

"Because *you're* the one making things much harder than they have to be."

"Hey, I just found out the two of you are part of this whole different world, okay? Not as much of a shock as it could've been, but give me a few seconds."

Ember and Cheyenne stared at him, then the halfling lifted her purple sparks and cocked her head. "All right, your seconds are up. Why are you working with the assholes powering O'gúl tech?"

"*Why?*" Matthew laughed wryly. "It's just business. And I'm not sure if you're calling them assholes because they're working with me specifically or because they're from Narnia or whatever."

"Ambar'ogúl," Ember offered.

He shrugged. "Okay."

Cheyenne killed the purple sparks in her hand and cocked her head. "So, you'll strike up a deal with a bunch of O'gúl loyalists, but you can't be bothered to learn the rest of the terminology, huh?"

"I don't understand why that's such a big deal. I thought all you magicals stuck together over here?"

Ember's shimmering violet eyes narrowed. "Are you serious?"

"Yeah." Matthew glanced at the fae and the drow halfling sitting in his living room, then snorted. "Hey, admittedly, I don't care about all the details. They came to *me* asking if I could help power these machines you seem so angry about because they're not supposed to work over here."

"You're helping the wrong magicals." Taking a deep breath, Cheyenne swallowed and forced her frustration back down where it belonged. *Maybe I should've asked Lumil to come with us.* "How did they know to come to you for all this?"

He frowned. "Guess I have friends in the right places."

"Yeah, so do I."

"Okay."

"You know what? You need to start talking and giving up some information." Cheyenne's drow magic flared through her, despite how hard she fought to keep it under control. "I get a little unpredictable when people don't answer my questions."

"I'm under no obligation to answer any of them." Matthew smiled. "Unless you pull out a warrant for that information or put me in handcuffs and drag me down to some Dungeons and Dragons precinct, that won't change."

"All right, that's it." Cheyenne lurched from the couch, a sphere of crackling black energy bursting to life in her hands. Matthew flinched back in his chair and stared at the ball.

Ember grabbed her wheels. "Cheyenne!"

"I tried, Em. I really did. If Matthew Thomas wants to play hardball, fine. I can play."

Ember's hesitation to say or do anything else made Matthew shrink

back even farther against the loveseat's cushion. "Are you serious right now?"

"She doesn't mess around with those things." Ember glanced at the black energy in her friend's hand. "So yeah, she's serious."

"If you hit me with whatever that is," Matthew muttered, "this won't work out well for you. Somebody finds me dead or severely injured in my apartment by something like *that*—"

"Yeah, you're right." Cheyenne took one step toward him and studied his reaction. *He's scared and completely serious at the same time.* "I'm not in the habit of attacking people who haven't explicitly done anything wrong. You're still sitting in a real muddy-gray area."

"I told you, it's just *business.*"

"Em, we have some rope in the apartment, don't we?"

Matthew looked at the glowing fae in the wheelchair. "What?"

Ember narrowed her eyes. "We're not tying him to the chair, Cheyenne."

"Fine. No magic. No rope. Guess I'll just beat the shit out of him until he says something useful."

"*What?*"

"No, you won't. Not yet." Ember wheeled toward the loveseat and shot the half-drow a stern warning look. "Cool it."

Cheyenne raised an eyebrow at her friend and snuffed out the energy sphere. *Okay, she's finally showing up to the party.*

Ember pushed her wheelchair as close as she could get to Matthew's loveseat and leaned forward to study his face. "It might not look like it with all the purple and pink and the glowing aura, but trust me when I say I'm just as pissed as she is to find out *you're* the one behind making our lives way more complicated than they should be."

"Ember."

"No, *I'm* talking now. You'll get your chance when I'm finished, and it better be nothing but all the right answers to every single question we ask you." The fae gestured at Cheyenne without breaking away from Matthew's blue eyes. "Because right now, I'm the only thing standing between this drow and your apartment being blown to pieces. After that happens, the whole thing's out of my hands."

"Jesus," Matthew whispered. "I thought you were the nice one."

"Funny. I thought the same thing about you."

He stared into Ember's fae-large eyes. "Okay."

Cheyenne leaned forward. "Okay, what?"

"Okay, ask whatever you wanna ask me. I mean, these are all private business relationships, but it's not like I have anything to hide."

"No, just that you're encrypting all the data about it under way too many layers."

"That's the way I have to do things." Matthew frowned at her. "You of all people should understand how dangerous technology and information can be in the wrong hands."

"The *wrong hands*?" Ember looked at Cheyenne and laughed in disbelief. Then she pointed at Matthew. "You're the one who *put* it in the wrong hands."

"Hey, I just helped write the programs. Put the resources I had into developing the code. These magic people told me the gear they brought from that other dimension was old-school and low-tech, and they wanted help getting it to work here. I *can* tell you the stuff they handed me in the beginning is *way* more advanced than ninety-nine percent of the stuff I've seen made in our own world."

"It's a portal to a connecting world," Cheyenne muttered.

"Huh?"

"Not a different dimension."

Matthew closed his eyes and shook his head in jerky twitches. "That's an irrelevant distinction, but okay."

"It's not irrelevant." Ember cocked her head, wrinkling her nose as she studied the cluelessness written all over his face. "And it sounds a lot like you writing it off as irrelevant is what got us into this whole mess."

"I still don't get it." He glanced at the magicals hovering in front of his loveseat. "What do my business' private transactions have to do with either of you? Beyond you somehow figuring out how to dig the connection up."

Cheyenne rolled her eyes and stared at the ceiling, gritting her teeth. "He has no idea."

"Obviously." Ember folded her arms.

"Who connected you with these magicals wanting Matthew Thomas to write programs that work with O'gúl tech?"

"My uncle."

"Your uncle?"

Matthew shrugged. "Yeah. I'm assuming you know about the Fantasy Realm, right?"

Ember snorted. "It's called Ambar'ogúl."

"What? No, not that place." Matthew rubbed his forehead and searched for the words. "The organization. Fantasy Realm on Earth."

She barked out a bitter laugh. "Matthew, someone's been feeding you serious misinformation."

"That's what my uncle's been calling it since he introduced me to these other weird-looking guys."

Cheyenne grimaced. "Are you serious?"

"Look, I said I'd answer your questions, but that one doesn't feel like a genuine question."

"Stop talking." Turning to face Ember, the halfling pressed her lips together and frowned. "He's talking about the FRoE."

Ember blinked rapidly and turned her head to shoot Matthew a sidelong glance. "Fantasy Realm on Earth?"

He spread his arms.

"That's the worst name for any organization."

Cheyenne snorted. "Well, we already know the FRoE's pretty lacking in imagination. Their poor choices don't surprise me anymore."

"Wait, you know them too?"

"Hey." Ember thrust a finger at him. "We're the one asking *you* questions. Who we know doesn't matter for this conversation."

Matthew chuckled nervously. "Don't you think that's a little one-sided?"

Cheyenne whirled back toward him. "Yeah, it's one-sided, 'cause you fucked up!"

"Whoa." He lifted his hands again and leaned back against the loveseat.

"Your uncle works for the FRoE, then?"

"No. He's a private investor."

"Oh, sure. Naturally." Cheyenne ran her hands through her white hair, the chains clinking on her wrists. "When did he bring you the magicals?"

"About five years ago."

Ember grimaced. "Shit, that's a long time."

"Yeah." Cheyenne squinted at their neighbor. *And we're only now just hearing about it and seeing this tech powered up. Someone's been sitting on this way too long for it to be about me passing the trials.* "And you just took their money and said you'd do what you could to help, huh?"

"That's business, Cheyenne. That's how I make a living."

"How wonderful for you. I'd say I'm sorry to burst your bubble, but I'm not." She pointed at the metal sphere again. "You're making a living off magicals who are sending tech like that, the tech *you* wrote programs for, into public spaces and *trying to kill people.*"

Matthew frowned. "Okay, now I can't tell the difference between the truth and you trying to intimidate me."

Ember swallowed with a pained frown. "You think we'd make up something like this for fun?"

"Honestly, I have no idea what you'd do. I have no idea who you *are.*"

"You tried extra-hard, didn't you?" Cheyenne raised an eyebrow. "I bet that's pretty disappointing for you right now."

"Yeah, a little."

"Okay, will you two just shut the hell up?" Ember shouted, extending a hand toward each of them. "Please."

Taking a deep breath, Cheyenne stepped aside to give all three of them a little more space.

"Matthew, we're not here to judge you as a person."

Cheyenne snorted. "Speak for yourself."

Ember gave her friend a long, intense warning stare, and Cheyenne turned away, scratching her nose. "We're here because that's exactly what's happening with all this tech. The magicals controlling them *are* trying to kill people."

"That's insane."

"And it's real." She raised her eyebrows. "Right now, they're only attacking other magicals as far as we know, but it's not that far-fetched to think the magicals running those machines will turn on humans eventually too."

Matthew tried to glaze over his disbelief with a smirk. "I can't even comprehend what you're trying to tell me right now."

Cheyenne scoffed. "You know, for someone who's supposed to be a genius in cybersecurity and a leader in like four different industries, you're pretty dumb."

"Now you're just being mean."

"Hey! Come on." Ember pointed at the halfling. "Cut it out. I'm serious. Look, Matthew, we've both seen these things in action. That metal ball on your couch came off an O'gúl war tank in action. And yes, it *did* attack us. I was almost killed in my sleep by a bunch of other machines that looked like beetles and had some nasty features, but this is all the same stuff. All the same technology you've been powering or at least connecting your programs to for the last five years."

"Don't forget about that thing that tunneled into Peridosh," Cheyenne muttered.

"Oh, yeah. That one almost got both of us too."

"And the fly in my classroom."

Matthew cleared his throat. "What's Peridosh?"

"Nothing you're ever gonna get to see." Cheyenne cocked her head at him. "We're not making this stuff up. A *lot* of innocent magicals have been attacked and hurt by these machines. Not just us, and it could've been a lot worse for a lot more of us. We can't hold it off forever, so you need to turn off your system like yesterday."

"No." The unsure smile on Matthew's face disappeared. "I won't throw away the last five years of highly advanced work successfully completed by my company. I don't care who you are or what you're trying to do. I won't just scrap the whole project."

"You really are stupid."

"Sure, maybe." The man's voice rose in volume as he tried to keep his composure.

Cheyenne scowled at him. *Either his voice is gonna break or he is.*

"Do whatever you want to my apartment, Cheyenne. I can replace everything in here."

When she took a deep breath and opened her mouth to reply, Ember quickly added, "Don't do anything."

"How else are we supposed to stop this, huh?"

"Well, it's not gonna be by tearing down Combined Reality, Inc. and these programs." Matthew sniffed and crossed one ankle over his knee again, but his casual ease wasn't convincing. "Besides, these friends of yours already have their own control centers at this point. We just update the system once a month and monitor it for issues. Occasionally, someone has a good idea, and we'll throw that into the mix."

"Well, stop doing *that*." Cheyenne shook her head. "Don't give these people anything *better* to work with. That's a good start."

"I can't make any promises."

"And I can't promise I won't come back here in the middle of the night and tie you up the way I wanted to from the beginning."

Ember hung her head and rubbed her temples. "I give up."

Cheyenne and Matthew stared at her, then the halfling blew out a heavy breath, puffing out her cheeks. "Just tell us who *we* need to go see to make it stop on their end."

He slowly looked at her, his nostrils flaring as if he'd suddenly developed a drow sense of smell. "You realize this is my *business*, right? I can't just give away this information without incurring serious losses, especially with *this* kind of business relationship."

"Yeah, I'm well aware. And you realize this is quite literally *the end of Earth as we know it* if you don't grow a pair and tell me what I wanna know, right?"

"Exaggerating the issue won't get you anywhere."

"I'm not exaggerating!" A burst of black churning energy flew from her hand before she could stop it and ripped into the armrest of the loveseat, sending up a shred of tattered upholstery and fluffy filling. She and Matthew stared at that hole. *Deep breath, Cheyenne. This isn't how you wanna handle it.* "Sorry."

He swallowed thickly and gave her a weak shrug. "Better that than me."

Cheyenne smoothed the hair away from her face and tried again. "Look, I've been fighting these things all week. I found a whole bunch of these machine parts being smuggled across the border, and now I know who's responsible for them being turned into weapons—weapons those magicals want to use on all of us over here, no matter what we are. I've seen a whole bunch of stuff you can't imagine, and we *have* to get to those clients of yours before they make that happen. You need to trust me on this."

Matthew wrinkled his nose. "Why?"

She glanced at the charred hole in the armrest and shrugged. "Because I hit the chair and not you."

Licking his lips in thought, Matthew glanced briefly at Ember, who stared at her lap in disbelief, then finally nodded. "Okay. And before you ask for clarification, yes, that means I will give you a name."

Ember jerked her head up in surprise. "You will?"

"Yeah." He started to stand and paused when he saw Cheyenne still staring at him. Then he spread his arms. "Is it cool with you if I go get my phone from the kitchen?"

"If that's what has to happen."

"All right." Matthew shot them each another hesitant glance, then stood and hurried around the loveseat to leave the living room.

"Don't take too long," the halfling called after him.

"I'm just getting my phone, Cheyenne. You can chill out."

She snorted and met Ember's gaze. The fae scrunched her nose and muttered, "I'm the only one who gets to tell you that."

"I know." Cheyenne glared at the wall separating the oddly sectioned living room from the kitchen and the rest of the apartment. "I'll let it slide this time."

"And if he does it again, I'll blast a hole in the other armrest."

Despite her growing frustration over the entire conversation, the halfling smiled. "You think you can do that?"

"Cheyenne, I have a whole spellbook. If you think I haven't already found something as dangerous as your drow fireballs, I'm happy to demonstrate."

"No, we're good."

Ember fought back a laugh and wheeled away from the armchair as Matthew's footsteps headed toward them again.

CHAPTER SEVENTY-ONE

"Admittedly," Matthew started as he scrolled through whatever contacts list he'd buried in his personal cell phone, "I'm sending you the info for a guy I seriously don't like."

"Huh." Cheyenne folded her arms. "Does that mean it's a good place for us to start?"

"Not necessarily." He looked at her once, then returned his attention to his phone. "But if any of these magic people are doing something shady with this system like you think they are, he'd be my first pick."

Ember closed her eyes. "Magicals, Matthew."

"What?"

"Call them magicals, not magic people. You sound like you have no idea what you're talking about, and it's hard to take you seriously."

"Oh." He gave her a sheepish smile and shrugged. "Sure, yeah. Magicals. Okay, so how do you want me to send this over?"

He and Ember looked at Cheyenne. The halfling stepped back. "I don't know. Go get a piece of paper and a pen or something."

"Or I could just send it to Ember."

"Please don't." The fae girl shook her head. "I don't want anything about this on my phone. And Cheyenne, don't even think about trying to convince us you don't have a whole bunch of stuff on *your* phone that keeps things hidden from anyone who looked."

Cheyenne rolled her eyes. "Come on. I wouldn't try to convince anyone of that."

"So, what's your number?" Matthew asked. "I'll text it to you."

She stared blankly at him until Ember smacked the halfling's arm. "Okay, fine. Hand it over."

Matthew gave her his cell phone, and she quickly typed in her number before chucking the thing back at him.

"Don't get any ideas about texting me or sending me a bunch of crap I didn't ask for, okay? This isn't a free pass."

Matthew scoffed as he transferred whatever information he had in a text. "Trust me. I'm not even a little interested in doing any of that."

"Good." She folded her arms and watched him until he finished and dropped his phone on the loveseat next to him.

"There. You have a name and an address and a few extra tidbits. That's all I can give you without tearing down everything I'm trying to do."

"Don't worry, Matthew. We won't topple your little empire just yet." Cheyenne snatched the metal orb from the couch and turned to leave, then paused and made herself look him in the eyes again. "Thanks for finally helping."

"Thanks for not tying me to a chair."

She nodded and headed for his front door as Ember took a deep breath and wheeled her chair around to follow.

"Ember, can I talk to you alone for a second?"

Ember stopped and met Cheyenne's gaze. The halfling opened the front door and gestured toward the hall. "I'm just going home."

She stepped into the hall and made a beeline for their apartment without bothering to close his door behind her.

Ember blinked and spun her chair again to look at Matthew. "What's up?"

"I'm just trying to help people. I mean, yeah, this is my business and my livelihood, and I have to do things a certain way to keep things running the way they're supposed to." He leaned toward her. "But I would never willingly enter into business with someone if I knew they'd use my work and my services to hurt people. You have to believe that."

Ember gave him a small, patient smile. "I *want* to believe it. Maybe you had no idea what was happening, but you have a lot stacked against you right now. I just hope you didn't give Cheyenne bad information she won't be able to use. For *your* sake, I mean."

"No, that would make me stupid, wouldn't it?"

"Yep." When he didn't say anything else, she turned her chair toward the door again.

"I hope this doesn't change things," he blurted after her. "You know, between us. Whatever that is. Because I *do* enjoy spending time with you the way we have been."

Ember looked over her shoulder and raised her eyebrows. "Honestly, that's the last thing on my mind right now. You've been nothing but helpful and decent to *me*, but all this? It kind of changes things, yeah. Just don't screw anything up, and maybe we'll keep hanging out. I don't know."

"Okay. Yeah." Matthew nodded, ducking his head and sliding his hands into his pockets. "Thanks for being honest with me."

"It goes both ways." Without waiting for him to reply, she wheeled across the hall and through the open door of her apartment on the other side. The last thing Matthew saw before Ember shut the door behind her was Cheyenne's glowing golden eyes locked onto his face.

"Asshole," she muttered, still glaring at the closed front door.

"Don't." Ember wheeled toward the kitchen. "We did what we went over there to do, and you got a name, all without having to blast things to pieces. Mostly."

"Yeah, but we don't know if this is the name we want. It could be useless."

"I know that." Ember flicked her hand toward the cabinet above the sink, which opened with a flash of violet light before one of their drinking glasses floated down from the cupboard and into her hand. She took it with her to the fridge to fill it from the water dispenser in the door. "We still can't assume that he's always lying to us."

"Em, we had to show him *this* to get him to tell the truth." The halfling gestured at her body, which was still in full drow form. "He's known about the other side and magicals being over here for at least five years, which is way longer than I expected, and we had to shove that in his face before he said anything."

"Well, just talking didn't work very well with you at first either, did it?" Ember took a slow drink of water, then gulped down half the glass.

"That's totally different." Cheyenne leaned against the back of the couch and folded her arms. "I wasn't supplying O'gúl loyalists with a *program* I wrote to help them power war machines. I wasn't involved in anything but trying to hide from everybody."

"All I'm saying is that you didn't tear down your walls until someone shoved proof into your face. It makes sense that that's what he needed too."

"I'm not a fan of comparing me with him."

Ember chugged the rest of her water and set the glass under the dispenser to refill it. "I know, but don't you think finding things we have in common with people we don't like is a solution? We both know you better than that."

Cheyenne stared at her friend, who now drank a lot more slowly. *She's not looking at me on purpose. I can take the hint.*

The halfling walked around the couch and the coffee table and slumped into the dry leather recliner. Then she pulled out her phone and opened the text with the file Matthew had sent her. *It looks legit. Time to find out.*

"You're not planning on hanging out with him again after this, are you?"

Ember's glass clinked on the granite countertop of the kitchen island before she wheeled back into the living room. "I have no idea. I *could* say it's none of your business, but that wouldn't be true, knowing what we know about him now."

"Right. And you don't know?"

"No. Now let's move on to the more important question, which is why you haven't called Corian yet to go after that guy."

"What do you think I'm doing right now?" Cheyenne wiggled her phone in front of her, then made the call to her nightstalker ex-mentor.

He picked up on the second ring with a gruff urgency. "Everything okay?"

"Whoa. Yeah. We're fine over here. You?"

"Spent all afternoon getting L'zar's fell-damn *audience* back home and making sure they're safe." Corian lowered his voice, his lips brushing the speaker on his phone. "I might kill him for doing that."

"Well, don't bring me into it. As long as everyone made it out of there today, I'd say we pulled it off. And I have some information for you."

"Like what?"

Cheyenne looked at Ember, who lifted her hands and slowly lowered them, mouthing "Gently." "I found the guy who wrote the program powering the war machines."

"Who is it?"

"The owner of a company called—"

"Hey!" Corian pulled the phone away from his mouth to shout. "If you guys seriously have to do that right now, you know how this works. Take it outside." He cleared his throat. "Sorry."

Cheyenne grinned. "Goblins?"

"No, it's the *other* pain-in-my-ass magicals who can't keep it together long enough to spare the rest of us from their constant nagging." The nightstalker sighed. "You were saying?"

"The company's called Combined Reality, Inc. Owned privately by ThomasSafe. Ember and I met with the owner, and he gave us the name of one of his *clients* who apparently has this software and the operating systems running the O'gúl tech."

"Wait a minute. You went to see the owner of this company without telling me first?"

"Well, yeah."

"Cheyenne, I don't have to explain to you how delicate we have to be with all of this. If you're running around blasting in front doors and asking questions that are likely to expose all of us then—"

"Jesus, stop talking and let me finish." Cheyenne stood from the recliner and put the call on speaker, not wanting his voice that close against her ear. When he didn't say anything else, she took it as the go-ahead. "We haven't been running all over town, okay? This guy just happens to live in our apartment building."

There was a loud click, and the line went dead.

Ember stared at the phone. "Did he just hang up on you?"

Cheyenne clicked her tongue in annoyance. "Yep. Without listening to anything I had to say."

"Is everything okay over here?" Ember yelped and jumped in her chair when an oval of shimmering light burst into existence three feet in front of her.

Corian stormed out of his portal, sidestepped quickly to avoid the fae girl's wheelchair, and headed for the front door. "Tell me where he is."

"Hold on." Cheyenne tossed her phone onto the recliner and took off after him. "Corian, wait."

"I am. I'm waiting for you to tell me where this sonofabitch is so I can wring every drop of information out of him before I wring his neck. What's his name?"

"No!" Ember wheeled quickly toward them, the violet light beneath her wheels lifting the whole chair enough to give her an extra boost of speed toward the front door. "You don't get to pop into the middle of our apartment like that to go storming after someone."

Corian spun around and raised an eyebrow, pointing at her with a hand tufted with light-brown fur. "I strongly suggest you don't let your new role as Cheyenne's *Nós Aní* go to your head. It's been eight hours."

"This has nothing to do with that." Ember gestured at Cheyenne. "*You* didn't bother to listen to her. And unless you're showing up like this to stop an attack, you seriously need to give us some warning."

The nightstalker turned his silver gaze on Cheyenne. "Sounds like you're starting to rub off on her, kid."

The halfling shrugged. "It works both ways. Not a bad thing."

"No." Corian nodded. "Tell me then."

"I'm not telling you where he lives. Not right now."

"I meant the information he gave you."

"Right." Cheyenne glanced at her phone in the recliner. "He gave me a name, two addresses registered under that name, a history of their in-person meetings, and a catalog of the services and various programs this Syno guy has been purchasing from him for a long time."

"How long?"

"I don't know. A couple of years."

Corian's nostrils flared. "Why don't I have this information right now?"

"You know what? You'd *have* it by now if you weren't jumping to conclusions and you took a minute to listen to me. I was about to text it to you but figured I'd call to explain first."

The nightstalker's lips twitched into a barely perceptible smile, one pointy tufted ear flicking against his light hair. "This sounds familiar, doesn't it?"

"Yeah, I get it. I used to be the one jumping to conclusions before I got all the information. Now we understand each other." Cheyenne went back to the chair and snatched up her phone to forward the text to him. "And now you have all the information."

"Does that include this company owner's apartment number?"

"That's not important," Ember said. "If we have to go back and talk to him, we will. But you should take your team and go look for this Syno first. If this information is good, you'll probably find one of their control centers."

Raising an eyebrow at Cheyenne, Corian clasped his hands behind his back. "*If* the information's good?"

She shrugged. "We're trying to take his word for it, okay?"

"I sincerely hope you made it perfectly clear what will happen if we find out he's jerking us around."

"Hmm, I don't know. Ember? Do you think we made that clear?"

The fae girl pretended to consider the idea. "Yeah, I'd say he's well aware."

"Good. I'll hold you to that. Both of you." Corian swung his finger from Cheyenne to Ember and dipped his chin. "We'd better not end up on another wild goose chase."

"We *get* it." Cheyenne gestured at the open space on the other side of the coffee table where he'd portaled himself into their apartment. "Go check it out. Unless you want us to come too?"

"No, you two should stay in tonight. Let the rest of the ceremony settle in. It has the potential for side effects."

Ember rolled her eyes. "Are you serious?"

Corian peered over the back of the couch at the scattered pages of Maleshi's spellbook. "Who's been working on spells?"

Cheyenne snorted. "Please. Like you don't know the answer to that."

Looking back over his shoulder, the nightstalker gave Ember a small, appraising smile. "How's it going?"

She folded her arms. "Better than Cheyenne, at least."

"That doesn't tell me anything."

"Okay, very funny." Cheyenne sank back into the recliner and crossed one leg over the other. "She's a natural. Created a tiny rainstorm over our chair." She gestured at the wet pool in the cushion of the other recliner. "And set up an alarm around the apartment."

"Really?" Corian dipped his head toward Ember. "I'm impressed."

"Thanks. It only works with other people in the hall, so maybe I should start working on something that'll go off right before nightstalker portals pop out of thin air."

"Maybe add a little warning shock too," Cheyenne added.

Corian ignored them both and stared intently at their front door. "I'm curious as to why you'd want an alarm to sound for someone out in the hall. Aren't there only two apartments up here?"

"Yep."

Ember looked quickly at Cheyenne. "We used it for the pizza guy."

When Corian gave the halfling a questioning glance, she gestured at the mostly empty pizza box on the coffee table. "It worked."

"I see." He gazed at the door one more time, then stepped away from the couch. "Then I'll get back to my phone, if everything looks good."

"It looks good. Just go check it out."

"I'll send Byrd and Lumil to take care of it. Maybe I'll join them. That way, there won't be any confusion over what we find."

"Great." Cheyenne gave him a tight smile and nodded. "Good luck."

"Mmhmm. Enjoy the rest of your night." The nightstalker's fingers moved quickly until a new portal shimmered open in front of him. He shot Ember one last sidelong glance, then stepped through the oval of dark light and disappeared before the portal closed.

Ember asked, "What was *that*?"

"I think we gave our neighbor away by talking about the alarm." Cheyenne rubbed the side of her face. "Sorry, Em. I guess it's easy to let something like that slip when I'm focused on keeping him from tearing this whole building apart."

"He's not going to. He'd better not."

"And the info on Syno had better be legit."

The apartment was silent until Ember chuckled softly.

"What's so funny?"

"Nothing."

"No, seriously. What?"

"You just stopped a *nightstalker* from pulling a Cheyenne Summerlin."

Cheyenne rolled her eyes. "I'm not that bad. I mean, it didn't take much to get him to calm down."

"Right." Ember chuckled and covered her mouth with a hand. "That's the funny part. When you get riled up, you're much worse than that."

"No, I'm not. For real?"

Ember burst out laughing, nodding as she leaned over.

Cheyenne thumped her head back against the recliner's cushion and grinned at their apartment's vaulted ceilings. "I'm getting better, though. Only left one hole in Matthew's furniture."

"That *is* a plus. I guess we'll see how long it lasts."

"Your support is always appreciated, Em." Cheyenne picked up her phone and glanced at the time. "Okay, it's after ten. Wanna watch another episode of that stupid show you're so into?"

"Ha. Which one?"

"I don't care."

Ember wheeled around the couch to take up her TV-watching spot at the far end of the coffee table. "But you *are* into watching TV. Maybe I am rubbing off on you too."

"Sure. Don't get too excited about it." Cheyenne pushed out the recliner's leg rest and stuck her hands behind her head. "I just want to stop thinking about all this, because tomorrow's Friday, and I'm not excited about stepping into a classroom in front of a bunch of under-grads to pretend like nothing more important is happening."

"Education is important, Cheyenne." Ember shot her a sidelong glance, then returned to scrolling through the selection on their giant TV.

"I never said it wasn't. Stopping these loyalists running the show behind all the war machines is just *more* important, and pretty much the only thing we can do until L'zar figures his shit out so we can make the crossing again and finally end this craziness."

"Well, who knows? Maybe teaching a class of undergrads will be a good distraction."

"Probably not." They both laughed, then Cheyenne picked her head up off the laid-back recliner. "Hey, you think you could make me kind of a reverse illusion charm?"

"Hmm." Ember squinted at the TV and kept scrolling. "For the halfling who can slip in and out of looking like two different people?"

"Yeah. Just in case something else happens while I'm teaching and I need to go full drow without freaking out my entire classroom."

"Oh, you mean like what that necklace did for you?"

"Kind of, but instead of turning off my magic, I need something that'll keep me looking like a human if I have to use magic." Cheyenne widened her eyes and thumped her head back down on the cushion. "I don't think I can convince them to close their eyes and meditate again just so they don't see me looking like a drow."

"You made them *meditate*?" Ember dropped her hand with the remote into her lap and stared at her friend. "In an Advanced Programming class?"

"Hey, I had to come up with something. It was either that or let that spy-fly thing buzz right out of there again to take what it saw back to its masters. Obviously, whoever's controlling the machines knew enough about me to look for me on campus. I have a hard time believing they won't try it again."

"Huh. Yeah, I can make you a charm for that."

"Thank you."

"Any objections to *Modern Family*?"

Cheyenne chuckled and waved a hand at the massive flatscreen. "Do your thing. I'll just veg out with you."

CHAPTER SEVENTY-TWO

The next morning, Cheyenne shuffled out of her bedroom, rubbing her cheeks and trying to focus her vision on her way to the bathroom. She stopped when she saw Ember sitting at the end of the coffee table with three different pages of the spellbook laid out in front of her. "Have you been sitting there all night?"

"What? Oh." Ember yawned, shook her head, and blinked quickly. "Nope. Woke up early for a head start, I guess."

"On that illusion charm for me?"

"Yep. I'm pretty sure if I stick all these spells together, it'll pretty much do what you want."

Cheyenne shook her head and continued toward the bathroom. "I don't know how you can look at that stuff and put it together in your head."

"Are you serious? It's just like adding a few layers of code to something, or extra levels to a stylesheet. Just with magic."

"Agree to disagree. But I seriously appreciate that you know what you're doing." The halfling stepped into the bathroom and closed the door behind her.

The second she stepped back out again, Ember grinned and lifted her hand. "Tada!"

"What?"

Ember wiggled the earrings dangling from her fingers and raised her eyebrows. "Your custom illusion charm."

Cheyenne barked out a laugh. "And you chose *those* earrings?"

"What? Come on, they're fun."

"I thought purple was *your* color, but okay."

Ember playfully rolled her eyes and looked at the two-inch earrings, which sparkled when she shook them again. "Well, I turned them into the charm you wanted, so this is what you get. You're welcome."

"Thanks, Em." Cheyenne held out her hand, and the earrings dropped into her open palm. "Purple *and* sparkly."

"Just shut up and put them on. If you're that worried about a pair of earrings cramping your style, don't put your hair up, and no one will see."

"This is ironic." Cheyenne removed the silver studs from her earlobes and slipped the charmed earrings into place. "It's always something with the ears."

"Yeah, because hiding pointy drow ears so people don't notice you're a halfling is totally the same thing as hiding a pair of sparkly earrings? You think people won't take your Gothness seriously if they see you wearing those?"

"No. I just don't do dangly and sparkly, but it's fine. Look, I put them on."

"Uh-huh." Ember folded her arms and watched Cheyenne unconsciously pull her black-dyed hair around her face to hide her ears. "The only thing that matters is if they work, so go."

"Right." Cheyenne drew her drow magic into being, the hot rush of it racing up from the base of her spine. She gazed at her hands, which were still as pale and human-looking as ever. "Feels like when I was wearing that pendant."

"Seriously, try some magic. Something small, though. You know, in case I missed a piece of the charm."

"You're not sure about this?"

"Of course I'm sure. I'm just saying." Ember shrugged, watching Cheyenne's open palms in expectation. "Go."

Cheyenne conjured a burst of purple sparks at her fingertips and grinned. "That's nothing like wearing the pendant."

"No, it's not." Rubbing her hands together, Ember nodded. "Okay, try something else."

The purple sparks flared in Cheyenne's hand before she replaced them with a sparking orb of black energy. The magic hissed in her palm, illuminating her pale, human-looking face with black and purple light. "This is weird."

"Yeah, but it's so cool. It looks like I just mastered combining three spells into your tailored illusion charm." The fae girl slapped the armrests of her chair. "You are one lucky halfling, you know that?"

"Compared to a few weeks ago, yeah. I'd say I have it pretty good." Cheyenne snuffed out the energy sphere. "Seriously, Em, thanks. This'll make things much easier."

"It better. You can pay me back by making coffee."

"Ha. Deal." Cheyenne headed for the kitchen but stopped when she heard her phone buzzing in her bedroom. "Crap."

"What?"

"Phone call. Then I'll make coffee. Promise." The halfling skirted around the furniture toward her room.

"I'm constantly surprised that you can hear half the stuff you hear."

"It's a gift and a curse," Cheyenne called as she darted through the door and snatched her phone off the bedside table to answer the call. "Corian. Hey."

"Turns out the business owner you're covering for gave us *mostly* good information."

"Shit." She spun and paced across her bedroom. "What happened?"

"We hit all three addresses last night. Whoever this guy is, he needs to update his records because the first place had been demolished."

"What about the others?"

Corian said, "Not that much better. We found a few pieces of gear left behind, but everything else had been packed up and shipped somewhere else. No clue where that is. And apparently, Syno thought it'd be super-hilarious to rig the place with a bunch of traps."

"You were attacked."

"Yup. A few wards that were easy enough to tear down and a handful of machines. They didn't put up much of a fight, though. Persh'al thinks they were programmed to respond to anyone entering the building. It didn't look like they had an active feed sending anything back to whoever's handling them, but we don't know for sure. And I'm not sure I'm a fan of that extra nugget of info you sent with that text about this company owner's affiliation with your other friends in black."

Yeah, that's one name for the FRoE. "He said it was his uncle."

"Either way, if the connection between that organization and Syno runs any deeper than a one-time business transaction a few years ago, it'll make things that much more difficult for us. We need to try again."

"We do. And we'll try again *after* I'm done teaching my class this morning."

"Cheyenne!"

"Nope. I'm not telling you where the company owner lives and leaving you to handle it your way when I'm not around. I've seen what happens to magicals when you 'try again,' and I seriously wanna avoid that this time. We'll go talk to him together when I get back."

"What if he still doesn't give us what we need?"

"Then we'll take a different tack, sure. But that's not gonna be the first or even second option, okay?"

There was a long pause on the line, followed by Corian's soft chuckle. "You're getting a lot better at this."

"At what?"

"Responding instead of reacting. It's good to see. Call me when you get home after your class, Professor Summerlin."

"Whatever." With a snort, Cheyenne ended the call and went to her dresser to dig around for a change of clothes.

Ember stopped in the doorway. "What happened?"

"Apparently, Syno thought it was a good time to clear out his buildings and set a bunch of traps for anyone wanting to snoop around the place."

"That's not good."

"Nope." Cheyenne changed quickly, tugged her hair out from under the collar of a plain black t-shirt, and crossed her room again to search through the pockets of the pants she'd worn a few days before. "So when I get back from teaching, we're gonna go pay Matthew another visit."

"Wait, Corian doesn't think Matthew lied to us, does he?"

"No, he said the information was *mostly* good. Just not good enough." Cheyenne found the folded slip of paper and unfolded it, dropping her pants back onto the floor. "But the timing does seem a little too perfect."

"Matthew wouldn't have called Syno to warn him. He said he didn't like the guy."

With a shrug, Cheyenne picked up her phone again and dialed the number written on the piece of paper. "I hope not, Em. But there's no way to know until we go talk to Matthew again."

"I'm coming too."

Looking up from her phone, the halfling met the fae girl's gaze and nodded. "Yeah. Of course."

"Okay. Good." Ember nodded at the paper in Cheyenne's hand. "What's that?"

"Maleshi's number. All this time and she just gave me her number a few days ago."

"What would *she* know about this?"

"No clue. I'm just hoping she'll be able to keep an eye on Corian so he doesn't try to find Matthew before I'm back. I wouldn't put it past him to do that."

"Huh." Ember wheeled away from the doorway, frowning. "I'll go make coffee."

"Oh, sorry."

"Don't worry about it. I don't have anything else to do right now, and I need caffeine."

As Ember headed into the kitchen, Cheyenne sent the call through to Maleshi and waited for an answer.

"Hello?"

"Hey, it's Cheyenne."

"Oh." Maleshi cleared her throat. "What's wrong?"

"Nothing immediate. Did you hear about this Syno guy with—"

"Control over a few war machines and a business deal with someone who apparently lives in your apartment building? Yeah, kid. I heard all about it. Got one hell of an earful from Corian."

"Yeah, he was ready to bash in a few heads last night." Cheyenne headed out of her bedroom and closed the door behind her. "At least I calmed him down enough so he could go check into those buildings instead."

"Did you call me to chat about this, or is there something else?"

Okay, abrupt and to the point. Got it. "I just wanted to know if you'd heard about what's happening, or any other information. And, I don't know, maybe you'll be better at convincing Corian not to go barging through apartment doors over here looking for this guy anyway."

"Well, if he told you he wasn't going to do that, I'd be seriously surprised if he went back on his word. Not his style, despite what you might think about the way we handle people who get in our way."

Cheyenne said, "Okay. So what's next?"

"Besides regrouping later to get better information?" The line filled with rustling and the quick zip of Maleshi closing her briefcase. "I'm going to teach my classes today just like any other Friday, Cheyenne. You should do the same. We're playing the game on both sides right now, seeing as your top-secret friends might be more involved in this than any of us gave them credit for."

"I know, but we haven't figured that out yet."

"That doesn't mean we don't have to be careful. Any slip-up on our part that might let this Syno or that scaly taratas or whoever else know we're on to them before it's time is a dangerous mistake we can't afford to make. So get to campus, teach your class, and we'll go from there."

"Right. Good thing I was planning on showing up there."

"That's an excellent choice, seeing as it'll keep you enrolled in the graduate program." Maleshi's light chuckle carried through the line.

"All right. I guess I'll talk to you later."

"Yep." The nightstalker IT professor hung up without another word, and Cheyenne slipped her phone into her back pocket.

"Any powerful insights from the general?" Ember called from the kitchen as the scent of brewing coffee hit the halfling's enhanced sense of smell.

"Pretty much the same thing. Wait. Keep waiting. Keep things running business-as-usual until we have more information and no other choice but to do something immediately."

"And that includes her?"

"Yep." Cheyenne lifted her backpack off the floor beside the couch and set it on the armrest to make sure she had everything she needed. "Even with O'gúl war machines tearing through the place and new portals popping up everywhere, General Hi'et is reporting for duty as a college professor."

Ember snorted, poured the first cup of coffee, and waited for the rest of it to keep brewing. "She sure did pick one of the last professions you'd expect of an O'gúleesh legend."

"It makes sense, though." Cheyenne gratefully took the first mug of coffee when Ember offered it. "She knows how O'gúl tech works over there. And after seeing what their stuff can do on the other side, yeah. Using human cutting-edge technology feels like playing with baby toys. Hey, good coffee. Thanks."

"Yep."

Cheyenne rifled through the pantry. "We need groceries."

"I'll just do a grocery delivery thing. Anything specific you want?"

"Just food." The halfling took another sip of coffee and glanced at the clock above the stove. "Shit, I gotta go."

"Forty-five minutes early?"

"I'm not gonna stand up and lecture to a bunch of skeptical under-grads on an empty stomach. Gotta factor in time for breakfast. That was a lot easier when I lived down the street from a gas station, come to think of it." She took three large gulps of the steaming coffee, then set the mug on the counter and went to grab her backpack.

Ember glanced at the still-brewing coffee, then snatched Cheyenne's half-full mug and got started on that. "Please tell me that's the only thing you miss about your old place."

"It's not, actually." The halfling grabbed her fancy new trench coat out of the closet by the front door and shrugged it on. "I had better neighbors over there too."

After gulping down the hot coffee to keep from spraying it all over the kitchen, Ember winced and laughed at the same time. "Fair enough."

"Speaking of neighbors." Cheyenne shrugged on her backpack and pointed at her friend. "Don't even *think* about paying Matthew another visit without me being there."

"Please." Ember rolled her eyes. "I don't want to be alone with him right now. Or at all, honestly. See you later."

"Yeah." Cheyenne slipped through the front door and locked it behind her. Before she headed down the hall toward the elevators, she cast a quick glance at Matthew Thomas' front door and frowned. *We'll be back soon enough.*

507

CHAPTER SEVENTY-THREE

She ate a breakfast burrito from a gas station on the drive to the VCU campus. By the time she pulled into the student lot and headed down the path toward the Computer Sciences building, Cheyenne still wasn't convinced it was a good idea to be here. *We should be talking to Matthew right now. Moving as fast as we can to bust those control centers. This is gonna get out of hand. I can feel it.*

She kept her head down and walked quickly, occasionally glancing up when a student shouted in surprise or laughed too loudly or ran too close in front of her on the walkway. *Something's wrong. Why can't I pin it down?*

When she reached the front door of the Computer Sciences building and grabbed the handle, a tingle of itching energy raced across the back of her neck and along her shoulders. Cheyenne turned and scanned the grass and the neighboring buildings, then jerked open the door and slipped inside. *Just keep paying attention. That itch means something.*

Getting to the empty classroom where she taught her Advanced Programming class ten minutes early didn't help the feeling of impending wrongness. Cheyenne pulled out her laptop and checked her email for something to do, but the only emails she had were from the students who'd turned their work in early for the week. She snorted and shut her laptop. "Overachievers."

The tingling energy raced across her neck and shoulders again, pulsing. She grabbed her backpack, pulled the activator out of the front pocket, changed to her drow form, and stuck it behind her ear. The sharp pinch made her eyelids flutter, then she gazed around the empty classroom and sat back in the chair behind her desk. *Nothing lighting up with this thing, so at least there's that. I sure as hell better be able to see what's happening. If it even does.*

"Morning."

Cheyenne glanced quickly at the classroom door and switched back to her human form as the first two students stepped inside. "Hey."

"TGIF, right?" The first girl who'd spoken let out a nasal giggle that ended in a snort. Her smile died when Cheyenne went back to gazing around the empty classroom. "Okay."

The undergrad students taking Maleshi's Advanced Programming class filtered quickly into the room, and at 10:31 a.m., Cheyenne stood from the chair behind the desk and nodded at the last kid to come inside. "Can you grab the door?"

"Oh. Yeah." The kid, who had a shaggy mop of dirty-blond hair, spun quickly and did as she asked before taking a seat.

I'm still calling them kids. They're only a year younger than me, if that.

"Okay. This is it. Just a regular class on a Friday morning." Cheyenne's eyes darted toward the door when the shadow of someone passing in the hall flickered across the narrow window. "Some of you are still working on the last tiny assignment from Wednesday, right?"

Her students nodded slowly, wondering what was up with their odd new instructor and sharing a round of confused glances.

"I'll take that as a yes." She slid her laptop aside on the desk and sat again. "Whoever hasn't finished that up yet, go ahead and take the rest of this class to do that. If you have any questions, I'm right here."

"What if we already finished it and turned it in?" The girl who'd laughed at her own lame joke leaned forward in her chair. "You did get my email, right?"

"Probably, if you sent it. I'll go through everything over the week-end. Everyone else, be sure to have it in by midnight tonight." *Right, like I'm gonna be going through assignments tonight.*

The girl raised her hand and slowly lowered it again. "If we already finished, what do you want us to do?"

Cheyenne laughed at that. "Whatever you want. I don't think I need to give you—"

The tingling energy raced across her back and shoulders again, and she sat up straight in the chair. *This feels familiar.*

"Give us what?"

"What?"

The girl shook her head, and the other students around her shifted uncomfortably in their seats. "You said you don't think you need to give us what?"

"Step by step instructions on how to use your time." Cheyenne tilted her head, wanting to shudder and roll the tingling energy off her back. "That comes standard with, you know, the fact that we're all adults."

Someone in the back row sniggered, and the eager student turned to glare at him. "Yeah, real adult."

Cheyenne swallowed. *What's going on?*

The next second, the activator flared to life with a burst of flashing lights and a blaring siren shooting right through her head. She grimaced and clenched her eyes shut, leaning over her lap at the sudden onslaught to her senses.

"Are you okay?" The girl with the half-shaved head who always sat in the front row leaned forward and tried to peer over the top of her instructor's desk. "Cheyenne?"

"What? Yeah, I'm fine. Bad headache just hit me." She could barely hear her voice over the blaring siren pulsing in her head. When she opened her eyes again, a blazing orange message flashed across the front of her vision.

Warning. Incoming threat approaching. Location pinpointed at forty yards southeast.

What the hell? Cheyenne pushed herself to her feet and turned to her right. A flashing yellow arrow blinked in the center of the wall, slowly rising and growing larger as the activator tracked the threat. She turned off the alarm with a thought and stepped away from the desk.

"I'm just gonna step out for a—"

The ground rocked and trembled beneath them, sending Cheyenne staggering sideways. The students shouted in surprise, clutching their backpack and laptops and looking wildly around.

"What is that?" someone yelled.

Cheyenne gripped the edge of the desk and caught her balance. "Earthquake, maybe."

"What kind of earthquake shakes like this?"

"Every kind!"

"This isn't an earthquake."

"Then what is it?"

The halfling ignored her panicking students and turned toward the classroom door. "I'm gonna go see what's happening."

The ground bucked again, and half the classroom erupted into screams when the overhead track lighting popped and sent a shower of sparks down on the room.

Cheyenne held out her hands and headed carefully toward the door, trying to keep her balance on the trembling floor. "Everyone just pretend this is one of those hurricane drills you had to practice in elementary school, right?"

"*What?*"

"Just duck and stay away from windows and doors. I'll be right back." She braced herself against the wall and jerked open the door. It cracked against the wall, and Cheyenne gripped the doorframe to keep herself upright.

"You shouldn't go out there."

The half-drow was already racing through the halls as fast as she could, trying to see through the furiously blinking lights in her vision. Multiple classroom doors flew open as she passed, letting out streams of panicked students and faculty, all scrambling to get out of the building. *That's not gonna help anybody.*

The activator's warning flashed wildly, filling her view with scattered descriptions she couldn't read while she focused on not falling flat on her face or being shoved against a wall by fleeing students. *That yellow arrow's getting bigger.*

An earsplitting groan rose from beneath the laminate-tile floor, bringing louder screams and more scrambling people into the halls. Then something loud cracked and split outside. Through the sliver of open door quickly shutting behind the last group of students to run outside, she saw a brilliant flash of multicolored light, punctuated by darting streaks of silver. "Shit."

The thump of a body hitting the wall around the corner in front of her made Cheyenne pause. Then a woman with dark hair in a rainbow tie-dye dress barreled around the corner and froze as the front door of the building clicked shut.

"Maleshi." Cheyenne raced toward the nightstalker posing as an IT professor, stumbling forward when the ground trembled again and brought another wave of startled and terrified screaming from people outside and inside the building. She steadied herself with a hand against the wall and swiped her hair out of her face. "Did you feel that?"

"Yeah, I felt it. What the hell's happening out there?"

"There's something coming." Cheyenne blinked against the bright flashes of warning messages darting across her vision.

"I meant what specifically, Cheyenne."

"I don't know." The blaring alarm returned in her head with full force, and she doubled over at the sudden deafening pain bursting through her head. "Enough, already!"

"Hey. Look at me." Maleshi almost fell into the halfling when she staggered toward her over another buckling earthquake. "What's wrong with you?"

Cheyenne pointed at her ear. "Activator."

"Seriously?"

Warning: Threat detected at the surface six yards southeast.

"Dammit. It's already here."

"Cheyenne."

"I said, I don't know! Come on." The halfling pushed away from the wall and darted toward the door, zigzagging across the hall as the ground bucked from side to side. Maleshi hurried close on her heels, and they both pushed the front door open before stumbling out into the bright mid-morning sunlight.

Two enormous mounds of dirt churned twenty feet from the front of the Computer Sciences building, ripping up grass and earth and sending huge clods flying through the air. The spinning corkscrew tips of O'gúl tunneling machines burst through the surface, the mechanisms roaring as the powered war tanks breached and toppled forward out of their tunnels.

"You've gotta be shitting me," Maleshi growled.

Students, staff, and faculty screamed even louder at the foreign contraptions of glistening black metal made their way across the lawn, spinning and rumbling forward as they churned and kicked up more grass and earth. Cheyenne hardly noticed the deafening chaos beneath the new rise of earsplitting alarms setting off one after the other in her head.

And the activator's yellow arrow didn't center on either of the O'gúl war machines.

"There's something else," she muttered, swiping twice across her vision just so the activator would get the message and turn off the damn alarms.

"Besides those things?"

"Yeah." The yellow arrow flashed brighter and brighter before a massive crack split through the earth between the two holes from which the tunneling machines had emerged. The ground shuddered again, and the fissure splintered toward the Computer Sciences building, rending the air with crack after deafening crack like magnified gunfire. Another blaze of shimmering light streaked with purple and green burst from the center of the widening chasm. "Shit."

"Just say it already!" Maleshi snarled.

"It's another portal."

"Did the activator tell you that?"

"No, but I've seen it before. I'll handle it. Can you deal with the machines?"

Maleshi shot her a quick glance. "That's the stupidest question I've ever heard you ask."

"Great."

CHAPTER SEVENTY-FOUR

Cheyenne darted into drow speed and raced away from the front door toward the splintering crevasse widening on the VCU campus. A fraction of a second later, she saw Maleshi enter the same plane of enhanced speed, hiking up her dress with one hand, slashing at the hem of it with her four-inch steel-like claws that had burst from the other, and running straight for the rumbling war machines.

The diggers only slowed against the magicals' enhanced speed until Maleshi reached them. As she brought her claws arcing down toward the blinking blue lights flashing at the spinning top above the corkscrew spiral of the first machine, the contraption turned its mechanical sights on her and unleashed a spray of green fire.

Maleshi dodged the attack with a hiss and brought her claws up against the side of the war machine instead. A grating screech of metal on metal erupted on contact, sparks flying. "What the hell? Since when did these things start moving as fast as us?"

"No clue," Cheyenne shouted, skidding to a halt beside the suspended burst of magical light rising from the crevasse. "You still got it?"

The digger groaned and opened a four-inch metal panel on its side before ejecting a rod tipped with razor-sharp pincers and spraying a burst of yellow magical attacks this time. Maleshi brought her claws down on the rod and severed it like a chef's knife through an onion. "Quit asking me and do whatever you need to do, kid."

The second war machine turned and headed toward the first, powering up for something clearly more intense with a low whine that quickly rose to a high warning pitch.

"Yeah." Cheyenne studied the crack in the earth and the light shimmering slowly in suspension. *Just reach out and feel for it. You've done it before.*

She closed her eyes and slid that sixth sense of her drow magic along the energy of the earth in front of her. *There.*

Hooking her fingers around it as if she were about to pull herself up on a ledge instead, the halfling took a lunging step back and pulled with all her strength. The ground trembled in protest, groaning and shivering even at her enhanced speed. Something like a scream erupted from the crevasse and startled Cheyenne out of her concentration.

"Cheyenne!" Maleshi shot a bolt of silver lightning into the second machine, lighting the digger up with jolting electric sparks. The second tank rose a foot off the ground and sprouted unfolding metal legs, using the two in the front to bat the nightstalker aside. Maleshi flew sideways and skidded across the grass, crouching to keep her balance.

The second war machine launched a massive ball of sparking yellow magic from an open hatch in the dome on its top. The attack struck Maleshi squarely in the chest and blasted her backward. This time, she landed on her back instead of her feet and snarled.

"I almost had it," Cheyenne shouted back, reaching out with her magic to feel for that ledge of the earth's energy so she could grab hold and try again.

"And these things might almost have *me*." The nightstalker scrambled to her feet as the diggers advanced on her again. "In case that wasn't clear, kid, yes. This is me asking for your help."

"Right." Cheyenne darted toward the machines, the activator lighting up their scrolling lines of code she now knew were O'gúl workings scrambled with Matthew Thomas' program. *That asshole's got a lot to answer for.*

The weakest parts of both diggers flashed the brightest in her vision, side panels, undercarriage, two small nodules on each of their fronts just above where the corkscrewing spirals emerged from the metal body. Cheyenne reached out for the first tank's closest side panel, her telekinetic energy heightened by the activator's precision as it peeled the side panel away with a shriek of ripping, buckling metal. The second tank's rotating dome swiveled toward the halfling, blinking in alternating blue and red, and opened five hatches to sprout five metal rods that looked way too much like gun barrels.

Shit. Cheyenne abandoned the telekinetic destruction and threw up a massive shield in front of herself as the tank opened fire with fell-green rounds of light. The rounds exploded on impact, blasting heat and a thick wave of green energy over Cheyenne's body as she fought to hold up the shield until the attack ended. *We're screwed without being able to move faster than these things.*

Maleshi ducked a swinging blow from the second tank's protruding legs, which had now rearranged themselves into long black blades with serrated edges. She brought her four-inch bladelike claws swiping up against the legs, only to be met with instant resistance and a shower of sparks. "Seemed a lot easier for you to rip these things apart yesterday!"

"It *was* easier yesterday!" Cheyenne gritted her teeth against the last of the green explosions, then darted around the shimmering black wall of her shield and sent two black energy spheres at the closest digger. The gun barrels swiveled again to face her. "Blast out what's inside."

"Inside *what?*"

"The part I just ripped off! And go for the head." The halfling ran back toward her shield, feinted away, and slid forward on her knees beneath the extended barrels stretching over the tank's body. The activator centered her telekinesis on all five rods, and she flung them aside, ripping wires and metal bolts and something that looked like a potions vial out of the digger's swiveling dome.

Maleshi ducked the hurtling gun barrels flying toward her and snarled, "That's the best thing you can come up with? Just get through the armor?"

"No." Cheyenne slapped her hands on the tank's side panel and felt a stronger burst of connection from the activator and her magic before she tried to haul the side panel away from its brackets. The metal body lurched away by half an inch and stuck fast again. "Go for the head!"

Maleshi leaped atop the digger attacking her, slashing at the metal spikes now pumping up and down along its back like motor pistons as she rushed toward the swiveling dome. She sent a bolt of silver lightning at the swiveling dome spinning fully around to lock onto her new position. The dome sparked and sputtered with yellow and red lights. "That's the head, right?"

"Yeah!" The halfling roared when the metal hull of the digger shifted its composition in tiny unfolding pieces and pierced her palms pressed against it with hundreds of needle-thin points. A burst of heat flared from her belly and the base of her spine as the activator flashed brighter and showed her the command to put everything she had into ripping off the panel. *Like I need prompting.*

With a shout of effort, Cheyenne torqued her body sideways and ripped the panel free with her telekinesis. Blood sprayed across the grass when the hundreds of needles peeled away from her hands and the panel hurtled away from her toward the crevasse in the earth. The ground wobbled under them in their enhanced speed. Staggering to her feet, she reached with her lashing black tendrils into the exposed innards of the tank. The coils of her drow magic bursting from her fingertips wrapped around the thick cables and razor-thin wires to rip them free. Green and orange sparks flew, and the small explosion at the digger's center rocked the machine sideways off one set of rolling tracks. The resulting magical shock jolted back up through Cheyenne's whipping tendrils and flooded her body with a sizzling burst.

"Ah!" She withdrew her tendrils and hissed, blinking against the minor static in the activator coil blurring her vision before it settled.

On top of the other tank, Maleshi leaped from one section of the machine's top panels to the neck, dodging the swiveling dome's attacks and sending bolts of silver lightning at the machine's head between intermittent slashes of her claws and bursts of sparks. "What the hell did they *do* to these things?"

"Made them better? I don't know." Cheyenne swiped her hair out of her face and glanced at her blood-smeared palm.

Another scream came from within the fissure opening within the earth. The halfling spun and headed back toward the edge of the newest Border portal, trying to erupt through the grass. The multicolored light shimmered in suspension, and the dark tip of a black stone pillar rose slowly from within the crack. *Nope.*

Cheyenne reached out again for that tension in the earth's energy.

Her activator noted the difference between the energy of the portal stone and the earth around it.

"Cheyenne," Maleshi said in a warning tone as chunks of shredded black metal hurtled away from the dome under her swiping attacks.

"If this thing comes through, we have a serious problem."

"So don't let it through!"

The half-drow let off a blast of crackling black energy straight down into the crevice at the first portal stone jutting through. The screaming intensified, and she hooked her magic around the earth's resistance and pulled again. With a massive groan, the fissure in the earth shrank inch by inch. Cheyenne staggered back, pulling her clawed hands toward her and snarling with the effort. The ground shifted again, and a massive explosion behind her almost made her lose her concentration again. Heat and flashes of green light bathed her back.

A ray of the portal's shimmering light erupted from the center of the closing fissure and shot straight up into the sky.

Maleshi delivered a final blow to the digger's dome. What was left of the metal shell fractured and finally ripped away, sending black metal shards in every direction before they slowed in the air, suspended in the nightstalker's and half-drow's enhanced speed. The mechanisms beneath the dome's shell burst into blue flames, and the digger let out a shrieking whine before that too cut out, and the broken machine lost power, crashing back to the ground. The nightstalker spun toward Cheyenne and saw the burst of light streak into the air. "You said you could stop it."

The portal ridge fought back and opened the crevasse again by another inch, pulling the halfling across the grass as she struggled to maintain her grip on the earth's energy.

"I'm *trying*!" A renewed wave of searing heat and tingling energy flashed from Cheyenne's core. The black flames burned behind her eyes and across her skin, setting her human-illusion ablaze with drow fire.

Maleshi's eyes widened. "Crown be damned."

She leaped from the back of the broken digger, sent a bolt of silver lightning into the machine Cheyenne had ripped apart, and ran toward the halfling. "Just don't let go, kid."

"Ya think?"

For the first time in countless centuries, General Maleshi Hi'et recoiled with a cold wave of alarm when she heard Cheyenne's voice, dozens of otherworldly tones speaking as one.

"Don't just stand there!" Cheyenne shouted, oblivious to the many-toned snarl in a spectrum of pitches erupting from her throat. She shot Maleshi a sidelong glance, the black flames dancing behind her eyes and shadowing her pale human face in dark light.

Maleshi blinked, and her momentary hesitation disappeared. "I'm on it."

The nightstalker's fingers moved quickly as she muttered her next massive spell. Then she clapped her hands together and spread them apart with a blinding burst of silver and pink light. The same pink shield wall she'd put up around the original unmonitored portal ridge rose from the chasm against the portal's shimmering light.

Cheyenne let out a final roar of effort and pulled with all her strength. Her grasp on the earth's energy held fast, and the activator measured the width of the crack in slowly decreasing increments. The fractured sections of earth slammed together with a boom like a hollow metal drum below the ground, and the portal's light behind Maleshi's shield wall flickered, dimmed, and winked out.

The activator beeped in her head and flashed a new update in bright yellow.

Detected threat contained. Volatile frequencies returned to normal levels. Shield application holding at 99%.

The thing measures spell effectiveness too?

The second Cheyenne's thoughts moved away from closing the portal ridge, the black fire along her skin snuffed out, and she staggered backward. "Damn."

Maleshi hung her head and stuck her hands on her hips, fighting to catch her breath. "That should keep things where they belong, for now, at least. Not sure how well it's gonna hold."

"Ninety-nine-percent," Cheyenne muttered.

"What?"

The halfling tapped behind her ear and brushed her black hair away from her face again, smearing blood from her fingers and palms across her forehead. "This tech has numbers for everything."

"I didn't know that was possible."

"Yeah, well, maybe it's just a halfling-using-O'gúl-tech-on-Earth' thing."

Maleshi snorted. "Sure. Maybe. Listen, I know this was a close call, but we need to do some serious cleanup right now before everyone else moving at normal speed starts seeing things they won't be able to figure out."

"I'm sure they already have."

"There's no reason to make it worse." Maleshi worked one more spell and finished it by pointing with both hands at the pink wall of her shield. The light disappeared, leaving behind a jutting mount of ruptured and mostly re-sealed earth stretching in a jagged scar across the lawn on the VCU campus—that and the two wide holes dug by the war machines. "At least they won't see *that*. Now, come help me move these damn machines."

"You can't make those invisible too?"

The nightstalker shot Cheyenne an unamused glance, her silver eyes flashing in the sun as they headed toward the broken machinery. "Of course I can. Gonna be a little hard to explain why a bunch of students and other staff keep tripping over huge, hard piles of nothing in the middle of the grass. We're just getting these out of the way."

"Right."

Together, they hauled the broken, mangled carcass of the first O'gúl digger tank across the grass and between the Computer Sciences building and its neighbor.

"Right here's good." Maleshi released her hold on the machine's outer shell.

Cheyenne held onto her end, her drow strength keeping that end of the digger slightly elevated as she stared at the nightstalker. "Seriously?"

"Not forever, Cheyenne. We're picking up the pieces, and as soon as we get that magical battlefield cleaned up, I'll make sure Corian gets his ass over here to help me with the rest. And I don't even know why I feel the need to explain myself to you. Let's go get the other one."

"You're explaining it to me because I'm not just somebody's yes-drow." Cheyenne dropped the hunk of O'gúl metal with a clank of loosened parts and followed Maleshi back toward the second.

"No one said you were."

"Then there shouldn't be an issue explaining a reason for something. I never said I disagreed with you."

"Great." Maleshi bent to lift the side of the second digger.

When Cheyenne stepped up next to her to help lift, the general leaned away quickly, blinking furiously as she stared at the bashed-in, shredded dome on top of the tank. "Did you just flinch away from me?"

Maleshi snorted and tugged on the war machine. "Just pull, halfling."

The machine left a trail of flattened grass in its wake as they dragged it behind the building to dump it beside the first. It clattered to the grass, and two blue lights flashed within the exposed side before a spear of black metal punched through the opening with a loud hiss.

Cheyenne clamped her blood-slickened hand around the extended pole and ripped it free with another spray of sparks and flashing colored lights. The broken piece of war machine slid through her slippery palm and thumped onto the ground at her feet.

Maleshi stared at it. "Effective. What happened to your hands?"

"Needles, I think. Or something." The halfling gazed at her palms. "This'll be fun to patch up. And by the way, you ignored my last question."

"Hmm."

"Seriously, why did you get all jumpy when you were next to me?"

"Stand back, kid." Maleshi cast a quick spell, staring at the remnants of the shredded war machines scattered across the grass. Each piece was encompassed in silver light, lifted two feet off the grass, and raced between the buildings toward where Cheyenne and General Hi'et were standing.

"Whoa." Cheyenne stepped aside and watched the black metal fragments clunk against the diggers' hulls when Maleshi's magic released them.

The nightstalker nodded, dusted off her hands, and cast another illusion spell over the remnants to render all the evidence of the war-machine attack invisible.

"All right." Turning toward Cheyenne again, Maleshi looked her up and down. "Fair warning, you're gonna feel like shit when you slow down into regular space-time again."

"What?"

"Take it from a war general who's done this a million times." Maleshi clapped a hand down on Cheyenne's shoulder. "It doesn't get better, even with an impressive track record like mine. Go ahead. The longer you stay in, the worse it gets."

Cheyenne glanced at the nightstalker's hand on her shoulder, and the woman removed it slowly. "Are you serious?"

"As serious as you'll be in two seconds, or whatever passes for seconds in hyper-speed. I'm right behind you."

With a groan, Cheyenne closed her eyes and slipped out of drow speed.

CHAPTER SEVENTY-FIVE

The second she fell back into regular time, Cheyenne couldn't feel her legs. They buckled beneath her and she tumbled sideways, barely managing to keep her face from hitting the grass. She rolled and hit her shoulder instead.

A heavy wheeze escaped her chest, but she couldn't form the words she wanted.

Maleshi cleared her throat. She now sat on the lawn beside the halfling and slowly lowered herself onto her back to stare at the blue sky. "What was that?"

"Why?" Cheyenne wheezed again and took a sharp, gasping breath. Her lungs exploded with tingling pain. *Am I coughing or choking right now?*

The terrified screams and shouts and the pounding of racing feet out of buildings and across the lawn took on more clarity beyond the muted pitch she'd heard at first.

Groaning, Maleshi slowly closed her eyes and swallowed. "The why doesn't matter, kid. Just the fact that it does."

The halfling managed to turn herself over onto her back, her hands thumping into the grass beside her. *I have to be seeing four of everything right now.* "Feels like being hit by a bus."

The general snorted. "Yeah, a bus that injects morphine into only half of you. Just give it a few more seconds."

Cheyenne blinked at the bright sky and finally got her breath back under control. The activator blinked in her vision, calm, silent, and ready for her next command. As soon as feeling returned to her arms and she could move them again, she pulled the silver coil from behind her ear and grimaced. "How did I not know about this?"

"There's a first time for everything." Maleshi pulled herself up into a sitting position and hunched over her lap. "My first time was during the raids at Holbrukfúrn. Of course, that was two dozen of us against five gremlin warrens, so moving just below the speed of light was pretty much the only way back then to not be overrun."

"Right. And my first time just happened to be with hybrid war machines that can move as fast as we do."

"Unfortunate, but yes." Maleshi pushed herself to her feet, then offered the halfling a hand up. "Once you can breathe again, it's pretty much downhill from there."

Cheyenne took the woman's hand and let the general pull her up. A brief wave of dizziness made her stagger, but she shook her head and it cleared right up. "So, now what?"

"Now we make sure that no one on campus was seriously injured. Or seriously traumatized."

"By an earthquake and a bunch of flashing lights shooting up out of the ground?" Cheyenne licked her dry lips and shot the nightstalker a sidelong glance. "I'm pretty sure everyone's traumatized."

"I meant by magic. We want everybody to feel safe, Cheyenne. Reassured. A little shaken up is fine, but people losing their minds over what they can't explain doesn't do us any favors. Then you and I need to make some calls."

"Sure."

"Here." Maleshi bunched up the ripped hem of her dress, glanced around them behind the building, then let out her glinting four-inch claws from within her illusion of human hands and slashed free two wide strips of tie-dye. "Wrap up your hands. I can grab you something later to help with all the punctures. What did you say happened?"

"That tank turned itself into an acupuncture board." Cheyenne wrapped her blood-smeared hands, grimacing at the sharp pain beneath the pressure.

"Sounds fun. We'll patch you up in a bit."

"I have darktongue salve in my backpack."

Maleshi blinked, a smile twitching at the corners of her mouth. "Have you *used* it before?"

"More times than I can count right now." Cheyenne tied off the temporary bandages and used the back of her wrapped hand to wipe off her forehead as much as she could. "And yes, I do prefer that short-lived agony to walking around with half-healed wounds all over me. I need my hands."

"Huh. You know, I always wondered if that masochistic streak just inherently came with being a drow. You definitely fit the description in that way."

"It's not masochism." Cheyenne snorted as they walked between the buildings and headed for the front doors of the Computer Sciences building. "It's pragmatism. No pain, no gain, right?"

"I understand the saying, kid. Just not the fact that darktongue is your first choice." Maleshi held the door open for Cheyenne before following her inside.

Three terrified students ran toward them down the hall and skidded to a stop when they saw 'Professor Bergmann's' ripped dress and Cheyenne's blood-smeared face and wrapped hands. "Oh, my God, are you okay?"

"All good." Cheyenne nodded and tried to skirt past them.

"Well, what happened out there? Is anyone hurt?"

"Not that we know of." Maleshi stopped to calm the panicked kids while the halfling slipped down the hall. "It seems like it's settled down now, but it's a good idea to check wherever you can to make sure no one else is hurt."

"Yeah. Definitely."

"We can do that."

"Good." The nightstalker nodded. "I don't think there's been any damage to buildings, but spread the word that people need to get out now, just in case."

"Okay. Thanks."

She nodded after them as they hurried away down the branching corridor. Then she asked Cheyenne, "Where are you going?"

"There's a whole classroom hiding under their desks right now," the halfling replied without turning around. "Figured I should tell them it's time to come out."

"Out back again in ten minutes, yeah?"

Cheyenne raised her hand and gave the nightstalker a wave of assent before turning the corner at the end of the hall toward her Advanced Programming classroom. She stopped when she reached the doorway and found chunks of plaster littering the hall. The door had fallen halfway off its frame, and her black Vans crunched across the debris when she stepped into the room.

"Holy shit. What happened to you?"

The halfling gazed around the room, where her students were crouched halfway under the rows of long tables or stood at the end of the rows where they'd braced themselves against the "earthquake."

"Fell on some broken glass." Cheyenne raised her bandaged hands. "All good, though. Looks a lot worse than it is."

"Does it hurt?"

The curious kid's friend elbowed him in the shoulder. "Dude, don't be stupid. Of course it hurts."

"What happened out there?"

"I thought I heard an explosion outside."

"Is anyone else hurt?"

"What do we do?"

"All right. Slow down." Cheyenne reached her desk and turned to face them. "I know everyone's freaked out. The earthquake's over. For now, it looks like everybody's safe, but we need to evacuate the buildings and get to somewhere safer."

"It's not safe here?"

"I didn't say that. This is just in case." The halfling blinked slowly and leaned against the end of the desk. *Mega energy drain. How the hell did she do this a million times?*

"Hey, you look like you're about to pass out." The girl with the half-shaved head slid away from where she'd crouched beside her seat and took two steps toward her instructor before Cheyenne lifted a hand for her to stop.

"Just tired. I'm fine. See this, everybody?" She gestured to herself and nodded. "Calm. Collected. Not panicking. Get your stuff and head for the other side of the campus, or go off campus the other way. There was some kind of ground damage right outside this building, so if anything *isn't* safe, chances are that's right here. *Go.*"

Her students bustled into action, swinging backpacks and messenger bags over shoulders and filing toward the classroom door. "You're coming, right?"

"Yeah, yeah. Right behind you, as soon as I get my stuff. Hey, if you see anyone else running around inside, tell them to get out too. Buildings can collapse after something like this." Cheyenne pretended to pack up her backpack as the room quickly cleared out. When the students' footsteps faded down the hall toward the front of the building, she slumped into her chair and pulled out the brown glass jar of darktongue salve. "You and I are gettin' to know each other, aren't we?"

The lid slipped more than once beneath the rags around her hands, but she finally got the jar open and quickly unwound the bandages. She stared at the thick, gooey white salve inside and gritted her teeth. *It's gonna suck no matter how I do it. Go all in.*

The second Cheyenne dipped three fingers into the jar for a giant scoop, the darktongue got to work on the tiny puncture wounds in her fingers. Growling, she pulled out the stringy goo and smeared it on her opposite palm before quickly rubbing the stuff into her hands like it was lotion.

She hissed as the searing pain of the darktongue worked its magic on her wounds. Still slathering the stuff around as much as she could, Cheyenne leaned forward and tried not to cry out at the pain burning through her hands. *Somebody's gonna think I got trapped under something.*

When she couldn't handle touching her hands any longer, she slumped over her lap, propping her forearms on her thighs and clenching her eyes shut to wait for the burning heat of instant healing to die down. Tears leaked from the corners of her eyes, and she hadn't realized she'd been breathing through clenched teeth until she had to open her mouth to take an actual breath.

"Holy shit," Cheyenne hissed through her teeth, her arms sore from the tension of bearing through the pain, and then all the discomfort vanished.

She opened her eyes and wiped her hands off with the rags enough to see the perfectly healed flesh of her palms beneath. *Sucks, but it works.*

She gave herself another moment to recover from the exhaustion and the suddenly vanished pain in her hands, then she closed the salve jar and stuck both that and the bloody rags from Maleshi's dress into her backpack. As she stood and slung the straps over her shoulders, a groaning shudder rippled through the wall of the classroom behind her. A thin shower of dust and plaster shivered down onto the rows of long tables stretching across the room, and Cheyenne headed quickly toward the door. *The earthquake's a lie, but the damage apparently is not. Time to get outta here.*

On the way to meet up with Maleshi behind the building, she only passed two other people in the halls. One was a faculty member darting out of an office with a briefcase in one hand and a hastily snatched-up laptop and a stack of thin binders clutched to her chest. The other was a terrified-looking freshman with his fly still unzipped as he staggered out of the bathroom and stared in shock at the empty hallway.

Yeah, that'd be the worst place to experience an earthquake. Cheyenne almost laughed but managed to hold it together. "You okay?"

"I don't know." The kid blinked at her, then looked down at his soaked pants and dripping shoes. "I fell over, and I think I broke something in there."

"In the bathroom?" Cheyenne nodded and pressed her lips together, trying not to visibly flare her nostrils at the smell. *Kid fell into the urinal.* "You'll be fine. Maybe go home and grab a change of clothes, huh? Or at the very least, just make sure you get out of the building and away from this area of campus just in case."

"Yeah." The shocked kid turned stiffly, arms spread by his sides as he waddled down the hall and left shallow wet footprints behind him.

She gave him a two-minute head start so as not to further humiliate him and hoped he was already out the front door by the time she reached it. He was. Cheyenne didn't see him anywhere when she skirted around the front of the Computer Sciences building again.

She stared at the closed-up crack that probably still held a burgeoning portal ridge beneath it and the two mounds of ruptured earth around the diggers' holes just in front of the fissure. *Man, that looks really bad.*

When she rounded the corner behind the building, Cheyenne slowed and tried not to trip over the invisible war machines on the thin grass. Maleshi stood beside her rolling briefcase with the metal handle in its perpetually upright position, her phone in hand. "With a minute to spare. Look at you."

"That wasn't a firm ten minutes anyway."

"You don't know. But I'm glad you didn't try to take some kind of drow shortcut, thinking you could solve all our problems on your own."

"What?" Cheyenne folded her arms.

"Just that you didn't waste any time. That's all."

"Yeah, that's not what you meant. Go ahead, General." Maleshi snorted at her former student using the nightstalker's former title, but Cheyenne only raised an eyebrow. "If you have something to say, better say it now and get it off your chest."

Maleshi glanced quickly around them and stepped closer. "I get that tensions are high, and you don't agree with every decision made by those of us fighting this fight for you."

"*With* me."

"Right. Yeah." The nightstalker dipped her head and lifted both hands in surrender. "With you. That being said, kid, I'm not a big fan of you and the fae going off on your own to interrogate someone for ridiculously sensitive information you couldn't even prove was legit first. *Without* telling the rest of us."

"That's what you're pissed about?" Cheyenne laughed and shook her head. "I don't need to ask permission to do something I know has to be done. And I'm not going to."

"Not asking permission, Cheyenne." The general returned her attention to her phone and pulled up the number she wanted. "Anyone who thinks they can control you by giving or withholding permission is a complete idiot."

Like the FRoE.

"I'm just talking about you telling us what's happening *before* it happens and not after. You don't know if we might have some tool or tactic or information that could help you do whatever you're trying to do. And no, I'm not talking about the tactics you've already made perfectly clear you don't approve of." Maleshi waited until Cheyenne finally turned her head and met the nightstalker's human-looking green eyes. "We're in this together—all of us. And I can tell you right now that L'zar's already screwed up enough on his own by going wherever he wants, doing whatever he wants, and leaving the rest of us to pick up the pieces because he never bothered to lay out a plan first. Even if it was just to say, 'Hey. This is happening. Gotta go.'"

The halfling chewed the inside of her bottom lip. "So he's been leaving the warehouse and putting us all at risk, then."

"No, kid. I'm talking about that drow's entire existence, from birth to holing up in that warehouse. We *want* to help you. Kinda hard to do when we don't know what's going on."

"Yeah, okay. I get it."

"Mmhmm."

"Seriously. I'll call next time I end up going after corporate CEOs to intimidate them into giving up the names of their O'gúl loyalist clients. Message received."

Maleshi scoffed, shaking her head and tossing her long, wavy black hair out of her face. "At least I know you're familiar with the specific instance. Now's the part where we call in everyone we know to clean up the mess none of *us* made." The nightstalker kicked at nothing but air with her brown suede boot, except it clanged against the invisible hull of one of the war tanks. "I'll get hold of Corian, and you call up your frenemy organization."

"What?" Cheyenne paused with her cell phone pulled halfway out of her pocket. Her trench coat rustled away from her back and hips when she tightened her grip on her phone and turned to face the destroyed strip of VCU campus beyond the front of the building. "Why the hell would I call *them* in for this?"

"Same reason you called them in for the new portal at your mom's. If anyone's mastered the art of containing these Border portals *and* keeping them hidden from humans, it's the FRoE."

"Yeah, and all the other Border portals are way outside populated areas for no humans to *see*."

"They won't see this one either." Maleshi gestured toward the scarred grass. "Thanks to you. And a little nightstalker magic, obviously."

"Obviously." Cheyenne pulled up Sir's number on her phone and stared at it. *No way am I pulling Rhynehart away from Mom's to come out here. This is gonna suck so much worse than last time.* Her finger hovered over the call button, then she looked at Maleshi with a grin. "Hey, good thing we both decided to show up and pretend to teach classes today."

"Ha. But we *do* teach classes. We just happen to be more than that." The general paused to shoot Cheyenne a sidelong glance. "You're not just pretending to teach, are you?"

"What? No, of course not. Hyperbole."

"Uh-huh." Maleshi made the call to Corian, and Cheyenne begrudgingly sent her call through to Major Sir Carson.

I wasn't gonna have time to grade assignments today anyway.

CHAPTER SEVENTY-SIX

"What do you want?" Sir snarled into the phone.

"A regular greeting over the phone would be a hell of a start." He paused for so long on the other end of the line that Cheyenne had to pull her phone away to make sure they were still connected. "You're not gonna like what I have to say."

"Tell me something I *don't* know, halfling."

She rolled her eyes. "Found another new *entrance*."

"Another?"

Cheyenne braced herself for the fiery explosion of cursing and items thrown across the FRoE officer's office, but this time, it didn't happen.

"I swear to every goddamn Dorito flavor, whenever shit starts splattering the walls, there *you* are, covered in it."

"All right, is that your way of saying you think this is my fault?"

"That's exactly what I think! So far, you haven't done anything to convince me otherwise, and that includes your infuriating proficiency at lying through your teeth."

"So you want me to just hand this whole thing over to someone else who'd like to use it? You know, I know a nice T-class family who could benefit from it."

"Goddammit, Cheyenne, you know that's not what I meant. Where is this fucking thing?"

"On the VCU campus, right outside the building I teach in."

"Oh, the Halfling Bullshit building. Yeah, I've heard of it." Something heavy slammed down, and Sir grunted. "Did you have to fight little kiddie monsters coming outta this one too?"

"No." She glanced at Maleshi, who paced six feet away as she spoke softly to Corian, the phone pressed to one ear and her pointer finger stuck into the other. Cheyenne smirked. "I closed it. Shouldn't be spilling out any monsters for a while."

"You closed it." Sir choked out a bitter laugh. "What does that even mean? These things come with a goddamn zipper now?"

"All just part of me being what I am. It's contained for now." Cheyenne swiped her hair out of her eyes and gazed at the lawn in the front of the building. "Look, what this new thing needs is someone to show up and reassure people that this was just an earthquake. Maybe keep an eye on it and do a little damage control. Your people *are* capable of that, right?"

"You have no idea what we're capable of."

This isn't going anywhere. "Will you send someone to VCU or not?"

"Already did. See? I can multitask and waste your time too."

Cheyenne hung up and slipped her phone into the side pocket of her new coat. *At least he took the information seriously.*

"How did that go?" Maleshi asked, bending to put her phone back in her briefcase.

"Exactly the way I thought it would." The halfling turned to face her. "But someone's on their way."

"How fun." The general took a short, discerning sniff of the air, then pointed at the ground beside her. "Come stand over here."

"What?" Cheyenne glanced around, looking for a reason to move, then slowly walked toward the nightstalker. "Is there a reason for needing to stand by you?"

The air behind her shimmered, and a portal opened right where she'd been standing. Corian stepped through a second later, frowning in his average-human-man illusion.

Cheyenne blinked. "Oh."

Corian glanced at her briefly with a quick nod, then turned to Maleshi. "Let's get to work, then."

"Oh, yes, let's." The general raised an eyebrow and stepped away from the back of the building, raising her hands to begin another spell.

When he approached Cheyenne's side, Corian leaned toward her and waited for Maleshi to work her spell. "You okay?"

"I'm fine. Got attacked, ripped some war machines to pieces, and closed a new portal before it turned VCU into another reservation." The halfling folded her arms. "Just another day in the life, right?"

He hummed in consideration. "Maleshi said the ridge and the tunnelers showed up at the same time."

"Yeah. That's not supposed to happen, is it?"

"None of this is supposed to happen." Corian stroked his hairless chin. "It raises some serious questions. Most importantly, whether this portal was intentional or just another massive coincidence."

"Doesn't feel like a coincidence anymore." Cheyenne looked at the dome of silver light flashing into existence around them as Maleshi finished her spell. Through the shimmering magic, she could make out the outline of buildings around them, cars parked in the back lot, and a handful of people moving quickly around campus to either investigate the strange new damage to the lawn or search for anyone who needed help and guidance getting out of the area. "I'm assuming this is just one more illusion."

Maleshi pointed at the seemingly empty air right behind the building's back wall, and the war-machine scrapheap reappeared. "One of the better forms, if I do say so myself. As long as nobody gets it into their head that where we're standing would be the perfect place for them to hang out for a while, we'll be fine."

"What about you?" Cheyenne asked her. "You think the portal and these machines showed up together on purpose?"

"No." Maleshi headed toward the junk pile as Corian opened another portal within the illusioned dome that was making them invisible. "That would imply both of them came from the same source, and that's not possible. Which we've already covered."

Corian's portal opened beside the pile of dead O'gúl metal. "Not to mention that these machines have to go through the hands of someone Earthside before they're activated. It feels like a coincidence when you look at it like that, and at the same time, it doesn't feel like a coincidence at all."

Maleshi snorted as she picked up the side panel of a digger tank. "When that happens, there tends to be another hidden power in play."

Cheyenne frowned. "You mean, like someone else manipulating the timing? Not the loyalists controlling the machines or the Crown on the other side?"

The general tossed the metal panel through the portal, where it hit the cement with a clang. "Someone else, sure. Maybe. It's not always a person stepping in where the interference isn't welcome."

Dragging the end of one machine toward the portal, Corian paused, looked at the halfling, and chuckled. "Don't look so confused, kid. You understand the concept."

The halfling cocked her head and raised an eyebrow at him. "You're seriously trying to write this whole thing off as fate? Or just some other universal power doing whatever it wants without any explanation?"

"Fate's one way to look at it." Maleshi tossed two more handfuls of broken machinery through the portal. "And yes, there are other *universal powers* doing what they want, as you so succinctly put it."

Corian chuckled again and resumed dragging the mangled war machine toward the shimmering oval of dark light.

"I don't see how that's funny."

"It's just an interesting take, kid. You ever think about what those universal powers might be?"

"Not really, no." Cheyenne stepped out of the way as Maleshi levitated the larger fragments of black metal and threw them toward their next destination. "Seeing as this is the first time I've ever had to ask the question."

"You could call it fate," the general continued. "Or magic. Or whatever force selected the location for each individual Border portal around the world that has stood in the same place for centuries."

"Come on. Magic isn't sentient." Cheyenne snorted. "The portals aren't, either."

"Maybe. Or maybe they *are* in a way we simply don't understand." Maleshi shrugged and fixed the halfling with her green eyes. "But if we weren't convinced before that you're sitting at the center of a *lot* of sentient attention, whether or not we understand it, we sure as hell should be by now."

Cheyenne blinked at the nightstalker woman and ignored the rhythmic drag of the huge, battered war machine as Corian pulled it through the portal. "I get enough shit from the FRoE about all this being my fault. I don't need to hear it from you too."

"I'm not blaming you for anything, kid." Maleshi leaned back against the second tank and folded her arms. "This isn't a matter of blame or whose fault it is. I mean, other than the bitch on the O'gúl throne. That one's got a lot to answer for. I'm just talking about the grander design. Not fate necessarily. L'zar's proven pretty unequivocally that the impossible can be made possible, or at least that there are loopholes within what everyone else wants to believe is a fixed course. An inescapable eventuality, right?"

The halfling wrinkled her nose. "L'zar only broke through that prophecy of his because he didn't *do* anything."

"Ah, but it was still his choice." Maleshi stood from against the war machine as Corian reappeared from the other side of the portal and headed toward her. "We've all made our own choices, whether or not they achieved what we wanted."

"I didn't *choose* to be part of this," Cheyenne muttered.

Corian bent and grabbed the underside of the second tank. "You choose every day to *keep* being part of it."

"Well, yeah. But you guys are trying to tell me fate or magic or whatever has some grand design in all this. How can me choosing to do anything fall under fate?"

The general snorted. "Well, then what *would* you call it?"

"Free will." Cheyenne spread her arms and leaned toward the nightstalkers. "After other people made their mistakes and forced me into being part of them."

Corian's lips twitched, and he released the war machine again before straightening and fixing Cheyenne with an intense gaze, even from behind his human-illusion charm. "You think you're responding to mistakes, huh? Do you know *why* your parents are who they are?"

"My mom doesn't have anything to do with this."

"Oh, yes, she does." Maleshi pulled her loose black hair away from her face and tied it back. "She *was* the one who birthed you, after all."

"Go ahead." Corian clasped his hands behind his back and eyed the halfling. "I'll wait for your answer."

"My answer?" Cheyenne looked from one human-appearing rebel nightstalker to the other and scowled. *They've lost it.* "My parents are who they are because L'zar couldn't keep it in his pants and wanted to keep playing god over humans and prophecies. His *mistake*, and Bianca fell for it. Her *mistake*. Forced me into being here, and I'm doing what I can with what I've got."

"Well, that's an accurate assessment of yourself, at the very least." Corian lifted his chin and raised his eyebrows. "But neither of them made a mistake the night they met."

"Why, because I'm some prophecy child of L'zar's?" Cheyenne scoffed. "No. I'm just the one he didn't go after *before* I passed the trials. It could've been anyone else."

"L'zar Verdys didn't choose Bianca Summerlin at random, kid," Maleshi added. "I'd go so far as to say he didn't *choose* her at all."

"That's exactly my *point*." Cheyenne sighed. "I have no idea where either of you is trying to go with this."

"Sure. Must be pretty frustrating when you can't see it all laid out in front of you like a line of code or an elegant program."

The halfling shot Corian a sharp glare.

"I don't mean that as an insult, kid." He shrugged. "That's just the way you are. That's the way L'zar is too, except he *does* see it all laid out like that. Don't get me wrong; that drow can't do much more than point and click behind a computer, but when it comes to magic and the threads tying it all together, he's rewriting the entire program. When you live as long as we have, you start to see the patterns, Cheyenne. L'zar found a new one with your mother, but he didn't *choose* her."

Maleshi took a deep breath. "The choice was already made for both of them. He found her simply by following the trail left for him by some universal power. Just like you've been following the trail of figuring out what the hell you're doing and how to keep making your choices."

"All right." Cheyenne waved them both off. "I'm not gonna keep picking this apart. Whatever L'zar did, it's done. We're looking forward, right?"

Corian chuckled and bent to pick up the edge of the war machine again. "Always have."

"Uh-huh. I think living as long as you guys have makes you crazy." The halfling shoved her hands into the pockets of her trench coat and turned toward the lawn on the other side of the Computer Sciences building. "Shit. They're here."

"Hmm?" Maleshi walked toward her and leaned sideways until her hair brushed the silvery dome hiding them to peer around the corner. "Do your FRoE friends usually move this quickly?"

"They do when they think it's important."

Corian barked out a laugh. "Sounds like they learned their lesson after ignoring you about those kidnapped kids."

"Smartest move they've made so far." Cheyenne nodded at Maleshi. "I should at least make an appearance and remind them not to screw this one up."

"Cheyenne and her mastery over the subtle art of negotiation." The general elbowed Cheyenne gently in the side and snorted. "That's bound to be a fruitful conversation."

The half-drow ignored the jest and glanced sidelong at Corian. "This won't take long, so don't disappear on me. We're not finished."

"No, we aren't."

Cheyenne checked for passersby outside the silver dome of Maleshi's illusion, and when the coast was clear, she stepped through it and headed toward the scar of the portal ridge she'd managed to keep from opening. *After this, Matthew Thomas and I need to have another serious conversation. Attacking me is one thing. Showing up at a school crosses a whole new line.*

CHAPTER SEVENTY-SEVEN

The team of FRoE agents swarming around the thwarted Border portal on the VCU campus looked like any other natural disaster emergency response unit. *Except for Sir. He might as well have a giant target painted on him.*

When the FRoE official caught sight of Cheyenne Summerlin in full human form and her new black trench coat, he muttered something to one of his operatives, then stormed toward her. "At the very least, I will give you credit for not running away with your tail between your legs, halfling."

"No, that *would* make me look guilty, wouldn't it?" She stopped and folded her arms to let him come to her.

The man's thick salt-and-pepper mustache twitched when he realized that, and he grimaced as he closed the distance between them. "I'm still not convinced you didn't have everything to do with this shitshow on a college campus, and I sure as hell don't need you hanging around trying to make sure we know what we're doing. We do."

"I wouldn't have told you about this if I didn't think you'd be able to handle it. And there are plenty of other people I could've called."

He snorted. "Tell me what else you know about this."

"Nothing." Cheyenne shook her head and studied the FRoE agents moving gingerly around the giant holes in the ground and inspecting the upturned ridge of earth where she'd closed the portal. "It showed up, and I stopped it before it could get any worse. *They* put on a pretty good show for anyone else who's watching."

"Well, don't expect a goddam song and dance, halfling. They're doing their jobs, and right now, that means keeping any curious know-it-alls from thinking this was anything more than an isolated earthquake. Not magic." Sir looked over his shoulder at the two massive holes in the ground. "What the hell made those things?"

Can't tell him about the machines, not if the guy who hooked Matthew up with O'gúl loyalists is investing in the FRoE. Cheyenne shrugged. "I don't know. Those were there when I got out here."

He gave her a sharp look and raised an eyebrow. "Bullshit. You have eyes, halfling. No way you didn't see something that big popping up out of the ground."

"You know what? I was a *little* busy trying to keep a whole line of jagged black rock with a *portal* inside it from sprouting up out of the ground."

"Yeah, yeah. Pat yourself on the back and go get a cookie."

Cheyenne folded her arms. "So, how are you gonna keep the magic part of this under wraps?"

"That's none of your goddamn business."

"It is if you don't want to look like a complete idiot when the person who handled it can't back up your story."

Sir sniffed and wrinkled his nose, his mustache brushing the top of his lip. "We're calling it an earthquake."

"Oh, wow. How inventive."

"Yeah, we'll figure out how to work around the kinks. For all intents and purposes, my guys over there are studying some other phenomena with isolated earthquakes. If any more of those damn portals pop up, people are gonna get suspicious about the ground shaking for no scientifically plausible reason. I put a media person on this to stick a lid on it before it gets screwed up any worse."

"I hope that's good enough."

"Of course it's good enough." Sir pointed at her. "As long as you don't try to step into the middle of it after this."

"Hey, I'm leaving it in your hands. The rest is up to you, 'cause it's your job to keep these things under control."

The man blustered, his face turning an alarming shade of red as his dark, beady eyes blazed. "You tryin' to come down on me about how I do my job, halfling?"

Cheyenne stared blankly at him. "Anybody ever say you have serious anger issues?"

"I don't give a damn about my anger or your feelings. Twenty-one years I've been doing this, and not *once* did any of it blow up on me like this until *you* wiggled your way into my organization and started fucking shit up like a goddamn tapeworm. And you still won't give me all the pieces."

She gestured at the closed ridge and his men squatting around it and poking at the grass. "I gave you another portal, *and* I kept it from opening in one of the worst places to have an active portal."

"And I'm this close to making you rip it the hell back open so I can push you through it."

"Good luck." Cheyenne turned and headed back toward the side of the Computer Sciences building. *Well, I tried.*

"Uh-uh. You don't get to just walk away from me like that, halfling. We're not done here."

She kept walking and didn't say a thing.

Sir stormed after her. "You think you run the show, huh? Let me tell you something, halfling. The only reason you're still on this side of the Border is that I let you stay. I could snap my fingers and have you sent right back to that magical fucking fairyland, and then you'd be in deep shit. Hey, I'm talking to you."

The second he brought a hand down on Cheyenne's shoulder, she spun away and clamped her hand around his wrist. Sir's eyes widened at the strength of her grip before she tossed his hand away. "Is that a threat?"

"Not if I'm goddamn serious about it. I've done it before when I had to, halfling, and I've had it up to here with your bullshit, tossing us what *you* think we should know and saving the rest for yourself. I know you're not telling us everything."

"I don't have to tell you *anything*."

"And I don't have to keep putting up with this. You know how many halflings make it back across the Border once they get tossed over? *Zero.* It doesn't happen."

"Then I guess I must be the first, so good fucking luck trying to hold that one over my head, *Sir*. I've already made the crossing. Twice. You don't have a single thing to dangle in front of me anymore."

The man blinked at her, rage and surprise numbing him into silence.

Cheyenne glanced across the lawn. "Look, we both know I don't owe you anything anymore. I've more than covered that debt for your guys not killing me the first time we met, and I could walk away at any second. But I'm not, because you people have the resources to handle this kind of problem, and new Border portals aren't good for *anyone* on this side, especially if they're unregulated. That's open season for a way bigger mess. And maybe I'm the asshole for assuming this, but I'm fairly sure you don't want this to boil over and blow the lid on your operations and your entire organization. Right?"

Sir growled at her and finally took a step back. "I don't need to answer that stupid question."

"Yeah, because we both know the answer. Maybe try some meditation or something, huh? Your decision-making isn't all that great when you get this pissed off."

He snorted. "Says the halfling who storms into secret ops without a goddamn clue about what's going on."

Cheyenne shrugged and stuck her hands in her pockets. "Hasn't happened again, has it? Something I'm workin' on too."

She turned away from him and headed back behind the buildings.

Sir scratched his head and spun to watch his guys taking stock of the closed crack in the earth and the giant holes. "Meditating," he muttered. "That's the dumbest thing I ever heard. Wonder if that'd do anything for my shit blood pressure?"

Cheyenne shook her head as she left the high-ranking FRoE officer to do what he was there to do.

When she rounded the corner of the Computer Sciences building, Maleshi and Corian turned away from each other and nodded at her in greeting. The general clasped her hands behind her back and cleared her throat. Corian stared at the sky, then looked down at his shoes in the grass.

"Okay, obviously I interrupted something."

"It can wait." Maleshi gave her a thin, unconvincing smile.

"Yeah, I know." Cheyenne glanced from one nightstalker to the other. *Barged in on their private moment. Not weird at all.* "So, I'm doing this your way now and *telling* you that I need to go have another chat with Matthew Thomas."

"Who?" Corian finally met her gaze.

"The owner of Combined Reality, Inc." The halfling shrugged. "Sure, the name he gave me was good, but obviously it wasn't good enough. Syno or someone like him is still sending those machines after me. To the *school.*"

"Well, they do know exactly where to find you now, don't they?"

Maleshi shot Corian a scathing glance, and he shrugged.

"I get it. All on me because I started firing magic at the first one and it locked onto my signature. Thanks for the reminder. Now I'm trying to fix it. If the Crown's asshole loyalists don't give a shit about keeping these attacks in magicals-only areas, we need to make sure this doesn't happen again."

A slow smile spread across Corian's face. "You're starting to sound like you know what you're talking about."

"Seriously?"

"Oh, shut up." Maleshi rolled her eyes. "We're already behind you on that one, kid. You don't have to convince us of anything, but it's good to hear you're ready to go all-in and give this another shot."

"To be clear, 'all-in' for me means going to his apartment and *talking.* Got it? Seeing a couple of nightstalkers in his living room might paint a different picture for the guy, but I'm serious about giving him another chance to fix his own mistake. You don't have to be best friends with the guy, but let's at least *try* to play nice until we know for sure he's not jerking us around."

Corian spread his arms and dipped his head. "I have no problem with that plan."

"Good." Cheyenne pointed at Maleshi. "I'm talkin' to you too, General. No slitting throats."

Maleshi said, "I'm happy to let you call the shots, kid. Mind telling us why this human writing O'gúl-tech programs is worth the trouble of playing nice?"

"I don't need a reason, and he technically hasn't done anything wrong, not as far as I can tell."

The nightstalkers glanced at each other in surprise, then Corian stepped aside to conjure a portal.

"What's that about?"

Maleshi grinned at the halfling. "What?"

Cheyenne wagged her finger between the general and L'zar's right-hand magical. "That secret little look."

"Like I said, Cheyenne. It's good to see you taking a stand and leading with what you think is the right decision to make."

"It *is* the right decision."

"No one's arguing with you there."

Cheyenne looked the woman over, then shrugged. "Okay, then."

Corian's portal opened in front of them, and the trio quickly stepped through it into the center of Cheyenne's living room.

Ember yelped in surprise when she turned away from the kitchen island and saw them appear from thin air. "Stop *doing* that."

"Sorry, Em. Kind of a time-sensitive thing."

"No kidding." Ember set her glass down on the island and wheeled toward them. "Are you okay? I heard about the earthquake on campus. It's all over the news. They're saying nobody got hurt, which is great, but the whole thing sounds weird, the way they're talking about it. I didn't wanna call you in case you were, you know, busy dealing with something other than an earthquake, which is a lot more likely, now that I think about it."

The fae girl paused, rolling slowly to a stop on the hardwood floor and staring at the three magicals standing quietly in her living room.

"What? What happened?"

"It wasn't an earthquake."

Ember's large violet eyes widened. "Then what was it?"

"New portal ridge popping up the same time as two digger machines came at me. Right there on the lawn for everyone to see."

"Are you fucking *serious*?" Violet light flashed around Ember's body, and she sucked a deep breath through her teeth. "That asshole gave us the wrong name just to save his stupid *business,* and those loyalist bastards got one more chance to do even more damage. That's it. We need to go back over there right now."

"Yeah, that was already the plan, Em."

"I'm gonna rip him a new one. Let's go."

Maleshi pressed her lips together to hide a smile and Corian cleared his throat, sending Cheyenne a curious glance. "Honestly, I have to say I'm surprised the two of you don't share the same elevated opinion of taking it easy on this Matthew Thomas person."

"She's a little upset."

"I'm not upset, Cheyenne. I'm pissed." Ember slapped the armrests of her chair. "And screw being polite this time. You guys can just port us into his living room, right?"

"His living room?" Maleshi propped one elbow on the opposite arm around her waist and tapped two fingers on her lips. "I feel like we're missing something."

"Yeah, that's probably the part about Matthew being our neighbor across the hall." Cheyenne glanced sidelong at Ember, who seethed in her chair, glaring at the couch. "And that he has a thing for Ember."

"I don't give a shit about whatever else he has except for the information we need to get rid of these damn machines digging tunnels under Richmond." Ember's gaze whisked toward the nightstalkers. "So let's go. Open a portal. Then I'm gonna let him have it."

Corian dipped his head and got to work conjuring their direct doorway into Matthew Thomas' apartment.

Maleshi leaned toward Cheyenne. "When she says, 'Let him have it?'"

"I have no idea what that means." The halfling shook her head. "This is a first."

"I like your fae friend, kid."

"Yeah, me too."

"Stop complimenting me," Ember muttered, shooting them both a brief glance before turning a fiery glare upon the dark light of the portal opening in front of them. "I'm trying to stay angry."

"Oh." Maleshi chuckled. "Well, if she has to try, I'm not worried about it."

Cheyenne shrugged and stared at the portal. "She *did* close the portal straight from Ambar'ogúl."

"Yes. There is that."

CHAPTER SEVENTY-EIGHT

Ember wheeled into the portal with a quick, furious shove. The violet light illuminating her hands and the wheelchair gave her an added boost of speed before she navigated around Matthew Thomas' loveseat with a drow-magic burn hole in the upholstery. "Matthew!"

A thump, the clatter of falling dishes, and the resulting shatter of glass across the floor came from the kitchen.

"What the hell?" He stormed around the wall from the rest of his apartment and stopped. "Ember. Jesus, what is that?" Matthew staggered back when he saw the dark oval portal hovering in midair inside his front door.

Corian and Maleshi walked through next, both having done away with their illusion charms to meet the owner of ThomasSafe in their true forms.

Matthew pointed at them and took another step back. "You're *cats*."

"Always the first observation," Corian muttered.

"At least he can see."

Cheyenne emerged from the portal behind them and folded her arms. "We need to talk."

"You know what? Take a seat." Ember pointed at the high-top dining table around the corner and the matching set of chairs that looked more like bar stools. "Sounds like you need a minute to find your voice, so go ahead and get comfortable. I'll talk."

"Ember." Matthew spread his arms and gazed at her with terrified eyes. "I didn't do anything."

"Now!"

"Shit. Yeah, yeah." He spun first one way then the other before remembering his dining table was six feet behind him. Stumbling toward it, Matthew tried to look back over his shoulder and watch where he was going at the same time. The urge to keep an eye on the strange magicals in his home won, and he staggered back, both hands lifted in surrender. "I don't know why you people just showed up like this."

He yelped when he backed into the closest chair and struggled to keep from knocking it over as he hastily pulled it away from the table.

Cheyenne raised an eyebrow while playing with the silver activator coil in her jacket pocket. *If that's an act, it's way better than last time.*

Ember cocked her head and stared at their neighbor. "I'm only gonna wait so long for you to sit."

Stammering wordlessly, Matthew scrambled onto the high dining chair. Twice, he almost slipped off, but he clutched the sides of the gray-painted wooden seat and gulped. "What is this?"

"This is what happens when you screw around with the wrong magicals, okay?" Ember pointed at Cheyenne and the nightstalkers without turning around to look. "They checked out that name you gave us—Syno. Turns out, the guy set traps at his locations and didn't leave a whole lot behind for us to work with."

"What?"

"He's gone, Matthew. And all his gear and his tech and the machines *you* helped him power with your fancy little program are gone too. That makes it look a lot like someone tipped him off about having visitors."

"Ember, I swear to you, I didn't say a word to Syno. I gave you that information to *help*."

"Well, it wasn't very helpful. It was the *opposite* of helpful."

"I don't understand."

"You don't understand because you don't stop talking!" Ember thrust a pink-tinged finger at him and leaned forward in her chair as she gazed at him. "Shut your mouth and listen."

Maleshi looked slowly over her shoulder at Cheyenne and raised her eyebrows, and the halfling shrugged. *Ember's badass is showing. Maybe we didn't need backup.*

"You wasted our time with *one* name that didn't get us anywhere, *and* you put thousands of innocent people at risk because you're worried about *incurring losses.* Two of those machines running on *your* programs showed up at VCU this morning."

Matthew stopped holding his breath and started panting. "What?"

"Yeah. Popped right out of the ground for everyone to see and started attacking people."

Cheyenne forced herself not to laugh. *Technically just Maleshi and me, but points for stretching the truth.*

"The only reason no one got hurt or killed in what they all think was a random and unexplainable earthquake was that Cheyenne was there to stop it." Ember grabbed the wheels and moved toward him until her knee bumped his sock. "We were nice last time. You need to give us the names of every single magical client you have who's been paying you for programs, software, tech support, supplies, or whatever the hell else you give them. All their information. Everything. And just in case you don't think I'm dead serious about this, take another good look at the nightstalkers standing behind me."

Maleshi grinned when Matthew's blue eyes settled on her. On cue, she lifted a hand tufted with black fur, and her glinting, blade-like claws shot out with a slicing hiss.

"What the fuck?" He stared at the deadly weapons and swallowed thickly. "You wouldn't just let that thing attack me."

"Not sure who you're calling 'thing,'" Maleshi tilted her head. "But I promise you I don't need Ember's permission for anything. I *am* here to back her up, though."

"This is insane." Matthew's foot slipped off the rung of the chair as he tried to push himself farther against the backrest. "You're strong-arming me. That's what this is, right? Hey, it's not the first time you people have tried something like this. Hell, it *is* definitely the scariest." He swallowed again and cleared his throat. "I can't in good conscience just give up that kind of sensitive information, not without proof."

Maleshi let out a low whistle. "Somebody's got their priorities mixed up."

With his hands clasped behind his back, Corian dipped his head toward Matthew and muttered, "We can change that."

"I said no." Cheyenne pointed at the nightstalker man before stepping into the dining room. "You want proof, Matthew? Sure. I'll give you proof. Where's your computer?"

"My what?"

"Come on, don't make me explain to *you* what a computer is." She pulled the activator coil from her pocket and stuck it behind her ear. Her eyelids fluttered as the tech synced with her magic and her vision, then looked around his apartment. She didn't need the activator's blinking lights to tell her that was his laptop sitting on the granite-topped island in the kitchen, but she couldn't mistake it for anything else.

Matthew tried to slide off the chair. "Wait, wait, wait."

"Sit!" Ember pointed at him, and purple light burst from her fingertip.

Matthew choked and scrambled back up in the chair again. "Cheyenne, seriously. You can't just show up in my apartment and start going through my things. This is a huge violation of personal space. Privacy. Basic rights. Hell, this is illegal."

"Yeah, what you're doing should be too. Too bad nobody knows anything about it, huh?" Cheyenne stepped around the kitchen island, her shoes crunching on the shattered glass in front of the sink, and opened his laptop.

"You might as well stop right there. I'll give you what you want if you can prove those other magic people used my system to threaten the school. Otherwise, you won't get anywhere with my computer. I've got passwords on everything."

The halfling looked up from the black screen as it cycled on and shot him a deadpan stare. "Please. You can't keep me out."

"This is ridiculous!" Matthew tried to go after her again before remembering the fae's finger pointed at his face and the nightstalker woman's deadly claws still extended from her fingertips. "What do you think you're gonna find in there, huh?"

"Your proof." Cheyenne studied the log-in screen, her eyes darting back and forth as the activator fed her what she needed to sign into Matthew Thomas' private laptop. *If I could take a screenshot of code, I better be able to pull up a lot more than that.* The log-in screen disappeared, replaced by his desktop screen and the background image. "Oh, hey. Good-lookin' dog."

"Yeah, she's my mom's. Wait a minute." Matthew's eyes bulged. "How did you—"

"Shh." Cheyenne held up a finger for him to wait. Her activator prompted her with every command she needed, and it only took a second of thought before the tech piece pulled up a mostly circular view in her vision of the grass right outside the Computer Sciences building on campus. It was a still frame, but the tips of both tunnel machines' spiraling noses were unmistakable. "Oh, yeah, here we go."

"What are you talking about?" Matthew's voice broke. "What are you doing? Hey, what is she doing?"

"Relax, will ya?" Maleshi shot him a playful frown. "If she's not throwing attack spells at your face, you've got nothing to worry about."

His mouth opened and closed soundlessly.

Cheyenne grinned when the activator prompted her with the option to download the video of her fight with the war machines onto Matthew's laptop. *I knew it. This thing does it all.* She accepted the prompt and had to log in again with an access code on the laptop, also provided by the activator, and hit download.

"All right, neighbor." She slid the laptop off the counter and carried it toward the table. Wiggling her eyebrows, she set the laptop down and snorted when he flinched away from her. "I did not expect you to get this jumpy. Just hit play and everything will be perfectly clear."

"What?" He glanced at the screen and the still frame at the beginning of the video. "Did you just download something?"

"Clearly."

"Great. I'm gonna have to run a system scan after this. Do you know how much valuable and sensitive information is on this laptop? Jesus. And you just took some random file and stuck it on my—ah!" He jerked away when Cheyenne leaned toward him, and she gave him a warning look before stabbing her finger down on the space bar.

"Watch the damn video, Matthew."

Slowly, he focused on the circular view of Cheyenne's fight with the war machines and the sprouting portal ridge. She'd scrubbed the audio on purpose, but it didn't matter. Everything Cheyenne had seen less than an hour before played out exactly as she remembered it on the thirteen-inch laptop screen.

Matthew's mouth fell open when a slashing, whirling Maleshi Hi'et came into view, complete with her four-inch claws and sparks bursting from the black metal diggers.

Corian leaned toward the general and muttered, "Did you know she was recording that?"

"No, Corian. I don't generally ask if a drow halfling plans on recording an emergency response to something like *that*." Maleshi squinted. "My guess is the activator."

"Didn't have that feature last time I used one."

She snorted. "The last piece of O'gúl tech you used was as much of a dinosaur as you are."

The recording ended with the final sputtering explosion of the last machine that ended the magical battle. Cheyenne propped her forearm on the dining room table and leaned on it. "There you go, man. Proof."

Matthew cleared his throat. "I don't believe it."

Ember shook herself out of her awe after watching the whole thing and folded her arms. "You need to start believing it right now, and then you need to give us those names."

"No, I had no idea this is what my system was being used for. This isn't what they told me."

"You mean, the O'gúl loyalists smuggling war machine parts over the Border, demanding to do business with you and refusing to take no for an answer were supposed to be the good guys? They did a number on you, didn't they?"

"They told me it was to help the other ones." Matthew scrunched up his face. "The other magicals."

"Dude."

He spun in the chair and looked down at Ember. "I am so sorry."

"Stop apologizing and give us what we need to stop this from happening again." The fae girl nodded. "That's the only thing that matters right now."

"Yeah. Okay, yeah. I can't believe this." Shaking his head, Matthew pulled his laptop closer and started clicking through files to get to the information he wanted. "I mean, I don't believe everything I see in recordings like that until I've had a chance to go through the data and look for tampering. You know, like video editing."

"I'm well aware of what you mean." Cheyenne glanced at Maleshi and Corian. Corian glanced away and turned to study the rest of Matthew's apartment so he wouldn't laugh.

"But that *she* was in there." Matthew gestured at Maleshi without looking away from his screen. "You can't doctor something like that."

"Well, feel free to pick apart that video file all you want." Cheyenne drummed her fingers on the table. "You won't find anything."

"I know, I know. I believe you." He opened a file and scanned through it. "Who am I sending this to?"

Corian stepped forward and set his cell phone on the table beside the laptop. "That server address, if you don't mind."

"Yeah. No problem." Matthew's fingers flew across the keyboard, and in under a minute, he jerked his hands away from the laptop and leaned back. "There. It's in there. Everything I have, I promise."

Ember shrugged when he looked at her. "You understand why we can't just take your word for it without checking."

"Absolutely. You guys go do what you have to do. I'll deal with this on my end too."

"By doing what?" Corian took his phone back and slipped it into his pocket.

"I can shut the whole thing down. Scrap the project. At the very least, deactivate the whole thing and archive it." Matthew lifted both hands and shook his head. "I don't want anything to do with it at this point."

"That's good to hear." Cheyenne nudged her fist against his shoulder and nodded. "Thanks for not making this as hard as it could've been."

He glanced at Maleshi's claws and swallowed. "Uh-huh."

The general chuckled. "Oh, don't look at me like that. I'm not the one you have to worry about."

"Yeah, it's a good thing we didn't bring Lumil along," Cheyenne added. "She would've been so disappointed."

"Thank you for your time, Matthew." Corian nodded and stepped away from the table to summon another portal.

Cheyenne and Maleshi walked with him and waited for the

doorway of dark light to open. Matthew glanced at Ember and finally got the guts to slide off the chair. "Ember, I had no idea."

"Not right now. I'm waiting to find out whether you're lying about it all over again."

"I didn't know it was this serious."

"We already had this conversation." Ember wheeled toward the other magicals and didn't look back. "I don't wanna have it again. Ever. If we don't show up in your living room in the next few days, it's pretty safe to say we got everything we needed. Thanks."

Corian's portal opened, and the nightstalkers stepped aside to let the fae girl wheel through and back into her apartment. Maleshi looked at Matthew and gave him a quick wink before disappearing. Corian didn't bother to say anything before he stepped through, and Cheyenne paused to point at her neighbor. "You can keep that video, but I'd be careful about letting anyone else see it. We can call a truce if you want."

"Yeah." Matthew nodded vacantly. "I'm cool with that."

"Sweet." The halfling stepped through the portal behind her friends, and the dark light shrank in midair.

Matthew stared at the empty space in his living room where they'd all just been standing and ran a hand through his hair. "I'm done taking clients on family recommendation. That's for damn sure."

CHAPTER SEVENTY-NINE

"Okay." Cheyenne spun to face the nightstalkers and spread her arms. "So, we wait for Persh'al to tell us where to go next, and then we hit hard. How long does that usually take?"

"Persh'al's fast, so we'll know where to start by the end of the day." Corian chuckled. "He's not happy that you cracked that tech from the last machine in less than twenty-four hours, but it won't stop him from getting the job done on his end. But you need to wait for my call, got it? We have to be careful now."

"Right. I'll wait for your call, and then I'll go in with you."

"No. I'm talking about the call when it's time to make the crossing again."

"What?" Cheyenne frowned. "When's that gonna be?"

"No clue. Waiting for L'zar."

"So, I'm out of the game now with these war machines? Just like that?"

The nightstalker shrugged. "Sorry, kid."

"No, no. That's not how this works." She snatched the activator coil from behind her ear and shoved it into her coat pocket. "I'm not the drow puppet who gets to fight off all the things coming after me just so I can wait around for everyone else who thinks they're smarter than me to get the rest of the job done afterward. I'm *in* this, Corian. I signed up. Made the crossing and everything."

"Yes, you did."

"And *you're* the one who told me not to keep sitting on the sidelines and to get involved."

He dipped his head. "I did. And now I'm telling you to wait for my call."

"Unbelievable."

"L'zar's almost ready to move. I can't tell you exactly when, but I know it'll be soon, and when he *is* ready, we need to make sure you're not busy fighting off something else coming for you. As far as we know, the loyalists controlling those machines aren't yet aware that you and Ember live in the same apartment. The wards we put up keep their systems from tracing anything back to you as long as you're here *inside* those wards. We need you to stay put."

"'Stay put.' What does that even mean?"

Corian was too busy conjuring another portal to answer her immediately. When he did, he raised his eyebrows and shrugged, one tufted ear twitching. "It means you stay in your apartment until you hear from me. As I understand it, you don't have any other obligations until Monday morning—assuming your school is up and running again after today's little incident, of course."

Cheyenne glared at him. "And what happens if L'zar's not ready to move before Monday?"

"Well, if that's the case, we'll reassess things when we get there. This is the safest place for you right now. Just get comfy." Without another word, Corian walked through his portal and disappeared.

Maleshi paused and gave Cheyenne a sympathetic smile. "You know he's right, and no, that doesn't mean you have to be happy about it. We're almost ready, kid. This close to the final step, things have a tendency to get dicey. So be ready."

"I've *been* ready."

"I know." Maleshi nodded at Ember and vanished through the portal two seconds before it popped out of existence.

Cheyenne clenched her fists and leaned against the back of the couch. Ember rubbed her forehead. "I didn't expect them to put you on house arrest after what happened this morning. I mean, at least it's a great apartment with a giant TV."

Shaking her head, Cheyenne stepped around the couch and headed for the stairs to the mini loft. "I didn't spend the first eighteen years of my life cooped up on Bianca Summerlin's estate just so I could let a couple two-legged cats imprison me in my own apartment."

"Right." Ember snorted. "Couldn't've said it better myself."

"I don't get why they can't just tell me what L'zar's trying to do. How much readier can we be? I mean, besides the whole part about having to go take down a cache of activated war machines." Cheyenne walked quickly up the iron stairs and sat in the chair in front of her wobbly desk.

"Sounds like they just wanna keep you safe."

"Yeah, *that's* obvious."

"Well, think about it. They've been fighting this fight against the Crown for hundreds of years, and then you come along, and you're half-human. That on its own is enough to make things even more complicated."

Cheyenne leaned sideways and met her friend's gaze through the iron bars of the mini-loft's rail. "You're telling me things I already know, Em. I'm hardly the most complicated variable in this whole thing."

"Ha." Ember wiped the smile off her face and cleared her throat. "Not being the *most* complicated doesn't make the situation *less* complicated. They don't wanna lose you before they get the chance to use you."

"Yeah, I get it." The halfling slumped in her chair and stared at the monitor's power button. "And I'm not gonna lie and say I don't end up getting into a whole bunch of trouble every time I go out to do something completely unrelated. So, full disclosure, I'm gonna sit here and sulk for ten minutes. When that's over, I guess we should have someone else do our grocery shopping and bring it on up, I guess."

"Already done." Ember grinned when Cheyenne looked at her again, then spun and wheeled toward the kitchen. "FYI, we have a lot more than pickles in the fridge now."

"Thanks, Em."

"Yep. Guess I better call the PT clinic too and tell them no appointment today. Honestly, I'm a lot less worried about missing a session than I was four days ago."

Despite her frustration, Cheyenne smiled and folded her arms. "Think that has anything to do with you standing on your own yesterday?"

"Maybe. Or maybe just the whole Ember-has-magic thing. I'm cool with it." She opened the fridge and moved the contents aside with quick bursts of purple light, searching for a snack. "Might be because my personal driver can't leave her apartment."

"If you hired someone to buy and deliver our groceries, I'm sure you can find someone to drive you to your appointment. Sorry it can't be me."

"Okay, first of all, I am tired of everybody apologizing to me. And more importantly, there's no way in hell I'm gonna call a random driver to come pick me up and drive me to my appointment and back, not after I've been riding around in that Panamera. Are you kidding?"

Cheyenne laughed. "Yeah, it's pretty hard to go back after that."

"You have no idea. From where I'm sitting, the passenger seat is *way* better. I don't have to focus on anything but the ride." The fae girl pulled out her phone to call the PT clinic and cancel her appointment.

Ten seconds into the call, Cheyenne's stomach growled furiously and didn't stop when she shifted in her chair. "Fine."

She stood and walked down from the loft, shrugging off her fancy new trench coat to toss it over the back of the couch.

"Oh, yeah. I'll be there on Monday. Not a problem, just had some transportation issues today. You can tell Dr. Boseley that I'm still feeling great. Yep. Thanks." Ember dropped her phone in her lap and looked toward the mini-loft. "I don't know why."

She jumped when Cheyenne opened the fridge door behind her, spun her wheelchair around quickly, and frowned. "Okay, let's make a rule about not zipping around at drow-speed inside. It's super creepy."

Grinning, Cheyenne pulled out a cup of yogurt and shut the door. "I just walked."

"Well, then you're quiet, and it's still creepy." Ember eyed the yogurt and wrinkled her nose. "Can you grab me one of those?"

"Yep."

"As I was saying, I expected the clinic to put up more of a fight about me not making it in for a third session."

"Well, Dr. Boseley knows what you are. Hey, maybe she even saw you stand up out of that chair and blast that creepy whoever-they-were back through the portal yesterday." Cheyenne tossed her the yogurt cup and shut the fridge. "She's probably not worried about it."

"Right." Ember pulled two spoons from the drawer and sent one sailing across the kitchen toward Cheyenne in a glow of violet light. "I'm not either."

Cheyenne plucked the spoon from the air, grinned at it, then pointed the utensil at her friend. "Not with neat little tricks like that. Nothing's stopping you now."

"Yeah, I'm getting pretty good at this magic thing a lot faster than I thought I would."

"Huh. Imagine that." The halfling stuck a heaping spoonful of yogurt in her mouth. "Almost like you were born with it or something."

"Okay, smartass."

Cheyenne turned with her yogurt toward the living room. "So, since neither of us is going anywhere, now what?"

"Movies. Lots of movies." Ember joined her roommate in the living room and parked her chair at the end of the coffee table. "We should do a marathon, like, some series that has more than four movies. Just blast through the whole thing."

The entry table whirred as the TV rose from its hidden compartment. Cheyenne held out her hand and wiggled her fingers at the remote. "If we're doing that, I'm picking the series."

"Great." Ember handed over the remote. "And you haven't seen much of anything, huh? The possibilities are endless."

The halfling stared at her friend with a surprised smile. "You are way too excited about this."

"Come on. I'm excused from grad school this semester, I don't have a job, and you're on magical house arrest. It's not like I have a lot of options."

"Yeah, that makes it sound great."

As Cheyenne scrolled through the movie options on the TV, Ember's phone rang, and she frowned at the number before answering. "Hello?"

"Ember, hi. It's Marsil. From the clinic."

"Yeah, I know. Hi."

"Hey. I'm calling because Dr. Boseley saw the note in her schedule today that you canceled your appointment. She wanted me to reach out and make sure everything's okay."

"Oh. Yeah, I'm fine. Just had a few things come up. Can't make it in."

"Everything's all right with Cheyenne too?"

Ember clenched her eyes shut and tried not to laugh. Cheyenne snorted. "She's fine. Just a little busy with some stuff if you know what I mean."

"Absolutely. Listen, if there's anything Dr. Boseley and I can do to help, don't hesitate to reach out. We're here."

"You're not just talking about PT, are you?"

Marsil laughed. "Correct. I mean that in the broader sense of 'stuff.' If you know what I mean."

Ember chuckled. "Sure do. We're good for now, but thanks for the offer."

"You bet. See you Monday, then."

"Okay." She hung up the phone, frowned, and tossed it on the coffee table. "So that was Marsil."

"Yeah, I know." Cheyenne smiled crookedly at the TV as she flipped through the movies. "I heard the conversation."

"Of course you did." Ember shook her head and dug into her yogurt again. "It's a little weird that I'm getting calls from my physical therapist's assistant about *you*."

"Only as weird as it was for them to be invited to that ceremony yesterday." Cheyenne shrugged. "Or as weird as anything else happening right now."

"You don't have a problem with that weird overlap into our personal lives?"

"Not really. Marsil and I are cool. The more friends we have over here, the better, right?"

"Huh." Ember narrowed her eyes. "You're sounding like a different halfling these days, you know that?"

"Why? Because I'm cool with a goblin named Marsil who calls himself George?"

"Okay, admittedly, that's a little surprising, but mostly it's that you don't seem to automatically hate everyone anymore." Ember laughed. "I mean, you just said having more friends is better."

Cheyenne rolled her eyes. "Yeah, well, I'm not trying to form a posse or anything. L'zar took care of that on his own. I don't know, maybe I'm just evolving."

"I wouldn't go *that* far."

"And *I'm* not a big fan of going deep into my psychological maturity right now. I'm trying to pick a movie."

"Uh-huh." Ember stared at the screen and whispered, "The *friendly* Goth Drow."

"Shut up."

CHAPTER EIGHTY

By 6:30 p.m., Cheyenne had had enough. "Why won't he give me a straight answer? Yes or no. How hard is that?"

Ember finished the last of the premade chicken casserole they'd had for dinner and set her plate on the coffee table. "Maybe 'cause you've been texting him nonstop for the last four hours."

"It hasn't been four hours." Cheyenne scrolled back through her texts to Persh'al and wrinkled her nose. "Okay, so I lost track of time."

"You're not making things any easier by annoying the crap out of him."

"*I'm* the one annoying *him?*" The halfling snorted. "I don't think so. If he'd quit giving me half-assed answers that don't tell me anything, I'd stop asking."

Her phone buzzed with a new text, and she opened it immediately.

'We're handling it. Positive results. I'm trying to work, so leave me alone.'

"What's it say?"

Cheyenne tossed her phone into her lap and thumped her head back on the cushion of the fully extended recliner. "That he thinks he's better than me 'cause he has a warehouse in DC and knows how to track magical frequencies."

Ember barked out a laugh. "That was *not* what he said."

"You don't know."

"Okay. Give me your phone."

"What? No. I need it."

Holding out her hand, Ember waved for the halfling to cough it up. "Not right now. If it rings, you'll hear it, but you need to get your head out of Persh'al's ass and try to think about something else."

Cheyenne blinked at her. "Did you just tell me to—"

"Yep. Come on."

"No."

"Cheyenne, give me the damn phone. 'Cause *I'm* tired of you texting him all the time."

The halfling laughed and shook her head. "Thanks, Mom, but if I want to annoy the troll, that's my choice."

Ember rolled her eyes and pointed at the cell phone. It lit up with violet light and darted into her outstretched hand.

"Whoa, hey! Not cool."

"Agreed."

"Ember."

The fae girl slipped the phone between her knees and pointed at it. "See? I'm not gonna go through your stuff."

"Oh, yeah. That was my main concern, that you might find something I didn't want you to see."

"Whatever. It's here. You need to quit obsessing."

Cheyenne stared at her phone, her lower jaw working. "You realize I have magic too, right?"

"Yep. Which you haven't even tried to use, so I'm thinking you wanted someone to take your phone. It's okay, you don't have to thank me. Being your best friend is a full-time job."

Closing her eyes, Cheyenne snorted a laugh. "I don't have anything to say to that."

"You're welcome."

The halfling tried to pay attention to their third movie in a row but couldn't get into it. "I don't get how so many people can spend all day watching stuff like this. Don't you get bored?"

"Nope." Ember snapped her fingers. "I'd love some popcorn, though."

"You put popcorn on the grocery list?"

"Duh. Only a giant family-size bag, but it's popcorn, and it gets rid of all the work involved in popping it myself."

"Yes. Sticking a bag in a microwave is such a complicated process. It takes real skill."

Ember tilted her head and gave her friend an exasperated glance. "It's not as cool as this." She raised her finger, and a purple light flashed in the kitchen. The cabinet door opened with a bang, and a giant resealable bag of popcorn sailed across the apartment to drop onto the couch beside her. Ember glanced down at the bag and shrugged. "Okay, I was going for my hand, but the couch is close enough."

"You're getting creative."

The bag rustled and squealed as Ember pulled it open before shoving her hand inside. "By necessity, halfling. Why push myself all the way into the kitchen when I can use magic to bring the snacks to me?"

"I don't have an answer for that. Also, I'm a little upset that I never thought about taking advantage of my magic for floating popcorn bags and stealing other people's phones."

"You've been a little busy. I get it." Ember stuffed a handful of popcorn into her mouth and crunched noisily. "Want some?"

"No, thanks." Cheyenne put the recliner back in its normal position and stood. "I can only take so many hours of vegging out in the middle of the day."

"It's not much different from sitting in front of a computer screen all the time."

"It's definitely different, Em. Nothing wrong with wanting to turn your brain off sometimes and watch things, but that's not what I do on a computer."

"Oh, that's right. You keep busy with all that super-important, highly secret halfling-hacker stuff."

"Pretty much."

Ember laughed and turned back to the TV. "Well, don't let me stop you."

"Wasn't planning on it." Cheyenne raced up to the mini-loft and slumped in the chair. *If Persh'al won't tell me what the hell's going on with those machine-driving idiots, I'll just have to look around and see if anyone else picked up on something. Just like Corian said, right? Follow the trail.*

She snorted and powered Glen up before punching the power

button on the monitor. Once she'd logged in, she got her VPN up and running, double-checked her security, and dove into the dark web again. The Borderlands forum didn't have much in the way of remotely interesting topic threads this time. Cheyenne scrolled down through title after ridiculous thread title.

I need help with a tracking spell to catch my boyfriend cheating on me.

Please advise in the proper preparation of human wafflecakes.

Did anyone else get the shits from Osna's grog this week?

"Damn." With a wry laugh, she shook her head and kept moving down. *If this is the biggest problem right now, Corian must be keeping their raids squeaky clean. Or at least silent.*

A private message popped up in the corner of her screen. "Who is this?"

EyeSee4U: I have something for you. Feel free to stop by if you're interested.

Cheyenne grimaced. *If this is some rando asshat trying to come on to me, he picked the wrong chick on the darknet.*

Squinting at the unfamiliar username, she leaned toward the rail. "Hey, Em."

"Yeah."

"Think you could toss me my jacket?"

Ember stared at the TV. "You want the fae in a wheelchair to get your jacket for you and throw it up into the loft?"

"Well, when you say it like that, it makes me sound like an asshole."

The trench coat lifted off the back of the couch in violet light and sailed up toward the mini-loft, where it came to a stop against Cheyenne's face with a rustle of thick fabric. She slowly pulled it down into her lap and stared at Ember. "I could say a lot right now, but I'm choosing just to say thank you."

The fae girl snorted. "You're welcome."

Pursing her lips through a smile, Cheyenne untangled her jacket and reached into the pocket for the activator coil. Then she hung the trench coat over the rail and attached the tech piece behind her ear. Her monitor instantly lit up with hundreds of code lines scrolling across her vision, and she focused on the private message from Anonymous Creeper.

This thing would've saved me so much time if I had it for Corian's dumbass scavenger hunt.

Cheyenne's finger swiped automatically in the air as she selected the different commands the activator gave her. In twenty seconds, the thing had pulled up a map of the central area of Richmond, and a red dot pulsed over a building she recognized.

"Ha. Apparently, the Oracle's good for more than cryptic prophecies, if that's what that was."

"Huh?"

"Nothing, Em." Cheyenne scrunched her nose. *I need to quit talking to myself.*

She tossed aside the map of Gúrdu's neighborhood in her vision and typed a reply to EyeSee4U.

ShyHand71: I had no idea you knew how to use a computer, raug.

Hitting the Enter key, she sat back. The reply was almost instant.

EyeSee4U: I know a lot of things. Specifically, the contents of one or two messages I think you'll want to hear.

ShyHand71: What kind of messages?

EyeSee4U: The kind that needs to be delivered in person. No offering necessary, hidna. Call it a freebie.

Cheyenne chuckled. *The raug Oracle wants to give me a free prophecy.*

ShyHand71: Is this the kind of message that can wait, or are we on a time limit?

EyeSee4U: That's for you to decide. I'm just the messenger.

The halfling dropped her hands from the keyboard and scoffed. *You think you're clever, don't you?* She glanced down at Ember, still glued to the TV, then at her phone nestled between her friend's knees. "Screw it."

ShyHand71: I'll head your way, then.

EyeSee4U: You know where to find me.

The message box disappeared from her screen before she could click out of it.

"Huh. Raug." Cheyenne left the Borderlands forum, closed down the dark web browser and her VPN, and decided to leave Glen running just in case. *Better sync it first.*

As soon as she thought it, the activator prompted her with the commands to send all Glen's alerts to a single number. When that was done in under ten seconds, she pulled off the activator, grimacing at the pinch behind her eyes. Grabbing her jacket, she headed down the stairs. "Em, can you do me a favor?"

"Depends."

The halfling snorted in surprise. "If you get any alerts from Glen, will you forward them to me?"

Ember tore herself away from the TV as Cheyenne shrugged into her trench coat. "What? Where are you going?"

"Got an invitation for a free raug prophecy."

"Didn't Corian—"

"Yeah, he did, but I can't handle just sitting around without being able to leave."

Ember shot her a curious frown. "You do that all the time."

"Sure, but it's different when I know I can step out whenever I want. Not a big fan of being locked up."

"Guess there's one thing that doesn't run in the drow family."

Cheyenne pointed at her friend. "Funny. Wanna come with me?"

"To see a raug? No, thanks. I've had enough crazy for one day."

"Okay." Cheyenne plucked her cell phone from between the fae girl's knees and stuck it pointedly in her jacket pocket. "What about any kind of charm that keeps my magic on the down-low while I'm out?"

Ember smiled at the halfling. "Are you reading my mind, or am I reading yours?"

"I don't know. That depends on what you say next."

"I was already working on it. Come here."

Cheyenne leaned toward her friend, and Ember whipped her arm back to land a vicious slap on the halfling's upper arm. A burst of purple light and tingling energy raced across Cheyenne's arm and chest. She straightened and rubbed her arm. "Ow. Did you have to slap it onto me?"

"No, the slap was for luck, and because we both know you probably shouldn't leave, but I can't stop you. By the way, if you use any magic or go drow mode, the charm's done. Then magicals will be able to find you."

"Then I won't power up anything." Cheyenne grinned. "Thanks. Oh, and by the way, let me know if you get any notifications, yeah?"

"From Glen?" Ember looked at the back of the computer tower in the mini-loft. "Why would they come to me?"

"'Cause I just synced them to your phone."

"You have a phone too."

Cheyenne cocked her head. "Yes I do, and it's back in my possession, thank you. I have a few small searches running. Just tiny stuff I put up real quick in case anything pops up about those war machines, their handlers, whether or not Corian's managed to take care of the problem."

"Seriously? You're monitoring *them* now?"

"Yes. And if you're thinking about lecturing me on the morality of said monitoring, I'll quickly remind you that Corian's been spying on me my entire life." Cheyenne grinned. "This doesn't come close to paying him back for that."

"Okay." Ember quickly shook her head. "But why did you hook your fancy computer up to *my* phone?"

"I'm going out to get a prophecy, Em. Something tells me an unexpected alert would ruin the mood. Who knows? Maybe even get in the way of whatever this raug thinks I should hear." Cheyenne stuck her hands in her pockets and paused. "Unless you're totally against the idea."

"Stop." Ember said, "I'll monitor your spy alerts from the computer you named Glen."

"Thank you."

"Wait, but what if there's something important? Texting you would interrupt you just as much as an alert."

"Right." Cheyenne fingered the keyring in her pocket and headed for the door. "But I trust your judgment. Only text me if something's life-or-death, okay? I mean, if anything even shows up."

Ember squinted at her friend. "Why do I have the feeling you set all that up just to distract me from the rest of my movie marathon?"

With a sharp laugh, Cheyenne opened the door. "I trust you. And I kind of like the idea of having a fae partner in crime keeping an eye on things for me."

"Uh-huh."

"And yeah, maybe you'll find another hobby you like a little more than watching movies all day."

Ember pointed at her. "If I want to watch movies all day, I'll watch movies all day. I'm a grown-ass adult."

"True. Then think of it as payback for magically stealing my phone. Bye." Cheyenne slipped into the hall and pulled the door quickly shut behind her. Ember's laughter followed her down the hall toward the elevators.

CHAPTER EIGHTY-ONE

Cheyenne pulled her black Panamera to the curb outside Gúrdu's apartment building. The high-pitched chirp when she pressed the automatic lock made her smile as she headed down the walkway to the building's front door. Her smile faded a little when she glanced at the browning grass in the corner formed by the walkway and the sidewalk. *That's where Maleshi puked her guts out. Great memory to bring up, coming into this.*

Two chickens clucked somewhere behind the building, but the raug's irritated magical neighbor didn't have an objection to the noise today. Cheyenne pulled open the grime-coated glass door and walked down the breezy hallway of the rundown apartment building. When she reached Gúrdu's front door, she paused for a quick glance around, then knocked.

The door opened immediately, a puff of dust raining down from the top of the doorframe. The huge raug behind it didn't seem to notice but stared at Cheyenne instead with glowing orange-brown eyes. His thick, muscular gray jaw worked on crunching a mouthful of something Cheyenne didn't care to know about. *Makes him look like a bull chewing his cud.*

"You're interested." Bits of black sludgy something spilled from the corner of his mouth.

She tried not to stare or let her nostrils flare at the smell. *Like copper and steamed broccoli.* "Wouldn't have come all this way if I wasn't."

Gúrdu grunted and waved a meaty gray hand tipped with thick, sharpened red nails. "Then let's get to it."

He turned away and left the door open for her. Cheyenne slipped into the dark, dusty entryway of the raug's large and neglected apartment, pulling the heavy metal door shut with a low echo.

Gúrdu's hulking figure disappeared between the dangling strands of wooden beads hanging from the hallway's ceiling. Cheyenne pressed her lips together when she saw the last four strands dangling without any beads at the end of the wooden rod. *Good thing Maleshi's not here with me this time to pick another fight with that thing.*

She swept away the clacking strands of beads and turned left into the long, wide room that stretched the entire length of his apartment. Low natural flames flickered in the lanterns hanging from the ceiling. Cheyenne almost tripped when her shoe caught on a frayed strip of fabric dangling from one of the dozens of cushions scattered across the dusty floor. She kicked off the clinging tatters and sent a puff of yellowed stuffing bouncing across the other pillows.

The large wooden platform at the back of the long room creaked and groaned beneath Gúrdu's tremendous weight as he climbed onto the stacked cushions of his Oracle's throne. Making her way toward him, Cheyenne paid more attention to where she stepped and ignored the dark shapes skittering across the floor beneath the cushions. "I'm guessing these messages you were talking about are more like prophecies, right?"

Gúrdu stopped chewing and swallowed his huge mouthful with another crunch and a wet gurgle. "It's dangerous to assume that type of thing, *hidna.*"

The warning growl in his voice made her stop ten feet from his platform. "My bad. You surprised me by sending me a message on the forum, so I will admit being a little hasty to jump to conclusions." Cheyenne cleared her throat.

The raug growled again, but this time it rose into a dark, heavy chuckle that echoed around the room. "You weren't nearly this hasty to back down the first time we met. You should see your face right now." A louder laugh burst from his meaty gray lips before dying quickly.

Cheyenne sighed. "There's nothing wrong with my face. You just like to screw with me."

He spread his thick arms in a slow, sweeping gesture. "I stood witness to the *Nós Aní* binding of the *Aranél*. It's a rare opportunity to screw with a drow, *hidna*." His lips peeled back in an eager grin, exposing yellow teeth with plenty of sludgy black food bits still clinging to them.

"Well, I'm glad you find that so amusing."

"I find many things amusing." Gúrdu's smile disappeared. "That doesn't include what you came to me to hear, just so you're not assuming anything else about this visit."

Cheyenne slowly navigated her way through the remaining cushions toward him and shrugged. "Kinda hard to imagine anything having to do with a prophecy is amusing."

"You're right about that." The raug's glowing orange-brown eyes fixed on the drow halfling as she found the least-disgusting cushion and lowered herself to sit on it. "Take off the charms, *hidna*. You have nothing to hide in here. Not that you *can* hide it, obviously."

"The charms? Oh." She quickly removed Ember's illusion earrings and stuffed them into her pocket. "Not much of a difference."

He studied her pale skin and black-dyed hair. "This time, you're not trying to be wholly something you're not."

"The first time, I was trying to get answers from a raug Oracle and figured showing up at his front door looking like a human wouldn't even get me inside."

Gúrdu chuckled again. "You're smarter than you look."

Cheyenne snorted. "Thanks. Are we gonna keep chatting like this is a social call? Totally up to you. I just put a few other things on hold so I could get over here for these messages of yours."

"Yes, doing nothing in your apartment must have been very disappointing to leave behind."

The halfling narrowed her eyes and lifted her chin. "If I didn't know you're an Oracle, I'd think you've been spying on me."

"All Oracles are spies, *hidna*. But for whom? That's the question so many greedy little magicals try to fit into the right box." Gúrdu's thick gray tongue poked between his lips as he slurped more gooey black leftovers from his last meal back into his mouth. "I spy for myself, and on occasion, for those I would like to see reach a certain outcome."

"Like me making the crossing with L'zar."

"That is one such outcome. Should we keep discussing my motives, or do you want to stop talking and receive the threads I've pulled out for you?"

Again with the thread-and-tapestry analogy. "Let's go with the threads."

"Hmm." Gúrdu reached out with a red claw toward the bowl of water on the closest table. The bowl flashed with silver light and hovered through the air before settling gently beside the raug's crossed legs. The silver tray came next from a different low round table scattered among the cushions on the floor.

And here's the part where he picks up all the sticks, dips them in the water, and eats them.

The Oracle grunted as he chewed, splinters of wood flying from between his mouth. He dipped his clawed finger into the bowl of water, then raised it to his forehead and drew a clear wet line down in the bridge of his nose, over his wood-flecked lips, and down to the underside of his chin.

"You will hear, *hidna.*" The bundle of dry twigs plinked onto the silver tray. "So many things have been woven around the *Aranél* of the new Cycle, and only one is worth sharing with you for free."

Cheyenne sat straighter over her crossed legs, listening intently. *Finally, someone's about to tell it to me straight, even if it's mixed up in a prophecy.*

"The threads are re-weaving, drow." Gúrdu swallowed his mouthful of sticks and closed his eyes. "Sometimes they snap. Sometimes when we thought they vanished, they reappear. In all my time of reading the weave, I have only seen one such thread unchanged. Maybe it means something. Maybe it's bullshit. But I am one of the forsaken who wishes to turn the Cycle anew. If you find anything useful in this, I'll be glad to know it helped you do what you're already preparing to do."

He's talking about making the crossing with L'zar again. That has to be it. Not gonna ask for clarification. Cheyenne pressed her fists into her lap and stared at the raug Oracle, who'd now fallen silent but for the slow, steady breath filling his massive chest and rushing out of him again like an ocean tide.

Gúrdu's next breath wheezed out of him as he set the backs of his gray palms on his knees. Then he gasped and opened his eyes. They were pure white now, seeing only the prophecy, but the flames in the lanterns hanging from the ceiling surged to two feet tall and took on the same eerie green glow.

"Blood bonds with blood. Blood flows both ways." The Oracle's voice rose in a thick growl in dozens of voices, echoing through the room as if they sat in a stone cavern instead. *'The black rivers of Ambar'ogúl thicken, waiting to herald the last scion and the first* phér móre. *The ancient ones howl in their shards of stolen prescience as the young ones are turned inside-out, outside-in. The heart rots. The heart beats. The heart will bleed in both ways."*

Gúrdu started swaying from side to side as he took another wheezing breath. The green flames in the lanterns flared again, whipping and sputtering in a wind that didn't exist anywhere else. A low, growling hum rose from the raug's throat.

"The Cycle will not turn for the Cu'ón *as was foreseen. It will break beneath the fires of return. She will shatter the bones of the darkpool cages and will not remain to see the world rebuilt. Blood runs both ways. To choose one is life. To choose life is chaos."*

A wet, hacking cough wracked the Oracle's chest. He struggled to draw another breath as his huge body trembled, every muscle taut and rigid.

Cheyenne gazed around the room. *This doesn't look good.*

"To shed her skin." Gúrdu coughed again, but his next breath never came. In its place was the same wet gurgle.

How do I know if this is normal or if he's choking on fucking sticks? She tightened her fists and leaned forward, ready to jump up and at least try the Heimlich if things didn't get better soon.

Then the raug's head whipped back, and a shrieking howl in all those otherworldly voices burst from his gaping mouth. *"The* Cu'ón *delivers his scion into ruin and decay. Blood bonds with blood. The* phér móre *is the sword. If it does not sail true, the scion will be their doom. The bridges and the river will both fall. Destiny runs both ways. The rot runs blood-deep. The rot shadows the bridges. The rot is her blood and her only path to claiming what was always hers from what he had no right to freely give!"*

Another howl came from all around them now. Gúrdu's body bucked and convulsed on his huge wooden platform.

"Shit." Cheyenne leaped to her feet. "Gúrdu? You can—"

"This is the only way! And you will tremble before the sacrifice, daughter of L'zar, daughter of the Cu'ón, *the Dark Grinning Weaver."*

Gúrdu's meaty hand jerked away from his knee and swiped across the room, sending out a spray of hissing orange sparks. Cheyenne leaped back over the cushions. "Hey!"

"Your blood will burn in the Heartfire. Your blood will ignite the cleansing storm!" The raug's other hand did the same, sweeping aside some unseen force but moving like someone else had taken control of a body that didn't fit. The flames in the lanterns blazed higher and burst at the center with black light as Gúrdu's gesture tossed the first two rows of cushions into the air with his uncontrolled magic.

Cheyenne batted aside a cushion that had flown at her and shook off the thick cobweb that clung to her arm. "Time to turn this thing off, Gúrdu. Can you hear me?"

"Your blood will bond to blood! Your blood runs through the heart! Cut out the heart! Cut out the heart!" The Oracle lurched forward and clapped his hands together with an ear-shattering boom. A ball of black fire churned between his palms when he drew them apart, the rest of his body still convulsing and making those awful sounds.

"That's it. We're done." Cheyenne slipped into her drow form and conjured two churning orbs of black energy. "Sorry in advance."

Gúrdu howled with dozens of voices and lurched forward again, his eyes and gaping mouth blazing with black fire as the flames between his hands grew larger, sparking with silver light. Cheyenne drew her arm back, meaning to throw an attack, then the dark flames in the lanterns roared into burning columns reaching toward the ceiling.

A loud crack came from behind Cheyenne, followed by a jagged streak of blinding silver light that raced for the prophecy-possessed Oracle. The shockwave made the halfling stumble forward, but she couldn't look away from the sight of Maleshi dropping back into normal time and sending a fist wrapped in silver light into the side of Gúrdu's face.

The screaming and howling cut off instantly, along with the Oracle's black flames and the dark fire burning in the lanterns. The entire room plunged into darkness, and in the sudden silence, the heavy breathing of all three sounded incredibly loud.

Normal yellow flames returned to the lanterns, lighting the room again.

Cheyenne blinked and swept her gaze around the room until she stopped at the Oracle's platform again. "What the fuck?"

Maleshi loomed over Gúrdu, who now lay on his back with his huge hands splayed out beside him. She straightened, smoothed her hair away from her face, and let out a long, hissing breath. "I've been wanting to hit this Oracle for centuries."

CHAPTER EIGHTY-TWO

G úrdu's gray, clawed hand lifted and swiped at the general's calf. "Don't even try." Maleshi stepped back and glared at him. "You deserved it."

"I wasn't finished." With a few light coughs, he groaned and pushed himself back up until he sat cross-legged on the cushions again, his eyes glowing orange-brown once more in the low light. "And you know better than to cut off the source before it's done."

"Spare me the pompous thread lecture, Gúrdu. You're not in any position to be meddling with shit you don't remotely understand."

"Oh, but I see all of it, Maleshi. I do understand." He wiped the corner of his mouth and chuckled at the nearly black blood smeared across the back of his hand. "And now so does L'zar's daughter, I think."

The general dismissed the raug Oracle with a sharp hiss and jumped off the platform. "Speaking of L'zar's daughter, you can put that away now."

"Yep." Cheyenne killed the black spheres of drow energy in her hands, then shoved them into her pockets and looked at Gúrdu. *If he had eyebrows, I might be able to read that expression a little better. At least I get a nod of approval. I think.* She glanced at Maleshi and shrugged. "Any chance you won't punch *me* in the face too?"

"You know, maybe I should." Maleshi spun to point a warning finger at Gúrdu. "This was the last time you pull one of these little stunts, got it?"

"She deserves to know, Maleshi."

"She deserves not to have her brain stuffed with cryptic tatters that could get her killed if she doesn't know how to untangle them the right way. She deserves not to be dragged into a deathflame show arena, you masochistic asshat." The general shot Cheyenne a quick, appraising look. "Come on. You'll figure it out eventually."

"Yes. We made sure of that, *hidna*. Didn't we?" Gúrdu chuckled and reached for the wooden bowl of water to pour it into his mouth. Water slopped over the sides in thick streams and splashed the raug's lap, his cushions, and the wooden platform. Cheyenne turned to follow Maleshi out of the room. "Ah. Only one thread unchanged, *Aranél*. Don't forget. That one's yours."

Maleshi stopped in front of the curtain of threaded beads and spun so quickly, Cheyenne almost tripped over herself to keep from running into her. "What the hell were you thinking?"

"Well, I was—"

"I've been around a long time, kid, but I'm not anywhere near senile. Didn't we talk about this? *Today?*"

"Yep."

"You put this *entire* cause at risk by heading out for a little joyride and a visit to the raug Oracle. Are you insane?"

Cheyenne raised her eyebrows. "Is that a rhetorical question?"

"Of *course* it's rhetorical!" Maleshi glanced into the long room full of pillows with a hiss.

I'm not gonna get in more than five words at a time.

"Or maybe it's not," the general continued in a low, threatening snarl. "At this point, I'm not sure I can tell the difference. *Are* you insane?"

Cheyenne widened her eyes and waited.

"What?" Maleshi looked the halfling up and down. "What are you doing? What's wrong with you?"

"I don't know. I seem to be incapable of finishing a—"

"You know what? You've got a lot of nerve... Oh." The general cleared her throat, stepped back, and nodded. "Go ahead, then. I'm not sure I have anything else to say that hasn't already slipped out."

"Okay." Cheyenne waited a little longer until Maleshi's glowing silver eyes finally rose to meet her gaze. *And we're a go.* "Look, I know you guys didn't want me to leave my apartment. I appreciate the wards. They work. Thank you. I left anyway."

"Mmhmm." The nightstalker bit her lip to keep from saying anything else.

"Ember made me a charm that masks my magic pretty much like the Heart of Midnight, only it broke when I went drow instead of me breaking it myself. So no, I wasn't driving around Richmond sending up magical smoke signals. I *have* learned a thing or two in the last few weeks, in case anyone was wondering. And yeah, I broke the charm because I have no idea what the hell just happened back there, and I was about to try blasting the raug out of it too until you showed up and sucker-punched him."

"Right. Well, don't worry too much about whatever you might've missed at the end there. Once a prophecy starts repeating itself like that, it's just running on fumes. Cheyenne, I have to ask what you gave him as an offering."

"Nothing."

"Because right now, it's…what? Nothing?"

Cheyenne shrugged. "He reached out to me on the Borderlands forum and told me he'd 'deliver a message for free.' Sure, he was vague about it, but it was pretty clear he had a prophecy about me—*for* me—and I figured it was something I could use to help us once we head back to Hangivol for this last hurrah. And then, yeah, he said the same thing when I got here."

Maleshi's silver eyes narrowed. "Did it make sense?"

"It was a prophecy. What do you think?"

With a snort, the general turned away and cast a new portal between them and the curtain of strung beads. "Then the rest is on you to figure out, and when you do, let's hope you figured it out *right*. I knew a *golra* once who misread his own prophecy and killed his healer brother. Turns out his brother could have saved him from the plague, which killed the *golra* two days later. And yes, we do get sick over here."

Cheyenne fought back a laugh. "Really?"

"Yes, really. Now, please. After you." Maleshi gestured toward the open portal, and Cheyenne peered through it.

"Go ahead. I'll drive."

"Nope. Sorry, kid. You, in the portal, now."

"No." Frowning at the nightstalker woman, Cheyenne stepped back and headed for the curtain of beads. "I'm not leaving my car. It'll take me like fifteen minutes to get— Hey!"

Maleshi's hand wrapped around Cheyenne's bicep before she jerked the halfling back toward her. "I'll take care of the car, Cheyenne. You *cannot* leave your apartment while we're getting the last few things together. Understand? No one's gonna be able to track you down inside an Oracle's den, but once you step through that front door, you might as well put up a post on magical Craigslist. Go."

"You need to let go of my arm."

Rolling her eyes, Maleshi released the halfling's arm, then lunged toward her and shoved her through the portal.

"What the hell?" Cheyenne whirled to glare at the general through the portal.

"Stay home. Keep your phone on you. We're almost ready."

The portal disappeared with a pop, and Cheyenne stared at the kitchen of her apartment. "Fuck."

"Lemme guess." Ember glanced over her shoulder with a grimace of sympathy. "You broke the charm, and your Probation nightstalker tracked you down."

"Yep." Cheyenne swung slowly around and eased toward the closest recliner before slumping down into it. The chair rocked back a few inches. "At least I got most of a prophecy."

"Oh, *really?*" Ember wheeled backward to get a better look at her halfling friend. "Now, this I've gotta hear."

"It's a bunch of jumbled crap, honestly. Except for a few things."

"Uh-huh." Ember propped her forearm on the armrest and leaned over it toward Cheyenne. "Such as?"

"Well, for one thing, this one had L'zar's name in it. Called him the Dark Smiling Weaver and the *Cu'ón.*"

"Okay." Ember's violet gaze swept in a thoughtful circle around their apartment. "That supposed to mean something?"

"Not by itself, but whoever or *whatever* was talking through the Oracle for this prophecy knew exactly who was listening. Called me 'daughter of L'zar,' and then something about the *Cu'ón's* daughter being the *Aranél*. Turning a new Cycle. Claiming rights that were always mine but not L'zar's to give away and a whole bunch of shit about blood and rot and fire."

"Ooh, very doomsday."

"Yeah. I think it was a warning."

"For real?"

"Yeah." Smoothing her drow-white hair away from her face, Cheyenne let her anger and her magic cool off and slipped back into human form. "I think L'zar wants to overthrow the Crown. Probably kill her. Maybe not. But all so he can take the throne and start a new Cycle as the new Crown."

Ember cleared her throat. "I mean, that was obvious when everyone's talking about rebellion and taking out the asshole drow on the other side trying to kill you first."

"Right. But all this other stuff about cleansing and burning away the rot and *my* blood being something different?" Cheyenne stared at the vaulted ceiling, turning what she remembered of the prophecy over in her mind. *Should've put on the activator and recorded it.*

Ember studied the halfling's profile and raised an eyebrow. "It looks like you already know the rest of what you're trying to say."

"Still obvious, huh?"

"Yep."

With a wry chuckle, Cheyenne propped herself up in the recliner and met her friend's gaze. "I'm just trying to decide if that's what I think this means, or if I'm just looking for more things to pin on L'zar so I have more reasons not to like him."

"Because you're starting to?"

"What? No. I don't know. Probably not. He's an ass."

Ember cocked her head. "And he's your dad."

"Please. You of all people know that's not an automatic exemption from being shitty."

"Sure. But *my* dad didn't lock himself up for three-quarters of a century to make sure I didn't die before breaking out of prison to keep making sure I didn't die. He just won't answer my phone calls."

Cheyenne barked a laugh and immediately shook her head. "Sorry. Sorry, I shouldn't be laughing at that."

"No, go ahead. I'll laugh with you. Ha-ha-ha. My dad's a selfish bastard who's given up on his only kid so he can pretend to be normal, and your dad's a selfish bastard who wants to overthrow an O'gúl regime and take you with him. At least he's trying."

Chuckling softly, Cheyenne shook her head. "There's that, I guess. But that's the thing about this whole prophecy, Em. I don't think it was warning me about L'zar taking down the Crown and winning this rebellion or whatever. I think it was warning me about him taking the throne to be the next O'gúl Crown. Obviously, he wants that too, but the death and destruction part? I don't know."

"Yeah, you do. Go ahead and say it."

With a groan, the halfling glanced at the ceiling again and let her shoulders sag. "I think that prophecy was telling me L'zar's not supposed to be the next Crown."

"Huh."

Cheyenne met her friend's gaze again and shrugged. "Seriously, Em. I think all that fire and rot and blood shit was a warning about what'll happen if I don't stop him after we've *won* or whatever. That he'll screw everything up just as badly if he takes the Crown and sits in her place."

"So, you mean what? You're gonna go help him win, and then you're supposed to kill him or something?"

"I don't know." Cheyenne shook her head and stared at her. "That's the thing. Prophecies are mostly bullshit, and the rest is impossible to figure out. I just don't know."

"Or *maybe* that raug's just trying to stir up trouble. Make you think you're supposed to do something, and this is just a way for him to screw things up."

"Maybe. But Gúrdu wouldn't have been at the ceremony yesterday if he was trying to throw a wrench in L'zar's rebellion."

"Well, there's that." Ember sat back in her chair and folded her arms. "What if it's another test? Like, to see if you freak out about this prophecy or if you just let it be and keep moving in the direction you were headed. Honestly, if I were you, I'd much rather believe the magicals who've been helping me and fighting with me over some half-assed prophecy mumbo-jumbo."

"Not a big fan of prophecies?"

"Nope. Granted, I'm just a fae who was born without magic but got it back by hanging out with you. I've never been the center of a prophecy, so I don't have anything to go on."

"Makes sense." They both laughed, and Cheyenne closed her eyes. *How much of this is real?* "Maybe that's the thing. That all prophecies are crap, and it all boils down to figuring out how to prove it. L'zar did that with his prophecy, 'cause here I am."

"Exactly. I wouldn't worry about it too much."

"I'm not worried." Smiling, the halfling drummed her fingers on the leather armrests. "It was seriously creepy, though. I think the guy had some kind of seizure or something. Then he started pulling up black fire and throwing pillows all over the place."

"Pillows?" Ember pressed her lips together to keep from laughing.

"Yeah. Instead of carpet." Both girls sniggered. "Maleshi punched the hell out of him to stop the whole thing. I thought she'd killed him for a second."

"From what I hear, raugs are ridiculously tough. And Oracles like to put on a good show."

"He succeeded." Cheyenne sat up straighter in the recliner and shook the entire event and the tangled prophecy out of her mind. *Worrying about this isn't gonna get me anywhere. I'm already skeptical enough about how we're gonna pull off this whole rebellion takeover.* "So, moving on. Did you get any alerts while I was gone?"

"Ha. Nope. Glen was fortunately silent, so I guess Corian and company are handling things pretty quietly." Ember frowned at her friend. "You need a distraction."

"Yeah, look how well *that* turned out."

"I'm talking about while you're here. Under house arrest." The fae pointed at Cheyenne's knees bouncing up and down rapidly. "You're fidgety and tense, and it's weirding me out. Stop it."

"Sorry." Cheyenne stilled her bouncing knees. "You're gonna suggest watching another movie to distract me, aren't you?"

Ember grinned. "Are *you* suggesting more movies?"

"Sure, I guess."

"Prepare to zone out, then." Ember played the movie she'd paused, and their apartment filled with the conversation from the characters on screen. Two minutes in, Cheyenne's fingers drummed in an urgent, jerky rhythm on the recliner's armrests. Ember shot her friend two warning looks before finally rolling her eyes and wheeling away from the table to head toward the kitchen. "Okay, I know what we need."

"Huh?" Cheyenne looked away from the screen she'd been ignoring. "Where are you going?"

"Grab the popcorn, halfling. Start eating. I had that delivery grocery person pick up enough ice cream to last us a month. I thought. Depends on how many pints you need to go through before you chill out."

The halfling burst out laughing. "Force-feeding me ice cream doesn't sound very relaxing."

"It will when you see what kind I got. And we're watching something fun. Screw the action movies and the creepy stuff. We need something stupidly funny." The freezer opened under Ember's violet light, and two pints of ice cream zipped down into her lap, followed by two spoons from the drawer. "You don't get to argue with me on this one, Cheyenne. Until we get the all-clear to leave the apartment, which is awesome and has everything we need, I'm calling the shots. Got it?"

"You know, I heard fae are especially skilled at getting what they want. Probably a bad move to argue with you."

"You have no idea."

A purple-glowing pint of ice cream and a spoon whizzed across the apartment and thumped into Cheyenne's lap.

CHAPTER EIGHTY-THREE

The next morning, Cheyenne lurched out of sleep, covered in a cold sweat. The echoes of her dream floated around her mind before she threw the covers off and climbed out of bed. "Screw all this 'blood bonds with blood' shit. The prophecies can suck it."

She burst out of her bedroom and headed for the bathroom beneath the mini-loft.

"Morning," Ember called from the kitchen. "I beat you to the coffee-making again, so don't worry about it. Whoa, you okay?"

"Not really." Cheyenne ran her hand through her black hair and stopped in front of the bathroom door. "More nightmares. More screwed-up prophecies about crap that doesn't make any sense. I'm thinking maybe I can burn it all out with hot water and steam."

"Okay."

"Coffee smells good." The halfling stumbled into the bathroom and slammed the door shut behind her. The sound startled her out of her grumpiness, and she turned on the shower with a grimace. *Ember didn't do anything. Don't take it out on her.*

Once the shower was running as hot as it would go, which still didn't feel hot enough, Cheyenne stepped in and let the scalding water pour over her. *I don't need to figure out what that prophecy means. I already know the Crown is tearing the other side apart. No shit, there'll be blood and fire and devastation. There already is. How am I supposed to stop it?*

An image of the Nimlothar tree from the ceremony two days ago flashed in her mind, overtaking her vision and her thoughts as it pulsed with purple and black light. With the pulsing light came a song in thousands of voices, a wordless tune that was a part of the tree and the life-force and the power inside it. Then the massive tree, the source of drow magic, gave a final pulse of light and darkened. The song became a scream, then thousands of screams. The base of the Nimlothar's trunk erupted in black flames, climbing higher and racing toward the branches and the purple leaves until the entire thing was consumed. The screams grew louder and more urgent, terrified and enraged. Beneath the Nimlothar tree, the earth buckled and shuddered with wide, pitch-black cracks that led down into nothingness.

"The phér móre *is the sword. If it does not sail true, the scion will be their doom."*

When the vision ended, Cheyenne found herself on her knees in the shower, both hands clamped over her ears, the drow-pointed tips of which peeked out above her fingers. She coughed, her voice hoarse and raw, water pouring down on her head and over her face. *Was I just screaming?*

"Seriously, Cheyenne, if you don't say something, I'm coming in," Ember shouted and pounded again on the bathroom door.

"I'm fine." The words left Cheyenne's mouth in a croak, and she cleared her throat and tried again. "I'm good, Em."

"Thank God." Ember closed her eyes. "You sure? I mean, I thought you were just blowing off a little steam until it didn't stop."

"Yeah, I'm sure. Sorry. I'll tell you when I'm done."

"Okay." Ember cast the bathroom door a skeptical glance, then wheeled back into the kitchen to finish making breakfast.

Cheyenne braced herself against the shower wall and stood again. Her legs shook when she straightened, but she forced her body under control and slipped out of drow form. *I'm so done with this.*

She quickly finished her shower, then turned off the water and stepped out. The bathroom was so full of steam, she could barely see the towel on the rack right next to her. The mirror was fogged up, and Cheyenne turned on the vent fan to help clear out the room. After drying off as much as she could in the steam, she wrapped the towel around herself and left the bathroom.

The apartment felt frigid after the bathroom. Cheyenne sucked in a sharp breath and headed quickly to her bedroom to change. When she dropped the towel and reached for her clothes in the dresser, she paused. *Crap. I just cooked myself.*

She gently rubbed the bright-red skin of her forearm and took a quick glance at her body. The rest of her was just as red and covered in a splotchy heat rash. Grimacing, Cheyenne tugged on her clothes, squeezed water out of her hair, and tied it all up in a bun she rarely wore. Then she headed back out into the living room and stopped to glance at the pile of the silver wrist chains she'd left in a heap on the bathroom counter. *Not today, I guess. The last thing I need is fashion chafing.*

Ember turned from the stove and directed two hovering plates of eggs and bacon toward the kitchen island. Once they'd settled gently on the counter, she looked up and saw Cheyenne heading toward her. "Whoa. I didn't think you were serious when you said, 'burn it all out.'"

"Yeah, I had something a little less intense in mind." Cheyenne poured herself a cup of coffee and took a long, slurping sip. "Sorry I freaked you out."

"Hey, it's fine. Some people sing in the shower, some people scream. I get it."

The halfling drank more coffee and leaned against the counter. "That wasn't part of the plan."

"What happened?"

"Apparently, I have visions."

Ember froze. "Visions."

"Yeah. It happened a few times before I passed the trials. When the Crown was actively looking for me, I guess. I saw some old crone's face and heard parts of L'zar's prophecy, but I'm sure that had more to do with the legacy box than anything else."

"And this vision didn't."

"Right. The box is already open. This one was a Nimlothar tree the way they used to be, I think, before the Crown screwed everything up. I saw it burn." Cheyenne shook her head before drinking more coffee.

"Yeesh."

The halfling slowly swung her gaze to meet Ember's. "With black fire."

"Oh." Ember shrugged. "I mean, you're not the only one who can summon black fire, right? Gúrdu did it."

"I don't think his was real. I'm sure it's a drow thing, though."

"Okay. So any drow could use it to burn a tree."

"Sure. Including me."

Ember shook her head. "You can't blame yourself for something that happened in a vision."

"No, I know. You're totally right. What I need to do is figure out what the hell it means and whether there's something I'm supposed to do about it. All this? The prophecy, the vision—it feels like a warning, and I have no idea why *I'm* the one getting it."

"Okay, hold on a sec."

"I didn't ask for any of this stuff, Em. I'm just trying to do the right thing. Help the other magicals on this side not get themselves in trouble when the other O'gúl assholes are running around stealing kids and blowing up marketplaces. All I wanted out of this was to get the orc who shot you, and instead, I'm part of this centuries-long rebellion that nobody's been able to fight because the idiot who knocked up my mom locked himself up just to see what would happen. L'zar won't even *fight* with us, and everyone still thinks he's the end-all-be-all to this whole thing. So I passed the trials. Awesome. I'm not just a clueless halfling who has no idea how to handle her magic anymore. Great. I could *do* something with that, and instead, I'm locked up in my own apartment, not helping everyone else, just like *he* did. I don't even know if what we're going to do once we cross the Border again is what needs to happen. I don't want prophecies and visions. I want shit to quit getting worse!"

The mug in her hand let out a soft pop, and she looked down to see a spiderweb of cracks spreading around the ceramic from beneath her hand, which had taken on the mottled grayness of her drow form without her knowing it.

"Shit." She set the mug down on the counter beside her and turned her hands over. "I'm halfway between drow halfling and Goth lobster now."

Ember snorted but immediately wiped the smile off her face.

"I had a handle on changing forms. Now I'm losing control and starting all over."

The kitchen fell silent, punctured by Ember slurping her coffee. "Did you get it all out, or do you need to vent more?"

Cheyenne puffed out her cheeks. "No, if I keep venting, I'll break something other than a mug."

"Okay. Now *I'm* gonna say a few things."

The halfling glanced at her friend, nodded, and looked down at her raw red arms and hands again as the patches of dark gray faded.

"First of all, you are *not* starting all over. Case in point, you didn't *shatter* the mug, and you didn't have to run away to hide your ears and wait for it all to settle back down. See? Look. Goth lobster."

"Jeeze."

"Sorry, but it's a perfect description." Ember set her mug on the kitchen island and nodded. "Seriously, Cheyenne. You're doing everything you can, and it *is* enough. One hundred percent. Look at what happened with Matthew, right? You went in there *twice* without using magic to fight your way to the answer. Okay, minus the one in his loveseat, but that's not the point. You *do* know what you're doing now."

"Except with that damn prophecy," Cheyenne muttered.

"Fuck the prophecies and visions. You're Cheyenne Summerlin. You're a drow halfling who's been to the other side and back again without being ripped apart. I mean, you're the only magical Earthside who can use that weird little coil tech, which makes you unstoppable. You *closed a portal ridge by yourself.* You don't need L'zar or Corian or Maleshi or the rest of them, but you're helping them because as far as any of us can tell, that is the right thing to do."

"I don't know if that's true right now."

"Listen, *you* are helping *them*, and everyone else. If you change your mind and back out, this whole thing goes to shit. They all know it. You know it. Honestly, you need to quit feeling sorry for yourself and just *be* yourself. That's why you do the whole Goth thing, right?"

"Because I like the way it looks?"

Ember scoffed. "Don't change the subject."

Cheyenne shook her head. "Sorry."

"Hey, the first time I asked you about it, you said you're Goth because you're not a quitter. There's no way in hell you're backing out of this now because you don't understand all the pieces. Got it?"

A slow smile bloomed on the halfling's lips. "Loud and clear, Em."

"Good. I made eggs and bacon, so eat it if you want. Or don't. Just stop trying to take on everyone else's problems." Ember pointed at one of the plates on the island, and it floated into her lap on a cloud of purple light before she wheeled herself into the living room.

"Coffee, breakfast, and a badass pep talk. Happy Saturday."

"Yeah, you're welcome." Ember laughed and dug into her food. "Don't expect it to be a regular thing."

Cheyenne grabbed a new mug to fill with the coffee from the one she'd almost shattered, then grabbed the other plate and headed into the living room to join her friend. "I don't expect it at all. But thanks."

"Hey, that's what a *Nós Ani* is supposed to do, right? Check their drow when they're making drow asses of themselves."

"Ha. I can always count on you for that."

"Damn straight, you can."

Cheyenne sat on one of the leather recliners and set her plate in her lap before starting with the bacon. *She's right. If I'm gonna get pissed off, I better make sure I can do something about it. No point otherwise.*

Five minutes into their breakfast, Cheyenne heard her phone buzzing on silent in her bedroom. "Oh, boy."

"What?"

"Phone call." She set her plate on the coffee table and hurried into her room.

"Is it Corian?"

"Yep." Cheyenne stared at his name on her phone, then answered the call and went back into the living area. "Hey."

"Hey. You still having a hard time with cabin fever?"

Of course Maleshi told him. "Not so much right now. I guess that depends on how much longer I have to stay here."

"Is today soon enough for you?"

She paused behind the recliners and stared at Ember.

"What?" Ember whispered.

Cheyenne shook her head and muttered into the phone, "To do what?"

"To make our move, Cheyenne. L'zar finally finished what he started

Earthside. Now it's time to finish what he started in Ambar'ogúl. Pack a bag and be ready to move. A light bag, but enough for longer than a day if we have to stay. And bring Ember. You'll need her."

"Wait, we're leaving today?"

"That's what I said, kid. In the next few hours. So buckle up." Corian hung up, and Cheyenne stared at her phone.

"Holy shit."

"Time to make the crossing again, huh?" Ember stared at her friend and slowly lifted a forkful of eggs to her mouth.

"Yeah. I didn't expect *that* to happen now. I haven't even been back Earthside for twenty-four hours, and now I'm doing it again."

"That was fast."

"No kidding." Cheyenne slipped her phone into her back pocket and took a deep breath. "He told me to bring you with me."

"*What?*" Ember choked on her mouthful and set her plate down on the coffee table. "No, no. I don't do Border crossings."

"Em."

"Uh-uh. That's a terrible idea."

"Okay. How about if *I* ask you to come?"

Ember rolled her eyes. "Now you're splitting hairs, and I still can't go with you."

"Why not?"

"Um, hello?" Ember slapped the armrests of her wheelchair and spread her arms. "Paraplegic fae isn't an advantage for any of you, Cheyenne."

"Yeah, and you broke through all that when you blasted that shadowy whatever-it-was back through the portal at the ceremony. That was all you. I'd be in the Crown's hands *right now* if you hadn't been there with me. Corian's right, Em. I do need you."

Ember clenched her teeth and took a deep breath. "So, someone's gonna *carry* me across the Border?"

"Whatever we have to do to make it happen, we'll do, Em. He wouldn't have said you need to come with us if he or any of the others thought there would be a problem."

"Just to be clear, I blasted that thing back through the portal out of pure instinct. I don't *know* how to fight."

Cheyenne folded her arms and smiled. "How do you think *I* learned?"

"Oh, jeeze." Rolling her eyes, Ember thumped back against her seat. "I'm not getting out of this, am I?"

"Nope."

The fae girl sighed. "And I can't convince either of us that I don't want to go. Making the crossing sounds like the worst thing most magicals could ever go through." Ember's smile looked more like a grimace until she looked at Cheyenne and forced herself to grin about it. "I *do* wanna go."

"Despite how creepy your smile is right now, I believe you." Cheyenne pointed at her friend. "We're doing this. Corian said a few hours and told us to pack a light bag in case we're over there for a few days."

"A few days." Ember ran a hand through her purple-tinted hair and puffed out her cheeks. "Damn. We're doing this."

"There you go. Let it sink in, then go pack a bag, I guess. This is it."

CHAPTER EIGHTY-FOUR

Cheyenne had her backpack mostly filled ten minutes later and dropped it on the couch to double-check the inventory.

Ember returned to the living room with a brown and green backpack in her lap and stopped on the other side of the couch. "What am I supposed to put in this besides a few clothes? I don't know what to be prepared *for*."

"Probably just clothes." Cheyenne glanced at the mostly empty backpack in her friend's lap. "Yeah, that looks like pretty light packing."

"Because it *is*. I feel ridiculous."

"Don't. I know a little more about what I'm doing because I've already been there, only this time is gonna be a lot different."

"No kidding." Ember peered across the couch at her friend's backpack. "What are *you* bringing?"

"Clothes. The darktongue salve."

"Naturally."

"The legacy box and the coin are down in the bottom somewhere. This." Cheyenne lifted the thick silver cuff L'zar had given her to keep her human side hidden from the native O'gúleesh. "Actually, I should probably just put this on."

L'zar appeared beside her at the couch's armrest. "Cheyenne."

"Oh! Shit." She leaped away from him and scowled. "You can't do that!"

Ember looked up from her backpack. "What?"

"I can, actually." L'zar's smile widened, his golden eyes flashing as he raised his eyebrows. "Packing for our final stand, I see."

"Wow. You're so perceptive."

"Cheyenne?" Ember spread her arms. "What are you doing?"

"I'm talking to—" Cheyenne gestured at L'zar and frowned. "You don't see him, do you?"

"Who?"

L'zar chuckled. "Did I open the *Don'adurr* at the wrong time?"

"Yes. It's always the wrong time for that. Stop talking." Cheyenne held up a finger toward the vision of her father he'd projected into her living room and met Ember's gaze. "L'zar's pulling his super annoying jump-into-my-head trick."

"Oh. Tell him to cut it out."

Trying not to laugh, Cheyenne looked at the image of L'zar and raised an eyebrow. "Corian said we're ready to go, and we're packing. What do you want?"

"Simply to remind you of one more important item." He gazed around whatever portion of her apartment he could see and narrowed his eyes. "By 'we,' you're referring to you and Ember, correct?"

"No, I thought I'd bring a few more friends along to spice things up."

"At least your thinking is sharp this morning. Do you have the *nalís*?"

"The tree pin?"

L'zar closed his eyes and took a deep breath. "It has a name, Cheyenne, but if that's how you think of it, then yes. The *tree pin*."

"Yeah, I have it."

"Make sure you bring that with you. I'm glad you haven't had to use it before now, or maybe even that you never thought to use it. We can add that to our list of last resorts."

"I have it, I said."

"Excellent." L'zar smiled at her, his golden gaze roaming over her face.

Dark Smiling Weaver, all right. She looked away from him, then glanced back and raised her eyebrows. "Anything else?"

"Hmm. No. I'll see you soon." He vanished.

Cheyenne snorted and returned her attention to stuffing the rest of the extra clothes into her backpack before zipping the whole thing up. "Of course he couldn't have just picked up a phone and let Corian send a message."

"What did he want?"

"He wants me to bring this charm he made me. The *nalís*."

"Ooh. Haven't read about that one yet." Ember leaned forward with an eager stare. "What does it do?"

"It opens an insta-portal to me from where L'zar happens to be. Emergency backup, I guess."

"He doesn't think you guys will be separated over there, does he?"

"I have no idea. I think he just doesn't want me to forget I *can* summon him whenever. Like, he's trying to convince me I need him or something. I mean, the *nalís* only works once."

"Maybe I can find something in Maleshi's spellbook to do kind of the same thing." Ember zipped up her backpack. "That would be awesome. Instant portals? Are you kidding?"

"I'm fairly sure you're not gonna find that charm in her spellbook, Em. Apparently, it's a drow thing, powered by nightstalker blood."

"Oh." Ember grimaced. "Okay, maybe not. *Really?*"

"Yeah. That's what powers the portal, 'cause nightstalkers are the only magicals who can summon portals."

"I *know* that part. It's just creepy that you carry around nightstalker blood in a charm with you."

Cheyenne chuckled. "I don't carry it around with me. I don't think it's that much anyway. Not nearly as much as the blood-tracking bombs the loyalists smuggled over here."

Ember shook her head. "That's taking it too far."

"Well, it sounds like Corian and the others took care of the issue with the war machines. That's what had to happen before we could make the crossing again. There's no way they just said, 'Screw it, we'll deal with those guys later.'"

"Huh. Fingers crossed."

"Okay, I'm gonna go get that pin." Cheyenne headed into her bedroom and searched her previously worn clothing scattered across the floor. She finally found the shirt she'd worn when L'zar gave her the pin and held it up to the light. *I'd completely forgotten about this thing. See? There's a plus side to not keeping up with the laundry.*

She removed the pin from the hem of the old shirt and attached it to the one she was wearing. "Guess I'm prepared now."

"Oh, *wow*." Ember's surprised voice came from the living room.

"Em?" Cheyenne shut her bedroom door behind her and stopped when she saw Maleshi standing between the coffee table and the wall of windows. "Hey."

"Hey." Maleshi turned and gave her an eager smile. "You ready?"

"I think so." Walking slowly toward the couch and her backpack, Cheyenne eyed the nightstalker. "Nice suit."

"You don't have to pretend to like it, Cheyenne." Maleshi rolled her shoulders back and smoothed down the front of her black and gray uniform jacket with a high, stiff, collar and two silver stripes slashed across the chest. Two patches with O'gúleesh symbols were sewn to the shoulders, and a line of smaller metals in various colors shimmered down the right side. "I know it's not like anything you're used to seeing over here. But where *I* come from, this uniform means something, so this is how they'll see me when Maleshi Hi'et returns to Ambar'ogúl."

Cheyenne's eyes widened. "Wait."

"Yes, I'm coming with you. Most of us are."

"Right. It's a party, then."

Maleshi turned her gaze to Ember and smiled. "The whole shebang. I'm glad you decided to come with us too, Ember."

The fae girl let out a wry laugh. "Not sure I have much of a choice."

"That's a load of shit. Give yourself more credit." With a firm nod, the general shook out her hands and lifted them in front of her. "Shall we?"

"Nothing else to handle before we head out." Cheyenne slipped into her trench coat, then grabbed her backpack and slung the straps over her shoulders. "Speaking of handling things…"

"Yes, Cheyenne, the information your terrified neighbor gave us was accurate, and yes, we did what had to be done in the last twenty-four hours to clean up that war-machine mess before we head out. Is that what you were wondering?"

"Yeah. What did you have to do?"

Maleshi shrugged. "We decided to follow your advice. A fun little cell for the loyalists heading their individual operations, and a *lot* of toys for Persh'al to pick apart at his leisure." The general focused on conjuring her portal, and Cheyenne glanced quickly at Ember.

They did listen. No slitting throats or handing out death sentences. For now.

The portal opened in front of Maleshi and she stepped aside, gesturing for Ember to wheel through first.

"What are you guys gonna do with them after this?" Cheyenne asked. "The loyalists."

"Honestly, kid, we haven't thought that far ahead. We have more important things to focus on now, and all of them require *your* head to be in the game." Maleshi's lips curled in a slow smile. "Which I'm assuming it still is. We can figure out what to do with the few dozen prisoners we locked up when we get back."

"Okay." Cheyenne nodded at Ember before the fae girl took a deep breath and wheeled through the portal. "Someone's keeping an eye on them, right?"

"Well, he's not happy about it, but he chose to stay behind, so the responsibility falls on him."

"Who?"

They walked through the portal into the warehouse. "Persh'al. I believe the best argument he could come up with against being a jailor for a day or two was that he only knows how to maintain computer systems, but I'm willing to bet his conscience will be enough to remind him to feed and water the magicals in the basement."

"I heard that," Persh'al called from the other side of the warehouse.

Cheyenne turned and froze when she saw the two battered carcasses of the digger machines they'd torn apart yesterday. "This was your solution for cleanup? Bring them to the warehouse?"

Corian chuckled. "I'm starting to run out of room in my apartment. The place can only keep so much junk."

"That had nothing to do with it." Persh'al stood from his chair on the other side of his computer table and pointed at the nightstalker man. "But here you are, trying to take all the credit again. After a few centuries, you'd think I'd stop being surprised by it."

"Or stop being so bitter about it, at the very least."

The blue troll waved Corian off and walked around the three tables connected in a squared-off U. "Everyone's trying to take credit for something, aren't they? And *you.*" He pointed at Cheyenne and cocked his head. "You stole all my thunder when you found the source of those programs, halfling. Half of me wants to rip you apart for that, and the other half wants to give you a fell-damn trophy."

"Thanks. I think." Cheyenne adjusted the straps of her backpack and shrugged. "The activator did most of the work."

"Obviously." Persh'al stopped beside the war machines in the center of the warehouse and folded his arms. "But you know how to work both, and you're the only one of us who can wear that thing and get any use out of it Earthside. I'm gonna give you this one moment of credit, and then I'm gonna ask you to please, *please* just let me keep doing my job over here. I'm the tech guy. You're the halfling warrior."

She snorted.

"No, seriously. There's a very firm line between our responsibilities. Quit steppin' into my bubble, kid."

"Good to see you too."

Persh'al grinned at her. "I know it's only been two days, but it feels like forever. And now you're going back."

"Yeah, I'm a little surprised you aren't."

"Nah. I've been on a battlefield, but I'm not cut out for this whole 'storming the castle' thing. In this case, that will be pretty much literal. Someone has to keep an eye on what happens when all of you make the crossing and the Earthside eyes on *us* go dark."

The back door squealed open as Byrd and Lumil stepped inside. "You're here already, huh? Nice."

Lumil cracked her knuckles as they approached the group gathered beside the machines. "Damn. I've been looking forward to this since the day you walked in here, looking all dazed and confused."

Byrd sniggered.

Cheyenne smiled at the goblin woman. "You mean, less than two weeks ago?"

"Fair enough. Been waitin' a long time to bring this fiery fist back to Ambar'ogúl, but yeah. After the last two weeks, halfling, I'm even more excited to be doin' it right next to you."

"Yeah, glad you're coming."

"Are you kidding me?" Byrd flexed his hands by his sides and cocked his head. "Wouldn't miss a battle for anything. Not the one that's coming."

"You mean, the one we're bringing," Lumil corrected.

"Hey, come on. How's that an important distinction right now?"

"Because it's *our* battle, and we're taking it *to* that bitch at the center of Hangivol." The goblin woman jerkily shook her head at him in disbelief, her short yellow hair flopping over her forehead. "The battle's not coming, *we* are."

"Oh, so that's what you're so concerned about? You think we'll mess the whole thing up if we don't talk about it the right way?"

Corian closed his eyes and let out a long hiss. "I'm gonna kill them."

"When the hell did you start caring so much about logistics, anyway?"

"Since you convinced me how *wrong* you are."

"Then how 'bout this? I like to fight! You wanna bring the battle now?"

"No!" Persh'al leaped toward them, waving his hands. "You do *not* get to fight inside. Those are the damn rules. And if either of you even thinks about throwing a single explosive punch, I'll whip you back into last century, got it? I'm still studying these machines, and I'm not about to let you two nagging greenskins screw that up. You break it, you buy it."

"Oh, that's interesting." Lumil widened her eyes. "You put a price tag on these things?"

"Yeah. Your life. So will you please shut up or get the hell back outside to settle it there?"

The goblins glanced at each other and burst out laughing.

"Uh-huh. Yeah. Very funny." Persh'al glared at them, then glanced at Cheyenne and waved for her to follow him. "Come on, kid. I wanna show you a little side project before you and the idiot squad head out."

"Sure." Cheyenne and Ember exchanged looks, then the halfling followed Persh'al back to his computer monitors on the center table.

Lumil jerked her chin at Ember and folded her arms. "You're coming with us too, huh?"

Ember cocked her head. "What tipped you off? Was it the backpack?"

Byrd burst into wheezing laughter, doubling over and pounding a fist on his thigh.

"I have no idea what *he* thinks is so funny." Lumil glared at him. "But I like the way you dish it out, fae. If I hadn't seen you at the ceremony the other day, I'd probably ask if you can dish out the same way in a fight."

"Well, I'm working on it."

"Uh-huh. You're not working on anything. You'll be fine."

Byrd wiped tears from his eyes and blew out a long breath. "Whew. You got me, fae. Keep that up. Helps pass the time while we're waiting for our practically immortal leader to make an appearance."

"Yeah, what's he doing in there anyway?" Lumil gestured at the closed door of the built-in office at the back of the warehouse. "You said we were ready to go."

Corian raised an eyebrow at her. "We are."

"So, what's *he* doing?"

"Meditating. You should try it sometime. Maybe then I wouldn't have to listen to you two pick each other apart."

Byrd snorted. "That's ridiculous. Meditating doesn't make you allergic to arguing."

Corian clasped his hands behind his back and turned toward the opposite wall and the chair propped against it. "No, but when you're meditating, you aren't doing or saying anything else. You're *quiet.*"

"Ha!" Lumil clapped her hands. "The nightstalker wants quiet, huh? Shit, if that's all he wants, he should've stayed home."

"Dude." Byrd looked at her with wide eyes and shook his head. "That's never gonna happen."

"Shut up."

CHAPTER EIGHTY-FIVE

Cheyenne leaned over Persh'al's desk to study the O'gúleesh code scrolling across his center monitor.

"You brought that activator with you, right?"

"Yeah."

"Good. Put it on real fast." Persh'al snorted. "Then I won't have to explain much at all, and we'll save ourselves a crapload of time."

Cheyenne pulled the silver coil from her pocket, changed to her drow form, and stuck it behind her ear. The syncing pinch made her eyelids flutter, then she opened them and focused on the screen.

The blue troll laughed. "For as much as I love that tech, I sure as hell don't miss the pinch."

"You get used to it."

"Ha, listen to *you* telling *me* what to get used to. Pshh." He swiveled his desk chair toward his keyboard and typed a few commands. "Okay, this is what I want you to see. Brand-new program, sort of. Fine, it's the reassembled parts of the system that CEO was selling like a stupid fell-damn human, but I added a few extra bits for this specific program. I'm assuming that thing translates for you even Earthside, yeah?"

"Oh, yeah." Cheyenne scanned the scrolling bits of O'gúleesh code rearranging themselves into the language she recognized. The activator gave her an overview of the lines she couldn't quite follow on her own. "Security system?"

"More like emergency broadcast. It just needs an endpoint." Persh'al pointed at her ear. "Which would be your fancy new toy. Think you can get that thing to upload this little nugget and sync up?"

She smiled at him. "Piece of cake."

"You know what? I love cake. Not so sure I love the smug look on your human-looking face right now. Which, by the way, is looking about as pink as your fae friend. You get a sunburn?"

Cheyenne turned quickly toward the monitor again and forced herself to focus. "Stayed in the shower too long. It'll go away."

"Uh-huh." The troll shrugged and sat back in his chair. "Go ahead, then. Work your tech magic."

"Got it." She straightened and shot him a grin. "Uploaded, synced, and ready to broadcast, looks like."

"*What?*" Persh'al vigorously shook his head and peered at the screen. "There's no way you just— Damn. Again, I can't decide between wanting to murder you or worship you. How did you get through all that in thirty seconds?"

"Just the activator." She spread her arms and stepped away from the table. "You saw me. I didn't touch a thing."

"I know. And I hate it."

"Hey, I didn't reassemble that O'gúl-human code mashup, either. That was manual on your part."

Persh'al kicked his chair away from the table and shook his head. "I don't need you to tell me what I did."

"I'm just giving credit where it's due, that's all."

"Uh-huh." The troll's orange eyes darted toward her, and his scowl melted into a grin. "Yeah, I know, kid. You get all the fun stuff, I get all the credit. I'm good with that. I better be, right? I'm stuck here while the rest of you get to rage against the Crown full-anarchy style over there."

She raised an eyebrow as she removed the activator and stuck it back into her pocket, then changed back to her human form. "I thought you didn't wanna go?"

"What? Oh, right. I mean, yeah, I *want* to go. It's just a bad idea."

"It was a pretty good idea for you to come with me two days ago."

"Yeah, but that was when it was just the two of us and I didn't have the half-crazy bossman looming over my shoulder." Persh'al nodded at the office in the back. It only took five more seconds of Cheyenne silently staring at him before he broke down and offered the rest. "Fine, you got me again. Yeah, there's more."

He glanced around, but the other magicals were involved in a conversation by the machines that had Ember and Maleshi laughing, Corian shaking his head, and Byrd and Lumil on the verge of a fistfight.

"Can I be honest with you, kid?"

Cheyenne held back a laugh. "Kind of impossible for you not to be, isn't it?"

"Okay, let's forget that you've got some kinda weird drow hypnosis thing going on and I can't lie to you."

"I didn't do anything."

"That's beside the point." He stepped toward her and leaned in as he lowered his voice. "I do wanna be there standing next to you when the Crown falls, kid. I want you to know that. And please don't try to convince me I should come anyway, 'cause the reason I'm staying isn't about me."

When he slowly lifted his gaze to look at her, Cheyenne nodded. *He's talking about Elarit.* "You think she'll understand why you chose to stay behind?"

"I have no idea. I hope she does. I hope she *can*. But I can't risk trying to explain it to her, and I can't risk going over there. Shit, kid, it's hard enough to keep anything from *you*. L'zar's a hundred times worse if you can believe it."

"Yeah, I believe it." She stuck her hands in her pockets and looked at L'zar's office-turned-private-room. "But she's part of this whole thing too. She's behind L'zar, not trying to stop him."

"Doesn't matter. Don't get me wrong, kid. Even if he found out before we take this battle to the Crown, he'd still let me fight. He'd let her fight too; pretend like he didn't know what was happening so we could all focus on the more important objective—the *only* objective in his eyes at this point. Afterward, knowing that I'd lied to him about cutting her off?" Persh'al shrugged. "I'd like to think he wouldn't do anything so terrible I couldn't live with it. We've been friends a long time. We've saved each other's lives more times than I can count. L'zar wouldn't hurt either of us if he knew she and I were still waiting for the day when we don't have two entire worlds between us, but he'd find some way to shame us for it. Most of that would fall on her, probably. I can't let that happen."

"Jesus." Cheyenne shook her head, unable to look away from the office door with her drow father somewhere on the other side of it. "So, we're following another dictator across the border."

"What? No. You've got that all wrong."

"Doesn't sound like it. He can't punish either of you for not letting him dictate who to be with or whatever."

Persh'al snorted. "Not a fan of that kinda relationship, huh?"

"I'm not *not* a fan." Cheyenne shrugged. "It's just not on my radar. Like, at all. But we're not talking about *me*, troll."

"Ha. Yeah, I tried."

"Why do you let him make those kinds of choices for you?"

Persh'al frowned. "I didn't. I went against his orders on this one, and that's on me. But why do I hand over the reins on everything else? 'Cause I respect him. I've followed him through more tight spaces than even Corian was willing to go way back when, and I honestly believe L'zar's got the interests of both our worlds as a high priority."

Cheyenne cocked her head. "But not the top priority."

"No. L'zar Verdys is his own top priority. We all know that." The troll snorted. "Doesn't mean he doesn't care about anything else, though."

"Sounds like we're replacing one shitty ruler with another shitty ruler who smells a little better."

"No way, kid." Persh'al stepped back and clapped a hand on the halfling's shoulder. "Here's the difference between L'zar and the Mother sitting on that throne. L'zar would separate Elarit and me if he found out, sure, maybe even forever. And he might throw an extra barb or two in there as a reminder to both of us that following orders is pretty much all we have now. Which I get. We'd move on and be fine, and that's the end of it. The Crown would invite us in and make us watch everyone we know get the magic sucked out of them and the flesh peeled off their bones."

"Jesus."

"Then she'd kill us both in some slow, fucked-up way that gave us a tiny spark of hope that we might be able to get ourselves out of it until we realized we couldn't. Then we'd be dead, everyone we care about would be dead, and there'd be no one left to stand up to it the next time the Crown decided her judgment was required. Do you need me to go into it in more detail?

"Nope. I'm good." Cheyenne swallowed and shook her head. "It's a damn convincing argument."

Persh'al laughed. "Yeah, against your statement that the only difference between them is that he smells better."

"Still. You're his friend, and you've had his back for a long time. It's not okay for him to dangle this kind of thing over your head."

"Well, he's got his reasons, and it's not the worst-case scenario. Who knows? If I can keep my mouth shut about it for long enough, maybe we won't get to the point where we have to admit lying about it." The troll spread his arms and raised his voice. "Maybe we'll all just live happily ever after with a bunch of rainbows and unicorns and sparkly shit until the deathflame brings the end."

The magicals gathered around the dead war machines turned toward Persh'al to shoot him curious, confused glances. Ember snorted. "I don't know what you guys are talking about, but if you're trying to get Cheyenne excited about something, that is *not* the way to do it."

Cheyenne grinned at Persh'al and nudged a fist into his shoulder. "I won't say anything."

"I know you won't. That's why you're going and I'm staying here." The troll sat at his desk and dove back into typing on his keyboard.

So, L'zar's not just a little better than the Crown. Sounds like night and day. Maybe that prophecy's not what I thought it was.

The door at the back of the warehouse creaked as it swung open, and L'zar stood dressed head-to-toe in light gray in the opening. He spread his arms and gave everyone that deviously feral grin. "Let's go fuck shit up, huh?"

"Wow." Lumil cocked her head and tried to keep a straight face while Byrd snorted. "I did not see *that* coming." Both goblins burst into hissing snorts of laughter. "Is that what you've been doing this whole time? Trying to come up with the perfect rallying speech?"

L'zar stepped out of the doorway, still grinning. "You'd like that, wouldn't you?"

"Oh, yeah. I'd love even more proof that you've officially lost your mind. Got any other nuggets of enlightenment for us?"

"Only that I fully expect you to put your money where your mouth is, Lumil."

"Ha!"

L'zar joined the rest of the magicals beside the broken war machines. He looked down at Ember and dipped his head. "Sorry for interrupting your packing this morning."

"Well, I didn't see you, so I guess it's fine." She looked at Cheyenne as the drow halfling and Persh'al left his table to join the others.

Corian folded his arms and watched L'zar intently. "You finished."

"Yes, I finished." The drow shot his *Nós Ani* a fleeting glance, then dismissed the whole thing when he looked away. "Which means the rest of us can officially start. I'm assuming everyone's ready."

"We've *been* ready," Byrd muttered.

"Yes, I think we're all aware of that."

Corian cleared his throat, casting L'zar occasional wary glances. "We're heading back to the portal ridge up north where we found the smuggled machine parts. Portaling this time, seeing as those machine parts and their former loyalist handlers are now in our custody."

"The Bull's Head can suck it." Lumil pumped a fist in the air.

"And if they do, it'll be in a cell." Corian raised his eyebrow at the goblin woman, who nodded and stared at the floor. "After what happened the last time Cheyenne and Persh'al made the crossing, we realize there isn't any way to predict what's going to happen this time. We might be separated. Hopefully not. We might come across something we've never seen before while we're passing through the in-between, so be on your guard, and don't get complacent. There's still a lot that could go wrong."

"Quick question." Ember raised her hand, then ran it through her hair. "So, I get that we have to stay together, be quick about it, on our toes, all that. Is nobody worried about me being in this chair? 'Cause that's gonna cause some problems with rocks, water, stairs, narrow spaces, and running. You know, the usual."

Maleshi and Corian looked at each other, and the general chuckled. "We heard you're fairly decent with spellcasting already."

605

"Well, thanks. But unless you know a spell that can make my legs work again, I'm not so sure whatever I can do will be helpful."

Byrd frowned at his fellow rebels. "Is she serious?"

"I didn't bring the wheelchair as a gag if that's what you mean."

Cheyenne pressed her lips together and rocked back on her heels. *This'll be interesting.*

"No, I didn't mean that," Byrd replied. "I meant, you don't need your legs to walk."

Ember's eyelids fluttered closed and she leaned forward, straining to keep her composure. "Say that again."

"We might have assumed you'd already realized this, Ember. What Byrd failed to explain is that there are spells that don't require working legs in order to move as if you didn't need that chair." Corian motioned for her to follow him away from the group where there was more space.

L'zar stared at them and slowly shook his head. "Is this necessary right now?"

"It'll only take a minute."

"I stepped out here ready to move, Corian. This isn't a fae magic class for beginners."

"Hey." Cheyenne frowned at L'zar when the drow turned to look at her. "Two minutes. She's good."

"I'm sure. That doesn't mean I have to wait patiently."

"All right, well, then just don't say anything." Cheyenne nodded at Ember as Corian taught her whatever spell she needed to learn. "I probably wouldn't be here now without Ember. We all know I need her, which means *you* need her. And, *I* was ready to go two days ago, but you sent me over there with Persh'al instead."

The troll rubbed his head. "No offense taken, kid. Don't worry about it."

L'zar dipped his head and stared at Cheyenne beneath darkening brows. "And your point?"

"My point is you're not the only one who's been waiting. And besides Ember and me, everyone else in this room has been waiting for *you* for a couple hundred years. This is two more minutes. Get over it."

The drow's eyes narrowed in a quick flicker, then he drew a deep breath and gave his daughter a tight-lipped smile. "Off to a good start, aren't we?"

Cheyenne shook her head and turned to watch Ember and Corian working against the far wall. *Persh'al wasn't kidding. L'zar Verdys' number-one priority is L'zar Verdys. That better not get the rest of us killed.*

A minute later, the purple light flashing around Ember's hands slowly lifted her from the wheelchair. Corian stepped back with a nod of approval. Maleshi clapped four times and folded her arms again. "There it is. Cheyenne wasn't exaggerating about her spellwork."

"Holy shit." Ember glanced down on either side of her to watch her feet stop an inch above the ground. "I did it. On purpose!"

Byrd snorted. "You shouldn't be casting spells any other way, am I right?"

Lumil elbowed him in the ribs and smiled at the fae girl.

"Okay. Kinda like standing, I guess." Ember looked at Cheyenne and opened her mouth wide in amazement. "This is real. What's next?"

"Just like walking." Corian nodded. "You just think about doing it."

"Just think." Ember floated forward and stopped, then burst out laughing. "Oh, my God. This is a thing. This works!"

"Excellent." L'zar closed his eyes. "Let's all celebrate by getting a move on, please and thank you."

"Ha!" Ember moved around the room, spinning to look at Corian, then floating in a small circle until she stopped at Cheyenne's side. "Damn. I almost forgot what it was like not to look up at everyone all the time. You're like a completely different person from this angle."

Cheyenne snorted. "You too."

"Yes!" Ember grinned at Corian, tears shimmering in her luminous violet eyes before she quickly blinked them back. "Thank you. This is better than…well, this is the best thing I can think of now, so just thank you."

"You're welcome." Corian picked her backpack up from the seat of the wheelchair and rejoined the group. "Keep your focus on that for now, okay? We'll see what happens if you have to use any of your other magic once we make the crossing. But Cheyenne *will* need you, so try not to get carried away."

She took her bag from him and laughed as she slid the straps over her shoulders. "Not possible. *Nobody* has to carry me, and that wheelchair can kiss my ass."

Lumil let out a startled guffaw as she doubled over, then straightened quickly and choked back more laughter with such force that her green face darkened.

L'zar rubbed his temples. "Someone open a portal so I can get out of this fell-damn warehouse."

"Need some fresh air?" Cheyenne narrowed her eyes at him when his golden gaze met hers.

Her drow father blinked slowly and looked away. "Something like that."

Corian eyed them both before summoning their portal.

L'zar looks like crap right now. I don't know, maybe I would too if I hadn't been home in a few hundred years.

The portal opened, and Corian gestured for the others to step through. L'zar stormed through first, anxious to finally leave the confines of another building holding him inside. Byrd and Lumil went next, followed by a grinning, floating Ember. Maleshi nodded at Persh'al before she disappeared.

"Give' em hell, kid." Persh'al raised his hand toward Cheyenne in a gesture she didn't recognize, middle finger curled into a loop with his thumb with his ring finger crossed over his pinky.

Despite the weird gesture, she nodded. "That's the plan."

Corian gave the blue troll a final nod as well before he followed the halfling through the portal and it disappeared behind them.

Persh'al spun to deliver a swift kick to the side of one of the broken war machines. Two blue sparks popped inside the mostly empty shell, and he leaped back, hissing. "Don't even start. You think I wanna be here with a pile of old-school junk? Lucky for me, I still have something to focus on."

CHAPTER EIGHTY-SIX

"This looks a hell of a lot better than the last time." Lumil cracked her knuckles as the group made their way across the clearing toward the towering portal ridge of black stone. "Who cleaned up?"

"No idea." Maleshi brushed invisible specks of dirt off the sleeve of her uniform. "Whoever it was stopped by before Cheyenne and Persh'al went through last time."

"And it wasn't us?" Byrd asked.

"Yeah, idiot." Lumil punched him in the shoulder. "We cleaned up all the cargo crates and all the bodies and took 'em back to the warehouse."

"Well, where are they?"

She snorted and rolled her eyes. "Not at the warehouse."

"General." L'zar turned toward Maleshi and gestured at the spires of black stone. "If you wouldn't mind."

"Apparently, this is my new specialty." Maleshi stepped forward and extended her hands toward the veil of shimmering pink light reaching into the sky from the center of the portal ridge.

Ember floated toward Cheyenne, staring at the tall columns in front of them. "This thing is huge."

"Yeah."

"Makes the one at your mom's place look like a baby."

Cheyenne snorted. "Maybe it is. This one's definitely been around a little longer."

"And you fought the crazy-ass monsters coming out of *this* thing?"

"I had help."

Lumil smashed a fist into her other hand, throwing up a shower of bright-red sparks. "And man, wasn't *that* a wild ride!"

Ember smiled. "Looks like you enjoyed it."

The goblin woman shook out her hand and chuckled. "More than you know, fae. I'm getting pumped for this one."

The pink wall of light flickered, then disappeared. Maleshi lowered her arms and turned around. "Well, there you go. The shield is gone. The portal's open. Time to get the hell off Earth, huh?"

Corian stepped past L'zar, thumping the drow on the back before he headed toward the portal ridge. "We walk through, and we keep walking until we're through the doorway on the other side. Don't stop. Don't change direction. And stay close together. Let's go." He waved them forward, and the group followed.

Ember exhaled quickly and shook out her wrists. "I'm actually doing this."

Cheyenne cast her a sidelong glance and smiled. "You'll be fine. Whatever's on the other side of those rocks is a hell of a lot easier to take down than last week. The rest of us can fight. You just keep floating."

"Ha-ha. I can fight too. I think."

"Well, if that's what's in your heart in the moment, go for it, Em."

They laughed softly before stepping up behind the magicals in front of them. Corian moved through the columns of shiny black stone first, and the rest of the group stayed close on his heels. Brushing her fingers against the thick silver band on her wrist, Cheyenne let her magic burn through her and slipped into drow form.

Cheyenne braced herself for the feeling of an elephant sitting on her lungs, but it didn't come. She kept walking, her gaze focused on the back of Lumil's yellow-haired head, and waited for the shift.

"Shit." Corian stepped through the other side of the stone columns where the woods started at the other end of the clearing and turned.

"Oh, come on!" Byrd thumped his fist against the last pillar as he passed it and stomped across the grass on the other side. "You get all hyped up, and this bastard portal rips all the fun right out of it."

Ember and Cheyenne passed through the ridge after the others. The fae girl looked at the rising black stone. "Let me guess: this isn't supposed to happen."

"No. It's not." L'zar stroked his chin and looked at the spires.

"Maleshi?"

"I had nothing to do with this one." The general folded her arms. "Just a shield. On and off. The portal was working just fine two days ago."

"And now it's not." Corian stepped back through the stone columns, but he came out on the other side just the same. "All right, first roadblock."

"Dammit!" Byrd stomped around the edge of the portal ridge to join Corian on the other side. "Giant stone towers shooting up out of the ground. *Roadblock.* That would've been hilarious if I wasn't so pissed off right now."

"Hmm." Corian's nose twitched as he scowled at the portal. "Doesn't do us any good to be pissed about it now. We need an alternative."

"Yeah, to a lack of a climax."

Lumil snorted. "Don't pretend like you have plenty of the opposite on a regular basis."

"What's that supposed to mean?"

"Can it, you two." Maleshi walked back through the portal ridge, and Cheyenne and Ember followed her. Only L'zar remained on the other side. "Our alternative is another portal. Which ones do we know?"

"Rez 19, to start." Corian folded his arms. "They've had a huge influx recently, so we'd be walking into a swarm of agents itching to see one of us screw something up."

"Rez 22 leads right into Ki'uali," Lumil offered. "Not where we wanted to end up, but it's something."

L'zar reached out and slowly tapped the closest column of black stone. A hollow, metallic ring came from it, and he frowned. "We're not going through a reservation portal."

"What?" Byrd whirled around to stare at him between the columns. "This is the only other one we know of."

"There's one more."

Cheyenne clenched her fists and stared at her drow father, who was suddenly and weirdly much more interested in studying the dead portal than in solving their problem. *Don't even think about it.*

The second she had the thought, L'zar's golden gaze flickered toward her. "In Henry County."

"No." Cheyenne shook her head. "No, we're not taking a field trip to the Summerlin estate. No fucking way."

"We don't even know where that one leads." Corian stared at L'zar as the drow moved slowly through the shiny black columns, brushing his fingers over each one he passed.

"It leads to Ambar'ogúl." L'zar stepped out of the stone columns and dusted off his hands. "Cheyenne proved that much."

"Yeah, but I didn't come out in the same place as everyone else. Maybe something weird happened in the in-between, or maybe that portal at my mom's house is a fluke. That's where I came out *after* Persh'al and I got separated." She shook her head. "I don't even know why I'm talking about that. That's not the point. We are *not* going out there."

L'zar turned his gaze on his daughter again. "If we don't go to that portal, Cheyenne, we don't get to Ambar'ogúl. Are you ready to throw it all away so soon?"

"There are hundreds of other Border portals all over the world. Pick one!"

"Ah, yes. Which reservation seems the most suitable for walking through the gates and saying, 'Hello. We've brought the fugitive your superiors are tracking down, plus seven magicals you don't have in your fell-damn system. Please let us through the portal you think you own.'"

Byrd snorted.

Cheyenne cocked her head, clenching her jaw as she tried not to lose it on the drow. "You walked out of Chateau D'rahl all on your own, L'zar. Twice. Don't tell me you can't figure out how to get past a few dozen rez guards who aren't looking for you there."

His cheeks twitched in distaste when he gave her a tight, unamused smile. "That's exactly what I'm telling you."

"Are you serious? A reservation full of FRoE guards is too much for L'zar Verdys to handle?"

Corian stepped toward her. "Cheyenne."

"Seriously? You guys show up at my mom's house and use the portal in her back yard? How the hell do you think that's gonna go over?"

"Well, we'd start by asking nicely." L'zar grinned, though the usual mischief didn't quite show through this one.

"Yeah, good luck with that." Cheyenne folded her arms. "Besides, there's a team of FRoE agents at that portal ridge too. Not reservation guards, but if they see L'zar Verdys strolling across the lawn, they're not gonna stop to ask questions."

L'zar spread his arms. "Then they won't see me."

"You don't take anything seriously, do you?"

"Hey." Maleshi nudged Cheyenne's arm and nodded at the other end of the clearing. "Can I have a minute?"

Cheyenne shot Ember an exasperated glance, then followed the general across the clearing for a private conversation. *Except L'zar will be able to hear all of it. Corian too, probably. No such thing as privacy.*

Maleshi stopped and faced the halfling. "I get what you're trying to do, kid."

"Yeah? What's that?"

"Protect your mom. And I don't mean from in-between monsters or magical earthquakes or war machines. From him." The general nodded at the group of magicals. L'zar had sat on the grass with his legs crossed beneath him.

"He's meditating. Great." Cheyenne rolled her eyes. "Yeah, I'm trying to protect my mom. She loses it any time magic or magicals are mentioned. And she drank almost an entire bottle of scotch on her own the day she showed me the Chateau D'rahl video of L'zar turning himself back in after their private New Year's Eve party. She's been dragged into this enough."

"Yes, she has, and none of us wants to involve her any further. But L'zar needs to keep his focus fairly centrally located, you might say. The Border reservations are too much of a distraction. Too much we can't control that could go wrong. And this portal isn't working."

Cheyenne ran her hand over the top of her head. "Yeah, I get it. I can't believe this."

"We'll make sure not to bother her." Maleshi nodded. "And it's not like we're heading that way for a social call. She won't even see us there."

"Yes, she will. Bianca sees everything." Rolling her eyes, Cheyenne shrugged. "I have to tell her we're coming. She deserves to know that, at the very least."

"Sure. Make the call. Both of them. You can get those FRoE agents to step aside for a few minutes, right?"

"I should be able to, yeah." Cheyenne pulled her phone out of her back pocket. "We'll see what happens."

"Thank you." Maleshi set a hand on the halfling's shoulder and gently squeezed. "It's a far cry from the worst that could happen."

"Yeah, and it still sucks."

Maleshi winked at her, then rejoined the rest of the group standing around the meditating L'zar.

Cheyenne noticed Ember watching her in concern, and she spread her arms. "Shot in the dark, Em."

"Fifty-fifty chance, right?"

Nodding, Cheyenne pulled up Rhynehart's number on her phone and made the first call. *Right. Fifty-fifty chance. Either I make this work and it'll suck, or today's the day everybody stops listening to me.*

Rhynehart picked up after the third ring. "Yeah."

"I need a favor."

"Oh, yeah? Figured you'd call me this time instead of going straight to Sir again, huh?"

Seriously? When does this end? "You're talking about the new portal at VCU."

"Damn right, I'm talking about it. I thought you and I had an understanding."

"We do, Rhynehart. I wasn't going behind your back, and the whole VCU situation isn't exactly a black ops thing. I didn't wanna bother you with something you would've just sent up the line to him anyway. I know you're up there at the portal at my mom's still, so believe it or not, I considered you quite a bit before calling Sir."

There was a slight pause on the other end of the line, then Rhynehart cleared his throat. "All right. What's your favor this time?"

"I need you to call your team away from that portal for like twenty minutes."

"Are you shittin' me?"

Cheyenne sighed. "Yeah, Rhynehart. I called you just to waste your time."

"Are you gonna tell me *why* my guys get an extra break all together without leaving anyone on rotation?"

"Because I'm asking you to do this for me. Tell them to turn away for twenty minutes. That's it. You can take them around to the front of the house for all I care, as long as they can't see anything in the back."

"I'd appreciate a crumb, halfling."

"Well, I'm sure you can figure out on your own why I'd want your team to leave that portal alone for twenty minutes. Beyond that, anything I tell you will just make it harder for both of us. Look, you said you trusted me to take care of my end of things. Please, Rhynehart. Just trust me on this."

His slow, frustrated exhale through his nose rustled against the speaker. "Fine."

"Thank you."

"When do I make this happen?"

"In the next five minutes. I'll text you when it's time to move them out of there. I have one more thing to take care of first, but I won't keep you waiting long."

"All right. If anything blows back on me because of this—"

"It won't. That's why I'm doing this the way I'm doing it—so nobody has to take the fall for something that shouldn't have fallout anyway."

"All right. I'll wait for that text." He hung up, and Cheyenne dropped her head all the way back and stared at the sky.

That sucked. This is gonna be even worse.

CHAPTER EIGHTY-SEVEN

Cheyenne pulled up her mom's cell number and forced herself to make the second call. Grimacing, she brought the phone to her ear and waited.

"Please tell me this is a courtesy call informing me that these agents on my property are being recalled."

Cheyenne bit her lip. "Hi, Mom. I wish I could tell you that, but no. And I'm letting you know ahead of time that you'll like this conversation even less than having those guys in the backyard."

"Well, thank you for the warning. I'm listening."

She won't be thanking me at the end of this.

"I'm not asking for permission, because I'll probably do it anyway, even if you refuse. You deserve to know ahead of time that I'll be at the house in a few minutes with some friends."

"Is Ember with you?"

Cheyenne almost laughed at that. "Yeah, Mom. Ember's here, and a few other people like me." *Spit it out and get it over with. The worst she can do is hang up.* "And," she added, gritting her teeth and clenching her eyes shut, "*he's* with us too."

Bianca didn't utter a word, and even with her drow hearing, Cheyenne couldn't hear so much as a whistle of breath from her mom.

"Mom?"

"I heard you."

"Okay. This'll be quick and quiet, no confrontations with the agents there. I made sure of that already. We're just heading out to the back-yard. A few minutes at the most, and then we'll be gone." *That's as much as I can openly say about walking through a portal into another world.*

"Yes. Brevity and silence are very much appreciated."

"I promise, Mom. We won't bother you."

"Oh, that ship has sailed, Cheyenne, but that's not the issue. I am perfectly willing to turn a blind eye to the presence of you and your friends on my property on two conditions."

Of course. "I'm listening."

"The first is that we never speak of this again, which works well for both of us, I should think. And the second is that you come inside to speak to me personally the instant you arrive. After that, whatever you and the rest of your party decide to do is in your hands, and I won't meddle. But I want to speak to you in person."

"Absolutely. I can do that."

"Good. Is there anything else?"

"Thank you."

"Don't thank me, Cheyenne. You said it yourself. You'd come here even if I refused. And you're right, I wouldn't be able to stop you. You know how I feel about this."

"Yeah, I do."

"Then you also know that despite my feelings and my personal opinions, I very much respect your decision to call me before any of it takes place. That can't have been easy for you."

Cheyenne blinked and turned away from the group of magicals so they wouldn't see her surprise. *Respect from Bianca Summerlin for pissing her off. The whole world's falling apart.* "Okay. Will you accept a thank you for *that?*"

"Yes, Cheyenne. That one I will accept."

"Thank you."

"You've earned it. I expect to see you at the front door very shortly."

"I'll be there."

Bianca hung up first, and Cheyenne took a moment to pull herself together. *I seriously hope a face-to-face talk will go as well as that did. Totally unexpected.*

She headed back toward the others. L'zar uncrossed his legs and stood in one fluid motion, settling his golden gaze on his daughter. "Time to go."

Cheyenne paused. "Yeah. Everything's ready."

A small smile lifted the corner of his mouth. "I'm much more used to being the one who handles the connections, Cheyenne. Still haven't figured out if I enjoy the experience of letting someone else handle it."

"I'm positive I don't enjoy the experience of taking you to my mom's house for that portal, but we're doing it anyway." She spread her arms. "Right?"

"Right." Corian lifted his hands. "Is now a good time?"

"Hold on." Cheyenne texted Rhynehart with one word.

Now.

She wiggled her phone with a shrug. "Just give it like five minutes. Oh, and by the way, I have to talk to my mom in person before we hit the portal. It won't be long, but that's the only way to keep her from losing it."

"More waiting." L'zar swallowed and looked at the sky. "My favorite."

Three minutes later, Rhynehart replied.

Clear.

She pressed her lips together and stuck her phone back in her pocket. "Time to go in."

Corian shot L'zar a quick glance before conjuring a portal straight into Bianca Summerlin's backyard. The drow stood stock-still, hands clasped behind his back and his eyes closed, breathing in a loud, slow rhythm through his nose.

Ember moved closer to the halfling and lowered her voice. "Everything okay?"

"Not really. Kinda weird that I'm more nervous about facing the wrath of Bianca than I've ever been about heading into a fight or even when making the crossing. Either time."

"Well, your mom's terrifying."

"Ha. Yeah. You know, she's never blamed me for being what I am. Not that she likes it, but she hasn't held it against me. This feels like she might."

Ember sighed as the portal opened in front of Corian and their group started walking through. "Guess you'll just have to find out, right? Not the end of the world if she blames you."

"True. I just don't think she'll be able to move past it if that happens."

"Cheyenne." Corian gestured at the portal. "Let's go."

She and Ember moved side by side through the oval of dark light and stepped onto Bianca Summerlin's well-maintained lawn behind the estate house. They stood in front of the much smaller portal ridge stretching between them and the edge of the forest.

"Okay." Cheyenne turned toward the house. "This'll only take me a few minutes. Shit!"

Out on the winding back veranda overlooking the valley and the backyard stood Bianca, a full glass of red wine in hand. She didn't move an inch while she stared at the group of unwanted magicals who'd appeared through a different kind of portal onto her property.

"What?" Corian turned, and the others followed suit to catch a brief glimpse of Bianca before she spun away from the veranda's railing and stormed into the house.

"She wasn't supposed to see us." Cheyenne grimaced and took off toward the house. "I'll take care of it. Just stay there."

I screwed this one up. Covered everything but the part about us not showing up in a car at the front of the house. How did I forget about that?

The halfling took the stone steps at the side of the house two at a time from the yard up the hill. The front door slammed shut, followed by a FRoE agent asking, "Ma'am, is everything okay?"

Bianca ignored the question and came storming around the side of the house toward her daughter. Her blue flats wobbled on the gravel when she rounded the last pruned hedge, but she didn't miss a step in barreling past and practically running down the stairs.

"Mom." Cheyenne stepped sideways and raised both hands in an attempt to stop her. "I'm sorry. This was my mistake."

Bianca didn't say a word but tried to sidestep around her daughter instead.

Cheyenne blocked her again. "Let's just have our talk. We can do that here, face to face. You don't need to go down there, okay? Let me take care of it."

Her mom stopped trying to step out of the way and looked Cheyenne's drow appearance over from head to toe with a furious gaze.

"I don't care if you look more like him than me right now, Cheyenne. I would recognize that man anywhere. Get out of my way."

Bianca didn't shove her daughter aside as much as she tried to barrel through her. Cheyenne stepped quickly aside to avoid knocking either of them down the stairs and watched her mom hurry across the lawn toward the portal ridge. *Yep. Worst-case scenario right here.*

She followed her mom, shaking her head when Corian and the others looked from Bianca to her halfling daughter. Then she realized L'zar wasn't with them. *Oh, great. He ran away again so he wouldn't have to face this.*

Bianca reached the group of magicals and gazed frantically from one face to the next. Then she stormed around them and checked the right-hand side of the portal ridge, then the left. "Where is he?"

No one said a word.

"I know you can talk, and I know you know who I'm talking about." The woman spun and glared at them. "I rarely raise my voice, but this is one of those moments. *Where is he?*"

Cheyenne slowed from her jog and stopped beside Ember. She clamped a hand over her mouth and watched her mom's fury in horror.

Ember leaned toward her to mutter, "Should she be out here?"

"I tried. The only way to stop her is to knock her out or tie her up. Nobody's getting away with that."

"Ms. Summerlin," Maleshi said gently, "I'm not sure this is the time."

"You're on *my* property, whoever you are. I'll decide what's the right time for my own choices. If you won't tell me where he is, I'll thank you to keep whatever you have to say to yourself." Bianca's chest heaved as she scanned the group of magicals, the other side of the backyard, and the tree line bending around the manicured lawn. Then she froze, grew rigid, and took a deep breath through her nose.

The last thing any of them expected was for Bianca Summerlin to whirl with her arm drawn back before swatting the air with every inch of her strength behind that blow. After a loud smack of flesh on flesh she stepped back, shaking out her stinging hand.

L'zar lowered the illusion making him invisible. He stood in front of Bianca, staring at her with wide golden eyes and rubbing the darker-gray splotch on his cheek, grinning like a lunatic. "Bianca. It's been a while."

"Oh, shit." Byrd lifted a fist to his mouth and coughed. "She just *slapped* him."

"Shut up." Lumil elbowed him in the ribs with a loud thump. The goblin hardly noticed as he stared with all the others at the unexpected reunion of Cheyenne's parents.

Bianca's jaw worked silently for a moment, then she lifted her chin and regained her calm, collected composure. "I don't want to know where you're going or what you're doing or why, but let me make this perfectly clear for you. If you don't bring Cheyenne back here at the end of it, I will ruin you."

Lumil sucked in a sharp breath. Standing on either side of Cheyenne's parents, Corian and Maleshi exchanged wary glances.

L'zar lowered his hand from his stinging cheek and dipped his head. "I have no doubt. Still, that's for our daughter to decide."

"No." Bianca took a step toward him and seemed to grow a few inches taller in her fury by sheer willpower. "She's nothing but a pawn to you, L'zar. Cheyenne is *my* daughter."

He searched her face, still grinning, then took a step back and spread his arms, bowing his head. But he didn't break away from her gaze. "I can't argue with you there."

Bianca looked him up and down, then spun away and walked three yards back toward the house before turning around and planting her feet again. One finger tapped the side of her navy dress pants, which was the only sign that she'd been furious enough to yell no more than two minutes before. Her gaze flickered briefly toward Cheyenne, and she nodded before having to look away again.

Never thought I'd see her embarrassed and vindicated at the same time. How the hell did she know he was standing right behind her?

L'zar motioned with a quick gesture for Corian to lead the others toward the unprotected Border portal. Corian and Maleshi moved past him, followed by the goblins, and then a hesitant Cheyenne and Ember. The drow turned back toward the mother of his halfling child and placed a hand over his heart. "Lovely to see you again, Bianca."

Her only reply was a bitter laugh and to further raise her chin without looking away from his golden eyes.

With a soft chuckle, L'zar bowed again and turned to step off her lawn and through the spire of black stone to enter the in-between.

Bianca Summerlin stood on her lawn and stared at the place she'd watched them all disappear. The only thing that broke her rigid vigil over the portal was the sound of Rhynehart's men returning after their twenty minutes were up. Rhynehart approached her slowly and gestured back toward the house. "Ms. Summerlin, I'm sorry to interrupt, but it's not safe for you to stay out here."

"I'm much safer standing here than whatever's on the other side of *that* thing." She shot him a quick sidelong glance, then stormed away from his agents across her perfectly green and exquisitely manicured lawn, scarred by the jagged spears of black stone that had taken her daughter.

CHAPTER EIGHTY-EIGHT

Cheyenne stumbled forward and bent over, propping her hands on her thighs as her lungs burned with their need for air. The rest of the group coughed and gasped, drawing in raw breaths after their painful welcome to the in-between. L'zar was the only one somehow unaffected by the doorway. He cleared his throat once and kept walking without so much as pausing for a deep breath. "We have a lot of ground to cover. Keep moving."

"Oh, my God," Ember wheezed, straightening to her full height and panting to catch her breath. "Is that supposed to happen?"

"Every time, yeah. I totally forgot to warn you. Sorry."

"No, no problem." The fae girl took a deep breath and stared around them at the landscape of nothingness punctuated by puffs of black smoke and the thick black fog covering the ground. "We were all a little distracted before stepping in here. Is that smoke?"

"No idea, Em. I'd give up trying to make sense of anything you see here. It's most likely not gonna happen. We just need to keep moving."

"Yeah." Ember floated steadily beside her, and both girls moved a little faster to make sure they didn't fall behind.

"I don't get it, though. How are we supposed to know where we're going?"

"That's the thing about it, fae." Byrd turned halfway around as he walked and spread his arms. "You just keep going and going, and if the madness or the monsters don't getcha on the way, ta-da! You get a prize."

Lumil grunted. "That's a stupid way to put it. It's not a prize if that's how this is supposed to work."

"Hey, for some people, not dying in this place *is* a prize."

In front of them, Corian growled softly as he scanned the landscape, which offered no discerning features to mark their way. "This is not the place for the two of you to spew your endless verbal diarrhea. Keep it up, and *you* won't get a prize."

"My bad." Byrd raised his hands in surrender and flinched sideways into Lumil when a mound of colorless earth released a geyser of black smoke into the air.

The party walked for a time impossible to measure, keeping the conversation down to a bare minimum as they focused on staying together and keeping a sharp eye open for attack.

Ember patted Cheyenne's arm hesitantly when a wet, slithering sound came from up ahead on their left. "What the hell was that?"

"Probably one of those weird-ass creatures. You guys hear that?"

Lumil stuck her hand in the air and flashed a thumbs-up without turning around. L'zar's response was to slow down enough for them to group tighter together.

"Keep your eyes open," Corian said, more for Ember's sake than anyone else's. "We shouldn't have too much trouble making a statement if these things show themselves and hit first."

The slithering sucking sound came again, then a dark, undulating shadow passed behind the drifting layers of black smoke moving across their path.

"Ha." Lumil jerked her fists down by her sides and summoned the spinning circles of sparking red light and magical runes around her fists. "Bring it. I'm gonna whup your monster ass."

"Keep walking," Maleshi repeated, her voice tense with annoyance.

One after another, dark shapes drifted behind the screen of black smoke, almost as if the shapeshifting creatures of the in-between were lining up to form an aisle for the party of magicals.

Ember swallowed and tried not to look at the wavering shadows. "So, we just keep going and wait for them to attack us?"

"Pretty much." Byrd leaned away from a particularly thick shadow on his right as they passed. "Sometimes they won't."

"Most of the time they do," Lumil added.

Corian hummed in thought. "We're not assuming anything about this crossing. Remember that. Everything's changing now."

L'zar led them farther across the nothingness of this partially existing realm between worlds. A creaking groan rose around them, making the invisible ground beneath their feet shudder. Then a gust of wind raced across the changing landscape and blew the thick black smoke away until only thin wisps remained.

Ember's eyes widened as she stared at the creatures all around them. "Oh, crap."

"Huh." Lumil gestured toward black tendrils as thick as tree trunks sprouting from the ground. The light of her magic-enhanced fists cast flickering red shadows on the tentacles' glistening surfaces. "We walked into a monster forest or a giant nest of black octopuses out of water."

"Will you quit waving those around?" Byrd tried to bat down the goblin woman's fists. "Genius idea to catch their attention with attack spells for gloves."

"What? I'm prepared. These things obviously know we're here, and they haven't done anything about it by now, so my guess is they're not gonna." The creaking groan rose again beside the goblin woman, and she turned to see a massive tentacle five times larger than the others rearing back before it swung down toward her. "Dammit. You jinxed it."

She leaped aside as the tentacle crashed to the ground where she'd stood. Lumil drew back one fist and smashed it into the tentacle. Another monster shrieked somewhere, and Maleshi spun with a hiss. "What are you doing?"

Lumil's other fist delivered a powerful uppercut to the underside of the tentacle as it peeled itself off the ground. Red light sparked across the thing's glistening flesh, and the ground trembled again. The goblin woman shot a quick glance at the general. "That thing attacked me."

Cheyenne and Ember raced forward. "I think we should pick up the pace."

The urgency in the halfling's voice made Corian turn around. "Why's that?"

"Incoming flying things." Cheyenne stuck her thumb over her shoulder. "Fair warning."

An ear-splitting screech ripped through the air before a thick black shadow sailed over the group.

"See?"

"Damn." Byrd gazed into the lightless gray sky streaked with black smoke. "I didn't know they could fly."

"They can do pretty much anything."

"Keep moving." Corian waved them forward. "Whatever comes at us, however it comes, keep moving."

The tentacles lining their apparent path shuddered, undulating faster as the group picked up the pace. Another monster wheeled overhead, hidden by the black smoke but casting a shadow through it.

"What are they waiting for?" Maleshi muttered with raised eyebrows.

"No point in trying to answer that question." Corian stepped away from a quivering tentacle. "The only thing we need to worry about is—"

A massive crack echoed through the in-between, and all the waving, trembling tentacles shot up into straight, rigid spikes lining both sides of the travelers' path. "Shit," Lumil whispered. "That's never good."

"It doesn't mean anything yet."

All at once, the rigid tentacles splintered, cracked, and shattered into thousands of tiny black shards. Like broken glass launched from an explosion, the fragments pelted the travelers.

"What the hell?" Cheyenne covered her head and kept moving forward at a crouch. Even as she walked across the broken pieces, she felt them moving along the invisible ground beneath her feet and around her ankles.

"They're shifting," Corian said. "Weird way to do it, but that's what's happening. Keep—"

"Moving." Lumil waved him off. "Yeah, yeah. We heard you the first thousand times, man."

Another shadow swooped toward them, and the flying beast decided to land. It crashed into the ground between L'zar and the nightstalkers behind him. The creature opened a beaklike mouth to reveal razor-sharp teeth and red sludge coating the inside and shrieked at the nightstalkers, making them reel backward. Glowing heat rose in the back of its throat.

"Lumil, *this* is being attacked first." Corian extended his claws on both hands and slashed the faceless creature's throat. The light and heat died, but the thing let out a deafening screech anyway.

Two more flying creatures landed where the tentacles had once stood, and the tiny scattered fragments of those tentacles clicked and clacked into place, assembling themselves like robotic pieces into new and larger shapes.

Like the war machines. Cheyenne summoned two churning orbs of black energy in her hands and waited for the monster-thing that looked like a bat with dozens of two-foot spikes on its back instead of wings to come a little closer. The bat hissed at her, and she sent one black orb straight into its mouth. It burst into thousands of shards again, and she kept moving.

Lumil smashed her fists into one of the flying creatures over and over, sending red sparks along the thing's flesh. It snapped at her with razor-lined jaws, and she brought her fist down on top of its head.

"Hey!" Ember jerked away from a tiny, thin tentacle lashing out of the black smoke to whip against her face. "Ugh. Get off me."

Cheyenne blasted the tentacle with her other energy sphere and grabbed Ember's wrist. "Come on."

A wall of dark flesh darted up from the ground in front of them and reared back, hissing. Cheyenne sent two more crackling black orbs into its open mouth, but they didn't do anything. The creature lurched forward and sprayed the air with hundreds of barbed projectiles. They bounced off Cheyenne's well-timed shield, and the halfling tugged Ember after her and around the attacking creature. Maleshi brought her four-inch claws up through the creature's side from behind, and it shattered too.

"Piece of cake." Byrd hurtled balls of bright-green fire into the floating masses of black shards as they tried to rearrange themselves. Each of his attacks made the creature start all over again until it finally spat a glob of black slime at his arm. "Ah! Asshole!" He shook off the slime and attacked faster.

Cheyenne blasted the creatures materializing in front of her, sending black energy spheres left and right. When the closest winged creature snapped its black-slobbering beak at Ember, the halfling's tendrils whipped from her fingertips and coiled around the thing's beak and its neck, and she jerked down. With a shuddering crash, the creature toppled sideways on the ground, giving Lumil the perfect opportunity to land a flying punch in its heaving side. The in-between monster exploded and fizzled away.

"Ha! There!"

Cheyenne faced the direction they were headed, and her eyes widened.

"Is *that* normal?" Ember squeaked.

"No clue, Em."

Byrd stopped when the massive creature rising in front of them cast its shadow across his body, and he turned too. Maleshi and Corian stepped toward each other, blocking the slavering beast with four gnashing sets of jaws from the goblins, Cheyenne, and Ember. Glowing red eyes spewing smoke rolled in the giant head. Between the night-stalkers and the creature stood L'zar with his hands clasped behind his back, which was turned toward the newest threat rising taller every second behind him.

"L'zar." Corian cleared his throat. "We have to keep moving."

Lumil growled. "If he's not gonna bash that thing to bits, *I* will."

L'zar's glowing golden gaze settled on the goblin woman, and he raised an eyebrow. "That's enough."

He slowly turned to face the snorting creature. All four of its mouths dripped with glowing black ooze. Its red eyes centered on the drow, and its jaws spread wide to bellow in four different voices. The force of that roar whipped L'zar's white hair away from his face and cleared the black smoke that had filtered back into the area.

L'zar stared at the creature without moving. He didn't even flinch when the thing came down with its open mouth as if it meant to rip him apart with each one. Two feet from the drow's head, the creature froze, shrieked in rage, and splintered into a million fragments that shot to either side of L'zar like he'd tossed them aside with his own hands.

The creature Byrd blasted with his green fire screamed and withdrew behind the black smoke. The rearranging pieces of black creature unfolded themselves and scattered. The flying creatures that hadn't been vanquished screeched and took to the air again.

Turning around to look over his shoulder at the rest of the party, L'zar dipped his head. "I'd say we're close."

Without commenting on the monsters, the drow gazed at the light-less sky and swung nonchalantly around again to continue in the direction they'd been heading.

"That's it?" Cheyenne muttered. "Did he even *see* those things?"

"I mean, he *did* stop." Ember moved quickly beside the halfling, searching through the trails of black smoke snaking through their party. "Other than that, yeah. Didn't look like he noticed anything."

"That doesn't make sense." Cheyenne picked up the pace, skirting around Byrd and Lumil until she fell in line between Corian and Maleshi, slightly behind them. "What was all that about?"

"We keep moving, kid. That's all this is."

"He didn't lift a finger to help us fight those things."

Corian shot a quick glance at her over his shoulder. "The beasts in this realm are the least of the threats we'll face today."

"Can he see them?"

This time, Maleshi turned to gaze at the halfling. "What would make you ask that?"

"Because L'zar looks like he's floating through la-la land up there. No reaction to us fighting or to that giant thing about to rip his head off in four different pieces."

Corian raised a finger beside his shoulder. "But it didn't."

"Yeah, and I wanna know why it and all the others scattered like that. Did you guys know that would happen?"

"Not explicitly, no."

"But you expected *something*."

"Hmm." Maleshi tilted her head from side to side. "Interesting line of questioning while we're crossing through, kid. Makes me wonder why you're so curious and why it can't wait."

Cheyenne snorted, blinking in surprise. "Because it's weird. It doesn't feel right."

"To whom?" Corian asked softly. "Looks to me like everyone else is feeling just fine about not having to fight those things."

"Well, everyone else is just passing through this place like regular magicals, aren't they? But I got *moved* by this plane to a different exit the last time I was here. The creatures *saw* me in drow speed, just like the last war machines. They knew I had the activator. Now L'zar's just breezing on by without a care in the world, and the things existing in here just give up. What's going on?"

Corian sniffed, his tufted ears twitching atop his head, and shrugged. "Must be in your blood, kid."

"No, that's not an answer." Cheyenne shook her head and peered at the tall shadow on their left. For a moment, she thought she saw the Nimlothar tree from her vision, then the black smoke thickened and blocked it from view. "And I'm sick of hearing about my blood."

The nightstalkers exchanged knowing glances.

"Be that as it may, Cheyenne, we have to focus." Corian peered behind them to check on the others, then centered his gaze on L'zar's broad back as the drow's long strides took them farther and farther through the shifting in-between. "This wasn't the portal we'd planned on crossing, so we're gonna have to adjust wherever we come out on the other side. File those questions away for another time when we don't need your head in the game with the rest of us, got it?"

Cheyenne looked at Maleshi, hoping the general would give her something more than that, but the nightstalker woman remained silent, facing straight ahead like she had her marching orders. *This isn't about them wanting to keep secrets from me. No, they're doing this 'cause they have no idea how L'zar's got that kinda grip on this place. They're blindly following the crazy drow.*

Ember floated faster to catch up with the group, falling in line on Lumil's left. "So, that's it, then? Just a quick fight that wasn't even hard, and now we have an open path?"

"Sure is what it looks like, huh?" Lumil shook her head. "*That's* what I call anticlimactic."

"Oh, please." Byrd hissed in irritation. "It's okay for *you* to say. Is that it?"

"I never said you couldn't say it. I was just commenting. Endaru's balls, goblin. Did your parents not give you enough battle clubs growing up? I swear, it's like you have this constant *need* for conflict."

Corian's four-inch claws extended in a flash, and the next second, Lumil found herself swallowing against the points of the nightstalker's weapons held against her throat. "Last warning. Keep up the bickering like a couple of suckling pups, and I'll finish what that noose started in Karu Ga'abil. Do we understand each other?"

Lumil glared at the nightstalker, who was at the end of his patience. Beside her, Ember stared at the huge glinting claws poking against the goblin woman's green flesh.

"We're good, nightstalker," Lumil muttered, her upper lip twitching in a sneer. "Takes two to tango, as they say. Don't tell me you're lettin' Byrd off the hook."

Corian's silver eyes flicked toward Byrd, who also stared at the silver claws against Lumil's throat. The nightstalker retracted his claws with a metallic ring. "I was talking to both of you. You just happened to be behind me."

He turned and walked swiftly to close the distance L'zar had gained on them, oblivious to the tension rising among his little band of rebels. Maleshi shook her head and chuckled.

The goblins, Cheyenne, and Ember followed close behind. Lumil tapped her throat, then jerked the collar of her leather jacket up around her neck. "Gonna take a lot more than manicured nails to get through *this* neck."

"You passed the deathflame once already, sister." Byrd clapped the goblin woman on the back. "He ain't gonna throw you into the fire."

"Yeah, I know. He's too much of a coward to try."

Cheyenne met Ember's gaze and nodded for her friend to join her behind the aloof nightstalkers. Ember looked at the goblins over her shoulder and whispered, "Are they gonna try to get him back for that? That will be a serious problem if we're all supposed to be on the same side."

"No, they're fine." The halfling frowned at the back of Corian's tufted ears. "That was his version of the way those two nag each other all the time."

"Huh." Ember swallowed and raised her eyebrows. "Nightstalker-intense all around, huh?"

"That's pretty much how they are."

"Shit. Good thing they're on our side."

Cheyenne cast her friend a sidelong glance. "Mostly, yeah."

CHAPTER EIGHTY-NINE

There's no way to tell how long we've been in here. Cheyenne gritted her teeth and trudged behind the nightstalkers following L'zar. No one had said a word for what felt like a long time because there wasn't much else left to say. *Except for how the hell L'zar can just walk around like he's taking a stroll through the park.*

Corian lifted his chin and peered around the drow leading them forward. "There. See it?"

Maleshi tilted her head. "Hmm. Moment of truth."

"Truth about what?" Ember muttered.

"Where in all the corners of the fell-damn Gape this portal opens on the other side." Corian let out a slow breath and nodded. "We're about to find out."

L'zar turned toward the rest of the group as they approached the door-sized rectangle of light floating freely within the in-between. A small, thoughtful frown creased his brows as he gestured toward the door. "Would anyone care to hazard a guess about this one?"

"You kinda put on a lid on that before we could start." Byrd scratched his head. "I'm not gonna *hazard* anything I can't see."

"Hmm." L'zar tilted his head, then turned slowly back toward the exit doorway. "Indeed."

"Okay, there's something seriously wrong with that drow," Ember muttered.

"That's what I've been trying to figure out." Cheyenne gazed around them and caught flickering shadows moving through the smoke. "We're still being watched, too."

"Oh, come on. I didn't need to hear that."

"Something tells me we're not having a repeat mock battle anytime soon."

L'zar stopped in front of the doorway and stared at it, tapping one long slate-gray finger on his pursed lips. "Corian, if I could—"

"I know." The nightstalker gave L'zar's back a not-so-gentle thump of encouragement before stepping past him to study the doorway. "We'll work with what we've got when we get there."

"Now I wish I'd paid more attention to the crone at Aelmhalk." Maleshi cocked her head. "She specialized in doorways. Though at the time, if anyone had told me I'd make the crossing twice in my life, I'd have ripped their heart out."

"Hmm. A refreshing reminder." Corian slowly reached toward the doorway.

The outline of the shimmering rectangle burst into black fire, the flames flickering in suspended animation as if moving through sludge instead of what passed for air in this realm. L'zar stared at the ground between his feet and the doorway. "Interesting."

"In more ways than one." Corian nodded. "I'll take point on this one. Unless, of course, General Hi'et would like to lead her return to the Motherland?"

"It's hardly a procession in a warlord's honor if she's at the head of it, don't you think?"

"Agreed. I had to ask." He gave Cheyenne a quick, reassuring nod, then stepped briskly through the doorway and out of the in-between.

L'zar gazed at the slow black flames around him when he stepped through next. Maleshi waved Cheyenne and Ember forward after him.

"Is it gonna feel like I'm drowning when we step out of here too?" Ember asked.

The general chuckled. "It's always better out than in. I suppose that's a universal saying."

"Great." Ember floated through the doorway, and Cheyenne followed her.

Maleshi, Byrd, and Lumil joined their group on the other side in quick succession, and the party stood at their unexpected destination in Ambar'ogúl.

"What the hell is this?" Byrd muttered.

L'zar stood rigidly alert behind Corian. His wide golden eyes were the only part of him that moved as he scanned the chamber of black stone in which they'd found themselves. Then he took a long, deep sniff of the air and growled. "I believe the last option left to us was very possibly the worst."

"Great." Cheyenne wrinkled her nose at the thick metallic odor hanging in the air. It covered something deeper and heavier—blood, a scent not unlike ozone, and a darker element she couldn't name. "I'd love for someone to just come out and say where we are."

Lumil leaned away from the warped reflection looking back at her. She lightly flicked the glass and grunted. "Mirror, mirror on the wall and all that, huh?"

Maleshi eyed the dusty, chipped mirror serving as a one-way exit from the in-between. "No fair queen in this hellhole."

"No way." Cheyenne blinked in the near-darkness lit by two blazing torches hovering against the far wall of the chamber. "Did the portal ridge at my mom's seriously lead us into the Crown's castle?"

"The Heart," Corian corrected.

"Sure. Whatever. This is it?"

"Yes." L'zar took another deep breath and finally started moving again. "This changes everything."

"Dammit." Byrd rubbed a hand vigorously across his mouth before trudging after the group. "Now all the timing's off."

"No, our timing was perfect," L'zar hissed. He stopped beside a dark metal table bolted to the black stone floors. The surface was scratched and dented in a few places, but that was nothing compared to the long-dried bloodstains on the metal and the stone below it. The drow spun and glared at Corian. "It was *perfect*."

The nightstalker glanced quickly at Cheyenne, then headed toward the drow and kept his voice low. "We'll make it work."

"We're too close, Corian. We're *way* too close. The first stage has been wiped off the table now."

"I understand, and we'll find a way to contact them. But there's no going back at this point."

"I don't want to go back," L'zar growled. "I want this done *right*." A purple light flashed behind the drow's eyes as he bared his teeth and curled his lips in a snarl. He breathed heavily in hiss after hiss. "We didn't come here to play it by ear."

"Well, it looks like that's what we have to do now. You're still under the Weave, and you're still running low. Don't let this undo what you spent the last week weaving through it, understand?"

"I'm not as weak-willed as you so comfortably think, *vae shra'ni*."

Both magicals turned quickly toward the other end of the chamber at the sound of footsteps descending a stairwell.

"That'll be the first pair of eyes, then," Lumil muttered.

"Quiet," Maleshi hissed.

The group waited in silence as the footsteps drew closer. A flickering green flame became visible in the stairwell across the chamber, then the magical carrying it, a short, round gremlin with scrawny limbs and a bulbous yellow nose, appeared at the base of the stairs. The gremlin sniffed the air and turned to look directly at the intruders. "What in the name of the Crown's vaulted hand do you think you're doin' down here?"

Corian's blast of silver lightning caught the gremlin in the throat, seared clean through, and burst against the opposite stone wall. The gremlin dropped with a gurgling choke, spilling the green fire like a dropped glass of water across the floor.

Shouts rose from the stairwell, and four more magicals in the same dark blood-splattered robes raced down the stairs. Maleshi and Corian sprinted toward them, Lumil and Byrd close on their heels. Cheyenne followed, shooting L'zar a scathing glance, which he didn't notice in lieu of the sudden appearance of a second metal table covered in dried blood. *He needs to cut this shit out right now.*

"Ember, can you keep an eye on—" A green dart like a crackling spear shot over the halfling's shoulder and barely missed the warped mirror on the wall behind her.

"Got it," Ember said even as Cheyenne snarled and entered the fray.

Five against four shouldn't have been an issue in this dark chamber that smelled like blood and fear. The Crown's appointed attendants in this place put up a much better fight than any dozen O'gúl loyalists Earthside. Two of them were gremlins who seemed to have mastered small bursts of teleporting themselves around the chamber. The other two were a skaxen and a shriveled goblin, neither of whom were any easier to lock on as targets.

Silver nightstalker light darted around the chamber as Maleshi and Corian took off after the yellow-skinned gremlins. Every three or four seconds, they'd catch up with one to throw or deflect a spell before the gremlins disappeared and reappeared somewhere else.

The skaxen leaped at Cheyenne, snarling and slashing with long, sharpened black nails at the ends of her orange hands. The halfling missed her first attack with her crackling orb of black energy. The skaxen darted from side to side, narrowly escaping Cheyenne's next attacks, then the orange-skinned magical headed toward the far wall.

Cheyenne paused when the skaxen skittered up the vertical surface like a spider, leaped to the adjacent wall, and kicked out to come at the halfling from a different angle. *That's new.*

She stepped aside and sent her black whipping tendrils to coil around the skaxen's outstretched claws. Then she dodged again and pulled the orange magical from the wall, tossing it into the closest table with a metallic clang. *How many of these torture tables are in this place?*

The skaxen scrambled to find a hold on the smoother surface and instead toppled to the floor with a hiss.

Lumil and Byrd took on the goblin together. It tossed small vials at them hand over hand that exploded in mid-air, sending bursts of blue sparks and stinging shards at them in billowing clouds. "Wall!" Lumil shouted.

"Heyup." Byrd's palms exploded, and a massive column of green fire roared up between him and the decrepit goblin. The O'gúl servant was blinded to Lumil sliding beneath Byrd's wall of fire to bring her red-glowing fist up into the goblin's gut. The chamber filled with a sickening crunch on impact, and the goblin sailed backward to strike the wall with a thump before slumping to the floor.

"Not bad, you backfield greenskin." Lumil leered at Byrd, then nodded toward Cheyenne, who'd gotten herself pinned against another metal table by the snarling skaxen.

"How 'bout it, kid?" Byrd called. "Need a hand?"

"Or a fist?"

Cheyenne grimaced at the foaming slaver dripping from the skaxen's mouth. The orange magical got in a deep slash on the halfling's upper chest beside her shoulder before Cheyenne finally managed to get a good grip on her attacker's wrist. She summoned a churning black sphere in the same hand and the skaxen lurched away, clutching the stump of her arm.

"Traitor!" the skaxen shrieked. "The Crown's fist will have your *nilsch úcat's* head on her serving tray!"

Cheyenne sent a roundhouse kick into the side of the bleeding, snarling skaxen woman's head. Her black Van collided with a crack, and the orange-skinned magical dropped to the dark-stained floor.

"Look at you." Lumil stalked toward her, nodding in approval. "All agile and shit."

"Just trained."

"Not by that guy though, huh?" Byrd nodded at Corian, who'd pinned the gremlin he'd been fighting to the wall, claws extended from both hands, one fistful piercing the gremlin's throat and the other through the magical's belly.

With a hiss, Corian ripped his hands free, and the gremlin dropped. Six feet away, Maleshi clamped her black-furred hands around the other gremlin's head and twisted sharply. The force of it snapped the yellow magical's neck and sent him flying toward another blood-stained metal table.

"No." Cheyenne grimaced at the nightstalkers. "I'm not sure Corian knows Earthside martial arts."

"Ha. *Arts.*" Lumil stopped beside the fallen skaxen, dropped to one knee, and sent a glowing red fist into her head with a wet, sickening crunch. She stood and shook the blood off her hand.

"Look at that." Byrd sniggered. "Red spinners, red fist."

Lumil snorted. "Yeah, I'm accessorizing. Shut up."

"What the hell?" Cheyenne stared at the skaxen's broken skull and everything that was once inside it. "I already took her down."

"No, you put that skaxen bitch to sleep." Lumil shook another spray of blood and whatever else off her hand. "I put her down."

"Why is all this necessary?" Cheyenne gestured toward the five bodies strewn around the torture chamber. "That skaxen wasn't going anywhere."

Byrd shrugged. "Not yet."

"Cheyenne." Maleshi moved swiftly toward her and shook her head. "This is the complete opposite of the day we found the smuggled shipments or even at your ceremony on Thursday. We don't get to take prisoners here."

"You don't get to kill them when they're down, either."

"Look, we're here, no turning back. You can be damn sure that if we left these O'gúleesh alive down here, the minute they came to, they'd be sounding the alarm and bringing the full force of the Crown's iron grip down on us."

"You don't *know*!"

"Hate me if you want, kid. Hate all of us for what we have to do. Today, it's them or us, and I promise you things won't change one fucking iota around here if you martyr yourself because you can't stomach doing what's necessary to get us where we need to go. You don't have to be a part of it on the same level if you have a problem getting your hands dirty, but do *not* bring this up before you and I are standing Earthside again. That's an order." General Hi'et narrowed her silver eyes at the halfling, then brushed past her and headed for the staircase.

"I don't take orders from you."

"You do today, halfling. Time to grow a pair. Move out."

Byrd and Lumil followed the general across the chamber, shooting Cheyenne brief sympathetic looks. Corian paused long enough to make sure no one but the rebel party was moving. Ember drifted quickly to Cheyenne's side and grabbed her arm to gently tug the halfling forward. L'zar swept his floaty, glazed-looking eyes around the chamber, then approached his daughter and nodded toward Maleshi. "I've missed having her around. I have to thank you for finding our general."

Cheyenne gritted her teeth and stepped after the others. "Yeah, you *should* be thanking me. All of us. What the hell's going on with you, huh? Quit standing around and help us fight for once. We need you!"

He turned halfway around to scan the bodies on the floor. "Obviously not."

"That's not the point, and you know it."

"Cheyenne, listen to me." They reached the base of the staircase and climbed at a steady pace after the others. Ember floated up the steps in a smooth line and tactfully didn't turn around to watch L'zar's short heart to heart with his daughter. His golden eyes blazed with the lucidity Cheyenne realized she hadn't seen in him all day. "If we want any chance whatsoever of getting you to the Rahalma so you can place your *marandúr* where it belongs, this is how it has to be done. I don't want to be useless, trust me, but if I play my hand too soon, we're fucked. I've done my part, and I'll continue to do it until it's time for you to do yours."

She studied the intensity of his gaze and hissed in frustration before storming up the steps. "You're just full of excuses, aren't you?"

"If it gets the job done, sure. Call it whatever you like."

If he keeps up this space-case routine, I'll end up calling it Gúrdu's prophecy coming true. We bring L'zar Verdys all the way back to Ambar'ogúl, and he's useless.

CHAPTER NINETY

When the party reached the top of the stairs, they found themselves in a circular chamber with a lot more magical light than the torture room below. The walls stretched up almost three stories around them, though the only doors existed on this level. Six massive doors of corrugated steel fitted with reinforced bolts closed off every entrance, and the circular room was empty.

Corian gazed around, his nose wrinkling in aggravation. "So far, so good, but it won't be long until someone figures out there's been a breach."

"They can figure all they want." Lumil raised her fist, swirling with sparking red runes. "Doesn't mean shit if they can't tell anyone."

"Well, let's hope that continues to be the case for as long as we need."

L'zar moved in a slow circle around the huge room, his footsteps echoing in muted whispers across the layers of dust. "We need to get a message to the Star."

Corian rolled his eyes before settling his gaze on the prowling drow. "How exactly do you suggest we do that? We planned for every contingency except this one. We would've had the resources at any other entry point, but we don't here."

"Let your mind out of its box, Corian," L'zar growled, his golden gaze flickering over the chipped black stone encircling them. "I'll get us where we need to go, but if the Star has no idea when or where our little rendezvous is supposed to take place, we might as well be walking into this stripped bare-assed naked as well as blind."

The nightstalker raised an eyebrow and didn't turn to follow L'zar when the drow circled the wall behind him. "You need to cool it."

"I know what I'm tempting. Do your job."

Closing his eyes, Corian took a deep breath, then headed for Cheyenne. "You have the activator?"

"Yeah."

"Put it on."

She pulled the silver coil from her pocket and held it toward him. "I don't wanna screw it up. You know a hell of a lot more about what you need than I do. I mean, we're in *your* house now, right?"

L'zar's bitter laugh exploded through the chamber before cutting out again, and he kept pacing.

"Not my house, Cheyenne. After as many centuries as I've spent Earthside, I'm willing to bet the entire mechanism of this place has rewritten itself far beyond what I can make out with what little time we have." He nodded at her outstretched hand. "That activator's got more of you in it now than anything else. You might as well be offering me your toothbrush."

"Oh, ew." Ember grimaced and turned away.

"Okay, that's the last analogy I expected you to use, but I get it." Cheyenne stuck the silver coil behind her ear, waited for the pinch and her eyelids to stop fluttering, then looked around the stone chamber. Her jaw dropped. "This is insane."

"What?" Ember drifted toward her. "You okay?"

Cheyenne scanned the stone walls, which only appeared to be stone. In most places, they were O'gúl metals, carrying the same frequencies, code, and tech-magic that had lined the walls and streets of Hangivol's outer circles. A few dark boxes remained in the walls where the stone hadn't been replaced, but those were few and far between. "I'm more than okay. It's like reading someone's mind, but that someone is a massive server network, and I'm standing inside it."

Maleshi snorted. "That was much better than your analogy."

Corian ignored her. "All right. I need you to find an access point for sending a message. This is going to a fairly specific location, though it'll be hard to pin down."

Cheyenne approached the wall and walked slowly along it, scanning the lines of code and letting her activator sift through it a thousand times faster. "Let me guess; that's because of the dampening wards L'zar put up in his secret rebel lair underground."

"Ha!" Lumil pointed at the halfling, then slapped a hand to her head. "How the hell are you reading all that in the fell-damn *walls*?"

"I'm not." Cheyenne's smile kept growing as she absorbed block after block of data. "I've been there."

That statement distracted L'zar from staring at the walls, and he turned to his daughter. The corner of his mouth twitched, then he resumed his dreamlike pacing.

"So, I can't get a message into the bunker." The activator lit up a trail of glowing blue code, illuminating it brighter than all others. She reached toward it and stopped. *Don't touch anything until you're sure.* Following the trail around the wall, she waited for the activator and her synced magic to find what she was looking for by feel alone. "Do they have any other endpoints set up with active tech? Right outside the wards, I mean."

"Over a dozen." Corian folded his arms and watched her. "That's the problem."

"Where are they most likely to come from when they *think* it's time to meet up with us?"

"Quadrant A4, Section 482C, Sub-section…" L'zar growled and closed his eyes, muttering to himself as he went through the jumbled routes of his memory. "Sub-section 87."

Cheyenne stopped beside the closest metal door in the wall and wrinkled her nose. "Mm."

"No, sub 86."

"Yeah, that looks right." Cheyenne lifted her finger toward the flashing point in the wall the activator had lit up for her with the Hangivol coordinates straight from L'zar's mouth.

The drow's eyes flew open and he focused them on his daughter, flashing a wide grin.

"Whoa." Ember patted her cheek and looked back and forth between

L'zar and Cheyenne standing on opposite sides of the chamber. "Is anyone else feeling out of the loop here?"

"Get used to it, fae." Lumil nudged Ember's shoulder gently. "When you're dealing with the drow, there's always a loop, and you'll never be a part of it."

"Huh."

Cheyenne firmly pressed the glowing point in the wall, and a shuddering jolt of energy raced up her arm and into the side of her neck. Her eyelids fluttered rapidly, and a surprised chuckle escaped her. "Oh, man!"

"See? Weird-ass drow stuff like that." Byrd pointed at the halfling. "If anyone else walked in on this, they'd think she's over there gettin' it on with the wall."

Lumil lunged toward him and raised her fist.

He shrank away and laughed, raising both hands. "Hey, hey. Not with the runes, huh? Come on. It's not like the rest of us haven't seen L'zar in his freaky fetish stages."

"You know what?" Lumil's open mouth closed when Corian cleared his throat. She stepped away from Byrd and slowly lowered her fist. "I'm dropping this."

"Okay, I'm in." Cheyenne stood there with her finger pressed to the wall, tapping into the massive mainframe of blended tech and magic coursing through the entire blueprint of Hangivol. "What's the message?"

Corian studied the halfling's blank stare and frowned. "Last-minute change unavoidable. New doorway in Heart lower pit. En route to the heart via…"

"Just put in our current location, Cheyenne." L'zar clasped his hands behind his back, his lips pursing in rhythmic twitches like he couldn't decide whether to frown or grin again. "That'll do."

"Yep. Then what?"

"Hurry. And that's the end of it." Corian glanced at Maleshi, who shrugged and went back to watching Cheyenne communing with the system disguised as a building. "The next part is a little trickier, kid. You'll want to encrypt this."

"Done."

"What?"

Byrd burst out laughing.

Cheyenne slowly removed her finger from the not-stone wall, sucking in a sharp breath when the river of energy seeped away from her neck and arm and left through her fingertip. Then she looked at Corian and shrugged. "Sent it."

"But did you encrypt it?"

"Yeah, triple-layered. I left a few clues, so they shouldn't have any problem figuring out the lock."

L'zar hummed in fascination and continued his pacing around the room. "Which is what?"

She glanced at him sidelong and tilted her head. "Thief."

A low chuckle came from L'zar, but he didn't say anything else.

Corian scratched the side of his head beneath a twitching feline ear. "This is something for the record vaults, Cheyenne. Which, if there *were* any pre-existing records of those attempting to do even half of what you just accomplished in two minutes, would be blown to pieces at this point. Well done."

"I mean, thanks. I didn't really try."

"Yes, and that's my point."

"Okay, so the Four-Pointed Star has our message." Maleshi eyed L'zar as he made another circle around the chamber. "Or they will, hopefully. That part's out of our hands. We need to keep moving."

"Ready to head out, General." Lumil gave Maleshi a weird, slanting salute.

General Hi'et eyed the goblin woman and shook her head. "Don't ever do that again."

Byrd chuckled, and Maleshi's silver gaze settled on him.

L'zar stepped into the middle of the chamber and turned in a slow circle, eyeing each of the metal doors. "This way."

"After you, then." Maleshi motioned for him to lead the way, and the group converged behind L'zar.

Ember joined Cheyenne with a curious frown. "That was some trick with the walls."

"Tell me about it. This'd blow your mind, Em. After all this is over, you should give it a try at least once. With your own activator, obviously."

"Oh, yes, obviously. I have no desire to come between you two."

"Very funny."

L'zar reached the door he wanted and waved his hand in front of it. The metal flashed a muted gray light, then rumbled open and slid sideways into the wall. Before it had finished opening all the way, the drow darted into the corridor, and everyone else filtered through after him.

He led them down one twisting passage after another, all of black stone. Only half of it in the narrow hallways was disguised magic-tech panels, and Cheyenne let herself take fleeting glances at the system code running through it all. *At least this way I'll be able to tell if someone sounds a silent alarm.*

Ten minutes later, L'zar held up a hand for them to stop.

"What's going on?" Ember asked as they pressed their backs against the wall and waited for L'zar to keep moving.

Cheyenne's drow hearing picked up different voices screaming and wailing somewhere in front of them. "You can't hear that?"

"No."

"Good. You don't want to." She grimaced and shook her head. *Sounds like the torture chamber in the basement isn't the only one they've got in this place.*

"We're about to walk into a rather large private gathering." L'zar looked over his shoulder and raised his eyebrows at Corian. "And it won't be pretty."

"No other route?" Maleshi asked.

"Unfortunately, no. This wouldn't be an issue if we'd come in where we were supposed to."

"It's not worth arguing about anymore, L'zar." Corian gestured at the branching corridor ahead of them. "Focus on what's possible *now*."

"One way into the courtyard." L'zar wrinkled his nose. "Through two walls, that entire joyous-sounding gathering, and the corridors branch off from there after that. If we get separated or anyone ends up losing their mind over what we're about to see, just remember that from here on out, keep turning right."

"That would just take us in circles," Ember muttered.

He leaned forward to meet the fae girl's gaze and smiled. "Not in Heart."

"Just say the word, then." Byrd nodded.

"Hmm." L'zar glanced down the hall again. "Lumil, you might be the better choice for getting us through."

"Oh, *yeah*." The goblin woman pounded her rune-encircled fist into the other hand. "I got this."

"Then stay close." L'zar took off down the next corridor.

Cheyenne's drow hearing picked up the growing volume of agonized screams ahead.

Ember swallowed, breathing faster as the group sped up. "What did he mean by 'lose our minds after what we're about to see?'"

"That wherever we're heading, it looks worse than it sounds, and it sounds bad."

"Fantastic. Too late to get off the next stop?"

"Nice try. The next stop is the last stop, Em."

CHAPTER NINETY-ONE

By the time they reached the massive metal doors of their only available route to the Crown's courtyard, everyone could hear the screaming. L'zar motioned them to a stop again and nodded at Lumil. "Thirty seconds, then have at it."

"You got it." The goblin woman raised both bespelled fists and approached the doors.

L'zar moved down the line and stopped in front of Cheyenne. "Make sure you're ready with the *marandúr*. If it's not immediately accessible, make it accessible. You won't have another chance after this to go through your things to find it."

"Sure." Cheyenne grimaced when a curdled wail seeped through the stone walls, punctuated by short, shrieking bursts of terror and agony. She slipped her backpack off her shoulders and tried to hold it and unzip it at the same time. L'zar grabbed the straps and held it up for her. "Thanks."

"Quickly."

She unzipped the main pocket and dug around in the bottom. When her fingers brushed the cold metal of the gold *marandúr* coin, she fumbled quickly to get a good grip, then pulled it out and flashed it at him.

"Good. Put it away."

Cheyenne stuffed the coin into her back pocket and frowned at him. *He's giving short-sentence orders, and I'm hopping to it. Never thought I'd be in a place where I trusted what he's saying. We'll see how long it lasts.*

When she finished, L'zar lifted her backpack higher and held it for her like a jacket as she slipped her arms through the straps. "Thank you, Cheyenne. I feel much better knowing you're as prepared for the next few steps as you possibly can be."

"Yeah, well, you know, I'm just doing it for your approval and shit."

He gave her a tired smile, and one of his eyelids drooped over a golden eye before he opened it again. "I'm sure neither of us wants that to be true. We're almost there."

Cheyenne couldn't help but offer a quick smile in return, then L'zar turned away and headed back toward Lumil and the metal door.

"You said thirty seconds, but I figured I'd wait for you to finish whatever that was." The goblin woman shrugged. "Go time?"

"By all means."

Lumil let out a whoop and charged toward the metal doors leading into the next room. Her fists flashed with the rotating patterns of blazing red runes, and she drew her arm back to lay into the door where it met the wall. Stone and metal shards and small, sparking bits of O'gúl tech flew in every direction. The screaming on the other side of the door didn't stop.

The rebel group charged after Lumil through the hole she'd punched in the wall. The goblin woman led the battle with a bellow, throwing punches at the startled Crown servants before the smoke and dust had halfway cleared.

Cheyenne summoned black orbs of sparking energy in her hands but paused when she realized what she was looking at inside the next chamber.

It was another circular room, this one with a massive round pool in its center. The pool was sectioned into six wedge-shaped metal cages rising two feet above the surface. Inside each cage was a magical chained to the metal bars above their heads by the wrists. Most of them dangled helplessly from their manacles as they shrieked and screamed and wailed nonstop, bobbing within not water but a black, bubbling, steaming sludge letting off the smell of rotting meat, cooking meat, and something distinctly floral.

Metal rods protruded from the bars, suspended on pulleys, every single one aimed at a caged magical. The last loyalist in dark-gray robes to notice the invasion by L'zar Verdys' rebel party got in one more good prod at the troll woman in the cage in front of him. His gloved hands wrapped around the metal rod and struck her between the shoulder blades. The tip of the rod sparked with blazing red light, the troll woman screamed, and the black sludge in her cage flashed with different colors before the brilliant blue steam rising out of it was quickly vented up into a clear glass bubble the same size and shape as the pool suspended from the ceiling.

This is where she takes their magic.

Cheyenne's fury boiled in her more violently than the black sludge in the pool. A roaring battle cry burst from her mouth as she charged the orc loyalist. He looked at her with a vicious snarl as she lashed out with her whipping black tendrils. They snaked through the bars of the troll woman's cage, coiled around the orc's neck, and jerked him forward. His face smashed into the metal cage three times before Cheyenne finally released him and darted around the large pool to finish the job.

The orc swayed on his feet, blinking and trying to regain his bearings. She curled her fist with a black energy sphere inside it and landed a cracking uppercut to the orc's startled face. He flew across the room, and the halfling raced after him.

A dozen servants of the Crown battled the rebel group inside the magic-stealing chamber, most of them goblins and skaxens. The orc Cheyenne blasted across the room a second time before turning to fight a snarling goblin wielding one of the magical cattle prods was one of two. She grabbed the rod before he could poke her with it and sent a concentrated stream of black fire racing across the metal. The flames ate the goblin's gloves in less than a second and started to consume him. The goblin screamed and reeled away, flailing as her drow fire did the rest of it for her. Cheyenne squeezed the metal rod with both hands and shattered the thick pole.

Then she turned toward her next fight.

Corian raced across the chamber in a flash of silver light and landed a powerful blow to the skaxen standing in his way, and the orange-skinned magical sailed into the sectioned cages. The top of the one he landed on broke beneath his weight, and he crashed into the black, steaming goo with a shriek. The chained magicals screamed and wailed as they jerked around, still attached to their manacles. When their skaxen torturer fell into the sludge, the prisoners stopped screaming long enough to watch him splash around in the substance, fighting for his life. None of them looked away until the skaxen had disappeared into the thick soup.

Ember and L'zar stood back from the battle a foot inside the hole Lumil had blasted into the wall. The fae girl's eyes were wide as she watched the Crown's servants racing across the room and leaping toward the rebels, attacking between snatching up various magic-stealing instruments and wielding them like weapons.

L'zar turned toward a metal shelf along the wall on his left, hands clasped behind his back as he studied the various supplies and ingredients stored there. He didn't seem to notice when a goblin crashed into the shelf two feet in front of him, jerking under the electric jolts of red light consuming him. Then the drow disappeared.

Byrd hurled balls of green flame into the fray, shattering beakers and vials, destroying the metal cages in the pool, and striking the O'gúl servants' faces and chests.

One massive ogre stood on the far side of the room, blocking the opposite exit. He was bare-chested except for an apron of slick, shiny black leather wrapped around his beefy gray torso, his flesh covered in burn scars and thick, slashing lines. A welder's helmet rested in the lifted position on his head, revealing his full sneer as he watched the battle.

His orange-red eyes settled on General Maleshi Hi'et as she ducked beneath a skaxen's attack spell of hissing green darts before bringing her glinting claws up to rip the other magical to ribbons from gut to gullet. Before the skaxen hit the floor, she whirled and saw the ogre.

"I'd heard a rumor," the ogre growled. "Never know what you can believe these days."

"I could say the same thing, Yarin." Maleshi bared her teeth and stalked toward him, undaunted by the spells and sparking weapons and blood flying around her. Her silver eyes burned with battle fury. "Looks like you got the promotion you were so eager to snatch up."

"Looks like you sold your honor for another furball and a washed-up prankster." Yarin swayed from side to side as the nightstalker general approached him. "You're finished, Hi'et."

"Well, we'll see."

The ogre chuckled darkly before bringing a meaty paw up to slam the welding helmet down into place over his face. Maleshi snarled and raced toward him, her four-inch claws flashing in the magical light overhead. Yarin waited until the last second before letting out a bellowing roar and heaving a massive plate of metal out of the huge cauldron beside him. Whatever it was meant to be used for, the plate now served as the ogre's shield. Sparks flew and blue fire erupted on impact as Maleshi slashed the plate. She darted in a silver blur around the ogre, lashing out where she could, and every time, she was met with a grunt and the ogre's surprisingly quick reflexes in blocking her.

Cheyenne raised an opalescent black shield in front of her and Lumil when the pair of identical-looking skaxens aimed two metal hoses at them and unleashed a yellow-green cloud of acrid smoke. The smoke materialized against Cheyenne's shield before dripping like syrup to the floor, eating holes in the stone and hissing madly.

Lumil grinned at the halfling, then spun out from behind the shield and raced toward the skaxens. Cheyenne blasted one in the face with a churning black orb and eyed the other skaxen, who had leaped away from Lumil onto a workbench. Glass vials and metal instruments crashed to the ground. Before the skaxen could get better footing to lunge toward the goblin woman, Cheyenne's black tendrils shot from her hands and wrapped around one arm and leg. She whisked the rat-faced magical off the table with a snarl and hurled the skaxen toward Lumil's waiting fist.

The crunch of breaking bones was masked beneath the other sounds of battle. The skaxen dropped to the ground, and Lumil cackled. "That's what I'm *talking* about!"

The battle died quickly as L'zar's band of rebels made short work of the Crown's servants. The only battle still raging was between General Hi'et and the ogre Yarin. He kept a firm grip on the metal plate serving as his shield. Maleshi darted around him, denting the plate and sending silver bolts of lightning at it, but she was unable to bring the ogre down.

Cheyenne wiped something wet and sticky off her forehead,

breathing heavily as she turned to watch the final battle. "No one's gonna help her?"

Lumil chuckled. "Better not, kid. Get in the general's way, and you might as well slit your own throat."

Corian retracted his claws from a gray-robed goblin's chest and turned to watch the other nightstalker battling the semi-armored ogre. Then he scanned the destruction littering the chamber, searching for survivors as the metal clang of Maleshi's claws on Yarin's shield echoed around them.

A thin, withered skaxen pulled herself from the wreckage beside the giant hole in the wall and the missing door. While L'zar's party watched Ambar'ogúl's greatest war general fight a shielded ogre, the skaxen crawled silently across the floor. She considered snatching up the motionless, hovering fae three feet away but thought better of it. Instead, the rat-faced servant of the Crown seized the opportunity and slunk out of the chamber, scrambling to her feet around the corner and racing down the hall to alert the Crown's Heart to what had come for them.

The second the skaxen disappeared to sound the alarm, Maleshi's claws shredded the metal shield in Yarin's hands and the thing broke clean in two. The ogre paused, his helmet moving between the twin pieces of metal in surprise. He reeled backward when Maleshi advanced again, but he wasn't nearly fast enough.

The general's clawed hand pierced the shielded visor protecting his face, then she jerked down. The ogre stumbled forward, roaring, before the nightstalker's other handful of piercing claws ripped into his chest. Maleshi screamed with effort and pulled her arms away from each other, shredding the metal mask and the ogre's chest until something crunched behind the visor and a gush of dark blood fell from beneath it.

The ogre hit the floor. General Hi'et stepped back, growling, and tossed her black hair out of her eyes.

"Feel better?" Corian asked.

"Well, it's a start."

L'zar materialized behind the fallen ogre and gestured toward the door leading to the corridors beyond. "By your leave, General."

"Cut it out. We both know I don't have a damn clue where we're going."

Ember floated toward the pool of bubbling black goo, her violet eyes swimming with tears. "We can't just leave them in there. They need help."

"Not anymore." Byrd sniffed and brushed glass shards off his shoulder. "These assholes were keeping their prisoners alive. My guess is the electric rods and something moving through those cages. Nobody's alive in there, fae. They've been left too long."

Ember scanned the faces of the tortured magical prisoners, looking for signs of life. "We don't know that. Can't we just check?"

"Your heart's in the right place, kid." Lumil patted Ember's back and steered her away from the pool toward the opposite side of the chamber. "We don't have time, and they don't have a spark of life left. Let them have their peace as they found it, huh?"

Ember turned over her shoulder to check one more time for movement, but that only came from the black bubbles bursting on the surface of the pool.

Cheyenne bit her lip and stared at her friend as the party gathered behind the exit to follow L'zar. *If she makes it through this and doesn't lose her mind, she can make it through anything.* The halfling gently took Ember's wrist and gave it a reassuring squeeze. "It's okay."

"No, it's not." Ember grimaced at her friend. "But at least they're not screaming anymore."

L'zar waved his hand across the door, which opened slowly to let them out into another series of corridors. "Keep up. Two minutes tops and we're at the courtyard."

He looked at Cheyenne and nodded.

Her hand went to her pocket and felt the gold coin's outline there. *And then I'll have to get this thing on a stupid table. Yeah, I'm ready.*

L'zar gazed at the top of the open doorway, then darted into the corridor to lead them through the Crown's fortress. The party quickly followed, racing against what little time they had left.

CHAPTER NINETY-TWO

The corridors got darker and narrower as they ran. Cheyenne tried to look straight ahead and watch where she was going, but the activator kept catching her attention with bright flashes of light racing along the walls beside her. The instant the activator alerted her to the fact that they'd been found out, a siren erupted from the walls, groaning and wailing like a trapped beast crying out in pain.

"Shit." Corian hissed as they ran behind L'zar. "Someone was bound to see us eventually. Sooner than we'd hoped, though."

"Don't stop!" L'zar shouted. "Just around this corner!"

A blaze of searing heat and roaring orange flames hurtled down the hall toward them. L'zar stopped at the front of their line, staring straight at the fire, but didn't lift a finger to do anything. Cheyenne gritted her teeth and raised a shield in front of him at the last second, sectioning off the corridor from floor to ceiling before the fiery attack reached them. The blaze flared and brightened with an angry roar as it churned against her shield, turning the stone and metal corridor into a magical oven. The rebels leaned away from the glaring brightness, bearing the heat and the deafening roar until the flames subsided.

Cheyenne hissed and let the shield drop so they could press forward. Maleshi turned briefly toward her as they ran. "Way to use your head, kid."

"Just trying not to lose it."

The alarm wailed around them, and the second they turned the final corner, they were met by a full contingent of orc soldiers, all with the Bull's Head embroidered on their black uniform chests, shoulders, and collars. The rebels hurtled down the next walkway, and Cheyenne almost stopped when she realized where they were.

They'd come out six stories above a massive sunken courtyard of black stone. The corridor they'd reached encircled the courtyard, open to the wide space in the center and separated by a narrow stone rail from the drop. In the center of the indoor courtyard stood the last Nimlothar tree, its gnarled trunk twisting up toward the domed ceiling far above. Gloomy gray light spilled onto the stone floors and the giant tree's twisted roots, which protruded from the broken stone around it. The Nimlothar pulsed with a faint dark light, its branches mostly bare but for the occasional cluster of frail purple leaves that looked as sick and twisted as the rest of the tree.

This is it.

Cheyenne spun toward the orc soldiers heading toward them along the narrow stone walkway around the courtyard and the next battle began.

Spells flew in every direction. Maleshi and Corian met the first line of orcs charging toward them, silver light flashing as they barreled through the snarling Crown loyalists trying to run them down. Orcs screamed as they dropped over the stone rail and hit the courtyard floor at the bottom. There wasn't much room for the other rebels to join the fight as the nightstalkers fought their way through the armed soldiers.

Footsteps pounded across the stone behind Cheyenne, and she turned in the opposite direction to see another wave of soldiers streaming from a second corridor opening onto the walkway. The first few caught sight of her and leered, then pounded meaty fists against their chests and broke into a run.

"Behind us too!" she shouted, summoning crackling spheres of black energy in both hands.

Lumil and Byrd turned and broke into matching grins of battle insanity when they saw the second group of orcs. "Excellent."

Cheyenne fired her churning black energy spheres, catching the oncoming orcs in the shoulders and chests. Two of them fell and were trampled by their fellow soldiers, who cared more about catching the invaders than the fate of their comrades.

"Cheyenne!" L'zar's hand wrapped around her wrist and jerked her into a recessed niche along the walkway. Lumil and Byrd met the next wave of orcs with red-flashing fists and bursts of green flame, laughing maniacally.

Cheyenne jerked free of his grip and glared at him. "I'm not hiding with you. I have to get out there and *fight*!"

"No. You need to get down there." He pointed into the courtyard. "Black metal table. On top of it is something that looks like an anvil. Get the *marandúr* into the bowl shape on top. That's the only thing you need to worry about."

From the opposite side of the courtyard on the fourth level came echoing shouts and the clang of weapons meeting. Bright bursts of lights lit the stone corridors, then a stream of magicals locked in battle spilled out onto the walkway.

"I can't let everyone fight for me."

"That's why they're here—to fight and buy *you* time to do what you came here to do. I'm right behind you. Go." He shoved her out of the recessed niche in the wall, and she caught herself on the stone rail.

On her right, a leering orc with a glistening scar running down the center of his face caught sight of her and summoned a crackling blue spear in his hand. He drew his arm back to throw, then lurched forward. The orc's eyes rolled back, and he fell onto his face on the walkway.

Behind him, Ember slowly lowered her outstretched hands and looked from the soldier's body to meet Cheyenne's gaze. "Turns out, I *can* fight."

"Em, I have to get down there."

"Yeah. Go. I'm good." Ember spun and shot shimmering darts of opalescent light into the orc army fighting the nightstalkers.

"Right." Cheyenne peered over the railing into the Nimlothar courtyard below. The Rahalma altar stood six feet from the base of the gnarled trunk. *How to get down safely? Six stories is a long way to jump.*

Across the courtyard, the second battle raged along the walkway. An ear-shattering bellow echoed around them before a hulking magical with gray skin and red fur barreled out of one converging corridor. Stone split and fell around Nu'ek's hulking shoulder as the *golra* squeezed onto the walkway and flung the Crown's soldiers down into the courtyard.

"They're here." Cheyenne turned toward the nightstalkers as she climbed over the rail and set her feet down on the other side. *"They're here!"*

L'zar's rebels spared a glance across the chamber to see the rest of Ambar'ogúl's defectors in the capital surging along the walkway. Lumil screamed a battle cry and pounded on anything within reach of her fists.

"Go!" L'zar snarled, ducking a swinging blow from an orc's monstrous sword. He lashed out with his fists and feet, pummeling the orc without using magic.

Cheyenne watched her drow father beating back his opponent with nothing but his bare hands, which moved in a blur of gray flesh. *At least he's finally fighting.* She glanced at the floor of the courtyard, gritted her teeth, and started to climb down. Fortunately, the stone walls that had stood at the heart of Hangivol for countless Cycles gave her plenty of hand- and footholds. Weapons and magic clashed around her as the drow halfling slowly descended.

From within a dark archway on the other side of the courtyard, a tall figure cloaked in fluttering black robes emerged. The figure's hands were clasped in front of it, hidden by the draping sleeves of the robes. The black hood concealed the features of the magical, but two golden eyes glowed within the darkness. The figure moved slowly across the stone, not heeding the battle raging above.

Cheyenne's foot slipped on the jutting stone beneath her and she shouted, clinging to the stones by her fingertips and forcing herself to regain her footing and her balance. A screaming orc dropped a foot to her right and slammed into the stone floor. She kept climbing down. *Just focus on this, and on not getting knocked off.*

A burst of crackling yellow and blue magic crashed against the stone wall on her left, pelting her face and arms with shards of black rock. She blinked and tried to blink the dust out of her eyes. When she glanced down again and saw how far she hadn't come, Cheyenne pressed herself against the wall and shook her head. *This isn't working. I need a faster way down.*

She looked as far as she could over her shoulder and eyed the gnarled, twisting branches of the Nimlothar in the center of the court-yard. *This is a real shot in the dark. I've been hit with black-magic sludge and bullets and almost had my hands melted off by war-machine spy beetles. This is a piece of cake.*

Summoning all the strength she had, Cheyenne lowered her grip to a handhold closer to her chest so she could bend her knees as she clung to the wall. With a roar of effort, she leaped off the wall with a powerful kick and turned toward the Nimlothar. Her black tendrils lashed from the fingertips of both hands, whipping through the air as she sailed toward the ancient drow tree. The tendrils of one hand missed the first branch, but the others wrapped around the next one down. Cheyenne swung from the branch, feeling it shudder and jolt beneath her weight. She scrambled to whip the tendrils from her hands around another branch and succeeded, but the force drew her back toward the tree's gnarled trunk way too fast.

Shit. Her eyes widened, and she spun in the air as much as she could to crash against the thick tree with her hip and shoulder instead of her face. The Nimlothar pulsed with a brighter purple light on impact, then fell still.

Grunting at the pain in her side, the halfling looked down at the courtyard floor and released her tendrils to drop the remaining twelve feet. She hit the stone floor and rolled, then picked herself up and shook off the pain before turning to find the Rahalma altar. The Nimlothar's massive trunk blocked the black metal table from view, but Cheyenne darted around it to look for the altar.

She skidded to a stop when she saw the black-cloaked figure walking slowly toward the center of the courtyard. *Great. I thought I was in the clear.*

The halfling stepped forward, staring at the two glowing golden eyes within the black hood as she summoned a black energy sphere in one hand and pulled out the gold drow coin with the other. Her fist closed around it tightly. *Here's hoping whoever that is doesn't know what I'm about to do.*

The figure stopped walking and slowly lifted their hands to remove the hood. The slate-gray skin and bone-white hair coiled in thick braids on top of the drow woman's head made Cheyenne's heart drop. *The Crown.*

The drow woman smiled as she stared unblinking at the halfling in her courtyard. It was a dead smile, amused but without sympathy. The Crown raised a hand shrouded by the sleeve of her black robes and flicked her wrist.

The courtyard filled with the rumble of moving stone and shifting metal. All around the circular courtyard, every space between the over-hanging wall and the floor of the walkway was sealed by thick, heavy walls of black metal dropping into place. One after the other, the walls clanged against the stone floor of the walkway, blocking Cheyenne off from the magicals fighting on the other side. The same metal doors dropped with an echoing bang to block off the other corridors on the courtyard's ground level. Two horizontal doors slid into place with a boom overhead, blocking out what little light there was from the domed glass ceiling at the top of the courtyard.

Cheyenne stood alone in the stone courtyard with the Crown of Ambar'ogúl, separated from the fighting rebels and the orc army. *Separated from L'zar.*

She turned quickly to search for any archways left open as the muted battle sounds faded behind all the metal walls. The only exit now was behind the Crown.

Turning toward Ambar'ogúl's dark drow monarch, Cheyenne bared her teeth. "Scared someone else is gonna come down here and help me?"

"Not at all." The Crown tilted her head and glanced up at the closed-off walkways far above them. "I merely wish for us to have a more private conversation, Cheyenne."

Cheyenne's blood ran cold, and she was vaguely aware of a sudden ringing in her ears. *I've heard that voice before.*

"You didn't have to come all this way just to speak with me, *hidna*, though I'm quite flattered." The Crown chuckled. "I did what I could to reach you before you were forced to go to all this trouble. For some reason, you didn't seem to want my help."

"I still don't." Cheyenne took another slow step toward the Rahalma. *Six feet away. I can make that.* "I never will."

The halfling darted toward the table. The Crown hissed and reached out with both hands, sending a wave of crackling black light barreling toward the halfling like a cyclone. Cheyenne stopped to throw up a shield against the whirling storm. Sparks and dark light spewed when the Crown's spell met her shield, then the spiral vanished.

"I see you're hasty." The drow woman dipped her head and grinned. "Don't be. We have all the time in the world."

Gritting her teeth, Cheyenne darted toward the altar again. This time, she was stopped by a blast of invisible force hurling her back. She staggered against it and felt the sharp bark of the Nimlothar biting into her back. The rushing spell pressed her against the tree, her white drow hair fluttering around her face and shoulders. Cheyenne roared and tried to peel herself away from the bark, but she couldn't.

No black fire either, or that vision comes true, and I'll be the drow-halfling fuckup who burned the last Nimlothar to the ground.

The howling wind of the Crown's invisible force cut out, but Cheyenne was still pinned to the tree. The Crown spread her arms and smiled. "Don't go anywhere. I just want you to stand there and listen to my offer."

"What *offer?*" Cheyenne spat. She glanced up at the sealed metal doors along the walkway. *L'zar said he was right behind me. Should've known he'd screw that up too.*

"An offer to join me, Cheyenne. You've been made a pawn in someone else's war, one that was never yours to fight. You belong in a seat of power, *hidna*. One like mine."

"You don't want to just give up the throne."

The Crown threw her head back and laughed. Cheyenne expected it to sound like an evil cackle, but it was one of the gentlest lilting laughs she'd ever heard. "I appreciate your ambition. I really do. I'm staying in *my* seat for quite some time, thank you. But I want to offer you a place beside me. To be my eyes and ears. To use the power you have to serve the Crown and the world that birthed you."

"Not gonna happen."

"Hmm. Did that grinning thief tell you he meant to bring me down?" The Crown's smile tightened into a grimace, her upper lip twitching. "Did he promise you power at *his* side when he returned to Hangivol to wrest my power out of my hands?" The drow woman lifted her hands and spread her fingers, wiggling them.

Cheyenne struggled against the force pressing her to the tree and looked down at her right hand. She opened it and summoned an energy sphere, but it flickered right back out again. *Fuck.*

"I understand L'zar Verdys can be immensely persuasive." The Crown pursed her lips, her nostrils flaring in disgust as she looked Cheyenne over. "But where is he now, hmm? He sent you into the heart of the throne *he* wants to take, and he won't lift a finger to help you. I've been trying to reach you since the second I felt your power here in this very courtyard." Gazing around, the drow woman widened her smile. "You didn't recognize my offers for what they were, and I can't blame you for that. The human world is rife with twisted truths, Cheyenne. Join me, and I will show you the *real* world in more clarity than you can possibly imagine. Leave L'zar to his little games on Earth, hmm? This is where the *real* drow belong."

Cheyenne stared at the Crown, her chest heaving. *She doesn't know he's here. She has no idea.* The halfling glanced down at the small, tree-shaped pin stuck through the hem of her shirt. *And I can't reach that thing.*

"I only have so much patience, girl." The Crown sneered, white teeth flashing in her slate-gray face. "Make your choice, and for the sake of full transparency, you only have two. Accept my offer, or I will feed the roots of that ancestor tree with your blood as I have done with countless others before you. Of course, the choice is up to you."

No other choice, right? I'm screwed either way.

Cheyenne swallowed and closed her eyes. When she opened them, she stared into the Crown's glowing golden eyes. "Show me then."

"Show you?" The drow woman's grin widened. "You *are* curious, aren't you? What would you like to see first, hmm? The way I've built this empire to bend to the magic I can show you how to wield? I would very much love to teach you."

"Show me how to kill L'zar."

"Oh!" The Crown's lilting laughter filled the courtyard again. "Even when you're trying to defy me, I can see that *is* something you want. We have that in common. He's always been a disappointment. We can start there, then."

With a flick of her dark wrist, the Crown dropped the immense force pressing Cheyenne against the tree. She stumbled forward and stopped, not daring to race toward the altar again. Not yet. "This'll be fun."

"Yes, it will."

Cheyenne slapped her palm on the tree-shaped *nalís* pin at the hem of her shirt. "*Abdur orzj*, L'zar."

The Crown's eyes widened, and a portal burst to life against the wall of the courtyard. L'zar barreled through it, his eyes blazing with purple light as he raised both hands toward the Crown, grinning like a madman.

"No!" The Crown's gaze darted between Cheyenne and her drow father. Her hands lashed out toward both of them at the same time, and dark light spewed from her fingertips. Cheyenne slipped into drow speed and ran toward the black metal altar, her fist raised high and clenched around the gold coin.

Even at enhanced speed, the Crown's attack moved quickly. A purple light flashed behind the portal, and Ember sped through it just before it closed. The rest of it happened all at once.

The Crown screamed as her dark-light attack met L'zar's blazing silver storm with a deafening crack. The drow woman's other attack curved to follow Cheyenne as she brought her hand down toward the bowl shape on top of the metal anvil. Ember spread her arms and blasted pale violet light from every inch of her skin at once. The fae's light consumed the Crown's attack before it could strike Cheyenne. The Nimlothar tree hummed and filled the courtyard with a bright white light so blinding Cheyenne couldn't even see her hand, but she felt the lip of the metal bowl beneath her fingers. *Please tell me I didn't miss.*

The Crown screamed.

CHAPTER NINETY-THREE

The blinding light and the echoes of the Crown's screams died at the same time. The only sound echoing through the courtyard above the muted din of the battle above them was the hollow metallic tremble of the gold coin spinning in the center of the bowl on the Rahalma altar. It wobbled and finally fell on its side.

L'zar pulled himself up from where he'd been blasted back against the courtyard wall and chuckled.

The Crown lay in a heap of dark robes on the opposite side of the courtyard from him. She sucked in a furious breath and fought with her cloak to free herself before scrambling to her feet. Then she whirled on L'zar and hissed, *"You!"*

Breathing heavily, L'zar pushed himself up off the ground, gave her a mocking bow with his arms spread wide, and grinned. "Hello, Ba'rael."

She snarled and studied his madly smiling face. "I would have *felt* you."

"See, that's quite amusing. Not having to deal with your shit Earth-side gave me an enormous amount of free time to study the Weave. It was perfect, really. My daughter passing her trials. Me, just two steps away from spinning the last stolen thread to shield myself from you. And you, of course, overwhelming in your urgency to rip through worlds in order to get to her first." He clicked his tongue and shook his head. "Now look at you. All accounts frozen, and not a drop of magic at your disposal."

Cheyenne pushed herself away from the altar and stared at the gold coin in the center of the bowl. It sparked, quickly melted, and was absorbed by the black metal. Two seconds later, every trace of it was gone.

Ember floated back slowly until she thumped into the wall, staring at Cheyenne. The halfling gave her a reassuring nod and returned her attention to the drow conversation.

"How dare you?" Ba'rael spat.

"Quite easily."

"I'll rip you apart, L'zar." The Crown stormed toward him, seething with rage, and raised both her hands.

"Ah-ah." L'zar lifted a long, slender finger and summoned a pulsing silver light at its tip. "If you fought *me*, Ba'rael, you'd be forfeiting *so* much more than your status." He threw his head back and laughed. "I *have* my magic. You'll just have to wait."

Ba'rael turned her furious golden eyes on Cheyenne. "You're as full of lies as he is."

Cheyenne shook her head in disbelief. "Yeah, and you might be crazier."

L'zar smoothed his disheveled white hair away from his face and chuckled again. "Checkmate."

The Crown gritted her teeth and gazed at the high walls surrounding them. She roared in rage and spun, stalking quickly across the courtyard before spinning again to pace the other way. "This isn't how it's done, L'zar."

"Oh, please. Don't tell *me* how to play the game. This isn't how *you* did it. Cheyenne isn't remotely capable of following in your footsteps."

"But she'll follow yours, is that it?" Ba'rael fumed and shot Cheyenne another scathing glare. "You've always been a bottom-feeder, and you're taking her down with you."

"I consider that a compliment." L'zar folded his arms. "A lot of wonderful surprises drift down to the bottom before anyone even knows they've disappeared. Don't worry. It might take some time, but you'll figure out how to navigate it."

The O'gúl Crown hissed, and her anger finally burst out of her in a scream. She doubled over and let it all out, fists clenched by her sides, until the echoing roar of the drow monarch's fury shook the walls and sent a few pebbles tumbling down around them.

The Nimlothar flashed with purple light, and one frail violet leaf broke from its stem and spun through the air like a throwing star toward the drow woman. The leaf's thin edge slashed her face, and Ba'rael's screams cut off in surprise. She staggered backward, slapping a hand to her cheek and glancing down at the blood on her fingers as the leaf fluttered to the ground.

"Can't argue with the tree, Ba'rael." L'zar burst out laughing, and the Crown stomping her foot on the leaf to crush it into dust only made him laugh harder.

Cheyenne watched them with growing wariness. *They're both insane. What the hell is this?*

When the Crown finished her tantrum, she straightened, smoothed a stray lock of white hair behind her ear, and lifted her chin with a deep breath. Her gaze flickered toward Cheyenne. "Name your price."

L'zar raised a hand toward the Crown. "I believe this is something that requires a little more discussion. We didn't come here with anything specific in mind."

Cheyenne and Ember shared confused glances.

"Fine. Let's discuss it."

The halfling looked at the metal walls surrounding the arches of the walkways above them and shook her head. "I'm not discussing anything until you call off all the fighting."

L'zar hummed in amusement. "Cheyenne!"

"I'm serious. Not while everyone's up there killing each other and we're safe down here." *I think.*

"Well, you have to agree it's a start." He raised an eyebrow at the Crown.

Ba'rael rolled her eyes and flicked both wrists toward the high walls. The metal doors slid back into place with resounding clangs, and dark light raced around the fighting magicals overhead.

Every one of them froze, suspended in various stages of attacking and deflecting. The courtyard fell eerily silent.

"There. It's been called off." The Crown spread her arms. "Satisfied?"

Cheyenne glared at her. "That's not what I meant."

"Well, that's what I'm willing to offer until the four of us come to some sort of understanding," Ba'rael spat.

Ember blinked and pressed herself farther against the wall. "Oh, I'm good. Just tagged along to help with the last part. You guys can talk without me."

L'zar and Ba'rael turned slowly to stare at the fae hovering an inch off the ground. L'zar burst out laughing and drew a hand down his cheek. The Crown's nostrils flared. "I wasn't talking about you, fae. You're lucky you're still standing."

Ember flipped the O'gúl Crown the bird, and L'zar lost it all over again.

Cheyenne stepped slowly around the altar to join them. Before she could ask who the fourth was, a drow with a short-trimmed white goatee in a scarlet suit stepped through the open archway behind the Crown. His white hair was tied back in a long ponytail, and his golden gaze drifted between Cheyenne and L'zar.

"Ah. Ruuv'i." L'zar spread his arms and approached the other drow as if he meant to wrap the man in a hug. The drow in the scarlet suit spared him a quick glance and looked away before stopping beside Ba'rael. "Pity. I was hoping for a more energetic reunion. It's been so long."

"Not long enough," Ruuv'i muttered.

"Do you mean to negotiate too, then? Perhaps sweeten the deal for yourself?" L'zar stepped toward them. "If I were you, I'd leave the guilty to her fate and free myself."

Ruuv'i's nostrils flared. "I stand beside her. Call it moral support."

Cheyenne approached the three other drow and snorted. "After everything she's been doing, looks like you failed at that job a long time ago."

"Ha." L'zar pointed at her and grinned at the two scowling drow rulers. "*And* she comes with a sense of humor."

"It's as boorish and crude as yours." Ba'rael shot him a condescending stare. "I find it tiring."

"Good. A tired Crown is willing to listen. Pure necessity, isn't that right?"

"Say what you came to say."

"Cheyenne and I have come back for her to place her *marandúr* on the Rahalma, Ba'rael. She will claim what's rightfully hers."

"You have no right to speak for her." The Crown looked at Cheyenne. "You're the one who delivered the *marandúr*. What do you want?"

I have no idea what this is about. Cheyenne nodded toward L'zar. "What he said."

L'zar sucked in a mocking gasp of surprise. "Look at that."

"You never walked through the fires, L'zar." The Crown whirled on him. "You never touched the waters beneath the bridge. None of this is for you to decide."

"Ah. You're forgetting the most important part, Ba'rael. Blood bonds with blood."

"*Blood* is not the issue, Weaver! You made that perfectly clear when you betrayed the Crown and chose the other world over this one."

"Well, my methods were a bit unorthodox, sure, but it worked out beautifully. For me, at least."

Cheyenne stared at them, no longer part of the conversation. *I heard half of this in the prophecy. If he says he wants to take her throne, I'm stepping in.*

"Be that as it may," Ba'rael said through clenched teeth, "you're forgetting one small detail. Your daughter might have made it this far, but she isn't finished yet. If her *Nós Ani* can't be at this meeting, I'm afraid you've both come all this way to waste our time for nothing."

Ember cleared her throat and drifted slowly away from the wall. "Nope. That's me."

The Crown's mouth fell open, then she whirled on L'zar with renewed fury. "You *knew* this would happen."

"I most certainly did not. That fae snuck through the *nalís* portal on her own." L'zar chuckled and nodded for Ember to join them. "I must say, I'm impressed. Apparently, we'd have lost without you."

Ember's pink-tinged cheeks burned a dark violet shade as she floated toward the four drow watching her. She stopped beside Cheyenne and pressed her lips together in determination. "She needed me."

Ba'rael's only response was a furious hiss as Ruuv'i looked Ember up

MARTHA CARR & MICHAEL ANDERLE

and down, staring for a moment longer at the inch between her feet and the stone floor.

"So." L'zar clapped his hands together. "The old laws stand, Ba'rael. The turn of a new Cycle is pretty much the only option you have now. Beyond death, of course, which we all know you remember quite well. I can't imagine feeding your predecessor to the deathflame is an easy memory to toss aside, no matter how long it's been."

Cheyenne bit her lip. *I would not be surprised if she started breathing fire right now.*

"Come on, then." L'zar spread his arms at the Crown. "You can give it up freely, or I can take it from you."

Ruuv'i's gaze whipped toward the drow thief.

Ba'rael let out a dark, bitter chuckle and pointed at L'zar. "You forfeited your claim when you turned your back on me, L'zar. The old laws no longer apply to you."

"Sure." L'zar bowed his head and held the drow woman's gaze. "But they apply to my daughter, and she's done everything required of her to fill the empty seat."

Cheyenne stared at him. "The what, now?"

"The seat, Cheyenne. Position. Throne. Would you like more synonyms?"

"No, hold on."

"Stop." L'zar lifted a finger and shot her an intense warning gaze. The Crown's lips curled into a predatory sneer.

Because if I say the wrong thing, we lose. Got it.

Her father clasped his hands behind his back and smiled primly at the Crown and the drow man ruling at her side. "Cheyenne has a fortnight to decide what to do with you. She'll take that home with her, and when she makes her decision, you'll hear from us."

"No," Ba'rael growled. "No! I demand an answer now!"

"Too bad." L'zar grinned at them.

"You're a disgrace," Ruuv'i spat. "You think you're the clever one, Weaver? You'll end up hanging from the flames when all this is over."

L'zar spread his arms and bowed again. "Don't we all?"

"Your path through the deathflame will rip you to pieces!" Ruuv'i shouted, thrusting a long finger at the drow thief. "Everything you think you've accomplished is nothing!"

"That's enough," the Crown snapped. Ruuv'i growled and clenched his fists, but he didn't say anything else. "A fortnight, then. That's plenty of time for both of us."

"If you say so."

Ba'rael looked at the frozen magicals locked in battle around the edge of the courtyard and flicked her fingers toward them. The bright light freezing the combatants shuddered and disappeared, and both O'gúl soldiers and rebel magicals stepped away from each other, swaying and blinking, disoriented.

"Hear me!" The Crown's voice exploded from the bottom of the courtyard and echoed more than loudly enough for everyone to hear. "Put down your arms and return to your posts. We are finished. So says your *Crown!*"

The orc soldiers cast their monarch confused gazes and slowly filtered back through the arches into the adjoining corridors, leaving the dazed rebels alone to recover from the spell from which they'd just been released.

"No one hurts them," Cheyenne said quickly, pointing at L'zar's rebels. "I swear, if you can't hold to that, you'll hear from me in sooner than a fortnight."

L'zar chuckled, and the Crown turned a disgusted glare onto the halfling. "You have no idea how this works, and you still invoke the old laws. I should have crushed you against that tree."

"Well, I'm a pretty tough nut to crack." Cheyenne raised her eyebrows at the Crown, and the drow woman gestured toward the now-open passageways lining the courtyard.

"Get out of my sight."

"Although neither of us is subject to your commands, Ba'rael, we will happily take our leave. Enjoy your last two weeks of semi-power." L'zar flashed her another grin, then gestured for Cheyenne to join him.

Ember fell in beside Cheyenne as they passed the altar and the last Nimlothar tree, which was still faintly pulsing.

L'zar leaned toward his daughter and muttered, "That was a valiant attempt but quite unnecessary."

"To keep them safe? Why was that unnecessary?"

"When you returned your *marandúr*, all of Ambar'ogúl felt it. Wait 'til we walk through the streets after this. Hangivol is going to be a very different place."

"Better or worse?"

"That depends. For us? I'd say things have vastly improved. Well done."

Behind them, the Crown growled and raised her hands, mumbling a spell.

"Ignore her. Keep walking."

"How much magic does she have left?"

L'zar tilted his head from side to side with a noncommittal hum. "Enough to poke around with a sharp stick. Not much more than that, though."

A green light flashed behind them, filling the courtyard. "L'zar Verdys, *Cu'ón* of Hangivol, Dark Grinning Weaver and O'gúl Blood Thief, I hereby banish you from the soil of Ambar'ogúl. May you never set foot in the heart again. May the deathflame consume your flesh and your memory if you dare press against the threads I now weave around the traitor!"

The green light flashed again and grew behind them. L'zar didn't bother to turn around when the Crown's spell hit his back, sending green lines of magic crackling across his flesh. He paused, shuddered, and chuckled softly. "Huh. Tickles."

"What just happened?"

"Keep walking."

"L'zar."

He nodded slowly and pointed at the archway ahead of them. "Pretty much exactly what it sounded like, Cheyenne. Once I leave Ambar'ogúl, if I try to come back, I'm a dead drow."

"She can't do that." Cheyenne started to turn around, but he grabbed her arm and squeezed with just enough pressure to get her attention.

His golden eyes flicked toward her, and he leaned closer. "Come on, Cheyenne. No skin off my back. I wasn't planning on staying long anyway. This world isn't big enough for her and me to inhabit at the same time, and I never liked my bitch of a sister anyway."

"Your *what?*" Cheyenne jerked her arm out of his grip, and he ushered her through the archway with a chuckle.

Ember stared at them both as she floated along with them.

"Oh, yeah. You're the rightful heir to the O'gúl Crown, Cheyenne, not just by challenge but by blood. Drow royalty and everything."

"No."

"Yes." They moved down the corridor, which was lit by loose magical flames hovering against the walls. "It can't be that hard to believe. Honestly, what we need is strong leadership on Earth, too. That'll be part of your decision anyway when you make it. There's time."

"And what kind of screwed-up decision is that?"

He clasped his hands behind his back and took a deep breath as he led his halfling daughter and her fae *Nós Aní* through the halls of the Crown's Heart. "Whether you'd like to take the throne in Ambar'ogúl or maintain drow royalty on Earth. Knowing you, I'd say you're capable of both, but there might be some blowback."

Cheyenne stared blankly at the stone floor in front of them. *What the hell am I gonna do on a throne?* "You can't be serious."

"I'm as serious as I'll ever be, Cheyenne. You're my daughter." L'zar glanced at her with the only smile she'd seen him give that didn't make him look insane. "You're the bridge between two worlds."

Overthrowing the O'gúl Crown is just the beginning. What happens next is a whole different game. Join Cheyenne as her adventures continue in *The Drow Grew Stronger*.

Get sneak peeks, exclusive giveaways, behind the scenes content, and more.
PLUS you'll be notified of special **one day only fan pricing** on new releases.

Sign up today to get free stories.

or visit: https://marthacarr.com/read-free-stories/

AUTHOR NOTES - MARTHA CARR
MAY 8, 2020

When it comes to trends, I tend to be very middle America. It will never matter whether I have a lot of money or none at all. What I like to wear, do, eat – the whole shebang – will never be the outer edge of what's to come, but instead a reliable barometer of what the masses of middle class are loving now.

That's how I know that my closet, which is three levels of sizes, is probably pretty typical. There was that short period around 2010 when it was all one size and a size I liked. Man, those were the days. I'd pass plate glass windows and sneak a peek just to see if maybe I was wrong and suddenly, I was not the size I always wanted to be. Nirvana. True to my middle class soul, it wasn't a tiny size, it was just perfect for me.

Just before quarantine I was on a tear, baking up a storm. I guess I actually was a little early on one trend. All the sampling of what I made lead to a lot of extra pounds and having to get out the largest set of clothes. When sheltering at home began, I kind of snapped awake to what I had been doing. And I wanted something good to come out of the weeks, maybe months of this life changing event. That and I read obesity could make surviving the virus a little more difficult. There was so much I could do nothing about, but here was at least one thing I could change - should change – and maybe get back to that one wardrobe again.

So far I'm down eight pounds, hard won and it feels good. I'm taking long walks the equivalent of a 5k, 3.1 miles, which gets me outside, helps clear my head and works toward that goal. I'm not into level number two yet but it's getting close and maybe by the time the world has righted itself again, I'll even be in level one. I can't wait to go shopping in my closet. The goal won't light the world on fire and in the scheme of things won't even change my life all that much. But still, worth doing and will make things easier just enough. I'll take it. More adventures to follow.

Going shopping in my closet.

Ok, now THAT is an interesting statement and not something I can do, or do well. A couple of years ago (more like four), I went through a phase where I would wear the same type of clothes every day.

I took the idea (modified for myself) from Steve Jobs, who was known for his black turtleneck, blue jeans, and New Balance shoes. In fact, many successful people wear the same clothes.

Why is that? The consensus is decision fatigue. If you get up at the same time, eat the same food, and wear the same clothes (you just buy many of the same products), then each day, you don't start off with decision fatigue.

For me, I didn't give two cents to what I looked like every day, so, I chose a black t-shirt (reduced the author-belly look), jeans, and whatever shoes I wanted for my normal outfit.

Then, I got "bigger," and the t-shirts got a little worn out. I went looking for larger black t-shirts and bought them in packs until I found out that wasn't a good thing. They were cheap and often got holes after a couple of washings.

Now my black t-shirt drawer was full of different styles of black t-shirts. Shit! I couldn't even get "wear the same clothes each day" to work for me.

Don't even ask me about jeans. When you do the math, my black t-shirt, jeans, and a pair of sneakers became something like one of seventy-two different decisions (six brands of t-shirts, four types of blue jeans, and three sneakers.)

Then, LMBPN went and purchased some collared Under Armour shirts, and I fell in LOVE with them. Not only did they hide the author-belly problem, they were a great fabric, had our brand, and were easy to choose.

Until my wife got tired of me wearing them all of the time.

It seems that my spouse might have wanted to see a husband with a bit of fashion sense (I have very little) and didn't approve of years of black, blue, and sneakers.

She found out I liked old-school metal and rock band t-shirts and bought me something like five one time. I knew right then that if she was willing to give me old-looking rock t-shirts, I needed to clean up my only black motif.

So I did.

I'm now wearing a *white* Under Armour LMBPN Publishing collared shirt.

Baby steps people, baby steps.

Diary June 14 – 20, 2020

So, Las Vegas is a little weird right now. You have pockets of people who are very Covid-19-aware around the valley area, and then you have the casinos. Some of the casinos are very Covid aware and more stringent, and others aren't.

No casino (that I've been to) mandates wearing a mask.

The Station Casinos shoot that temperature gauge at you when you enter their establishment but are pretty open after that.

Caesar's Hotel and Casino (for this latest weekend) was packed with people, and they try to encourage social distancing, but occasionally people get a little close together—and by occasionally, I mean all of Friday night.

I can't speak to Saturday or Saturday night since I didn't get to continue playing. My budget was used up, so I worked and slept most of Saturday, catching up from some mixed up sleep during the week.

I'm at the Green Valley Hotel and Casino. Sitting in the food court, I can see at least twelve people playing on the casino floor. The mask to no-mask ratio seems to be about even, except for the person who has a mask, but is smoking, so the mask is pulled down.

I'm going to count that as a no-mask.

Here in the food court, the mask ratio is about one person with a mask to twenty without one.

We are fifteen feet from the slot machines.

I get why those of us in the food court have no masks (and there is no difference when I go to regular restaurants. Once a person sits down at a table, the masks come off almost immediately.)

I think I will be about done with these updates starting next week. Enough of my diary entries have dealt with Covid-19 and Las Vegas, it's time to just…talk about other stuff.

Like books, maybe?

Sometimes, it's hard to remember what readers want to hear about in our (author and publisher) lives. I eat, sleep, and breathe publishing and stories at this point in my career, and what's normal to me (and seems like would be boring to you) is probably not.

As always, THANK YOU for reading our stories. We would not be able to create the wonderful stories without readers like you supporting us!

Ad Aeternitatem,

Michael Anderle

CONNECT WITH THE AUTHORS

Martha Carr Social

Website:
http://www.marthacarr.com

Facebook:
https://www.facebook.com/groups/MarthaCarrFans/

Michael Anderle Social

Website:
http://www.lmbpn.com

Email List:
http://lmbpn.com/email/

Facebook
https://www.facebook.com/TheKurtherianGambitBooks/

OTHER BOOKS BY MARTHA CARR

Series in the Oriceran Universe:

THE LEIRA CHRONICLES
I FEAR NO EVIL
REWRITING JUSTICE
SCHOOL OF NECESSARY MAGIC
SCHOOL OF NECESSARY MAGIC: RAINE CAMPBELL
ALISON BROWNSTONE
THE DANIEL CODEX SERIES
FEDERAL AGENTS OF MAGIC
SCIONS OF MAGIC
THE UNBELIEVABLE MR. BROWNSTONE
THE KACY CHRONICLES
MIDWEST MAGIC CHRONICLES
SOUL STONE MAGE
THE FAIRHAVEN CHRONICLES

The Terranavis Universe

THE WITCHES OF PRESSLER STREET
THE ADVENTURES OF FINNEGAN DRAGONBENDER

BOOKS BY MICHAEL ANDERLE

For a complete list of books by Michael Anderle, please visit:

www.lmbpn.com/ma-books/

All LMBPN Audiobooks are Available at Audible.com and iTunes

To see all LMBPN audiobooks, including those written by Michael Anderle please visit:

www.lmbpn.com/audible